VADIM: THE COMPLETE TRILOGY

CLUB XXX NOVEL: CONTROL, CORRUPT, & CONQUER

LANA SKY

CONTROL

Control

Control By Lana Sky

Copyright © 2020 by Lana Sky
All rights reserved.

No part of this publication may be reproduced, distributed, or
transmitted in any form or by any means, including photocopying,
recording, or other electronic or mechanical methods, without the prior
written permission of the author.

This is a work of fiction. Names, characters, businesses, places, events and
incidents are either the products of the author's imagination or used in a
fictitious manner. Any resemblance to actual persons, living or dead, or
actual events is purely coincidental.

Cover Design and Interior Formatting by Charity Chimni
Proofreading by Charity Chimni

ACKNOWLEDGMENTS

Thanks so much to everyone who supported this draft along the way, including the many beta readers who provided encouragement along the way! Please keep in mind that this story includes dark, graphic, and explicit content matter that is not suitable for readers under the age of 18—or for readers who are uncomfortable with the following subject matter: explicit sex, mentions of sexual abuse, mentions of child abuse, graphic depictions of violence, and mentions of self-harm.

CHAPTER ONE

When delving into the world of sexual promiscuity, it's totally okay to have *one* glass of wine beforehand, just to calm your nerves. Two is fine too. Okay, three—but there's a benefit to every sip of alcohol far beyond the use as a mental crutch.

Or so I tell myself.

For one, I'll be nice and loose for whatever millionaire I manage to snag on my first night on the prowl. Depending on how well it goes, I'll be closer to scratching the big-ticket item off my bucket list—joining a secretive, exclusive sex club. Through that act alone, I'll be giving my ex-husband the ultimate kiss-off, while indulging in years of repressed sexuality to boot.

Win, win.

Telling myself that makes it easier to down my fourth glass as I scan the offerings milling about the exclusive "Gray Bar" of Hotel Six—the most exclusive venue within ten miles of the area's major airport. It's a forty-floor haven for millionaire businessmen with too much money to spend and not enough time to look for a relationship lasting beyond a few hours. In theory, it should be a sexual revolution Mecca.

In reality, it's slim pickings tonight, go figure. The one night of the week I finally managed to gather up the nerve to assemble an outfit that—in the right lighting—makes me look like I almost belong here. Enough that I was able to slip past the stern-faced bouncer before he could do a double take.

Though, maybe I should have tried my skills on him first? The old guy could have been a nice warm-up for my rather lacking talent of seduction. Frowning, I do the math on my fingers. Six months since my divorce from Jim was final. Three years since we last had sex. Minus the odd dildo every now and again, I haven't been laid in…

Too damn long. Sighing, I let my fingers fall to the table before me and tap the polished wood with my hot pink nails. A normal person would try online dating, or maybe troll the grocery store for some horny single dad with a fetish for one-night stands to ease her way back into the dating pool. A normal person.

I, however, decided to skip the queue and jump into the big, wide world with a bang. Literally. Why feign interest in a long-term relationship or play the roulette game with STDs when you can aim right for the jackpot—exclusive millionaire sex clubs like the kind my uncle Conroy used to gossip about after one too many brandies.

The millionaire part is beside the point. Three big ones, actually—safety—both physically and health-wise—privacy and most importantly…kink. Weird, crazy kink. Enough to drown out say, seven or so years of a lifeless marriage and boring, missionary sex so lame that a nun wouldn't consider participating as breaking her vows.

Yes, Tiffy, I tell myself. *You're on a roll. A horrible, fruitless roll.*

An hour in, and I have yet to be approached by one of the three men occupying the lounge in addition to me. It must be the slow hour for rich bachelors.

One potential prospect sits at the bar, his back to me. A curtain of dark hair obscures most of his face, but he's scrawny. Too scrawny. *Next.*

Sighing, I shift my attention to another potential victim. Aged approximately seventy years, with a beautiful head of balding gray hair, he's only a moderately more appealing candidate. I bet rich old men have plenty of experience to draw from, though. Viagra can be a heck of a drug—and hell, to make their trysts last, those over sixty probably extend the foreplay too.

Bonus points.

Not that I would know how to recognize extended foreplay if it slapped me in the face. Jim thought oral sex was sinful—unless on the rare occasion he had two beers, it wasn't Sunday, and I was the one willing to open my mouth.

Stop it. I shake my head to clear away the negative thoughts—no more dwelling on the past. I'm the new and improved Tiffany Connors. No longer bitter about years of youth wasted. No longer hating on my prudish ex-husband. No longer sexually repressed.

So very sexually repressed.

I crane my neck to the corner of the room where the third and last potential victim sits thrumming through a magazine. The fact that it's Vogue, paired with his impeccably tailored suit, sends my gaydar pinging hard. *Strike three.*

After yet another sip of wine for courage, I cycle back to bachelor number one, the guy at the bar. He's not my type, but what's the harm in trying? Glass in hand, I leave my booth and approach him, praying to God I don't trip in these heels. It's the first time I've worn anything but neat, respectable flats in nearly a decade—yet another example of jumping headfirst into my new carefree life.

Forcing my lips into a friendly grin, I sidle up to my target. "Hello," I purr huskily—or at least I try to. "I'm Tiff."

He inclines his head toward me, and my eyelids flutter in shock. I'm so caught off guard; I nearly let my sexy rouse slip in favor of gaping at him.

He's pretty. Freakishly so. An angelic nose anchors his delicately crafted features—like a masculine but beautiful doll. Pale skin conforms to his high cheekbones and strong jaw. Jesus almighty, I've never seen a sexier jaw. Eyes so dark, I feel the need to strike a match take me in with little reaction, and my brain runs wild trying to decipher them. Is he bored? Surprised that I've approached him?

A half-empty glass of whiskey sits in front of him and nothing else—a testament to the brooding businessman stereotype.

Score.

"Gorgoshev," he says in a voice so rich my tongue dampens, my throat contracting. He has an accent I can't place. Russian, given the name? No. Something more musical. French? I'm too distracted to put much effort into narrowing it down as he extends his hand toward me.

And it's as beautiful and slim as the rest of him. My nails look garish against his porcelain skin, and I'm ten times more self-conscious. Way to make a first impression. If he already doesn't think I'm a dumb bimbo, I'm halfway there.

"Do...do you come here often?" I ask, flicking my hair over my shoulder. I must flick too hard because one of my hoop earrings smacks off my chin, and I nearly slip from my stool.

A cool hand catches my wrist before I can lose my balance completely, anchoring me in place.

"T-Thank you," I stammer, smoothing my fingers over my skirt. He moved so fast. Already he's back to nursing his whiskey as if he never budged at all. "I've probably had way too much wine."

I groan internally. The fact that I acknowledge drinking at all is a sign I've definitely had too much wine. Surprisingly, Mr. Pretty doesn't seem to mind my sloppiness.

My heart races the more I watch him, and I dare to hope this could be working. He's handsome enough, and yes, he may be freakishly thin, but I can work with it. Jim—no, not thinking about him. *My ex,* has the body of a college linebacker five years beyond his prime, so I'm not picky.

Smiling wider, I try to engage the non-cheating, non-asshole person before me in conversation. *Say something smart, Tiff.* "Is Gorgoshev your first or last name?" I wonder.

Kill me.

"Last," he says, either oblivious to the stupidity of the question or he must get it a lot. "I'm not inclined to give out my first name to strangers." A playful smirk shapes his mouth, softening the rejection hidden within his words. *Touché.*

"I'm Tiffany Connors," I blurt. It could be the wine talking, but something about him makes me curious enough to extend the conversation, all embarrassment aside. "Age twenty-eight. I like long walks on the beach. I can assure you that I'm not a serial killer—"

"And I'm sure you carry quite the reputation in finance to commandeer a private booth in such an establishment," he says over me.

I clam up as my cheeks catch fire. Smart man—*too* smart, it seems. "I…I…"

"Relax." He cocks his head back and takes a small sip from his drink. "You're the first woman under fifty to come in here alone—" He meets my gaze directly, and my heart lurches. "Pardon me for being curious."

"Oh, yeah…" I flick my tongue along my lower lip, weighing the benefits of further engagement. He seems nice, but his lack of ogling my tits or trying to feel me up leaves me puzzled. Navigating the dating world beyond high school is a brand-new experience for me. Are we in good territory? Bad? Should I cut my losses and move on to an easier mark like the bald guy across the room?

Decisions. Decisions.

Jutting my chin, I decide on the spot to cut the bullshit and go for the balls. "Maybe I'm not a financier," I confess, eyeing him through my lashes. "Maybe I'm interested in something a lot more fun than comparing business ventures. What do you say? I'll show you mine if you show me yours."

A part of me cringes inside—the good, God-fearing part of me that wishes I was wearing a nice sweater instead of a dress that exploits my cleavage to hell and back. After two years, it's still hard to shake the old girl.

But as Mr. Gorgoshev's eyes flicker from my face down to my collar, I suddenly can't hear anything but the hard swallow contorting my throat. Good girl Tiffy can put a sock in it.

"Vadim," he says. "First name."

"Vadim," I parrot, playing with the syllables. I probably sound more tipsy than sexy, but a thrill runs through me anyway. I swear his eyes narrow slightly. So I say it again.

"Are you alright?" he wonders, a black eyebrow raised.

"Huh?"

"Your voice. It sounds strange." Frowning, he takes another sip of his whiskey while I pray I might sink through the floor and die. Just when the mortification becomes unbearable, he flashes one of those disarming grins. "If I didn't know better... I'd think you were coming on to me, Ms. Connors."

A teensy bit of my panic gives way to an excited flutter in my belly. "And if I am?"

He seems to mull it over, his dark eyes gleaming. "Then I would have to say..." With undeniable interest, his gaze flits over me a second time, and my heart lurches. "How much?"

"M-Much?" I eye my glass of wine and feel my nose wrinkle. "To be honest, I haven't really been paying attention to the number of glasses I've—" My brain realizes what he's implying before my mouth does. The second I do, my teeth slam together as a horrible wave of mortification washes over me, so intense, so paralyzing that it brings with it a sensation of déjà vu.

Like the day I strolled past my beautiful white picket fence, in my old beautiful life, and walked up the porch of my beautiful house. And then I found my once beautiful husband sitting at the kitchen table beside his beautiful whore. The joke had been on me. After seven years of changing myself to please him, he'd decided to spring for a younger, newer model.

And together, they had presented their case for a divorce.

I told myself I'd never feel like that again. Not ever. Not even at the mercy of the mysterious figure I once considered fucking.

"I've offended you," he says, the second I lurch from my stool. "Explain."

Something in his tone forms a wall against the indignation prickling through my skin. It's like the world just shifted, and even though I'm the one insulted, he's managed to turn the tables.

"What makes you think I'm—" I glance at the bartender nearby and lower my voice, horrified. "A prostitute?"

His brows furrow, and once again, I feel like I'm the asshole. "You're beautiful," he points out in a tone that makes my brain sputter and anger go poof. "I'm not your type. I can tell by your body language—" He nods toward my legs, which were neatly crossed with my hands folded over them. "You'd be positioned toward me if I were. Therefore, a beautiful woman, in a lounge meant only for business professionals, confronting me directly even though she's not sexually attracted to me..." He smirks, letting the obvious hang in the air.

As Uncle Conroy would say, *"That's check and mate, Tiffy. Know when to quit."*

"Check please," I call to the bartender, fighting to keep my voice calm. "I'm sorry, I should go—"

"So soon?" I stiffen as, once again, his tone catches me off guard. Not insulted, I think. Just curious. "Whatever your price, I would have paid it," he adds offhandedly. "I have time to kill before my next flight."

I falter as two realizations clash in my brain. One, he really does think I'm a prostitute. Two, he's boldly stated his interest in sex. With me. Now. Sex, complete with a graceful escape built-in by way of him being guaranteed to leave afterward.

My irritation dissipates instantly. I feel like a kid who had Christmas literally fall into her lap.

"You could name your price," Vadim continues, sparing me another glance. He lingers this time, allowing a hint of appreciation to seep into his gaze where it lacked before. He's not my type—he was right about that. But there is something about him that makes me do a double take, paying particular notice to his mouth. It's just so damn pretty. His lips look soft too.

And my brain jumps straight into X-rated territory because restraint is a foreign concept to this new and improved Tiffy. He's probably amazing at oral. Not that I'd know what oral—amazing or otherwise—from anyone feels like. But that's the point of going on a sexual adventure, isn't it? The thrill of discovery.

"I should have known better, I suppose." Vadim sighs wistfully, his mouth quirked in another teasing smile. "A beautiful woman, approaching me in a lounge primarily inhabited by men older than this brand of scotch, at a particular time when I was considering finding myself a companion..." He stands and fishes a handful of crisp bills from the breast pocket of his suit, placing them onto the counter. "Of course, it was too good to be true."

He steps past me, emitting a scent of booze and cologne that hits my nostrils like a punch. It's so deliciously male. So…sexy.

Without thinking, I'm already following after him. "If I was a…" I can't even say it. "What would you think my 'price' would be?"

"Honestly?" He looks me over, his frown thoughtful. "A grand for the four hours," he says—but from his tone, I can tell that it's not a boast. It's an honest gosh darn guess.

"R-Really?"

"You're confident which betrays a familiarity with high-class clients," he deduces, stroking his chin as if interpreting me is a task requiring his full concentration. "I'm sure your agency keeps a list of your references, and judging from your outfit, you have the financial stability to be discerning."

My outfit. It's one of the few things I splurged on with my first few alimony payments. A hot pink faux fur jacket with a genuine *Sergio Demassi* red silk cocktail dress that cost so much money I couldn't even look at my bank account after. My shoes are vintage Chanel in a rare royal purple I managed to score from one of my mother's socialite contacts. As far as jewelry, well, the diamond necklace was a present from Uncle Conroy from about ten years back, but it still cuts a striking figure with the right outfit. One could say I'd gone overboard. On the trip here from my less exclusive, more modest hotel across town, I'd caught plenty of women glancing at me with barely concealed smirks.

I hadn't even blushed. Who cares? I'm free, and freedom comes with the ability to wear whatever the hell you want. And apparently, some rich, beautiful man thinks that I'm worth a grand for just four hours. The joke's on them.

"Wait!" I don't even realize he's halfway across the bar until I finally regain my senses enough to choke out a strangled, "Thank you."

He cocks his head, his steps slowing. "Please tell me you've reconsidered?"

Biting my lip, I think through my options. Explore this avenue a little more or go crawling back to my hotel room? Or, take my chances with baldy across the way. There is no competition.

"Come sit." I sink back onto my stool and crook a finger, beckoning him with a confidence that sends my inner Bible-self reeling. "You didn't even finish your drink."

I snatch up his glass before the bartender can clear it. Held beneath my nose, the smell packs a punch. It's well beyond the cheap stuff a teenage Tiffy might have smuggled from Mommy and Daddy's drink caddy. It's the good stuff. Very good. *Uncle Conroy-trying-to-impress-wife-number-six-with-his-wealth* good.

"You could finish it for me," Vadim suggests, appearing by my side. Dutifully, he regains his stool, copying my position with his back to the bar. "I should keep my head clear. I have a meeting in not too long."

Curious despite myself, I take a sip and promptly sputter. It tastes like nail varnish. Damn expensive, quality nail varnish.

"So, you're just passing through? Where are you headed?" I ask, my ears still ringing from the booze. Way, way more dangerous than a glass of wine. *Slow down, Tiffy,* my inner voice warns. But that voice isn't face-to-face with a man so pretty it hurts. I find him sexier the more I appraise him. After another tiny sip of whiskey, I'm wondering why I ever considered him unattractive in the first place.

There's something about his eyes that I find the most enticing. They're…shadowed. Like he has an invisible wall up, and I'm only seeing a sliver of what lurks underneath —what he wants me to see. And right now, he wants me to see a sheepish, devastating smile.

"Have you ever been?" he wonders.

"Huh?" Another sip of whiskey and my brain is practically buzzing. He could have drugged it, or so says the rapidly diminishing voice of good Bible-Tiffy. But I doubt it. You can't disguise a roofie in classic, rich bourbon—another one of Uncle Conroy's pick-up lines. God, I need to get out more.

"You asked where I was headed," Vadim points out, his voice soothingly deep—stern enough to anchor my floating brain. I shiver as he drags a finger over the back of my hand, and excited goosebumps erupt. He feels electric. "'The East coast. Then onward to the south of Italy,' I said. 'For business, not pleasure, unfortunately. Have you ever been to Europe?'"

"Oh!" Had he really been speaking all this time? I try to look away and form some semblance of a conversation. "Italy? No. But I did some of my schooling in the south of France."

"Really?" He sounds so amused. The tipsy, redhead "prostitute" summered in Leon for a while. Go figure.

"My mother insisted," I add with a giggle, facing him again. "She thought it would culture me."

All it did was put me on a crash course for a quickie marriage and a one-way ticket down heartbreak lane, smack-dab in the middle of wasted potential central.

"Does thinking about it upset you?" Vadim wonders. His voice is starting to sound way too suave. Persuasive. Enough that I might begin spilling my guts rather than offer them up to any millionaire in exchange for a lesson in kink.

"You said I might have spared you the effort of looking for a companion," I murmur to distract him, kicking my legs out as I observe him again. Damn. My eyes linger over his face this time, and my next breath catches in my throat. His eyelashes go on for days, his lips alarmingly pink. Again, my brain turns to dirty, dirty things. But a part of me almost feels ashamed for putting him in that light—even in my imagination. He looks so innocent.

"For the night, yes," he says, continuing the conversation and putting my assumption to the test. A wicked grin ignites his soft features, enhancing their intensity. "I have a few agencies I prefer to choose from. I can have my records sent to you via any method you prefer. As long as you are on regular birth control and clean, I prefer not to wear a condom."

I almost choke at how blunt he is about a subject most people in my life would clutch their pearls at the horror of discussing. More than that, he makes it sound so… orderly. So business-like.

Awed, I find myself murmuring, "You do this often?"

He nods, and I'm instantly suspicious. Someone so pretty, presumably rich, and yet he hires escorts rather than troll for celebrity arm candy? I smell bullshit. He's young enough—early-thirties I'm guessing—that a desperate actress would hitch her wagon to him in a heartbeat and supply all the sex he could ever need.

Unless relationships aren't his style.

"I prefer the ease of it," he says after a moment, seemingly proving my point. "Less hassle. Less potential for any… mess. Simple and clean."

Simple. We have that desire in common. I inhale sharply, nodding in agreement. Yes, this could work… Only, there is one tiny matter that might prove to be a hitch. "What if I'm *not* a prostitute—"

"Escort," he corrects.

"Escort then." I'm amicable to the name change—it sounds so much classier.

"If you agree to my conditions, then who am I to tell the difference?"

"Conditions?" My eyes narrow. That sounds like a potential speed bump. For instance, Uncle Conroy's "conditions"—which sent him burning through six consecutive marriages—are that he enjoys threesomes, booze, and little else. Since he's one of the few millionaires I know personally, I'm hoping his proclivities don't serve as a template for the lot. "Like?"

"Hmm." He reaches out and gently pries the nearly empty whiskey glass from my hand. Then he downs the remaining sip in one go. I gape, riveted as his throat works to swallow. Meeting my gaze, he slams the glass onto the counter, resembling a cowboy throwing down a gauntlet. "Come to my room and find out for yourself."

I stop breathing. Could it truly be so easy? A sexy businessman on my very first attempt?

Don't look a gift horse in the mouth, Uncle Conroy would warn. *Take your shot, girl. Luck doesn't strike twice.*

"Where to?" I murmur, rising to my feet.

His eyes widen—have I caught him off guard? Perhaps not. Already, a beautiful, mischievous expression erases anything else. He cocks his head and stands, offering his hand to me. "To a diversion," he says. "But first things first…"

He pulls a cell phone from his pocket, and with a series of swipes, he brings up a screen that he tilts for my inspection. It takes me a second to interpret what I see— medical records, digitized for easy access. In crisp, clinical jargon, they proclaim him to have a clean bill of health.

"Oh!" I reach into my purse and withdraw a folded slip of my own dated, printed records, drawn up by my PCP just last week, along with a copy of my birth control injection administration. He looks them over and nods.

"Shall we?" Even as he smiles that charming grin, I sense a warning in his words—that of a firm boundary being drawn between us.

He's offering up a diversion. Nothing more.

And nothing less.

The rest of the Six turns out to be even fancier than the lounge—not that I manage to take in much of it, considering that I can barely walk in a straight line. My heels have absolutely no grip against the plush, lush carpeting of the upper floors. I flounder gracelessly. When I nearly careen into a potted plant, a stern figure captures my wrist, pulling me against his slender frame for support.

"Easy," Vadim murmurs near my ear as I melt into him, relishing his body heat. "Are you alright?"

"Better than alright," I slur with growing determination. The alcohol running through my veins just makes me more eager for whatever Mr. Pretty might have in store. With the added bonus that if I'm terrible, or if he's terrible, or if everything is terrible, I probably won't remember by the morning.

Win, gosh darn *win*.

"It's here," Vadim says, stopping before the only door lining this hallway. When we exited the elevator we turned down one of four halls. We're on the topmost floor of the hotel. The level reserved only for the crème de la crème. Rooms more expensive than most people's mortgages.

Rooms well beyond my modest target price range of *"millionaire with thousands to blow on kink."*

"Are you trying to impress me?" I giggle, patting his chest. It's surprisingly firm, and I fan my fingers over him in curiosity. Despite his slender shape, I suspect he's solid muscle underneath. "Very funny. Where are you really staying?"

I'd already scoped out the hotel layout before infiltrating the lounge. So I know for a fact that the business and executive suites are between the tenth and thirtieth floors.

This floor sports just four suites, all exceedingly exclusive. Visiting princes and dignitaries' level of exclusive.

"Here." Vadim shoots me an odd look while reaching into the breast pocket of his jacket. He withdraws a silver key card and swipes it through the reader beside the sleek, modern door.

And it opens.

"My, oh my." I cover my mouth with my hand as I stagger forward, too curious to pretend to be unimpressed by luxury—I'd read in an online guide that to snag a rich guy's interest, pretending to be unfazed by his wealth is a must. Though Uncle Conroy seems to enjoy any pretty woman he can woo with a Rolex, so to each their own. "You must be quite the businessman to afford this. Don't tell me I'm in the presence of a millionaire."

I have the impression that Vadim intentionally stands back, allowing me to lead the way inside.

"Billionaire, perhaps," he says with a charming laugh that obscures if he's telling the truth or not. I hear the door close behind us, and his footsteps echo, advancing. "Please pardon the mess," he murmurs near the nape of my neck.

It's decided. He is officially sexy. Sexy in both appearance and in his mannerisms. The mess he's referring to seems to be a single black leather briefcase left open in the entryway of what appears to be a branching suite, complete with a spiral staircase leading to an upper level.

"Holy beans," I mutter, craning my neck back to take in the vaulted ceilings and modern architecture. "Do you always stay in the most expensive suite when you're just 'passing through' town?"

He laughs again, and my skin tingles at the sound. Actually tingles. Either that, or I am beyond tipsy and inching into drunken mess territory. Whatever, I'll worry about the consequences later.

"I have a standing reservation for convenience's sake," he says, as though it's completely normal to book a hotel room for a few hours. Could he be lying to impress me? Most likely.

Do I care?

No.

"I bet the bed is huge," I suspect, flicking my gaze toward the staircase. I slink over to it and palm the railing, feeling ten times braver than I had just minutes ago. I look over to find Vadim watching me, his dark eyes unreadable.

"Do you prefer missionary?" he inquires.

I turn away as my cheeks burn. *Stop it, Tiffy.* I'm no longer the repressed prude, but an unleashed sex kitten. For good measure, I pinch myself on the wrist.

"You know what, I've been dying to try something new," I purr, whirling around to face him. "I'm sure you have tons of experience to draw from."

That makes him smile one of those secretive grins. "I may…"

"Like?" I shed my coat as I wait for his response. It's warm in here. Too warm. Sweat is already misting over my skin, and the faux fur clings to my fingers as I set it aside.

Vadim is still standing, watching me.

"I'll let you set the pace," he says dismissively. I frown only to lose my train of thought as he runs a finger along his collar, loosening it. He's even pretty underneath the tailored fabric—his chest gleams like marble, hairless—

but there's a flaw so glaring I sway at the sight. A jagged scar claims the left side of his throat, clawing down to his shoulder. With his collar done up, I'd missed it before.

"What happened?" I blurt out.

His eyes flicker, suddenly icy. "A minor accident." A deliberate note in his voice conveys a chilling bit of doublespeak—*so don't concern yourself.*

Fair enough.

Shaking my head, I refocus on the rest of him and try to recall his first directive. Set the pace.

Okay. Meeting his gaze, I attempt to advance toward him, slow and steadily like I've seen women do in pornos. But those women weren't drunk, most of them weren't wearing stilettos, and their costars weren't fully clothed, observing their every single move.

I stagger, and he practically teleports to my side, just in time to grab my arm, righting my balance before I can fall.

"I'm beginning to wonder if I might be taking advantage of you, Ms. Connors," he says, sounding annoyingly serious.

I giggle—one of those stupid, tattered drunk-girl giggles. Oh, dear, it's happened again. Well, it's too late to back down now.

"I'm fine," I insist. "In fact…"

Grab the world by the balls, Uncle Conroy would say.

So I drop to my knees and fumble for the fly of his slacks. The first thing I notice is how luxurious the fabric feels— very expensive. My second realization is how he stiffens. His body tenses beneath me, and I jump back as if burned.

"It's alright," he snaps, but irritation taints his voice like clouds obscuring a dazzling sun. Sudden and alarming.

"Sorry," I murmur, peeking up at him. "I just really want to see your—" I have to physically bite back the word "manhood"—my mother's term drilled into me since childhood. This moment calls for something dirtier. "Cock," I say instead, loving how filthy it sounds. "I really want to see your cock."

His expression shifts, neutral once again. I probably caught him off guard by how sloppy I am, and I make a concerted effort to gently brush the fastenings of his pants.

"Can I?"

"You may," he says, playful instead of serious.

I bite my lip as I work at a delicate silver clasp. With some finagling, I get it open and tug the waistband down his hips. Solidly cut muscle greets me, and I inhale in appreciation. He is *built*—as if chiseled from stone. I could cut myself on the ridges of his hips and defined thighs. But again, something detracts from the otherwise perfection.

"Are you hurt?" I ask, fingering a small, white patch placed on his abdomen, right over his hip. A thin, clear tube snakes from it, apparently connected to a rectangular device, roughly the size of a deck of cards that he withdraws from his pocket.

"Oh," I say, recognizing the device for what it is—an insulin pump. "You have diabetes?"

One of the little girls at my church had a pump, though far less high-tech than his seems to be. As I watch, he removes the patch, taking out the cannula as well. A frown tugs on his mouth as he turns and sets the device on an end table. Annoyance?

"Cold feet?" he wonders as I hesitate.

I blink, and my brain switches instantly back to sex. "I'm anything but cold," I murmur, returning my eyes to the prize—a pair of black boxers is the only remaining thing shielding him from me now. "No… I just want to savor this moment for a sec."

Impulsively reckless or otherwise, this is *it*—my moment. My first time ever sticking to a plan—no matter how outlandish—and seeing it through simply because I wanted to.

It feels damn good. Too good.

Everything is falling into place so perfectly. Usually, that only heralds bad news. Either I passed out in the lounge, and this is all a vivid hallucination, or something bad is on the horizon to dampen this moment. Either way…

I don't want to turn back.

Vadim stands utterly still as I work my fingers beneath the waistband of his boxers and tug. The moment I see all of him in full, stark glory, disappointment crashes through me so painfully I groan out loud.

This definitely is a dream.

"Something wrong?" he wonders, still so damn unaffected. Amused, even. "I must admit I'm rarely met with this reaction by the opposite sex. Though sometimes shock is expected."

"I'm sorry," I say earnestly. "I... I've just never seen a beautiful cock before."

And I've seen a lot of them. In porn, obviously, but still. Those enormous, suspiciously always erect penises were at the high end of my wildest expectations for what endowments I might discover along my new sexual adventure. But for the most part, I've kept my hopes grounded at least in the "better than Jim" range. Not too stubby, not too short, and way more willing to be placed in my mouth.

Vadim takes those mild expectations and crushes them.

"Beautiful?" Something in his tone makes me glance away with difficulty from his hips to his face. A fleeting expression shapes his features, resembling anger more than appreciation. He purses his lips a heartbeat later as if to disguise the reaction. "I'd love for you to explain, pretty girl."

My brain spins at the heated way he says that nickname. His voice drops to a lower octave, enhancing the mysterious notes of his accent. It. Is. Beyond. Sexy.

My eyelids flutter as I settle onto my knees and approach him with a single outstretched finger. When he doesn't recoil, I brush the uppermost edge of the thatch of dark curls shielding the main prize like some glorious curtain.

"It's so long," I say huskily, surprised that my voice actually sounds sexy this time. Not faked. "And…perfect," I add, inching a fraction lower. "And *pierced.*"

A metal barbell goes right through the crown, topped on either end by a round bead *just* large enough to seem more tempting than intimidating. It's so deliciously sinful. So kinky.

I almost can't handle it.

"A modified Prince Albert," he explains in response to my unanswered question. "And no, it won't hurt you. That seems to be commonly asked in this situation."

By pansy fools, I decide. My only driving thought is curiosity as to how he'll feel inside me. "I've thought about getting pierced before," I tell him absently—a secret I've never spilled to anyone. Ever. "It's so pretty."

This is the extent of my vocabulary at this moment. Because all I really want to do is taste him. Part my lips around him. See how deep down I can let him go. Things I have never thought about a bodily appendage before—not even Jim's.

My eyelids get heavy, and I lick my lower lip, mulling over an angle of attack.

"I wonder what you taste like," I whisper, and I swear I see him jerk, a web of veins becoming more pronounced throughout his length. The reaction sends up a ping of alarm—does he not want me to suck him off?

"Up." He crooks a finger beneath my nose, startling me with the authority in his voice. My gaze darts to him, and I nearly sigh in relief when I catch that slow, lazy grin shaping his mouth. Not anger this time. "I've shown you mine," he explains. "Now you show me yours."

"Oh!" My brain switches gears, happily turning to something that might excite me almost as much as fellating him. Exhibiting myself for him. I lurch to my feet so quickly that I trip, and he has to grip my waist to steady me.

"Easy does it." His voice... It's so pretty when heard up close. His baritone inspires shivers that dance down my spine and shimmy in my belly. So very nice. I lean against him, straining on tiptoe to bring my nose near the crook of his shoulder. He stiffens again, but lets me inhale a whiff of him.

And it's like someone lights a match right between my legs. A noise rips from me I've never heard myself make before, and I wiggle free from him just enough to tug at the skirt of my dress.

"Allow me." He spins me around and finds the zipper nestled within my freshly blown-out hair. One tug and the fabric gives enough for me to scramble from it. I barely get my arm free of a single spaghetti-strap sleeve when a sudden tension on my hair makes me stiffen, my lips parting, spine arched. He's grabbed a handful, it seems, using his grasp to control my movements.

Like some sexy sort of leash.

"Stop," he commands in a voice so rasping my bones quiver as if made of jelly. "Allow me."

With effort, I force my hands to my side, painfully aware of his presence. My lungs ache, infected by his heady scent. His fingers are so, so soft, tracing a path from my shoulder, down the center of my back to find the zipper again.

"You have beautiful skin," he praises, sounding surprised by the fact. But his fingers brush a raised scar along my lower back, and I'm the one cringing from him this time.

"Beautiful? I've just had amazing surgeons," I insist. "It's from a boating accident and was nowhere near as painful as it looks."

But that's a dangerous topic, far too serious for my brain to comprehend.

"I have even better tits," I tell him, jutting my chest. "Not surgically enhanced, mind you."

He chuckles, and I relax into him again. Taking the hint, he slips his fingers beneath the fabric of my dress, discovering the secret that I'm not wearing a bra underneath. Or underwear.

A devious idea sneaks into my brain, and I'm too reckless to resist. As my dress falls low enough to expose the top of my butt, I inch into him just a fraction. Enough to catch his startled grunt.

"Again, I'm waffling on whether or not you truly are an escort," he grates. Gosh, I love the sound of his voice. It's like music. Sexy, disorienting music so unique it transcends any genre. "It seems you've come more than prepared."

"I'm just super horny," I confess, my breaths quickening. Something about him inspires honesty from me I'd never explore around anyone else. "Super *super* horny."

The sexy voice is back, practically vibrating from my throat. His slow-moving fingers finally reach my belly, and I can no longer be patient.

"I'd love for you to touch me," I whisper, grinding on him more. The pathetic amount of friction is like gasoline to my sex-starved brain. I want more. More more more.

"And yet another strike in the 'not an escort' column," he muses. "You, pretty girl, are far too disobedient."

"Disobedient." I toy with the word between my tongue and giggle at how silly it sounds—considering that the opposite term had been my sole defining attribute for the better part of the past decade. The good obedient housewife. Good, obedient Tiffy. Subservient, oh so likable and so depressed, she contemplated suicide at least once per week—screw obedience.

"I've upset you." Vadim snatches on my hips, turning me to face him. His dark eyes skim over me, but a part of me buzzes faintly in alarm. His expression doesn't match the concern in his voice one damn bit. He looks too… excited. Like discovering my ticks is a fun, thrilling game.

So I rake my fingers down the front of his chest and lower my gaze to his cock. It's slightly more erect, thicker than before, those veins even more pronounced. He's aroused by this. Giddy triumph surges straight to my brain. I'd clap my hands if they weren't too busy relishing the feel of him. So sturdy. So very solid.

"I want you to finger me, please," I tell him, barely able to keep my eyes open. "Pretty please. I've been dying for it."

Another low, amused chuckle. I'm entertaining him. But a part of me loves the thrill of being on display—no cares given.

"Touch me," I beg, taking it a step further. "I bet your fingers feel amazing."

"Show me how, pretty girl." He shoves me back, and I have no chance in hell of preventing the fall. Luckily, I land on something soft that conforms to my shape—a leather couch. With enviable grace, Vadim steps forward, forcing my legs to part to give him room. With him looming above me, I feel smaller than ever. Something delicate at his mercy. Or disposal.

"Show me," he repeats, grabbing my wrist.

I gasp as he guides my hand between my legs and my thighs part on command. Years of both secret and more recently, regular masturbation have made me an expert at it. With the right mood and setting, I can get myself off in no time flat. In some ways, it's become a chore. Flick, flick. Twist, twist. Boom, there goes Tiffy.

But this…

Having a beautiful man's dark, beautiful eyes track my every move is an experience unto itself. Already soaked, my folds part easily with one brush of my forefinger. But the sensation—it's *lightning*. My head rears back as my teeth skewer my lower lip, trapping a moan inside.

A new record. No amount of porno or dirty reading material has ever gotten me this close, this fast. My fingers still, and I'm almost terrified to move. How pathetic would it be to get myself off so quickly?

But if anything, Vadim doesn't look disappointed. His eyes gleam as I part my legs and risk slipping one finger inside me. My body convulses as nerves explode despite my attempts to stave off the pleasure. But I fight the spasms just to watch him.

Holy hell. No man should be able to look like this. Aloof, and yet at the same time ravenous. Like a vulture who knows that the antelope writhing in agony before him is almost ready to feast upon. Almost.

He just needs to let it die first.

"Please touch me." I'm whining as I inch my finger deeper inside me while stroking my clit with my thumb. Usually, it takes a few good strokes to get me going. Now? "Oh gosh—"

Vadim moves with a calculated focus. One of his hands grabs my thigh, wrenching it higher as he palms his cock with the other. It's a sight unlike any other—his piercing glows, electric amid the swollen crown. No porno could ever compare to this, watching him angle himself against me.

My eyes roll as he slams forward, thrusting inside me with no preamble.

And I nearly come off the couch. He's so big. One thrust takes him deep, so deep. I cry out as my body grips him so hard I swear I can feel the outline of each one of those pulsating veins—every curve of his piercing.

And it feels beyond good.

My brain boils more with every thrust. Any semblance of coherence my thoughts possessed dissolves. I claw at him, nails drawn, urging him deeper, harder—to give me everything.

But when glimpsed through my heavy eyelids, he looks more determined than ever. Like a doctor carefully doling out an allotment of medicine. Just enough to do the trick.

But never enough to overload.

Never enough to lose control.

I'm aware of it—the boundary he maintains even as I tremble around him, gasping for breath. How he grips the back of the couch as if to maintain the same, consistent rhythm as he thickens inside me, demanding more…

That he denies himself of claiming.

And when he growls through his own release, he doesn't throw his head back in triumph. Instead, he grits his teeth, cutting off the noise. Closes his eyes, cutting *me* off.

"N-No!" I arch into him, letting my body grip him so ravenously we both cry out. "I want to see you. Please…"

His eyes reopen, but they're dark. Detached. Disconnected.

He withdraws abruptly, letting me slump against the couch. A lazy smile shapes his lips before panic can even set in fully—but it persists, nonetheless. This horrible sense that I've done something wrong. Offended him somehow.

Or that for him, real no-holds-barred pleasure was never part of the deal. As if reading my mind, he steps forward, his gaze softer. But his frown persists, ruining the façade he puts up. I'm five seconds from salvaging my pride and leaving altogether when he cups my jaw, tilting my head back to easily meet his gaze.

"Beautiful," he says, his voice deep.

And I let my brain turn off, ignoring those tiny warning signs urging me to run.

Somehow, we wind up on the floor with me on top of him, his hands on my waist. I marvel at the beauty of his body, feeling up whatever parts of him I can reach. Even his scar. Despite its jagged appearance, the skin feels surprisingly soft to the touch—like silk.

"You're so pretty," I tell him, barely able to feel my tongue.

He found another bottle of wine from somewhere, and it tastes even better than what they served downstairs. Dangerously sweet, enough that I'm already on my second glass.

You're a mess, Tiffy, a part of me scolds. But being a mess is surprisingly fun. Alcohol enhances every sensation to the nth degree. I giggle, relishing the tingling, tightening feel as my body recovers. But Vadim is watching me, eerily alert. Again, I can't shake this tiny voice warning me that he's almost too alert. I don't remember seeing him drink though he lazily pours more into my glass without bothering to sit up.

Whatever. I'll worry about that later.

"Tell me something," I slur to distract from the feeling. "Something you've never told anyone ever." When his brows furrow skeptically, I stroke my finger along his chin and add, "I can assure you that there is a fifty percent chance I won't remember any of this by tomorrow."

Another dizzying chuckle escapes him. Gosh, he could drug someone on his voice alone. "Only fifty? I hate to break it to you, Tiffany, but you are thoroughly sloshed."

I concede to that assumption with a nod. "Yeah. Which makes show and tell even funner!"

"Why don't you start?" he suggests. Extending his finger, he tucks a stray curl behind my ear, lingering near the lobe.

"Okay…" I suck in a breath and exhale it in an involuntary giggle that ruins the gravity of this moment. Here goes nothing. "I *did* scope you out on purpose," I confess. "I'm not a prostitute—but I do want something from you."

His eyes practically glow, smug. As if he knew as much all along. "Money?" he guesses. "Clout? Protection from an abusive spouse that has you on the run?"

I snicker and raise my hand to tick off each debunked assumption one by one. "First, the abusive spouse is long since divorced. Second, I have all the money I need. And clout—" I burst into cackling laughter and lose track of which finger I was on. "What does that even mean?"

"Power," he says seriously. "Men in my position possess plenty of power. Some seek to manipulate it for themselves."

"Hmm." I hum, brushing my lips along his throat. His scar is surprisingly the softest part of him, and I linger over the contours of it, daring to sneak a taste with a flick of my tongue. "I *love* how power sounds when you say it. Your voice is so sexy—"

"You are overly affectionate when you're drunk." I frown at the obvious distaste in his voice, but when I scan his expression, I don't find anything but a humored smirk. He's so good at hiding himself.

I should be worried about that, I think.

Or I can take another sip of wine. Smacking my lips, I set my glass down and nearly knock it over.

"I *am* drunk," I confess, sadly. "The cat is out of the bag. Such a poor little pussy. It hasn't been out in ages—"

"So, what was it you wanted from me?"

I shiver, easily distracted. His breath even smells nice, deliciously warm, tinged with whiskey. "I was hoping you were part of a sex club," I confess against his chest. "Like, the really debauched, really exclusive kind with pillories and such. Super taboo, kinky sex. The kind only rich people can have in utter confidentiality."

Something weird happens. His face… It's like he knew exactly what I would say down to the last period. But then drunk Tiffy mixed-up the script, catching him off guard. Even worse, irritating him. My stomach drops to the floor, and I rush to clean-up my own mess.

"I'm sorry—"

"You think you can survive in such a club?" he wonders in a tone that chills me, all ounce of humor gone.

"Maybe," I say quickly. "But I've survived seven years of boring, milk toast sex and utter misery, so I'm ready for a challenge. Joining a place like that is on my list," I add with solemn seriousness.

"List?" He raises an eyebrow, still so tense. Edgy.

Sighing, I try to find the right words to explain. "My 'no one owns me, fuck all list.' It has five items—"

"Just five?" he counters, and I snicker. Is that amusement I detect?

Raising my hand, I start to tick them off. "Yes. Dress how I want. Fuck how I want. Live how I want. Eat what I want. And no relationships."

That last one is a new addition, but he relaxes beneath me. For whatever reason, I think I've given him the right answer. To what question? He's so mysterious—I wonder if I'll ever know.

"But I feel bad for profiling you," I add, tapping his nipple. Mentally, I try to stop myself from using the word "beautiful" to describe the dusky peak. But it is. Gosh, he's like some alternate version of Adonis come to life. "I now think you're very straight-laced," I say, treating the term as a compliment. "I don't think you belong to a kinky, Godless sex club—"

"Oh, but I do." His upper lip quirks into one of those quick, devious grins. "One of the most debauched in the country, in fact. Though I will admit that I've let my membership lapse."

"R-Really?" My eyes go bug wide, and I scramble into a sitting position, straddling his slender hips. "Do they do orgies?" I wonder, practically squealing with excitement. "Do they do bondage? BDSM? Exhibition? Gang bangs?"

Kid, meet candy store. If I somehow manage to remember this in the morning, I'll never stop speculating.

"I don't know the menu offhand," he admits. "But you never asked me what my confession might be?"

"Oh, yes!" I extend my fist toward him as a makeshift microphone. "Mr. Vadim Gorgoshev, what secrets are you hiding?"

"I'm not on my way to a business meeting," he says. That's right—he did mention leaving for a flight soon.

I flutter my eyelashes. "So, where are you going?"

"My brother is throwing a party." His tone makes it sound about as appealing as an execution mixed with a root canal.

"I take it you two don't get along?"

His lips twitch into a sly grin. "One could say that."

"So why go?"

He seems to be pondering that exact question. Whatever answer he decides on, he doesn't say out loud.

"Well, at least you got to have some fun before you leave." I shift, shamelessly rubbing my nipples against his chest, loving the sensation that sparks in response.

"Fun?" He raises an eyebrow. "You aren't going to stroke my ego and tell me it was the most mind-blowing fucking you've ever experienced? All in the hopes of weaseling an invitation to the club out of me, of course."

"It was definitely the best I've ever been fucked." My wistful tone could convince even a blind man that I'm not lying. "But... You held back." I make my finger dance down his abdomen, able to sense the subtle tensing of his body. He maintains that invisible wall between us, even as we lie drunk on the floor, utterly naked. "It's fine, though. I'm sure you have some kind of control freak mental hang-up that makes it hard to let loose. I get it. God knows I do. It's probably for the best."

Mindless, emotionally-charged sex is a unicorn I'm better off not chasing.

"You gave me what I wanted, so thank you very, very much…" I trail off as I finally notice his expression. Dark eyes narrowed, lips pursed in contemplation. I've annoyed him again.

"I mean it," I insist. "It was amazing—"

"Come with me," he says.

My poor, drunk brain can't compute a response. All I can think to say is, "Where?"

The grin returns, playfully stern. "To the party, beautiful."

I smile inwardly at the new nickname. An upgrade from pretty. Then smart, good-girl Tiffany manages to get a stranglehold on lusty-Tiffy just long enough for me to ask, "You want me to meet your family?"

It sounds suspicious. *Very* suspicious when paired with the fact that I can no longer get a solid read on him. His teasing grin could hide a million ulterior motives.

But when his fingers find a lock of my hair and toy with it, I forget a teensy bit of the paranoia.

"It's just a party," he says—though were someone to tell that to my mother about one of her carefully crafted soirees, she just might reach for a kitchen knife with murderous intent. Something in his tone robs all sentimentality from the term, at least in this instance.

"Admittedly, it's in another city, but I'm willing to fly you there and arrange for your transportation back, all at no expense to you."

"Could you even get a ticket this late? You're leaving in…" I glance at a clock hanging on the wall, and a panicked bit of despair leeches into my tone. "Roughly one hour."

So darn soon. Thus ends Tiffy's first foray into sexual exploration. And darn was it fun.

"Come with me," Vadim insists. "It's a private plane, so no ticket required. We'll get in by the morning. You can have the day to shop. The party is in the evening, and you can be on a flight back before the night ends. And," he adds, presumably to present the tempting carrot to my desperate mule. "In exchange, I'll grant you an exclusive membership to my club. Granted, it's in Fair Haven, on the East coast, so you will have to find your own way back, should you decide to utilize it."

I pout and roll off him to contemplate my options. He's managed to present a multitude of both tempting and grounding proposals in one go, all neatly wrapped with a bow.

A whirlwind day to distract from having to dip my toe in the businessman waters again.

A guaranteed trip back.

A membership to a bona fide sex club.

And, a shopping trip thrown in, presumably all-expenses paid.

But the part I find surprisingly bracing is his casual acknowledgment that we're done after that. No contact, and should I one day wander into his sex club, it will be on my own dime and time.

Fair enough.

"Will we have sex again?" I wonder. I'm shocked by how much I'm hoping for a yes. A chance to experience him again and give my fellatio skills another go. A chance to see what might lurk beneath his invisible mask.

"No," he says, dashing my hopes. "I don't mean to offend you, but I don't think you're my type. I hope I didn't give you the wrong impression."

I wince. His rejection hurts more than it should, though it certainly explains a lot. His amusement. The invisible wall. The fact that he stopped short of handcuffing me just to keep me off his cock. There certainly is a bit of irony to it, though. I started this night uninterested, only now I can't get his smirk out of my head. Or those eyes. Or his scent…

Leaving now would be the smart, responsible thing to do.

"What would my shopping budget be?" I ask him instead.

He chuckles. "The sky is the limit."

Somehow, I keep my eyes from bugging out. Humming in contemplation, I tap my chin, thinking it over. "Tempting, tempting…"

"But you still aren't sold?" He rolls over and captures my chin, making me face him. Eyes glittering like coals, he takes me in from my hair all the way down to my still curling toes. "What can I do to seal the deal?"

I sigh, suddenly exhausted. The alcohol is finally taking its toll on my brain, dulling my senses and making me sluggish. Finding the strength to answer him at all is a challenge, but one I feel obligated to accept. "Fine. Tell me what about me changed your mind."

Because he *had* been interested. I could tell from the way he looked at me in the bar—that quick, fleeting glance when I started to walk away.

"You don't like redheads? My tits are too small?" I fondle said tits morosely. "I can handle it. Promise." I lift my pinky in solemn solidarity.

"Don't take it personally," he scolds while propping his chin on his fist. The elevated position allows him to stare down on me, unreadable as my eyelids grow heavier by the second. "Personal preference is no insult."

"I know that." I'm pouting, but I'm far too gone to care. "Still want to hear it, though."

"You're too unpredictable," he says. "I prefer my trysts to be…uncomplicated."

"That's it?" I roll my eyes, and they wind up closing for good. I'm too exhausted to open them again. "Talk about a shitty reason."

"Oh?"

"Yes," I snap, suddenly irritated, though the word comes out a slurred mixture between a whine and sigh. "No one *likes* the predictable. It's just that some men can't handle not controlling everything from their lifestyle, to when they come. I'm talking from experience," I add, in case he decides to challenge me.

But he doesn't.

Confusion spurs me to muster up just enough strength to crack open one eye to observe him.

And I gasp. He's angry. Truly, unashamedly angry. Fire crackles through his eyes, gathering in the corners of that supple mouth. I suck in a breath, recoiling.

"I don't think you'd like how I handle the unpredictable," he warns. My heart throbs in the face of it, my nerves zapping.

It's the sexiest, most alarming thing I've ever seen.

And it's the sight that haunts me as I finally pass out.

I groan, torn between writhing in agony and regretting the life choices that led me to this point. This point being lying on an unfamiliar bed, craving Tylenol with every fiber of my being, and cursing the effects of alcohol to hell and back.

The fact that I don't know where I am or how I got here can be addressed later.

At the moment, all I can do is peel my eyes open and scan my surroundings for any hint of immediate danger—and, or, a bathroom. *Bingo!* In a blurred sea of navy blue walls and blinding windows, I spot an open door that looks promising enough.

Somehow, I stagger to my feet, feeling out for whatever I can find to steady my balance. When my bare toes finally leave plush carpeting for what feels like cold tile, I sink to my knees and crawl toward a porcelain basin that has never looked so beautiful before.

From my murky teenage recollections, I remember that the easiest way for me to cure a hangover has been to vomit. Purge whatever is left in my system and then crawl into a steaming hot shower until the life returns to my limbs.

The shower in this bathroom is a huge, imposing rectangle of glass. An LED panel seems to control it but appears to need the wisdom of an electronics engineer to utilize it. Groaning, I press buttons and curse until water gushes in from about ten thousand showerheads. It's freezing cold, and I scream as the spray hits me.

But it will do.

Time to collect yourself, Tiffy, the stern, good-girl part of me warns, fully resurrected. *Try to remember what happened. How big of a mess do you need to salvage this time?*

Hmm... Well, I vaguely remember scoping out someone handsome at the bar. Very handsome, the tingle in my belly tells me. But I can't escape the sense that something was wrong with him. So wrong that he's no longer an option— not that I was looking for anything long-term anyway.

We went to his room, I think.

And then... We had sex. Which explains why my pussy is throbbing like hell, and my lips feel swollen. We had very good, very impersonal sex. Then we talked for what felt like hours, and I agreed to come with him...somewhere.

Gosh, what was his name? Gorgo? Vlad…*Vadim.*

And he, apparently, is nowhere to be found. Nice.

"You brought it on yourself, Tiffy," I scold myself out loud. My teeth are chattering, and once I feel coherent enough to form a more solid thought other than—*holy crap what have I done*—I fiddle with the panel until the water turns off, and then I crawl out of the stall.

The bathroom itself is enormous. White marble creates a crisp, clean color scheme that makes me feel like something dirty and unwanted that slithered in through the drain. I'm still wearing my beautiful, now ruined "sexual revolution dress," though I don't know where the faux fur jacket is, or my shoes for that matter.

Using the wall for balance, I manage to wrap a towel around myself and reenter the room I woke up in.

Make that, the *executive suite* I woke up in. A massive bed dominates the center of a sleek, modern room composed of navy walls interspersed with floor to ceiling windows that display a skyscraper laden view of a city. A vast, industrial city a world apart from sleepy Main Oaks, California.

Thrown over a leather armchair in the corner of the room is my jacket, with my shoes neatly placed on the floor nearby. The place apparently comes with its own soundtrack as well—a persistent, high-pitched ringing…

Oh. I spot a silver phone on a glass end table near the bed and warily approach it. "H-Hello?" I whisper after bringing the receiver to my ear.

"You're awake," a musically accented voice remarks. "Good. You slept in later than expected. You have only three hours to find something to wear. Our budget will remain as discussed."

"B-Budget?" I frown, rubbing my forehead. "I'm sorry… who is this?"

A low, devious chuckle serves to kick start my memory. *Vadim.*

"I believe you should avoid mixing your liquor with wine from now on, Ms. Connors," he says, playing with the syllables in my name. "I'll be around to pick you up at six. In the meantime, I've informed the hotel to allow you unlimited use of a town car and driver. Feel free to shop where you like. The driver has a card for you to use. My only stipulation is that you find something sexy. The more revealing, the better."

"Sexy?" My breathing hitches as I take the card as though it's made of glass. Memories are starting to come back to me, one in particular that still smarts. "I thought you said we weren't going to have sex."

"We aren't," he states matter of factly. "But my brother surrounds himself with a certain type of crowd. I don't want you to stand out."

Fair enough. "Where are you?" I wonder, gazing from the window. "Where are *we?*"

"Fair Haven," he says as though I asked him what color the sky was. "As for where I am, I had some business to see to. Until tonight. Oh, and if you need to change your dress, I arranged to have an outfit bought for you. It's in the closet."

He hangs up, leaving my brain reeling. Frowning, I stumble around the room until I find a sliding wooden door that conceals a walk-in closet. Inside, on a single hanger hangs a lone white sundress. It's not too shabby, though a bit conservative for my tastes. My new tastes anyway.

I slip it on and wrestle some semblance of humanity into my hair and splash water onto my face. When I reach the hotel lobby, I'm surprised to find an aura that feels more exclusive than the Six. Gold walls and polished black floors convey decadent luxury. A concierge even comes to meet me right at the elevator.

"You must be Ms. Connors," he says warmly. "William is already bringing the car around. Can I get you anything while you wait? Coffee? Tea? A glass of wine, perhaps?"

Still suffering from my current hangover, I nearly choke. "N-No thanks."

He ushers me into a private booth as I wait, and when the driver arrives, he professes his intent to wait for me as long as required.

A smile tugs on my mouth for the first time as I enter the back of a sleek silver vehicle.

This might be fun.

CURSING, I attempt to swipe my room key through the reader while juggling an armful of shopping bags. Finally, success! I kick open the door and hop inside, only to scream as my eyes settle over a figure glowering in the center of the sprawling suite.

"I told you six," Vadim snaps. He's already dressed in a sleek ebony suit, tailored to perfection. His dark curls conform to his skull, slightly mussed. Capping off the look is a blood-red tie that betrays a hint of the daring nature I've come to suspect he regularly suppresses. "We're going to be late…"

He trails off when he notices the army of bags at my disposal.

"Hear me out," I plead, holding up my hands in a gesture of surrender. "I couldn't decide what to wear. And then traffic was hell. And…" I fish through my bags and brandish a luxuriously wrapped package in triumph. "I got your brother a gift. And his wife, if he has one." I wield a second gift in my opposite hand and smile as sweetly as I physically can.

"He has a fiancée," Vadim grunts, still surly.

So I resort to plan B and start to shimmy out of my dress. "Don't hate me until you see the options," I say in a rush. "Option one—" I snatch a garment from a black bag betraying the name of a designer I used to worship back when I had the lack of brains and excess funds to spend on clothing. A deep shade of navy, the slim-fitting cocktail dress sets off the red in my hair and conforms to my shape. Sexy, but modestly so.

"No," Vadim says, observing me with a frown. "It is a party, not a church service."

"Ah." So maybe life with Jim is harder to shake than I thought? No matter. Skipping to another bag, I dig out my second option.

"No," he growls before I can even pull it on—a black, moderately more revealing mini dress.

"Okay. Big guns, then. Now when you said sexy, I hope you meant…stripper. Because that is this dress." I reach for my final option, and his eyes narrow thoughtfully. When it isn't met with instant rejection, I tug it on, wrenching the tiny frock down over my hips.

It's a *not-safe-for-work-fuck-me* dress in Jessica Rabbit scarlet with her flair for the daring. A bold, plunging neckline reveals the globes of both my breasts, and the view extends almost to my navel. The back is equally low cut, but given the quality of the fabric, it's admittedly more high-class escort than stripper.

"This will do," Vadim says. He lunges forward and grabs my wrist, dragging me from the room before I can even get my bearings.

"W-Wait—"

"We're late," he growls. He must not have been kidding about things being tense between him and his brother. I only manage to slip on my heels and grab the two presents before I find myself tugged into the elevator, dragged from the hotel, and promptly shoved within a scarlet sports car waiting out front.

Vadim takes the wheel, still scowling.

I feel drawn to tap his shoulder once, my frown apologetic. "I'm sorry," I say as he pulls into traffic. "I'm terrible with time management. Jim—I mean… Some people used to say I'd miss the rapture because I'd just have to go back and grab the perfect tube of lipstick to wear through the holy gates."

He doesn't laugh.

I try another tack. "Do you live here in Fair Haven?"

Still no answer.

Sighing, I sit back in my seat and wring my fingers together. "If you're angry with me, you might as well just yell about it. Otherwise, I'll talk and talk to fill the silence. I can't stand it to be honest. I would rather be boiled alive than—"

"So it wasn't the wine that made you so talkative." His tone is so cutting, I wince.

"*Touché*, Mr. Gorgoshev. I… Are you okay?"

He's shivering, his body vibrating over the seat. His teeth chatter, but his eyes are narrowed and focused.

I fumble with the dials on the console until the heat kicks on.

"Maybe I should check for a fever—"

"I'd prefer it if you stopped talking, please," he says, still devastatingly polite.

I fall silent, stung for reasons I can't name. For all of his surliness, I hate the fact that I might have disappointed him.

It isn't long before we pull up before what I assume is the entrance to a private stretch of property along a waterfront, just beyond the city limits. Without a word of warning to me, Vadim strikes the button that lowers the window on his end.

"I was *invited*," he says, but his voice is sharper than the low, delicious hum I'm used to. It's cold, and the contrast has me sitting straighter in my seat. He's speaking to a man who came seemingly from nowhere, dressed in black to blend in with the shadowed surroundings. An earpiece is attached to his left ear, which he fingers while murmuring something too softly for me to make out. Then he nods us forward.

"You can go."

A smug, icy expression dominates Vadim's features, exaggerating the harsher lines of his face and diminishing the softness. I'm tempted to try probing him again—something more than my tardiness has to be bothering him—but then I spy the structure looming before us at the end of a long driveway, and I promptly lose my train of thought.

"Holy crap, it's beautiful," I murmur.

The house is far from the gaudy, showy properties I grew up in and among. The architecture alone conveys wealth, but subtly. Warm light emanating from within highlights the stone base with rustic accents of wood and beautiful, arched windows displaying a snippet of the home's interior where several people mill about a wide, spacious room.

Excitement sneaks in, nibbling away at any lingering doubt. While navigating a surly millionaire—sorry, supposed *billionaire*—is a new experience, if there's one thing I know, it's parties. Juggling the presents in both hands, I watch Vadim exit the car, and I let loose a relieved sigh as he crosses to my end and opens the door for me.

"I'll be good, I promise," I tell him with a smile.

But he isn't even looking in my direction. He eyes the house up ahead as though it's a battlefield. One he's willing to dominate at all costs.

A shiver of unease runs through me as I follow him, finding my balance in my new—and higher—stilettos. A paved stone path leads to a wide porch at the front of the house. We've barely managed to mount the first step when the door flies open so brutally it slams into the wall and ricochets off with a sound like a gunshot.

Startled, I jump and nearly trip off the steps entirely, but Vadim's hand captures my hip, righting my balance.

"You dare come here?" a man demands, his voice heavily accented and booming like thunder. I have to crane my neck back to take him in; he's so tall. So huge. A wall of muscle, he nearly consumes the entire doorway, barely leaving space for the startled people standing behind him. He radiates fury, his expression so cold I'm instantly chilled and find myself inching closer to Vadim.

Not that he's a beacon of warmth at the moment—he's trembling even more than before.

"Let him in, Maxim," a softer, less stern voice commands from within the house. A British accent plays with the speaker's pronunciation, making every word sound stern yet polite. "Tell me, is causing a scene really worth it? Now? Here?"

Maxim, presumably the big man, finally stands aside. Light from inside the house spills out, illuminating the long blond hair streaming down his shoulders. Angular features craft a handsome, if stern, face, and his eyes are so dark, they seem to feed on the shadows.

"If it breaks the tension, I invited him," the British speaker insists. A dark-haired man steps forward, wearing a gunmetal gray suit. He's alluringly handsome, but something in his gaze makes me look away rather than ogle. Wolves are pretty too, but even I know better than to make eye contact with one.

"Come, Dima," he adds. "I'm sure you came here only to celebrate with us."

I know a warning not to piss on the couch when I hear it. Usually, said warnings are directed toward me. *Be good, Tiffy. Don't fuck this up, Tiffy. Just be fucking normal, Tiffany!*

"I'll try to be on my very best behavior," Vadim simpers. The shift in his personality is even more palpable now. I glance over to find his eyes flashing, ignited with that mischievous gleam times a million.

Uh, oh. A part of me warns. *What the hell have I stepped into?*

All I can do is follow all three men into the house where I quickly realize that—one, it's just as beautiful as the outside. Two, if sexy was the dress code, then I'm the only person who got the memo.

In addition to the three men, two women linger on the outskirts of a massive, open floor plan living room. Both wear modest and yet fashionable black gowns presumably tailored to their individual preferences. A slender brunette wears hers slightly short, but with a conservative neckline while a striking blond models a slightly longer design with fashionable sleeves. Though, strangely, she looks just as uncomfortable as I feel being here, her large eyes darting between all three men.

It doesn't take me long to realize what might be guiding their fashion choices—the presence of children. Small ones. Bigger ones. At least six in total stand scattered throughout the room. A little boy with huge brown eyes takes one look at me and scampers over to a small girl with long sandy hair. "You can see her boobies," he stage-whispers to her.

And I feel slapped. Used. My entire body tenses up with the realization that he urged me to dress this way on purpose. To cause a scene. Prove a point. It's happened before—being the girl who arrives to a party braless in a thin white T-shirt because she was stupid enough to fall for the "It's a charity wet T-shirt contest" line.

Humiliation washes over me in crippling, searing waves, and all I want to do is sink into the floor and die. Old Tiffy would have. She would have crumbled to pieces and run from this room in tears. She would have berated herself for being so stupid. So weak. She would be an easy target.

But I'm not her anymore.

Reigning in the shame takes all of five seconds. I jut out my chin into the air, square my shoulders, and plaster a charming grin on my face the likes of which would make my mother proud.

"Oh gosh, I am so sorry," I declare, laughing politely. *Haha, silly me.* "Poor Vadim tried to warn me that this dress might be a bit much, but I didn't pay him any mind." I turn to him and playfully slap him on the forearm—hard. If he notices the hostility, his expression doesn't show it. "If it isn't too much trouble, could I borrow a jacket or a shawl?"

"Here, Miss." An older gentleman steps forward and shrugs his own suit jacket from his shoulders, offering it to me.

I shimmy into it, balancing my gifts. I can sense Vadim watching me from the corner of my eye, the bastard. Smiling harder, I turn the charm up to eleven.

"You must be the brother," I exclaim, turning to the dark-haired man. It's a logical guess, considering his hair color, but when I glance at the blond man, I realize my mistake. No two creatures could possess eyes that shade by accident. "My apologies. *You* are the brother," I declare, turning to him. Smiling prettily, I extend my gift and force myself to meet his cold, piercing stare. "I'm Tiffany. Thank you so much for inviting us. We picked out something small to show our appreciation." When he doesn't take the present, I laugh nervously. Desperate for an escape, I set it down on a nearby end table instead. "And your fiancée must be..." I pivot and spot the two women again. The blond eyes me, her expression unreadable, but the brunette looks as uncomfortable as a deer in the headlights. *Bingo.*

"You must be the fiancée!" I cross to her and nearly sigh in relief when she accepts the gift.

"I'm Francesca," she says softly. Her voice lacks an accent, at least, but she's young. Really young. I do a double take of Vadim's brother, and I have to fight back the inner judgmental voice wondering just how young she truly is.

"Well, I'm so sorry we made a scene," I say, returning to Vadim's side. He's rigid, unmoving even as I grasp his hand and shamelessly dig my nails into the palm of it.

He'll pay for this later. Oh, he will so pay. But for now, I know it's better to play my part and bide my time. No one will ever make a fool of me again, out of spite or otherwise.

"So, what are we celebrating?" I ask.

The two brooding men share a look.

"An engagement," Vadim says before either one can offer up an answer themselves.

"Lovely!" I clap my hands, my smile beaming. "Congratulations!"

I swear everyone flinches.

But I take the awkward tension as a challenge. I will survive this, so help me, God.

Or I will gleefully take Vadim down with me.

CHAPTER SIX

When it comes to parties and how to play them to their fullest, there is no match for a mansion born, cotillion raised Connors socialite. I learned from the best—Genevieve Mackenzie Adalynn Connors, who operated her events with me balanced on her hip while juggling a serving tray and a hospitable smile.

She had the grace and charm required to turn any hostile gathering into a soiree so warm and welcoming; she could sow world peace if the room were big enough. Emulating her, I only manage to simmer what tensions lurk between these men to the barest minimum—and I'm nearly sweating with the effort.

Dinner is an awkward lesson in how to juggle the tersest small talk with a grin and a funny quip.

"So when is your wedding?" I ask, referring to the supposed reason for this "party."

Maxim and his fiancée share a searching glance. "Soon,"

he says in a tone that makes me scramble for my glass of wine. "It will be a *private* affair." His eyes slice in Vadim's direction with chilling intensity. I have a feeling he won't be getting an invite.

"What a shame," Vadim replies, his teeth bared. "I was so looking forward to witnessing the nuptials. Some might say we'd thought to never see the day you'd settle down with *one* of your women."

"I've always preferred intimate ceremonies," I blurt in a rush, parrying the incoming blow from Maxim before the man can even open his mouth. Across the table, poor Francesca's cheeks turn blood red though the children innocently chatter amongst themselves, oblivious. Thank God. "I wish I'd had a small wedding," I add wistfully. "Maybe a destination one?"

At least then, I could look back on the memories fondly. Instead, my only recollections consist of sweating in a massive gown bought on my parent's dime while being paraded before what seemed like the entire parish. That day, instead of marital bliss, my main takeaway from the experience is the memory of the pain from holding a fake smile in place for sixteen hours.

I'm so lost in the nostalgia that I barely notice the rest of the conversation has gone silent. Good. As far as social landscapes go, this one is my most challenging battlefield yet. I feel like I'm juggling knives. One wrong move, and everyone gets stabbed in the eye.

But I manage, with no assistance from the very man who brought me here.

Something happens to him in the presence of his brother. Something dark that festers within him, seeping out in cold, icy sarcasm and glittering, unreadable eyes.

It's the eyes that unnerve me the most. His wall is back in place, higher than ever. Insurmountable.

"At least you're dressed fucking decently," his brother hisses as we get through most of the first course. "Have you grown bored of crawling in the shadows, luring children away?"

The British man, Milton, lifts his hand and pinches the bridge of his nose.

"I have," Vadim replies with a manic grin. He's still shivering, more noticeably than before. I can't resist slipping my hand into his pocket, hoping to provide some warmth—but he recoils from me so violently he jolts the entire table.

"This has been lovely," he says, lurching to his feet in an enviable display of grace. "Sadly, we must be going."

"Awww!" The little girl whines from her spot near the end of the table. "You have to go now?"

"Ainsley…" Francesca cuts her gaze in the girl's direction, her tone a warning.

Undeterred, Ainsley pouts. "I wanted to show you my pony, Uncle Dima."

"Some other time," he says before taking a gallant bow.

"Wait." Milton inclines his head toward Maxim. Something wordlessly passes between the two of them. Then Milton turns to Vadim. "Dinner," he says. "Neutral territory. Next week?"

Vadim says nothing and starts from the room, leaving me to follow. At the door, I return the jacket to the older man, and by the time I leave the house, Vadim is already at the car.

With his back to me, he palms the door. "You survived." He has the nerve to sound surprised at that. Impressed.

"Fuck. You," I spit, utilizing the dirtiest word in my newfound freedom-vocabulary. When he whirls around, an eyebrow cocked in amusement; I lose any shred of restraint. Leveling him with my nastiest glare, I go off. "You used me. You dragged me here, for what? To make your brother think you disrespected him by bringing some stupid slut around his children? To his home? What the hell is wrong with you?"

"Plenty." His jaw clenches, his expression icier than ever. "You earned this, I suppose," he says, flicking something at me too quickly to catch. Thin, rectangular, and silver, it lands at my feet—some type of business card. "When you make a reservation, use my name," he states. "Otherwise, you won't be allowed entry."

I eye the card again, recognizing it for what it is. The price of my humiliation, it seems—entrance to some exclusive sex club.

"You know what? Screw you!" I flip him the finger and start down the driveway, staggering in my heels. "Do you know how you made me feel?"

"Inconvenienced?" he guesses in that cutting tone. "The feeling was mutual, I can assure you—"

"Sabotaged," I snap, whirling to face him. "Insulted. Humiliated. Hurt. I told myself a long time ago that I would never let anyone ever make me feel that way again."

Go figure. I've failed in that respect.

"Consider it practice for when you bare yourself before strangers who only want to fuck you," he suggests. "I do hope you enjoy the amenities. I hear they're quite debauched."

My cheeks flame and something inside me snaps. "Practice? Oh, trust me, I don't need any practice. After that night with you, I'm *desperate* to be ogled by someone who doesn't think he's too good to have his cock sucked."

His eyes widen and narrow in quick succession. Did I hit a sore spot? Gosh, I hope so.

"Does this get you off rather than fucking?" I wonder, gesturing around us with a harsh, cackling laugh. "Bringing me all the way across the country to what? Get under your brother's skin? Hurt some sleazy slut who had the nerve to approach you? Well, sorry to break it to you, but I'm fine, Vadim. I am more than fine!" I stroll past him and stoop for the business card, brandishing it like a hard-fought trophy. "You know what, I will go get ogled by strangers, and I'm going to enjoy every fucking minute of it! I'm going to fuck as many men as I can, too. Suck every last cock that will have me, and then…" My chest heaves, my body radiating anger, and I have to gulp down enough air just to keep going. "I'm going to compare every last one of them to yours. How they feel. How they taste. From now on, I'm going to keep a running tally of all the bastards who fuck better than Vadim Gorgoshev could ever dream. Choke on that while you're on your private plane."

Card in tow, I keep marching down the driveway, blinking rapidly. *Almost there, Tiffy,* I plead with my inner waterworks. *Just a little more. You can make it.*

"Oh, and don't think you've stranded me or that I'll be crying out on the street tonight," I shout back to Vadim. "Call and have the hotel switch the room over to me. I can pay for it. Have a good fucking night, Vadim. I hope you run into a beautiful escort, one-hundred percent your type who fleeces you for all you're worth."

"You really think you can walk back to the city?" he wonders in a voice like steel.

I flick my hair over my shoulder and walk faster. "Watch me."

He makes a sound between a grunt and scoff. Not even a full minute later, his sports car is racing past me, leaving me in the dust.

I wave at him with none of the decorum befitting a well-bred lady.

Then I suck in air, wobble on my heels, and the tears start coming down hard. I must get lost—enough for someone from the house to take pity on me. It isn't long before another car pulls up alongside me. The driver is the same kind-eyed figure who let me borrow his jacket.

"Can I give you a ride, Miss?" he says, his tone polite.

I sniffle and nod, climbing into the backseat.

Then I endure the ride into the city, plotting the next phase of my adventure—shameless, sexual revenge.

CHAPTER SEVEN

I can't actually afford the hotel room by myself. Realistically, anyway. I can last about three days tops, and that's if I completely decimate what little savings I have. I could always call my parents, but I've suffered enough of their pity to last a lifetime. Besides, I'd rather not deal with Daddy bribing me to come back home or hear my mother cry about "the state of my only little girl's life" one more time.

So I approach the front desk, ready and willing to swallow the cost no matter the pain.

"I'm sorry," the hostess informs me, frowning at her computer screen. "It looks like the room has already been paid in full for the week, complete with an open tab for room service."

I frown. Could Vadim be planning to claim the suite for himself? What a dick. He might already be there right now, screwing some blond escort submissive enough to fit his preferences.

"You are listed as the room's primary occupant," the hostess adds, scouring her records. "Ms. Connors, correct? It looks like the change was just freshly made. About an hour ago. I could always refund the card on record—"

"No." I turn on my heel and head for the elevator, squashing all doubt. "Thanks for your help."

I reenter the suite to find my bags where I left them and everything else in place, though neatly arranged, the bed turned down by some over-eager housekeeper.

So this must be Vadim's idea of the ultimate kiss-off. Leave me in an unfamiliar city. Pay off the incredibly expensive room he stuck me in. Leave without a trace.

And I thought Jim could be an asshole.

Dejected, I sink onto the bed and sob in earnest. I let out every ugly, choking, nasty cry and allow the tears to stream down my cheeks in earnest. Then I find the remote to a flat-screen TV hidden behind a pair of black curtains hanging across from the bed, turn to the music channels, and find the most upbeat pop imaginable. I play it as loud as I dare, shed my dress, and then hop into the bathroom and face myself in the mirror.

Years wasted in a loveless marriage can teach a girl a lot of things. Like that, no one—no gosh darn one—is worth losing your self-respect for. No one can make you feel any lower than you allow them to, and no one should ever rob you of your smile.

I smile now, displaying my teeth at the exhausted woman before me.

"You are confident," I tell her. "You are bold, and vivacious, and sexy. And—" A new addition to my mantra, but ad-libbing is all part of the exploration of freedom. "You are going to march into that sex club and own the darn place! Vadim, who?"

I manage to work the shower properly and then crawl into bed, feeling fresh and renewed. This might be a setback, sure.

Or it could be the real start to my adventures in sexual freedom.

I wake up and order from room service, half-convinced that the card on file will be declined, and Vadim Gorgoshev will have the last fucking laugh. But not even ten minutes later, my meal arrives steaming hot and I feel bold enough to write a generous tip on the napkin afterward with a message to charge to the account.

After changing into the blue dress from my shopping spree, I head down to the concierge and request assistance in finding a flight straight back to California, ASAP. Sure, I told Vadim I'd go to his little sex club and orgy myself silly. But that was just a boast made in the heat of the moment, right?

"I've found two flights, Miss," the concierge says, drawing my attention. "Both don't leave until tomorrow morning. Should I book one for you?"

"There isn't one sooner? Tonight, at least?"

He shakes his head apologetically. "I'm afraid not. Though, if you're looking to kill time, I've been informed that you are still authorized to use the town car should you require it."

"Alright, I'll take the earliest flight. Thanks anyway." Frowning, I accept the booking information he gives me and then return to the room, feeling more trapped than free.

But then I spot it. It being a platinum, no-limit, fancy smanshy credit card that Vadim gave me for my dress. I could have sworn I'd returned it to him. Even thinking about using it now would be both illegal and reckless. Not to mention petty as hell.

Minutes later, I'm in the town car, directing William to the shopping district I'd scoped out yesterday. I find my favorite designer—whose clothing I couldn't afford guilt-free, even while on my parent's tap—and I march in, guns blazing.

I buy the sexiest dress I've ever seen in my entire life and shoes to match. And the purse. And the complementary faux fur stole and diamond-studded belt.

It's the outfit heist of the century, and I'm fully resigned to have the card declined as the salesgirl goes to ring me up. It's the thought that counts—one last screw you to the bastard who hurt me way more than I'd like to admit. Not just the whole *"I used you to embarrass my brother and his family because I am a dick"* thing. Maybe my irritation has less to do with that and more to do with…

The whole *"I don't want to fuck you, or get sucked off by you, and by the way, you're not even my type"* thing.

Hurt pride is a vengeful, nasty animal—one best soothed with lots of retail therapy.

"I'm sorry," I blurt as the saleswoman returns, brandishing the card. "My husband probably cut me off. It's for the best—"

"Having cold feet?" she wonders, glancing at my spoils of war. "It went through, but if you like, I can cancel the charges?"

"No!" I lurch to my feet, my thirst for vengeance suddenly renewed. "I'll take them all, please. And let's throw in one or two of those brooches to match. And I'd love to see your jewelry collection. And how about some more shoes?"

WILLIAM DRIVES me to the address listed on Vadim's little sex club calling card, and my cheeks burn the entire trip. My heart skips too, partly terrified, partly excited.

I don't know what to expect when the car finally comes to a stop before this mysterious Club XXX.

A place that looks like the gate to a sleek, exclusive corner of hell, isn't it. My mouth falls open as I take in the remote building formed of bold, eye-catching lines. It's a gothic mixture of the macabre and the modern. Turrets stab at the indigo sky, creating a striking silhouette against a forested backdrop. The entrance itself consists of stone columns framing a black door, trimmed in glittering gold. A stone path leads to it before forking into a massive circular driveway like some beckoning gesture.

Any doubt I felt dissolves as my lips part into a massive grin. Color me impressed.

I approach the door warily, discovering no doorman or bouncer waiting to deny entry. It's as if the act of palming the handle itself is the only method required—a dare all on its own. *Are you even brave enough?*

I hold my breath as I push my way inside, entering a world of black marble and gray walls ripped right from my most deranged fantasies. Granite floors accent the circular foyer, making every footstep echo times a thousand. There is no sign, it seems, proclaiming "sex rooms this way." Just three silver Xs adorning the space above a curving archway across from the entrance serving as the only advertisement. Two other arches frame it, each leading off into different directions.

Pulsating music emanating from the leftmost one serves to cast a mysterious aura, and all I can do is see where it takes me.

I follow a wide hall to another archway and discover my first clue that the place isn't entirely deserted. A man stands beside it, dressed in a black shirt and slacks. Authority radiates from his stern gaze and, without thinking, I hand him the business card.

"Vadim sent me?" Why I make it a question, I have no idea.

He looks it over and then nods, presumably giving me permission to enter.

Here goes nothing…

I take a few steps forward and nearly faint. What at first looks like a typical—though decadent—lounge turns out to be so much more on second glance. A long ebony-topped bar dominates one end, and an L-shaped stage divides the room in half on the other. Crowning the space is a row of floor-to-ceiling windows providing a view of the darkness beyond.

And it is better than I could have hoped.

Décor consisting of black leather with bright drops of blood-red accents crafts such a sexy allure I almost squeal. The icing on the cake, however, is the clientele milling about the massive room. Everyone here makes my red party dress from last night look like a nun's frock in comparison. Beautiful women wear strips of leather and silk masquerading as dresses while men shamelessly parade in a mixture of suits or less.

I instantly feel oddly...at home. When an elegantly clad server comes to take my jacket, I relinquish it eagerly. And with renewed determination, I delve into my newly found freedom.

I know firsthand that the absolute worst thing you can do to someone is pretend that they no longer exist. Not in the petty, childish way you might ostracize them on the playground. No. This level of indifference requires skill and tact. You acknowledge the person, of course. You simper and utter all the right niceties as if they were anyone else—that's the key to it. As if they were anyone else. Someone meaningless without a string of memories attached to them.

Someone whose name didn't require remembering.

Someone worthless. Thus, such is the ultimate blow I swore I would never ever inflict upon someone no matter how much I hated them.

Until now. Hate has nothing to do with it, just pride. So the icy cool businessman came to see how I would play in his world? Well, I can thrive, regardless of his presence.

Let him watch and learn.

He arrives just when I start to let my guard down enough to take a stool at the bar. Acclimating to a debauched club is a surprisingly gradual experience. One can't merely jump in and star in a six-person gang bang right out of the gate. Fitting in requires confidence and finesse—like the time when I felt old enough to enter the sauna at my parent's country club. I couldn't let my unease show on my face or Barb—a bitchy socialite who liked to gossip in said sauna— would have sent me out on my butt the second I entered.

No. I had to play the game and meld seamlessly into the background. Which I've been doing here, until now. It's not like I'm waiting for him to show up—but the entire room notices when he does.

Dressed in a black suit tailored close to his frame, the bastard arrives with an aura comparable to a king making an entrance with a full retinue. Though alone, he oozes… ownership. Like he's too good to step foot in this club, let alone fuck anyone in it. He's merely here to observe, for his own entertainment.

And it seems I may be his main attraction. Is his aim to gloat? His eyes dart in my direction, and I turn away, keeping my smile intact. Inside, I'm seething, and when the bartender appears before me, I order my Achilles heel.

"A sangria, please," I say. "Don't water it down."

He nods, and then I scan my nearest surroundings for someone, anyone. I told him I was going to spend my night sucking cock. Well, darn it, that's just what I'll do. On my third perusal of the room, I notice a man advancing in my direction. Dressed in a tailored suit, he's probably a businessman and disgustingly rich.

When he raises a sensually questioning eyebrow, I simper in response. *Target acquired.* I beckon him over with a wave just as my Sangria arrives to provide my reckless impulses extra ammunition.

He's tall. Blond. Not my type, but why does it matter? His body isn't bad to look at, and when he smiles, he's easy on the eyes if a bit older than I would have aimed for.

"I'm Tiffy," I tell him, extending my hand.

"Geoff," he replies in a husky baritone. "Pleased to make your acquaintance—" He breaks off suddenly and smoothly withdraws his hand. "I'm sorry. I didn't realize you were here with someone."

"Huh?" Following his alarmed gaze, I look over my shoulder and stiffen. Perched on a black couch nearly halfway across the room, Vadim sits facing my direction, a whiskey glass in hand. Judging from his casual, relaxed position, I don't think he's moved or said anything to give the impression we were together—but the expression on his face…

I feel a tug in my belly as if an invisible hook has caught the flesh and yanked. It's certainly not how he looked at me in the Six lounge, that's for darn sure. Mocking. Daring. …Possessive?

Easy, Tiffy, my inner bitch warns. *Eye on the prize.*

I blink innocently and squint at the aloof billionaire. Then I sigh and shake my head. "I'm sorry, but you're mistaken," I tell Geoff, turning back to him. "I've never seen that man before in my life."

"Oh." He frowns, confused, only to blink in shock when I palm his bicep, testing the give of the muscle. He's no surprisingly-built, slender waif, but he feels solid enough. Satisfied, I shift toward him and let my eyes glaze over, my smile warm.

"I'm here all alone," I tell him. "Keep me company?"

He grabs a nearby stool and pulls up beside me while I sip frantically on my sangria. By the time he brushes my hand, drawing my attention, my confident grin is back in place.

"Come here often?" he wonders, while internally, I cringe at what had been my tired and worn pick-up line not too long ago. Had it sounded so darn cliché when I said it?

No wonder Vadim lost interest.

Still smiling, I shake my head and eye him through my lashes. "This is my first time," I say, utilizing my sexy purr once more.

He falls for the bait hook, line, and sinker. His hand grazes my thigh as he grips the edge of my stool and tugs me closer to his.

"I could tell," he says confidently. "You look fresh. There is nothing like your first time, eh? I'm curious as to how a girl like you even found your way in a place like this."

Gag. Maintaining my simpering grin suddenly takes more effort, my teeth clenched. "I know a guy," I say.

Geoff raises an eyebrow, impressed. "You must have friends in high places. I feel like I had to sell my soul just to get an invite. The owner is selective as hell."

I file away the information for later. For some reason, I suspect he isn't referring to Vadim, given he didn't seem to recognize him. Who could his business partner be, I wonder?

"There are several owners actually," Geoff adds. "But Maxim runs this part of the club. If you're here, I assume you've heard of its reputation?" He glances me over, lingering on my cleavage while I take another sip of wine to disguise my shock.

Maxim owns this? His brother. I risk sneaking a glance at Vadim, more confused than ever. Zap! Our eyes meet with a jolt—it's like he knew I'd look at him. Knew I'd jump and turn away just in time to catch him sipping from his glass.

Damn it.

"Are you alright?" Geoff tucks a piece of my hair behind my ear, his tone concerned.

I nod, fighting to stay focused. "I'm fine." To prove it, I fixate stubbornly on his mouth, refusing to look anywhere else. Even as the back of my neck prickles with the uncomfortable knowledge that someone is watching *me*, daring me to notice.

"I'm looking for a teacher," I murmur, inclining my head to display my throat. "I'm very, *very* eager to learn."

"Good," Geoff murmurs, his smile dashing.

This is good. Better than good. Barely ten minutes in, and I've successfully infiltrated my first sex club. I even scored my first test subject. All is well.

As far as my list is concerned, *check, check.*

So why the hell am I shaking?

"I could oblige you," Geoff says with a resonating laugh. "I take it you don't have a private room yet?"

I sit forward, curious enough to ignore everything else. Private, he says? Whatever it is sounds absolutely delicious. I decide on the spot that I must experience one before the night's end. "No," I say. "For now."

"Good." He grabs a napkin and fishes a pen from his breast pocket. After scribbling a number onto the corner of it, he hands the napkin to me. "Come join me when you've finished your drink. I'll head up first and...prepare it for your first lesson." He looks me over from head to toe, and any other day I would be elated by the attention. Actual, lustful male attention.

As it stands, all I feel is…anxious. My palms are slick, my heart racing. I must still be hungover.

"Let me walk you out," I suggest as Geoff starts for the exit. I step up to him, linking my arm with his. "So, I can see which direction you go."

We start for the main hall and nearly run smack dab into a man who seemingly appears from nowhere to rudely block our path.

"Pardon," Geoff hisses.

I merely smile sweetly and pat the stranger on his arm as I would do for anyone who nearly ran me over. "Excuse me," I say, slipping past him.

Deep down, I sense something in the atmosphere shift—a warning drop in the air pressure like the kind that proceeds a bad storm. Oblivious, Geoff runs his fingers down my arm and then enters the hall, heading for an archway opposite the club floor.

"There are the stairs," he tells me. "The rooms are on the second floor."

"Ah," I nod and flutter my eyelashes. The second he's gone from view, I retreat to the bar and down my sangria as if it's the antidote to nerves. I'm not approached once. When I finally finish, I enter the hall while telling myself with every step that I can do this.

I had sex with one stranger on a drunken whim. What's another? And hopefully another?

But this pang in my chest won't ease no matter how many ways I envision sucking off Geoff. The stairs he referenced lurk at the end of another hall and curve to join a split-level landing that overlooks the main foyer, unseen from the first floor. The rooms themselves must be behind a row of polished, ebony doors. Geoff's is apparently near the end.

Sighing, I square my shoulders and march forward. *You can do this, Tiffy. One step after the other...*

Or not. A hand grabs my arm, and someone drags me into a room at least four doors away from Geoff. Stunned, I wrench away from them and whirl around, a scream poised at the back of my throat.

In the end, it escapes my lips as a hiss instead.

Vadim glowers, looking so beautiful it hurts. His eyes are even more electric, his jaw clenched, his posture broadcasting authority. It's such a contrast to his icy, closed-off persona from the other night. I feel my throat dampen.

At least before I remember that I hate him.

"What do you want?" I demand when he doesn't speak. "To have me mentally scar a few more children?" I gesture to my outfit—it's ten times more revealing than my ensemble from last night. A black, skintight mini dress leaves little to the imagination, and two slits on either side go up so high they might as well touch my armpits.

"You came." Vadim's eyes rake over me, dark and unreadable. I came—and he doesn't sound too thrilled about that. Why? Did he really think I'd run back to Cali and let him keep his little club all to himself?

"Leave me alone," I snap, ignoring how his gaze lingers over my partially exposed breasts. Turning on my heel, I march for the door.

"Wait—" He grasps my wrist, yanking me right back.

"What?" I whip around to face him again, snatching my hand back. "Why are you even here?"

"Curiosity," he grates coldly, though I get the sense that he responded to me without thinking. His attention is otherwise consumed—rapt, his gaze traces me again, and I can't suppress a shiver in response. "I wondered if you were serious," he murmurs, eyeing an exposed sliver of my hip. "Or..."

"Ha!" I throw my head back for a nasty laugh. "Or if I was bluffing? Oh, I was *so* serious. Bachelor number one is already lined up. Curious as to how you stack up? Stick around, and you just may find out."

"I...apologize," he grits out, as if it physically pains him to admit as much. "If you were offended."

"Offended?" I don't know whether to laugh at him or give him the finger. "You treated me like a stupid slut. Of course, I was offended. Now get out of my way!"

"*Ta gueule*," he hisses, shifting to block my path once more. "Let me speak—"

"Don't you dare cuss at me in another language," I snarl, recognizing his tone though I don't understand the term. French? "And listen to you? I think not. Now, excuse me, stranger whom I've never met before. Stop following me." I wave him off with a haughty flick of my fingers. "If you don't mind, I'm about to get laid—"

"Wait!" He snatches my forearm the second I take a step toward the door. This time I lash out, gasping as my hand bounces harmlessly against his chest. He steps into me, grasping my chin. Before I can react, his lips capture mine, silencing me with a brutal kiss that leaves my mind reeling.

It's…hot. Really hot. He grips my hips, his fingers fanning out. Then he breaks off and shoves me toward a leather chaise. I lean over it, scrambling to find my balance.

But he's already behind me. His fingers plunge beneath my skirt, and a vicious sound rips from his throat.

Again, I've forsaken any panties, a fact that he takes advantage of with a swift, deliberate thrust of what feels like his thumb.

Holy crap. My startled moan rings out. This isn't like how he touched me before. Gone is the mocking, persistent wall. His finger trembles with barely concealed restraint.

Like it's taking everything he has in him not to rake with his nails. Shove inside me. Grip. Mark. Hurt.

The worst part? Something sick inside of me kind of wants him to.

"Are you going to just tease me again?" I wonder mockingly. "Fuck me half-assed and then kick me to the curb?"

He goes rigid, and I chuckle in triumph, scooting away from him.

"I thought so. Now, if you'll excuse me, I have a *real* fuck waiting to be experienced—"

He grabs me hard, shoving me face down against the leather. Panic prickles through my nerves, but a stronger emotion keeps the fear at bay for now. Excitement.

The hands wrenching up the skirt of my dress aren't polished and mocking anymore. They ruthlessly feel along my skin, palming my ass. I hiss in irritation when they withdraw only to…

Thwack! My eyelids flutter as fire sears through my left cheek—the kind of pain caused by only one act.

"D-Did you just spank me?" I question through clenched teeth, horrified. As if in apology, his palm cups me again, smoothing over the stinging flesh. He withdraws…only to assault the same spot again. Harder—*definitely* a spanking.

My mouth waters at the realization, my knees buckling. Throat rasping, all I can think to say is, "Do it again…"

He doesn't. Instead, he must grab a chunk of my hair, using it to yank my head back. I whimper as the pain sears through my scalp. It actually hurts.

It hurts so good.

Sweat mists my skin as I arch my hips, seeking out more contact. Touching. Anything. Disappointed when he doesn't deliver a single caress, I scoff, my laughter harsh.

"Are you going to fuck me with your wall up?" I taunt him, rolling my eyes up to the ceiling—the only thing I have a clear view of from this position. "Sorry, Vadim. Been there. Done that. Got the postcard and it wasn't all it was cracked up to—"

"*Merde.*" The foreign word rips from him as he tests me with his thumb, finding me dripping. "You enjoy this?" he mutters, his voice rasping with confusion.

Enjoy? My brain takes that word and runs with it, translating it from brooding billionaire speak to English —*won. Trapped. Conquered.*

I made him come here, to a venue he seems to hate, run by a brother he loathes. I've reduced him to this—a creature ruled by lust, too far gone to hold back. He'll take what he wants.

I whimper at the telltale hum of a zipper being undone. The hiss of shifting fabric. Then I feel him pulsating against me, and my brain threatens to turn off for good.

"I thought I'm not your type," I tell him spitefully, even though he feels so good I almost hate myself for trying to deter him. He's a delicious conduit of heat, prodding my lower lips, feeling thicker than before. Intimidating. One experimental buck of his hips forces him a fraction inside me, drawing a groan from my mouth. But when he thrusts for real, I can't silence a scream.

He goes deep, lacking his previous restraint. His next thrust is even harder. Ruthless.

It's everything I never knew I wanted, and my brain can't cope. I go blank, drugged on the sensation as he manipulates me like a rag doll, driving in so fiercely my teeth chatter with the violent motions. Somewhere at the back of my mind, I know he's snarling in frustration, spitting out a mixture of English and that other mysterious language.

While my mewling, throaty cries easily overpower him.

"Is this—" His hips slam into me, rocking my body against the back of the couch. I have to scramble like I'm trying to crawl over it, just to find enough stability to push back, ridding every stroke he has to give. "What—" Another thrust. "You wanted?"

A *punishing* thrust nearly robs me of my voice. Gasping, I answer him mindlessly. "Yes, yes, yes. So good. More, more."

I stimulate my inner muscles to grip him hard, testing his resolve. If anything, the challenge seems to spur him into snatching my hips, yanking me into him. Groaning, he works to shove past each rippling, grasping contraction. His cock swells, sowing friction that has my toes curling in my heels.

I think my brain explodes.

The next thing I know, an orgasm is tearing through me so strongly I can only grit my teeth and ride it out, wave after brutal wave. Even in my daze, I sense the moment he seems to pull back. Come to his senses. Try to reassemble his wall before it's too late.

"No!" I wiggle my hips shamelessly, humping him like some porno star. "Come in me, please, please, please."

He swipes his hand over my lower back—hesitating? Then he grips me hard, his nails sinking in. All I can do is seize the edge of the couch and hold on as he bucks into me, grunting. Groaning.

Then he shudders, and it's like I can track the tension building within him, riding up his cock and finally exploding from him in reckless, ruthless waves.

And it's the most amazing thing I've ever felt. Tears spill down my cheeks, my grin wild, my laughter shrill with triumph.

But then, somewhere within the come down, I realize…

I just fucked a human switchblade.

I don't know how we got here. *Here* being my hotel room, I think. I barely remember leaving the club. Entering a fancy red sports car. Having someone practically drag me into an elevator. Then, stripping my clothes and frantically trying to undress someone else— who stubbornly refused to remove more than his suit jacket and undo some of his shirt buttons. We stumbled into the bedroom afterward, and…

Hmm. Everything's starting to blur and run together— but who cares?

I now have two glasses of wine, one in each hand. A beautiful man lies beneath me while I straddle him on a massive, luxurious bed. It's heaven on earth, even if a part of me whispers that it's a lie.

"You're mean," I tell Vadim seriously. So sexy and so mean. "What you did was really mean. I shouldn't even be talking to you!" I lift my arms in indignation and wind up sloshing wine over the sliver of his chest bared by his partially undone shirt. *Oops.* Before a single drop can stain the tailored cotton garment, I lower my mouth to his pec and lick him clean. All better.

"Mean," he echoes, sounding amused once more. He stares up at me, his gaze crystal clear. I doubt he's taken a single sip of the wine he procured for me. No matter. That just means there's more for me.

"Yes!" I nod. Then I giggle. "Spanking me was very mean, but in that case, you have my permission."

"I should do more than spank you." He's frowning, his gaze distant. "My brother rarely speaks to me," he adds, gripping my hips to steady me while I continue to bounce in place. "Never has he reached out genuinely. Not once. This morning, he sent you a present—well, I'm sure his fiancée had a hand in it, but your name is on the box."

"Presents?" I perk up and scan the room. "Where?"

He nods to indicate a glass table positioned near the windows.

With a giddy squeal, I shimmy to the edge of the mattress and allow him to assist me by taking my wine glasses. Staggering on jellied legs, I find a beautifully wrapped package complete with a small handwritten note.

Thank you for the thoughtful gifts, someone had written. *Francesca and Maxim.*

I marvel at the simple gesture. Maxim may be scary as hell, but maybe there is some hope for him yet? At the moment, I'm tipsy enough to give even the Devil himself the benefit of the doubt.

"How sweet!" Feeling like a kid on Christmas morning, I rip into the package and gape at the present within. "Oh! It's so pretty." And luxurious too—a beautiful ruby-colored shawl made of silk. I drape it around my shoulders and find something else tucked within the box. "They sent you something as well." I lift the navy colored piece of fabric and unfurl it, revealing a very nice tie. Lurching to my feet, I spin around only to find Vadim behind me. He eyes the strip of fabric as though it's poisonous.

"So skeptical you are." Giggling, I loop the tie around his neck only to instantly regret the finished effect. "Blue is so your color," I tell him, annoyed at that fact. Navy enhances the depth of his gaze, making his eyes seem even more intense than usual. No fair.

"Do you make a habit out of manipulating people into giving you what you want?" he wonders grudgingly.

I bristle at that. "Not uh! It's the first rule of engagement." I lift my finger, about to school him on the proper gifting protocol, otherwise known as social norms. "Never arrive to a party without a gift for the hosts. Always shower them with adequate compliments. And…" I trail off, frowning as my thoughts turn fuzzy. "Something about always asking for seconds, even if the food tastes like ass, I think. Can I have my wines back, please?"

He frowns, so surly. "I'm starting to wonder if I should cut you off…"

I gasp in mock horror and snatch one glass right from his hand. "Never! I'm free, and no one can tell me what to do, remember? Not even you. It's on my list."

To prove it, I skip over to the window and admire the view of the city outstretched below, like a smattering of diamonds. If I stand at the right angle, I can make out my reflection—tall, butt-naked, swaying in the shadow of a larger, more enigmatic figure.

"Come here." I beckon Vadim until he reluctantly steps forward, and then I sigh. "We look so sexy together." And we do. Fire and embers. Light and dark. "What a shame that you're so mean."

"Why shouldn't I be?" he counters. His hand smooths over my hip, and I arch into the contact. Then he stiffens as if he realizes only now what he's done. Touch me of his own free will.

"Mean?" I prod before guzzling from my wine. I resurface pleasantly buzzed and add, "Because it's mean!"

"In my world, you learn quickly that it's better to be on your guard," he muses. His words nuzzle the nape of my neck, and he's even closer. "People seek out others only to gain something they want. I'm just prudent enough to ensure that more often than not, I get my desired win first. Consider that *my* version of a list. The first rule is to always anticipate the selfishness of others. The second someone believes they have what you seek, they own you."

It sounds so cutthroat. So darkly sexy.

"I didn't want anything from you," I point out, draining my glass. "I mean, I did, but mainly I wanted to do things *to* you. Sexy things. You wouldn't let me."

A low hum resonates through his chest, and I nearly drop my empty glass.

"Will you let me do them now, I wonder?" With a mischievous grin, I slink around, grinding my body into his, relishing the stern, impassive reaction. His obvious restraint makes the thrill so much better than what I figure Geoff's lust would inspire. Lust is boring. But Vadim? He's unpredictable, proven to snap once pushed to his breaking point.

So I *push*, bracing my hand on his chest to urge him back, back, back until he has to sit on the edge of the bed, staring up at me with a questioning gaze.

"I wanted so badly to suck you off," I announce, licking the rim of my glass for emphasis. From the corner of my eye, I watch him tense, his nostrils flaring, eyes narrowing. Holy crap. My inner thighs clench, and I fight to ignore the reaction. "I wanted to take you deep," I add, intrigued as his breaths quicken in response. "So deep. I wanted to practice all the new skills I've read about. It wouldn't have been perfect, but I'm sure it would have been good." I'm still violating my wine glass shamelessly.

I lick all the way around the rim and then swirl my tongue through the opening while holding his gaze. "Your size is impressive, but I'm sure I could have deepthroated you."

He sits forward, flattening his hands over his knees, his legs parted ominously. "Kneel."

A thrill of excitement runs through me so quickly I almost fan myself. Instead, I turn my back to him as I consider complying or crawling into bed and waiting for my hangover to kick in. All it takes is one look at him in the reflection on the window for me to bend—slowly— and set my glass on the floor.

When I stand and face him again, he's still wearing the same hard, unreadable expression. But as I sidle over to him, a muscle in his jaw quirks.

"Kneel?" I parrot him innocently. "Like this?" Stopping short just beyond his reach, I sink gracefully to my knees, my head bowed. When I gather the nerve to peek at him, he's unmoving, his eyes flashing. He's too proud to even command me.

But there's a distinct bulge tenting the front of his slacks, too tempting to resist, my pride be damned. I crawl to him, licking my lips in anticipation. When I finally come close enough to reach for the fastenings of his pants, he doesn't shy away.

Trembling with the anticipation, I unwrap him with far more care than I did my present. I peel the fabric back slowly, all while squeezing slightly to test the hardness lurking beneath.

He grunts, sounding pained. His clenched teeth betray that he's trying his damned hardest to suppress any noise at all. I'm not so composed.

"Gosh," I murmur, once his cock is freed. "So, so pretty. So beautiful." I kiss the smooth, bulbous end for emphasis —and I think Mr. Vadim nearly comes out of his skin.

That's all I do at first—feather kisses up and down his length, the more of him I coax free. I even tease the ends of his piercing. He has his own unique taste that I find myself craving, tainted with remnants of me. Should be gross in theory, I suspect. In reality...

"We even taste good together," I murmur to him, in case he was wondering. What a shame he can be such a dick. Mournfully, I flick my tongue along the underside of him, testing the give of the largest, pulsating vein surging beneath. I think I could come from this alone—exploring him lazily, drunk off both sex and wine.

But now it's time for the finale. I honestly don't know where to start—the women in pornos make it look so easy. Letting impulse guide me, I part my lips around the crown and swirl my tongue. But then it's like the second my mouth closes over his shaft, instinct kicks in.

An electric impulse jolts down my spine, guiding my movements. Slow at first. Then harder, using my hand to pump his length where my mouth can't reach. He hardens darn near instantly, thickening to make even taking his tip a struggle.

But I'm eager to keep going. Try harder. Please him as much as humanly possible. Because when he moans…

A choir of singing angels couldn't compare to the sound. Nothing else in the world could ever come close to this man, grunting in pleasure, fisting his hands through my hair like he's losing his mind just as rapidly as I am.

"*Merde*," he swears throatily. "*Je n'ai jamais…* Fuck."

Spurred on by the reaction, I lunge into him, taking him further. More. Deepthroating him isn't an option, but maybe one day. I could learn to let him in, down my throat—and the mere idea of it sets me off like a match striking gasoline.

My fingers jab between my legs, seeking out my clit as I suck, caressing him with my tongue, urging him in wordless moans.

And then it happens. He goes rigid, his fingers practically tearing out my hair. His cock jerks against my lips, and then I feel it. Taste it.

His release, coming so quickly, he couldn't hold back even if he tried.

Holy, freaking crap.

My eyes roll into the back of my head as I work to swallow. But it's too much. *He* is too much. Excess dribbles down my chin, speckling my tits, and I've never felt filthier. And it feels so, darn, good to be filthy with him. Better than good.

And I could cry with the conflicting emotions washing through me as I back away from him, gasping for air. "See how good it can be when you give me what I want?" I tell him accusingly. "I give you what you need…"

Something he might contest, I realize once I meet his gaze. Rather than dazed with ecstasy, he looks so…angry. Furious, even. Color paints his elegant cheeks, tightening the corner of his mouth and enhancing the darkness of his irises.

Abruptly, he stands, letting his pants fall down to the floor. One by one, he kicks his legs to shed the garment completely, then he advances and palms my skull, sinking his fingers through my hair. A gentle tug warns me to rise along with him, craning my neck back. He forces my head near his, his breath fanning my lips. Tension builds the longer his dark eyes scour mine.

The good thing to do would be wait and see. But I can't. His nearness feels so darn tempting. I'm the kid in the candy store all over again. Straining his grip, I stand on tiptoe and brush my lips over his. Again. He frowns, resisting me as I nudge his more firmly, urging them apart. Thinking quickly, I flick my tongue along his lower lip. Success. He opens his mouth, nipping me in return, and…

It's sin.

Kissing him is a new realm, so different from the sex. He can shield himself from me, even while railing my brains out. But like this? I'm poking through a crack in his wall when we're like this. Eager to explore, I palm both sides of his head and wiggle my hips into him. His hair feels like silk, his body perfection. My brain swims, overheating, oozing out of my mouth as mindless nonsense.

"You feel so good," I murmur against his parted lips. How can *anyone* feel so good?

But it's as if my excitement flips a switch in him. *Bam!* His wall goes up in record time, forcing me to withdraw completely or risk having my tongue sliced in half by the falling action. His jaw hardens against me, his head cocking, that cold expression returning.

"You hate when I praise you," I point out, waggling my finger at him in disapproval. *Bingo.* His gaze darkens, withdrawn, and mistrustful. Sighing, I flounce away from him and dive onto the bed.

"Sorry to break it to you, Vadim—" I roll over to face him and deliberately suck in a lungful of air. His brows furrow as if he's reading my mind, and he starts forward, mounting the mattress in my wake. "You fuck REALLY GOOD!" I scream it at the top of my lungs, cackling as he grips my chin to silence me. I look up at him, enthralled by the planes of his face and those gorgeous freaking eyes. And his mouth, still wet from our kiss. I wonder if he's one of those guys who hates tasting the results of sex. That could explain the hot and cold action to an extent. But no. Even as I watch, his tongue traces a dangerous path from one end of his mouth to the other.

And my toes curl helplessly.

"You should put your mouth on me," I tell him, pleading. "Just once. To make up for hurting me. I'd love you then, forever and ever."

"It only takes oral sex to buy your love?" he wonders mockingly.

"My love? No!" I push on his chest, thrilled when he lets me manipulate him onto his back and straddle him. Between my legs seems to be the one position where I feel like I have the advantage. He's easier to read from this angle. "My love would cost a lot more than that. Like, the entire new Chanel spring collection in every color levels of dedication. But for now, to buy my *maybe* forgiveness, I'll settle for you telling me why. Why did you go through all of that trouble for something so spiteful? It would have been way easier to just pick up a real hooker on your way there."

"Why?" He shrugs and palms my hips with both hands, keeping me in place. "My brother brings out the worst in me," he says.

As if that explains it. Though maybe it does. I know firsthand what it's like to have someone bring out the parts of you better left buried. Jim is my case and point.

"What happened between the two of you?"

"It's a story that isn't worth retelling," he says with one of those devious, secretive smiles.

"What about the other man? Milton?" I ask. "Who is he?"

His smile wavers. "A friend. More of a brother to me than Maxim in so many ways. Some could say we grew up together…"

He sounds so wistful. Honest. I marvel at the rare hint of vulnerability, and like a vulture, I can't resist nibbling.

"Tell me more?"

His expression glazes over, and like magic, the wall comes back up. "There isn't more."

I frown and poke him in the center of his chest. "Where are my wines?" I wonder, glancing around the room.

"You drank one," he reminds me. "I left the other…over here." He shifts beneath me and reaches for a nearby end table, withdrawing my glass from the edge of it.

"Thank you very much," I simper, holding out my hand for it.

"Should I do the responsible thing and pour it out, I wonder?"

I gasp in mock horror and lean down to steal a sip right from the rim. "It would be a sin to waste such a perfect vintage. But maybe I should slow down just a tad…"

He obediently sets the glass aside while I roll off of him and stare up at the ceiling. For whatever reason, he remains beside me.

"You know, if you kept me around, I could smooth things over between you and your brother in no time flat." I snap my fingers for emphasis.

"I would hate to dampen your enthusiasm," he remarks, "but I doubt even your skills could help much in this instance."

He sounds so sure of that. Disappointed, even?

"Never doubt the skills of a basic bitch from California," I tell him solemnly. "It's a damn good thing we aren't compatible. A mere week with me, and you'd wake up to find your bachelor pad now a pastel hell designed by Laura Ashley, and that you and your brother have a weekly golf game every Sunday."

"A tempting future," he murmurs. The weird part? I can't tell if he's being serious or not.

Rolling onto my side, I tap his jaw with the tip of my finger. "But you'll never have it," I tell him.

"Is that so?" His voice drips down to that amused, delicious murmur and something inside me quivers. Fearful? Excited? I can't tell.

"You'll have to buy my forgiveness first, and I don't see any Chanel bags. Besides." I scoot away from him and shimmy beneath the covers. "You'll pull your mysterious billionaire act and disappear before the morning, which is just fine with me because I have a plane to catch. Try not to let the door hit ya on the way out," I add with a forced yawn. "I'm a light sleeper."

"And if I decide to stay in the room that *my* accounts are paying for?" he wonders tonelessly.

"You won't." True regret slips into my voice before I can help it. "That would require letting down your wall, dear Sir. Something you seem to have trouble doing around me."

Even now, he's playing along, saying the right things. But something tells me that's all he's doing—playing. The real Vadim hides behind an ironclad façade, and I only see glimpses when I taunt him enough into coming out.

Sure enough, I sense the mattress lighten, suddenly devoid of his weight.

"It would be a shame to waste this room since it's already been paid in full for the entire week," he muses.

I burrow deeper beneath the blankets and pout in secret. "Maybe you'll find some escort to play with while I'm gone?"

"I may."

I peek from beneath the blankets and watch him leave every bit as inconspicuously as he had arrived at the club. Dominating the entire room.

And then stealing the air with him, making the world feel chilled and suffocating in his absence.

I wake up too hungover to function. All I can do is moan in agony and stumble into the shower. Ritual healing performed, I can start to piece together the events of the previous night, all while trying not to die in utter mortified shame.

I had sex with Vadim again. Technically twice. Once in an alarmingly rough display, I'd pour over later, and then again when I finally got to fellate him for real.

And what an experience that was. I feel like a child who discovered that Santa, magic, and the Tooth fairy are all real—but surprise! You can only see them on a particular full moon, at midnight, only if you stand on one foot and squint in the right spot, and it's already the morning after. The opportunity has sadly passed, never to return again.

Unfair.

The smart thing to do would be to get on the first plane back to California and put this whirlwind excursion behind me. Luckily, I have a flight leaving in…soon, I think. Frowning, I shimmy into a towel and run through the room, searching for the itinerary documents I had the concierge print out for me. I'm panting by the time I find them, and when I reconcile the time of my booked flight with the current time flashing on the LED alarm clock by the bed, I groan in despair.

"Damn it!"

A second later, the phone rings, and I lunge toward it, hoping beyond hope that it's an airline representative offering to hold the plane just in time for me to race across town and board.

"Hello?"

"Morning," a suave voice replies, and I bite down a groan. So sexy. So smug. My heart pangs as my belly clenches—two polar opposite reactions. "It seems you've decided to occupy the room another day after all."

"W-Wrong," I stammer while collapsing onto the end of the bed. "You've just caught me in the middle of packing. I'm on my way to the airport. My flight leaves soon."

"Wrong," he counters smoothly. "Your flight has been canceled. The next plane doesn't leave until tomorrow morning. All of this, you would know if you were already at the airport for your eight am flight, or if you were awake for any one of the ten wake-up calls, the hotel receptionist attempted to place to inform you. I'm alerted by email when you don't answer, you see. It appears that punctuality is not your forte, Ms. Connors."

I sigh in defeat. There's no arguing with that. "I can't help wondering if you got me drunk on purpose, Mr. Gorgoshev. If you wanted to keep me here so badly, you could have offered me the use of your private jet," I point out. "I would have gladly graced you with my presence for at least another day."

But now? I'd consider renting a car and driving cross country myself just to get out of his orbit.

"Where are you?" I ask him before he can reply. "Attending to more mysterious business meetings?"

"Something like that," he says. "I'm in the process of interviewing women."

My nose wrinkles. That's a weird way to phrase it. "For a secretarial position?"

"No. To be my wife."

I hang up automatically and back away from the phone as if burned. *Ouch. Ouch. Ouch.* I never knew rejection could sting so badly, and I've survived a messy divorce fit for tabloid fodder. Gosh, it's not even what he said that makes my stomach roil as if I'll vomit. It's how he said it. So mockingly. So matter of fact. *I'm interviewing women to be my wife*—which is a weird concept within itself—*but hahaha, Tiffany. You may have fucked me and sucked me, but you aren't even on my shortlist.*

Not that I would want to be, because what kind of person interviews marriage candidates? Someone so jaded and mistrustful he has an invisible wall built up wherever he goes.

And now I'm forced to spend another night in the same damn city as him.

Chin up, Tiffy, my inner bitch snarls. *Remember those promises you made to yourself? Put them to the test bitch! Start with your morning routine—let no one ever get you down.*

Right. Blinking back any tears, I find the music channel on the television and turn up the volume. Today's choice is vulgar, offensive feminine rap, and I loudly chant along to the lyrics while sifting through my past impulse purchases for something to wear. It is as I enthusiastically prattle along to the words, "Y'all men ain't shit," that I'm struck with a glorious revelation.

Fuck Vadim Gorgoshev—not literally but figuratively. He's left me in a gorgeous hotel suite, with room service already included, and I have not one but three designer gowns to choose from, membership to a sex club, and time to kill.

Geoff may have been a false start, but no worries. I'll find someone even better to fuck me senseless until my flight in the morning, Vadim and his new wife be damned.

Grinning, I settle on the black option he'd rejected as my party ensemble. Then I blow my hair out into loose waves and find the reddest lipstick from the handful I picked up the other day.

"You look gorgeous, Tiffy," I tell the bombshell beaming at me in the mirror's reflection. "Now go knock 'em dead."

I STROLL into the hotel bar as if I own the place. Screw private businessmen lounges or exclusive clubs. I'll take whoever I can get. It's being picky that got me into this mess in the first place.

With my shoulders back, head held high, I stroll into the sleek, modern setting feeling more confident than ever— and I almost run right back out.

This time of day, there are slim pickings as far as available men go—but one of the most eligible and hands down the most handsome of the prospects, sits at a table smack dab in the center of the room. I'll have to walk past him to reach the bar at the back, but that's not the worst part.

Seated across from him, as beautiful as if she stepped off of a runway, is a slender brunette with tousled curls, perfectly applied makeup, and a modest two-piece suit ensemble in a delicate shade of ivory. Paired with Vadim, they look like some sexy, uber-rich power couple, and my confidence plummets through the floor.

Damaged pride almost drives me away. Almost. But then I make my grin as wide as I can and approach Vadim's table casually. *Very* casually.

Thinking on the spot, I wave at him, brimming with enthusiasm as those dark eyes narrow in suspicion. Skipping to his side, I lean over him from behind and place my hand on his shoulder. He stiffens instantly, even more so as I bring my mouth near his ear and murmur loud enough for his table companion to hear me.

"Baby, when you're done with your meeting, I'll be waiting for you at the bar. Kay?" My voice comes out the chirpiest, peppiest imitation of a Cali airhead, and I couldn't be more pleased. Winking at the startled woman, I kiss Vadim right on his clenched cheek. "Don't work too hard."

Still grinning, I march to the bar where I promptly order my favorite vice and try not to die in utter shame. So the man who fucked my brains out—twice—is now interviewing marriage candidates right underneath my nose? I'm not jealous. Not in the slightest. After two sips of my wine, I'm not angry, either.

Especially when a hunky redhead in a dashing suit claims the stool next to me. "Is this seat taken?" he wonders, his blue eyes twinkling.

I clear my glass to the side and give him a more thorough once-over. "Not at all." He isn't bad for a last-minute option. He's certainly muscular enough. Who cares if his eyes aren't flashing with mystery, and his smile isn't dazzling?

I'm over the brooding, aloof thing, anyway.

To prove it, I stick out my hand, my expression simpering. "I'm—"

"Not taken, I hope," the man says, his gaze fixed beyond me.

"Huh?"

He chuckles, but there's a nervous quality to the sound. "Please tell me that the man staring daggers at me isn't your husband or something."

Husband, he says?

I laugh loudly as I extend my hand again. In a voice clear enough to be heard from the main lobby, I declare, "Oh no, I am *soooooooo* single. My name's Tiffy. What's yours?"

He rattles off a boring answer like Ben or Sam. Then he proceeds to spend the next ten minutes regaling me with tidbits of the stock exchange market. At the same time, I muster every ounce of control I possess not to turn around. And I don't. Even when an alarming warmth falls over my shoulder—the kind of pressure that could only belong to a masculine hand.

"*Baby*, I'm done with my meeting now, so you can stop provoking me. Kay?" a man purrs into my ear, his voice such a dead-on imitation of my Cali drawl that I do a doubletake. Dark eyes meet mine, sparkling with amusement—and something harder, promising punishment. "Tell the nice gent you're sorry for wasting his time," Vadim scolds, switching to his normal tone. Then he reaches into his pocket and withdraws a wad of cash that he offers to Ben, Sam—whoever—presumably as reimbursement for my second glass of wine.

Confused, the man takes the cash and backs off. "Sorry, man."

Once poor Ben or Sam has escaped the bar intact, I whirl to face the figure already perching onto the vacated stool beside me.

"Provoking you?" I parrot innocently and sip from my drink. "Is that what it's called when you're minding your own business, enjoying your time alone?" I pout and flutter my eyelashes. "My bed is so very big. I'll get lonely if I sleep in it by myself."

He frowns, his gaze dimming, and something that could be regret diminishes my feeling of triumph. No fair. He had to go and make things serious.

"Your wife candidate is gone?" I wonder, my tone slightly less nasty. After scanning the room, I don't find the woman anywhere. "Was she too brunette for your tastes? Too '*unpredictable*?'"

"Too jealous," he says in a deadpan tone. "She demanded to know why I was interviewing her when I have such a beautiful girlfriend." His frown lets me know that the words aren't his. Knowing that doesn't kill the fluttering butterflies that come to life in my stomach, though. "Had you not hung up on me, I would have further explained my motives," he adds, deliberately dangling a carrot before my nose.

Am I curious enough to take the bait? *No,* I decide, taking another sip of my wine. But then I remember how beautiful he looked, paired with a taller, more exotic looking woman, and a muscle in my jaw twitches.

"What motives could possibly explain interviewing marriage candidates?" I fold my hands neatly over my lap and feign interest. Internally, I'm struck by his appearance more than usual. The planes of his face seem bolder, his eyes darker. Even his hair looks glossier. Frowning, I try to pinpoint the source of the change, and then I find it—in addition to the ebony suit that I'm beginning to suspect is his signature look, a pop of color stands out in stark contrast. His shirt, a rich navy blue. I have a sudden flashback of me drunkenly informing him that blue is his color.

And it freaking is.

"Are you alright, Ms. Connors?" he wonders, his brows furrowing. At the same time, he strokes the edge of his collar, deliberately drawing my attention downward. "You seem distracted."

Rolling my eyes, I attempt to regroup. "Don't tell me the aloof bachelor is looking to settle down," I snipe. "Newsflash, that typically involves having to touch someone more often than giving them a kiss-off."

"In theory," he smoothly replies. "Luckily for me and my 'aloofness' this has nothing to do with romance whatsoever. I'm merely seeking a business arrangement."

"Oh?" I find myself inching closer to him while sneaking another sip from the rim of my glass. "A marriage of convenience?" I glance him over and nod with judgment. "You look like the type. You want your wife on call for public appearances with an agreement to freeze her eggs in case you desire an heir. No fucking required."

I sound so disappointed. Poor Vadim's future wife. He wouldn't want to endure the many, many, *many* sessions of sex it might take to conceive a baby. Halfway through, he'd close up out of nowhere, erect his iron wall and leave her high and dry. She'd be better off with a turkey baster. It would certainly provide more stable emotional support.

"You seem very interested in what duties I might desire in my wife," he points out.

I scoff and sip from my wine. Ignoring him would be the smart option—but I just can't help myself. "With your dazzling lack of imagination, I'm sure I have a pretty good idea already."

He chuckles, and I stiffen. Damn him, he can sound so carefree when he wants to. So…normal. So disarming.

"You have such a good idea of my intentions, and yet I doubt you would even make it through the interview process."

Low burn. I eye my drink and half-heartedly consider throwing it on him. Then I down it in one go and slam the empty glass onto the counter. Meeting his gaze directly, I fashion my most beautiful, charming smile. "Try me."

He stands without hesitation and approaches the table he left vacated. He moves so assuredly that I can't help feeling like a rabbit clumsily caught in a hunter's snare. I'd been so busy chasing my own tail that I didn't even see the trap coming.

"Change your mind?" Vadim calls without turning around.

I slink over to him, feigning disinterest with a bored sigh. To save face, I stall by circling around him before claiming the seat the brunette had occupied. My nostrils wrinkle, and I fight to stifle a frown. I can smell her perfume—cheap, knock-off designer.

"Ms. Connors, is it?" Vadim has a stack of papers placed before his spot. He leisurely rifles through them and looks up, eyeing me up and down. "I'm afraid your attire isn't at all appropriate," he scolds. "Did you even read the requirements?"

I squirm, unsure if he's joking or mocking. Probably both. It's so hard to tell with him. Biting my lip, I once again contemplate leaving—but the thought barely has time to form before I find myself leaning over the table instead. His quick glance downward reveals that my dirty trick hit its target—he definitely notices my cleavage, straining against the black silk of my dress. The effect is even more revealing if I arch my back in just the right angle.

So I do.

"I could go and change," I murmur innocently, deploying my sexy drawl. "Though you should loveeeeee this dress. *You* bought it."

"About that." He shifts, suddenly serious. "Your total came to—" he rattles off a number so insanely enormous that I instantly suppress it from my memory. "Would you like to repay me in a lump sum or in installments?"

I wrinkle my nose. Stealing from him was never my intention. Needling him a little? Totally. Still, even if it makes my throat go dry, I can't refuse him outright. "I do remember being promised a shopping spree in return for my accompanying you to ruin your brother's party—"

"That was for one dress," he clarifies, smoothing his finger along his collar. "Not four, a pair of shoes, a fur stole, a purse, two brooches and—"

"I'll return them, then," I say, dismissing him with a wave of my hand. "I kept the tags on. No harm, no foul."

"You won't." He laughs at the absurdity of such a proposal. "You had the driver circle around for hours until you found the exact store you wanted. Judging from your eventual tardiness, you spent even more time combing through each collection, picking your favorites. You may not be punctual, but I can tell you don't do things half-assed, either. To use that word, you so endeavor to abuse, you *love* those garments."

My heart races, panicked. I feel so personally insulted. So…known. He read me like a book, so expertly, he didn't even have to run his fingers through me to do it. No fair.

I try to salvage my pride with a toss of my hair and a bored sigh. "It's not like I could take them on the plane with me, anyway." *Lies.* I'd already run through the logistics hell of how to perfectly smuggle all four dresses, a purse, a pair of shoes, a fur stole, and two brooches into one of the customary wrapping boxes small enough to fit under my plane seat. Rather than admit defeat, I find ammunition to lob over the figurative net right back at him. "Most men would see the sex as more than enough payment."

He doesn't even flinch. "Yes. What was the rate I offered you? A grand for four hours." He extends one of his hands before him and eyes each finger. Reaching some internal conclusion, he looks up, jabbing his gaze right into mine. "It would take years for you to pay off such an investment."

Losing was never my forte. I suck at it, actually. Desperate to change the subject, I jab my finger at his stack of papers. "Ask me your stupid interview questions, then. I'm sure a man who can waste money on a fake wife can spare a few grand on some clothes." A few *hundred* grand, to be exact.

For whatever reason, he doesn't go in for the kill. Not yet, and my spine tingles with the painful reality that he has me by the balls this time.

"Do you have any relevant experience?" he wonders. Again, he utilizes that rich, unreadable tone that makes it hard to tell when he's serious or not. *Not,* I decide.

"I have seven years of it," I say, folding my hands onto the table. "All spent within an unhappy, loveless marriage. One could say I am an expert in the faking marital bliss arena."

He shuffles his documents, his expression unreadable. "What is the extent of your education?"

High school—the fancy boarding school variety, but with grades not worth bragging about. I find myself composing a different answer. "I taught Sunday school for five years. I'd make the good, wholesome breed of wife."

He raises an eyebrow, but I meet his skepticism shamelessly. I'm not lying. I'm not ashamed either. Teaching—even in the rather limited aspects of biblical commandments—is one of the few moments in my life with Jim I don't regret.

"Have you ever considered children?"

I wince. "Next question."

Something falls across his expression, hardening it. "No." He sets his pages aside and braces his hands over the table. "I'm afraid that question is non-negotiable."

I squirm. "And if I don't?"

He shrugs. But I can tell what will happen just from his rigid demeanor. He'll lose interest. Close up. Erect that stupid wall. Maybe I'm just too bored to let him retreat so soon?

"I *wanted* kids," I croak, hating how hoarse my voice sounds. "Once. My body had other plans. Besides, I'm fine with being single, and children mean no more frivolous expenses anyway. It's best for everyone."

"Money is no expense where I am concerned." In some ways, it resonates more like an insult than a simple statement. How dare I even question? His hypothetical wife would have the best of both worlds, of course. A billion icy, brooding children and the wardrobe fit for a queen.

I hate her already.

"What is it you even do anyway?" I demand, scouring him with a more critical focus. Barely in his thirties, he couldn't have climbed too far up the corporate ladder. An heir of some kind? No. I grew up around boys with silver spoons stuck up their asses—though mine was shoved firmly in my mouth, so who am I to judge—but he doesn't fit the template. He's too cold in his dealings—a creature with nothing to prove to anyone. "A stockbroker?" I say, taking a guess out loud. "Venture capitalist?"

"To make it simple, let's say that I dabble in pharmaceuticals," he suggests. "A few strategic patents have made me a very, *very* wealthy man."

"Like?" I prod, curious enough to risk irritating him.

But he shrugs, unperturbed. "Are you familiar with Eingel Industries?"

I'm not. Still, it sounds prestigious enough to assuage my skepticism. "Smart as well as loaded—" I nod in approval. "I'm sure your future trophy wife will be very pleased."

"You have yet to ask me directly what it is I seek from my…wife."

Haven't I? I decide to cut the bullshit and take him up on the dare. "Why, oh, why would you want a wife, Vadim? Something tells me, it isn't to fuck."

"I seek a particular arrangement," he says cryptically. "To achieve that, I need to go through government officials, and in that capacity, I must present a certain…image to make the right impression."

"How did I know you wouldn't tell me outright," I mutter. "What do you want so badly that being a mere bachelor wouldn't get you?"

He shuffles his papers and elegantly tucks them within a leather briefcase he had placed by his feet. "I would tell you," he says without looking up, "had you actually passed your interview. I'm sorry to say that you failed."

Heat sears my cheeks. *Score: two Vadim, nil Tiffy.* Time to cut my losses and scurry away to lick my wounds.

"I'm leaving." I stand and turn my back to him, robbing him of the chance to inspect my reaction in full. "Enjoy your wife hunt. May you both find eternal bliss. I plan to find something *internal*." I start for the doorway, forcing my chin high into the air. "Maybe I'll run into Sam in the lobby? I have time to kill before my flight, after all."

"His name was Joshua. And you can wave to him on your way upstairs," Vadim replies. "Because you won't have time to engage him in conversation."

My steps falter. "And why is that?"

"Because you need to change into another one of your stolen dresses. I've decided to take you to dinner."

My mind reels. He's *decided*. It sounds so damn insulting that I puff up instantly incensed. And at the same time, it seems so damn intriguing. So damn…commanding. First spanking. Now, this. The man is insane.

But damn, I may love it.

"I don't remember agreeing to anything of the sort?" I crane my neck to eye him from over my shoulder.

And I instantly regret it. Holy crap. His eyes blaze, a muscle in his throat jerking freely.

"You'll come," he says. That's it. As if he's so damn sure I wouldn't dare refuse. It's only when he finally deigns to eye his watch that I realize I've stood here all this time, gaping at him open-mouthed. "I'll give you an hour to change," he says as though bestowing some precious gift upon me. "Wear something I haven't seen you in before. I'll meet you in the lobby."

"You are so full of shit," I blurt incredulously.

He merely inclines his head as if considering the phrase. "I've filled you as well," he finally counters in that deep, relentless murmur. "But it wasn't with shit, was it?"

My mouth falls open even wider, and I have to make a mental note to close it. Turning on my heel, I storm for the main lobby. Before decorum can rob me of the gall, I stick up my middle finger in a princess-style wave as I go. "Fuck off, Vadim."

But damn him. The way he said filled. It does strange things to my head and conjures dangerous, explicit memories. Like him swelling inside me on the verge of release—and then the eventual sensation of being flooded by him. Consumed by him.

CHAPTER ELEVEN

I sway on my way into an elevator, and I nearly run into the suite in a desperate bid to escape thoughts of him. Dinner, he says? Hell no. I'm going to pack for my flight, order a million wake up calls, and do whatever it takes to ensure that I make it on time. I'm going to…

Scream and race out of the room as if electrocuted. My heart pounds as I warily tiptoe back inside, unwilling to believe my eyes.

My first coherent thought is that the bastard stalled me on purpose, knowing all along that someone was in my room unloading boxes upon boxes placed throughout the master suite. A stack lies before the bed and more dominate the glass dining table by the window. Not just any boxes either, but a classic, iconic black box wrapped in signature white ribbon…

Chanel. So much Chanel that I fear I'm hallucinating. *Obscene* amounts of Chanel. He must have spent a literal fortune. Either that or he's playing a sick, awful joke at my expense.

So, of course, it's the latter.

Sighing, I fight to control any excitement that may be bubbling beneath my skin as I approach the nearest stack and lift one of the boxes. It's heavy enough to prove that it's not filled with air, at least. But when I peek inside…

I sink to my knees and wind up cooing over the most beautiful purse I've ever seen. It matches the ebony dress I discover next. And a pair of similar shoes, and then a collection of delicate jewelry. Jackets. More shoes. More purses.

And then it clicks. The bastard bought the spring collection. The most iconic, eye-catching pieces, to boot. Gosh, just last month, I'd drooled over the lineup, trying to talk myself into flirting with bankruptcy just to buy a single purse. Maybe a pair of shoes?

In person, every piece is more beautiful than I could have ever imagined. All I can do is strip my black dress and try on a new, light pink one with worshiping reverence. In a daze, I discover a full-length mirror on the closet door, and I admire myself from every angle.

Then I try on another ensemble. And another. Another.

It quickly becomes apparent that he didn't settle for just teasing me with a few new dresses. He bought entire outfits down to the last finishing detail. I recognize more than half from the runway, and something he said to me echoes in my brain as I model yet another gorgeous dress —wear something *different,* he commanded me in reference to his dinner.

The bastard.

I get lost in the task of trying to find which dress—of many—I'm aching to test drive first. The pink? The blue? An innocent sheer white?

I'm barely halfway through my options when the door to the suite opens, and a lanky, smug bastard strolls in.

"How did I know that this would be the cause of your delay?" He gestures to the mess of tissue paper and cardboard coating nearly every inch of the floor. His neutral expression doesn't quite match the surliness conveyed by his tone. He's not entirely angry, just amused.

And what he said finally registers in my brain. *Delay?*

Only now do I realize that it's nearly pitch-black outside. I'd turned on a few lights to better illuminate the details of each garment, so I barely noticed. Concerning his dinner date, I'm about four hours too late.

I try to apologize, I think, but all I manage to muster is a pained groan as I model another black dress and promptly fall in love. Thinking quickly, I skip through the minefield of clothing and grab a checkered style boy bag from the chaos. When slung over my shoulder, it completes the outfit so perfectly I gasp, and my eyes roll back into my head.

"You truly feel this way about a few items of clothing?" Vadim wonders. He's seated on the bed, watching me, his gaze unreadable.

"Clothing?" I sound so horrified by such a dismissive term. "This is *art*." But even as my heart soars with affection for every beautiful piece, my inner bitch has to dampen my mood. "But I can't keep it." It nearly kills me to even suggest as much out loud. *Kills.*

"Is that so?" His eyes flicker dangerously as he blinks without an ounce of mercy. "I could return it…"

"You should." I last all of five seconds before I break down shamelessly. "No, please! I have nothing to wear, thanks to you—" My suitcase is somewhere in an abandoned hotel room back in Cali. Considering that most of that clothing consists of conservative holdovers from my life with Jim, I'm more than ready for an upgrade. Biting my lip, I twirl and sigh in admiration of how amazing this dress alone makes me look. Even he has to appreciate the effect. And after all, I deserve a reward for putting up with him. He's been so darn mean.

"What will you give me for it?" His low, husky tone makes me swallow hard.

Too terrified to look at him, I observe my reflection more intently than ever.

"I would offer you my body, but we both know that you aren't particularly interested in that." I should leave it there and salvage what little I have of my pride by throwing every last item in the trash. Reflexively, my fingers grasp the strap of the purse, but I can't seem to budge. "What would you want?" I finally demand.

"I want you to accompany me to dinner," he says.

"Is that it?" I frown at his tone. The audible hesitation doesn't match the ominous way he uttered that word. *Dinner.* Curious, I crane my head back to peek at him.

He's staring into space, his mouth more tense than the smirk I'm used to.

"Dinner," he repeats. "With Milton…and my brother."

"Oh." I look away and finger the skirt of my dress. Even an idiot could catch the reluctance lurking beneath his level tone. "Well, I… Wait, that dinner isn't until next week!"

"Monday, in fact," he clarifies. "A timeframe that I'm sure gives you more than enough opportunities to utilize my bank account in your quest for revenge."

I whirl on him, hands on my hips. "Pray tell, Vadim, you aren't trying to keep me here yet another week?" I sound playfully alarmed, but inside I'm panicking. Could I survive another week in this man's orbit? One look at his quick, devious smile, and I have my answer.

Hell no.

"You can keep the Chanel," I say a bit more seriously this time. I carefully shimmy out of my dress, fold it, and return it to one of the boxes. "Now get out of my bed. I need to get up early tomorrow."

I stroll toward him, vaguely aware of the fact that I'm butt naked—underwear, ironically, hasn't been a priority during any of my few shopping sprees, and my only pairs are in said lost luggage. Circling around to the side of the bed opposite him, I make a show of yawning and lie on my side with my back to him.

"Goodnight—"

"And here I was assuming that the entire Chanel spring collection was the way to your heart."

I scoff. "I would have to be an idiot to let you anywhere near my heart." I'm startled by just how genuinely I mean that. Already something in my chest feels...off. I don't care what it takes—tomorrow, I leave.

"Nothing might change your mind?" he wonders, still so deceptively neutral. A different woman might make the mistake of assuming he's bored, even. Just prolonging this conversation to kill time. But I'm beginning to realize that time is the one commodity Mr. Vadim Gorgoshev doesn't spend frivolously.

And that icky feeling in my chest grows tenfold.

"No," I say smoothly. Then my brain catches up and has the nerve to contradict me. "Fine. What might change my mind? I want a straight answer from you for once. I want to know your secrets. And—" I wince as my stomach growls loudly enough for him to hear. "I'm hungry."

When he doesn't reply, I roll over and rise onto my knees, only to find him seated close to the phone, a glossy black brochure in hand. "Room service?" he inquires, switching to his deeper, more professional baritone. *"Parlez-vous Français? Très bien."*

He presumably proceeds to order from the menu, only he's speaking entirely in French. Given that up until now, everyone in this damn hotel has spoken nothing but unaccented English, I recognize the act for the power play it truly is. A display purely meant to disarm me.

Finished, he sets the phone down and then inclines his head as if I'm the one intruding upon his stolen room. "You were saying?"

I want to be angry. Deviously, spitefully angry. Something about him makes me more reckless instead. So it's mind games he wants to play?

I shuffle toward him, still on my knees, and then I shamelessly drape myself over him from behind, bringing my mouth near his ear. He stiffens predictably—score one for me—but an answering shiver ripples down my spine, and the score evens out. I love how solid he feels against me. So strong. I can lean all my weight against him, and I have no doubt that he can handle it.

Snap out of it, Tiffy.

"*Baby*," I murmur, adopting my ditzy wifey drawl from earlier. "I might consider staying if you tell me all of your deepest, darkest secrets."

"Like?" he wonders.

I swallow. Ask him something profound and personal? My tongue has a different aim in mind. "Why do you have your penis pierced?"

We both glance down to the center of his slacks. Is that a slight bulge I see? My cheeks heat, and I'm not sure if I enjoy the idea that he may like feeling me against him as much as I do. Or, it could be a trick of the light.

"Why? Control," he says simply. "To prove that I alone can exert ownership over my body."

I frown. It's a surprisingly deep and profound answer. I figure most men in the same position would mention something about wanting better orgasms. Intrigued, I shift around him to straddle his lap, spreading my legs directly over that suspicious bulge. Persistent heat firmly nudges my core, and I flinch in response. Not a trick of the light, after all.

Fighting to stay focused, I rise up just enough so that I can look down on him, and I quirk my lips into my own mischievous smile. "Do you think I should get my clit pierced, baby? I, too, am known for my exemplary self-control."

A muscle in his jaw twitches even as his dark eyes remain carefully blank. "I don't think you could handle the pain, *baby.*"

"Oh?" *Bastard.* I lower myself hard, relishing in the low grunt that rips from his throat. His hands capture my hips automatically though he doesn't guide my movements—deliberately, I suspect with an internal giggle. My first aim is to change that. "I can handle anything," I insist while rocking my hips to tease that bulge further.

Within seconds, however, the tables turn. Needling him becomes less important than feeling him. Moisture dampens my inner thighs and at the back of my mind, I know it's shameless to tease him, when I could wind up ruining his expensive clothes in the process. But logic melts away like tissue paper against the waves of pleasure just grinding on him inspires. If I shift in the right direction, the friction of his pants scrapes over my clit. It's brief, fiery bliss. A little wiggle in the other direction, and the sensation is enhanced tenfold.

And I'm not the only one loving this, it seems.

His eyelids flutter, his jaw tightening by the second. A hint of something dangerous flickers across his irises, gone before I even have the sense to fear it. Sense being the operative word.

He feels so damn good. My thoughts dissipate, and what little remain turn to sex. What it would feel like if he fucked me from this position. How his piercing would feel pressing against the innermost parts of me. Each devious thought seems to take control of my hips, making them move faster. Slower.

As if from far away, I register a sudden knock on the door of the suite, followed by Vadim's surprisingly guttural command, "Come in."

"H-Huh?" I vaguely register the door opening before a tall man in a suit strolls in, a silver tray balanced on one hand while he holds a bottle of wine in the other. Our unfortunate room service deliverer.

He takes one look at me—straddling Vadim completely naked—and nearly drops both items onto the damn floor. Not to mention that the sea of partially opened Chanel boxes makes the room a hell he's forced to navigate like some weird, fashion-focused game of twister. Finally, he makes it to the dining table and unloads his burden before he practically hops back to the entrance of the suite.

"Add a grand to the tab for the gratuity," Vadim says as the man bows and closes the door.

"Mean!" I grind on him mercilessly, desperate to ruin his fancy smanshy pants by way of payback. My traitorous body makes that task ten times easier to accomplish—the tailor-made fabric is already soaked. My brain is in la-la land, and I'm too far gone to stop. I could come like this, I realize happily. I wiggle my hips in the hopes of spurring that inevitability on faster. He might have the last laugh, but at least I'd salvage something from this. Something I suspect will be well worth the hassle. Tempting heat creeps through my belly, spurring me on. I'm so close already…

And right when I'm on the very edge, he grips my hips, wrenching me off of him.

"No!" I claw at his shoulders, trying to find my way back onto his lap.

I'm no match. Utilizing effortless strength, he stands, keeping me at bay with a single grip on my arm. Then he pivots. I land on my back, staring up at him stunned as he rips the belt from his slacks and tosses it aside. My mouth waters when he unfastens his pants next, freeing his cock. It's more than just a little hard now, pulsing and erect, his piercing gleaming.

I spread my legs, alarmed by how his eyes fixate on me in response. He's anything but disinterested. Even the thought of having him touch me makes all of my logical brain malfunction. The needy whore takes over.

"Please…" I arch my hips, presenting myself to him. "Please. Please—"

An uncharacteristic grunt rips from him. Tearing off his suit jacket, he mounts the bed and grabs my thigh, yanking me closer. My heart pounds as my ass comes precariously close to slipping off the edge of the mattress.

Before I can even fall, he catches my thigh, positioning himself against me. Those dark eyes find mine, flashing and furious. Have I pushed poor Vadim to his limits again?

Good. I writhe, stroking myself up and down his length, feeling him strain even as he grits his teeth. The reigns of his restraint are stretched thin, I suspect. Seconds from snapping entirely.

So I do the good, respectful thing and palm his hips, sinking my nails in.

"*Merde!*" He bucks, entering me so mindlessly deep that I lose track of everything but the need to drive him deeper. Take more.

I beg for him, slurring each request in increasingly explicit tones that would make me blush in my right mind. "Fuck me. Yes. So deep. Please!"

I come off the mattress, nearly climbing up his body just to enhance every thrust. My moans drip into his ear, my nails grazing whatever parts of him I can reach.

"So good. So good. So good—"

Suddenly, he rears back and feels along the mattress until he finds something long… His belt. I stiffen, alarm battling the lust turning my brain to mush. "W-What are you…"

He takes my hands, bringing them together. Then he wraps the length of the belt around them both and ties it tight, binding me. Restraining me.

And the fact of him robbing me of the ability to even touch him does something weird to my head. I'm boiling. He grates out another foreign curse, rocking his hips as if to stave off his release—but he can't. He's thickening inside me, setting off a chain reaction that boils my blood and has me screaming. Never have I ever come so hard in my life. My toes curl, my back arching off the bed, my body rippling around him like a vice.

It goes on and on and on. When I finally come down, I'm murmuring senseless praise that makes him shudder.

"So good. So good. Please more. Please. Please."

He withdraws from me so violently it hurts. I moan, struck dumb with shock only to find myself shoved onto my stomach as his weight pins me from behind. Again, he slams in, still rock hard.

But this angle…

Everything feels enhanced to the nth degree, and I cry out throatily in pleasure. It's like he knows me from the inside out. How to create the most toe-curling friction. What spots to press. How to move. How to stop, leaving me quaking on the very edge of sanity.

Just when I'm about to tip over, he hisses out something too grated for me to interpret. A curse? His hand falls over my ass, squeezing hard. Then he withdraws and then rapidly brings his palm down, resulting in a stinging slap.

Again.

Again.

"Never," he snarls in a tone I've yet to hear from him. "Never wanted to chastise a woman. But you…" Another smack makes me writhe into the contours of his hand, extending the contact. "You demand to be punished."

"So punish me," I blurt. Or at least, I would if I was in control of my brain enough to adequately transfer the command to my mouth. I moan instead, rocking into his next tentative thrust.

I feel like I'm burning alive.

My only salvation is the relief that comes from release, and I slavishly chase it. Eventually, he regains his brutal rhythm, driving me across the mattress with each wrenching thrust. Ultimately my upper body is left leaning over the edge of the bed, and I'm staring dazedly at the floor as he finally groans and his cock thrums against my battered walls.

Somehow, I manage to twist around to watch him, and I promptly rocket to cloud nine all over again. With his head thrown back, throat cording around a groan, he looks so beautiful it hurts. His hooded eyes meet mine, and I'm shocked at what I find swirling within them. Pleasure mixed with hesitant relief.

Like he didn't think it was possible to feel *this* good.

This free.

Like sex—despite his obvious prowess—is a novel experience to him, he's only recently discovered.

In this brief second, he looks at me like he's never come this hard or for this long…

For anyone.

And I know as a logical part of me reforms and urges a warning that I need to get my ass back to California. As soon as possible.

He is the most dangerous man I've ever met—and I'm enjoying that way too much.

CHAPTER TWELVE

"I love this wine!" I brandish my third glass at Vadim and open my mouth for the forkful of pasta he amusedly shoves into it. "And I love this food," I murmur in ecstasy, my eyes threatening to roll.

We're in bed again. Together. A bad idea, but I'm drunk, so who cares?

He's naked, lying beside me with a plate of lukewarm pasta between us, and a bottle of the amazing wine propped up on a pillow nearby. I wiggle my sore limbs, stretching as I watch him sample his own much smaller bite of pasta.

"You have such a beautiful mouth," I gush mournfully. "What a shame you won't get to use it on me before I leave."

I'm surprisingly devastated by the idea. To drown my sorrows, I sip more of my wine and distract myself with the contours of his abs instead.

"You're perfect," I tell him, brushing my fingers along his right pec. "It's unfair you're so beautiful."

His eyes cloud over, stormy and distant. "And you are still so affectionate after a glass or two of wine," he remarks, his annoyance palpable.

"Why do you hate when I praise you?" I drain the rest of my glass and set it aside. Then I prop my chin on my fist and observe him critically. "Every time I say anything nice about you, you get so surly and mean."

"What is praise, and what is…leverage?" he counters.

"Ah, I get it." I roll my eyes knowingly. "The big bad rich, handsome billionaire has become so jaded to compliments and the schmoozing of others. He can no longer trust who truly wants him or his money. Am I correct?"

He nods in capitulation. "Though it is not always money."

"Hmm." I stroke my chin, mulling over the sheer depths of his paranoia. To live as such with a body like his. It must be hell. "I can't speak for anyone else, but typically when a woman climaxes on your cock while screaming about how good you feel, she most likely means it."

It's the wine making me so tactless. But why stop now? I fumble for the bottle and add pointedly, "Since I'm never going to see you again after tomorrow, allow me to get it all out now. I love how you look. So sexy but so understated, requiring a second glance to register the full effect. And—" I try to pour myself a fresh glass and wind up spilling more wine onto myself than anything. Sighing, he's forced to assist me, manipulating the bottle with his much steadier touch. In triumph, I take another sip and settle against a mound of displaced pillows. "I love your mouth. I love your eyes, especially—I never know what you're thinking. I love when you spank me…" I trail off as I notice him staring far more intently than before. "And, I love your voice. I really love your cock. It's perfection. And I *love* your piercing—"

"Enough to copy me?" he wonders, swiping his finger along my belly.

I reflexively clamp my knees together at first. Then, emboldened by another sip of wine, I spread them, revealing every inch of the flesh in question. At the back of my mind, I marvel at how comfortable I feel in front of him. I panic at it. I felt dirty in anything less than a conservative negligee around Jim. He made me feel as if his lust was my sin. But Vadim?

He makes lust feel as heady as alcohol, mine alone to enjoy. To get drunk on.

And it feels so good to get drunk.

"You would pierce this?" he wonders, eyeing my anatomy skeptically.

"I would," I boast. "For a price."

He frowns, unimpressed. "You would mutilate yourself just to please another?"

"Oh, I've been curious about it," I admit with a shrug. "I've heard it can make you orgasm like that—" I snap my fingers for emphasis. "But I'm so horny that I could make myself come while thinking about a wet paper bag. But you? I have a hunch that you would *love* to see me pierced."

Not that he ever would because I'm leaving in the morning. He knows I'm going. Even as his eyes take on a thoughtful, dangerous gleam, he knows it…

"I'd let you have a say in every part of it," I add, casually sipping more wine while playing with fire. "The size. Placement. I'd even let you pick the metal—"

"Silver," he says absently. "Of the highest quality. And you seem perfectly suited for a VCH."

"Oh?" I lift an eyebrow and run my tongue along the rim of my glass. So much for his aversion to kink. He sounds fairly knowledgeable in this arena all of a sudden—too knowledgeable. A part of me can't help wondering if clitoral piercings is a subject he regularly tackles with his one-night stands. Or just me. For instance, if he only started researching the topic not long after our very first meeting when I drunkenly expressed interest in it? A dangerous thought that requires another tasting of wine to wash it down.

"What's a VCH?" I ask, turning to a much less risky topic.

"A vertical clitoral hood piercing," he says, his gaze flashing and devious once more. "It's well known for increasing stimulation during sex."

I suck in a breath, intrigued. But then I remember the caveat making this entire conversation moot. "What a shame that I'm leaving tomorrow—" In six hours, to be exact, judging from the flashing numbers on the console by the TV. "If only you were nicer to me. We could have had so much fun." In very real disappointment, I down the rest of my glass in one go.

"Hypothetically speaking, what would your price be?"

"Hmm." I cast him an appraising glance, though I already know my answer. I've been thinking of it obsessively ever since the first damn time he slapped my ass. Even now, I'm growing wet at the prospect of it and just how much I'll be denied when it comes to him and sex. Therefore, I have no guilt in blurting out the truth. "My price? That would be *you*, Mr. Vadim. I'd want you to—"

Both of his eyebrows go up in shock as I proceed to lay out a detailed list of all of my fantasies when it comes to kink. All. Of. Them. Bondage. Being pilloried. Much more "chastisement." I mention the one time I briefly considered nipple clamping but chickened out. Orgies. Exhibition. Being blindfolded and gagged. And then a whole list of items so X-rated I immediately block them from my memory the second I utter them.

By the time I finish, Vadim actually looks shocked. Not merely amused. Shook.

Score two for Tiffy. Utterly pleased with myself, I lean back further against the cushions supporting me, displaying the breasts that I just admitted I'd wanted clamped, teased, and tormented.

"We would have to wait to do the really fun stuff until after the piercing healed, of course," I add, taking this ball and running far with it. "That could take... I don't know—"

"Four to eight weeks," he supplies. "About the same length of time it would take to special order the apparatuses you so cleverly described. Even if I paid the rush fee."

Again, he sounds far too knowledgeable on the subject. Even I know when to back down at the last minute.

"Yes, well, it will never happen." I lean over to place my glass and plate on the nightstand. Then I proceed to shimmy beneath the luxurious blankets. With my back to him, I yawn for real and make a show of closing my eyes. "Nighty night. See you again, never. Try not to make too much noise on your way out. I'm a very—"

"Light sleeper," he finishes, but I can't escape the sense that it sounds more mocking than insightful. Like he knows some delicious secret I don't regarding my sleep.

Back off, Tiffy.

"Night!" I slam a blanket over my head and settle down in earnest. Before I drift off, I send up a prayer that I'll wake up in time to catch my flight. *Amen.*

And that once I land in California, I'll magically forget all about Vadim and his kink.

Amen, amen.

A girl can dream.

CHAPTER THIRTEEN

I wake up with roughly two hours to get dressed and hustle to the airport—which is the good news. The bad news is that I wake up so content that I think I'm in a dream at first. A dream so sensual and relaxing that it couldn't possibly be real. It stars my naked body and someone's hand on my ass. A hand composed of slim fingers that involuntarily stroke me every now and again as if its owner can't keep his hands off me even in his sleep.

That's why I woke up. I'm so damn horny that my brain couldn't cope, instinctively knowing that something is horribly wrong. Because the hand is very real, I realize as I tentatively arch my back and said fingers grope me in response. Not to mention that the owner's smell is so damn signature that there is no mistaking his identity.

It's *Vadim's* hand.

Crap. I blink my eyes open to the darkened hotel room. Someone drew the courtesy blinds closed after I went to bed. That same person, no doubt, rearranged the pillows and neatly tucked the blankets over us both. My mouth drops open. The bastard had the sheer gall to climb beneath them with me as if we were a normal couple after a normal night of normal sex.

The worst part is how damn beautiful he looks. Watching him deeply asleep should be a crime against humanity. He looks so...vulnerable for once, with his dark lashes fanning his cheekbones and his curls framing his face like a corrupted halo. But that vulnerability lasts up until the moment my gaze falls over his mouth, still fixed in that surly, mistrustful line. Even in his sleep, the man has his wall up.

Get out of here, Tiffy. I tear my gaze away from him and creep into the bathroom. There I take the quickest whore bath imaginable, and then I find my way through the dark to fish out the one outfit I refuse to leave behind—a black, red, and white checkered tweed suit and skirt ensemble with a frothy white blouse to go underneath. For good measure, I find a beautiful black clutch too incredible to risk abandoning. Then I tiptoe toward the door of the suite in a pair of black block heels.

A sigh of relief escapes me once I clear the minefield of clothing boxes. Paces from the door, I eagerly reach out for the handle, and I'm home free.

Until a deep, sexily husky voice rings out, "I'm afraid to inform you that your flight has been canceled."

I whirl around to find Vadim still in bed, a lazy smirk playing over his lips, visible even in the dark. His eyes practically glow with amusement, and I flick the nearest light switch, robbing him of the mystery of shadow to hide behind. The action backfires—gosh, he looks more mouthwatering in the dim glow cast by one of the bedside lamps. The sight of his bare chest makes me groan—the gleaming, chiseled panes practically demand further exploration. With my fingers. With my mouth.

I shake my head to clear the thoughts, blinking to refocus. "W-Why? I mean, how do you even know that?"

He extends his arms and casually laces his fingers together behind his head, leaning back against the pillows. "Because I took the liberty of canceling it."

Shock makes me sway, all tension of my potential escape dashed. I feel along the wall until I reach a leather-backed chair and collapse onto it.

"Why?"

"Why?" He inclines his head, an eyebrow raised. "I don't typically allow people to steal from me."

I scoff. "You don't own me." But he does own this dress. And this purse. And these shoes… Clearing my throat, I rush to add, "And you can bill me for the clothing. I'll pay it off."

Internally, I'm screaming. Realistically I *could* pay it off… if I sold my body for a few years into sexual slavery. Even my trust fund wouldn't cut it, nor my alimony. Theoretically, I could always ask my parents to cover maybe a teensy, weensy fraction—a few grand at least. But the guilt would eat me alive, so that's a no.

Sexual slavery it is.

"Money was not the agreed upon price," Vadim says, his tone scolding. My ass smarts in memory of his "punishment," and I hate myself. How is it possible for someone to switch from icy cool to sexy dark so easily? "I will take my payment in full," he adds as if aware of his effect on me.

"Payment," I grouse. "Dinner with your brother? Are you that afraid of going alone?"

What I intend to sound taunting lands with a thud when he nods.

"Yes," he says unapologetically. "I am. Maxim and I can rarely occupy the same space without…unpleasantries."

Minus the one night I accompanied him, and we scored two presents out of it. Sighing, I lean forward and tap my chin as if mulling over the prospect—which I'm not. A week is far too long to stay here, away from home. Far too long to stay within the orbit of such a dangerous man. I've already lost my brain around him—twice. No siree can that happen again.

"You're considering," he remarks as if reading my mind. "Tell me what will put you over the edge."

I grit my teeth, still contemplating the idea of running down to the front lobby and begging the concierge to find me any flight leaving within the hour to anywhere but here. If only his voice didn't make the demand sound so damn tempting.

"I'll need underwear," I point out. "I mean, I would, *if* I were staying—which I'm not."

He nods. "Fair enough."

"But not just any underwear… Lingerie. French-style from Atelier Noir. An assortment of course. Bras, panties, and full sets." Gosh, I can barely keep the excited squeal from my voice. Designer to the rich and famous, the items from Atelier Noir are legendary in both style and price. I once made the mistake of looking up the cost of a bra and panty set I'd admired in a magazine and promptly fell into a weeklong despair at the price.

"Done," he says. A devious part of me wants to drop an average price point of the garments and watch him squirm—but the longer I observe him, the more I suspect that he already knows the cost and then some. Either way, he's prepared to pay it.

"You drop obscene amounts of money on your one-night stand, and yet you clam up the second she says anything nice about you." I raise a skeptical eyebrow, crossing my legs.

"Clothing, money, and even lingerie is a physical exchange," he explains, sounding like some stuffy professor—not that I had ever gone to one college class to know the difference. "Compliments, on the other hand? Praise? Those are delivered with only one goal in mind. Manipulation." He's staring off into space, no doubt glowering at the memory of all the prior women who dared to compliment him.

"So cynical!" I lean forward and eye him with renewed scrutiny. "I've changed my mind. You know what will make me stay? You praise *me*. Something nice and personal—you've called me beautiful before," I add before he can say as much. "But that doesn't count."

"Why not?"

I frown, uncomforted by the answer. "Because it's not a real compliment," I say. "It's an assessment. You can call me beautiful, but it doesn't require any personal engagement on your part. I want you to dig deep, Vadim. For instance…" Licking my lips, I sweep my gaze along him and settle over his waist. "I've told you that you have a beautiful cock, that I enjoy it—but have I told you why? It's so damn good that I think you've adopted it as your primary personality. Dick."

He chuckles, and I inhale at the genuine sound. "Praise. That is all it will take for you to stay?"

"Well, I do need new underwear." I glance forlornly at the brand-new, priceless skirt I'm already in danger of ruining. Lately, sex has been on my brain more often than not—making up for lost time and all that—but never to this extent. Being around him has me in a perpetual state of arousal, and I hate myself. "But yes. Offer me a real, heartfelt compliment, and I'll stay. Until Monday. After that, you're allowing me the use of your private plane to go back to Cali so that you can't 'cancel' any more commercial flights."

He frowns, looking surlier than ever.

"I can start, if you want?" I say sweetly. "Watch and learn —I love your cock. I love how you fuck when you lose yourself in the moment. I love it when you slap me on the—"

"The things you say." His frown deepens, his brow furrowing in aggravation. "Am I really to believe that you were a Sunday school teacher?"

"Amen," I say solemnly. "But whether you believe me or not doesn't matter to me. I don't spend my life concerned with the intentions of others like you do."

Minus, of course, those of the dangerous, enticing billionaire who toys with me like a bored owner tossing his hyper puppy a bone every now and again.

"Now give me what I want," I prod. "Or I'll go to the airport right now and find a pilot to screw. *That* will get me a ride home, I'm sure—"

"Since you're already dressed, we'll do breakfast instead of dinner," Vadim says. He shoves the covers back and stands.

And my brain short-circuits.

Unsurprisingly, he's still naked, and my eyes feast upon his body when glimpsed in full. His cock is breathtaking, of course, stiff with morning wood—but his ass. Damn, his ass. I nearly groan out loud as he turns around and bends to pick up his discarded clothing from the floor.

"Is that agreement, I wonder?" he asks without turning around.

"H-Huh?" I blink, struck dumb. The man was crafted by the Devil himself. Slender and lean, the one part of him that isn't solid muscle, is balanced on top of his muscular thighs. Plump and firm, it looks so damn squeezable that I have to clench my hands into fists just to stop from reaching out.

"I asked if you were going to be agreeable and join me for breakfast or if you were going to insist I jump through some kind of hoop first?" he says, turning to face me, his clothing slung over one arm.

Dick.

"Praise me," I demand, rising to my feet as well. "Or I'm leaving. I mean it—"

"You..." He eyes me as if hunting for something he can find to compliment me on. When the seconds tick by, heat sears my cheeks.

"Well, don't try too hard," I snap. "You might give yourself an aneurysm—"

"Your smile is...decent," he says finally. "Satisfied?"

"Thanks," I croon, displaying the smile in question. "With a little bit more training, I'll have you an expert in bedroom talk."

For his next conquest, of course. Because by then, I'll be in Cali crawling under another businessman. Or maybe a doctor.

"I need to change." He strolls to the door, unabashedly bare. "Preferably before you attempt to sneak away, thus committing theft. Though I am sure you are above such devious actions?"

I shiver as he passes me, and it takes everything I have to keep from ogling his ass a second time.

"I'm not," I admit. "The second you leave, I'm running headlong to the lobby. Try and stop me."

"Is that so?" He eyes me from over his shoulder, his smirk firmly in place. Casually he dons his shirt and suit jacket and then slips into his pants. The only missing item is his belt, which I think is lost in the bed somewhere. Rather than hunt for it, he enters the hallway, and I follow him, more than ready to attempt my escape.

I expect him to head for the elevator, or maybe the stairs. Anything but across the hall and casually fish a keycard from his pocket. One swipe, and the door opens.

"You rented out the suite next to mine?" I stammer open-mouthed.

He enters the suite, and his voice reaches back to me. "You mean—I rented out two suites adjacent to each other? Then yes. The fact that you manage to occupy one serves only as a testament to your remarkable ability to take from me what you may."

"Oh, really?" I storm after him, shocked to find a suite every bit as spacious as mine. The only difference is the obsessive, painful level of neatness that I suspect goes far beyond the hotel cleaning services. There isn't so much as a used napkin lying around, and all of his clothing appears to be neatly unpacked and stored within the walk-in closet. He enters it and proceeds to undress while eyeing his options.

I shimmy past him and gain an up-close look at what essentials a billionaire might think to pack in his travel wardrobe. Lots of black, for one. A multitude of simple, but crisply tailored suits and a boring arrangement of ties. Though professional attire isn't all that I find dangling from wooden hangers. Tucked at the very back is an array of insultingly plain sweatshirts when compared to the quality of everything else.

"A gym rat?" I suspect out loud. That would certainly explain his remarkably fit shape. Biting my lower lip, I flick through the nearest selection of suits. Tucked amongst all the black is a collection in a deep, rich shade of navy, and I'm too tempted to resist.

"Don't tell me your style has changed within the space of five seconds," Vadim murmurs as I strip the suit from the hanger. "I must say that I'm curious as to how a masculine style would look on you."

I suck in a breath but push the thought out of my mind instantly. Wearing his clothing is way too intimate. "Wear this," I demand, whirling around to shove the suit at him. "Eww. Not that!" I playfully smack his hand away as he reaches for an ebony selection instead. "This one."

I hold the jacket up to his chest and instantly regret the selection. "Maybe not."

Like a shark sensing blood in the water, he snatches the garments from me and tugs them on as I watch, increasingly terrified by the overall effect.

Damn, damn, damn. Blue is so his color—to an alarming degree. It enhances the darkness reflecting in his eyes and brilliantly plays off the paleness of his chin. The only thing that could possibly enhance the look more is…

I scan the space for it, and my eyes fall over a tie organizer hanging on the opposite side of the closet. Sure enough, shoved at the very bottom in an array of muted colors is a navy one made of silk. My fingers shake as I loop it around Vadim's neck.

"So much better," I confess. "You're far too handsome to avoid color."

"Is that so?" He's frowning as he adjusts the tie, deftly tying it. "Will you make me buy myself a wardrobe next?"

I flinch at the surly tone, but he presents a tempting possibility. "Maybe," I say, my voice distant as I picture how he'd look in red. My throat goes dry.

"So…breakfast." Forging a change in subject, I slip past him and re-enter the bedroom. "Where are you taking me?"

I steel myself for some insanely expensive restaurant or a McDonalds—knowing him, either option is within the realm of possibility, chosen primarily to catch me off guard.

"Downstairs," he says, surprising me. "I have a standing reservation. It will, however, serve as a business meeting as well."

As if to demonstrate as much, he crosses to a briefcase placed beside the entrance and lifts it. "After you."

"Business?"

He doesn't give me an explanation as I follow him out into the hall. We take the elevator down to the lobby, and within minutes, we're herded to a beautiful table in the back of an elegant French restaurant.

"Are you French?" I ask him as I claim the seat across from him. I notice that the menu is in French and paired with his display from last night, I think he enjoys flaunting his bilingualism before me.

"My mother was," he admits, opening his menu to scan the pages. "And it is my preferred culture of the many I grew up immersed in."

"Military brat?" I say, taking a guess. He certainly has the stone-cold emotional range of someone who grew up with a hard ass, drill sergeant parent.

He looks away, and his gaze turns distant. "No. Not quite."

"You don't like to talk about your childhood," I surmise. "That could be a good thing. Mine was so boringly typical that there isn't much to talk about."

"Oh?" Real interest flashes across his features.

"My dad was an investment banker," I admit. "My mother was a glorified housewife—but damn good at it. My uncle Conroy runs one of the largest vineyards in the country, and I had the typical, milk toast, country club, basic bitch white girl upbringing."

And there is no shame in that.

"But you were married..." He busies himself with pouring water from a pitcher into two glasses, but I sense that he's very interested in this topic.

"For seven years," I say tiredly. "I met him the day after I got drunk at a high school yacht party and flashed my tits to a group of guys who took pictures. Then I fell off the upper deck and sliced open my back. Wine is my Achilles heel."

More so whenever he is involved. "My parents were scandalized. My Dad was terrified I'd be ostracized, and my mother couldn't stop crying at the thought of me being labeled a dirty slut. So, I panicked. The very next day, while bandaged and high on painkillers, I joined a bible study class at my private school, and there I met James Andrew Walker. Jim for short. He told me I was pretty, I told him I was born again, and with my newly reformed attitude, no one could judge me for my hellish lapse in judgment. My parents were happy. I was happy, or at least I thought I was…"

"The marriage was unhappy?"

I nod. Then I shake my head. "Not necessarily at first. We dated for a year before then, but… It was like nothing I did made him happy. How I dressed. How I acted. What I did. Didn't do. I couldn't conceive on *his* timeframe—" I don't go into the details, and luckily he doesn't ask. He just listens, as watchful as ever. "I couldn't have sex the way he wanted. Every day spent with him made me feel like some dirty, disgusting, worthless failure. He was prominent in the church, you see, so I always had to be a 'model wife' for his congregation. Apparently, I failed, because one day, I came to our beautiful home and found him waiting for me with his beautiful secretary whom he'd been sinning with in secret for a year, I think. This, after we were basically separated already so he could 'reevaluate things.' The newer model was pregnant, so divorce city for me. Marital bliss for them."

Saying it all out loud hurts more than I would have anticipated. My eyes burn, and blinking rapidly can't keep one rebellious tear from breaking loose.

"After that, I told myself that I would never, ever beat myself down for anyone else. I would never change who I am to please anyone. If I want to run off on a crazy sexual adventure, then damn it, that's what I'll do."

I look at him, expecting the judgment I'm so used to seeing reflected at me these days. All he does is nod in silent agreement—and in a way, his acceptance is so much worse.

"What happened between you and your brother?" I ask, turning the tables. "You weren't close growing up?"

"You could say that." He's distant again, staring off beyond me. "We weren't close, and for the most part, we grew up apart—he lived with our grandfather after our father's death. Then our uncle…" Disgust colors his voice, making me suspect that he doesn't care very much for that particular family member either. "Even so, we were very much reminded of each other's existence."

"Ah. A sibling rivalry." Lucky for me, I was an only child, but I saw firsthand how nasty sibling battles can go. Uncle Conroy has two sons who constantly vie for his favor. "Let me guess. You were the good twin, and he was the bad?"

"I was the reminder," he says softly. "Of everything he never wanted to be."

"Beautiful, smart, and stubbornly brooding?" I wonder playfully.

He blinks and refocuses on me. His expression is skeptical rather than amused. As if he can't quite understand why I'm trying to joke with him.

"Order something sexy for me in French," I command, spotting our waitress arriving just in the nick of time. "Something sweet."

My heart stops at the devious gleam flashing through his gaze. After scouring the menu for a few more seconds, he turns to our waitress, opens his mouth, and proceeds to utter the most panty-melting stream of words I've ever heard someone speak before. In English or otherwise.

Well, almost. Nothing tops his grunted slip-up from last night, but this comes close.

I smother a groan and try to disguise how my cheeks set on fire by looking down to read my own menu. Once he's finished, I sneak a glance at him through my lashes and hiss in irritation.

He's smugger than ever.

"I've taken the liberty of ordering you a selection of items," he explains, gathering up the menus for the waitress to take. "I will discover which you prefer to dine on the next time you find yourself drunk and hungry while in my bed."

I nearly choke, and I rush to take a sip of water, clearing my throat. "Sorry to break it to you, Vadim, but you won't enjoy having me in a bed with you ever again. Because we aren't having sex again," I feel the need to clarify. "Ever."

He raises an eyebrow, deliciously confused. "You mean to deny yourself of my beautiful cock?"

No fair. I gasp, my brain stalling. When my thoughts come back online, all I can think to utter is, "You're damn right. I'm starting to think that I need to guard myself carefully around you."

Fire flashes through his gaze. "I would never hurt you," he growls—and at the back of my mind, I take comfort in that. Though Jim had said the same thing at one point.

"Not like that," I say softly. "More like… I think you enjoy playing mind games with people, while keeping them at arm's length. Which is fine, I guess. I just don't think I can last on your emotional merry-go-round for long."

Admitting something so honest should feel more alarming than it does. There's just something about him. His face, maybe? I feel so safe when it comes to our conversations. *Which is why you need to run far and fast, girl,* my inner-bitch warns. *Preferably now.*

"Keeping people at arm's length," he murmurs, another amused smile tugging on his mouth. "Usually, I am the one left feeling as though I am on that…merry-go-round as you put it."

"Oh?" I prop my chin on my hand and eye him more closely. His expression remains as neutral as ever, though, on second glance, I notice that his eyes are more hooded than usual. He's recalling his past again. "Your brother?" I guess. "Family? Other businessmen? Frankly, I can't imagine any woman with a functioning libido wanting to keep you at any length, even if you can be a total dick—"

"You asked about my upbringing?" he counters. Something inside me tingles, and I sit forward, suddenly rapt. He was vague about his past before for a reason. The fact that he's bringing it up now makes me feel that something made him change his mind.

"The way my brother and I were raised could be described as a competition," he explains. "Our every waking moment was spent being compared to each other. Who was faster? Stronger? Smarter? Over and over again. Such antics take their toll over time. In many, many ways, I did not measure up to Maxim."

He's so blunt about it, and yet this one fact explains so much about him.

"That's why you hate when I praise you," I say, awed at the realization. "You're so used to being picked apart that your brain can't fathom the concept of a harmless compliment."

"I wouldn't call your words harmless." He shoots me a glance that makes me rush to take another sip of water.

"You mistrust anything that isn't strictly transactional or negative," I add, confident in my psychoanalysis. "The fact that I think you're beautiful, sexy even, with the body of a God makes your brain explode."

"Should an ex-Sunday school teacher speak such blasphemy?" he taunts.

I shrug him off. "Baby, I've decided to no longer be offended by your dickishness. I'm just going to train you as any decent woman would."

His smirk grows, stretching across his pink, tempting mouth. "Train me?"

"Oh, yes!" I clap my hands together at the enormity of the task ahead. "You'll soon come to enjoy my compliments. I think you might even start to crave them, you beautiful man."

"Is that so?" He sits back in his chair and cocks his head to give me a thorough once over. "And these compliments will come without us having sex?"

A challenge, for sure, but one I'm still up for accepting. "Yes," I say with a nod.

"What a shame…" He strokes his finger along his jaw, his gaze reflective. "I was so looking forward to discovering just how you wanted me to use my mouth."

I nearly fall out of my chair. For a horrible second, my thoughts devolve to a frantic mantra of *unfair, unfair, unfair!* When I finally regain my senses, our waitress has returned to set an entire spread of various dishes before us.

Vadim takes the time to name every dish in that drool-worthy accent.

"How did I know you would go for the cream first?" he muses as I grab a fork and shove it into a delicious looking white substance served with jam.

Everything tastes beyond amazing. I sample each dish, circling back to a few in particular, aware of him watching my every move. I've cleared my plate twice when I finally push back from the table in defeat.

"Now what?" I ask as he dabs his mouth with his napkin. Between the two of us, I've eaten seventy-five percent of the meal, but he's barely touched what little items are on his plate. Before I can point out the discrepancy, he shifts his focus to something behind me.

"Now, my business meeting is here." He reaches into his pocket while I glance over my shoulder and spot an older woman wearing a gray suit, her brunette hair pulled back into a severe bun. "What price would you put on having full access to my accounts for the evening?" Vadim questions, his tone suddenly serious.

"H-Huh?" My brain nearly crashes again at the thought of what I could buy if unleashed for several hours. More clothes. More shoes. Maybe I'd take him up on that threat to buy him a new wardrobe? Something tan, or navy, or red. Surprisingly that seems more appealing than the rest.

But then I finally notice the object he has trapped between two fingers and I recoil in alarm. It's a wedding ring. So he wasn't lying about the fake wife.

"Are you insane?"

"Whatever amount you think you could spend, double it," he suggests, but he doesn't extend the ring to me. I have to reach out and take it.

Which I won't. I can't. I…

"Mr. Gorgoshev?" A woman calls from paces away as I finally relent and lunge for the ring. It lands on my palm, and I slip it onto the finger that—until now—had been proudly bare.

Sweat slicks my neck as Vadim stands to greet the woman, and I race to copy him.

"Ms. Anderson, is it?" he says to her warmly. "This is Tiffany, my fiancée."

"P-Pleased to meet you," I stammer while shaking the woman's hand.

She looks different from the typical businesswoman, or even an industry professional for that matter. Her clothing is strictly utilitarian, and the briefcase she carries has seen better days. As she sits, she shuffles through said briefcase and withdraws a stack of documents.

"Ah, yes," she says, furrowing her brow as she reads. "You've applied for permanent residency it looks like. We'll need to do a preliminary house visit, of course, but given the circumstances, I'm sure we can seek placement within a couple weeks. And out of courtesy to you, we can arrange a meeting with the previous family. Your lawyers have assured me that you seek to expedite this case as much as possible?"

"Yes," Vadim nods. In the blink of an eye, his entire posture has shifted. He sits taller, which has the effect of lengthening his body overall and making him seem even more commanding than usual.

Watching him, I quickly lose track of the complicated business terms as they repeatedly discuss placement and a challenging case. Some kind of business he's hoping to acquire? Eventually, the meeting ends as both Vadim and Ms. Anderson stand and shake hands.

"Great. And it looks like you've already secured a property here in the city! If you're okay with everything as specified, then I would love to schedule the first preliminary visit by the end of next week, perhaps?"

"That will suffice," Vadim says, nodding. "I will do everything within my power to ensure that it is perfectly suited."

Smiling, Ms. Anderson walks off. I'm so distracted by watching her departure that I don't notice until it's too late the hand that settles over my lower back.

"A decent performance, *baby*," Vadim murmurs against the column of my throat. "Though next time, try not to drool of utter boredom, *oui*?"

Startled, I swipe at my mouth. Did I?

His laugh reveals that once again, I fell for one of his mind games. Hahaha.

"I should renegotiate my price, adding a deduction for every time you stared off blankly into space, but alas, we have an agreement. Feel free to try your hardest to drive me into bankruptcy. I assure you that you cannot."

"Is that so?" Challenge accepted. My mind reels with the most expensive, exclusive stores I'd never dream of shopping in before. But as Vadim leads me across the lobby to the concierge, I have enough sense to ask. "What was so different about that meeting that you needed a wife present? I'm sure you've made plenty of deals as a bachelor to get where you are."

His jaw twitches—something I'm starting to realize may be his one and only tell. He's hiding something.

"Ms. Connors is to have unlimited use of the town car, this evening," he says to the concierge without addressing my question. "Adieu."

I watch him go, mildly curious. Halfway across the lobby, he pauses and rummages through his jacket pocket.

"I almost forgot this," he calls back to me without turning around. He brandishes a small object between his fingers, forcing me to cross over to him to retrieve it—his credit card. "Spend unwisely," he says, starting off again. "Let's see how much damage you can do."

Challenge accepted. I'm already mulling over what style suit might compliment him the best as I meet my driver out front, and we head toward the shopping district. But at the back of my mind remains this niggling sense that I just missed something.

Something vital.

Something he was willing to bargain unlimited use of his credit card and the promise of a shopping spree to distract me from.

I return to the hotel just before midnight in a different vehicle from the sleek, compact model I left in. Halfway through the outing, the poor driver stuck with me had to call for backup and switch out his smaller model for a Range Rover.

Regardless, my purchases are practically spilling out of the SUV. So much so that I have to run to the front desk to request assistance. But the second I give my room number, the hostess raises an eyebrow.

"I'm sorry, Miss," she says. "But it looks like you were checked out at least…" She scrolls through her records. "At least five hours ago. The room has already been cleaned."

"W-What?" Panic grips me so fiercely I have to brace both hands on the counter. *Deep breaths, Tiffy. You still have the bastard's credit card, unless he's already canceled it…*

"Oh! It looks like there was a note left for you. Your

husband wanted you to know that he had your things sent home and that he'll be waiting for you there."

"Home?"

She scribbles an address onto a slip of paper. I read it warily, half-expecting to find the listing for the Hotel Six back in California. Instead, I don't recognize the street address or the location.

I try to hand the page back to the hostess. "I think there's some kind of mistake."

"No mistake," she insists. "Our driver will be able to see you home. Thank you so much for your stay, have a wonderful night!"

In a daze, I stagger back out to the car and hand the slip of paper to the driver. Minutes later, we're leaving the city, heading in a direction that seems vaguely familiar. A view of a gleaming body of water pierces a calmer landscape dotted with trees and the average home made of stone or wood. As the driver turns down a long, winding driveway, it clicks.

While this isn't the exact same house his brother Maxim lives in, the one we're pulling up to now looks eerily similar—no doubt within the same location if not the same neighborhood.

It's sprawling, more modern with a winding driveway and acres of neatly manicured property. It's as if someone wanted to copy the coziness of Maxim's home, but applied the crisp, overly neat style of Vadim. The resulting creation is both breathtaking and imposing.

"Allow me to help you with these, Miss," the long-suffering driver insists as he helps me out of the backseat. Between the two of us, we manage to carry most of the packages to the front door, which opens before I can even form a fist to knock.

"Such a late hour," a man suavely remarks. "I was just about to retire to bed and assume you'd used my accounts to charter your own private plane."

"I could do that?" The marvels of men with money. Shaking my head, I try to focus. "What the hell is this, Gorgoshev?" I step forward, barging into the entry, and I drop my packages right there in the middle of an open foyer. While the house may somewhat resemble his brother's from the outside, the inside is all Vadim.

Cool, neutral colors—beige, gray, white, and black. Incomprehensible cleanliness. And then the chaos that comes with me and my five thousand shopping bags.

"Thank you for seeing her home," Vadim warmly tells the driver while tucking a large wad of cash into his palm. "Goodnight."

He heads to the door to see the man off while I take the opportunity to march through the first level of the home. It is massive. A large living room overlooks a view of the water, glistening in the moonlight. Within the same open floor plan is a gorgeous kitchen complete with stainless steel appliances and a double oven.

"Don't tell me you cook as well?" I call over my shoulder, sensing him within earshot.

He chuckles. "No. I had it installed anyway, just in case my fake wife would enjoy the feature. I made sure to cover the cliché basics of what most women supposedly like."

"Wrong." I stick out my thumb and point it to the floor. "I hate cooking."

"Fair enough. It will make for a beautiful focal point during our meals of delivery," he says as I coincidentally pass a sleek bar counter that serves as the bridge to a dining room positioned near a row of massive bay windows. Not far from it is a small lounge complete with black bookshelves already stocked and a neat, official-looking study.

"You really just moved in?" I ask. He makes it look so easy when I can barely organize myself out of a suitcase.

Rather than answer, he trails me until I circle around to the front of the house, my tour completed.

"I suppose you can help me carry these upstairs." I gesture to the mountain of packages. "The brown ones are yours. Any other color is mine."

"The brown ones..." He eyes the mostly brown pile of bags and shoots me a quizzical glance.

"I wasn't sure of your size, so I had to guess," I say, ignoring the implications conveyed by the prospect that I may or may not have spent more time shopping for him than myself. "You can leave mine by the door since I won't be staying here long."

Though should I even consider staying here at all? Spending the night in a fully populated hotel with a dangerously sexy billionaire is one thing. Holing up with him in his private, sprawling mansion is another thing entirely.

But by the time I mount the topmost step of the modern staircase leading upstairs, I promptly forget all about logistics and decency.

"Oh my gosh," I exclaim, spinning in a circle to take in the architecture. High ceilings. Gray, textured walls, and black wooden floors create a sleek, impressive effect so different from my perfect, white-picket-fence dream home. The hall branches into two ends, leading to two separate wings of the house. I start toward the right side, finding a short hallway lined with just two doors. I reach for one, and Vadim makes a sound in his throat that stops me in my tracks.

"That one is private," he says, but his tone makes me bite back a taunting retort. He sounds on-edge for once. Nervous?

A part of me warns that he could be hiding the bodies of his previous fake fiancées in there. Either way, I back off, letting him have this one round.

Turning on my heel, I begin to explore the other wing. The first door I open predictably leads into a massive master suite, but unlike the hotel's more classic décor, this one reads him down to the last detail. Gray walls. Navy accents. A huge bed—far too big for someone intent on living alone.

"Another feature to tempt your fake wife?" I wonder while running my fingers over the navy bedspread.

"No," he says in a deadpan tone. "The closet, however? Well, you be the judge."

An excited thrill has me nearly running to the door he indicates with a curt nod. Sure enough, I find a magical realm of possibility in the form of a closet so big it spans not one, but two entire rooms, each one decked out with plenty of storage for both practical use and display.

He must have it organized into two sections. The first belongs to him, already stocked with a selection of boring, professional attire. The second is mostly bare despite a small collection of neatly arranged Chanel and my previous purchases. What had seemed excessive in the hotel room now looks pitiful, barely taking up a full rack.

"Your future fake wife is a lucky woman," I admit, my heart panging with longing as I spot a full wall of shelves that she could dedicate to purses and shoes alone. Not to mention her ring—for the first time, I inspect the jewelry sparkling on my left hand in full and bite down a groan. The only terms my brain can come up with to describe it are *gorgeous, big ass, diamond.* With difficulty, I turn away and catch him watching me, his devious gaze as unfathomable as ever.

"Chop-chop!" I clap my hands commandingly. "Go fetch my purchases, please. It's time to give you a makeover." I eye him with a raised brow, surprisingly excited to see how he'll look in what I picked out. "We'll cover the basics first," I warn as he strolls into the hall, seemingly unbothered at being bossed around.

"Oh?" he wonders. The subtle, taunting inflection in his tone makes me gulp, but this time I'm prepared with a devious trick to regain the upper hand.

"Undies," I call after him, grinning from ear to ear. "You need a full shakeup from head to toe, baby. Maybe the constriction caused by those horrible boxers is what's making you so mean?"

He laughs, and I sway, knocked off balance. Something tells me that this little plan will backfire.

Spectacularly.

CHAPTER FIFTEEN

In theory, buying him a full range of *tidy-whities* with the intent of having him model them for me sounded fun. Like harmless, mischievous fun while ensuring that I maintain the upper hand in our strange, transactional relationship.

The second he steps from the closet wearing only a pair of black, low riding boxer briefs that, though tight, the salesman at the high-end boutique insisted were more comfortable than going bare, I realize that I've failed.

Game. Set. Match.

"Judging from how your jaw is on the floor, I assume you find these to your liking?" he suspects. Before I can think to stop him, he turns around, displaying his perfectly supported ass, and I can't contain a groan.

"T-Take those off," I spit out, making a mental note to steal every pair of the style I bought and return them. No future fake wife deserves to ever see him in something so sinful.

"Now?" He slips his fingers beneath the waistband, and I practically lunge from the bed and race past him, entering the closet with him on my heels.

"I want you to try on a suit," I decide, spotting a selection he had already partially unpacked. Neatly tucked within a custom garment bag is a rich, brown suit of impeccable quality. Well, almost impeccable. "I had to settle for standard sizing since I don't know your measurements, but they offer custom tailoring, so I took the liberty of including that in the price. Don't have a heart attack when you see the bill."

"I've seen it," he says, coming to stand at my shoulder. I shiver as he reaches around me to finger the sleeve of the suit, testing the quality. "My estimations were on the higher end, but you came close."

I grit my teeth, hating the warmth that spreads through my belly at his nearness. "Was that praise I heard you utter, Mr. Vadim?"

He doesn't answer, and desperate to change the subject, I turn to face him and size him up.

"I'm pretty sure I guessed correctly," I decide, scanning his chest. "Over there are dress shirts."

Obeying my instructions, he promptly unpacks ten shirts in varying colors, ranging from gray to a golden shade of yellow. I made sure to spring for multiple fabrics, including silk and cotton as well. He eyes them all without a word of either agreement or dislike, but his fingers linger over a light blue selection more than the others.

"Blue and brown?" I cock my head and bite my lip in concentration. "An atypical pairing, but let's try it."

He proceeds to dress as I watch him shamelessly from a corner of the closet. When he finally inclines his head for my approval, I think I'm in danger of fainting.

"I need to ban you from wearing blue," I blurt, stunned by how the color animates his features, making his smirk ten times smirkier. "We're done modeling for now." As he takes off the jacket, I re-enter the bedroom, my head spinning. "Where am I going to sleep—"

"I am done modeling," Vadim says, alarmingly stern. "As for you. I insist that you show me at least one of the purchases that rang up to over ten grand at *Atelier Noir*."

I nearly die hearing him mention that number out loud. To a normal person, it's more money than could be feasibly spent on a purchase as frivolous as underwear. But to him, money literally seems meaningless. I don't think it's a front either. He says the numbers with no inflection. Ten dollars or ten grand doesn't mean anything to him either way, and I wonder just how much money he truly has. I'm probably better off not knowing.

"Don't tell me you're ashamed of your selections?" he prods, knowing right where to aim to make me react.

"Fine!" I start toward the doorway, but he clears his throat.

"They're in here." He points to the closet, but I don't have the energy to argue. I'll remove them later.

Sure enough, in the other section of the closet, I find my comparably small arrangement of purchases. My first thought is to try on the more boring, practical bra and panty set I'd gotten. Sometime during my search through the packages, I change my mind and settle on the most daring and risqué.

Jim would die if I ever wore something like this for him—and not in a good way. Die. Come back to life and then restructure his sermons about the dangers of the flesh and how wives are inherently sinful creatures. I chuckle out loud, but it's too close to the truth to be a real joke.

Given Vadim and his damn wall, I picture him eyeing me with no emotion, unmoved by the design either way. So I take my time to ensure I provide him with the full effect.

I strip my Chanel ensemble and hang it. Then I gingerly slip into a sheer emerald green bustier adorned with a dozen hand-sewn ebony roses that decorate the plunging neckline. Admiring myself in the mirror is a surreal experience. I've never felt sexier or more beautiful. A part of me despairs that—for now—this outfit will go woefully unappreciated.

No more sex with Vadim under any circumstances. That doesn't mean I can't needle the hell out of him, though.

"It's a shame we won't be fucking," I declare as I strut into the bedroom, my hips swaying, head thrown back. "Because this little ensemble demands I be…fucked."

Revenge slips from my brain the second I take in his expression. He changed while I'd been in the closet, stripping his suit for that flattering pair of briefs. I must have caught him off guard, in the middle of sitting on the bed. He's frozen mid-crouch, his eyes fixated on my body. A jolt of electricity runs through me as he rakes his gaze up and down the length of me. The poor man doesn't even have the time to rebuild his wall.

I can track every minute reaction transforming his features within the span of a few seconds. A raised eyebrow at my nipples, prominently on display. An appreciative swallow as he roves downward to my practically invisible thong. But then he keeps going down, tracing the curve of my hips and the shape of my thighs, then up to my shoulders and my own throat contracting around a quick swallow.

Our eyes meet, and I realize that I never stopped advancing toward him. In response, he finally moves, lowering himself onto the edge of the mattress as I draw closer. Any second, I expect him to throw his wall back up. Break this spell I can't seem to snap out of as long as he looks at me like…*this*.

With hunger and no ounce of restraint.

My fingers fly up to the neckline of my ensemble, and some reckless impulse makes me finger the thin strap sleeves, pushing his reaction to its limits.

A low hum escapes him as he leans back, taking me in like a man having a world-shattering revelation. One of the *"Holy shit, I'm forever changed"* variety. His eyelids flutter the more I toy with the straps until finally, I let them both slip from my shoulders, sending the neckline plunging.

And he finally moves.

His hands grip my waist first, drawing me into him. Our lips meet next, tongues clashing as my brain goes on hiatus. I wind up straddling him, wantonly rubbing my chest against his, gasping at the friction of the lace over my nipples, enhanced by the heat of his skin. Soon enough, he has the brassiere off and his fingers grope my breasts, kneading them ruthlessly.

"The way you feel..." He trails off, his voice a guttural rumble.

Maybe it's a good thing he doesn't finish that thought? A burst of wetness coats my inner thighs, and I don't think I could survive a second more of him speaking like this.

As if to spite me, his mouth finds my ear as he groans, shifting beneath me so that his legs part, a firm bulge pressing against my mound. "The least I should do is taste you," he murmurs against my flesh. "If we can't fuck."

Total mental shutdown. I'm struck dumb as he lifts me off of him and manipulates me onto my back. All I can do is prop up my upper body on my elbows and watch as he crouches at the foot of the bed between my splayed thighs.

Anticipation builds to a painful degree. As if knowing that, he takes his sweet time trailing his fingers up to my hips and finds the waistband of my thong. One gentle tug and I writhe to assist him.

His lips part as his eyes meet mine. Then he lowers his head and…

I'd imagined what it might feel like to have his mouth on me. Reality takes those fantasies and dashes them. So much for the idea of him partaking in tentative, sensual licking.

He stiffens his tongue, instead plunging it inside me so swiftly I cry out and nearly jolt from the mattress. It's like he's too eager to even play the game he seems to relish in —taunting.

He *takes*. It's a sensation so different from anything else. Silk in lieu of steel, conforming to my every curve and contour. I stiffen as he traces my outer lips, displaying an almost feral attention to every detail. Tasting me in hungry flicks and searing breaths. Panting, I draw my knees up beside him, nonsense spilling from my mouth. Pleas. Praises. Curses.

He is too good at this. Too adept at manipulating his tongue to strike all the right spots. My clit. Then downward, teasing my entrance. Then inside swiftly. Then up again. Such skill betrays that he *had* to have done this before.

But then a growl rips from him, vibrating all the way down to my core. One of shock—like a kid experiencing the taste of candy for the first time. Poof, a glutton is born.

And I'm at his mercy. His hands grip my thighs, nails piercing my flesh in a startling burst of pain. Trapped, I can only squirm as he lunges, applying more pressure. More vigor. More of everything.

My body goes off, climaxing so viciously I barely hear him groan above the sound of my racing heartbeat.

"The taste of you," he grates, sounding crazed. "*Incroyable.* Never get enough…"

And he keeps going, long after I come once. Twice. Again. Soon, I'm shaking, my body drenched in sweat, voice wavering and broken.

"Please. No more… I can't—" Fireworks explode down my spine as he suckles at my clit, drawing out the stimulation to an almost painful degree. "*Vadim!*"

"Addicting woman… I *will* pierce this," he rasps in between nips, and I nearly go off all over again. At the last second, he draws back, leaving me teetering on the edge. Our gazes meet, his unfocused, glimpsed through slits, and I gasp for breath. He looks insane. Mad.

So desirable, it hurts.

"Please." I part my legs eagerly as he steps forward, wrenching his briefs down his hips. His cock juts to attention, so thick my eyelids flutter at the sight.

He doesn't hesitate to mount me, shoving in so deep I come again. And again.

Lost in a haze of pleasure, I hear him curse, his hips slamming over mine. Like gasoline poured onto a roaring inferno, the sensation of his release flooding my sheath sets me off yet again.

I cling to him, clawing at his back, marking him as brutally as he fucks his pleasure into me, still moving until his cock finally softens.

Spent and breathless, the reality doesn't kick in until I'm staring up at the ceiling, aware of him partially on top of me, his mouth on my throat.

So much for no sex.

CHAPTER SIXTEEN

I am so royally fucked. Literally and figuratively.

I wake up beside Vadim again—this time with one hand on my ass and the other on my tit. I lie facing him, his arm around my hips, his body relaxed, his face utter perfection. My heart pangs as I blink my eyes open to see him, bathed in the glow of early dawn.

I drink him in, barely able to keep from touching him. My brain is still drunk off the sex, and dangerous thoughts creep in. Like how good it feels lying beside him. His posture alone conveys that he feels the same way, relishing our carnal attraction. Lust isn't an affliction he's forced to suffer. If anything, he has to surrender to it.

But how long can I stomach this before I get hopelessly addicted?

It's like he's always reading my mind, even while unconscious. He stirs, his eyes opening, as a part of me warns that it's already too late. Those dark irises take me in leisurely, still unfocused from sleep. A groan rips from him as his tongue traces a path along his lower lip.

"You are so beautiful."

And he means it. He truly thinks I'm beautiful enough that he slips up and breaks his most stubborn social rule. A frown shapes his mouth as he realizes what he's done, and he rolls onto his back. Both of his hands withdraw from me, and I can practically see him rearranging the bricks of his invisible wall.

"Don't be mean to me." I shuffle forward and mold myself against him. The logical part of my brain is screaming, but I don't care. Rejection is a pill I can't swallow right now. Not when I can still feel him inside me, and my brain is still churned to mush. Jim always pushed me away.

Vadim sighs but relents to the contact. Reluctantly, his arm slips beneath my waist again, and I wiggle into his touch, overwhelmed with relief. A pity cuddle is beyond his comfort level—I know that. But he endures this one anyway. Later, I'll go over the repercussions.

Now?

I'm dizzy, and clinging to him seems to be the only way I can ground myself.

"I loved having you go down on me," I confess against his ear. His jaw twitches, but the depth of his expression is hard to make out from this angle. Good? Bad? "I love how you felt," I continue, letting my eyes drift shut as his heat thrums through me, more relaxing than the world's best wine. "I love when you lose control. I love when you fuck me wild—"

"Enough to stay?"

"Hmm?" I peel one eye open only to find him staring at me intently, all traces of lust erased. He's serious.

"Enough to let me pierce you?" He slides his hand along my thigh, raising goosebumps.

I sink against him again and let out a dreamy sigh. "Enough to consider letting a trained professional pierce me, yes." I may even mean it. Just thinking about how a piercing might have enhanced my pleasure last night?

I'm beyond tempted.

That seems to placate him enough that he relaxes beside me. We must drift off like this. When I come to again, I'm lying naked with the sheets kicked down to my ankles and the space beside me glaringly empty. Confused, I roll over to catch a half-naked Vadim strolling across the room, wearing only a towel slung over his waist. Dripping water, his curls hang freely, and I have to clamp my knees together as I take him in.

"You showered without me." I sound devastated by the fact.

Frowning, he doesn't seem to realize why.

I flip onto my back, but I don't bother to cover myself with a sheet. "Letting me suck you off in the shower should have been your number one priority after last night," I point out. "Fair is fair."

He chuckles, strolling toward the closet with renewed confidence. "The things you say…"

"Are you leaving?" I sit up and finally reach for the end of the comforter, drawing it around me. A row of floor-to-ceiling windows provides a bird's eye view of the surrounding landscape. It looks to be early in the afternoon, though cloud cover and a light rainfall make it harder to pinpoint a time for sure.

"I have some errands to run," he admits. Then almost hesitantly, he adds, "You are welcome to join me."

"Really?" I bound from the mattress before he can change his mind.

"The bathroom is through that door," he says, nodding toward a polished, silver one in the corner of the room. I step through it only to enter a dream world formed of stainless-steel fixtures with the main attraction being a clawfoot tub positioned near a view of the water.

It's also infuriatingly modern.

If the shower at the hotel confounded me, this one leaves me hopelessly confused as to where to begin—it's a panel built into the wall in the center of a huge stall enclosed by glass. In the end, I give up and call for help.

An amused Vadim appears at my shoulder seconds later, dressed in the brown suit and blue shirt ensemble he modeled for me last night. His breath tickles my shoulder as he explains how to operate the shower. Once I have the water pressure set to my liking, I lather up, only to realize that—rather than leave the bathroom—he's seated leaning against a row of marble-topped counters, watching me bathe.

A sly smile tugs on my mouth. I feel like some concubine at the mercy of her captor—and I abuse his attention to the fullest. Closing my eyes, I toss my head into the spray and shamelessly stroke myself with a washcloth. Up and down. Between my legs. I pay special attention to my breasts and the curve of my ass, turning around as I do so that my back faces my audience.

Even above the relentless roar of the water, I still hear his groan.

When I finally finish, however, and step from the shower, he's gone. I have to pad across the room and grab my own towel from a silver rack. Before any real disappointment can set in, he reappears, a strip of fabric slung across his arm.

"I can't risk you spending hours to dress yourself today," he says by way of explanation. He unfurls the fabric, revealing one of my new dresses.

"Do you think green is my color?" I ask, eyeing the selection skeptically. It's an eye-catching A-line day dress with a modest neckline and black buttons rimmed in gold going down the front. I may have picked it out to wear on my own, but the color is suspiciously close to that of the lingerie I wore last night.

Sporting a smirk, I drop my towel and pull the dress on. Ever the smart ass, he also supplied me with a pair of lace panties it seems—but no bra.

"How scandalous, Mr. Gorgoshev," I scold as I prance past him into the bedroom, and my nipples promptly harden at the shift in temperature.

I can't help feeling like the joke is on me, though, as he follows behind and swears under his breath. "*Merde.*"

Apparently, this dress hugs my ass in a way he appreciates.

Tit for tat.

Downstairs, he fishes a pitcher of orange juice from the fridge and proceeds to pour two glasses. On the counter, someone already laid out a cold spread of delicate glass bottles of jam, a bowl of fresh fruit, and a basket containing an assortment of bread from croissants to a baguette.

"Did you leave these out all night?" I wonder, shooting him a curious glance.

"No," he says while handing me a glass of juice. "Ena did. He doubles as both my security and my chef when the urge strikes him. He makes himself scarce, and I specifically requested he stay out of sight to avoid startling you. The presence of security can sometimes make those around me uneasy."

"Ah." Given how much money he likes to throw around, a highly trained security team makes sense. Is it creepy that some stranger had access to the property without me knowing? A little. "I'm guessing that Ena was responsible for delivering my Chanel the other day?"

He nods and picks through the breadbasket, settling on a piece of the baguette. "As I mentioned, I told him to make himself scarce, but sometimes he gets persistent when he believes I'm not eating enough."

"Because of your diabetes," I deduce softly. Reaching out, I playfully tug on his sleeve, surprised when his mouth twitches into a fleeting smile. "Don't tell me you're one of those workaholic men who recklessly disregard their health in their pursuit of the almighty dollar."

"Not quite." He trails his fingers across the lid of a light-yellow jam as if mulling over whether or not to divulge more about himself than he already has. "Sometimes, I may go days without eating if I am not reminded. It's not a conscious choice, mind you."

"Oh?" I watch him, my throat thickening. Could he suffer from an eating disorder?

"When I was a child… Meals did not come regularly." He deftly opens the jam bottle and slathers a healthy amount onto his bread slice. "I learned to suppress my hunger to escape the torment. And with insulin in short supply, doing so probably saved my life in the long run. Even in my adulthood, I've found that it's been difficult for me to revert from that mindset."

Building horror tempers my curiosity to ask him more. I don't like how he looks whenever he recalls his past. He isn't reminiscing over wonderful Christmases and holidays spent on his uncle's vineyard, that's for sure.

Guilt stings as I regret ever needling him at all. To lighten the mood, I snatch a croissant and proceed to shove half of it into my mouth.

He eyes me quizzically, his upper lip quirking, and boom. He's distracted.

"Try not to choke," he warns, dabbing at the corner of my mouth with a crisp white napkin. "I may have use for this throat yet." He grazes the quivering column with his thumb, and my brain threatens to go offline again.

"The things you say," I scold once I manage to swallow.

He laughs and gathers up the assorted breakfast items, carrying them to the glass dining table. The mysterious Ena must have been the one to set the table for two, as well as put a neat stack of newspapers near the place setting Vadim claims for himself.

"Is this how you impress your other women?" I taunt as he lifts the topmost paper from the stack and proceeds to flip through it. "Proving yourself to be a worldly and knowledgeable businessman?"

He doesn't look up from his task, but his mouth quirks. Another smile? "I prefer to brush up on the current events every morning. It is my routine."

"Ah." I stuff my face with another bite of bread and settle in to watch him. He skims through the major sections of the paper, paying attention to the world news and politics before heading to the business section. As he reads, his expression shifts from thoughtful, to concerned, to neutral again. When he finally thrums through the last stack, he looks up as if surprised to find me still here.

"You aren't bored?"

"No," I admit truthfully. It shouldn't be this damn enthralling just ogling someone as they go about their simple routine.

His smirk returns, and he downs the rest of his orange juice before standing.

We cut through the back of the house, passing through a doorway that opens into a spacious garage containing three vehicles in varying degrees of flashy. The most conservative is a black van. Then a gray compact car, and then finally the cherry red sports car he drove to his brother's house. In some ways, they remind me of three distinct personalities. The surly, mysterious Vadim, the cold Vadim, and the warm, slightly unpredictable daredevil who spanks women in one moment and manipulates them the next.

"After you." He ushers me into the passenger's seat, and within minutes we're heading toward the city.

Our first destination is a tall, sleek office building in the heart of a mass of skyscrapers clawing at the sky. A simple logo adorns the front façade—three emerald-colored circles interlinked beside a crisp font read *Eingel Health Industries*.

"Is this your company?" I ask as he parks in a reserved space at the heart of a parking garage at the base of the building.

"One of them," he says. "I no longer have a role in the day-to-day operations, but my share of the stock allows me to utilize an office in the American headquarters whenever I'm in town."

"A hotel room in California. An office here in Fair Haven. It seems as though you bounce from city to city, Vadim." Though the woman from his meeting yesterday did mention that he only recently bought his house.

"I've yet to find anything worth keeping me in one place for too long," he admits while we enter a polished lobby and take an elevator to the top floor. As if in afterthought, he adds, "Anything that requires me, anyway."

And yet, all of a sudden, it seems, he's gotten the urge to buy a fake wife and purchase a sprawling mansion near his estranged brother? I contemplate asking him as much, but I can almost see the invisible bricks of his wall threatening to fall into place the second I push him too far.

So I bite my tongue and follow him down what appears to be an executive suite guarded by a single secretary seated behind a desk. She eyes Vadim and then does a swift doubletake, nearly falling off of her chair.

"M-Mr. Gorgoshev! We weren't expecting you. It's been so long since your last visit—"

"Over a year, I think," Vadim says with a charming grin. Jealousy prickles through my belly, though when I scan his expression, it's the neutral detachedness I've come to expect from him.

"Yes, a year," the secretary says solemnly. "Your office is just as you left it. I'll have fresh coffee sent in immediately."

"For two," Vadim adds before taking my hand. I warily follow him past the secretary and into a spacious office that looks fit for a CEO—not a "casual investor" who hasn't bothered to visit this place in over a year.

"Were you on an extended vacation?" I ask him playfully as he claims a leather armchair placed before a polished wooden desk while I collapse into a matching seat before him.

"Something like that." He looks away. *Thunk*. Before I know it, the wall has come down between us. I'm surprisingly stung—more than I should be. Cracking him takes so much effort. I'm not used to being the aggressive party in any relationship.

Not that this is a relationship.

Still. I can't resist testing one of his invisible bricks for any hint of weakness.

"How long were you in Cali for?"

He frowns, stroking his chin. "A month? Two months? The days tend to blur together. I was here not too long ago, but that trip was not for business."

Ah. I nod. "So, what made you want to come back now?"

Especially after a year of absence.

His smile turns cold. "One could say…complications within my family. But I'm here for good. At least if…"

"If?" I prod, leaning forward. We're in a tug of war, I sense—fighting over the position of one of his bricks. I'm pushing hard, but he's fighting just as relentlessly to keep it in place. With a sigh, he sits back, and something gives.

I win this round.

"There is something I want," he says carefully—deliberately vague, but it's a start, so I bite my tongue. After a few tense seconds, he rewards me by speaking some more. "Something I want enough to fight for, even if it means staying in this God-forsaken place. I won't let anyone stop me. This time, Maxim won't drive me off."

A stupid, careless part of me wants to suspect that he means a relationship. A relationship he might have spontaneously discovered with a certain redhead. But that's not it. His expression radiates emotion for once—a raw, feral energy that makes me shudder. Whatever his goal is, it requires him to fake a wife and risk living within his brother's volatile orbit to attain it.

And maybe I'm a teensy bit jealous.

"Can I have a hint?" I ask sweetly.

He blinks and looks up as if remembering I'm even here. Then he casually tugs open a drawer on his end and fishes out a silver pen. "I need to work."

His tasks this time stretch well into the early afternoon. Again, I think I should be bored, forced to watch him, left with no other entertainment. But damn, even watching this man pour over reports and make phone calls is riveting. It's almost like observing a ballet dancer gracefully in his element—a master at work.

Eventually, he puts his papers away and seems to take pity on me because he stands and extends his hand to help me to my feet as well.

"Lunch," he explains, leading me out into the hall. I expect him to take me back to the car, but instead, he turns into a large boardroom set with a spread fit for a king. "I took the liberty of having a few things delivered," he explains while guiding me to a seat near the head of the table while he takes the one across from me.

"I think I recognize that brand of wine," I say cynically, eyeing the infamous bottle of vintage that had been my kryptonite back at the hotel suite. "Are you trying to ply me, Mr. Vadim?"

"Yes." He sits back further, threading his fingers together. A part of me quivers, recognizing that I'm on an unfair playing field. This room, this location is an arena best suited to give him the advantage.

So, like any sore loser, I play dirty. I yawn as if bored and reach up to flick open the topmost button of my dress. Then another. Another. The barest tease of cleavage is enough to dampen his smug grin to acceptable levels. All is fair in war, after all.

"There is something I want to discuss," he says, cutting to the chase.

"Yes?"

"You teased me about being pierced before," he begins, laying one of the most dangerous topics on the table. "Were you serious?"

"Yes," I blurt automatically. A sexy piercing would be the introduction to the kink I've been fantasizing about. My relationship with him aside, why should I let a harmless fling stop me? Especially if he's planning on paying for it.

"But," I add, still eyeing the table. "I want to renegotiate my previous price—"

"Anything." The heat in his voice draws my attention, and I sorely regret facing him directly. I got my wish. His wall came down, but I'm no match for what I find lurking beneath it. Dark eyes heavy-lidded and focused, a jaw clenched to brooding perfection and pink lips slightly moistened by a slithering tongue. There's no way to describe the reaction other than raw, naked lust.

"You really want me to do this," I whisper hoarsely. Should I be horrified? I'm not. I'm freaking thrilled. My mind skips ahead, imagining him, teasing some delicate silver piercing with his teeth. Even the thought makes synapses in my brain explode and fire at random.

"Yes," he confesses without shame. "I... I would love to pierce you."

Holy hell. I have to keep from fanning myself, and all I can think to blurt out is, "Why?"

He sits back, eyeing me objectively. His gaze flickers down my torso, settling where the table obscures. "I am intrigued... No. I *love*—" his tongue fumbles with the word, betraying how little he must say it. If ever. A part of me feels oddly pleased that few women probably ever hear him utter it in this husky, dangerous tone. Overall, I'm more alarmed than ever. "I love the idea of you entrusting yourself to me."

Heat pools beneath my legs so hotly my brain has trouble catching up. But when it does, I blink, snapping from the daze as something clicks.

"You mean, *you* actually want to pierce me?"

He raises an eyebrow as if the concept isn't totally insane. "I would prefer to be the only one to pierce you."

I shake my head. "Sorry, but I can't just let anyone put holes into my nether regions." There are some lines even I'm not willing to cross. "Anyone but a trained professional."

His mouth quirks into an expression of utter sin. "Luckily for us both, I am a trained professional."

I scoff. "Really? For real, or did you just learn by watching videos online or something?"

His murky gaze offers no insight, and I feel stunned, more off-balance than ever.

"Let me guess," I spit in exasperation, "you pierced yourself?"

His smile falls flat, betraying a hint of vulnerability, and my eyes go so wide I'm sure they'll pop right out of my head.

"You did? You pierced yourself!" I scramble upright and circle the table until I reach his chair.

"There are cameras," he warns in that unnervingly neutral tone. But I don't care. I straddle him anyway, forcing him to push back from the table to give me enough room. If there are cameras, I figure my hunched frame shields how my hand slithers between us, finding the front of his slacks.

He watches on in cautious amusement as I tug open his fly and slide my hand beneath the fabric, cupping his shaft. Surprise, surprise, he's hard, pulsing against my palm. But foreplay isn't on my mind as I drag my thumb across the crown, gently—very, very gently—probing one of the protruding silver beads capping the bar of his piercing.

"Why on earth would you pierce yourself?" I croak, still stroking him. But he already gave me the answer, didn't he? For control. To exert ownership over himself that no one else could. Why might he be driven to such an extreme? I shouldn't want to know.

"I may or may not have been in my right mind," he confesses, his eyes narrowing further with every hesitant brush of my thumb. Maybe I should stop touching him like this? I can't seem to.

"*You*, on the other hand, I will treat with the utmost care," he promises, his voice thickening, making my tongue moisten. Damn, he makes being stabbed through with a needle sound…irresistible. "I will even numb you first so that you feel no pain."

"No pain… You pierced yourself *raw*?" I blurt, my voice so loud anyone passing by could hear me. "Baby!" I cup his jaw with my free hand, forcing him to meet my gaze. He stares back blankly, as if he can't quite decide why I care. Deep down, I don't know why either, but the thought of him hurting himself—because that's the only way to describe it—makes me…

Ache in ways I never have.

"Tell me why," I whisper, running my lips over his jaw, sensing it stiffen. Then soften. "I'll let you put as many holes in me as you want, *just tell me why.*"

"My feelings have changed over time," he says carefully, his gaze growing distant. "But I would be lying if I claimed that my original goal was anything other than…mutilation."

My heart lurches at the thought of it. Someone so lost, so tormented that driving a needle through his own penis was the only way he could regain control. Over his body. Over himself.

Voice rasping, I murmur, "Why?"

"I thought it would make me unappealing," he confesses tonelessly. "Grotesque. That no one could derive pleasure from it. No one would ever crave it—me—honestly. I could track their intentions then. Anyone who claimed otherwise, obviously had ulterior motives. I would be on guard."

Such a freaking man. So paranoid, he would turn his own penis into a lie detector. A faulty one at that.

Overwhelmed, I release him and twist around until I face the world looming beyond a row of full-length windows. The city stares back, cold and lifeless. Why he would choose to settle here, of all places? I can't imagine.

Or maybe that's the point? Denying himself of beauty and pleasure is starting to seem like his defining trait.

"*That's* why you rejected me after the first time we had sex," I deduce out loud. "I called your cock beautiful."

"A lie, of course," he admits, his breath hot against my ear. "Or so I thought at the time."

"And now?" I crane my head back, my chest tightening at how tormented he can seem in one brief moment—and then hard the next.

"I may be warming up to the idea that you have a very warped sense of attraction."

Ass. I hiss in annoyance, but I find myself leaning into him, bracing my back against his chest, allowing his mouth the nuzzle the crook of my shoulder.

"Is that why you want to pierce me?" I wonder, almost fearing what he might say in response. "To mutilate me—"

"Never." A growl rips from his throat, vibrating with indignation. One of his hands lands over my thigh, radiating a power that makes me feel deliciously small. At his mercy. "On you? Such adornment could *only* be beautiful."

He treats that word so reverently, laving it with his tongue, making me wish he would say it over and over again. Or not. His cock is pulsing against my ass, spurring an answering wetness to coat my inner thighs. Cameras or not, I can't resist rocking against his hardness, teasing a groan from him.

"Do I have your answer?" he grates through clenched teeth.

I only need to think for a second before I'm nodding. "Yes. You can pierce me. I… I *want* you to pierce me. But when?"

He grips my hips and gently lifts me from his lap, chuckling in a low, lethal tone. "I will pick a time most agreeable to me. I don't think I'll tell you, though. Not until I'm good and ready."

"Ass!" I manage to stand on trembling legs, and he rises as well, smoothing his hands over my hips to help right my balance.

"Yes," he murmurs while sliding his palm down to the back of my thigh. "Ass. You have a lovely one, I must say."

My face heats, my thoughts threatening to boil once more. "Is that a compliment, Mr. Vadim?"

He doesn't answer. His hand reluctantly leaves my ass only to capture my wrist, steering me after him down the hall and back into the office. He heads past the desk, opening a door that leads to an executive bathroom, complete with its own marble fixtures and walk-in shower.

"Impressive," I mutter as he guides me back against a row of counters placed before a pristine mirror. He spins me to face him, and I suck in a breath at what I find when I meet his gaze.

Fire.

The brooding businessman has dropped his wall again. Heat sears through my belly, enhancing the moisture already trapped by the fabric of my lace panties. I arch my back, clamping my knees together.

A twitch in his jaw reveals that he's well aware of my actions.

"I do believe there is some policy on the books that cautions against the CEO or whatever you are trapping innocent young ladies within bathrooms—"

His lips settle over mine firmly—and yet hesitant. As if he's testing out what a kiss might feel like in this context. If I had an ounce of self-control, I'd remain still and let him explore in peace. But I don't.

My fingers sink through his hair, pulling him into me as I adjust my hips, teasing the front of his pants until he's panting, his eyes unfocused. He reaches out, snatching my wrist, and guides my fingers to his still open fly. I don't think he even realizes what he's doing.

I cup him fully and sink to my knees, relishing how he groans, his hands settling over my scalp.

"I would like to make an addendum to our previous arrangement regarding the piercing," I hum, letting my breath wash over him. His piercing jumps, his body rigid.

"Anything," he rasps in that beautiful, enticing way.

I extend my tongue, tapping his thickening crown. "I want to know everything about you," I confess, lapping at a bead of fluid that weeps from him. My core clenches, my breaths thinning. Despite my faked confidence, I'm rapidly in danger of a total factory shutdown where my brain is concerned. For some reason, this matters, though. Saying this out loud, knowing he can hear me. "Everything. The good stuff. The bad stuff—" I capture the topmost silver bead between my thumb and flick it gently. He rocks on his heels, hissing something I don't understand. French? "I want to know about your past. What you do for fun. Everything." I take him into my mouth, swirling my tongue around the pulsing head of him.

A grunt revs in his throat as his nails tease my scalp. Could the icy businessman be losing control? Gosh, I hope so.

I bob my head and suck harder to encourage him. His piercing feels electric every time my tongue strikes it, his vibrating moans intoxicating. I'd always been intrigued by fellatio, but I never knew giving it could feel so…

Empowering.

I have him in the palm of my hands—literally. His balls swell, his body quaking, and his grip becomes insistent.

"Not…in your mouth," he grates.

But I can't resist. Like a child with a treat, I devour him with vigor. Deepthroating him isn't in the realm of possibility now, but I take him as far as I can, giving him a taste of what it could be like. What *we* could be like.

Fire. Sizzling, crackling, pulsating energy.

My throat is already contracting the second the first taste of him floods my mouth, and this time I drink him all the way down.

Panting, he slumps against the counter, comfortably crushing me between it and his muscular thighs. Pleased with myself, I rear back to watch his face as he stares down on me, his eyes wide. He's having another world-altering revelation, I suspect. Still breathing heavily, he reaches down and strokes my bottom lip, chasing a stray bit of moisture.

"Insolent witch," he rasps hoarsely. "I didn't want to risk… Should I punish you for disobeying?"

I nod, a part of me way too eager to take him up on that threat.

But he stands upright with an urgency that displaces some of the lust. He adjusts his pants and helps me to my feet. With a wet paper towel, he cleans me up, and we escape the bathroom together, then the office entirely.

Minutes later, we're back in the car. He drives with one hand while the other finds mine, capturing it. I marvel at the sight of our combined fingers, my heart racing.

"More work?" I wonder, as he lazily merges into traffic.

He shakes his head. "I'm done for the day. I'm thinking of heading home." His eyes flicker toward mine, and for once, I know exactly what he's thinking. Dirty man.

I can't deny the idea of crawling onto him the second we enter his house is very tempting. I'm still on edge, and at the back of my mind, I realize that I never actually came in the bathroom. I didn't even notice. Somehow, watching him had been more than enough to satisfy me in the moment. And now, I crave something…more.

A taste of him more intimate than even his literal taste.

"I want you to take me somewhere," I tell him, flipping our clasped hands so that I stroke the veined back of his. "Somewhere special to you. I wasn't kidding before."

And maybe that should scare me. The more I learn of Vadim Gorgoshev, the more I forget my internal promise. This is all just fun and games. Nothing serious. I'm not falling for him after barely a week.

I'm not.

"You really want to know?" he wonders, his voice suddenly cold, devoid of heat. I stiffen, alarmed, and sit straighter in my seat. "Then I'm afraid there is something I haven't told you about. Someone."

I choke down a panicked swallow. Someone? A real wife he has hidden in a storage shed somewhere?

"Who?"

He sighs, and casually manipulates the steering wheel, leaving the main street altogether. "The love of my life," he says simply. "It's time you've met her."

CHAPTER SEVENTEEN

I want to vomit until he parks before a building on the outskirts of the city—presumably the home of his supposed true love. As soon as we exit the car and I inhale a familiar, musky scent, some of my panic eases, replaced by grim amusement.

"Don't tell me your true love lives in a barn?" I ask as he leads me into a wide, spacious stable overlooking a vast expanse of green pasture.

"Oh yes," he says with a stern nod. "This is her kingdom, and here is the queen..."

I gasp as he leads me to a stall where the most beautiful white mare I've ever seen immediately sticks her head over the low door. She whinnies in greeting, her eyes gleaming at the sight of Vadim. True love in its purest form.

A love that seems wholly reciprocated.

"And here she is," he gushes, stroking her ivory mane. "My Zzazza. My sweet." He brushes his lips along her cheek. "The only girl to ever claim my heart."

"Should I be jealous?" I wonder as I creep forward and offer my hand for her to sniff. Money must not really be an option for him. She's gorgeous, and her "kingdom" appears to be a massive stable housing only her and two other horses, each within their own spacious stall.

"Who is this?" I ask, spotting a darker, chestnut face eyeing me from another stall.

"Donali," he explains, reluctantly leaving Zzazza. "And that handsome gelding is Markesh. All beautiful. All who own a piece of my soul."

"You own this entire stable?" I ask incredulously.

A sly smile shapes his mouth, and his eyes gleam in a way I've never seen, resonating warmth. "I rent it out to a few students who give Donali and Markesh all the love they could ever need. But my girl Zzazza? She is all mine." He returns to the mare, rubbing her affectionately. "But I have sorely neglected her. For that, I apologize, my sweet."

"Don't tell me you haven't seen her in a year?" I move to stand by his side, watching as he showers the horse with murmured praises and generous petting.

Something that could be guilt darkens his gaze as he withdraws from her with a sigh. "Ena has been keeping you company in my absence, hmm?" She knickers as if in agreement. "I told the old bastard to take you out at least once a day."

"She must be a dream to ride," I say.

A small smile shapes his mouth. "That she is. It's been far too long since we've taken a nice long one, hasn't it?"

Something about how he tailors his voice for the horse alone makes my chest feel tight. Awe? Maybe more jealousy too.

"We could now?" I suggest, only to realize that a dress worth several thousand grand and a tailored suit probably aren't the best items of clothing to wear horseback riding.

Vadim scoffs. "Most women would be horrified at the prospect of smelling like an animal and risk breaking a sweat." His eyes glitter playfully, and I puff myself up, placing my hands on my hips.

Challenge accepted.

"Is that so? My mother bred thoroughbreds for fun when she wasn't playing the socialite housewife. You should be worried if your riding skills will even impress me. If I had suitable clothing, I'd have you take me out in a heartbeat. We could always ride naked," I add, savoring the faint color that paints his cheeks even as his expression remains stubbornly neutral. "But that might offend your workers' sensibilities."

"Luckily for you, I keep a spare set of jodhpurs here," he says, leaning in close, his breath hot on my neck. "And I am more than willing to display my skills for your judgment."

I crane my neck back and meet his gaze with a lazy smile. "You're on."

HE IS AN AMAZING RIDER. Balanced in front of him, I can sense every slight shift in his posture as he guides the horse beneath us down a winding path through a vast range of fields. He and Zzazza move so beautifully in sync it's as if they're reading each other's minds.

And maybe I'm more than a *little* jealous now.

I had wanted him to *tell* me more about himself, but I'm starting to realize that this way is so much better. Seeing it for myself. Feeling the air whip through my hair as a powerful, massive creature moves beneath me primarily of its own will. It's an illusion of control built mostly on trust, and I think I understand a fraction of his obvious passion for it. And once again, my impression of him is turned on its head.

We return to the stables far too soon and change into our regular clothing. Night is just starting to darken the horizon by the time we approach the house.

"You head in," Vadim says as he pulls into the garage. "I have some things to attend to. I'll be back soon."

His hand lingers over mine as I reluctantly leave the car, holding me until the last possible second.

"Where are you going?" I ask, suspicious.

He laughs. Such a sinful sound. "I think you enjoy it more when you can't anticipate my actions," he says smugly. "I'll be back soon."

He drives off, and I watch him go with a frown. The man is starting to know me too damn well. Enough for me to admit that he's right—I enjoy the thrill of his mystery now more than ever.

Sighing, I enter the house, relieved to find the door unlocked. I can't help but pout as I wander the spacious interior all alone. I could have begged him to take me, but even I can take a hint. He wanted to be alone.

Probably to head to some hotel bar and troll for another fake wife.

Knock it off, Tiffy, warns my inner bitch. *You're getting too involved with him. If anyone should be leaving, it's you.*

I should. I even linger near the staircase, toying with the idea of running upstairs, packing a few things, and then escaping into the dead of night with only a note left for him on a pillow or something equally as dramatic.

Instead, I keep moving, heading for the kitchen in a frantic search for wine. I round the bar counter and promptly scream as my eyes fall over a figure rummaging through the fridge.

He's bulky, dressed in a scarred black leather jacket and jeans. A blunt mop of dark hair frames an angular, round face set with almond-shaped brown eyes. The man's tan skin enhances their color to a piercing degree as he inclines his head to observe me. Unimpressed, he returns his attention to the fridge.

Assuming a thief would show more discretion in front of a potential witness, I try to think of another explanation for his appearance. Then I remember. "Are you Ena?" I ask as the man turns, closing the fridge door with his hip. In his arms is an array of more fresh fruit that he arranges onto the counter. My heart stutters as he snatches a knife from a nearby drawer and promptly halves an apple.

"You," he says, his voice gruff and heavily accented with a dialect I can't place. "Mr. Vadim eat—" He points to the fruit before lifting an orange and cutting it into slices. "Yes?"

"Y-Yes," I croak, warily inching toward a stool. "You want us to eat—"

"No. No." He faces me fully, his eyes narrowed. "You *make* him eat—" Again, he points to the food. "Or his brain goes." He adjusts his thumb and forefinger into a terrifying imitation of a gun. Then he presses the tip of it to his temple and mimes pulling the trigger. "You make him eat. Yes?"

"Yes," I insist, my voice rasping.

"Good." He marches to a nearby cupboard, surprisingly light on his feet despite his girth, which isn't entirely composed of muscle. His build reminds me of a Sumo wrestler, and I realize why Vadim might use him as a bodyguard.

He opens a cupboard and withdraws a wooden bowl. As he neatly arranges the fruit inside it, I contemplate how rude it might seem if I escape upstairs. Not out of fear—mainly to hide. There's a tension in his body that unsettles me in a way I can't explain. I doubt he'd hurt me, but I get the sense that I am sorely not welcome here.

And not just in this house, but Vadim's orbit in general.

"You go to brother dinner?" Ena grunts the second I start to shimmy in the direction of the hall.

"Um…yes," I stammer. "With um, I think his name is Maxim and—"

"He should not go." He slams his knife onto the counter and storms to the sink to wash his hands. "Brother makes Mr. Vadim go crazy," he adds once he shuts off the water. "He goes for you."

I blink. "I'm sorry?"

Hissing in disgust, Ena whirls to face me, and there's no mistaking the raw anger lashing toward me like a whip. "You are toy in brothers' game—" He jabs a finger in my direction. At the back of my mind, I register that he only has three remaining on his right hand. "You go. He stays. So go." He points in the direction of the front door.

I'm too stunned to say anything. By the time I regain control over my mouth, Ena is already stomping through the kitchen, heading toward the exit himself. "You bad for Mr. Vadim," he says coldly. "You go. He better."

A second later, the front door slams behind him.

Overwhelmed, I reclaim my stool and bury my face in my hands. Maybe the disgruntled bodyguard is right? Playing this game with Vadim—no matter how fun it might be in the interim—is only going to end badly. His idea of a relationship seems to extend about as far as his credit card limit and as for me…

I'm not looking for anything serious. Because doing so would be a total betrayal to my new, improved independence freshly reclaimed after years stuck in my marriage with Jim. After nearly a decade, what do I have to show for it? A trail of broken dreams, wasted potential, and no survival skills to speak of, other than living off a mixture of my trust fund and alimony.

Jumping into another relationship—real or otherwise—could only be deemed as unhealthy at best. Pathetic at worst.

It's not like I'm falling for him, the beautiful, sexy, billionaire of unknown wealth who delivers the best sex I've had to date. That would be recklessly irresponsible. So it's a good thing I'm not thinking about him right now, wondering what the hell he's getting up to without me.

I'm not.

To distract myself, I mentally catalog all my potential outfit pairings utilizing my new wardrobe. I don't even notice that someone is behind me until it's too late. They touch my shoulder, and I nearly jump out of my skin.

"I didn't mean to startle you," a voice like sin drips into my ear. The owner's trademark smugness proves that yes, startling me was exactly his intention.

My eyes narrowing, I whip my head around, startled by his charming grin. That ride did wonders for him. His eyes gleam, and his posture seems relaxed for once. Even his smile looks more natural and less like a mask anchoring his wall.

I'm instantly on guard.

I sniff the air and find myself scanning him for any hint of lipstick or perfume—any trace of another woman. Because I'm an insane, irrational cow who has no right to be jealous. When I finally notice the object balanced on his palm, I wrinkle my nose in suspicion.

"What is that?"

A box, it seems. Light blue, wrapped with a white ribbon that makes it suspiciously resemble a present.

His grin widens. Then he notices something on the glass dining table and crosses to it, setting the small box aside. "Good. I've been waiting for this to arrive."

So his henchman's visit wasn't all about food, I realize. Ena must have left the small brown wooden box for him. "I met your little friend," I tell him dryly. "I don't think he likes me much."

"Ena?" He raises an eyebrow, too intent on inspecting the box to pay me much attention. "He doesn't like anyone. It's why I've kept him on for so long. He senses who a person truly is at their core and compromises himself for no one. There isn't a more honest man in the world."

I swallow hard, recalling his insinuation that I'm nothing more than a toy. "How long has he worked for you?"

"Over a decade," Vadim says offhandedly. "But I've known him longer. Ena is gruff, but I'll make sure he avoids you. Don't worry about him. What you should concern yourself with is this..." He beckons me closer, and I warily comply, coming to stand by his side.

Aware of me watching, he takes his time opening the box, revealing an interior lined with black silk, containing a single, silver object nestled in a specially shaped cavity. It's oval-shaped, about the size of my thumb, and crafted from delicate material.

"What is it?" I ask, unnerved by the bold way he strokes the edge of the container. "I will admit that I was much more impressed by the delivery of a lifetime's worth of Chanel."

Undeterred by my ungratefulness, he reaches into the box and withdraws something else. "This came with it," he explains, revealing a larger, square-shaped object of the same material. The only thing of interest it seems to contain is a silver button built into the center. He presses the button.

A low hum comes from the box as the small object begins to vibrate. Suddenly it clicks, and my thoughts dissipate.

"You ordered this for me?" The mixture of both awe and terror in my voice shocks me almost as much as it seems to please him. His teeth flash, his eyes practically glowing.

"You wanted kink?" he questions, his tone gravelly in a way that makes me shiver. "Let us see if you truly have what it takes. I will admit that I originally didn't have much interest in the subject, but I have started to conduct my own research."

I rock on my heels, my brain spinning, thoughts in disarray. I don't know what shocks me more? The fact that kink was supposedly never on his radar before I goaded him into spanking me, or the fact that…

He's been learning. For me.

"And what have you discovered?" I wonder, batting my eyelashes at him innocently.

That telltale muscle in his jaw twitches, and he lifts the silver vibrator from its box.

"I've learned that control is a defining factor of these… relationships. As is trust. I want to test just how much control you can exert over yourself in the quest for fulfillment. And how much you can trust me to always give you what you need."

No man has ever lived up to the term "panty melting" so thoroughly. The inside of my legs chafe as I take an involuntary step toward him. I don't think I've stopped aching since the office. Boldly, I slip my hand around his neck and sidle up to him, pressing myself against his rigid frame. I'm not the only one aroused. Despite our little oral session, he's straining against my hip. I grind against him slavishly, watching as his eyes glaze over, his tongue tracing his lips.

"You want to sexually torment me?" Again, I sound equally alarmed and excited. I can't keep a tendril of curiosity from my tone either. One little silver dildo has never seemed so intimidating.

"No." He shifts, capturing my chin to force me to face him. "I want to explore your limits. Once I learn them, I can better exploit them."

I suck in a breath. "You aim to *manipulate* me?"

He chuckles and lowers his mouth to my ear. "I aim to pleasure you. More than any other. Do you accept that proposal?"

"So what?" I finger the still vibrating object balanced on his palm and shudder. Even picturing it inside me is... dangerous. "We play with it?"

"No." He steps into me, his stance suddenly clinical, like a doctor about to perform a procedure. "You keep this inside you—" He lowers his hand to my hip, pressing enough for me to feel the vibrations through his skin. *Holy heck.* I grip his forearms for balance, my brain melting. "Until I give you permission to remove it."

I rear back to meet his gaze, my mouth opened in horror. "On?"

"Not constantly." I sense him inhale as he brushes his mouth along my throat, tasting my scent. "However, I will have the remote on me at all times, to be utilized at my discretion. You will be surprised by the range. My main request is that you refrain from touching yourself. At all. Only I may have that privilege. Understood?" His fingers slip beneath my skirt, trailing up my thigh, and I nearly buck into his hand just to find relief.

"So wet," he murmurs in approval. "But this game will not commence tonight. This will be merely the preliminary round."

I frown. "Not even one little orgasm for me?" I arch into him, pressing my breasts against his chest. My hips seem to move of their own accord, grinding, teasing.

With difficulty, he pulls back, leaving only his hand against me. "No," he says thickly. "Do you trust that I will make it good when you finally do experience release?"

Do I trust him? All it takes is the memory of his tongue on me to come up with an answer. "Yes…"

"Good. The other stipulation is that you cannot remove this. I will know if you do."

He guides me back and taking the hint, I lean against the table, spreading my legs. Observing him crouch before me, his head disappearing beneath my skirt is an experience all in itself. Orgasming without touching myself only a few days ago would have seemed like a pipe dream. Now? I arch my back, gasping in anticipation.

My clit is already swollen, demanding attention as the smooth surface of the toy grazes my lips.

Vadim makes a low sound in his throat. "So beautiful you are," he praises. "So eager already. Can you wait for me to savor you?"

I nod, feeling like a child undertaking a chore in the hopes of a treat. And even his slow, careful insertion of the device is a sensual delicacy almost enough to make up for the lack of his fingers. It's so light, I barely feel it, but the vibrations when felt internally…

I grit my teeth, my eyelids fluttering, and my muscles jerk, making me squirm. I'm vaguely aware of him rising to his feet before me, watching my reaction.

Finally, the sensation abates, and I can breathe again.

"Holy…crap…" I'm panting, my body slick with sweat. A wicked grin shapes my mouth even as I contemplate the daunting prospect of enduring this at his discretion for only God knows how long.

"Too unbearable?" Vadim wonders, sounding irritatingly level.

I shake my head. But I can't resist asking, "If I'm a good girl, will you fuck me fast?"

His smile. It's so sinful, so wicked. My toes curl even as my thighs twitch, too aware of the pressure building between them to risk coming together.

"I will fuck you," he promises, copying my filthy language. "All in good time."

I pout, rolling my eyes. "So, what will we do until then?"

"Dinner," he says, smoothly, clearing the table. I note that he tucks the smaller, baby blue box he'd teased me with earlier into his pocket. "It dawned on me as I drove back that I haven't fed you since lunch."

A lunch that we never actually enjoyed, thanks to me.

And I'd been too caught up in the whirlwind day to notice. With a pang of guilt, I recall what Ena said about making him eat. The fact that he seems to take effort on his part to remember normal meal timeframes proves just how little he must eat normally.

"Are you going to cook for me?" I ask as he steps behind the counter and opens the fridge.

"No." He opens a drawer that I assume is the freezer and withdraws a slim, rectangular metal container. The space seems to be full of at least six other similar boxes. After closing the drawer, he places the container on the counter and lifts the lid, revealing a neatly proportioned meal of baked chicken, vegetables, and rice.

"Equestrian. Chef. Damn good in the sack. Is there anything you can't do?" I wonder, partly impressed, partly irritated.

He laughs and places the container in the oven. "I share your thoughts on cooking. You should be complimenting Ena. He continues to make these things for me, though I rarely eat them before they spoil."

"So far, my competition for your heart seems to be against a fake wife, your bodyguard, and a beautiful horse. Can't a girl catch a break?" I'd been speaking without thinking. It's only when I see his jaw clench that I realize how stupidly reckless I was.

Mr. Vadim, the guarded, mistrustful businessman, doesn't seem to want a relationship with me either. Great.

In silence, he opens a cupboard and withdraws two glasses and a familiar bottle of wine. As the food warms, he returns to the table and pours two glasses.

I take a seat across from him and promptly drain over half of my glass in one go. The moment the buzz creeps to my brain, I forget all about my discomfort.

"Why aren't you married?" I ask him, folding my arms before me. "For real?"

He looks away and slips his hand into his pocket. *Zap!* I nearly lunge from my seat as waves of pleasure rip through my core in a relentless, pulsating rhythm. I lose track of everything, trying not to scream as it goes on and on... When it finally relents, I slump against the table, breathless, my chest heaving, nipples erect to the point of pain.

And the bastard is standing before the oven, removing the steaming container. "Food's done," he says. "I hope you have an appetite."

I gape as he divides the food between two plates and places one before me. Smiling, he sits on the opposite end of the table and casually slices off a piece of chicken.

"Don't let the food go cold," he scolds.

I eat warily, constantly on edge. My mother once tried fence training her Pomeranian with a shock collar, and in this moment, I feel for the poor thing. Only more wine can soothe my nerves.

"Dinner with your brother is in two days," I point out, sounding breathless. "What happens after that?"

He shrugs and chews on a bit of vegetables. "I have many talents, but I'm afraid that seeing into the future isn't one of them."

My upper lip quirks even as real irritation sears through my nerves. Bastard. "It looks like you're learning to have a sense of humor, at least."

He smiles, one of those rare, authentic grins. Again, I can't shake the sense that whatever happened today changed him. Shook something loose in him that leaves him sitting languidly, clearing his plate for the first time since I've been with him. Maybe it was going to the stables? I let him show me something special to him.

And now I only want more. Another sip of wine firmly shoves me from borderline tipsy into drunk territory, giving me the courage to probe him despite the risk of sexual torture.

"If I wanted to stay after the dinner, what would you bribe me with?"

I'm boasting, of course. There's no way I'm actually considering it. Not even as his eyes cut up to mine, darkly suspicious.

"What would you want?"

"Hmm…" I mull it over, making him wait. "Tell me what *merde* means," I say, picking a harmless target first.

Those dark eyes fixate on me mercilessly. "It could be translated as 'shit,'" he finally admits, taking another bite of his food—seconds. "An expression of frustration, you might say."

And one he seems to love spilling around me. I puff up, oddly pleased to have pushed him to such a breaking point. Cursing doesn't seem like his go-to vice. I've made him utilize it.

"What about *ta gueule?*" I ask, no doubt butchering the phrase he'd hissed at me while in the club.

"It means 'shut up.' Is that all you want?" he prods before I can retort, his tone mocking. "Translations?"

"No." I meet his gaze and lick my lips. "You buy me a horse as magnificent as Zzazza so that we can have an honest race between us to settle who the better rider is, once and for all. I have a feeling you'll be the one to *'ta gueule.'*"

He laughs, his eyes sparkling. "If such a creature existed, I would have no trouble procuring him for you."

"When did you get her?" I ask, presumably another easy topic.

But I'm wrong.

His face falls, his wall erected in a heartbeat. "When I was lost," he says softly. "On the verge of death. She…she brought me back to life."

"Oh." I want to ask him more. I bounce in my seat, weighing the risk. Screw it. I start to, "Tell me—"

"We should head to bed." He stands and grabs our plates and—sadly—wine glasses and places them in the sink.

"I'll help." I grudgingly rise and cross over to assist.

Bzzzz. I howl and grasp the counter, my legs turning to jelly as searing pleasure builds, fed by incredible friction. No matter how tightly I clamp my legs, it builds. Builds. It's almost too much, going on for too long. Pleasure turns sharp, honed to a painful, aching need, and I have to physically stop myself from reaching into my panties just to find some relief.

Finally, it stops, and I'm on my knees, shaking against the side of the counter.

"I'll meet you in bed," Vadim says, strolling for the staircase at a leisurely pace. "Ten minutes should be enough time for you to prepare, correct?"

Prepare? "But where am I going to sleep—"

A teasing jolt has me yelping though it only lasts a second. A warning, I suspect. Its intention is clear—I'm sleeping with him. In his bed. Again.

When I'm able to walk without staggering, I practically run up the stairs and into the bedroom. My cheeks heat as I pass him stripping beside the bed, and I enter the closet, grabbing a more conservative bit of lingerie—a black negligée. Then I race into the bathroom, wash up— dragging a cloth gingerly between my legs—and I finally approach the bed with minutes to spare of my deadline.

Yawning for his benefit, I wrench back the covers and climb onto the mattress beside him as if I'm not intimidated by the idea at all.

Sleeping beside him without the aid of a lusty stupor to explain it.

Sighing, he copies me, but he doesn't remain on his end for long. Shock runs through me as his hand lands over my hip, wrenching me against him. Effortlessly, he folds over me from behind, preventing any hope of shimmying away during the night. It's the most dangerous concept of spooning one could ever envision.

"Goodnight, *baby*," he murmurs against my scalp. "Try your very best to get some sleep."

And I go alight with the threat.

CHAPTER EIGHTEEN

Vadim Gorgoshev is a sadist.

I barely drift off before I'm jolting awake, gasping in agony. Those vibrations return with a vengeance, ten times more intense, given how sensitive I already am. What felt like a nine on the pleasure scale before is cranked up to twenty.

I'm gasping to smother any moans, writhing beneath the sheets. Nearby, a sturdier body lies innocently motionless, even as a moan finally succeeds in escaping my throat. Moisture coats my inner thighs, spiking the air. Despite my neighbor's rigid stance, I sense him inhale—even in my addled state.

And it somehow adds to the building inferno like gasoline.

I'm trembling when the pleasure finally eases.

Cautiously, I fall asleep.

Only to be startled awake again.

Over.

Over.

Over again.

I lose track of how many times it happens through the night. Enough that I'm barely coherent when dawn light displaces the shadows, and Vadim moves from his spot, looking infuriatingly refreshed.

"Sleep well?" he inquires before strolling toward the bathroom.

I can't even answer. I'm too busy contemplating how much shame I'd feel if I admitted defeat right in this moment and rubbed myself off. I never knew that arousal could be this painful. This…intense. My clit is my brain's sole focus, demanding relief. Anything.

"I have work at the office," Vadim says, returning fully dressed. His crisp ebony suit bolsters the reality that it's already late in the morning. I'm losing track of time, my brain is so scrambled. "I don't know how late I'll be," he adds, drawing my attention back to him.

I suck in a breath as he leans down and plants a kiss on my sweaty forehead.

"I will see you later tonight."

My heart lurches. "T-Tonight?"

He leaves the room without a reply, but I don't trust my legs to attempt to follow. I shimmy to the edge of the mattress instead and tentatively brace my foot on the floor. *Buzz!* Another torrent of vibration makes me curl into a ball, and I scream for real. Fuck him. God, I want to. I need to. I can't…

Think.

Desperate for some kind of distraction, I stumble into the bathroom and try to shower.

Buzz.

Buzz.

Buzz.

It's too much, and I wind up trembling naked on the cool marble floor, seeking out what little comfort I can find. My body is a slave to my libido, heightened to an insane degree. Something about the toy's design must make it so the pleasure provided is incredible—but never *quite* enough stimulation for an orgasm. The result is some hellish sexual purgatory.

And at the back of my mind, I'm praising Vadim as a horrible sexual genius asshole—I got my wish. Debouched kink times a thousand.

My nipples are rock-hard, my hair matted with sweat, my thoughts sluggish. My only remaining goal is to not get myself off. Even if it means I cry in torment, feeling real tears stream down my face as the toy buzzes. On. Off. Again.

The bastard wasn't lying about the range of his remote. It's like I can time each bout, using what I witnessed of his schedule yesterday as a guide. He's read his newspapers. Remembered me. Struck his button. Drank his orange juice and ate his breakfast. Button. Drove to the office. Button. Went through reports. Button.

Button.

Button.

I know I can't survive another fucking minute when the sensation has me wavering between lucidity and utter insanity. If I somehow manage to reach a phone and call him, would he come? But I won't. Fuck him and his game. This torture. In defiance, I crawl back to the bed and climb onto the mattress, guiding my hand down my belly. But something won't let me bridge that final inch.

And as if sensing my flirtation with rebellion, Vadim hits his fucking button.

I'm senseless, screaming. Cursing. I don't even hear the thud of quickly approaching footsteps until their source is standing over me, his voice a gentle hum.

"*Merde…* Are you aching for me?"

It's like my brain is torn in half. The first part can only register his scent. His nearness. I unfurl my limbs and nearly jump from the bed onto him. He's wearing a black suit, and I clumsily rip at the fabric of his pants.

The other half registers the genuine awe in his voice—mingled with that ever-present suspicion. The latter lasts only as long as it takes me to claw at the fastenings of his pants.

"My beauty." His voice alone enhances my torment, in addition to the reverent way he strokes my damp hair and tries to meet my gaze. It's too much. Too much intimacy in this moment. He's having another revelation, but I'm too far gone to wonder about what.

To care.

"P-Please." I can barely speak, my voice high-pitched and broken. "Vadim, please—"

"Lie back." He brushes my hands away and quickly unfastens his pants himself. My entire body rocks at the sight of his cock. Pulsing, completely erect, so thick, I can't imagine how he's not as mindless as I am. Though maybe he is… A muscle in his jaw twitches, his eyelids lowering as I spread my legs.

"Incredible," he grates—real, unforced praise. With his gaze fixated between my thighs, he mounts the bed and slides his hand between my legs. I nearly levitate as his fingers enter me, focused on a task other than providing pleasure. There must be some trick to removing the toy, requiring a gentle, teasing bit of manipulation. Then, he yanks, ripping the device free, and I howl with relief. The next second I'm splayed beneath him, and he's finally easing inside me.

My eyes roll back into my head as I convulse amid a sensation too intense to name at first. *Electric. Punishing pleasure.* One orgasm quickly blends into another. Another. Another. All I can do is cling to him and ride every dizzying wave, sobbing his name until I lose my voice altogether.

I never knew it was possible to crave someone so much. To feel so much hedonistic gratification, it becomes unbearable. Agonizing.

It's only when he rears back and slides his hands beneath me that I realize he hasn't moved since that first thrust. His eyes meet mine, his lips parting, voice relentless.

"You waited for me, didn't you?" Again, he sounds thoroughly shaken. As if he's come to some massive, world-altering conclusion. Something that I think should terrify me. All I can do is rasp his name in confirmation.

I waited.

And he pulsates, his jaw clenched. "You knew that only I could ever give you this." His eyes darken as he grips my hips and snatches me to him.

I moan, my back arching, toes curling. How is it possible to be filled so completely? The sensation floods up through my body, straining my very skin. I'm bursting at the seams, so weak that I'm helpless when he rocks his hips and thrusts again.

Again.

He moves hungrily, grunting, his eyes fluttering shut as he goes deep. Deeper. Fathomlessly deep.

It's more than I can take. All coherent thoughts vanish beneath a wave of ecstasy so potent that I know with a horrifying certainty that no one else could ever give me this. It's the insanity brought on by the toy talking. Inspiring this crazed understanding that no one else will ever feel this good. I would never let anyone else reduce me to this.

I praise him wordlessly, driven by an instinct I can't name to stave off the next release I feel building. Not until I sense him stiffen, his cock pulsating inside of me, his voice a throaty rasp.

"You will come with me," he commands as if reading my mind, connected to me in every way. "Come for me, beauty."

And I do so screaming.

His release floods me like an antidote to a pain I didn't even realize had been festering inside me. I surrender to him, letting him fuck out the rest of his release until we both collapse in a boneless mass. His arms encircle me, dragging me against his chest so that my head rests against his shoulder as I gasp to catch my breath.

It's a slow, surreal descent from cloud nine. I can't stop shaking as my body registers normal sensations again. The coolness of the room. The heat of him. The fact that the sunlight streaming in through the windows betrays that it's either late in the morning or early in the afternoon.

So much for him returning tonight. A cocky smile quirks my lips—I wasn't the only one in agony, it seems.

"Are you alright?" Real concern edges his tone as he strokes my arm, sensing every quaking twitch of my muscles. He sounds so hesitating, truly worried for me.

With what little strength I can muster, I tilt my head back to meet his worried gaze. Once he sees my expression, his lips part into a dazzling grin.

Panting, I tell him, "Best…idea…ever."

CHAPTER NINETEEN

We sleep for what feels like an eternity but turns out to only be a few hours before hunger drives me awake. I roll over to face him only to find him already watching me through hooded eyes.

"I love the way you sleep," he declares, his voice a shallow rasp.

My aching pussy throbs, and I groan, so sensitive that even his voice seems liable to set me off.

"I love the way you come for me," he adds mercilessly, teasing his fingers through my hair. "I love the way you sound. And…I love that you trusted me to pleasure you."

I sigh, my lips stuck in what seems like a permanent, if tired, grin. "You are affectionate when you're sprung," I tease him, my voice hoarse. Gently, I stroke his chest, marveling at the softness of his skin. "I love the toy you had made for me. I love the game we played—"

"Enough to do it again?" he wonders, an eyebrow raised.

An ominous shiver runs through me as I decide upon my answer. Yes. I would. Turning into him, I brush my lips along his collar, tasting him. "I want to play many games with you."

"Your wish is my command." His smug tone warns me that the vibrator wasn't his only custom-made item in the works. Does that scare me?

"You are excited," Vadim suspects, stroking my chin. "Does my kink please you?"

I roll onto my back and languidly stretch out my sore, aching limbs. "I *love* your kink. But I really need to shower, and I'm starving." I crawl toward the end of the mattress, but he stands before I even make it halfway.

"No." Stern steps bring him to my side. Before I know it. I'm in his arms, cradled to his chest. "You are to be pampered," he says while carrying me into the bathroom.

My grin grows wider. "Is that what you learned from your research?"

His wicked smirk warms me more than the temperature he sets the shower to before setting me onto a marble bench built into the wall of the stall.

"My research has taught me many things," he explains as he returns to my side, laden with bottles of luxurious looking bath soap and fresh washcloths. "That you are to be pampered and rested in between our games, for one—"

He lathers up a cloth with the sweetest smelling soap I've ever smelled and washes my legs, starting at each ankle. "And that I am to never push you too far. And that ensuring your pleasure should be my main desire. *Never to hurt you.*"

I swipe my fingers through his wet hair, loving the feel of it. Like silk.

"It seems I'm in good hands," I say, spreading my legs so that he can continue his ministrations unabated.

The man takes his time, bathing every inch of me until I feel so boneless, I doubt I could walk on my own. Not that I'm given the choice to. He dries us off with a towel and then carries me back into the room. With a secretive smile, he sets me on the freshly made mattress before he wanders into the closet. A few minutes later, he returns dressed in a pair of sweatpants and with one of my less revealing nightgowns—an ivory one made of silk—slung over his arm.

The man even dresses me, resisting any attempt I make to help.

"I will bring you food," he explains as he pads to the door, leaving me splayed on the bed.

"More food of Ena's?" I playfully taunt.

He chuckles rather than answer.

And I go to war within myself. This is going too far. Too fast. An intimate bath and breakfast in bed take this liaison far beyond a one-night stand. The fact that we're well beyond one night makes that clear as well. I should be doing whatever it takes to cement the boundary between us, and when I hear his steps approach, I'm ready to remind him of the unescapable facts—this won't last. It certainly isn't real. I need to return to California.

But then he rounds the corner, strolling through the doorway, and I forget my train of thought.

"From your stunned silence, I can assume this meal is to your liking?" he wonders innocently while advancing sporting a silver tray piled high with sweets and delicacies on one hand while holding a bottle of wine in the other.

The good wine.

Too stunned to argue, I scoot over to make room, and it isn't long before I'm eating right from his hands. I groan with utter content as I sample a chocolate-covered strawberry.

"I *love* when you pamper me," I declare as my eyes glaze over.

He chuckles, and his fingers dance over the tray of desserts in search of another treat. "I'm beginning to suspect that chocolate is your weakness every bit as much as wine is."

I nod, relaxing into him. He sits with his back to the headboard while I lie in between his legs, leaning against his chest. Spoiled, tipsy, and with my brain still mush from earlier, I'm in no state to filter myself.

"What made you come after me?" I ask, thinking back to that night at the club. My teeth descend into my lower lip as I picture it. The very first time I pushed him past his boundaries with marvelous results. "I thought I wasn't your type?"

"You aren't." He's frowning even as he says it. Before I can fully tense, he lowers his mouth to my ear, his breaths thick and hesitant. "Maybe that's a good thing… Or bad," he adds, "considering my finances."

A self-satisfied grin tugs on the corner of my mouth. "Tell me."

He sighs as if thinking it over. Then he picks a small, bite-sized piece of cake from his tray and brings it to my mouth. As I chew, he says, "You challenged me." His tone deepens, making it sound so novel to him. A foreign concept. "I've offended women before. Some left. Others threaten to ruin me, or extort me for money…" His eyes take on a cold gleam, betraying that sadistic hint of his personality. I pity the poor woman that ever thought she could take advantage of him. Something tells me, he more than ensured they regretted that decision. He relished in it. But then he cocks his head, his mouth tilted downward. "None have ever threatened to compare my sexual prowess to that of a sex club's full roster before," he admits, brushing his finger along my exposed shoulder.

I shrug to hide my blushing cheeks. "Could you see yourself wanting a real relationship with a woman you don't have to bribe?"

Beneath me, his chest rumbles with a thoughtful hum. "Could you see yourself in a relationship so soon after your divorce?"

I squirm, unnerved by how easily he saw to my main source of hesitation.

"I don't know," I admit. "In theory, I want to say no, but in practice? I suppose there could be someone out there worth exploring something deeper with, no matter the time frame."

And yet, I'm frowning. The thought is surprisingly unnerving, far too serious for my drunken brain to contemplate, so I crane my neck back and open my mouth.

Taking the hint, he places an exquisite looking piece of chocolate onto my tongue. I groan, sufficiently distracted, all thoughts of losing my newfound independence forgotten.

"Do you ever see yourself getting married again?" Vadim asks, unwilling to let the subject drop.

Damn. I take my time swallowing and then shrug. "I don't know—"

"What about children?" His voice shifts, taking on a deeper, more cautious tone. Something about his reaction triggers a part of my brain, but I'm not sure why. Maybe recognition? It's the same wistful, guttural way he spoke about his horse, betraying a deeper emotion I can't comprehend just yet.

Which leads to a more important question—does he want children?

"No. I… I don't want children," I confess. If I did want to pursue a relationship with anyone, it's best to get that out of the way. "I don't."

He stiffens, and my cheeks catch fire. It's the same reaction I've grown used to, and one of the main reasons why I've avoided my parents, in addition to loathing their guilt.

Your biological clock is ticking, Tiffy, they gently remind at every opportunity. *You don't want to be alone forever. You would make a wonderful mother.*

"It's not like I hate children," I add in a rush. "I love them. So, so much. I always wanted to be a mother too, but when I was with Jim…" I close my eyes, combating an unexpected prickling sensation—that of tears threatening to form. "He was kind of a Nazi when it came to setting the timeline of when he thought we were 'ready.' In short, never. He'd spin the tired old excuses about having enough money or time, but the truth was he never wanted a baby. Not with me, anyway. But as these things usually happen, I got pregnant unexpectedly." I suck in a breath as the pain rises up swiftly, striking like a punch to the chest.

"You don't have to say anymore," Vadim warns, still cradling me in his arms. Maybe it's his warmth that makes me brave enough to keep talking?

"I was so happy," I croak. "Everyone says that, but I can't explain… I truly was so ecstatic. My relationship with Jim was a bust, but with this new baby? I would be the perfect mother. I would do anything…"

"What happened?" Vadim prompts, his voice soft. I look down, surprised to find that he grabbed my hand without my realizing it. His thumb strokes my palm, and I find that it's easier to continue now—when I've never spoken about this to anyone. Not my one-time therapist. Not my parents. Not even Jim.

"I have some pre-existing medical issues, so I knew it was a risk from the start. I prayed for a healthy pregnancy, anyway," I add thickly. "I promised that I would be perfect, just as long as everything went well. Jim wasn't happy, but for the first time, I didn't give a damn what he thought. I was happy. I was confident I could do it alone if I had to, and that was enough. But…" I sigh, and tears fall, impossible to keep at bay. "I woke up one morning, barely four weeks in, and I knew something was wrong. I went to the hospital, they told me there was no heartbeat, and… I can't explain what that felt like. I can't. I don't think anyone can ever understand unless you sit there watching some stupid machine refuse to pick up what you know in your heart should be there. It's devastating. It is world-altering. But at the back of my mind, I always knew that it was probably a blessing. I couldn't do it. I wasn't ready."

Case and point? Jim got the privilege of becoming a parent before I ever could—a "fuck you" from the universe if there ever was one.

Vadim's silent, but I suspect he's thinking again, mulling over the best way to phrase his next question. "You've never considered adoption?"

I shake my head. "I had a friend—well, a member of the church—who adopted through foster care, and it was a magical experience. That is until the drug-addicted mother attended a few classes and decided she wanted her baby back. All it took was one overzealous judge to mandate visitation, and the adoption was undone. I can't go through that pain. I can't…"

"I'm sorry."

Something in my heart rips open, and I can't stop the vicious onslaught of tears. His judgment I could handle. Maybe a scoff, or an eye roll, or a gentle reminder that loss happens and I should get over it or some bullshit like what my therapist—who lasted a week—tried to shove down my throat. His understanding is a balm on an infected, blistering wound, and it burns like disinfectant.

"What about you?" I croak, wiping at my eyes. "Are children in your future?"

He goes rigid again, and I shiver as his fingers trace a path up to my wrist. "Too personal? I'm sorry—"

"I was abused as a child." He says it so tonelessly that it takes my brain a second to process it. When I do, horror washes over me so heavy I can't suppress it. I gasp. A million of his little nuances flash through my mind, cementing his claim. His piercing. His mistrust. His initial approach to sex.

And I suddenly feel like the biggest bitch in the world for pushing him. Taunting him. Dragging him from his comfort zone without a damn given to anyone but myself.

"Oh, baby…" I reach for him, lacing my fingers with his free hand.

"I won't go into the details," he adds, his tone eerily level. Robotic almost. "But whatever form or manner you can envision happened, most likely did."

I twist around and stroke his jaw, my eyes brimming with even more tears. He looks so cool again, so distant. But this time, his wall is down, and I can sense the monstrous effort on his part that must take. To let me in. To allow me to feel the tension rippling through him.

"Children of my own was never something I envisioned." A cold, slow smile shapes his mouth. "But it seems the universe enjoys taunting me by challenging my past perceptions."

"How?" I ask hoarsely.

He shakes his head—a topic for another day, I suspect.

"You'd make an amazing father." I sound mournful as I admit it. To gauge his reaction, I turn around as I sink against him. "You're patient. Gentle…"

"You can be so sure despite knowing me for only a week?" he questions skeptically, throwing his arm over my hip.

I nod. "Yes. Call it my special gift—" Either that or a major character flaw. "I'm good at reading people. *Too* good. I knew within two days that Jim was a self-centered, abrasive asshole. I just ignored the warning signs. But you? I find myself trying harder just to ignore the *good* things. So yes, I have no doubt that you'd make an amazing dad."

Given the empathy evident in how he cared for his horse alone, a child of his would grow up both spoiled and cherished beyond measure. And he deserves a woman who could give him that future.

"I've upset you," he says as I roll off of him.

"No." I shake my head as I climb from the bed and stand on shaking legs. "I'm fine. I promise."

I just feel the need to put distance between us, any way I can. I wind up in the bathroom, slumping over the counter. My eyes are bloodshot, my bottom lip trembling. Self-pity?

No. The pain ripping through my chest has everything to do with guilt. Vadim is such an infuriatingly stubborn, guarded, mysterious man. And the more time I spend around him, the more of him I'm starting to crave. My instincts are warning me to run far and fast. Before it's too late and I do something stupid.

Like jump into another relationship with someone I barely know.

I splash cool water onto my face and then reenter the bedroom with a lazy grin. He's still propped up in bed, watching me warily.

"Are you alright?"

"Yes." I skip to his end of the bed and climb onto the mattress—directly onto him. He grunts in shock, capturing my waist to keep me steady. I plant a drunk kiss on his jaw and keep kissing my way down his chest until the tension drains from him completely.

"I love being with you," I confess, somewhere near his navel. "May your future fake wife burn in hell."

He leans back and meets my gaze, an eyebrow raised. "Is this your way of telling me that you plan on escaping after tomorrow night?"

"Tomorrow?" Belatedly I remember dinner with his brother, my supposed reason for staying this long. "I guess our arrangement will be over, then."

"Will it?" That dangerous gleam ignites in his gaze, setting the hairs on the back of my neck on end. "You've been so intent on leaving that you have yet to ask yourself—will I let you go? I think you might very much enjoy bondage play."

Excitement bubbles in my belly at the mere thought of having him shackle me. *Snap out of it, Tiffy.*

"You won't want me around for very long," I say, shifting my position to nuzzle his neck. "One month of my spending, and you'll cancel your fancy card and send my ass right back to California."

"I doubt that." His voice deepens into a richer, thicker baritone and my toes curl in response. "I've had more entertainment watching you squeal in excitement over a few dresses than I've ever experienced through my wealth.

"Mmm." I purr, wiggling against him. "Keep talking dirty to me, and I may let you play with that damn toy again." I spare a glance at the hated object, resting on his nightstand, freshly cleaned.

"Dirty?" he echoes, pressing me against him. "Stay with me after tomorrow night, and I will show you the world I could offer you."

My breath catches as my brain spins with a million possibilities. More shopping sprees. More carefree mornings. More impromptu horse rides and casual dinners. An abundance of kinky sex.

"You are considering it," he accuses while laughing that buttery laugh.

"I am," I confess. "But you shouldn't want me to. I think I might be…bad for you." I frown, even as I say it. A selfish part of me wants to immediately take the words back. Why can't I chase him, even if our ultimate aims aren't compatible? Maybe I could change my mind. Maybe…

"Bad for me?" He laughs in that sinful way, and his hands creep up my ribcage, cupping my breasts. He groans as my nipples harden and traces their peeks through the fabric of my negligee. "You have been terrible for me—" He flicks his gaze up to mine, watching my reaction. Something in his heated expression makes me suspect he didn't intend the confession as an insult. "I've been distracted from my work. Rather than just a few hours at a time, I find that I've been sleeping through the night these past few days. Not to mention, I'm considering meeting Maxim *without* the aid of an armed guard. You have thoroughly demolished my routine. I'm sure you are pleased with yourself."

My grin returns wider than ever. "So pleased." I brush my lips over his, relishing the feel of him. He's so soft, but so dominating the second he pushes back, urging my lips apart for his tongue to slip between.

The kiss is sweet at first. Then hungrier until I'm lying naked beneath him, and he's palming his cock, his eyes unfocused, our breathing labored.

I part my legs, and he easily sinks inside me.

One thrust takes me so high I go right past cloud nine and straight up to ten.

And even as I quake amid the aftermath, I know that I'm already well past the danger zone of becoming addicted to him.

CHAPTER TWENTY

I wake up in his arms, and we spend most of the morning lying in bed, talking about nothing in particular. It's surprisingly easy to share his space and enjoy his nearness. I could never pass time like this with Jim. Not that he would give me the time of day regardless.

Vadim? He acts as though his business and unknown meetings can wait. As if letting me nuzzle at his throat is worth more than anything else. And the giddy, childish joy goes straight to my head.

"When will you pierce me?" I wonder, nestling against his chest.

A low, shocked grunt resonates from his throat. "You are eager for it?"

I purr and nod, surprised by that fact almost as much as he seems to be. "I'm *so* eager for it. I'm sure you have it all planned out, and I like where your brain goes when you 'research.'"

He chuckles, his gaze thoughtful. "I think you will enjoy the ultimate result, but I am not quite ready yet."

I pout. Then I remember the looming deadline that is tonight, and some of my giddiness diminishes. "Ena warned me about you," I admit. "He said that your brother makes you crazy, and that I am just a toy in whatever is going on between you two."

"Is that so?" His tired sigh ruffles my hair, and he gently smooths the stray strands back into place. "Ena is…let's just say, protective of me. He has earned that right. But I have learned that eighty-percent of the time, he's as overzealous as a worrisome mother."

"And the other twenty percent?" I ask.

His mouth twitches into a reluctant frown. "While he may be overzealous, he is usually never wrong. In this case, I believe precedent may be coloring his perception —" He runs his hand down my back as if in reassurance. "Maxim brings out the worst in me, and Ena knows that better than most."

"How did you meet him?" I inquire next as I trace a path from one perfect nipple to the other. "He doesn't strike me as the type to stroll into one of your offices wearing a suit with a resume tucked under his arm."

"No." His second sigh resonates through my skin, more wistful than the first. "He saved my life. And I don't mean it in the sense that he stopped a bullet for me, or prevented my murder—which he has, many times. I mean it in the most primal sense of the phrase. He saved my life. I met him at a time when I had nothing. Was nothing. For that reason, I will always humor his quirks. Though I may have to remind him that not everyone is so tolerant of his bluntness."

"Tell me?" I risk asking even as he stiffens, his gaze turning distant. "I know I'm prying—and if you don't want to, I won't push it. But I want to know. I'm willing to listen."

I sense his wall wavering, threatening to solidify against me. Driven by an impulse I can't name, I brush my fingers through his hair and cradle his jaw. Finally, he blinks. When his gaze fixates on mine again, it's more intense than ever.

"I was property once," he says bluntly. "Take that as you may. I can't…" He swallows hard, shaking his head. "Some things I won't relive in full. Do you still want to hear it?"

"Yes," I croak without an ounce of hesitation. "I'll listen to whatever you're willing to tell."

"I was property," he repeats. "Little more than a slave but without the benefit of even that title. My worth registered in the tens of thousands, and yet at my core? I was worthless. Soulless. I was nothing."

My heart pounds as an ominous foreboding makes me settle against him, pressing my ear to his chest. Despite the obvious pain in his voice, his heartbeat is sluggishly slow. Too slow. As if his body is completely disconnected from the horror in his mind. Tremors ripple through him, reminding me of the way he shook around Maxim. It's like he's freezing from the inside out, even as his skin blazes.

"My last 'owner' possessed acres of property in some European country, untouchable by the authorities. They called him 'the collector' and he more than lived up to that name. Animals. Weapons. Vehicles…people. He loved horses, you see. He had stables filled with them. And when things got unbearable, they were my escape."

The detachedness of his voice creates a horrific picture. One so sickening, I can't even envision it fully—a nightmare far beyond my picturesque upbringing in southern California.

"The bastard would send his goons after me, and more often than not, I'd be severely punished," Vadim says. "But for whatever reason, when all else in life had lost any appeal, that haven remained tempting enough for me to risk seeking it out at every opportunity. One horse, in particular, drew my notice. A young filly who the stable hands had deemed 'incorrigible'—" He smiles in that rare, genuine way that makes my heart ache. "She retained her spirit despite their attempts to break her, and was prone to lashing out and biting."

"Zzazza?" I say softly.

He nods. "She never attacked me. Not even the first night I snuck into her stall to hide, bloodied, and broken. Whenever anyone came by looking for me, she'd snarl and bite, but never at me."

"How did you escape?"

"One day, my 'owner' decided that I was a liability worth eliminating. He had me beaten within an inch of my life and called in one of his guards to finish the job…" Something terrible constricts his features. A raw pain, unlike anything I've ever witnessed. The type of agony that can only be experienced to understand—a loss of yourself. "I begged for my life," he confesses hoarsely. "Like an animal, I begged. Pleaded. Sobbed. I will never understand why then—I had been through worse before. Never once did I plead. But I did, even though I knew the guard would laugh and kill me anyway. I had resigned myself to death. But I was wrong…" He frowns as if still stunned by that fact. "The guard aimed his gun at me, and then turned it on my bastard owner and pulled the trigger. There was no hesitation in him. No ounce of wavering or struggle. He merely made a decision, and that was that. He helped me escape, and since then, he has never made a decision I do not trust."

I swallow hard, my eyes burning. "So maybe I can try to be nice to Ena a little," I say with a watery laugh.

"He is one of the few men I trust in the world," Vadim swears. "And he makes a mean chocolate cake if you do manage to get in his good graces."

"Ah, so the man prefers chocolate as well," I say, filing away the fact for later.

"I enjoy many things," he says, sliding his arms around my waist, drawing me even closer. Near my ear, he murmurs, "Many of them new revelations."

"Such as?" I wonder smugly.

"Such as kink," he says, his voice deepening. "I never knew sex could be so…stimulating."

My breathing hitches. I can't shake his previous confession. Did I really push him too far?

"In a good way," he adds before I can fear the worst. "It can be…pleasurable." He pauses as if fighting to find the right words. "I am not used to that experience."

And yet, he hires escorts seemingly on a regular basis. Does the lack of connection—paired with his obvious joy of manipulation—make it easier for him, even if pleasure isn't his main goal? It's an admittedly cold way to approach such an intimate act. No wonder he'd been so alarmed by my enthusiasm the first night we met.

"I never knew that research could be involved," he adds with a rasping laugh. "That, too, I have come to enjoy."

My grin expands across my face. "Do you *love* our kink?"

"With you, I do. I may even come to love your filthy mouth. The things you say."

"Little me?" I turn to face him and flutter my eyelashes. "I would never say anything vulgar! Like that, I really, really want you to fuck me. Now. Hard."

His eyes narrow as he snatches me to him and promptly rolls over, trapping me beneath him. "Challenge accepted."

CHAPTER TWENTY-ONE

Far too soon, night starts to fall, and we reluctantly leave the safety of the bed for reality. He enters the shower while I comb through the closet and compile two outfits muted in nature—a black suit for him, and an ebony dress for me—fashioned with a modest neckline this time.

I pick out his tie as he gets dressed, and I approach him cautiously, looping it around his neck. "Nervous?" I ask, trying to make my tone more joking than serious.

His eyes darken, gazing into space beyond me. "You asked me once why I did it," he says, his voice so cold I shiver as I twist the tie in on itself. "Why I brought you across the country just for a dinner. Why? You were unpredictable." He slowly lowers his eyes to meet mine. "In my world, those who subvert my expectations have been the only ones I can trust... Don't assume my sole reason was to humiliate you."

I digest the confession slowly, swallowing hard. "I guess I should take that as a compliment, then?"

But I don't. Ena. Zzazza. It feels far more than normal praise to join the ranks of those precious few. Far more vital—and terrifying. I'm getting the sense that those Vadim deems worthy of his attention don't leave his orbit so easily. Like his brother…

"Did Maxim subvert your expectations, too?" I ask softly. Gosh, I can't even look at him. Psychoanalyzing someone like him is a dangerous game to play—but it makes sense. A man so calculating doesn't waste his effort on those who he feels aren't worth the time, family or not.

Not even if they flirt with his hateful side more than most.

Rather than reply, I sense his finger graze my cheek in a simple, lingering caress. When he withdraws, I'm shivering more violently than before. "Get dressed."

Once I'm ready, we head down to the car, and I sense a shift the second he claims the driver's seat beside me. The wall is back up, and the contrast in his demeanor is stark —his eyes darken, his knuckles white as he grips the steering wheel tightly.

"I wonder what's on the menu?" I say in a last-ditch attempt to spark some of the previous humor that had bubbled between us only a few hours ago.

He doesn't laugh or respond, for that matter. I suspect he didn't even hear me. He sits stiffly, hunched over the wheel, his jaw clenched in stubborn silence.

"Baby?" I touch his shoulder, surprised to find him shaking. "Vadim—"

"I'm fine." He shrugs me off, and I choke down any other attempts at conversation, turning my attention to the road. Rather than his brother's house, we head toward the city and eventually arrive before a familiar, impressive building.

The kinky sex club. A strange place to have a family dinner, that's for damn sure. Rather than say as much out loud, I follow him inside. It doesn't register until I spot the familiar surroundings of dark walls and floors that this is the same bar I entered—only now, it's been completely rearranged.

Gone are the scantily clad patrons and oodles of sensual atmosphere. Instead, a long dining table dominates the center of the room, set for six. The tall man, Milton, stands to greet us, followed by the beautiful blond from the party as well.

I sheepishly offer my contribution—one of my precious bottles of vintage. "We brought wine." I make my smile as wide and charming as I'm physically able to. The blond hides her answering grin.

But no one else even cracks a smirk. Still, I take it as a small win. At least *someone* has a sense of normal dinner-party etiquette.

Vadim's brother remains seated beside his young fiancée. His eyes fixate on us, narrowed to slits. Even while dressed in a suit, he radiates feral energy that makes it shockingly easy to picture him lunging across the table at any moment, fists poised to deal out a blow.

"You had the nerve to show up," he growls, his accent thick, his voice booming. "I thought proposing this fucking farce was an elaborate joke on Milton's part."

"What can I say?" Vadim shrugs, and a cruel smile replaces his playful one. "You could have always rescinded the invitation, dear Maxim," he counters.

"It wasn't his bloody invitation to rescind," Milton cuts in, eyeing Maxim with a heated stare fit to light a fire. "Please, sit."

I follow Vadim's lead, taking the seat beside him. As I look up, I realize that we're on an island unto ourselves. Everyone else is seated on the opposite end.

"This looks lovely," I rasp, eyeing the steaming trays of food placed at intervals throughout the length of the table. Roasted meat. Vegetables. My fingers twitch as I spot my bottle of wine, but I suppress the urge to lunge for it.

This isn't about me or my nerves. They're nothing in comparison to the man beside me. He's still shaking, and real concern makes me grasp his hand, squeezing tight. Sweat beads across his forehead, and Ena's warning invades my thoughts. When was the last time he's eaten?

"You have some damn nerve coming here, I will give you that," Maxim snarls, palming the table. His hands are massive, the knuckles scarred and battered. "Did he tell you?" He turns his piercing gaze to me, and I flinch, sliced through. "Did little Dima mention that he kidnapped a child. Held her hostage while her sister panicked, thinking the worst. Did he tell you that?"

Alarmed, I look at Vadim, and I barely recognize him. He's ice-cold, his wall an ocean between us. The skeptical, twisted part of my brain races through the reasons why someone might kidnap a little girl—none of them heartwarming. Especially when paired with what he mentioned of his past…

"Did he?" Maxim presses, his tone so fierce I can't resist replying.

"No," I admit hoarsely. "He didn't tell me that."

"And did he tell you that he threatened my life? That he likes to play God with his money? That he is a snake—"

"What a lovely dinner," Vadim says, his grin wicked. He pushes back from the table and stands. "I'm afraid I'll have to take my leave—"

"I'm not done with you." Maxim lurches to his feet as well. "Did you tell your whore that she is nothing more than a puppet in your quest to mock me?"

The woman beside Maxim lowers her head as my cheeks catch fire. I feel slapped. My lips are already parting as I attempt to stammer out a reply.

But another voice cuts over me. "Enough." Very softly, Vadim murmurs, "I suggest you choose your words more carefully, Maxim. Whore is a strong word to use in your circumstances."

The brunette's eyes blaze, her chin set stubbornly, and Maxim rocks onto the balls of his feet, opening his stance.

"Get the hell out."

Milton stands then, "*Maxim—*"

"Gladly." Vadim snatches my wrist, yanking me to my feet. "We were just leaving—"

"Good. I hope you've had your fun playing copycat. What next? You hire some children to reenact my life in full? You are pathetic."

Vadim stops short, his teeth clattering together, his eyes like ebony fire.

"Copy you?" he wonders coldly. "By womanizing and terrorizing? Don't kid yourself. Hire children? I've known my limits in ways you can't even imagine. I was not so reckless as to gamble a young life to placate my 'whores' or assuage my ego—" He cocks his head and smiles that beautiful, breathtaking grin. It's wider than ever, quivering at the edges. Meanwhile, his eyes blaze, a chilling ebony.

"How long before your happy little family falls apart by your own making?"

"Son of a bitch!" Maxim's arms ripple with tension as he starts to circle around the table. "Is that a threat?"

"Maxim," Francesca says, rising from her chair. Her eyes worriedly trace his shuddering frame, but if I'm not mistaken, he stops short, his breaths thundering from his chest like growls.

"Get out," he snarls.

"Why should I?" Vadim counters. "I do own part of it, after all."

"An oversight." Maxim shoots a glare in Milton's direction, implying something I suspect. Vadim mentioned that he owned part of the sex club—but I'm realizing that partnership may not be mutual on Maxim's end. "One I will soon rectify if I have to beat a 'recusal' out of you. You think I'll let you weasel your way into my life? My club? You should have stayed in the shadows, rat. Sniveling in secret suits you better than playing the part of a man!"

He lunges, but Vadim doesn't move. He doesn't even blink. I've never seen him like this. Enraged. Frozen. Paralyzed. Social etiquette would dictate I try to smooth things over—but something in my brain snaps, and all of my social conditioning goes right out of the darn window.

"S-Stop!" I step forward in the path of the advancing man, though Milton is already behind him, placing a restraining hand on his shoulder.

"Have you forgotten what we discussed?" Milton says quickly, his grip tight as he glares at the back of his skull. But Maxim's clearly too angry to see anything other than Vadim in his firing line.

"Leave him alone," I rasp anyway. "We're going—"

"Ah, so you've trained her to defend you," Maxim sneers, his mouth a fearsome snarl. "One would think you'd repulse any woman with an ounce of sense. It must be the money. Pathetic. I hope you reward her well for this stunt."

My vision blurs as anger sears through my skin. I think something in my brain snaps, robbing me of any semblance of decorum. I don't even realize I'm speaking until my voice echoes back to me, high-pitched and bitchy.

"What the hell is wrong with you?" A better question would be—why am I so angry? Why does the sight of Vadim standing rigid make something inside of me tear open and bleed? I can't explain it. I can't suppress it. Facing down Maxim, I grit my teeth and square my shoulders, unafraid. "All he wants is a relationship with you! Can't you see that?"

I can. I can acknowledge the effort it took for him to even come here. His barely concealed confusion that I had scored a customary present from his brother, who only seemed to treat him with hate. I don't know what lurks between them. Heck, I don't even know the man beside me. But with my hand in his grip, I can't seem to back down, even as he tugs me toward him, his voice a slap, "Come. We're leaving—"

"Why are you such an ass to him?" I demand, though I've heard the horrific actions mentioned. Kidnapping. Threats. But Vadim's scar looms vibrant in my mind. His pain when he speaks of his past. The longing he doesn't even seem to realize whenever he brings up his brother. Is it all rooted in hateful malice? No. I don't think so.

"Do you have any idea how much he just wants to be accepted by you?"

Maxim blinks, his nostrils flaring, eyes widening.

And I have my answer.

"You don't do you? You don't have a clue—"

"*Tiffany!*"

I flinch in response to Vadim's tone. It's icier than I've ever heard it—a stranger's, adrift on an island to himself. "We're leaving. Now."

He releases my hand and storms toward the entrance, leaving me to follow.

"Dima," Milton calls after him. It seems he's about to go after him, but the blond takes his hand and stops him, her eyes pleading with something I can't even begin to understand. Only now do I realize that everyone is staring at me. Open-mouthed. All I can do is spin on my heels and chase the lanky figure marching steadily toward the red sportscar out front.

He holds out the door for me, but as I pass him and enter the passenger's side, I suck in a breath, chilled to the bone. He's *angry*. Furious.

My heart pounds as he claims the driver's seat, his expression a mystery in the dark.

"Did you really do it?" I croak as he slams on the gas, sending us careening down the driveway. "Did you kidnap a little girl?"

I don't sound anywhere near as horrified as I should. Maybe because I already know the answer before he clenches his jaw, his gaze fathomless.

"Yes."

He did. A man who seems to enjoy needling his brother through any means had no qualms with using a child as a pawn in their game. But is it really so simple?

"Why?" I ask, struggling to understand.

He shrugs, and his haughty chuckle should give me my answer. "Take your pick of one of the many horrific explanations circling your brain," he suggests coldly. "You know my past. I'm sure you're jumping to that conclusion—"

"Don't you dare." I square my jaw and shift to face him though he doesn't look from the road once. "Don't insult me. Don't shut me out. You did it. I'm willing to hear why. So tell me." Something in how he stiffens makes me add, "I know you wouldn't hurt her… You wouldn't."

Maybe it's naive, but when I picture him with Zzazza—his affinity for such an innocent creature—I can't see him hurting a child, not even to spite Maxim. Even as I watch, he flinches at the insinuation, betraying his own disgust at the accusation.

"You didn't," I insist, surer of that by the second. "I want the truth."

"I…" He deflates, his posture wavering. "I wanted to know," he finally confesses, his voice soft. "I wanted to know."

"What?" I whisper. Gathering up enough nerve, I tentatively stroke his forearm. He's as rigid as stone, stiffening against me. "Tell me."

He laughs, and his wall comes up in record speed. Stunned, I recoil, withdrawing from him.

"Don't pretend like you aren't suspecting what I know you are—"

"Stop it!" I lower my hand, this time resisting the impulse to recoil. "Stop pushing me away."

"Why?" he counters, more harshly than ever.

"Because I know you," I say simply, though deep down, I know how false that statement may be. But in some ways, it's not. I feel it in a way I've never been so sure about anything before. Jim was an asshole. Vadim is far from it—though he likes to play the part of one. "I don't think you would hurt a child. Not with the way you treat Zzazza—and if you did, I think Maxim would have killed you," I add with a hard swallow. "You had to have a reason, and I'd like to think it's deeper than trying to spite your dick of a brother."

He goes silent, still stewing. Still brooding. Still so very angry.

But as his eyes flicker from the road for an instant, I sense for the first time that I'm not who he's angry at. Not by a longshot.

"I wanted to know," he reiterates, his voice a hollow rasp. "If I… How… If I could be around her. If she could sense that I was broken. If I had made the right choice. And I did then. I know I did. I *know*." His voice breaks, conveying such pain…

Tears prick my eyes before I can fight them back, drawn by the fierceness of his reaction.

"The choice to what?"

"To leave her," he says, devoid of any emotion. "To abandon her. I let her go. I had to… I had to."

I don't think he's talking about Maxim's little girl anymore —or anyone I'm familiar with. Another woman? I don't have the heart to ask about her now. He's more distant from me than ever.

"Vadim?" I brush my hand along his forearm.

He wrenches away from me violently, and the car jolts sideways with the force of his reaction. I brace my hand against the dashboard as he navigates through the city, and after what feels like an eternity, we finally reach his home.

He parks and leaves the car before I can get my bearings. I'm forced to trail him into the house, unsure of whether to even stay.

Vadim is gone. His body may be here, but his soul is eons away. I risk whispering his name, but he doesn't even look at me. He crosses to the bar and hunches over it, his face in his hands, his body trembling.

"You should eat something," I suggest, taking a tentative step forward.

"I need to be alone."

His tone is a slap. Confused, I turn to the stairs and hurry up them without letting myself reconcile the fact that I should leave. Staying at all is foolish. We aren't in a relationship. He owes me nothing.

And I'm not responsible for soothing his boo-boos or fighting his battles. I tell myself this even as I enter the closet and exchange my dress for an ivory nightgown.

When I approach the bed, Vadim isn't there waiting for me.

He doesn't come up the stairs when I lie down, either.

And I remain awake, listening for him until I finally hear his steps resonate…

But they depart the house entirely.

And a door slams in his wake.

CHAPTER TWENTY-TWO

He doesn't return by the time dawn creeps across the horizon, and I drag myself from the bed and venture downstairs. It's eerily silent, and the excessive neatness of the house stands out in stark contrast to the chaos of storm clouds building beyond the windows. On second appraisal, the place looks barely lived in.

There are no pictures. No personal knickknacks. Despite my sex toy, I don't think I can name anything in the house that stands out as remotely unique.

The man is living in a dollhouse.

And yet I sense that he picked it—specifically this location—for a reason. To further torment his brother? Out of some unhealthy interest in the children Maxim lives with? Or is it more than that?

Something to deal with *her*. The person he mentioned abandoning. Someone from his past?

Jealousy, that vicious thing, nibbles away at my resolve. From his tone alone, I sense *she* mattered to him more than I could ever dream to. I've never heard his voice so… broken before. So vulnerable and raw.

So imperfectly human.

I'm tempted to venture up to the room he warned me against. Maybe the answer lurks in there? I shrug off the thought, though.

My past is an animal I feel comfortable dredging up only on my terms. I sense he might feel the same way.

So, I'll wait, and stew in self-pity instead. Ena was right. I'm an idiot toy, and I couldn't even do something as simple as make sure the darn man ate. I picture him wandering mindlessly, his blood sugar dangerously low— or high. And it's all my fault.

Cooking was never my forte, but I enter the kitchen and find myself fishing ingredients from his surprisingly well-stocked kitchen. This must be Ena's realm. I try to tread carefully as I dump a handful of ingredients into a bowl, too distracted to measure properly. I merely work on autopilot until I pour some semblance of a batter into a cake pan just as the front door opens, carrying a familiar scent.

I shove my cake attempt into the oven and race from behind the counter. Vadim is already entering the kitchen, still wearing his suit from last night, his face haggard. His eyes take me in, and gradually his wall lowers.

I pull out a stool and silently urge him onto it. Sighing, he complies, shifting to face me as I circle the counter.

I'm painfully aware of his eyes on the back of my neck, tracking my progress as I wash each dish and return them to their rightful spot. By the time I'm done, a promising smell issues from the oven.

I check on my cake and warily pull it out. When I turn holding my offering, Vadim raises an eyebrow.

"Breakfast," I say awkwardly as I set the cake before him. "It won't taste as good as Ena's, but you need to eat something." I hunt for a fork, stab it into the center of my cake and warily offer it to him.

He meets my gaze for so long my legs have gone numb by the time he finally accepts the fork and takes a bite.

"It's good," he lies, struggling to choke down my creation. To my shock, he drags the cake closer to him and goes in for another bite.

A relieved sigh nearly robs me of balance. I have to brace my hands against the counter just to stay upright. "I'm sorry," I blurt. "I shouldn't have run my mouth. I shouldn't have said—"

"Don't." He sounds so tired. "Don't ever apologize to me. You've earned that right. No one—but perhaps Milton— has ever defended me like that against him," he adds thickly. "No one."

He makes it sound so momentous—arguing with an, albeit very scary, dickhead who seems determined to rip him down for whatever reason. He's having another one of those revelations, I suspect—but this one is dangerous, because I think I'm sharing the same moment of awe.

Such a beautiful, broken man who doesn't realize he's worth defending. Protecting.

"Don't shut me out like that again," I whisper. I'm begging. "Don't. You scared me."

"I know." He looks away and rakes a trembling hand through his hair, his expression pained. "I know…"

"Next time, I just won't force-feed you a horrible cake that may or may not give you unintended food poisoning, either."

His lip quirks, forming a shadow of that trademark grin. "Next time?"

"Yes," I say, deciding something momentous on a moment's whim. There's no turning back now. "I want a relationship with you. A real one, if you're interested, that is…"

He looks away, and my heart seizes up. Panic, unlike any other, grips me tight, and I realize just how badly I do want to explore something with him. Something beyond sex. Something real?

"Do I want it?" he echoes softly. His slim fingers flatten over the counter as he stands. "Turn around."

I frown but comply, sensing an urgency that warns me not to question. His breath fans the back of my neck as he approaches me from behind and smooths the hair from my neck. Something flashes before my eyes, and I sense a coolness settle against my throat. I reach up instinctively and gasp as my fingers fall over a delicate, silver chain.

"Vadim," I whisper, my voice shaking. "It's beautiful."

A diamond necklace beyond my gold-digging dreams. It's decadent and yet delicate, and I know without even having to ask that it must have cost him a fortune.

"You didn't have to buy me anything," I start, but his hand settles over my shoulder, making me fall silent.

"I know…" At the sound of his voice, I spin around to find his gaze stormier than ever. He strokes my cheek, cradling my jaw against his palm. "Think of it as a down payment in my quest to earn your affections," he adds. I notice that nearby a baby blue box rests on the counter. The same one he'd taunted me with the other night.

A tiny prickle of unease stabs in my chest—the same feeling I got when he thought I was an escort. Beautiful or not, the gift is yet another subtle insinuation that our interactions are only ever a transaction to him. He once claimed that communication was merely another form of manipulation. Does he think I'm only interested in him in exchange for bribes and toys? Even his brother had insinuated as much.

"You don't like it?" He frowns and copies me by eyeing the box. "I can return it—"

"No!" Shaking my head to banish the doubts, I lean forward, letting my lips settle over his. "Don't return it. But I do have rules," I confess as his lips part against mine, and his hand slides around to the back of my skull, dragging me close.

"Oh?" He chuckles, his eyebrow raised. "Do state your proposal clearly."

I reach down to finger his tie. "I want you to be open with me," I murmur, loosening the silken strip. "I want you to trust me. I want you to be kinky with me whenever I command."

"Ah, very tough conditions." He draws back and grasps my hips. I arch into him. Gosh, I hadn't realized just how much I'd craved his touch. A night without him and already the withdrawal was unbearable.

"I want to comfort you when you're hurting," I whisper, my eyes closing. "Don't shut me out. You are not repulsive to me. I… I want you—"

He silences me with a kiss so deep my head spins as I relax into his arms, letting my hands roam his body as my hips seek out the firmness straining the front of his slacks. He feels so good against me. I can't get over it.

Drunk on his scent, I match his vigor and palm him through the fabric of his pants, drawing a beautiful groan from his throat. And yet, he captures my wrist, preventing me from freeing him.

"Ena will kill me if we soil his kitchen," he grates, guiding me back toward the doorway. "I think it's about time I came up to bed, anyway."

"No." At the base of the stairs, I slide my fingers beneath his jacket. "I need you now."

He stiffens as I tug at his pants, only to watch me with dawning understanding as I drag them down his hips and free his cock from the confines of his briefs. He's hard already, stiffening against my touch. His hands cinch my waist as he pivots, pressing me against the wall while I eagerly wrap my leg around him.

He enters me slowly, and I savor the way my body adjusts. Like I was made for him. Designed to conform around him—so expertly, he fits me like a key sliding into a specially crafted lock. My eyes flutter shut, but he strokes my chin, forcing me to meet his heavy-lidded gaze.

"Stay with me," he murmurs while thrusting so darn deep. "I need you to look at me, beautiful. Stay with me."

He's pleading as his eyes scan mine for something—though I'm not sure what. Something that makes my head rear back, my eyes threatening to roll. Only for them to fly open in shock as he withdraws, leaving me aching and gaping.

It's only after my gaze returns to his that he starts to move. Again. Harder. More.

"So good," I tell him, sensing now more than ever that he needs to hear this. Know this. "You feel so good, baby. So good. So good."

He grunts, snatching my hips toward him, altering his angle of attack.

I cry out, gasping iterations of his name as my nails sink into his hair. I know even as my body clamps down around him, trembling with release, that I'm far beyond the danger zone when it comes to him. I think I've been past the point of return for days now.

I burry my mouth into the crook of his shoulder, stroking his back as he slams into me, inching my body up the wall with every thrust. I never knew sex could be like this.

Raw.

Real.

Intoxicating.

We're experiencing something more than just a sharing of bodies. Something primal that makes me cling to him long after my orgasm rips me apart.

So much for finding a billionaire to screw for the weekend. Vadim Gorgoshev has shattered those simple expectations. This moment cements that whatever we share is already far beyond that.

And far more than my sexual adventure is at stake.

I'm falling for him.

Hard.

And from this height, I don't see any soft landing in sight.

HE BATHES ME AGAIN, massaging my limbs while I lie prone on the shower bench at his mercy. The water has long since stopped running—triggered by an automatic shutoff from what I could tell. A warm haze of steam bathes everything in a soft, dreamy blur, misting our skin and fogging our glass surroundings.

We're in our own private universe, one I never want to leave.

"Your body is a masterpiece," Vadim says, his voice a low rasp. I shiver as he drags a rag across my lower back as if memorizing every divot and curve.

"Why, Mr. Gorgoshev!" I exclaim with mock alarm. "Is that a compliment? Dare I say praise?"

He smiles, and it's breathtaking. I make a mental note to never allow him near his asshole of a brother again. No one is worth making him lose this smile.

"Or should I call you Dima?" I wonder, recalling the moniker Milton and his brother used.

I instantly regret the suggestion as his face falls flat.

"No," he says, stroking up the curve of my spine. "I… I love the way you say my name."

My grin is a mile wide, and I attempt to practice my sexy purr, "You mean like this? *Vadim.*"

He nods, his nostrils flaring. "Like that."

I roll onto my back and observe him leisurely, drinking in every inch of his gorgeous frame.

"Will you pierce me now?" I wonder as he turns his attention to my torso. He skirts the cloth between my breasts, traveling down over my belly.

"Now?" He releases an appreciative sigh as his gaze lowers to my legs. "Perhaps," he says. "You still want this?"

I grin wickedly. "More than ever."

Something equally feral alights his gaze as he stands and pulls me into his arms. Cool air assaults us both when he finally opens the shower stall, and we forsake the warmth for a brisk return to the real world. On his way into the bedroom, he grabs a handful of towels and dries me off before letting me crawl onto the mattress.

I twist around, reaching for him. "Are you going to do naughty, sexy things to me before I'm pierced?" I wonder, my voice giddy.

"I—" A crisp, musical tone cuts him off. Confused, we both turn to the nightstand where his cell phone rests. It dawns on me that I've never heard it ring before. The novelty of the fact makes him frown, and I suspect it's not by accident. Few people must have that number, their calls unavoidable. "I have to take this," he says reluctantly, crossing over to the end table.

I lie back and watch as he casually answers, only for his posture to shift drastically in the space of a heartbeat. He hunches over, gripping the end of the table, his voice hoarse. "T-Tomorrow? No, I understand. Yes, I am still interested. Placement?"

He exhales raggedly, tearing his hand through his hair, and I rise up to my knees, concerned.

"What's wrong?" I ask when he finally hangs up.

He averts his gaze, his expression drawn tight. His stupid wall comes up, up, up, and I feel like a madwoman desperately trying to tear it back down.

"No! Don't!" I shuffle toward him and loop my arms around his neck, pressing my body to his. "Don't shut me out. You don't have to tell me everything, but just give me a hint. Don't shut me out."

"A hint?" He sounds so damn exhausted. I lean back, pulling him onto the bed, forcing him to lie beside me. He stares up at the ceiling while I straddle him, stroking his cheek. Finally, his eyes refocus on me, and hesitation transforms his features. He almost looks like a stranger again. Some new man with new secrets to uncover. "I will need my fake wife tomorrow," he confesses.

Jealousy rises up so swiftly I can't suppress it—until I remember. I don't recall him actually hiring anyone to fulfill that role. In fact...the ring is still on my finger, so comfortable there I'd forgotten I've been wearing it all this time. Leaning down, I claim his mouth and drag my fingers down his front.

"Me," I tell him sternly. "I'll be your fake wife." I simper, pleased with myself, but his frown deepens, his gaze still distant.

"There is something I need to tell you," he says seriously. "But I don't think you'll stay if I do."

I shudder at the thought of what. A real wife that he needs a decoy in order to divorce from? Legal trouble, and he needs a wife as a character witness? My brain churns through the possibilities, but I can't think of any dire enough to make him look so…

Torn.

I come to a decision too quickly to parse through the consequences. "Then don't tell me," I say, sealing the request with a kiss. "Not yet. I think I can handle anything—but murder, a secret army of bastard children, or my participation in a ponzi scheme—" I break off as he jolts upright, knocking me off of him.

Dazed, I roll onto my side and watch him. He's cradling his face in both hands, his expression stricken.

"I said something wrong," I whisper, reaching for him. "I'm sorry. What did I say—"

"Nothing." He stands and marches into the bathroom, his shoulders hunched against me. "I… I'll be back."

I slump against the pillows, blinking as my eyes burn. I'm stung by the whiplash of his reaction, but more than that, I'm worried. For him. He's flickering like a candle flame now more than ever. I don't know which direction to swing in to match him. Playful? Serious? Sensual?

I still haven't decided by the time he reappears in the doorway, his hair dripping, his face damp. I imagine him standing over the sink, splashing water onto his face until he regained his trademark composure. His dark eyes flicker to me, wholly unreadable.

"Stay," he commands before entering the hallway, his footsteps resonating. Puzzled, I wait once again in anticipation of which way the flame of his mood will dance. Seconds later, his voice drifts back to me, "Come."

I stand and follow after him on unsteady legs. He's just down the hall, in the closed room directly adjacent to the bedroom. The space beyond is just as massive though sparsely furnished. Cardboard boxes are stacked in one corner, each one large and sufficiently mysterious. In the center of the room is a leather chaise with a sheet draped over it. Nearby is a metal folding table upon which is an array of neat, surgical-looking supplies set on top of another white cloth.

Standing with enviable grace, Vadim tugs on a pair of gloves with his back to me.

"Are you ready to accept this?" he wonders, his tone sin.

I quiver, my heart racing with excitement. "Ready to accept what?" I ask innocently as I continue to close the distance between us.

So maybe he wasn't lying about being a trained professional. His setup looks sterile and organized with clinical precision.

"Impressive," I murmur, stroking his shoulder. He cocks his head back, a quick, tempered smile playing over his lips.

Whatever upset him before is apparently forgotten.

"Sit," he commands, gesturing to the chaise. "I need to examine you."

A thrill runs through me as I practically hop onto the surface and lie back while lifting my nightgown up to my hips. He turns to survey me, his gaze narrowed with focus. Shyly, I spread my legs, giggling as he sucks in a breath. Yet overall, he maintains his steely, doctorly presence.

"Have you ever been pierced before, Ms. Connors?" he wonders while unfolding a medical drape that he places over my abdomen.

"Just my ears," I reply.

A low sound resonates in his chest as he urges my legs apart and instructs me to bend my knees. "*Merde*," he grates, an unprofessional term. Not that I care. The expression on his face… It's enough to make me bite my lip and consider putting this off long enough to seduce him. His eyes are wide, his lips parted and deliciously pink. I inhale as they move, his voice a low hum, "You are so beautiful."

I'm drunk off his baritone, dizzy already. Having him peer between my legs is surprisingly more comfortable than I feel it should be. More intimate. He eyes me appreciatively but in a way that doesn't make me feel like a piece of meat. What was that word he used?

Masterpiece.

I shudder as he guides me further into the correct position. Then he changes his gloves to a fresh pair and swipes a cool liquid over my mound, fighting to regain his professional composure.

"You will feel some pain," he warns as he turns back to his selection of tools. He lifts something delicately with a pair of tweezers and holds it up for my inspection. "Is this fitting enough to meet your expectations?"

"Oh, Vadim," I breathe as I take in the delicately curved piece of metal—the female equivalent to his barbell piercing. "It's beautiful."

I watch eagerly as he manipulates his tools and captures the tiny hood of flesh above my clitoris. But as I hold my breath in anticipation, his doctorly persona slips.

"Tell me you want this," he commands in a gruffer baritone, meeting my gaze. *This.* That dangerous word contains so many unspoken entities, each one hinted at by the ferocity making his eyes seem to glow.

And I don't hesitate. "I want this."

Wordlessly, he guides a needle through a corresponding tool and then sets the piercing in place. The needle drives in easily, but despite any numbing he may have used, the pressure is uncomfortable as hell. I grit my teeth, hissing at the sensation. Thankfully, the discomfort quickly fades into awed admiration as I watch the piercing mark my flesh. A statement of independence if there ever was one. A slight bit of pressure exists but isn't unbearable, and as Vadim guides me to my feet, I don't feel too much discomfort.

"No tight clothing for the first week, at least," he warns, as any professional would. "To err on the side of caution, no rigorous sex for the same timeframe either. Four to eight weeks at most is the typical healing timeframe."

I pout. "But what shall I tell all of the many horny billionaires wrapped around my finger?"

He frowns as if seriously mulling it over. "Tell them that you are taken," he suggests, pulling me into his arms. "That you are *owned*."

"Owned?" I play with the word on my tongue. It surprisingly doesn't sound anywhere near as degrading as it should. More than that. Powerful. Owned the way the moon owns the strength of the ocean's tides—both drawn to each other in an inescapable, magnetic pull. "There is one billionaire in particular who demands satisfaction," I tell him, standing on tiptoe so I can whisper into his ear. "I don't think he'll want to wait a whole week to enjoy me."

"Oh?" his tone lowers to that dangerous, devious baritone.

I nod, sliding my tongue along my lower lip. "Oh, yes. I suppose I'll just have to find other ways to pleasure him in the meantime. Starting with…" I blurt out an array of x-rated suggestions, and he laughs, throwing his head back, his eyes gleaming.

"It's a good thing I took the liberty of special-ordering a few apparatuses specifically for that occasion." He gestures to the boxes in the corner, and my eyes go wide.

"A kinky room, just for me? Why Vadim, I didn't know if you had the imagination in you."

"And then some," he warns, his upper lip quirked. "You'd be surprised what a quick Google search and an hour's long consultation with one of the world's most renowned sexual experts can accomplish…"

CHAPTER TWENTY-THREE

It isn't until midnight that he turns distant again. I catch him brooding through half-closed eyes, and I doubt he's even aware that I'm watching him. His brows are drawn together, his expression stricken. Two slim fingers massage his temples to no avail. With every passing second, his frown deepens, enhancing the uniqueness of his face that lends to sadness so well. To torment.

I start to reach for him, but he turns away, lying with his back to me. And I know that whatever is bothering him has everything to do with our newfound relationship. Regret?

But why?

I'm too terrified to seek out an answer now. Not freshly pierced and drunk off lust. I drift off instead, and it's morning when I finally startle awake.

"I need you dressed."

I look over to find Vadim exiting the closet, already wearing a suit. Over his arm is an array of brightly colored fabric that must be an outfit for me.

"Please," he urges, spreading out a tweed coral skirt and ruby blouse onto the end of the mattress.

"What's going on?" I blink my eyes to adjust to the harsh daylight as I sit upright. My piercing aches, but not in an overly painful way. More like a giddy reminder of the hedonistic pledge I made to both him and myself—owned. My brain melts at the memory, and I almost miss what he says next.

"My…meeting." He cuts his gaze to the door and tugs at his tie. "They are almost here."

He's nervous, I realize. It's such a contrast to his usual icy cool that it takes me longer to process it.

"Okay." I bound into the bathroom and wash up quickly. Then I change into the clothing he specified, puzzled by the overall effect—modest, yet fashionable. The perfect perky wife to his cold businessman. When I stand beside him, I envision the picture we make.

And I freaking love it.

A posh businessman and his classy, yet sexy wife. My heart aches as I realize just how much I enjoy the thought of it. Being his, displayed on his arm. Belonging to someone who seems eager to show me off rather than make me wilt in his shadow.

I smooth my hand down his shoulder, startled when he pulls away.

"I need to tell you—" He breaks off, his body angled away from me so that I can't see his face. Puzzled, I reach for him again.

"What's wrong?"

He cocks his head and moves swiftly toward the hall. "They're here."

They? I follow him warily, lingering in his wake. Downstairs, a stern-faced Ena stands guard near the foyer. The two men share a glance, conveying a silent understanding. As Vadim nods in approval, Ena opens the door, revealing the woman I recognize from his lunch "meeting" the other day. Today her outfit is an olive green two-piece suit ensemble with a modest-fitting jacket and skirt.

"Good morning," she says with a tight smile, stepping inside. "I'm so glad you could accommodate us at such short notice. *We* are glad. Aren't we, Magdalene?"

Vadim descends the final few steps and crosses to her, his voice deeper and more tense than ever. "Of course..." He trails off as a smaller figure appears beside the woman.

And I nearly fall down the rest of the stairs.

The girl—so small she can be only six or seven at most— looks like a living doll she's so beautiful. Curling black hair frames a face set with delicate features. *Familiar* features.

That nose. That chin. That surly, brooding frown. I can't even believe it at first—but as I blink, I realize my eyes aren't lying. The only difference between her and the man standing a few paces away are her eyes, a bright, vibrant blue.

But there is no mistaking the obvious. Genetics are a strange animal—two people couldn't just strike the same biological jackpot by chance.

This little girl is his. She has to be…

His *daughter*.

And I realize—just like I did the night he used me to taunt his brother—that once again, I've been a pawn in his game. A fool. Because any relationship he claimed to want with me was based on nothing more than a twisted lie.

CORRUPT

Corrupt

Corrupt By Lana Sky

Copyright © 2020 by Lana Sky
All rights reserved.

No part of this publication may be reproduced, distributed, or transmitted in any form or by any means, including photocopying, recording, or other electronic or mechanical methods, without the prior written permission of the author.

This is a work of fiction. Names, characters, businesses, places, events and incidents are either the products of the author's imagination or used in a fictitious manner. Any resemblance to actual persons, living or dead, or actual events is purely coincidental.

Cover Design and Interior Formatting by Charity Chimni
Proofreading by Charity Chimni

ACKNOWLEDGMENTS

Thanks so much to everyone who supported this draft along the way, including the many beta readers who provided encouragement along the way! Please keep in mind that this story includes dark, graphic, and explicit content matter that is not suitable for readers under the age of 18—or for readers who are uncomfortable with the following subject matter: explicit sex, mentions of sexual abuse, mentions of child abuse, graphic depictions of violence, and mentions of self-harm.

CHAPTER ONE

There is a reason why, when most people climb from their rock bottom, they tend to promise themselves some variation of—*never again*. Never will they reach that low point again, and especially not at the whims of someone else.

Only a fool like me would promptly forget those internal vows the second they fall for a pretty face with a nice wallet. *And* incredible sex. That's the hurtful part—in exchange for a few welcomed distractions, Vadim Gorgoshev made me disregard my list.

My creed.

And I fully deserve the reality bitch-slap coming my way. Ironically, said slap is delivered in the form of a child so beautiful it almost hurts to look at her head-on. With every passing second, I'm reminded of the man standing nearby who manipulated me into this position.

And deep down, I know that I can't even truly be angry with him.

Not when I'm the idiot who failed myself.

"I'm so glad that you and Magdalene can finally meet in person," a dark-haired woman standing in the doorway says warmly. I vaguely remember her name as being Ms. Anderson—the subject of one of Vadim's so-called "business meetings." Now, her real identity is painfully clear as she places her hand on the girl's shoulder and urges her forward with a gentle nudge—*social worker.* "Say hello, Magda," she prompts.

Magda. A creature so small, her limbs are more delicately shaped than even Vadim's. Pale skin enhances her frailty— gosh, she really could be a living doll. A doll dressed in hand-me-downs. I recognize the ill-fitting shape of her simple black shirt and gray skirt—an anomaly I file away for later. Looking at her, it's hard to focus on anything else but the unease setting my face on fire.

A thin headband restrains a mass of wayward curls, but stubborn strands have slipped through anyway to frame her cherub cheeks. Curls every bit as stubborn as her frown. It's like looking at a mini-Vadim, scowling at the world, mistrustful and calculating. Even of her father, it seems. Her eyes flicker over him, devoid of recognition, and confusion mingles with the anger building beneath my skin.

"Magda..." Vadim's voice is a rasp that tugs at something inside me, even as fury simmers hot. He takes a step forward and extends his hand only to let it fall when she crosses her arms—deliberately, I suspect. "Welcome," he grates, letting his hands dangle uselessly at his sides. His eyes dart around the room as if hunting for anything he could direct the conversation to. Lost, he stammers. "Welcome home. I mean, welcome to—"

"It's okay," Ms. Anderson says gently, displaying the patience that I assume comes with her profession. "We hope this will be a great home for her, too. Care to show us around?"

"Of course." Vadim lurches into motion, guiding them through the lower level. Like a sleepwalker, I find myself straggling behind them, watching. Lurking.

It's selfish—I know it is—but my brain plays a horrible game. It takes the features of that beautiful little girl and taunts me with who her mother might be. What she looks like. Someone so alluring that a man as tormented as Vadim took an interest in her. He was careless with her. He trusted *her* with his child.

A child whom, as of five minutes ago, I didn't even know existed.

I stare as they move in a stiff, awkward progression through this clinical, sterile mansion. Magda's appearance alone creates a stark contrast that makes her absence from Vadim's life painfully apparent. Nothing from the color scheme to the sleek architecture lends itself to the idea of a child visiting, let alone living here. But does she? I recall one word Ms. Anderson stated, and my perception is turned upside down for a second time—*placement.* As in adoption?

No one offers up any other explanation. As the small procession makes its way into the kitchen, Ms. Anderson abruptly turns back to the foyer. "I think I'll step out for a minute," she says with a small smile. "I'll grab some paperwork from the car, and you three can use this time to get acquainted."

She leaves, and "us three" take up various positions across the kitchen like opposing generals in a silent war. Vadim hovers near the dining table, his expression stricken. He can't seem to take his eyes off her, Magda. She stands by the bar counter, her arms crossed, her eyes suspiciously narrow.

Gosh, seeing the two of them nearly side by side…

It's breathtaking how identical they look—both in manner and appearance. Simultaneously they embody the two halves of Vadim's personality I've become the most acquainted with. The vulnerable, raw part of him that calls to the empathic part of my soul. And the calculating, vengeful mastermind always one step ahead. With every second ticking by, that selfish, pathetic hurt in my chest digs deeper, biting into my very core.

"Hello, Magda," Vadim manages to say, once again attempting conversation.

She purses her pink lips in a deliberate show of silence, flicking her gaze throughout the room.

"Are you okay?" Vadim adds, and I do a double take. I've never seen him so…off-balance. So out of his element. Helpless, he rakes a hand through his hair, his eyes lacking their calculating cool.

Though Magda seems to possess more than enough for both of them.

"Am I going to live here now?" Her voice is soft, as cold as his can be but lacks any accent. "When I leave the Robinsons?"

"Y-Yes." Vadim fumbles for a chair and sits on it, facing her. "If that is what you want—"

"So, you are a foster family?" Her eyes shift in my direction, inspecting me from head to toe. In some ways, it's the most thorough dressing-down I think I've been subjected to. With a sigh, she turns her attention back to Vadim and cocks her head. "You don't *look* like a foster family."

"Or more," Vadim says thickly. "If that is what you—"

"I hope everyone is getting acquainted," Ms. Anderson declares as she enters the room, a briefcase in tow. "We can go over some of the paperwork, and then Magda, you can visit for as long as you'd like."

"Can I wait in the car?" Magda asks.

"Already?" Ms. Anderson's bright smile strains at the edges. "Don't you want to get to know Mr. Vadim and Ms. Tiffany?"

Magda's blue eyes flash with a hint of emotion that vanishes before I can identify it. "No." She neatly clasps her tiny hands and marches into the hall. A second later, the front door slams shut, and Ms. Anderson collapses onto the nearest chair with a heavy sigh.

"I'm sorry. Magdalene is a wonderful little girl—so brilliant. I mean, you don't know the half. But I won't deny that she has proven to be…challenging lately, especially for her current foster family. Two years ago, and things were wonderful, but it's as if since her illness… Well, she decided to go from a sweet, respectful child into—" She seems to remember her current surroundings and breaks off. Clearing her throat, she shuffles through her briefcase and extracts a handful of documents. "Her placement with her current family ends on Monday," she explains. "They've decided to move back to Michigan after the end of the term, though they did request a meeting with you at your earliest convenience. If it's not too soon, Magda will be ready for placement with you as soon as Tuesday. It is unusual to move so quickly in the process. Still, after the whole teddy bear incident—" she breaks off again and coughs to disguise the action. "Anyway, with the term ending, and Magda's unique health concerns, it could be a challenge to find a suitable family. Thankfully, I see here that you have passed all of the relevant courses."

"Health concerns?" I hear myself croak.

"Yes." Ms. Anderson nods. "She suffers from insulin-dependent diabetes, so she requires a strict dietary regimen and a provider qualified enough to assist with monitoring her sugars regularly. And I'm sure you're aware of the unfortunate setback last year, so her health is a significant factor in finding the right placement. She is also unusually gifted, as you might have been able to tell. Her intellect can make her interactions with some adults…unnerving. For that reason, she requires a very stimulating education that, coincidentally, one of the schools here in Fair Haven, is able to provide. She even received an anonymous scholarship to cover the costs for the duration of her entire schooling, so you can see why keeping her here would be a priority."

Vadim says nothing, his gaze distant. Perhaps he's ruminating over those few key words. *Intelligent. Challenging. Unnerving.* Or, like me, he's marveling at the fact that the description of that child could have easily fit *him*.

"Excuse me," I blurt, unable to hold back any longer. "Where is her mother? Her birth mother?"

"Her m-mother?" Ms. Anderson blinks and glances at Vadim. "Magdalene was discovered abandoned at the age of five, left right on the steps of an orphanage." She shakes her head sadly. "We, unfortunately, have no real information on her birth parents. Adoption would be the aim of this placement, as we have already discussed with Mr. Gorgoshev."

"Of course," Vadim grates, his gaze averted from me. The wall is back up, and I seethe at that, perhaps irrationally. Maybe it's selfish to want something more from him now

—some shred of emotion to cling to. Regret? Smugness? *Something.*

"Excuse me." I turn to the door, moving quickly. "I… I have a horrible headache."

Only now does a familiar voice call out, "Tiffany…"

I falter despite myself. He has the nerve to sound hoarse. Tortured. I hear his chair move, but I shake my head. "Don't," I say firmly as I start for the stairs. "Do not follow me."

I make my escape into the bedroom, and I don't stop until I'm barreling into the closet, snatching items from hangers at random. The fact that I own nothing here really doesn't matter in the grand scheme. I selfishly take handfuls of clothing—both his and mine—and shove whatever I can into one of his briefcases. When the case is stuffed to the brim, I take it and march down the stairs. As I descend the final steps, I catch him ushering Ms. Anderson from the door. The second she's gone, he closes it, his back to me.

"Tiffany…"

"What?" I throw the briefcase at him, and it lands harmlessly at his feet. He doesn't even flinch. "Get out of my way."

"What do you want me to say?" he demands, and I stiffen at his tone. The harsh, bitter cadence is a damn near match for Magda's. Their anger is as chilling as their hostility, erected like an invisible brick wall against anyone who dares approach them.

Even if that person has their heart laid bare.

"What should you say?" I hiss incredulously. "Maybe that you have a daughter!"

He's silent, his hand on the doorknob. Despite my anger, a tiny bit of unease bites through, making me falter in my descent. Would he really try to keep me here? Trap me here?

To rebel against that very possibility, I force myself down onto the next step. Then another.

"You have a daughter, and you *abandoned* her," I add to twist the knife, parroting the word Ms. Anderson had used. "You put her in foster care? So now what? You yank her back out? Is that what you wanted your fake wife for? A decoy to game the system to regain custody of your own child? Answer me! I swear to God—"

"She doesn't know I exist."

My shoulders deflate at the raw pain in his tone, and dizzying confusion displaces some of the anger. "So why…"

"I didn't know she did either until two years ago," he explains, turning to face me. His eyes trace the floor rather than meet mine directly. He cradles his temples in the palm of his hands, his jaw clenched. "One day, someone went through great lengths to slip me an envelope that contained only the picture of a five-year-old little girl and her location in an orphanage upstate. I only had to see her face, and I knew. Those eyes…" He shakes his head, clearing away the memory. "There was nothing else—no information on who left her or why. I arranged to have our DNA matched, but the results were no surprise. Afterward, I intervened to have her brought here, where she could receive an education. I secured her safety…"

The raw pain in his voice makes me sway, and I grasp for the banister, gripping it so tightly my knuckles whiten. At the same time, I grit my teeth to keep my expression from faltering. "You learned of her years ago, but you let her go into the foster care system?"

He flinches, leaning against the door as if it's the only thing keeping him upright. "I didn't know what to do. I… I couldn't take care of her—not then." He sounds so earnest about that. His tone, paired with Ena's vague hints of his mental state, makes me wonder just how unstable he had to be at that point.

It doesn't take rocket science to come up with the answer —so unhinged, he didn't trust himself around his own child.

"And her mother?" I descend another step but don't approach him.

He meets my gaze, and I know whatever he's about to say is anything but a lie. "I can't explain that right now. You need to trust me on that."

But I can't. There's something in how his eyes shift, darkening in that way he does when his wall is up. When he's hiding something. When he's pushing me away.

"A one-night stand?" I prod. Somehow that possibility stings more than him having a genuine relationship. I couldn't convince him to let me suck him off during our first meeting, and yet some other woman managed to snag his child in one go.

Lucky her.

"No," he says, confusing me further. "It is…complicated. More than you can imagine." His jaw clenches in that telltale hallmark of when he's reflecting on that which haunts him the most—his past. As angry as I am now, I can't seem to broach that topic.

So, I do the next best thing and march over to my makeshift suitcase. As I stoop for the strap, his voice rings out.

"Don't."

"Why not?" I hiss, placing my hand on my hip instead. "Give me one reason why I should stay? I didn't sign up for this. You may enjoy treating people like toys, but I won't serve as your smiling Barbie so you can acquire some poor little girl—"

"I can't do this alone. I *can't*." His voice is so guttural each word resonates in my bones, sinking deep. "I can't do this by myself, and I've worked too damn hard to secure her placement. I… I need your help. It's why I wanted to hire…" He grits his teeth, his expression grim with determination. "Stay. I'll give you whatever you want—"

"I want honesty!" I snap, but my voice rings out hollower than I'm used to. Broken. "I want you to tell me more than the basic, generic damn answers. Tell me the truth!"

"I will," he counters, raising his tone to match mine. "I will. But you yourself stated that you had a perfect childhood. I was not so lucky. So do not doubt that my sole concern is Magdalene, and I will do whatever it takes to ensure that she is safe with me."

"Is that a threat?" I try to sound nonchalant—like I'm not afraid. But when he looks as he does now…I am. His eyes blaze, ruthlessly determined.

And not for the first time, I'm forced to reconcile the fact that I have no idea what he's capable of.

"Stay with me," he commands, his voice slightly softer. "I cannot risk losing her to some bureaucratic miscalculation. I've worked too damn hard… The sacrifices I've made for her? You think I've betrayed you, fine. But understand that I can't risk losing her placement. I *can't*."

And he's begging me to prevent just that from happening.

"Fine." Overwhelmed, I lift my hands in surrender. "I'll stay until she's placed with you—but I'm leaving after that."

He sighs in relief. "Thank you—"

"But that is all you're getting out of me," I say over him, desperate to put distance between us—any petty way I can. "Forget our 'relationship.' There isn't one. And I suggest you find somewhere else to sleep. Don't touch me. Don't talk to me. I don't want anything to do with you."

"*S'il te plaît*! Just listen to me…" A groan escapes him, so pained, it stops me right in my tracks. "Tell me what I can do to earn your forgiveness."

"Nothing!" I snarl. Why am I so angry? I still don't know. Or maybe I just can't admit it, even to myself—a stinging pinch in my chest reveals the answer anyway. Jealousy. Jealousy. *Jealousy.*

It festers on a million different petty observations. Like how he listened to me pine for a child I'll never have, while hiding his own. A child connected to him in ways I suspect he's deliberately not revealing—her mother's identity, for one. *Those eyes,* he said in that hollow tone reserved only for those who matter most to him, like his horse Zzazza. *I only had to see her face, and I knew. Those eyes…*

The mere thought of him withholding something from me hurts in ways I can't explain. Tears spill from my eyes as I whirl to face him, my voice scathing, "I escaped a marriage with one self-centered asshole. I'll be damned if I'm jumping into another with someone ten times worse, fake or not. Jim didn't pretend to be anything other than a prick. So, fuck off, Vadim. I suggest you continue your search for a fake fiancée."

I turn on my heel and leave him there. Storming into the bedroom, I slam the door behind me so fiercely the sound echoes like a gunshot.

Then I sink onto the bed and cry in earnest, like I haven't in a very, very long time. Shoulders shaking, voice breaking, full-throttle sobs. It's a pity party, for sure. I can admit that. But it's surprisingly painful to go from wanting someone so much—despite every last warning sign—to knowing that it's better to have nothing to do with him.

And yet still craving him all the same.

Hope can be such a bitch.

CHAPTER TWO

I'll never forgive myself for who I became during my marriage—a doormat. Not only did Jim completely obliterate my self-esteem, but he convinced me during the process that it was entirely my fault. For so long, I believed that lie…

And one of my promises to myself after the divorce was that no one would hurt me and walk away scot-free ever again. Thus, my list was born—the series of goals I've managed to uphold despite a lifetime of failed ambition and broken dreams.

And the most important one? No relationships.

Being spurned by someone like Vadim is exactly what I deserve for forgetting that key vow. For ever forgetting that *my* needs come first now. Always. While the good lord encouraged forgiveness, the Bible did mention that little thing about an eye for an eye.

Therefore, I intend to gouge out Vadim Gorgoshev's

entirely guilt-free. Step one? I wake up alone and enter the closet with only one goal in mind—finding the most revealing, skin-tight, sluttiest ensemble I can without risking the integrity of my piercing. Screw it. I wear a lacey, see-through bustier and short black tweed skirt that rides up my hips, avoiding pressure on my healing flesh.

Later I'll reflect on the utter stupidity of letting a virtual stranger pierce my nether regions in the first place. At the moment, revenge is a far more appealing animal. To enhance my look, I leave my hair down and skip a bra entirely.

Mr. Billionaire eat your heart out.

No one will ever again make me feel worthless, as if my only value is at their disposal.

I am a queen. So, I do my makeup in the style of one, and when I finally leave the room, I'm ready for war. Irritatingly, I don't find my opponent when I venture downstairs. In the kitchen, all I discover is a lone croissant resting on a plate beside a bowl of fresh fruit. As subtle a peace offering that a smug bastard could present without eating crow.

Whatever. I ignore it in favor of scouring the rest of the house in search of him.

I toy with the prospect that he didn't sleep here at all, ceding this battlefield to me—but then I spot him in the study, slumped over his desk. And a teensy, tiny bit of doubt creeps in, poisoning my heart with...concern.

Gone is the calculating, smug businessman. This creature, with his eyes closed and features gaunt, is the epitome of exhaustion.

My fingers twitch rebelliously. Anger takes a backseat for a split second, surrendering to the emotion only he can inspire in me. I have a sudden urge to smooth the hair back from his face and encourage him to go to bed.

I take a step forward… And a tendril of light from the window enhances the planes of his face—and how identical they are to his daughter's. My anger renewed, I loudly storm back into the kitchen and slam my way through cupboards and drawers until he appears in the doorway, his eyes bloodshot. His gaze settles on my face first, his lips parting. "We need to talk—"

"Or not." I down a glass of orange juice as I snatch up the croissant and head for the stairs.

He doesn't follow me, and I spend the rest of the day avoiding him, too terrified that the sight of him may make me break.

And after seven years of cowering, I *refuse* to break.

Sleep provides only a brief reprieve. As soon as dawn creeps over the horizon, I steal a pair of masculine sweats from the closet and a set of tennis shoes for good measure. Desperate for fresh air, I head downstairs, but I barely make it through the front door before I sense him behind me.

"Where are you going?"

Gosh, he sounds more haggard than yesterday. I turn to face him and once again feel my resolve being tested. His dress shirt is rumpled, suspiciously resembling the one he wore two days ago. His pants are a wrinkled mess, and his hair sticks out at odd angles—no doubt assaulted all night by raking fingers. He looks so tired. So worn.

With difficulty, I flick my gaze from him and escape into the chilly, dawn morning.

"I'm going for a walk," I tell him coldly. A part of me flinches at my tone. *Chill out, Tiffy.* Again, I can't understand why I'm so angry. Why a sick part of me thrills at making him flinch. Survival instinct? Maybe. I'll guard my heart at all costs from him, even if it kills me. "Don't follow me," I add as I slam the door.

Driven by nervous energy, I explore his property with a singular focus and find myself surprised by how big it is. And at the same time, just how empty it seems. He must control acres and acres, their boundary defined by wooden posts placed at seemingly random intervals. The house itself overlooks a wide pool set in gray stone as well as a private dock and a vacant boathouse. There's even an empty, lonely stable at the back overlooking a view of the waterfront.

It's a home that any little girl would dream of living in, and yet it's almost entirely devoid of anything she might want to do. There is no playground. No dollhouse. No sea of toys to drown herself in.

It's as if the man found the perfect blueprint for a family home but had absolutely no clue how to fill it. And now the clinical emptiness of the house makes more sense—he's stuck, torn between who he is at his core, and the man he seemingly *wants* to be.

A father.

If I weren't so angry with him, I'd gently suggest he work some color into the décor. Build a swing set and maybe a garden for her to play in. Does he even have a room picked out for her?

Yes, I suspect, recalling the one upstairs that he requested I avoid. But something tells me that even it is empty. Was he expecting his fake wife to lend him expertise in that arena? It sounds so stupid—a man like him with so many resources could easily hire someone to help him design a little girl's room. At the same time, it fits. Vadim is so cripplingly self-conscious, he wouldn't trust anyone to help. Not even me, the woman who bared her soul to him. Who claimed to want a relationship with him.

Who now hates him.

I reinforce that last statement as I return to the house dripping sweat, only to find an unfamiliar vehicle in the driveway—a stocky, serviceable minivan. When I ease open the front door, a sharp voice reaches my ears, and I hesitate over the threshold, straining to listen.

"…so, you can see why we were concerned," a woman says, her tone shrill and haughty. "We love and nurture children of all ages, shapes, and sizes, but I hope you are prepared for that girl."

"She can be…unusual," a man interjects, his voice slightly more tolerable, almost apologetic. "That's what you meant to say, right, honey?"

Rather than sulk upstairs like I should, I follow the conversation into the kitchen, drawn by the tone. It's far too serious than I figure a typical visit would be—not that Vadim seems like the afternoon brunch type anyway.

I find him seated at the table, impeccably dressed in an ebony suit. Across from him are two strangers—the minivan owners, I assume. The woman wears a hideous sweater ensemble, her blond hair pulled back severely into a bun, while the man wears a faded suit and sports a thinning brown mustache. They certainly don't look like the type to consort with a billionaire in his private estate.

Unless…

They're Magda's current foster placement.

As I falter near the doorway, the woman looks at me, her gaze honed sharp. "Oh, is this your wife?"

"Tiffany," Vadim says by way of explanation, though he isn't looking in my direction. His gaze is solely focused on a pile of documents scattered before him—the supposed topic of this meeting. "These are the Robinsons," he adds, his tone crisp. "Magdalene's current foster family."

Ah. I struggle to resume my fake wife ruse and force a grin, tucking my wild hair behind my ears. In a heartbeat, I channel my mother, my anger pushed aside—for now. "Pleased to meet you," I say charmingly. "I apologize for my appearance. I must have lost track of time."

"Oh, it's no worry. And I don't want to be rude…" Mrs. Robinson wrings her hands together, her lips pursed. The judgmental part of me recognizes the expression for what it is—a pent-up busy body about to unload. "It's just, I have to ask, did Angela tell you *everything*? I know Magdalene is only a child, but I insisted upon a higher level of care for her. Perhaps…psychiatric in nature. I know it's not politically correct to insinuate—"

"I am fully prepared to take her," Vadim says sternly. It's strange. His entire expression is a carefully constructed mask of utter politeness. But something in his gaze makes me shiver. I step forward, claiming the chair beside him.

"Yes," I say, squaring my shoulders in a show of solidarity. "We're ready."

Poor Mrs. Robinson swallows hard and shifts in her seat, laughing nervously. "Yes, well… Honey, tell them." She nudges the man beside her. "Tell them about the *incidents.*"

"Magda has only been with us a year, mind you," Mr. Robinson admits with a heavy sigh. "And she had already been through so much, what with her health problems. We knew she'd need some time to adjust—"

"She's terrorized the other children," Mrs. Robinson blurts out, folding her hands over the table. "She's damaged property. There's this teddy bear she came with. Well, recently, we discovered that not only did she rip its head off, she then broke into my embroidery kit and sewed it back together with red thread! It's ghastly. We think it was a threat intended to frighten the other children." Horror laces her tone, her voice shaking. "She's incredibly isolative. She won't let you help her with anything. Not her hair. Not with bathing—"

"She's independent," Mr. Robinson cuts in with another apologetic frown.

His wife scoffs. "She's stubborn. The teachers at her school say she hasn't attempted to make any friends—"

"Some children can be shy in social settings," I interrupt, driven by an instinct I can't name to defend a child I don't even know. Internally I scold myself—despite the irritation prickling in my chest, these people can't be all terrible. Can they?

"*That* girl isn't shy," Mrs. Robinson says with a sniff. "And with the cost of her education, you would think they'd try harder to drill some social skills into her curriculum."

"Is that so?" A muscle in my jaw jerks, and I feel my smile twitching. "Well, children do learn by example."

Mrs. Robinson's brows furrow. "I'm sorry?"

"I…" Thinking fast, I try to smooth out my response. "As a teacher, I learned that it's unfair to subject everyone to the same standards."

Somehow, I maintain my polite tone—but it must crack, because both Robinsons flinch. *Good.* My hands are clenching, I realize, my nails digging into my palms. With difficulty, I flatten them against the table, keeping my grin firmly in place.

"Her grades are exemplary," the husband admits with genuine awe.

"That's the thing. She's intelligent to an uncanny degree," Mrs. Robinson says, her nostrils flaring. "*Too* intelligent. She likes to sing creepy little songs in foreign languages— but she refuses to say what they're about. She carries that terrifying bear everywhere she goes. I assumed it was damaged at first and tossed it into the rubbish bin, and she threw a tantrum so fierce we had to call Angela over just to soothe her. A few weeks ago, Richard noticed that someone had been breaking into his office at night, using his work computer. The other children wouldn't dare. When we looked at the search history, we noticed that whoever used it had been looking up drug companies. One of them manufactures a medication Richard takes for a heart condition. What if she was trying to find out some way to—"

"Thank you for coming." Vadim stands and gestures politely toward the foyer, his posture stiff. "I would hate to keep you, given that you are so busy with your other children. I appreciate you stopping by."

"Yes, thank you," I snap, matching his tone as I rise to my feet. From the corner of my eye, I see his hand twitch as if aching to take mine. At first, I deliberately flatten my palm against my side—but then something makes me relent, grasping his.

Together, we start for the foyer, leaving the couple to follow.

Stunned, they blink in unison and share a quick glance. Then they hurry past us as Vadim opens the door.

"Angela is a wonderful social worker," Mrs. Robinson adds as she lingers over the threshold. "I'm sure if you wanted to look into another child…"

That's it. I feel my mask slipping, my grin flattening. If I didn't understand Vadim's determination to gain custody of Magdalene before, I do now. While unsure, he'll strive to be a better provider to her than these people could ever be.

As if he's reading my mind, a muscle in his jaw twitches, and Mrs. Robinson promptly scuttles after her husband. I join him in watching them leave, my thoughts swirling. On the one hand, they seem like the breed my mother used to loathe back in Cali—overly conservative busybodies. At the same time…

The child they painted seems well beyond the skill set of an ex-Sunday school teacher and an emotionally withdrawn businessman. Does he have any idea what he might have gotten himself into? I glance at him, surprised to discover that...*yes*, he does. His jaw is set, more determined than ever.

And in that lone expression, I see a hint of his daughter, and any doubt dies. Two creatures, easily misunderstood, requiring patience to read. Understand. Love. My fury returns, but wavers the longer I watch him, imagining him with Magdalene, unraveling her own guarded layers. The second he catches me staring, his expression softens, his voice rasping, "Tiffany, wait—"

But I don't. Releasing him, I turn and head straight up to the bedroom, my heart racing.

Damn. Damn. Damn!

CHAPTER THREE

I t shouldn't be so hard to maintain my anger toward him. Within the space of a few minutes, my thoughts have turned from *"make him pay"* to… *"listen to him, you stubborn bitch."* Fighting to regain my resolve, I shower and change into a sinfully revealing negligee and a barely visible thong that by some miracle doesn't snag on my healing piercing. Both make for impenetrable armor in this silent war, and when I strut back into the hallway, I'm determined to win the last battle at all costs.

And I nearly run into Vadim. But he's…different. It's as if the pleading man from downstairs transformed into a stranger in an instant. A disinterested stranger. His eyes skim over me with barely any notice as he promptly enters a nearby room.

And I nearly trip as my head whips around, tracking him. *What the hell?*

The room is the same one he pierced me in, I see as I follow him, driven by sadistic curiosity. What could distract him from his groveling?

Redecorating, it seems. The leather chaise is now against one of the walls, the medical instruments vanished. One of those heavy boxes lies open in the center of the room while Vadim rummages through it, apparently assembling something. It's large and black made of wood. A table?

Square-shaped and about waist-high, it contains a divot with a soft cushion covered in red fabric and two silver fixtures on either side. A detail so unusual, I find myself inching forward just to make sure my eyes aren't playing tricks.

Nope. The closer I come, the easier it is to identify those objects, positioned upright, made of silver rings —manacles.

And something inside me is brutally savaged by a wave of jealousy so fierce I sway.

"Preparing for your new fake wife?" I ask nastily, grasping for any form of retaliation.

He doesn't even look at me. Instead, he peers at a white booklet that I assume must be instructions. Then he adjusts something at the end of the odd platform with a silver wrench. He's changed, stripping his suit for the white dress shirt and slacks. The look, paired with his current task, makes something inside me quiver, my throat dampening. *Damn.* He makes a buttoned-up Mr. Handyman look sexy.

But I'm not fooled.

To prove as much, I stomp loudly downstairs and steal one of Ena's meals from the freezer. I eat while scowling and contemplate taking one of his fancy sports cars and attempting once more to send the poor man into bankruptcy.

Instead, I find myself bounding right back upstairs and towing the boundary of that mysterious room. He's still here, assembling yet another unknown wooden structure. Sweat glistens on his brow, and he's left the first few buttons of his shirt undone, exposing the scar along his throat. He looks so intent on his task, he doesn't seem to notice me until I strut boldly to the platform.

Up close, I start to get an inkling of what it might be, and my heart skips a beat. The red cushion is the ideal size and width to comfort a woman's torso if, say she happened to be leaning across it—and those manacles are in the perfect position to capture her wrists and keep her immobile.

Like some sexy, taboo pillory.

My heart sinks, poisoned by yet even more jealousy. I swear, my vision goes green. I can't help myself. Like any scorned creature, I attempt to go right for his jugular.

"Nice to see that your research into kink won't end with me," I say coldly, placing my hand down within his line of sight. I can't stop myself from fingering the curve of one of the manacles as burning hot envy unfurls in my chest. So much for his supposed ignorance when it comes to kink. He seems to be well prepared to welcome his next conquest and indulge her fully. "I hope your new fake wife is a prude—"

He snatches my wrist before I can truly process the action. With an easy display of strength, he flattens my palm against the platform. *Clink.* The manacle encircles my wrist and stunned, I tug, surprised when it doesn't budge.

"What the hell?"

He grabs my other wrist and secures it within the other manacle just as quickly. Then he backs away from the platform entirely, escaping my limited view. Panic sends my heartbeat racing as I crane my neck, desperate to track his movements.

"What the hell are you doing? Vadim!" My voice rings out, trembling with a hint of uncertainty. "Vadim!"

Within seconds, he reappears directly across from me, dragging a black stool behind him. Calmly, he sits, placing his hands on either knee. Our gazes meet, and a tendril of unease races down my spine. I'm suddenly aware of my new piercing, grazing my clit, enhancing the burning sting I've barely grown accustomed to. But it's anything but painful. Stubbornly, I strive to ignore the sensation in favor of baring my teeth at him.

"Get me out of this!"

He cocks his head to the side and leans back on his stool. I sense that he's waiting for something—like a dog trainer waiting for the naughty mutt to remember one command or the other.

"You fucking bastard!" I strain at my binds, hissing in exasperation. "Let. Me. Go!"

Something unreadable flashes through his dark eyes, and I stiffen, falling silent. A subtle softening of his jaw is my reward, and I watch, riveted as he lifts one of his hands and lowers it to his fly.

With envious dexterity, he has it open in seconds, palming his cock. *Holy crap.* He moves slowly in firm, deliberate strokes that have him hardening in a shocking display that leaves me gasping.

"W-What are you doing?" I try to sound angry, but awe laces my tone instead. *Shit. Shit. Shit.* I *want* to seethe, and rage, and scream.

But he is impressive even from this angle. His piercing stands erect, swallowed by the swelling flesh until the rounded ends of the barbell are all that remain visible.

Well aware of my drifting attention, his eyes ruthlessly seek mine out as he manipulates his straining cock. Stroke after stroke leaves him pulsating, but his expression remains unchanged. Unreadable. Cold. Undeniably sexy…

No. "S-Stop!" I shake my head and struggle against my binds, making the metal clang. "What the hell are you doing?"

He *does* stop, his hand stilling, his gaze unmoving. For seconds. Longer. Unbearably long. I squirm, my lips parting for another demand.

The second they do, he starts to stroke himself again, rendering me silent. As my lips close, he strokes faster. Again. Soon, his entire body is rocking with the motion, his cock straining in his grasp. Beautiful doesn't even begin to describe the sight. Any words die in my throat as his hand moves even faster. Surer. The longer he pleasures himself, the more I lose my train of thought.

Men like him don't exhibit themselves lightly. It's an intentional display, I suspect. Meant for me alone. To tease me. Shatter me. Chastise...

And it's cruel, unusual punishment. I'm senseless, lost in the whirlpool of conflicting emotions. Shame. Rage. *Need.* Musings of anger quickly turn to imagining how he would taste, let alone feel if I tried to take him from this angle. As if reading my mind, he stands, letting his pants fall down to his ankles, baring himself completely. Slowly, he advances, his hand still moving, muscles straining beneath his skin.

I don't even realize that my mouth is already open until he cups my chin, tilting it so that I'm forced to look up at him. His thumb traces my lower lip as he bucks his hips. And I don't hesitate.

A groan rips through me as his taste explodes over my tongue, and I eagerly lap at the crown. My eyes roll, and I forget all about hating him. Fellating him on the bed was one thing. But this…

It's so different.

The angle forces him deeper, and I have to tilt my throat to better accept his length. Bound and immobile, all I can do is take whatever he's willing to give. Just the tip at first. Then the full crown. More. More.

More.

I gasp in exasperation as he pulls away, but then our eyes meet. As if in warning, he caresses my cheek before guiding himself in, in, in.

My eyelids flutter as I struggle to handle this much. He's throbbing against my tongue, so thick I can barely close my lips around him.

And it's utter perfection.

I hum in contentment as he rocks his hips, feeding me more, precious bit by precious bit. My wrists strain against the manacles as pressure builds between my legs, seeming to center right over my piercing. I start to whimper as he cradles my cheek while easing more into my mouth, barely teasing the back of my throat.

Then he withdraws again, leaving me gasping.

Before I can even protest, his fingers work to part my hair as he encircles my position. His other hand finds my waist and toys with the waistband of my thong. I shiver. The slightest pressure teases the piercing and sets off a tidal wave of friction, unlike anything I've ever felt. Unprepared, I writhe, torn between clamping my knees against the heat or opening myself up to him further.

"How did I know this method would reach you when words don't?" He sounds so damn smug. I hiss, only to trail off as he teases me again with another gentle swipe. Another and I moan in hapless surrender.

"You wore this to tease..." His voice is a guttural shadow of his usual neutral cadence. Still calm, but nowhere near as disarming. Lust lurks in the vicious tone, heightening the heat building in my blood. "Didn't you?"

I shake my head, gritting my teeth against a reply as I struggle to remember my anger. "Go to hell—"

I gasp as his finger slips between my legs, teasing the moisture gathered there. "It's working," he grates. "Consider this me teased to the point of madness..."

A part of me stiffens, aware of my healing piercing—but the pain doesn't hurt, and I'm reckless enough to writhe, just enough to test my limits. More pressure sets me ablaze.

And it's too tempting to heed common sense warning me to stop.

I wantonly rock my hips, seeking out the contact. In response, he teases me with the tip of one elegant finger, and my brain explodes. I buck against him, seeking out more.

I'm denied. The finger withdraws only to tug my thong down my hips entirely. Cool air tickles the heated flesh, and I shiver as his touch finds my ass, kneading the right cheek.

"So beautiful." He practically groans the praise, his voice thickening. "So wet. Beg me for mercy, and perhaps I'll grant it."

Even as his groping fingers churn my brain into butter, I manage to cock my head back and laugh. "Beg? … Screw…you!"

His hand withdraws only to strike again in a stinging burst of pain—he spanked me. My tongue moistens my lips as my thoughts go on hiatus. His palm is already stroking the pain away, but just as I relax, he smacks me again. *And again.*

"I will redden this flesh," he promises darkly. "That's what you want, isn't it? My beauty, so damn stubborn. I warned you that only you have ever driven me to *this*. Chastisement." Another smack makes me lurch against my binds, a whine trapped in my throat. "Do you require more?"

Yes. "N-No," I attempt to hiss. "Get off—"

Unbearable friction teases my mound—thick, pulsating pressure rubbing against me, carelessly close to my piercing. I go rigid, my thoughts self-destructing. The resulting pleasure is almost too good. Too dangerous. My brain can't handle it. It wipes itself blank, a slave to the whims of his movements. His sadistic game.

Groaning, he parts my lower lips around his shaft, sliding through my wetness only to pull back. Again. Back. Again.

It's maddening.

My lips seem to move of their own accord, spitting out pleas my brain never approves of.

"Please," I whisper, arching into him as much as I can. What I'm begging for? I don't know. Just that I need more of…this. His touch. His appreciative grunts as I eagerly buck into his fingertips. More of him.

"You want me inside you?" he wonders, his tone a rasp.

I can only nod, too far gone for shame. "Yes—"

"You know I can't." He rocks against me anyway, and my eyes roll it feels so good. But he never goes deeper than the slightest, taunting bit of pressure. Out of concern? My piercing is on fire, but in a way that only enhances the pleasure shooting through me in an electric pulse.

"Please—"

"You want relief?" His tone softens even as his grip on my hair tightens sharply, tugging. The act forces my head back, wrenching my gaze to the ceiling. "Do you want to come, beautiful?"

I nod mindlessly, wiggling my hips for more.

"Please…"

His cock disappears, leaving me so aching I cry out. Another pressure eagerly replaces his full length—smaller and more persistent. His thumb? He eases the tip inside me before going deeper.

And my binds are the only things keeping me from levitating. *Piercing. Pleasure.* Those two words dance through the remains of my lust-addled brain. Holy goodness, I never knew that even fingering could feel this good. The slightest penetration enhances the pressure swelling over my clit—one teasing thrust and combustion.

My orgasm rips through me so fiercely I don't even realize it's happening until I hear my own cries echoing back to me. My nails scrape against the wood beneath them, my body trembling with ecstasy.

"I told you once… You are *owned*," I hear Vadim claim, his voice gruffer than ever. Possessive. *I should fear it,* a part of me warns. At the moment, I'm too far gone to care.

"Owned," he continues, still stroking me from the inside out. "Cherished. Chastised." *Smack!* Another blow to my ass makes me lurch onto the tips of my toes, my core rippling, my brain mush. I lose track of the words spilling off my tongue—just that they would make me blush were I in my right mind.

"Please, please, please—"

He strokes through my hair, murmuring praises as his cock returns, pressing insistently at my mound. My clit is on fire, a searing warning—but all concern of healing timeframes leaves my brain.

"Please!"

He bucks his hips, entering me with such a smooth, controlled thrust that only my sheer wetness drags him as deep as he goes. From the outside, my sore flesh isn't touched at all. But from the inside…

I scream as pleasure tears through me in unbearable waves. Almost too much. Tears sting my eyes, and I slump, mindless as he takes me so, so gently.

"Beautiful," he says, his breaths feathering, thrusts strengthening. "So beautiful… *Mine.*"

I'm boneless when he wrenches himself free and hisses through his own torturous release. Fiery heat spills against my lower back, and my eyes flutter as my brain rockets to cloud nine all over again.

When I finally regain my senses, I'm no longer bound. His fingers trace patterns up and down my arms as his grated voice sinks into my ear.

"So good," he praises. "So beautiful when you come for me… So beautiful."

I face him on jellied legs. Our lips meet. Teeth gnashing, tongues grappling for leverage. I'm in his arms before I know it, grinding against him without a damn for my healing piercing.

"N-No!" Seemingly with difficultly, he pulls back and shoves his hand between us, preventing me from further stimulation. Then he snatches my waist, lifting me into his arms completely.

Dazed, I go limp as he carries me into the master bedroom and then the bath, and finally into the shower. He strips us both of our remaining clothing. Then, one-handed, he programs the water and sets me on the bench, blocking me in with his body to keep me seated.

"Let me clean you off, beautiful," he demands, as the water lashes down.

But I rub my legs together shamelessly, imploring him. "I want more." I barely recognize my voice, rasping with lust. Never in my life have I so wantonly craved anything else. *More.* More pain mixed with pleasure. More teasing. Taunting. *Everything.*

I'm drugged on a kink I never knew existed. And deep down beyond the ecstasy, I know I should be terrified that he holds the keys to it all.

"You'll have more than enough when I'm through with you." He chuckles and sinks to his knees before me, brandishing a cloth and a bottle of soap. I shiver as he pries my legs apart and inspects me, frowning. "But not tonight," he adds sternly. "You need rest. Now stay still so that I can clean you."

A pout tugs on my lower lip, but I'm quickly distracted by his touch as he guides the cloth carefully over my aching frame. It's dizzying how seamlessly he can go from spanking me, to bathing my limbs with the utmost care.

Almost as quickly as I can go from hating him, to practically purring in his arms. In my right mind, I'd be more alarmed by that, I think.

As it is, I go languid beneath his ministrations, and watching him is almost enough to make up for the lack of stimulation. When he's done, he tosses the rag aside, shuts off the water, and returns with an armful of towels that he bundles me in.

Minutes later, we land on the bed, and I eagerly snuggle into him, nuzzling against his chest. "I'm sorry for being such a horrible bitch," I confess, my tone surly.

He sighs, wrapping me in his arms, pulling me close. "You weren't completely horrible."

"Hey!" I playfully slap his chest only to copy his sigh as I eye him through my lashes. His serious expression remains unchanged, even as he strokes through my damp hair. I find myself observing him in full, from the pale skin of his chest to the jagged shape of his scar. I reach out, brushing my finger along the edge of it. It's so long, stretching from his ear down to his collar bone.

I can't even begin to imagine what might have caused it. An accident? Something more violent?

Without offering up an explanation, he lets my finger dance along his skin, but from the set of his jaw alone, I know instinctively not to ask him about it. Not yet, at least. Instead, I turn my attention to something a bit more imminent.

"It's a good thing that you're building a playground just for me," I point out softly. Now those mysterious boxes in that room have a newer significance. "But you need to build one for Magda."

He stiffens, inhaling sharply. I'm finding that it's getting slightly easier to read him. I can peg this reaction to one cause in particular.

"You don't want to talk about her," I surmise. "Not yet."

"No..." He shakes his head, his expression tense. "I will. But this... It is painful for me. I just need time."

"At least you're being honest with me." I reinforce the praise by brushing my fingers down his chest. "That's all I'm asking for. You don't need to tell me everything—but I need to know *something*."

"And you will." He captures my hand and brings it to his cheek. "Just know that... I want this," he confesses hoarsely. "More than anything. I want my daughter to be with me. I want to be a father to her. I want..."

"What changed within two years?" I ask gently.

He frowns and seems to shrug in the same instance. "She almost died," he says. "Last year. She became very sick—

an infection entered her bloodstream. You've heard of her condition? It makes any prolonged sickness far worse. She became septic and eventually required a machine just to breathe. For ten days, I spent every minute wondering if I'd lose her for good."

"God…" I picture her frail, fragile appearance and shudder at the thought of her on a vent. I know firsthand how it feels to lose a child—even if I've never met my own—but I can't imagine that level of torment. Thankfully. Swallowing hard, I struggle to form words. "That's awful." I squeeze his fingers tightly, unsure of what else to do. Or say. The only obvious course seems to be just listening—and I suspect that's exactly what he needs. To talk.

"It was the first time I'd seen her in person," he admits, staring ahead, his face blank. "I held her. Sang to her. I touched her cheeks… I watched her fight for her life. But the second she grew well enough to breathe on her own, I left her…" He sighs. "And I did not handle the guilt well." A small, tired smile alludes to the tumult of emotions he only ever lets me get a glimpse of. "One could say I went off the deep end afterward. Only Ena could keep me from doing something foolish—" He frowns at the memory, and I don't have the heart to explore that statement further. Sighing once more, he shifts, holding me more firmly against him. "When I finally came to my senses, I was resolved, however. I *knew* that I had made the right choice. I would continue to fund Magda's education and expenses from afar, but I would keep my distance—it would be better for us both.

And I did stay away. Even when events beyond my control forced me to return to this city, I stayed away from her."

"Then what made you change your mind?"

"Maxim," he says coldly. "I had spent months talking myself out of claiming my own child, and in the meantime, Maxim had taken six under his wing, none of them his. It was as if, once again, my 'legitimate' brother was flaunting that superiority right in my face."

"So, you decided to officially adopt Magda?"

"I have no legal claim to her as it stands," he says. "To give her the best life possible, I need to go through the proper channels and jump through whatever hoops the government insists I may. My resources can achieve many things, but, in this case, I cannot rely on them. And while I know that she is biologically mine, for obvious reasons, I cannot claim as much without proof and documentation. For both her sake and mine, this is the easiest way."

"Is that why you wanted a fake wife?"

A lazy smile shapes his mouth for a fleeting moment. "I was interviewing mainly childcare workers," he admits. "Entirely for Magda's sake and not my personal enjoyment. It seems I settled on a candidate the complete opposite to what I initially thought."

"I do have childcare experience," I grudgingly point out.

"I lucked out then," Vadim says, still running his fingers through my hair. "If you will stay, that is. I apologize for not being upfront before."

"It's not like you didn't try," I admit as I parse through my memories of the past few days. There were a handful of moments where he definitely tried to confess something important—and I had obliviously shrugged him off. "But if we are to do this, then no more secrets..."

Even if admitting them out loud stings like hell. Facing him, I force a serious note into my voice. "I need you to understand right now that I'm not sure if I'm really ready for a serious relationship with a child involved. No, actually, I know that I'm not—not that you are either. Magda is your main concern now."

I nod along with my own logic. Laying out such boundaries now makes sense. Exposing myself to a man whose emotions run hot and cold is one thing. Opening myself up to a child, in the same way, isn't fair to either of us.

"I understand," he admits, but when I crane my neck back to observe his face, he's frowning, as surly as ever even with his eyes half-closed.

"But we can still have sex," I add, feeling no shame in making that demand. "At least until Magda is placed with you permanently. After that, we're done. That is what is best for everyone."

Mainly myself, and the struggle of reconciling my newfound lust with my own internal promises. My list. My rules. My creed.

He doesn't mention whether he agrees or not with that assessment. He's silent for so long that it isn't until I look back at him that I realize why—the poor man fell asleep.

CHAPTER FOUR

I wake up just as the sky is setting beneath the waterfront below. It's evening already, though I still feel exhausted beneath a level of sex-drunk energy. Yawning, I disentangle myself from Vadim, and I have to pinch myself just to keep from watching him for hours. His two-day exile from bed resulted in poor sleep, apparently. He's unconscious, his chest rising and falling in a slow, easy rhythm that shatters the guarded persona he so regularly presents to the world.

He's mine like this—a dangerous thought I can't seem to shake. Hoarding his beauty to myself, I take my time lightly stroking the panes of his chest, my mind racing ahead to all the dirty ways I could explore him further.

Eventually, his welfare takes precedence as my own stomach growls in hunger. Sighing, I leave the bed and tiptoe into the closet to steal one of his shirts, opting for more coverage than my lingerie in case I find Ena lurking downstairs. Then, I enter the kitchen to find it empty, and

I fix up one of the freezer meals, dividing it among two plates. When I return upstairs, I'm juggling a bottle of orange juice for him and wine for me.

I move cautiously, only to trip over the threshold, and I wind up dropping my wine. It lands with a thud that could wake up the devil himself. Crestfallen, I look at the bed, and sure enough, Vadim is stirring, a lazy hum rumbling in his throat.

"Breakfast?" he wonders, sounding so darn husky my toes curl. His eyes are surprisingly mistrustful, suspicious even. Might I have laced his juice with poison, I imagine him thinking. Do I truly forgive him so easily?

I smirk to feed his paranoia, and a lazy grin shapes his mouth in response, his jaw softening.

"Dinner," I correct, inching forward to set our plates on the bed. I lift a fork from his and stab at a piece of steaming meat. Then I shift onto my knees and crawl toward him. "Open."

He does so with his own amused smirk, allowing me to feed him the first bite. I gape as he chews, and I rush to drag his plate closer and offer him something else.

"I love pampering you," I murmur as he opens his mouth for more.

"I will turn you into a domestic yet," he teases, making my heart skip. "First, I'll get you addicted to my cock, and then I'll have you trained to enjoy feeding me. You'll be far too sprung to leave."

He sounds so confident. Too confident, making the boast sound more like a promise than anything else.

"Is that so?" I scoot back and grab my own plate, sampling a few roasted veggies, leaving him to feed himself. "I'll have you know that I don't think I'd make a very good soccer mom."

Something in my tone makes him shrug the blankets from his frame and stand. I stare as he stretches his bare limbs and pads into the bathroom. I follow him and wind up leaning against the doorway as he steps into the shower.

Cocking his head, he meets my gaze, his eyes flashing. "What was that you promised me once?" he wonders. "Something about sucking me off to show your gratitude…"

"Devil!" I grin wickedly and finger the buttons of my borrowed shirt. "Only if you ask me nicely."

His gaze fixates on my mouth, and I shiver as his tongue traces his lower lip. "I would very much enjoy feeling your mouth on me."

I'm naked within seconds, practically running toward him. The shower spray bastes us with gentle pressure as I follow him to the bench and drop to my knees. Our eyes meet and something unspoken shoots between us, as jolting as electricity.

I take him in without hesitation as he sinks his fingers through my hair, groaning in approval. Eager to push his reaction to the fullest, I grip the base of him, gasping as he thickens, straining against my touch.

The pleasure is so intense my eyes threaten to roll, but… A part of me panics with the increasing realization that watching him watch me is ten times more explosive than any impending orgasm. Our eyes meet again. I lick him. He jumps. I suck. His grip tightens, his eyelids fluttering.

So, I do it again.

And again.

His wall is down, his gaze open, and all I see is a man so beautiful it hurts, looking at me as though I'm a goddess. Desirable. Cherished.

And yet still kept at arm's length.

Still, it's beyond anything newly-divorced Tiffy could have imagined just a few days ago.

I close my eyes, overwhelmed, and put all of my focus into pleasuring him, feeding off the throaty groans that broadcast his enjoyment. Deeper. Rasps. Grunts. I worship him, teasing him with as much of my throat as I dare.

And in the end, I relish his release, drinking him down—every last drop.

It's too good. Panting, I rest my face against his knee, seeking out the comfort of his touch. The sensation of his fingers over my heated flesh feels too damn soothing. A salve I've gone my whole life without needing, healing a pain I never realized ached until this moment.

Dangerous thoughts, Tiffy. With difficultly, I pull away.

"I will forever live in regret of denying myself this," he says. I look up to find him leaning back against the wall of the shower stall, his hair mused, his expression shifting amid another earth-shattering revelation. His fingers graze my cheek reverently, smoothing back my damp hair, and I can't resist settling against him again. "I love the way you suck my cock."

I feel myself blush as my tongue chases every remainder of him from my lips. "Careful, Mr. Vadim. That almost sounds like praise."

He laughs, stroking me absently, his expression utterly content. "Take it as you will, Ms. Connors. I look forward to indulging your other fantasies."

"Oh?" I perk up, my brain skipping ahead. "Such as?"

He chuckles deeply and cradles my jaw, urging me to meet his gaze again. "I will show you," he promises. "I will build you your playground as you call it. But in return? You lend me your expertise."

I raise an eyebrow and rise up to straddle him, inching as close to him as I can. His arms encircle me, forming a cocoon of warmth against the shower spray. "My expertise in what?"

"Children," he says simply. His mouth settles in the crook of my shoulder, nipping. Sucking. "You help me with Magdalene," he commands in between teasing nibbles. "Help me make this place a true home for her—" At least he has insight into his current anti-child décor. "Do this for me, and I will ensure that you are sufficiently sprung."

My toes curl.

"And if I refuse?"

His hand slides boldly between my legs, and I inhale, my thoughts spinning. "You won't," he smugly surmises, *barely* grazing my piercing. "My money may not impress you, but I know what does. You've just had your first dose of the day," he reminds me as my face heats further. "I will keep you well supplied. As long as you help me. Anything else can be discussed at a later date. I just need you to promise me this."

I stroke his chest, more touched by his confession than I care to admit out loud. When the man engages in his limited pillow talk, my senses combust. But when he's open? Something in my heart starts to bleed, and I'm worried that it's not entirely a bad feeling.

"I'll help you," I tell him, smoothing my fingers across his rock-hard pec. "I'll help you with your daughter."

He captures my chin, tilting it so that our lips meet fiercely. I moan into the kiss, arching against him, frowning when he pulls back.

"What's wrong?"

"First, I need your help with something else," he tells me, brushing his lips across my jaw in a series of featherlight touches that make my eyelids flutter. "Something marginally less important, but still requiring urgent attention."

I frown, confused. "What?"

That grin. It's so quick and devastating in its prowess. A flash of white teeth paired with a hint of mischief in those dark eyes. I'm dumbstruck.

"Come." He stands, pulling me along with him even though we're both naked. My involuntary shiver must be what makes him take a detour to the closet where he snatches one of his shirts from its hanger and dresses me in it. "I think I prefer this to…"

He breaks off, his throat clenching, and I beam in triumph and finger the tip of his starched collar. On me, the shirt strains over my breasts, and I have a feeling he can see my nipples protruding against the material.

New sexy outfit idea? *Check, check, check.*

"Oh, Mr. Vadim. Are you saying that you *like* to see me in your clothing?" I twirl for his benefit and relish in his savoring moan.

"Witch!" He grabs my wrist and spins me around to face him. Ravenous, his eyes rake over me, settling on my chest. He can *definitely* see my nipples judging from his appreciative swallow. "I think I love you in my clothing," he confesses, his voice rasping.

And I'm more aware of my piercing than ever, hovering dangerously close to my clit. So on fire, it's nearly unbearable.

"But, you may be too distracting." He slides his fingers beneath my collar in search of the topmost button and swiftly undoes it. Then another. Another. Soon, the garment is hanging open, exposing my torso, and some of the heat in his gaze simmers to a liquid lust that makes me sway. "Much better," he declares before finding a shirt of his own.

I follow him from the room and into that infamous space the next door down. My breath catches as I spot the pillory, and my brain loses track of everything but the prospect of doing it again. For longer. With more spanking. More intensity. More.

"Finish your homework admirably, and I will reward you," Vadim says thickly as if reading my mind.

"Homework?"

"Furniture," he declares. "For her room…" Without explaining further, he crosses over to that corner of stacked boxes and easily lifts a massive one from the nearest row. He brings it to the center of the room and places it down. Wiping his hands, he nods to a section of the room I hadn't noticed until now.

"My laptop is there," he says, indicating a small, neatly arranged collection of items. A pillow. A folded blanket. A laptop. A stack of clothing. My throat constricts as I pad closer and recognize the small corner as where he must have stayed during his exile from the master bed—in addition to his study—though I suspect his laptop and briefcase saw much more use than the pillow and blanket did.

"You can use it to do your research," he adds.

Nodding, I grab the laptop and obediently bring it toward him as he opens a box with a silver knife. He logs me in and opens up a browser before returning back to his main task. I peek over his shoulder and watch on excitedly while he rummages through a carefully packed arrangement of black wood.

"Another toy?" I wonder, a thrill in my voice.

"Attend to your assignment, Ms. Connors," he scolds, eyeing me from over his shoulder. "And, I will attend to mine."

Challenge accepted. I hunker down with his laptop and try to decide where to begin. I don't feel the need to ask him for direction, at least. He wants me to help him prepare the house for Magda. Predictably, I do a cursory search for girl's bedroom ideas only to find myself distracted as Vadim rolls up the sleeves of his shirt and casually lifts massive piece of wood, after massive piece from the box and begins to assemble them using the white instruction manual as a guide.

The man has skill. He works methodically, utilizing his hands in a graceful display to manipulate the various pieces and screw or hammer them together. My cheeks flame as he looks up and catches me spying.

"Ten minutes in and you haven't spent millions? I'm disappointed, Ms. Connors," he chides playfully.

I scoff. "Watch me."

I return to the screen, peering through an endless array of furniture listings and design styles. I'm observing a promising pastel color scheme when something flashes across the screen. An email alert? I frown as I scan the subject heading.

"You speak Russian?" I ask, vaguely recognizing the unfamiliar shapes of the Cyrillic alphabet from a brief lesson on the Bolshevik revolution in high school.

"What?" Vadim looks up sharply, setting his tools aside. He grabs the laptop from me and quickly scans the contents of the email. Whatever he reads makes him curse, and he slams the computer shut, turning on his heel. "I'll be back," he says in a tone that warns me not to follow.

Seconds later, I hear his voice drift from the bedroom. He must be on a phone call. "You want to play peacemaker?" he demands in a scathing tone. "Keep your dog on his leash. I've restrained myself where he is concerned because *you* asked. I've gone to your dinners, and played your game, but if he dares to play his games with me, I'll end this war for good. I'm warning you both, Milton—" he pauses as if allowing the person on the other end to reply.

Whatever they say makes him laugh. "It seems that someone's been digging around my holdings in Moscow," he adds. "Who else but Maxim? Unlike him, I've kept my enemies in check. How much more am I supposed to sacrifice to keep little Maxi sated? Rest assured, I'll give him a friendly warning to keep his distance. *Adieu.*"

He must hang up, because he's entering the room a heartbeat later, his expression haggard. Spotting me, he clenches his jaw and returns to his scattered tools.

"Change your mind?" he asks as he snatches up two long pieces of wood and secures them to a rectangular base. "You can still use my computer—"

"No," I say, still stunned by the ferocity I've just witnessed. It's like he flips in some ways, flicking between these two halves of his personality. My mind is burning with questions—what has his brother done now? But something inexplicable warns me from asking.

So I don't.

"I'm just reassessing," I say instead. "I think it might be better to make these purchases in person. Find something special. Do you even know what she likes? Dislikes?"

He looks down, his jaw tight. "There is a list in the documentation from her social worker," he admits.

"You've read it?"

He stares off into the distance and slowly nods.

"We'll look for things together, then," I suggest, rising to my feet. The real world lingers beyond this room, but I'm selfish. Childish, even. I'm desperate to extend this moment, and I cross over to him without a second's hesitation, looping my arms around his neck from behind. "Tomorrow we'll go out and buy some things for her in person. Do I still get my treat?"

He stiffens, but then cups my hips, and any previous tension eases. "Remember when, during your explicit proposal of your demands in exchange for a piercing, that you requested a swing?"

He makes it sound so harmless, but I squeal in utter debauched delight. It's a relatively effortless gesture on his part, but it betrays an intent that leaves me giddy—more debauched kink. My eyes trace the contours of the rectangular base, and I slowly begin to recognize the makings of a sexual swing set. Just for me.

"I love how you make my fantasies come true," I murmur near his ear.

He strokes down my hip, and I sense again that something unspoken is being transferred between us. Something hot and sensual that makes me back away.

"Let me be your assistant?" I ask as he turns to face me.

He smirks and directs me to a leather case containing silver tools. I perch beside it and hand him tools one by one at his request. I think he manages to work for a solid hour in peace before the pressure building between my legs becomes unbearable. Being with him is forcing me to rethink all the turn-ons I'd had before now.

A man wearing only a dress shirt, screwing pieces of a sex swing together? *Check.*

Said man glancing at me every few seconds with hooded, lusty eyes? *Double check.*

And when he stands and rakes his fingers through a mane of curls glistening with sweat, I shrug off my own shirt and sidle up to him, easing a silver wrench from his grasp.

"I want a demonstration," I murmur, stroking my fingers along the partially built swing. Then I inch the same hand around to his abdomen and boldly stroke downward. "A taste of all the dirty things you plan to do to me on it?"

In exasperation, he turns to me and captures my chin, his grin dangerous. "I'll never finish at this rate," he says, eyeing my front.

I shamelessly display myself for him and cup one of my breasts, thumbing the nipple. "You could always say no," I remind him.

His eyes narrow as if he's processing the idea. The next second, he's stepping into me, his mouth finding mine, his hands gripping my hips. One harsh tug brings my pelvis against his.

I take that response as a yes.

CHAPTER FIVE

I wake up dazed, lying on a hard surface. The floor? Beside me rests a warm, tempting body that I greedily nestle against even as my eyes open and blink to adjust to the dim light. *Oh.* I vaguely recognize the budding sex room, complete with the partially-built swing looming above.

And beside me is Vadim, his cheek resting on the open manual and my heart practically melts. No man has ever looked sexier and I can't resist stroking my fingers along his jaw until he opens his eyes.

"Your playground will take months to achieve at this rate," he says tiredly. I arch into him as his arms encircle me, drawing me closer.

"Good," I say with absolutely no regret. "In the meantime, we can build one for Magda—but I promise I won't strip naked while you work on *her* swing set."

He chuckles at that, sounding skeptical. "When do you want to begin your search, oh expert?"

I glance at the gray light coming in through the window and wiggle away from him, climbing to my feet. "Now."

I help him up and lead him into the shower where I risk a small delay to reward him for indulging me. Together we dress quickly—him in a plain black suit and I settle on a dress in a matching color—and, after a quick breakfast, we take the sports car into the city.

I lean into him, stroking his arm while my brain plays some frantic warning about my own boundaries. My own deadline. My own red lines—I told him this would end soon. After Magda is settled, I need to leave. It will be best for everyone.

"Having second thoughts?" Vadim asks as I pull away from him and focus my attention on the window nearest me.

"H-Huh?" I look over, but he doesn't appear anywhere near as distraught about us ending this as one might assume.

"I assure you that I am not a good shopping companion," he confesses. "Are you sure you can't manage alone?"

Oh. I brush my fingers along his forearm and squeeze the rock-hard muscle lurking beneath. "I need your strength," I insist. "I plan to put your skills as a handyman to use."

"Handy, you say…" His upper lip quirks as he scans the road. "There are people I can hire for that."

"No." I marvel at the authority my own voice packs. "I want *you* to do it. Some things we can make exceptions for, but you should have a hand in this."

He doesn't respond but his eyes take on that far-away darkness. Desperate to change the subject, I lean down and fish through his briefcase until I find a blue folder containing a stack of neatly printed documents. I can tell even as I spread them over my lap that they have been well-perused before me. The edges are dented from what I suspect were a pair of slim fingers flipping through them over and over. Still, I feign ignorance as I spot a small but detailed list.

"She likes blue," I read, awed by that preference she unknowingly shares with the man beside me. "She enjoys reading. She likes to play chess. She enjoys—"

"Swimming," Vadim finishes before I can. "Playing in the park. Boats. Her favorite food is buttered toast. She also likes horses." He speaks with such a confidence that I don't even have to glance at the paper to know he's memorized them by heart.

And the fact that his home contains both a swimming pool and a stable, as well as a boathouse takes on a new meaning. One that leaves me stunned.

"*That's* why you picked that house," I say, returning the papers to the briefcase. "I thought you wanted to be a dick to your brother, but it was for her."

His lips contort into a small, beautiful smile that reveals just how exhausted he is. How many nights has he lost worrying about this? Far too many I suspect.

"I cannot be faulted if Maxim also has an interest in child friendly real-estate. Not to mention that I've owned…" He trails off, his jaw tight. "Contrary to Maxim's egotistical view, my life does not entirely revolve around spiting him."

I recall the phone conversation I overheard last night, more disturbed than before. What trouble might be building between the brothers now?

Today probably isn't the best time to dig for answers on that subject, however.

"It's a beautiful house," I say, gently steering the topic to safer waters. "But together, we'll make it perfect for her. I promise." I interlink my fingers with his free hand, squeezing tight. He risks taking his eyes from the road just long enough to eye our clasped hands.

"Together…" He says the word as though it's a novel concept. One he's never applied to his life before and again I seethe in jealousy at whichever potential wife he may have picked. No one will help him like I will.

But then you'll leave him, a part of me snipes. *You plan on skipping out as soon as you can, you heartless bitch.*

"Have you decided where to attack first, Ms. General?" Vadim wonders once we reach the city proper.

I latch onto the distraction and tap my chin, humming thoughtfully. "No. But I did find a custom boutique online. Everything they sell looks insanely expensive yet beautifully crafted. Let's start there."

He chuckles. "Let's see if you can reach my expectations. With my accounts at your mercy, I should be nearing bankruptcy by the evening's end. I hope you won't disappoint."

"You're on," I declare, with upmost confidence.

But something tells me that the stakes of this little venture may result in more than just his finances being at risk. Like my resolve for one.

And my boundaries, too.

AFTER A MORNING SPENT SHOPPING, we have lunch and then take a detour to a high-rise that I recognize as one of his offices. Eingel Industries reads the name emblazoned on the corridors as he leads me inside.

"I need to grab some legal documents," he tells me. "I'll be just a moment."

And yet, he didn't have me wait in the car or come here himself. Could this be a reclusive billionaire's attempt at transparency? My heart flutters, unsure of how to accept this deliberate turn of events.

As a good thing, I decide.

"I'll wait out here," I suggest, spotting a pair of glass doors that appear to lead into an enclosed courtyard. Vadim nods and sets off while I venture out into a small, beautiful garden brimming with carefully cultivated bushes and flower beds. A bubbling fountain ties the peaceful scenery together but when I spy a golden plaque my heart constricts as I read the simple phrase inscribed on it—*Hiram Gorgoshev Memorial Garden.*

A family member of his? Given what little he's revealed about his past, I'm not even sure if I should risk asking.

I'm instantly aware the second he steps out to join me. It's as if the entire atmosphere shifts. Thickens. Mellows.

A lazy smile is already playing on my lips even before I feel his hands on my waist as he comes up behind me. "My accounts are settled," he murmurs against the nape of my neck. "You may continue to spend as you please."

My brain reels at that, considering that—together, based mainly on his input—we've already spent a small fortune on enough furniture and small knick knacks to please any seven-year-old.

"I'll turn you into a shopaholic yet," I declare, spinning around to face him. He looks so freaking pretty in the pale, overcast daylight. Like a fallen angel finally remembering to unfurl his wings after an eternity of damnation. Hopeful.

I hate myself for daring to mention, "This garden… It's beautiful."

He shoots me an odd look, an eyebrow raised. "Do you think she'd want one like it?" Before I can reply he slips an arm around my shoulders and steers me back through the building, out to the car.

"A garden would be a nice touch," I say, letting the subject drop.

As we pull away from the building, his eyes linger on it, and for a split second, his expression slips. Raw pain distorts his features and I want to kick myself for ever bringing up the subject.

Whoever Hiram Gorgoshev was to him, I suspect he doesn't think on him with quite the same hostility he utilizes toward his brother or his past.

But he isn't ready to talk about him either, and I can't help but wonder why.

CHAPTER SIX

"A little to the left," I command while leaning against a wall of newly purchased pillows, all still wrapped within their plastic packaging. Before me stands Vadim, musing over the correct placement for a scenic portrait.

"Here?" he asks, moving the ivory frame slightly to the left.

"Maybe to the right," I say, but I'm admittedly not staring at the painting but something far more enticing just a few feet below. I'm caught when he turns around and catches me gawking.

"Are you referring to the painting or my ass?"

"Both," I confess sheepishly. "You're sexy when in interior designer mode—the room looks beautiful."

And it should—the combined effort of over twenty hours of work, building and painting with a night spent sleeping on the floor to boot. The space he had chosen for Magda was originally beautiful with a perfect view of the water and the surrounding property—though utterly bare. At its core were the basics for a girl's dream bedroom, however. A bay window, complete with a window seat, conjures the image of a father reading bedtime stories, and the bed we picked out is made of a luxurious pale wood.

"I would have died for a room like this," I tell him, meaning every word.

"Would you have?" A grin ignites his wary expression, battling the exhaustion and streaks of baby blue paint still speckling his cheeks. I suck in a breath, horrified. My sore piercing—thank God it isn't infected or damaged despite my throwing the healing instructions to the wind—throbs in a delicious tempo in tune to my racing heartbeat. "You're going to rock the single father trope."

"Single?" He tilts his head, stroking his chin with fingers reddened from assembling furniture for hours on end. Something feral seeps into his gaze, eating away at the playful demeanor until... God, he looks too damn serious.

I jump as he pivots, setting the picture aside, and advances toward me, his gaze crackling. The faster I move, the wider his strides become until he's gained on me. With the tip of his finger, he tilts my chin back, forcing eye contact.

"Single is not something I foresee for myself," he murmurs, stroking my jaw in a devastating, toe-curling swipe. "Not anymore."

"Haha." I inhale sharply and take a small step back. "Planning on another wife so soon? At least let us have our fake divorce first," I say, attempting a joke. It falls flat —my voice is a hoarse whisper, and Vadim doesn't laugh.

"Not quite…" He advances again, ruthlessly pinning me against the wall, until I have no choice but to quiver against him. His gaze is too damn intense, demanding in a way that makes my hips arch despite my protests, my pulse thready.

"No new wife. No new woman—" his sly, devious grin makes me exhale sharply, contrasting with the way he sweeps his touch down to my throat, each fingertip radiating possession. All the while, his gaze remains honed, sharper than ever. Determined. "I think I have denied myself of happiness for too long. I think I'd like to renegotiate our options."

"N-No." I shake my head, attempting to turn away. "I told you. This won't work—"

"You did." He captures my cheek against his palm, urging me to face him again. "But I suggest we renegotiate those terms. In fact… I insist upon it."

"No!" I sound exasperated, and again I try to escape from around him—but he shifts to block me at every turn.

"Vadim." My heartbeat falters as I brace my hand over his chest. "Please don't," I croak. "Please. I don't want to ruin this."

He blinks, and just like that, he flips his internal switch. He's neutral again, the fire gone. All I sense from him now is ice-cold calm. "As you wish."

He returns to the wall and picks up the frame, relentlessly hammering it into place within seconds. I watch him, wary for reasons I can't explain. His insistence isn't what unnerves me. It's my own—and fear of things not working out isn't what makes me want to run far in the opposite direction. No… I find myself stroking the fake ring on my finger as I grapple with the truth—I'm terrified by how good things *could* be. So good. And I don't know if I can face the disappointment if that fantasy never comes to fruition.

My time with Jim taught me that relationships, for the most part, *always* fall apart.

I'm so lost within myself that I barely notice when Vadim leaves the room for good. It isn't until I find myself searching for him that I finally register his absence. Alone, I stand and pace the room, marveling at the small touches that his money alone couldn't buy.

For one, he mixed two shades of blue to find the perfect hue to accent the wall above her bed. He found trinkets and books to fill her shelves, picked out without my input. Each detail reveals the depth of a devotion I doubt even he is truly aware of.

He wants his daughter with him. He craves her happiness. And I can't come in between them before they even have the chance to connect.

Right?

To distract myself from pondering the answer, I gather up the loose pieces of trash strewn across the room. Then I unwrap the pillows and dress them in the crisp, baby blue sheets we picked out together at a boutique downtown. I adorn the bed with them and add a matching comforter and ivory woven throw blanket.

All in all, it's a room any little girl would love.

Left with nothing else to do, I have no choice but to face the world beyond this room. And the conversation I sense lies in wait the second I do. Warily, I creep down the hall toward the bedroom. There, I find Vadim standing in the center of the space, his face in his hands, his back to me. Seeing him in torment makes me ache in ways I never have. Like my heart is on fire, and only his nearness can put it out. To do so, I'll risk bending my own rules, just a little. I can't help it.

"Let's forget what we said," I suggest, approaching him. "I don't want to fight. I don't—"

He spins around, capturing my wrists, drawing me close. A shudder runs through me as our lips connect, tongues meeting hesitantly. Closing my eyes, I sink into the kiss, letting him overpower me with forceful, deep strokes. Too forceful. Devouring. I'm dizzy when he pulls back, and I blink my eyes open, gasping for breath.

He's flipped that internal switch again, suddenly ablaze with an array of emotions too obscure to name outright.

"You've ruined everything," he tells me, his eyes darker than ever. Furious. Resigned. Terrifying. As I stiffen, he caresses my jaw, his expression pained. "You give me a taste of what it could be like... How could I not want more?"

"Huh?"

He leans in without explanation, taking my mouth with a ferocity that leaves me breathless. I cling to him, buffeted back as he surges forward. Without warning, he shoves me down, forcing me onto my back.

I look up at him, dazed, my throat tightening as he reaches for his pants, easily tugging them open. Fire shoots through me, and my brain goes blank as my legs spread apart. Only a frantic warning at the back of my mind makes me gasp out, "Wait—"

"You feel it, don't you?" he inquires with that smug confidence as he rips his pants down his legs and frees his cock from the boxers beneath. My teeth seize my bottom lip at the sight. He's erect, his piercing gleaming, precum wetting the pulsating crown.

So beautiful.

And *dangerous*. I recognize that look in his eye. That cold, calculating expression. The same one he sported after tormenting me with the silver toy and locking me in the pillory.

Punishing.

"You feel it," he repeats too quickly for my sluggish brain to keep up. "This…rightness. Don't you?"

I nod—anything to keep him pleasuring himself with those firm, confident strokes. Only belatedly do I register his words and the husky way he delivered them. Like a prayer. Something sacred he doesn't confess lightly.

Only in worship. Reverence. Desperation.

"Vadim…" My brain swims as I try to sit up and muster my tongue into forming some semblance of coherence. "We need to talk about this—"

He moves, cutting me off as he leans over me, bringing his pelvis dangerously close to the heat building between my legs. I writhe shamelessly, forgetting my train of thought all over again. But it's important, I think. Something about boundaries. Reinforcing them. And if I don't…

Things will go way too far.

"No relationship," I insist as I arch my hips to meet his anyway. But he pulls back. My wrists are in his grasp before I know it. He spreads them apart, forcing my arms above my head. Suddenly, a firm pressure replaces his grip over my left wrist, and I hear a subtle snap! Dazed, I crane my neck back and find a strap of leather tethering that arm to the bed.

"W-What are you—"

Snap! My other wrist is immobile as well, impossible to move.

Alarmed, I look down, too stunned to fully process my predicament. Manacled again? "Vadim…"

He shifts his weight, settling between my legs, but his eyes hold my attention this time, even as my body radiates with his nearness. He's never looked clearer, more intense. Intent. Like a dog insistent on having his bone, no matter the cost.

"So beautiful," he praises, sweeping his gaze along the length of me. I nearly jump out of my skin as he strokes his thumb down my chest. Even through the fabric of another one of his borrowed shirts, my skin ignites. "I had everything planned, but you."

I mull over that calculating term. *Planned?* Desperate to regain my focus, I experimentally tug my arms.

"You won't get free," he tells me as he stands, leaving a gaping absence where his heat used to be. "They are custom made from a craftsman in Germany. Specifically designed for your measurements. I can assure you that both are of the highest quality and designed to be tamper-proof."

I frown as my gaze fixates on his cock, my body quivering. "Why tie me up?"

His smile…

It steals my breath in a startled gasp as an ominous pressure begins to build in my belly. Lust, fed by *this* despite my own insistence. Aware of every tendril of heat, a devious gleam sets his dark eyes alight, making them glow. He's more beautiful than ever.

"I aim to convince you to change your mind," he says. "I respect your concerns. I do. But I do not think I should let you cling to them without hearing my perspective."

He releases his cock, and I bite back a groan. What an amazing perspective.

Snap out of it, Tiffy! Sex isn't the only defining factor of a relationship. If it were, we'd be golden. But there's so much more.

"I can't be a mother," I tell him, jumping right to the heart of the matter. "Helping you keep her is as far as I can go. No more. I can't. You know why. Please respect that."

His expression falls flat, and it's a double-edged sword. Some of the lust churning my thoughts to mush dissipates —but in return, guilt descends like a sucker punch. The man has me tied to a bed, but the idea of disappointing him alarms me more than anything else. Maybe because he's being open for once, hiding nothing from me.

Not even his pain.

"I'm sorry," I whisper.

He turns away, shielding his expression, and I strain my binds, my legs flailing.

"Wait! Don't go!"

He leaves anyway, slipping through the doorway without a second glance. Before I can even panic, he's back, and in his hands is an object that makes my eyes go wide.

And my stomach drops right through the floor.

"No," I whisper, in panicked horror. Flailing, I strain at my binds to no avail, my voice rising in pitch. "No… Don't."

Heedless of my pleas, he stalks forward, brandishing the object that makes me gasp, partly terrified, partly… excited. It's a silver dildo, similar to the remote-controlled one. But larger. Longer. Thicker.

I clamp my knees together as he advances toward the bed, shaking my head.

"No. No. Vadim!"

The bastard doesn't wrench my legs apart like a brute. He caresses me instead, smoothing his fingers up and down my hip, barely touching my skin. Over and over. The gentleness with which he does so is such a startling contrast to the intent etched within his hungry features that my brain doesn't know how to process it. A part of me lurches into his touch while the other fixates on that damn silver toy.

"I won't hurt you," he swears, his voice a persistent, soothing hum. "I will never hurt you."

And I believe him, even as he lowers that toy between my legs.

"Look at me," he commands. When I do, I almost can't breathe at the intensity I find in his gaze. He eyes me like I'm something more than just beautiful. Cherished. Desired. My thoughts spin again, threatening to scatter.

But when a cool, firmness nudges my lower lips, I balk.

"Vadim, please…"

Pressure. Pressure. Thick, filling pressure. Shock robs me of my voice as my head rears back. Deep down, I know that he's using the toy, easing it inside me bit by bit.

"So beautiful," I hear him grate as my muscles relax to adjust. "So wet for me. Trust me, beautiful. I will never hurt you."

Because he wants to kill me instead.

This toy is deadly. I can sense the subtle differences from the last one the second he breaches me with the rounded tip. After a few days, the shape and feel of his cock are etched into my brain. How it stretches me pleasurably. The friction he can achieve with just one stroke.

And this toy…

It's *him*. In almost every fucking way.

"Yes," he says in response to my puzzled expression. Gently, he smooths the hair from my face and leans over me, trailing his lips along my sweat-slick forehead. "Another custom request," he adds near my ear. "You ask for pleasure, I aim to deliver."

He shoves his hand—driving in the toy in the process—and my brain goes on hiatus. Too much. Too fast. My eyes roll, my breaths shallow as my body conforms to the foreign object—familiar, yet different. Nothing in the world could ever serve as a substitute for him, and in so many ways, the toy feels worse. The pressure only heightens the lust throbbing between my legs. My inner muscles clench in vain, demanding the real thing. It's sadistic.

It's torture, beyond kink.

It's exquisite.

"D-Devil," I whisper as my senses reassemble, and I realize his intent. Drive me insane.

"Angel," he praises, still petting my dampening hair. "So beautiful. Tell me you'll stay with me. That I can give you what you need, *oui*?"

"No," I counter forcefully as my eyelids flutter—but he nudges the toy just enough to press against my gripping muscles, sowing incredible friction. I have to gulp at the air to survive the rippling contractions. "Can't…"

"You can," he insists, maddeningly calm. "In a few days, you've made me rethink my entire life's trajectory. I think you can readjust your stubborn beliefs. Tell me you will."

But I have. I've thought of what life could be with him, even playing house with a child who doesn't even know he exists. It sounds sick on paper. In reality? It could be so very good, and I'm terrified by just how appealing it seems.

Because every sense in my brain is telling me that nothing could ever be that good. Run away. Disengage. Kill that hope now before it festers.

"You belong with me." His voice. It's sin, falling into a deep, smooth cadence that renders me gasping. "I told you once to ask yourself… Would I ever let you go? From the moment you leaped on my cock as though it were a treat, I knew you were mine. You *will* be mine."

He sounds mad. Too serious. This isn't a game anymore.

Unease rises up to combat the pleasure swirling around my brain. "V-Vadim, please—" I cry out. At the back of my mind, I realize why—he shoved the toy in deeper.

"I never knew sex could be like this," he says, sounding miles away, and yet at the same time, his voice resonates through my brain as if implanted there. "More," he adds hoarsely. "I never knew. You think I'd let you go so easily?" He laughs as my eyes flutter to him, and I barely catch a devious grin before he thrusts the toy again. Deeper. Harder.

My back arches, jerking off the mattress. "Vadim!"

"I never knew it could be like this with another person," he adds, his voice rasping, eyes heavy-lidded. "Tell me, do you deny it?"

"Yes," I croak, only to gasp as he wrenches the dildo free.

"You don't feel the same?" he wonders, his tone mocking. "Should I leave you like this?"

I shudder at the horror. "No! No!"

"Then tell me…have you ever felt this with anyone else? This pleasure?"

The toy returns, easing inside of me, and my eyes roll at the sensation.

"No," I murmur before I can bite the word back.

"Tell me how good it feels."

He stills again, and it's like my body takes on a will of its own. My hips sway, seeking out more pressure. More depth.

"Tell me," he insists, threatening to pull back.

"G-Good!" I whimper in relief as he slams the toy home. The pleasure hits like a wave. My brain goes blank, and I hear my mewling cries echoing off the walls. "So good."

"Damn, you're beautiful," he says thickly, and I moan in response. "So beautiful. So wet for me. Do you ache for me?"

I nearly scream as he jerks the toy. "Yes."

And it's true. I'm throbbing in a way that I never have. On fire.

"Tell me how badly."

All I can do is whimper. "Please—"

"Tell me."

"I need you. I need you."

"Fuck, you're incredible." I realize somewhere within the shambles of my brain that it's the first time I've heard him curse like this. Truly unrestrained. Wild. A creature unleashed from his own constraints. "Look at me, beautiful."

With difficultly, I refocus on him, and my heart stalls. He looks magnetic. Powerful. Like a predator, looming above dying prey. "Tell me… Tell me you need me. Say it—"

"I need you," I croak, shameless. "Please."

"Tell me I can have you." He leans down, brushing his lips against my quivering throat. "Tell me I deserve you."

My brain reels at his tone. Guttural. Broken. Teasing aside, this is far beyond sex. Too far.

"Vadim—"

He nips, rendering me silent. "Say it. I deserve you. I… I am *owed* you. No one can take you from me. Not him. Not God. No one."

"Vadim, listen—"

A scream rips away any other coherent words I might say. My spine arches off the bed as ecstasy explodes through my body. Buzzing. Persistent vibration…

The toy is electric, and he's just turned it on.

"Stay with me," he urges, his tone radiating authority. "Stay with me, beautiful. Look at me."

My eyes stream, throat rasping as I meet his gaze. He looks so open in this moment. So raw—and the intensity building within me only strengthens. A brutal orgasm is looming, one so devastating I almost fear it.

"I will have you," Vadim swears. He withdraws the toy, setting it aside, and I moan wordlessly as he settles over me, his cock throbbing against my inner thigh. "I will keep you. I will own you. Say that you're mine."

He thrusts in so deep I think I lose consciousness. When my senses return, I'm gasping, dizzy and dazed, clawing at the sheets as he slams inside of me.

I cry out his name as my body convulses over and over. He's steel, pulsating against my inner walls. And yet, as stern as ever, his voice drips into my ear, murmured like a prayer. "Come for me, beautiful. So wet. So perfect. Tell me you need this. You need *me*."

I comply in whimpers and groans, too far gone to speak logically. As he moves, I lose track of time and space. Of how many times I come.

It's pleasure beyond any physical understanding. I'm drugged, overwhelmed, drowning in him. But even in my dazed, broken brain, I take note of when he groans, his throat cording, hands grasping my hips.

He throws his head back, groaning my name as his release floods me in fiery waves.

And I know that my attempts at putting distance between us were pathetic, pitiful lies. Much like our very first meeting, I was never in control.

Not really.

He's always had an alternate plan, one I suspect I'm barely aware of even now. All I can do is surrender to the chaos and try to swim against the current.

Or drown.

"You are *mine*," he declares, collapsing against me. "And I will take what I am owed..."

"Did I hurt you?" Vadim asks, his voice a low rasp.

I'm in his arms, too weak to move. At some point, he must have released me from the manacles because my arms are free, trembling at my sides. With what little strength I can muster, I shake my head and rest my cheek against his shoulder.

"No," I tell him as he strokes my back with so much gentleness it leaves me reeling. "No, you didn't hurt me."

"I'm sorry," he adds, brushing his lips across my damp forehead. He doesn't say for what. For sexual torture? For pushing my fragile boundaries to their limits? For a part of his plan, I'm woefully unaware of?

"I do want you," I croak, letting my eyes shut as exhaustion barrels through me, mixed with guilt and regret. All of it creates a tumult so vast, the only way through it is to just talk. "I do. I'm just afraid. I don't want to disappoint you or *be* disappointed. I've been through too damn much… I can't be disappointed."

He laughs so deeply that I force myself to open my eyes merely to see his face. He's eyeing the ceiling, his lips contorted into a tired grin.

"I've never had a relationship, so perhaps that fear isn't entirely misplaced…"

"Never?" I can't hide my skepticism. I'm practically in a coma after a bout of ruthless, vicious sex. Does he really expect me to believe that no other woman has experienced this with him?

No, I realize with growing awe. He doesn't care either way, because it's the truth. A rare hint of vulnerability shapes his expression, betraying just how uneasy he is at opening up to me. Which further reinforces the gravity of the fact that he's doing so at all.

"What did you call me?" he wonders, grimacing at the memory. "Mean? I call it prudent. Most people don't seek more from me than what they want in the moment. What they can gain. My brother sees me as a burden. To Ena, I am a partner. Even Milton sees me as a scared little boy he's sworn to protect. As for women? I've never experienced more than sex."

"Their loss," I rasp, letting my face fall against his chest, utterly spent. But a part of me bristles at his boasts. Someone like him—so used to using manipulation as a tool—might see those relationships in such stark terms.

But a partnership without true concern doesn't result in someone stocking the fridge of their employer just to ensure they eat. And Milton... I saw how he intervened between him and his brother. Someone who didn't care wouldn't do that. Could a man be so blind as to the genuine love of those around him? Woe to any woman who dared to broach the topic. "I think I should be pleased to be the recipient of your pent-up lust," I add, changing the subject to safer waters.

"Thirty-one years of it," he declares, sliding his hand down my back. "Why shouldn't I demand more? I am tired of waiting for my turn."

His turn?

"You make me explore things I never thought possible," he adds with a subtle hint of inflection that makes me quiver. "I *will* break you down... I can be persistent when it comes to that which I desire. You have been warned."

Does he truly mean that? My aching body shivers at the possibilities. I could cry at the potential, and yet my toes still curl, ravenous for more.

"I love being with you," I confess, lulled by the thrum of his heartbeat. "I just don't want to hurt you."

"You hurt me?" He laughs again, this sound more beautiful than the first. "I think I can suffer whatever pain you can dish out, as long as you perform your unique way of currying favor afterward."

"Ah." I lift my lips, pleased that he seems to enjoy my "ways" as much as I do. "And just to think, a few days ago, I had to fight you to let me suck your cock."

"A foolish man, then," he concedes. "Such a fool. But he is thankfully in the past. Stay with me, and I will learn plenty of ways to both pleasure you and explore the use of your mouth."

He pulls me closer, holding me so tight it's just to the point of painful. For some reason, it's easier to write off his words as boasts made in the heat of the moment. Nothing more. Even as his gaze burns with searing intensity…

He's bluffing.

"Promise?" I say, testing that assumption despite my better judgment.

"I will," he declares as if to shatter that hope. "No promise necessary."

I WAKE up to the sensation of peace, unlike any other. One so deep and so encompassing that I assume I'm dreaming at first. No one's arms could possibly feel this safe. This warm. This comforting.

I open my eyes, expecting a fantasy realm of unicorns and ponies and other fantastical dreamworld things. Instead, I find a man so beautiful he can't be real. My heart despairs until he opens his dark eyes, and his expression matches mine. Fearful with diminishing hope. There's no way this can be real.

I snuggle into him, attempting to extend this moment for as long as I can only for him to stiffen. Gradually, his frown softens, his eyes losing their unease. I shiver as his fingers part my hair, smoothing through the strands as he sighs, utterly relaxed.

This may not be a dream, after all.

"Morning."

I moan at the sound of his voice, husky with sleep. "Morning," I whisper in response.

So yes, this is real. Vadim, holding me against him, our bodies still slick with sweat, the bedsheets twisted around us. Pale dawn light bathes his skin in a soft glow, making him seem more ethereal than ever. My beautiful, tormented angel so convinced he doesn't deserve happiness.

He has to take it.

All of last night comes crashing back in one go. My ultimatum. His sensual, torturous response. Something in my expression must change because he stiffens, betraying breathtaking concern. Horror, even.

And I do nothing to reassure him. Slowly, I brace my hand against his chest and push back, wincing as my body throbs with a mixture of lingering lust and bone-shattering exhaustion.

"I'll never forgive you," I tell him, my voice breaking. "Never."

His throat constricts as he reaches for me, stroking my cheek. "I'm sorry. Are you in pain?"

I snatch his hand, wrenching it from my face. Then I manipulate the digits until the longest finger is extended, and I eagerly brush it with my lips, stroking my tongue across the tip. He looks horribly confused, this beautiful man, torn between arousal and alarm.

I deign to put him out of his misery and suck on the very tip of his finger just once.

"How dare you keep that toy all to yourself," I scold him, still too weak to put real effort into my mocking tone. "I'm starting to think I should demand you come clean about all of your new custom goodies."

He chuckles and gingerly slips his finger from my lips, drawing me closer. "I plan to keep you well satisfied on the real thing," he says, and sure enough, I sense him hardening against my belly. "That substitute shall only be deployed in emergencies."

"You see my potential leaving as an emergency?" I question, my voice soft.

He brushes my jaw, his lips firmly closed. "You're shaking," he finally declares, eyeing the length of me with a frown. "It seems another round of pampering is in order."

He shrugs the sheets from his body and stands. A heartbeat later, I'm in his arms as he heads for the bathroom. When we pass the window, I eye the morning sky and remember our unofficial deadline.

"Today is the last day before she comes," I declare. "I guess my playground will have to go under lock and key."

If he hears me, he doesn't respond. Instead, he drapes me carefully over the bench in the shower and proceeds to clean me off with more care than should be possible. After my few relationships—mainly with Jim—it blows my mind that someone can treat another person with such reverence. I feel like an idol worshipped by him. Revered by him.

And for a second, I can forget my rules—just for a second.

Determined, he bathes every inch of me with utmost gentleness. I'm riveted just watching him inspect me, awed by every part of me.

"You make me feel so beautiful," I murmur as he wipes the lather from my limbs and bundles me in a towel. "I love the way you—"

"My beauty, so full of compliments," he says while carrying me back into the bedroom. "You're inflating my ego. I've spent years fighting to keep it in check."

Rebelliously, I reach up, brushing my fingers along his jaw. "You deserve praise," I say, meaning every word. Perhaps that suspicion is what drives him to doubt the motives of those around him, even if they obviously care. "I give you permission to be as cocky as you want."

He makes a thoughtful sound in his throat as he settles me on the bed. He switched out the sheets, I realize, replacing them with a fresh set. "Cocky enough to think I can claim you?" he counters.

I sway as our gazes connect. It should be illegal for someone to look so…ravenous. And yet in the same breath, utterly restrained—all that tension tethered to a hair-trigger.

"Tell me you want me," I whisper, toying with that dangerous, fragile line.

With a feral expression, he snaps it. "I *crave* you."

To prove it, he leans down, making me feel so small in his massive shadow. Our lips meet, teeth gnashing with the ferocity. It isn't long before I'm beneath him, writhing for the pleasure only he can provide.

"Vadim, please—"

He slams into me before I can even finish voicing the plea. I hum in ecstasy, grasping for any part of him I can reach. My nails pierce the flesh of his forearms, but he moves, capturing both my wrists and pinning them flat to the bed.

Will he shackle me again? My heartbeat picks up at the prospect, but he merely entwines our fingers as our gazes reconnect. Somehow this tethering is more intimate. I feel even more helpless, rendered with no protection from the emotions spilling between us with every thrust. I grip him in return so tightly my hands shake.

My eyes threaten to roll as he rocks into me, taking me with a skill that dissolves every coherent thought, leaving only heat behind. Desire.

Panting, he brings his mouth near my ear, rasping, "You are mine."

I come around him, gasping his name.

And I let myself toy with the idea that his ownership may not be such a bad thing…

My list be damned.

CHAPTER EIGHT

We spend most of the morning in bed before finally venturing downstairs to eat one of Ena's frozen meals. Afterward, we put the finishing touches on Magda's room, hanging the final remaining pictures and arranging her blankets.

Just after midnight, we wind up in bed, our limbs entwined. I drift off cocooned in his arms, but the second I wake up, I know that everything has changed.

It's as if the air has become tinged with some unfamiliar scent, shifting the careful dynamic between us. Vadim rises from the bed without a word, his back to me, his fingers tearing through his hair. I roll onto my side and watch him, my heart swelling with too many emotions to decipher.

Today is the day everything between us changes. For better or for worse?

"We should get dressed," he says, his tone too neutral to give me an inkling either way.

He enters the closet and begins rummaging through the hanging clothing.

"The blue one," I tell him. "With the tie your brother brought you."

He shoots me an odd look, but as I crane my neck and sit upright, I see that he's complied, tugging on the navy suit with a black dress shirt.

I stand and follow him, stretching my sore limbs.

"The emerald dress," he tells me as I start to appraise my options. "With the cream jacket."

"An interesting color profile, Mr. Gorgoshev," I remark while I pick out the items in question. Once fully dressed, I eye myself and sigh in resignation.

Not only is the man sexy as hell, but he has an eye for fashion to match.

"I look like a very respectable fake wife," I say, surprised by the overall effect.

He comes to stand beside me, his expression approving. "Thank you for doing this for me," he says, leaning in to press his lips against my forehead. "I promise to find a safe place to reassemble your playground so that you may enjoy it fully."

I practically melt, and only the faint reminder at the back of my skull keeps me from trying to strip him naked —Magda.

Together, we enter the hallway, but as Vadim ventures downstairs, I take a detour to the next door over and peek inside. Sure enough, all of my charming apparatuses have vanished, leaving the room starkly bare. Surprisingly, I'm not too heartbroken as I descend the steps and enter the kitchen.

While we wait, I force feed Vadim a croissant, and I'm in the middle of goading him into drinking a glass of orange juice when a knock sounds at the front door.

He doesn't move. I'm the one who has to stand first and take his hand, leading the way to the front door. My heart pounds as I reach for the doorknob, only to have Vadim beat me to it. Gradually, he pulls the door open, revealing a smiling Ms. Anderson.

And beside her, is a little girl who looks as though she'd rather be anywhere else.

"Good morning!" Ms. Anderson beams and ushers the girl beside her inside. "I hope we aren't too early."

"N-No." Vadim shakes his head. Then he turns his attention to a small gray suitcase resting on the paved walkway. "Is that all of your things?"

Magda meets his gaze without flinching, her blue gaze electric. "The decent things," she says in that lilting voice. She steps forward, examining the foyer with an unreadable expression. God, the parallels between her and the man beside her mount up by the second.

The intensity of their gaze. The way they move, holding themselves with utmost confidence. Even their distaste, visible in how they purse their lips, their eyes narrowing.

"This is where I'm going to live now?" she asks.

"Of course, honey." Ms. Anderson chuckles nervously while Vadim grabs the suitcase, bringing it inside. "We… we talked about this, remember? Mr. Vadim and Ms. Tiffany are your new placement."

"Hmph." Magda turns her gaze to me, her arms crossed. She's carrying something crushed to her chest. White. Small. It isn't until she turns that I recognize the object from a different angle—an ivory teddy bear. Only…

"That's an interesting toy," I croak. No wonder the Robinsons were so disturbed.

Magda looks down while Ms. Anderson's cheeks promptly turn ten shades redder.

"His name is It," the girl declares, brandishing the bear by its head. A head that looks as though it's been ripped off at one point, only to be crudely sewn back on with a series of stitches in garishly red thread. "I don't really like him."

"Yes, well, Magda is very creative," Ms. Anderson explains with a nervous laugh. "Especially when it comes to her toys."

"Ah… Creative." I swallow hard and cut my gaze to Vadim. His expression is more guarded than ever.

"Well, I have my morning free," Ms. Anderson says quickly. "I would love to stay and help Magda get settled. I—" Frowning, she reaches into her briefcase as a musical sound begins to chime. A cell phone apparently. Pressing it to her ear, she says, "This is Angela. Oh, really? Now? But… No, I can be there—" she hangs up, frowning. "I'm so sorry. I planned on staying, but I just received an emergency call to attend to another case. Do you think you'll be fine if…"

"Yes," Vadim says hoarsely. "We'll be fine."

If she's convinced by his tone, Ms. Anderson's wary grin doesn't reveal much either way. With a small smile shaping her lips, she stoops down beside Magda and shakes her hand. "Be good. You all have my number if you need it. Even you, Mags."

"I won't be needing it," Magda says with steely confidence. Her eyes continue to skim around the room as if taking stock of every single tile in the flooring and divot in the wallpaper.

"Well, goodbye." Ms. Anderson leaves, and it's as if she takes some of the air in the room with her.

The absence of a third party makes this all way too surreal. A mini female Vadim is prancing around haughtily while the original, older Vadim stands rigid in the corner, watching her.

And then there's me, ogling them both with an increasing sense of panic. More than ever, I'm starting to sense what I was afraid of all along, that niggling suspicion that I don't belong here. I don't deserve to belong here.

Navigating awkward social situations in the past has taught me that the only way to banish such an emotion is to force some small talk and hope for the best.

"I… Um, why don't we show you to your room?" I croak, to break the silence.

Magda cocks her head at me, her gaze skeptical. "My *own* room?" she prods in that eerily charming yet cold cadence. "I don't have to share it?"

"No." I force out a strangled laugh. "Who would you share it with, sweetie?"

She eyes me directly and blinks once. "You. Aren't you the other guest in the house?"

I grit my teeth in shock. My gaze cuts to Vadim, who hasn't budged from his spot. He shakes his head, raking his hands through his hair.

"No," he croaks. "She's not—"

"Let's show you around," I say, jutting my chin with what I hope passes for poise. I start for the stairs. Within seconds, Vadim is by my side and, in our wake, resonate tiny, hesitant footsteps that trail behind during the entire ascent upstairs.

When we reach her room, Magda toes the threshold, eyeing everything with barely any expression. "It's okay, I guess," she declares after a few weighty seconds of silence. "I just wish…"

"What?" Vadim steps forward, suddenly animated, his jaw clenched. It's as if the prospect of disappointing her does something to him internally. Shatters him.

Magda sighs and tosses It onto the bed, unconcerned as his floppy head rebounds off the headboard. "I just wish it was yellow," she says, folding her arms over her black pinafore. "I hate blue."

"You do?" Vadim's expression further constricts. "But, Ms. Anderson—"

"She must have lied." Dismissively, she shrugs her shoulders and moves to stand before her window. Her fingers ruthlessly clutch at her forearms, but I don't miss how they twitch. Like someone aching to jump onto the window seat and peer through the glass in awe of the view. Or run their fingers through the fully stocked bookshelf. The more I watch her, the more I'm convinced. She's Vadim's through and through.

Meaning that every word and action is calculated and intentional. And right now, for whatever reason, she *wants* to see his guilt-ridden expression reflected off the window glass. In response to the sight, her small chin lowers, and her fingers grip her arms tighter in triumph.

"We'll let you get settled in," I suggest, reaching for Vadim's hand. His is shaking though his expression reveals nothing but cold, careful blankness.

"What would you like for dinner?" he asks, his tone level. "You can ask for anything. You may have it—"

"I'm not hungry." Whirling on her heel, Magda marches over and snatches her suitcase right from his grasp. She starts to place it down beside the bed only to notice something that makes her eyes widen as she pauses mid-act. "I have my own bathroom?"

My ears perk up. For a second, that haughty chirp cracked, revealing a hint of true excitement. As if aware of her failing façade, she kicks the suitcase over and sighs with the utmost nonchalance.

"Yes," Vadim says, though I don't think he noticed. He's too busy watching her. Gaping at her. If I'm stunned by the similarities in them both, I can't imagine what he must be feeling. "All of this is yours. Everything. And we can have the color changed tomorrow—"

"I'm tired." Magda crosses over to the door and grasps the handle. "Can I take a nap?"

Vadim blinks. "Of course."

"Okay." She proceeds to close the door, forcing us to scramble out into the hall. The resulting slam resonates through the walls.

I look at Vadim. His expression is more controlled than ever, crafted to avoid displaying a hint of real emotion. But he can't hide from me—not anymore. Confusion haunts his eyes as they meet mine, alluding to a pain he desperately scrambles to hide.

"Let's go see about lunch," he says.

I follow him into the kitchen, where I'm surprised to find the fridge and cupboards magically stocked with food fit for a child and not just enough sustenance to keep a reclusive billionaire alive. Ena's even made a series of new meals to fill the freezer, it seems. Color coded, to boot— blue lids contain the usual meat and vegetable entre that Vadim appears to prefer. Yellow, on the other hand, looks to be an array of child-friendly fare from chicken nuggets and fries to vegetables cut in all sorts of appealing shapes.

"I have got to get myself a henchman," I say as I examine another carefully crafted meal.

Vadim eyes me with the hint of a smile threatening his serious frown. "I have a feeling you'd be a lot more demanding than I am. Ena would love you as an employer."

"Maybe I'll rethink keeping my distance from him," I propose. "That is, if he can forgive me for forgetting to feed you before your standoff with your brother."

Vadim's grin falls flat, and a sudden thought makes me reach for his hand, stroking the back of it.

"Does he know?" I ask. "Maxim. About…"

"No," Vadim says, his teeth bared, eyes cold. "And as far as I'm concerned, he doesn't need to."

"He is her uncle," I say, but I'm not sure if I mean it as a question or a statement. I know firsthand that relationships, no matter how close, can dissipate overnight. Titles mean nothing. You can go from someone's wife one second, to a stranger the next—and vice versa apparently.

In search of a distraction, I turn my attention back to the freezer and rummage through the prepackaged meals. "I think I want chicken," I declare, deciding for us both.

Dutifully, Vadim places the platter in the oven while I stand on tiptoe to rummage through the cupboards above his head.

"I also think this occasion calls for a little daytime wine. Yes?"

He shoots me an amused look that makes my breath catch.

"I think I should buy shares in this company," he says while reading the label of my cherished vintage. "You must singlehandedly keep them afloat."

I simper. "What can I say? It's in my blood—" I break off as I spot a small figure watching us from the doorway, her arms crossed.

"There is a pool," she says carefully. Her tiny frown and stern gaze take on a harder edge, as if she's fighting to seem as disinterested as possible.

"Oh, that's right," I say, recalling the list Vadim and I had poured over. "You like to swim. Right?"

Magda says nothing, turning her attention to Vadim, who cautiously meets her gaze. It's like something unspoken passes between them, and they both promptly turn away, their jaws clenched.

"Never mind," Magda says, shrugging. "It's too cold to swim, anyway—"

"It's heated," Vadim says. He skirts the counter and advances toward her. "You can swim whenever you'd like. As long as I, Tiffany, or another adult is present."

Magda's lips twitch, but she forces a curt nod. "Okay."

"And there are acres of property," Vadim adds, ushering her into the foyer. I follow them at a distance, but close enough to hear him add, "We're having a playground built there—" he points to a section of budding construction visible through the row of windows in the living room. "And there is a boathouse if you're interested in going onto the water. And a stable…"

I'm so distracted watching them. I barely notice the muffled thud of advancing footsteps until the front door trembles beneath a thudding blow. Another. Then, as we all watch, the door flies open to reveal a hulking creature resonating so much rage he almost seems inhuman.

Maxim. His dark eyes fly to Vadim as he forms his hands into fists, and boldly crosses the threshold.

"Is this a game to you?" he demands, his accent so thick I can barely understand him. "Buying this house. Flaunting your ownership. To taunt me? I should—"

He plows into the foyer without seeming to notice the small figure nearly trampled in his path. Magda's eyes go bug-wide as her mouth contorts into a startled o-shape. I don't even think she manages to scream before she turns on her heel and runs.

But her target is already halfway to her. Without hesitation, Vadim snatches her into his arms, crushing her to his chest.

"Get out," he growls, holding his daughter protectively close. I've never seen him like this—eyes flashing, expression lethal. "Now."

Maxim falters, his body deflating as shock disrupts his furious features. He blinks, looking from Vadim, to Magda, and then me.

"You sick son of a bitch," he says incredulously. "You think this is a family? Where did you find her, huh?" He jerks his chin at Magda. "Off the fucking street? Did you kidnap her too—" He breaks off, and I have a sinking suspicion why. Magda, from the safety of Vadim's arms, glanced at him fearfully, turning far enough that he could see her face. A near mirror image of *Vadim's* face.

I can't describe the expression that befalls him next. As if struck, he staggers back a step, his massive body swaying before he manages to right himself, his gaze puzzled.

"Get out," Vadim snarls. "Now, so help me God. Don't make me resort to other methods. *Leave.*"

Maxim's nostrils flare as his lips open and close wordlessly. Then, without so much as a parting threat, he turns and barrels through the remains of the door.

"Ena," Vadim calls the second his brother disappears from view.

The stout bodyguard enters the foyer as if conjured from thin air, his expression gruff. "*Now* I secure perimeter?" he asks in his halting drawl. Simmering anger laces his tone, and I suspect I'm witnessing the tail end of an argument. Something to do with the property and securing it. Maxim had been able to waltz right through the front door—because Vadim had intentionally kept his security at bay?

Whatever his reasons for doing so, I assume they've quickly changed. "Yes," he says with a nod. "No one comes close without you handling them personally."

Ena nods and puffs up, satisfied. He crosses over to the remains of the door and inspects the damage. The confidence with which he does so makes me suspect that intervening after a violent situation isn't exactly an unusual occurrence for him.

Vadim steps back, moving toward the kitchen. His voice reaches me, a soothing, persistent hum that chokes my heart.

"*Chut, ma douce fille,*" he murmurs, stroking Magda's dark hair. "*Tout va bien. Tu es en sécurité...*"

He rocks her against him with such a gentle motion that I doubt he's even aware of it. She clings to him, her face in his chest, her tiny hands gripping him so tightly her knuckles are white.

He continues to speak to her in French until she finally draws back and wiggles free of his grasp. Her face is beet red, I notice as she turns and marches past me, storming up the stairs. A second later, presumably, her bedroom door slams shut, the thud resonating throughout the house.

"I'll kill him," Vadim says, but his tone is far too serious. He means it.

Thinking quickly, I approach him and lace my fingers through his hair, planting my lips against his collar. "No, you won't." I smooth my hands down his front and finger the very end of his tie. "You're going to help me make lunch for Magda. Then you're going to have Ena secure the property, hmm? And later, you will think of a *humane* way to confront your brother."

He stiffens. Cautiously, I feel his fingers sink through my hair as his arm encircles my waist, holding me close.

"*Oui*—yes," he says, his accent thick. I file away another quirk of his for later reflection—he switches to French when overwhelmed, or protective, which gives a greater semblance to the words he murmured to me the other night. *Tell me you'll stay with me. That I can give you what you need, oui?*

Overwhelmed, I draw back and turn my attention to the freezer. "Nuggets, or broccoli and cheese shaped like dinosaurs? Which do you think she'd like?"

He makes a low sound in his throat as he inspects his options. "I never was a fan of food crafted to look like other forms of food," he says skeptically.

"Nuggets, it is!" I hand him the container to heat up while I head for the stairs, skirting Ena, who found a set of tools from somewhere and is working on the door with vigor.

My heart skips as I approach Magda's room though I'm not sure why. Perhaps because I'm breaking another one of my impromptu rules—stay out of this. Let Vadim get to know his daughter in peace, no matter how awkward a process it might turn out to be.

So much for that.

"Magda?" I gather the nerve to knock on her door and gingerly push it open.

A sweet, soft melody drifts out. Halting. A song? The foreign words are uttered with meticulous care. French? It has to be. Every syllable is pronounced in an accent fitting enough to match Vadim's—but overly careful as if parroted rather than fluent mastery of the language. Lost in concentration, she's standing on the window seat, her hands braced against the window while her bear sits propped against her feet. She sings mindlessly while scanning the horizon with such an inquisitive expression I stop short.

She goes rigid and whips around to face me, her eyes narrowing. The song dies mid-phrase, and she crosses her arms once more.

"Can I help you?" she asks, her tone shrill but polite.

"Are you settling in okay?" I warily step inside the room. Her suitcase is open, various items strewn across the bed. A few pieces of clothing, a worn looking leather-bound book, and another stuffed animal, though one lacking the signs of surgery that It sports. Beside the lot is a small pink carrying case that looks as though it's seen better days.

The moment my eyes settle on it, Magda jumps from the window seat and crosses to the bed. Meeting my gaze, she deliberately grabs her belongings and shoves them back into the suitcase, slamming it shut.

"I'm fine," she says. "Thanks."

"Okay." I force a smile and turn for the door. "We'll be just downstairs, and we made lunch—"

"I'm not a baby, you know." Gone is the façade of politeness. Her tone is so cutting that I can only think of one comparison fitting enough to match the icy hostility —the insistence of a certain billionaire that I wasn't his type, for instance.

I turn to face her, sensing my eyebrow raise. "I didn't mean to imply that you were."

"Who are you anyway?" She appraises me with a haughty flick of her chin, her arms crossed. "You're not married to him. Even if you do have a ring on." She nods to my left hand, and I clench said fingers into a fist, caught.

My cheeks flame, but something prevents me from backing down. Instead, I advance a step toward her, keeping my tone level. "And if I'm not?"

She bites her lower lip and seems to mull it over. Then she smiles, and it's such a beautiful match to Vadim's. The one he wears when his aim is cruel. "Did you read my file?" she asks sweetly, batting her eyelashes. "My last family, the Robinsons, are moving to the other side of the country, just to get away from me." Her smile grows wider as if she's utterly pleased with that fact.

But her eyes are every bit as expressive as her father's, revealing the truth in snippets that require deciphering.

"I don't know what I did to scare them so much," she says, throwing her hands into the air. "Maybe it was when I tried to microwave the cat?"

Any other time, with any other child, I'd be rightfully disgusted. Fearful, even. Maybe I should be in this case? I don't know what it is about her gleeful, ghoulish expression that makes me perch on the end of her bed and cross my legs casually.

"Is that all?" I ask, an eyebrow raised. "I once threatened to turn my father's prized stallion into glue. I even looked up the number for what I thought was the glue factory. Then I ran away with a duffle filled with barbie dolls and an entire box of pop tarts."

She blinks, caught off guard.

"I didn't make it far, mind you." I extend my fingers, inspecting the pink polish. "I was barely past the tennis courts before I chickened out. Besides, I didn't really want to hurt old Dauntless, anyway. I just wanted to make my parents squirm." It's an odd story to relay so bluntly. Something I predictably wouldn't tell most people on our first meeting.

Magda frowns, unsure of how to process it.

"Did the Robinsons do something to you that made you want to make them squirm?" I ask, free of judgment.

She purses her lips. "No. But what if I want to make *you* squirm?"

"Hmm." I think it over, then I lean forward and meet her gaze head-on. If I'm not mistaken, she flinches and takes a small step back. "Then try harder. I may look like a dumb bimbo, but I too, went through a hellion phase. Whatever you're thinking, whatever you're planning—trust me, baby, I wrote the book."

She wrinkles her nose, seemingly more confused than ever. "Why?" she demands.

I shrug as if the answer is obvious. "I wanted attention. I wanted to make my dad feel guilty. I wanted my mom to stop day drinking and look at me. I was bored. What made you want to provoke the Robinsons?"

Her piercing eyes narrow further. "You're weird," she declares, returning to her suitcase. She wrenches it open, and one by one withdraws what seems to be her few personal belongings. Displaying another one of Vadim's quirks, she meticulously folds a cream-colored sweater and reaches for an orange shirt.

"We can take you shopping if you'd like," I say, volunteering the use of Vadim's magic credit card. "Do you like dresses? Pants?"

She doesn't answer, preferring to sort her few outfits, leaving her book and stuffed animal on the bed. The case she grabs last. "This has to go in the fridge," she says with all of the maturity of a miniature adult, not a seven-year-old. "It's my insulin."

"Okay. We'll throw it in when we go downstairs. How about we speed things along?" I reach for a neatly folded jacket. "I can help you put these away—"

"Why?" Her tone isn't quite as hostile, but her dark brows are furrowing, her frown skeptical. God, it's so much like interacting with Vadim. Someone constantly on guard, mistrustful of any hint of kindness. For a horrible second,

I wonder if his daughter's upbringing was even a fraction as horrific as his. Then I push the thought away and tug the jacket from her grip, moving toward her closet as she watches on in shock.

"You have beautiful hair," I tell her, ignoring the question. "I can braid it for you tonight, if you want. I used to love when my mom did that."

"But you aren't my mom," she snipes almost in a singsong tone.

I ignore the bait and snatch an empty hanger from one of the many rails lining her very own massive walk-in closet. My brain skips ahead, envisioning all of the various clothing items she'll need to stock it with. Pajamas. Day clothing. Night clothing. Dress-up clothing. If dressing her father was a challenge, I assume she'll be just as surly to shop for. A challenge I'm willing to accept.

"Here," I tell her, holding out my hand for the sweater in her grip. "Let me put your things away. Then we'll go get some lunch, huh?"

So surly. So wary. To my surprise, she reluctantly steps forward and relinquishes the sweater. As I hang it, she reappears with the rest of her clothing balanced in her arms.

"What's your name?" she asks almost grudgingly as I arrange her clothing according to color.

"Tiffany."

She accepts the introduction with a sniff. "I'm hungry."

I hang her last shirt and switch off the light. "I think the food should be ready. Let's go check."

She follows as I descend the stairs and enter the kitchen to find Vadim at the counter, dividing the contents of the platters between three plates. While I stow Magda's pink insulin case into the fridge, he looks up, his expression almost panicked. *Help me*, I imagine him begging were he desperate enough to do so out loud. *Don't leave me.*

I smile to reassure him.

"I hope you like nuggets," I tell Magda as I take a seat at the table.

She claims the one across from me but frowns as Vadim places a plate down in front of her. Warily, she nudges a nugget with the tip of her finger before taking a hesitant bite. Ena's cooking must win her over because all reluctance drains from her face, and she doesn't need any more prompting.

I watch her, so distracted by the sight of her that I barely notice as Vadim sits beside me. Pretty soon, we're *both* staring at her, his beautiful little girl, unaware of the nearness of her biological father. Or how much he loves her already. His fingers twitch as she reaches for a glass of water as if he has to stop himself from grabbing it for her. When she finishes her food, he's already racing across the kitchen in search of a napkin.

"Am I still going to my school?" Magda asks, pushing her plate aside.

"Yes." Vadim offers her a napkin that she doesn't take. Awkwardly he sets it beside her and circles the table to reclaim his seat. "After the break. Don't worry about any disruptions."

"Okay," she says, eyeing her tiny fingers. "And I can have new clothes?"

"Anything," Vadim rasps.

Magda fixates her steely gaze on me. "And *you'll* take me?"

"If you want," I say cautiously. "We could go tomorrow?"

She shrugs and sips from her water. "Okay."

I don't think I'm the only one who misses the fact that Vadim is pointedly left out of her invitation.

"Can I go up to my room now?"

"Y-Yes—" Vadim barely gets the word out before she's skipping merrily across the kitchen. Her tiny steps echo as she marches up the stairs, and once again, her door slams with force.

Vadim sighs, his jaw clenched, his gaze on the table. One of his hands forms a fist over the glass surface, the knuckles whitening.

I gingerly cradle his fingers with my own and lean down, kissing the rigid peaks. Then I feather another kiss over his wrist, up to his collar. Higher, until I finally reach his lips.

"You did good," I insist as his mouth remains stubbornly closed. "You did so good—"

"Have I?" He withdraws from me and stands, tearing at his hair with both hands. "I need to work," he says. "I'll be in the study."

I watch him go, more conflicted than ever. Can I withstand two switchblade humans battling their emotions? My heart throbs in a way that gives me serious doubt.

CHAPTER NINE

Left to my own devices, I pour myself a fresh glass of wine and decide to take my chances exploring the outside of the house. A small glass door near the back of the kitchen leads onto a stone terrace surrounding the private pool. Beyond, stretches the waterfront lined by a rocky beach that conjures the potential for plenty of warm, fuzzy memories to be made. The more I take in the view, the more I feel for my beautiful, tormented Vadim. The poor man had to have envisioned the same images I am.

Magda, playing in the pool or skipping happily by the water. Her, fishing water toys from the boathouse or racing off to the stable in the distance. Him, showing her how to ride his white mare, Zzazza…

As if summoned by the thought, I sense the door open behind me as a looming figure steps onto the terrace. "I come with an offering of contrition."

I turn to find Vadim exiting the kitchen, a wine glass in tow. Beaming, I gladly accept his token. "You are forgiven, peon," I tell him, taking a sip.

He settles against me from behind, his hands capturing my waist. It's such an intimate position—I should balk, I think. Maybe I'm too tired, lulled by the promise of wine? Or I'm lying to myself, desperate to escape the obvious. It feels so *natural* being with him like this, and my ever-present list feels further away.

"Thank you for staying," he says against my scalp.

Gratitude nearly knocks me over, and I hastily take a second sip of wine to steel myself. "Don't mention it."

Together, we watch the sun scuttle across the horizon, each of us envisioning a million potential uses for the beautiful property. Will any of them ever come to fruition? Who knows?

I, for one, am willing to hope for as much.

Eventually, I bring myself to brush my hand along his forearm. "We should get ready for dinner," I suggest, though a part of me wishes I could spend the night in his arms, just enjoying the vastness of his property.

As if to spoil the potential of that ever happening, we both turn as the sliding glass door is noisily wrenched open from the inside.

"I'm hungry," Magda declares, her tone flat. She scans the waiting pool and the waterfront beyond with feigned disinterest. But her eyes linger over the bay, in particular, a rare gleam of hunger coloring her irises. Just as quickly, it vanishes, snuffed out with a surly pout. "I'm really hungry."

"What would you like? Whatever you wish," Vadim says, moving toward her.

She crosses her arms, her lips pursed thoughtfully. "The Robinsons never let me have pizza," she says.

"Because of the carbohydrate content," Vadim explains, following her into the kitchen. "We need to be careful about how much we consume and always make sure to cover our meals with enough insulin."

"We?" She stares as he lifts his shirt, revealing the tubing of his pump. He uses it so rarely around me, I've almost forgotten the device's existence.

"*We*," he reiterates. "Luckily for us both, I know of a pizzeria that creates an amazing low carb pie. Name your toppings."

She thoughtfully taps her chin. "Cheese and pepperoni."

"Done." He pulls a cell phone from his pocket and steps aside to phone in the order while I back into a corner and watch them both. There is something so beautiful in seeing them interact together, each cautious in their own right.

When he's done on the phone, Vadim approaches the fridge and grabs a pitcher of orange juice. "Set the table?" he asks Magda.

She doesn't agree out loud, but she gradually moves to the cupboard he indicates and accepts the three plates he gives her.

I don't inch forward until the table is set, and Vadim is pouring three glasses of juice to place at each setting. "What else do you like in addition to pizza?" he asks her.

"Cake," she says, and I get the sense she's deliberately provoking him.

With an adept social grace, Vadim doesn't even seem to notice the bait. "I know of a bakery as well that makes a delicious cake. What else?"

She proceeds to play a devious game of naming foods that are not diabetic-friendly, while he patiently counters each one with a sugar-free alternative. It's as if he studied the list of foods a child may crave and ensured that he had a ready supply of options for her.

In fact, I'm sure that's the case.

Finally bored, Magda proceeds to tap her slender fingers along the table. Noticing the act, Vadim asks, "Do you play any instruments?"

She wrinkles her nose. "Maybe."

"I loved playing the piano when I was your age," he says softly. "When I could find one."

"The Robinsons didn't have a piano." She folds her arms, her chin jutting.

"I can get you one." He makes it sound as simple as snapping his fingers. "And lessons, if you'd like."

She mulls it over, and I half-expect her to refuse. I think a part of her wants to. But like him, she's too curious, drawn to an opportunity to tackle something new. While Vadim chooses to research BDSM, she'll warily accept his offer of musical training.

"Okay."

"I'll make the arrangements first thing in the morning."

We sit in awkward silence until the pizza arrives, courtesy of a gruff Ena who manages up what I think might be a smile once he spots Magda. We eat together, saying nothing until finally, Magda sets her plate aside.

"I'm tired," she says.

"Do you need someone to tuck you in?" Vadim starts to stand, but she shoots him a look so withering he falters.

"I'm not a baby," she says, her nose in the air. She flounces from the room and up the stairs. Predictably, the door slams.

"Give her time," I say, approaching Vadim from behind. I run my fingers over the muscles of his back, sliding around to his front. When I toy with the waistband of his pants, he sucks in a deep breath.

"Restraint is one skill we will both have to learn," he says hoarsely.

"I know." I nuzzle the back of his neck even as my fingers obediently withdraw. "Just know that I find you trying to be super dad incredibly sexy. I wish to do all sorts of naughty things to you when little ears are finally asleep."

"Oh?" He turns to face me, an eyebrow raised. I shiver as he draws me close, letting my body mold against his. "What kinds of things?"

"Well…" I stand on tiptoe and murmur a list of sordid, X-rated options into his ear. "And that's to start."

"You are insatiable." He runs his fingers down my back as his eyes lower to mine. "And patient. And… I couldn't do this without you."

A part of me despairs at the fact that he actually seems to mean it. "Yes, you could," I argue. It's the truth. "She's resistant to you, but that's because you're both so alike. In no time, you'll have her madly in love with you. Just like —" I manage to physically stop myself from saying more by slamming my hand over my mouth.

His eyes narrow, and he snatches the fingers in question, drawing them away. Something between us shifts from sizzling lust to a smoldering heat I feel deep in my core.

"Madly in love," he says as if tasting the words for the very first time. "Like?"

"Sir!"

We break apart as Ena storms into the kitchen, his expression sterner than ever. "Visitor," he says to Vadim.

"Mr. Hood. I let him in?"

I look at Vadim in awe as he seems to physically bite back a groan. Finally, he nods. "Yes. Let him in."

Ena races off, and Vadim turns to me, cradling my cheek against his palm before I can pull away.

"Check on Magda for me?"

"Okay," I concede without prying as to who this mysterious visitor might be. I can't resist placing a soft kiss along his jaw—just one.

Upstairs, I find the door to Magda's room ajar. True to her insistence on the fact, she *isn't* a baby, more than capable of getting herself ready for bed. She's already dressed in a pair of pajamas, her damp curls hanging down her shoulders as she moves about her room, dragging It by his floppy, reattached head. When she spots me staring, she eyes me without comment, glancing me up and down with a flick of her unnerving eyes.

"Goodnight," I say, closing the door behind me as I reenter the hall.

"Wait."

I return to find her rummaging through an end table for an object that she marches toward me and offers up without a word. A worn, wooden hairbrush.

Like a princess used to dolling out commands, she sits on her bed with her back to me.

"Braids?" I suggest as I dutifully approach her and smooth my fingers through her thick ringlets. Gosh, her hair is every bit as beautiful as her father's. I brush through it all gently and arrange two plaits when she doesn't offer up a complaint either way.

As soon as I finish the final braid, she lurches to her feet and snatches the brush. Then she climbs under the blankets, tucking It under her arm.

"Goodnight," I murmur as I escape this time without a word from her.

A small smile shapes my mouth as I return downstairs. Before I remember that, I shouldn't be doing things like tucking my one-night-too-many-stand's daughter into bed. If anything, I should be putting distance between us.

And her father.

The man whose voice alone makes me quiver, even now as he speaks to someone else, his tone low and strained. "…I didn't know until two years ago. For obvious reasons, it's not something I'm eager to discuss."

"*That's* why you went off all that bloody time," a man replies, his accent distinctly British. "I thought it might have been because your old partner died, but… You didn't think to ask for fucking help?"

"I thought it was best to keep her separate from me," Vadim says. Even from this distance, I can picture his expression—tortured, guilty eyes, and a tight frown. My heart aches, and I long to run my fingers through his hair until his devious grin returns in full. "I've changed my mind since."

"Why?" the other man demands. I think I recognize his voice—*Milton.*

A low sound issues from Vadim that could be a laugh from a normal man. "Why not? If Maxim can become father of the year, I can't? My daughter is at least *mine.*"

"But how? Don't tell me you knocked-up some woman and just left her. That's not like you."

Vadim's silent for so long. Finally, he sighs. "Do you remember my last owner?" he asks, his tone gruff. "The one they called The Collector?"

"I remember him, the sick fuck," Milton snarls. I imagine his handsome visage twisted with anger, his dark eyes narrowed. "I remember the rumors as well. Don't tell me…"

"They're true." Vadim sounds so cold. So distant. A stranger. "He had that name for a reason. His *collection.* He always spoke of breeding his favorite toys, be them animals, or…"

I'm drawn forward three more steps before I have the sense to stop at the base of the staircase. Their voices must be coming from the study—I don't see anyone in the foyer or the living room.

"He must have stored his samples in a place where they were spared from the purge. I'd thought I'd burned everything else to the fucking ground."

"Samples?" Milton's tone conveys enough horror for us both. "Fuck! Do you know who her mother is? And how could his *samples*… Maxim said she's young. That bastard died over a decade ago."

"I don't know why or how she was born," Vadim admits. "As for her mother… I do have one hunch. You might even remember her."

"Another 'favorite?'" Milton asks, hissing the term.

"Her name was Irina." I've never heard Vadim's tone so detached. Broken. "Magda has her eyes. If I would consider anyone an ally in that world, other than you… But most would not understand our relationship," he adds. "With your convenient knowledge in psychiatry, I think you'd deem it something along the lines of… *Unhealthy codependency with anti-social attributes.*"

"Oh?"

"You know what it's like," Vadim says softly. "When you question your own humanity. When you crave validation and power so badly, you'll do anything to find it? Confide in *anyone.*"

"I understand," Milton says, his voice a rasp.

"Irina and I were more partners than anything else. In manipulation. Deception. Seduction. We made a game of it. Stealing tokens to prove who was the better player. Looking back, I think it was the only way we could survive. She disappeared before I gained my freedom," he adds. "Whether she was killed or escaped, I never found out. But now I suspect she left on her own. Left me behind. To her, it would be just another part of the game."

"And your child?" Milton presses. "Is she part of the 'game'? Have you tried to find her, Irina? You cite my 'psychiatric' experience, which you gladly make use of. And yet, in all of our sessions, you've never mentioned her."

"I don't know," Vadim says in a tone that makes something inside me throb. "If she is alive…she's deliberately concealed herself from me. When I found Magda, she had no documentation. No birth certificate. It's like she appeared out of nowhere, but the doctor who did her first examination claimed that she had been well-fed beforehand. Well-groomed and her vaccinations appeared to be up to date. The only abnormality was that her diabetes was dangerously uncontrolled."

"Could she have been planted?" Milton wonders. "Where you would find her."

"If Irina is her mother…" He trails off in that way he does when he's mulling something over. Something puzzling like the prospect of me leaving, or a woman who may or may not be the mother of his child. "Why have I never mentioned her? We all had our ways of coping," he adds softly. "She could see those around her as creatures to protect or toys just as easily. When she left, there was no point in dwelling on her. She would *want* me to dwell.

And now? I don't see her abandoning Magda without a reason."

"A fucked up one from what it sounds like," Milton hisses. "I have to ask. Was… Was she part of the trade, your girl?"

"No," Vadim says, and I sense them both release sighs of relief. "Her examinations revealed no sign of abuse. She's had a relatively normal upbringing. No matter her origin, I will protect her."

"And you won't be alone in that." The heat in Milton's tone challenges Vadim's own assurance. *"Milton sees me as a scared little boy he's sworn to protect."* But duty is a very different animal from unquestionable loyalty. "Can I see her?" he asks.

"She's sleeping," Vadim says. "Maybe tomorrow. But she doesn't know who I am for now. As far as she's concerned, I'm her new foster placement."

"Damn." Milton whistles. "Do you plan on telling her?"

"Maybe. When the time is right."

"And here I thought Maxim could be a secretive prick. He hides his women from me. You hide your children. What a friendship we all share."

"You know I trust you more than anyone," Vadim says, sounding closer. Advancing footsteps force me to scamper up the stairs just as the two men appear in the foyer, advancing toward the front door.

"And you deserve to meet her," Vadim adds.

"And Maxim?" Milton draws up beside him, fingering the collar of his crisp, ebony suit. "I hear he didn't make the best impression."

"*He* won't be coming anywhere near her," Vadim says coldly. "I tried with him. But he's proven more than once —he isn't worth the time. As far as Magda is concerned, he's a violent stranger who barged into her home and scared the hell out of her."

Milton frowns. "For what it's worth, he didn't mean to scare her."

"The fact that he's saying as much through you and not in person is all I need to know." Vadim's gaze darkens, closed-off. "He will never see her again."

Milton shrugs as Vadim opens the front door. "I hope you change your mind," he says before stepping out into the darkness. "That little girl needs all of the family she can get. You know better than anyone else that one can't be too picky when it comes to that subject."

He leaves, and Vadim closes the door after him, sighing. Rather than escape before he catches me eavesdropping, I take a moment to ogle him. His shoulders are rigid, his profile the picture of brooding unease. As I watch, his constricted expression softens as his lips part, his voice rasping, "My beauty," he calls to me despite my hiding place. "So cunning. So sly. How much did you hear?"

I step around the corner and descend the stairs, my chin jutting in defiance. "Enough to know I deserve to be punished." I force a smile, praying that I seem nonchalant enough to have missed the trigger points of his conversation. Like the mysterious Irina who shares Magda's electric-blue eyes. Naughty questions persist on the fringes of my brain anyway. Such as, *did he love her? Is he hoping she'll return?*

I could ask him.

I should…

But I can't.

His gaze is far too guarded, and I don't have the heart to shatter my ruse. I saunter to him instead and grab his tie, stroking the fabric suggestively.

"Should I be spanked for my insolence?" I wonder, making my voice low enough so that it won't carry upstairs. "Or do I deserve a harsher chastisement?"

Vadim cinches my waist in both hands, yanking me closer. I finger his collar while his mouth finds my ear, nibbling at the lobe. "You deserve the world," he growls in a tone that makes my head spin. So insistent. So confident in that regard.

A world of his making. A sinful, kinky paradise in which I'm at his mercy—helpless as he pulls me down the hall and into his study, taking care not to make too much noise. I smother a moan as he strips me, leaving the façade of his perfect fake wife on the floor before he spreads me over his desk and doles out my punishment.

I nearly scream as he latches his mouth above my piercing, thrusting with his tongue until I'm incoherent. This is true torture—having to stay silent amid the tumult of pleasure he gives me. Ruthlessly, he gives it. Over and over until I'm wracked with sobs as tears stream down my face in my quest to smother all noise.

I praise him with drawn nails raking through his hair instead. With orgasms that leave him groaning in their wake. Limp and panting, all I can do is lie helplessly as he stands and frees his cock from the confines of his slacks.

I take him deep on the first thrust, hissing in pleasure, my eyelids fluttering. I don't know if it's the location, or the tension that comes from sneaking around but I come damn near instantly, and he isn't far behind, snatching me to him as he spills inside me.

We come back to clinging to any part of each other we can reach. As my breathing returns to normal, I find his ear, my voice a whisper.

"I feel sufficiently punished," I tell him.

He chuckles and draws back to stare down on me with those haunting, brooding eyes. "Enough to repent?" he wonders, stroking the hair from my face. "For ever wanting to leave me?"

I nod even as a part of me warns me to back down. Avoid. Salvage our one fragile boundary. "I believe your torturous methods are making progress with this prisoner," I confess despite myself. "For better or for worse."

"Better," he insists, drawing me into his arms while scanning the floor for our scattered clothing. "This is better."

And he sounds so damn confident.

I almost believe him.

CHAPTER TEN

I blink my eyes open, unsure of what drew me awake in the first place. I'm on the bed, I think, judging from the softness beneath me. Weak sunlight pours in through the window, illuminating the empty space beside me—Vadim is gone.

Sighing, I slump against a pillow, stroking the silken sheets he'd laid on beside me. Kinky sex is a drug unto itself, but I don't think anything tops being held by him. Falling asleep to the sound of his heartbeat while his breaths ruffle my hair. This man will be the end of me, in a way Jim could only dream.

Fuck the list. With every passing second, I'm growing resigned to my fate—but that doesn't mean I can't enjoy every fucking minute.

I halfheartedly scan the rest of the room though I sense without having to check that he isn't here. Sure enough, the doorway to the bathroom is empty, as is the rest of the room…

Or not. I bolt upright, clutching the sheet to my front as my eyes blink to bring the tiny figure watching me from the foot of the bed into focus.

"M-Magda?" I croak.

She's fully dressed, her dark hair neatly brushed back behind a scarlet headband. Another black pinafore over a white shirt makes her look like some tiny, less demonic version of Wednesday Adams. At least until I spot the once decapitated bear dangling from her arm.

"Are we going shopping today?" she asks, unconcerned as I scramble to make sure I'm fully covered and that any silver toys are hidden from view.

"Um… Where is your fath—Mr. Vadim?" I ask.

She shrugs. "I don't know. It's six a.m.," she adds. "I've been up since five."

And Vadim's been gone since then? Frowning, I try to pinpoint any time during the night when he could have left, but I can't remember. Facing Magda, I'm left with no choice.

"Well, um, why don't you go into the closet and find me something to wear, huh? My stuff is on the left-hand side."

She frowns but obediently scuttles off, and I take the brief freedom from tiny eyes to race into the bathroom and jump into the shower. I wash off quickly and thank God that Vadim had the sense to stash a few robes here, hanging on a hook near the shower entrance. I select a black one that smells like him and shimmy into it. When I return to the bedroom, I find Magda sitting patiently on a leather chair by the window, nearly swallowed by a sea of hot pink faux fur perched on her lap.

"You actually wear this?" she asks, lifting what appears to be the sleeve of my favorite jacket between two fingers.

"Yeah." I gently take the jacket from her grasp, discovering a purple, frothy dress underneath. Frowning, I eye them both, impressed by the potential. "Interesting color choice, Ms. Magda."

Her expression doesn't reveal either way if she picked the clothing on purpose or as a joke. When I pop into the bathroom to change, I'm stunned to find a flattering ensemble. Bold. Daring. Fluffy. The perfect outfit to tackle the challenge this day is shaping up to throw my way.

Magda, however, doesn't seem very impressed. She crushes It to her chest while sweeping her gaze over me with abject disinterest. "I'm hungry."

"Okay…" I exhale nervously. *Don't panic, Tiffy.* If I'm lucky, Ena packed away some breakfast in one of his prepared meals. "Come on. I'll make you something to eat."

Downstairs, I quickly discover no luck in terms of the prepackaged breakfast department. Luckily, Ena seemed to have countered such a lack by stocking the pantry with more—relatively healthy and carb controlled—colorful cereal than I think I've ever seen stocked in a grocery store at one time. After Magda picks out her preference, I make her a bowl and watch her eat while chewing on a croissant. She has a pump I quickly discover as she slips it from the pocket of her pinafore and programs her dosage of insulin.

"You need any help?" I ask.

The humorless look she directs my way is all the answer I need.

Within a few minutes, it's painfully clear that Vadim isn't down here either. Neither is he in the study when I gather the nerve to creep down the hall and check. Again, I wrack my brain, trying to remember anything from last night that might give me a clue as to his whereabouts.

I remember…

Warmth. I can recall the sensation of soft lips nudging my throat in reverence and a husky voice murmuring praises, even while half asleep. *"…beautiful. So beautiful. Mine."*

And then I remember a sudden chill as he pulled away. A noise in the distance. A phone call? He'd left the bed to take it, I think, speaking in a hushed tone.

How did I forget this before? My lust-drugged brain is sluggish with the details, and I rub at my temples until bit by bit more snippets return. He'd sounded…worried, I think. His tone had been gruffer than usual, deepening by the second. I think he'd been frantic afterward, moving through the dark, throwing on clothing.

How in the hell had I missed that?

"Did you hear me?" I blink and refocus on the source of the soft, irritated voice. Magda watches me frowning with her hands neatly folded beside her now-empty cereal bowl. "*Now* are we going shopping?"

"I…" I glance around, unsure of where Vadim even keeps his car keys, let alone any necessary numbers or emergency information in case we need them. "We should probably wait for your fath—Mr. Vadim to come back—"

"Mr. Vadim no come back." The stern grunt comes from Ena, who appears at the mouth of the kitchen, his arms crossed over the front of his battered leather jacket. "He busy. I take."

"You'll take us shopping?" Magda stands and smooths her hands down the front of her crisp pinafore. Taking It by his mangled head, she warily approaches Ena. As haughty as a little queen's, her voice reaches back to me, "Can we go now?"

"I guess…" Though I'm tempted to prod Ena for more details. Maybe I would if he didn't deliberately seem to avoid eye contact with me. As I approach him, he sticks out his hand, grudgingly offering me a single, small object.

"Mr. Vadim said to give you this."

This being his fancy, smanshy credit card. Only when I scan the name printed on the front, I nearly faint. It's mine. Or a version of mine, at least: *Tiffany Gorgoshev.*

"We go now," Ena says, snapping me from my shock. He waddles to the front door with Magda prancing in tow.

And I wonder if I'm already in far too deep.

ONCE WE REACH the downtown shopping district, I fight to push all concerns for Vadim out of my head. It's surprisingly easy once I enter the first boutique, and it becomes readily apparent that, for all of her reserved surliness, Ms. Magda may harbor a secret love for fashion.

More than once, I catch her gazing longingly at the smaller versions of the adult designs adorning various mannequins. After our personal saleswoman shows us to a private dressing room, I decide to put my suspicions to the test.

"Well?" I sit casually on a leather chaise and sip from a glass of customary wine—I'd argue with Vadim about the credit card later, but being married to a billionaire at least on paper certainly has its perks. "Show me your favorite outfits?" I dare her.

And for once, Magda squirms, her lips pursed with unease. I catch her gaze dart to an outfit near the back of the boutique that draws even my interest—a turquoise sweater dress with a bold, black collar and a matching headband.

Shopping for a little girl is a different animal from what I'm used to. Everything is too damn adorable, screaming to adorn tiny limbs. My brain skips ahead, picturing her any one of several designer fashions, complete with a cute hairstyle to match.

Reign it in, Tiffy, I scold myself.

"What kinds of clothing do you like?" I ask, desperate for a distraction.

She shrugs, crossing her arms. "The Robinsons never took me shopping," she says, her nose wrinkling. "I just got the old clothes."

I picture the smug Mrs. Robinson with a renewed rage.

"Well, we have the time." God only knows where Vadim's gone. "Let's see what you've got in terms of style, kid."

When the saleswoman returns to our corner, however, I take the lead and point her to the turquoise outfit, much to Magda's shock. "We'll try that one first."

Magda stares on in silence as the woman brings her the garments in the correct size. Her frown remains stubbornly in place as she creeps into a dressing room. But as she reappears minutes later, I clap my hands, pleased.

"You look beautiful! Turn around." Much like her father, blue is so her color. The hue enhances her eyes and alights the small, fleeting smile that shapes her mouth before she realizes it and frowns in earnest.

"It's…decent," she says crisply. "Just okay."

"*Okay*," I parrot with a knowing wink. "We'll take that one," I tell the saleswoman without bothering to hear the price.

"Now, what about that one?" I point to a red ensemble hanging across the showroom with an adult set to match. "We can both try it."

Magda says nothing, but when the saleswoman returns with the chosen clothing, she enters the dressing room beside the one I claim.

And I start to hope that this may not end in flames.

It isn't until well after nightfall that we return to the house. By the time Ena and I approach the backseat and fish through the mound of shopping bags gathered there, Magda is fast asleep. She's small enough that I can easily carry her inside while Ena extends our tense truce by gathering up our combined purchases.

She's so beautiful, I'm mesmerized with every step it takes to enter the house. She has Vadim's long eyelashes that ghost her delicate cheekbones. Her glossy hair is freshly blown out into soft waves—courtesy of a trip to the salon after shopping—and her newly painted nails cling to It even in sleep. Something tightens in my chest the more I watch her while gingerly stepping over the threshold.

A day spent with a seven-year-old should sound horrifying in theory—had it been with most of my Sunday school class it would have been. But she's such a strange, unusual creature. I'm afraid I may be as intrigued by her as I am by the figure pacing anxiously in the foyer, his expression constricted.

"Thank God," he says, advancing toward me. "You're back."

I can't get a read on his expression as he leans in to press his lips to mine. Then he turns his attention to Magda and cradles her head gently while lifting her from my arms.

They make a breathtaking picture together. Him, in a dark navy suit, his hair slightly mussed as if he'd spent most of the day raking his fingers through it. Bundled in his arms, she looks like a doll wearing an ebony faux fur jacket and one of her new dresses—a gray slip with white applique flowers decorating the hem.

"You can kiss your billions goodbye in about ten years," I inform him softly. "I'm afraid to inform you that your daughter has all the signs of a budding shopaholic. Trained by yours truly, she's going to spend you out of house and home if you aren't careful."

His upper lip quirks into a pained smile as he smooths the wayward curls from Magda's face. "I'll just have to work harder then," he murmurs. "If I am to support *both* of your habits."

Both. I don't argue with that as he heads upstairs, entering Magda's room. He sets her gingerly on the bed while I scour her closet for a worn pair of pajamas. Something she said earlier makes my heart ache, and her few meager belongings take on a new significance. I don't say anything to Vadim though as we gently undress her and ease her into a nightdress. He tucks her beneath the blankets afterward, smoothing them over her with heartbreaking care. After ensuring that It is tucked in as well, we escape her room and instinctively head downstairs, putting as much distance between her and us. It's only when we're in the kitchen that I feel safe to talk again.

"She told me her foster family only gave her hand-me-downs," I say as we settle in at the island counter.

Vadim frowns, stroking his jaw. "That can't be right... I gave them access to an account specifically for her—with more than enough funds. Under the guise of a donation, of course. They've been making regular withdrawals."

"Well, they haven't been spoiling her, at least," I say halfheartedly. Inside, I'm more than happy to permanently vilify the Robinsons. Good riddance. "She was like a kid in a candy store today. Where were you?" I try to phrase the question as innocently as I can—but his reaction catches me off guard. He stiffens, his gaze distant.

"You took care of her," he says thickly. "Thank you."

I shiver as he reaches out, brushing my cheek in a gentle caress. His nearness is almost enough to make me bite back more questions. Something is bothering him. I can sense it in his eyes and what he doesn't say. His hands shake, and his paleness betrays that he hasn't eaten recently, if at all today.

"Let me make you some dinner," I say, turning to the freezer in search of one of Ena's meals. "Magda and I already ate. I made sure to check her sugars, and I took her to a restaurant with low carb options."

Though the latter part is entirely due to Ena, who seemed to know a list of suitable options by heart.

Vadim watches me as I select a chicken and veggie dish and heat it up for him. Minutes later, we trade places as I watch him dig in.

"She's a weird little girl, your kid," I tell him wryly. "She loves fashion, though I think she didn't want me to notice. She loves turquoise, especially. And black. I hope you don't mind, but we got our nails done, and that's the color she picked—"

"Thank you." He looks at me with such an expression. It steals my breath away and makes my skin catch fire in a strange, inexplicable way. Like I'm burning alive from the inside out, but it's a fire I wouldn't extinguish for the whole world.

"You say that like it was hard," I counter. "Being around her. Being around you."

Mayday, Tiffy, a part of me warns.

But his façade slips again. Whatever kept him away today is still haunting him. Distracting him. He looks so... tormented. The same, closed-off man I met in a hotel bar with his invisible wall firmly up.

When he clears his plate, we wash the dishes and eventually migrate into his study, where he claims the chair behind his desk. The second the door closes behind us, I sidle to him before I can stop myself and climb directly onto his lap, toying with the end of his tie. He sucks in a breath, his gaze cutting up to mine. Those dark eyes of his are endless—soul-sucking. One look and I'm captured, a slave to his whims.

"Tell me something sexy," I command, eager to distract him.

"You will stay," he says on cue. His hands encircle my waist possessively, tethering me to him. *Trapping* me with no hope of escape. "I will keep you here, beauty. You are mine."

I don't argue. Instead, I press my lips against his jaw and slide my hands down his chest, resting them over where I know his heart to be. "Be honest with me, and I won't be able to leave. So... Where were you?"

"Business," he says, brushing his lips over my forehead. "Though that's not everything. I..." He sighs, pulling back to face me directly. "This time of year is difficult for me."

"Oh?" Driven by the raw emotion in his voice, I force the lust to the back of my mind. "Tell me?"

He frowns. Then he stands, lifting me onto his desk. Stepping between my legs, he keeps me pinned in place, his captive audience.

"It's nearing the anniversary of…" Something in how his expression constricts makes me able to guess the answer.

"Your escape?" I say hesitantly when he doesn't explain.

He nods. "One day, I will tell you more. I swear to you. But…"

"I understand," I whisper, even though inside I'm torn. Could the mysterious Irina play a role in the pain of this anniversary? God, it's too selfish to consider, let alone mention out loud.

Instead, I settle against him, resting my mouth against the crook of his neck. Soon enough, I'm kissing my way down his collar bone, feeding off his startled—yet encouraging—grunt.

He claimed to have never had a relationship with a woman—but that's the scary part. Relationships could be categorized and forgotten. But true, rare connections went deeper than such a word. They were insidious, everlasting, even after the recipient of such feelings vanished.

They lingered, never disappearing.

And no one else could ever fill that void.

CHAPTER ELEVEN

The next morning, my wakeup call comes in the form of a contented sigh that fans across my shoulder in a burst of heat. I open my eyes to the man lying beside me, so beautiful in half-wakefulness that it hurts. Overnight, whatever had been bothering him seems to have vanished. His devious grin makes a triumphant return as I snuggle into him with a matching peaceful sigh.

"Morning," I murmur.

He strokes his fingers through my hair, marveling at the reddish strands. "Morning. A very good morning." He shifts, revealing a hardening erection that strains against my hip. I murmur in sympathy and slither beneath the covers to test just how rested he is.

Minutes later, he's fully awake, sitting on the side of the bed with a reluctant frown. "Early start today," he says before standing and heading into the bathroom. "I have some deliveries coming."

"Oh?" Though the logical part of my brain warns me against getting too excited, I can't help it. I sit up, licking my lips at the possibilities.

Until he rains on my parade with a stern frown. "None for you. Well, maybe one is for you, but please don't try to fuck it."

I laugh at his serious tone and scramble from the sheets to join him, standing naked before the shower as he washes down. I don't know who, between the two of us, is enjoying their view more. He groans like a man at his whit's end when he finally leaves the shower to find me leaning against the countertop, fondling my breasts.

"You'll be the death of me," he whispers, eyeing me from head to toe. Then he shakes his head, and I sense him struggle to contain at least some of his lust. Enough for him to escape into the bedroom without lunging for me. "I can't afford a delay today," he insists while scrambling into the closet. "Some of these deliveries are time-sensitive…"

He seems to lose his train of thought as I prance toward him, my hips swaying. I manage to steal a five second's detour worth of a kiss before he breaks away, cursing and snatches a shirt from a hanger as if it's armor against my charms.

"Please," he grates. "Give me this morning to be level-headed, and I promise I'll reward you later. After your punishment."

Satisfied, I get dressed beside him, and we venture downstairs to find the first of his "deliveries" already being carried across the foyer by a team of workers. Ena stands nearby, directing them with curt, one-word instructions.

"Vadim." I grasp his hand and stand on tiptoe to plant a kiss along his jaw. "She'll love it," I tell him.

He strokes my cheek in return, his gaze distant. I suspect he doubts that very statement, still stuck on her obvious hostility.

"Check on her for me?" he asks as if hesitant that I'll refuse.

"Of course." I risk teasing him with another quick peck, and then I head down the hall and cautiously enter Magda's room. She's still dead asleep, her tiny chest rising and falling with every soft breath. The semblance between her and her father doesn't end when they sleep. Though… Something about Magda's button nose makes her expression less tormented than Vadim's. More calculating. Even in slumber, it's like she's still thinking, still planning.

A trait of her mother's? It's a cruel thought that doesn't leave me as I circle the bed to stand in front of her, copying our positions from yesterday in reverse.

"Morning, sweetie," I say until she opens her eyes, frowning at the sight of me.

As if oblivious, I approach her window and pull back her curtains, letting in the fresh sunlight. Then I rummage through her end table until I find the wooden brush and climb onto the bed beside her.

"Which of your outfits shall you wear today?" I ask her, while extending the brush before daring to touch her. It's only when she doesn't cringe out of my reach that I gingerly stroke through her thick curls and smooth them into place. "The turquoise dress? I loved that one."

She doesn't say, choosing to crush It to her chest instead while she endures my brushing. Once I'm finished, I smooth her hair back and enter her closet in search of a headband. Ena—I'm starting to wonder if he may be more of a Saint than a devil—somehow managed to not only unpack every purchase from yesterday, but he arranged them by color and even stocked a glass cabinet with every accessory. I strongly consider extending our truce as I pick out a black velvet headband and turn to find Magda behind me, observing her options with a frown.

In the end, she settles on the turquoise sweater dress with a pair of leather Mary Janes. The resulting look is too darn cute—a little princess, grumpy beneath the weight of her crown.

"I'm hungry," she declares afterward, tugging on my hand. While I marvel at the fact that she's touching me at all, she manages to drag me into the hallway. Downstairs, Vadim had the piano placed near the back of the living room by the window.

The second she spots it, her lips part into a smile she can't contain. "That's for me?" She runs over to the instrument and tentatively strokes the polished surface.

Vadim stands beside her, his expression slack with relief. "Yes," he says, stooping down beside her. "It's yours. I'm still arranging your lessons, but do you want to try it out now?"

She nods, and he lifts her onto the bench and settles down beside her.

I find myself inching closer, riveted as he begins to play a soft, jaunty melody before showing her where to place her fingers to achieve the same sound.

Single Father of the year. My ovaries swoon, but then a part of me resents that statement. *Taken* man of the year, it insists. *Mine.*

Rather than immediately quashing the thought, I get lost in their interactions, skipping ahead to imagine dangerous variations on this very scene. Me seated beside them, for one. Another child with his curls perched at his shoulder. Another. Another…

Snap out of it, Tiffy.

"I'll make us something to eat," I whisper, excusing myself into the kitchen. I rummage through the freezer and attempt to heat up one of Ena's meals. In the end, I get distracted and creep right back to the boundary with the living room.

But they're gone.

Confused, I search the rest of the lower level, finding it deserted. Did they leave? By the time the food is fully heated in the oven, they haven't returned. I fish out the container and divide the food between three plates. Just as I bring them to the table, a tiny figure races from nowhere, snatching for my hand.

"Magda? What's wrong?"

Her eyes are bug-wide, but all she does is tug until I warily follow her through the foyer, out the front door and around to the side of the house. There, at the end of the massive driveway, Vadim is unloading his latest delivery. At least now, his suggestion regarding my present takes on newer significance.

A gorgeous white mare nuzzles at his neck as he strokes her ivory mane.

"Will you welcome your new family members?" he asks, while enduring Zzazza's ruthless affections.

Magda looks on, spellbound, but when a worker guides another animal from the back of a white trailer, she releases me and races over.

"Is he mine?" she exclaims in response to the beautiful chestnut pony prancing at the end of a pink lead rope.

"*She* is," he says, reaching out to pat the small horse. "Her name is Dasha. Will you care for her with all of your heart?"

She nods solemnly and inches forward to touch the pony herself. As the filly sniffs her fingers, she smiles for real this time, completely unaware of the expression. And it's breathtaking.

"And for you." Vadim turns his attention to me, his voice lowering. "It took me a while to find a creature to fit your specifications. Does he suffice? His name is Magnus."

I gasp as a second worker leads another horse from the trailer. Majestic and completely ebony, he's the second most beautiful creature I've ever seen. The first watches me intently, gauging my reaction.

"He's incredible," I whisper, advancing toward the beautiful stallion. He watches me with lipid eyes, snorting as I extend my hand for him to smell. I can't even begin to imagine his cost, and the enormity of the gesture makes me sway.

"Shall we show them to their new home?" Vadim asks, speaking to Magda.

She nods, and together, they and the workers lead the horses down the path toward the stable. I watch them go, sensing the need to hang back this time. I can only pray that Vadim can continue to make progress without me. Still, my thoughts are solely focused on them as I return to the kitchen and continue setting the table. It seems, however, that a pony delivery may appeal to Magda more than chicken nuggets.

Sure enough, after an hour passes, I venture out to find them in the stable. Near the one apparently earmarked for Zzazza, Vadim holds Magda by her waist, high enough for her to brush the mare's ivory mane.

His eyes meet mine from over her head, brimming with a tenderness that warms my heart. I keep my distance until Magda spots me. It's like a switch is flipped, and being caught near Vadim is a slip in her façade she can't maintain. She wiggles from his grasp and backs away, crossing her arms.

"Can I ride my pony whenever I want to?"

Vadim frowns, and as if his hands mourn the loss of contact, he braces both against Zzazza's broad back. "You can with supervision," he says. "Either myself, or Mr. Ena. Horses are beautiful creatures, but they can be dangerous."

She nods and exits Zzazza's stall, extending the distance between them. And I know she has no clue as to the pain that slices through him like a knife. I can't stop myself from approaching his side and covering one of his hands with my own.

"Can I go to my room now?" Magda asks.

"Yes," Vadim rasps. "You can."

"Make sure you grab some lunch first before you head up," I call after her.

The second she's out of earshot, I loop my fingers around his neck, burying my face against his shoulder.

"I'm trying," he says hoarsely. I notice his hands withdraw from Zzazza and curl into fists. "Like hell, I'm trying. But I feel like she's putting up a wall every time I get somewhere."

"Give her time." I stroke my fingers down his front, sensing the muscle lurking beneath the tailored fabric. "I think you're wearing her down."

"I think I'm worn down." He captures my hand, bringing my fingers to his mouth. Our eyes meet as he brushes his lips over my knuckles. He eyes me reverently, like a man lying prone before an altar, desperate for mercy.

It's too darn intense. Awed, I stroke through his hair, driven to give him some kind of reassurance, even against my better judgment. "I'm here with you," I tell him. "I've got your back."

"Just my back?" His sly smirk makes me chuckle and arch into him, wrapping my arms around his neck.

"When do I get *my* day of special deliveries?"

"You've gotten them," he says cryptically, his gaze unreadable. "If you are a good girl, I'll let you unwrap them."

In the absence of prying eyes, I kiss him, groaning as his lips part against mine, and his tongue matches my own thrust for thrust. It feels so good, stealing these moments with him. I shamelessly tease the erection hardening beneath his slacks, but with a groan, he backs away.

"I would have you on the ground," he swears in a tone that makes my toes curl. "Naked beneath me. But—"

"With our luck, Magda would come skipping in," I finish for him. "I understand, Mr. Dad."

Chuckling, he takes my hand, and we return to the house together. Up above, a smattering of dark clouds thickens, promising a storm—the first drops of which start to fall the second we escape into the kitchen.

Magda's plate is missing from the three on the table, and Vadim and I eat in silence. He's brooding again, I suspect, stressing over her reaction to him. A reaction that confuses me the more I think about it. Apart from Maxim, Magda had been…challenging, fitting the term Ms. Anderson used, but when it comes to Vadim, it's as if she deliberately stops herself every time she starts to soften toward him.

Like she's *refusing* to soften toward him. Curious as to why, I place my dirty plate in the sink and head for the stairs. "I'll check on her."

In the hall, a strange haunting tune teases my ears, drifting from Magda's room. That foreign lullaby.

"That's beautiful," I say, finding her slumped on her bed while tossing the hapless It into the air. "Did you learn that at school? What language is that?"

She frowns and lets the bear fall onto the bedspread. "No." Rolling onto her knees, she eyes me warily as if deciding something on the spot. "Will you play with me?" Her defensive tone makes me suspect that it's a request she's used to having denied.

The Robinsons and their ineptitude strike again.

"Of course." I sink onto the bed beside her and kick out my legs. "What will we play?"

"Tea party," she says innocently. "I'll be the queen, and you'll be my loyal subject." She looks me dead in the eye as she adds. "And I'm going to poison you."

"YOU'RE SUPPOSED TO BE DEAD!" Magda shrieks in indignation, her cheeks pink. But her lips twitch, fighting a grin she ultimately succumbs to as I writhe, still in the midst of my "death throes."

"I *am* dead," I tell her mournfully. "Or maybe I'm not? Maybe I'll…" I shoot to my feet and lunge, my fingers drawn, aiming for her armpits. "I'll stage a coup and decide I'm the new queen!"

"N-No!" she exclaims between giggles. "You can't!"

We collapse into a heap, laughing hysterically before I even register how odd that fact is. She's laughing, batting at my hands as I tickle her ruthlessly. It's such a strange, unexpected moment. I can't explain what it feels like.

My shock must match Vadim's as he appears breathless in the doorway, presumably assuming the worst from Magda's high-pitched shrieks. "Are… Is everything okay?" he asks, his hair mussed, his suit ruffled.

Just like that, Magda falls silent and sits upright, her frown firmly in place. "I'm tired," she says.

Sure enough, the sky is darkening. We've spent almost a full day already though it feels like snippets of time.

"I've made dinner," Vadim says softly.

We follow him downstairs, and Magda makes a show of picking at the food on her plate, though in the end, she eats a majority of it. Then she heads back up to her room with Vadim and I hot on her heels.

"Do you want me to brush your hair?" I ask her, unable to resist tugging on the end of one curl as she climbs onto her bed.

She seems to hesitate. Then she shakes her head, her eyes on Vadim. "I'm not a baby."

"Okay." I stand and join Vadim, closing her door behind me.

"We'll be here if you need us," he says.

I can't stand his tormented expression as we head to the bedroom. Literally. The only way to salvage my selfish pain is to close the door, lock it, and boldly strip my dress as he watches. I saunter to him slowly as he backs up toward the bed and sits on the edge, waiting for me.

I straddle him and kiss him as deeply as I craved to in the stable. When he relaxes, I slide my hand down between us and grip the erection throbbing inside his slacks, freeing it. Sinking to my knees, I worship him, taking him into my mouth as deep as I can.

I relish in his groans and the reverent way he strokes my hair even while on the verge of pleasure. I'm so drugged on the moment, that I'm tempted to break my one last rule. Drawing back from him, I breathe against the pulsating head of his cock, watching his piercing jump.

"I could stay…"

Mayday. Too far! I look up in horrified anticipation of how he'll react. Gloriously. Like I said, the most beautiful, magical words in existence. Eyes glowing, he fists his fingers through my hair, guiding me up so that our lips meet.

"Again," he commands against my mouth in a tone radiating authority. "Tell me I can have you."

Too dangerous. Too…wrong. Right? We barely know each other. A few short weeks can't be enough time to breach such a raw, intimate boundary.

Not even if he's begging and desperate, his hollow eyes open, craving affection no matter how small. In this moment, I can't deny him. Not of a lie. Not anything.

"I'll stay," I whisper, brushing my lips over his once. The phrases he demanded I repeat while manacled on the bed return to the forefront of my mind, ample fodder to feed his pleasure. "You can have me. I desire you. You deserve—"

He shifts, trapping me beneath him, and I surrender to his thrusts as he slams inside me, moving in a brutal rhythm. The entire time, I continue to speak to him, my voice rasping, my thoughts scattering.

We collapse breathless and spent beneath the sheets. Before we even fully come down from the high, he's dragging me into his arms.

"Don't regret now," he warns, his tone gruff. "I know I need to earn those words. But hearing them? I will pay any price to hear you say them again."

"No price," I insist tiredly. "Just honesty." Something that's been on my mind all day chooses now—of all times —to resurface. "Why did you leave her, really? What made you think you couldn't take care of her?"

Just from how he interacts with her, his nurturing instinct is wholly intact. Something deeper must have shaken his confidence. A hint as to what shapes his expression now— raw, unbearable pain.

"My real surname isn't Gorgoshev," he admits—an unsurprising admission given his accent. "My mother never gave me one, and my father denied me his… I was worthless, a bastard unworthy of belonging to any family. I never envisioned starting one of my own."

I brace my hand over his forearm, my throat tight. No man should sound so depreciating—especially not him. So beautiful, so intelligent. Can't he see that?

No, I suspect, reading his stricken gaze. He can't. He's blind to that aspect of himself entirely.

"Back when… In my captivity," he says hoarsely, "we had no say over our clients, mind you. I'll let you interpret that statement as you may. Reading people became a strict criterion for survival. I was adept at it. Until one day, a man came before me who wasn't like the others. He had been promised a luxurious getaway on my employer's estate—which in reality was a setup to frame him, allowing my employer to use his presence there as blackmail. This man was a professor, and a researcher in a prominent biotechnical company. His knowledge and skillset made him a tempting target for those in the realm of garnering black-market information. In pharmaceuticals. Genetics. Biotechnology. You'd be surprised the price such knowledge can fetch."

I listen to him in silence, my heart throbbing at his clinical, detached tone. He almost sounds like he's reading from a script, not recalling his own past in chilling detail.

"The man's name was Hiram Gorgoshev," he says. "And rather than utilize his power to abuse me, he saw through my act. We were well trained, you see, expected to lie to our clients, creating the façade that we were willing participants rather than the victims we were. Slave owners, you see, cringe in abject horror when faced with their victim's chains—but as long as they're hidden out of sight, they can sleep at night." Real emotion colors his tone—disgust. Rage. Hatred so searing, I flinch as if burned.

Reflexively, he grips me tighter, preventing me from pulling away, even if I wanted to.

"Hiram *saw* me," he says. "He spent his time with me reciting the laws of physics rather than refuse outright and risk having me beaten. He sacrificed his own leverage just to ensure that. I didn't understand the risk he took back then. I had no idea…" A rare, broken smile shapes his lips for a fleeting moment. "He even offered to help me escape —but I couldn't. Not then."

My brain mulls obsessively over his potential reasons why. For Irina?

"When he finally did leave, he slipped a piece of paper into my hand with an address on it," he explains. "But it wasn't until a year later that I finally gained my freedom."

"And you went there?" I ask, craning my neck to better see his face.

He nods. "I wound up before a modest estate in Germany, wearing rags, my mental state in ruins. I think at that point, Ena had to force-feed me bits of bread during the trip, or I would have died from starvation by then. When Hiram saw me, shivering on his doorstep, he brought me into his garden. Gave me a cup of tea. He offered his home to me so that I could rest… And I don't think I left once for six whole months." A muscle in his jaw twitches, and he strokes the flesh with the tips of his fingers. "And that entire time, he kept me fed. Clothed. He let me heal my fractured psyche, and when I was ready to reenter society, he gave me his name. More than that. He used his connections to get me a world-class education more comprehensive than what the children of some dignitaries are privy to. He guided me to a prominent position in his own company, Eingel Industries, which was a fledging, but promising, venture. When the time came, he ceded control to me, and even when my wealth far surpassed his, never did he ever ask me for anything. Not once. I think… He was the closest thing I've ever had to a father." He sounds confused, even as he says it. As though it's a realization he's only *just* come to. "He was the one who helped me navigate Magdalene's sudden appearance," he adds. "Nothing ever caught him off-guard, not even her existence. He encouraged me to gain custody of her, in fact. When she was sick, he was preparing to come on the next flight from Munich just to see her. That bear she has? That came from him. His idea anyway. But in the middle of her illness, he died suddenly of a heart attack, and I couldn't even leave her side to go mourn him."

"That's why you dedicated the garden, the one at your building," I say, my eyes widening as everything clicks into place. "For him. It's your way of saying goodbye… I'm so sorry."

"Maybe it worked out for the best." He shrugs. "I wasn't ready then."

But for some reason, I doubt that he truly believes that. Maybe it's just easier for him to reconcile it.

But the reminder of his vigil over her bedside triggers a thought I can't seem to suppress. "When Magda was sick… Did you ever sing to her?"

He frowns, lowering his mouth to my forehead. "That is a strange question to ask after sex."

I have to croak out a laugh at that. "I'm serious. Humor me. Did you?"

He purses his lips, thinking it over. Then he nods. "Yes. I think I sang to her. Some silly song about a group of hens. It was the only thing to come to mind—"

"Was it in French?" When he raises an eyebrow, I add, "Sing it to me?"

He sighs, but slowly, his voice forms the words of a lilting melody. He sounds rougher, and reluctant, but I can barely smother the shock dawning on me like a blow. It's the same song.

"Satisfied?" Vadim asks playfully when he finishes. "Though I will admit that in terms of ways you might seek to exploit my devotion, forcing my humiliation via song was fairly low on my list."

"You said she was on a ventilator," I say, referring to Magda. "But was she awake at all? Is there any way she could have heard you?"

His expression darkens. "No. She was in a medically induced coma. The moment she regained consciousness, I left."

"But you were there for days," I point out.

He nods. "Over a week. Day and night. She wasn't placed with a family then, so I could pull the right strings to have access. Why are you asking this?"

I bite my lip, torn between telling him my suspicion or staying silent. It's a stretch, yes. But so is the fact that a seven-year-old who's only grown up in America could know the same obscure French melody about "a group of hens" sung perfectly in tune to his halting rendition. Though…

As much as it stings to admit, she could have learned the song from anywhere.

"What made you sing that to her?" I ask him. "Why *that* song?"

His eyes go distant, and I fear I might have gone too far. Softly, he says, "My mother used to sing it to me. I was so young… I have no idea how I've remembered it. As for why? I don't know. What else could I do? I read to her, sang to her, recited the laws of physics as Hiram did for me… And yet I couldn't even face her the moment she got well. I ran. I left her. What good is a fucking song now?"

He releases me and rolls onto his side with his back to me. "Goodnight."

I nestle into him, melding against his rigid contour even as he stiffens against me. I stroke my fingers down his forearm, finding his hand and capturing it. Then I settle my mouth against the crook of his neck and inhale him deeply.

"I think it meant more to her than you know," I tell him. "Your presence meant more to her. I think that you don't need to spend thousands on ponies or pianos to buy her affection. You have it. But she's as stubborn as you are. Trust that she'll come around. I think you're connected to her, more than you know. She feels it too."

In fact, I suspect that Magda may know far more than she's led him to believe...

If he feels the same, he doesn't admit as much out loud. Maybe it's easier for him to ignore the small, subtle signs?

I let him have this one victory and remain silent. God knows he's earned it.

I DON'T KNOW what startles me awake. Just that I wind up blinking through the darkness as Vadim stirs beside me.

"Did you hear that?" he asks, his voice sharp with concern.

It's enough to make me shrug off exhaustion entirely and sit upright. Together, we strain through the silence until…

"Magda!" He lunges from the bed, stopping only to grab a pair of boxers before peeling into the hall. I follow him, snatching a robe for myself. The further I go, the more apparent the sound becomes—sobbing.

Magda's. She's huddled beneath her blankets, her face buried in the crook of her arm.

"*Ma chérie*," Vadim murmurs, switching on her light. He crosses to the bed and crouches down, stroking her hair until she faces him. "*Qu'est-ce qui ne va pas*? What's wrong?"

Redness paints Magda's cheeks, and I can almost see the battle within herself. To recoil from him even as a part of her is lulled by his soothing tone. There's no denying his concern. No ignoring the fact that he would do anything in this moment to help. She can't resist.

"It," she says, though she looks at me as she does so. "I lost him. I think he's out there." She points to the window where a flash of lightning illuminates the landscape, making her flinch.

"Is that all?" Vadim stands. "Stay with her," he tells me as he enters the hall.

Sighing, I sit on the bed beside her. She lets me pet her hair, and I try not to notice as she inches closer to my side. It might break the spell. Together we wait as the storm rages beyond the window until finally, heavy footsteps ascend the steps, and a soaking wet Vadim reappears.

"Is this what you were looking for?" he asks, brandishing a relatively dry It by one of his floppy arms.

Magda sniffs and reaches for him, swiping away any lingering tears with the back of her hand. She cradles the bear to her chest, and Vadim's expression softens in a way I've never seen. Hopeful.

At least until she catches him staring and flings the bear violently across the room.

"I don't want him anymore." She burrows beneath the blankets, drawing them over her head. "Can you get out, please?"

"Yes…" Vadim retreats, his expression stricken.

I remain behind just long enough to switch off the light, but as I close the door behind me, I notice a tiny figure crawl from the bed and dart across the room for a small object that she crushes to her chest.

These two will be the death of me.

When I reenter the bedroom, Vadim is sitting on the edge of the bed, his face in his hands. Eyeing me through his fingers, he exhales an exhausted chuckle. "What was that about her softening to me?"

I sigh in sympathy and join him, leaning against his shoulder. "I need to ask you another seemingly pointless question."

He grunts. "Oh?"

"How did you explain the bear?" It's a weird question on the surface, but not so weird when her attitude toward him is taken into context. I know firsthand that she has other stuffed animals she has yet to mutilate. But that one she vandalized. *That* one she carries with her everywhere. The only one she sleeps with at night and panics if she's without.

"I'm sure they told her it was donated by a nurse," he says offhandedly.

But what if she already knew that it hadn't been? What if that one bear mattered to her so much because she knew its original source. And through that very same bear, she loved tormenting said source.

"We should get some sleep." I crawl up the mattress and slip beneath the covers. "I need you well rested for tomorrow."

"Tomorrow?" Vadim wonders as he follows me, snatching me into his arms.

"Yes," I say, arching into his touch. "Magda needs some toys. You're taking us shopping."

Put a shopaholic and a shopper-lite into any Boutique in the fashion district with an unlimited credit card, and chaos will ensue. Put a man desperate to buy his daughter's affections into a toy store—a man with no concept of money or boundaries—and watch as they fall into a silent power struggle that I'll be lucky to survive without getting slung across a cash register myself.

By the time Magda makes her way toward the store's extensive doll section, I feel compelled to put my foot down.

"She doesn't need one of every doll, Vadim," I scold.

Following dutifully in her wake, he eyes me the way I figure a kicked puppy might, and I march forward, prepared to put him out of his misery.

"Magda." I crouch down beside her and meet her calculating gaze. She's wearing a burgundy ensemble that enhances her eyes to an almost painful degree. With her curls held at bay by a matching headband, she looks every bit the little princess she must think she is. The only flaw in the façade is that battered, deflated teddy bear clutched to her chest. "I want you to get something you really want. Something you'll play with every day."

She frowns, mulling over the request. But as I hoped, she seems to take it as a challenge rather than a demand.

"That one." She points to a particular doll high up on a shelf. Behind me, I sense Vadim already scrambling to find a salesclerk to retrieve it. It's one of those porcelain frilly dolls decorated in an ivory Victorian-style costume with a straw bonnet and huge reddish curls.

Vadim pays for it on the spot and removes it from the box, handing it to her. I watch in awe as her lips part into one of those rare, incredible grins. Meeting my gaze, she says sweetly, "I'm going to call her *Biphany*." She pats the doll's head lovingly, shoving her bonnet down her face in the process. "She's an orphan, poisoned by the queen. And everyone hates her."

"Magda…" Vadim sounds horrified.

I, however, raise an eyebrow. "Is that the best you can do when it comes to a backstory?" I feign a yawn and rise to my full height. "Boring. I bet you can come up with something better."

She pouts, the gears in her brain ever whirling.

When we finally leave the store—with about only half of it in tow—Vadim takes us out for lunch, where Magda makes a show of refusing anything from the menu he suggests to her. In the end, she winds up drinking only a milkshake, and pointedly ignores him for the rest of the trip.

It's taking its toll. His usual enduring patience wears thin. His eyes turn hollow and distant. When we return to the house, he lingers in the garage to carry the bags while Magda marches inside, It slung under one arm and Biphany under the other.

I follow her into the foyer and watch her dump her toys on the lid of the piano before climbing onto the bench.

"Why are you needling him?" I do my best to sound as nonjudgmental as possible. I'm not angry with her. Just curious.

She taps a piano key, letting the note play out. "Because," she says, just as heavy footsteps approach from the direction of the garage. Her head cocked, she whirls around and meets my gaze directly. "I hate him."

A heavy thud draws my attention to the corner of the foyer, where Vadim stands amid a pile of fallen shopping bags. As I watch, his wall comes up too quickly to stop. His eyes darken, his expression rigid. Without a word, he gathers up the bags and carries them upstairs.

I watch him, my heart aching. I almost start after him, but tiny arms go around my waist, keeping me in place.

"I like *you*," Magda says, her face in my hip. "You don't lie like other grown-ups." She draws back and snatches my hand, tugging me after her. "Can we go see my pony?"

"Okay." I follow her, my heart in my throat. We venture out to the stable and spend time brushing down Zzazza and the other horses under the watchful eye of Ena, who appears from nowhere to stare from the shadows—on his master's orders, I suspect.

"Can I ride?" Magda asks as we approach Dasha's stall.

"You could ask Mr. Vadim to teach you?" I suggest, hopefully.

She gives me a look that sums up her thoughts even before she utters a terse, "Never mind."

We settle for cooing over Dasha from afar. When we return to the house, an incredible smell reaches my nostrils the second we step inside.

"Don't tell me you've decided to add chef to your list of accomplishments," I exclaim in response to the sight of Vadim standing before the counter amid a variety of vegetables and ingredients in various states of preparation.

"Have a seat," he says without turning around. "Name your drink preferences, both of you."

"Wine for me," I blurt, alarmed as he turns around, his expression blank. Is he still hurt by Magda's hostility? *Yes.* I can see the hurt coloring his irises, but he's smothering that pain for her sake.

Turning his attention to the tiny figure climbing onto a stool beside me, he tentatively asks, "And for you?"

She frowns. "Orange juice."

"As you wish." After fulfilling our drink orders, he continues to cook, filling the room with incredible smells, while I attempt to prod what little information I can from Magda.

"What do you like to do with your friends?" I ask in between fortifying sips of wine.

She folds her hands with It perched on one side of her, and Biphany on the other.

"I don't have friends," she says. Her surly tone could betray the words as yet another lie meant to provoke, but her eyes tell a different story. A hint of vulnerability creeps through that unnerving blue and something in my heart throbs, rubbed raw. "I don't *need* friends," she adds firmly, rephrasing it.

"What about hobbies?" I ask. "Do you have any of those? Do you like to read? Play games?"

She strokes her chin and nods with sudden seriousness. "I like to plan world domination." *Damn.* She utters that declaration without even a hint of mocking inflection.

"Oh, goody!" Feigning nonchalance, I clap my hands together. "Then, to get started on your merry way, you need to beat me at the one game perfect for world domination training."

She eyes me skeptically. "What game?"

I wink and rise from the table to approach the lone figure slipping in through the glass door leading out to the terrace. Ena eyes me the way I figure one might either a hungry lion advancing toward them or a diseased rodent.

Writing it off for the greater good, I lean near his ear and make one whispered request.

I can't tell from his surly expression just how he processes it. Finally, he nods. "I be back."

I watch him scuttle off, utterly pleased with myself. I'm even more pleased by the results Vadim comes up with when he finally leaves the kitchen to adorn the dining table with platters of steaming, amazing looking food.

"Fresh vegetables, salad, and homemade garden burgers," he declares, indicating each platter with a wave of his hand. "Let's eat."

One bite, and I groan in appreciation. "This tastes incredible."

Even Magda seems impressed enough to endure his physical nearness as she samples a burger with delicate bites. By the time we finish the meal, and Vadim has cleared the table, Ena arrives as if on cue, brandishing my sole request.

Barely suppressing a grin, I rise to my feet and accept what turns out to be a rectangular board game infamous among my family's gatherings.

"You aim for world domination?" I ask Magda. "Let's see what you've got, kid. Try your hand at the ultimate decider."

I slam the game board onto the table as Magda and Vadim share puzzled looks.

"Monopoly?" He reads from the gameboard lid as though he's never played.

And I'm alarmed to realize that he might not have. Neither of them may have.

"You poor innocent fools," I tell them mournfully. "Prepare to have your butts kicked by the real estate queen."

CHAPTER FOURTEEN

An hour later, I realize that, though untested in the ways of Monopoly they may be, both Vadim and Magda are fearsome opponents. I wind up going bankrupt early on, and the game quickly shapes up to be a brutal war between their two growing fictional conglomerates.

"I think you're a sore loser," Vadim remarks in response to my pouting. In the same breath, he completes his purchase of yet another block of hotels, extending the reach of his empire.

"Am not," I hiss in indignation while fulfilling my new role as banker. "I'm just hoping that Magda kicks your butt and keeps your ego firmly in check."

As if to rise to the challenge, Magda promptly proceeds to buy out an entire strip. I'm so impressed I ruffle her curls and beam at Vadim. "Long may she reign! Can you defeat the queen?"

What unfolds next is a long, hard-fought battle, but in the end, Vadim concedes with a groan while I shower Magda in a flurry of paper money. Her tiny lips twitch, resisting a smile that gradually unfurls despite her best attempts to squash it. And her pride only seems to grow as Vadim stands and bows to her grandly.

"Your majesty." He extends his hand to her. After a brief moment of hesitation, she places her small fingers over his, allowing him to help her stand on her chair while we continue to shower her with accolades.

"What do you wish to claim as your prize?" Vadim asks her, his eyes gleaming.

Magda doesn't seem to need even a second to think it over. "Can you teach me to ride my pony tomorrow?"

If possible, Vadim's eyes glow, brimming with hope. "As you wish."

It's a moment so real, so very genuine. I don't think my heart can contain it, and I start to play that dangerous game. Wishing. For more. For him. Them. This.

Stop it, Tiffy.

My only hope is that something happens to shatter this moment before it becomes too potent to ignore. But in a cruel twist of fate—coming in the form of advancing footsteps—I get my wish tenfold.

Vadim reacts first, his expression darkening as I turn to find Ena marching into the kitchen with a taller figure in tow.

"Mr. Hood," he announces gruffly. "He come. Already cleared."

Apparently, Milton doesn't require the same security reserved for Maxim. His expression wary, the British man steps forward, dressed in a gunmetal-gray suit and a blood-red tie. His dark eyes go directly to Magda, widening as he takes her in.

But she pales and nearly falls off the chair in her scramble to get down. She winds up jumping, but rather than onto the floor, she flings herself at Vadim, who catches her seemingly by instinct, holding her close.

She copies the same stance she took in the presence of Maxim—her face buried against his shoulder, her knuckles white as she grips him tightly.

But this time, Vadim strokes her back with a sigh. "It's okay, *ma chérie*. This is…Uncle Milton." His voice conveys nothing but soothing warmth though his eyes tell a different tale. He looks like a man who came close to claiming a pile of gold, only to have it slip through his grasp at the last minute. And he eyes Milton as though he's the force that made said fortune vanish.

Unperturbed, the other man boldly steps forward. Almost before my eyes, it's as though he transforms, softening the harder, angular stance of his rigid posture for a softer, friendly appearance. Even I'm fooled, almost forgetting the imposing figure he so regularly presents as. Smiling warmly, he says, "You must be Magdalene. I'm a friend of your… Mr. Vadim's."

Sensing the danger has passed, Magda squirms from Vadim's arms and scrambles away from him, her cheeks pink. She eyes Milton warily but doesn't move to take the hand he extends her way.

Without missing a beat, he uses the same hand to reach into the breast pocket of his suit jacket and withdraws an enormous lollipop even the surliest child couldn't resist. Case and point, Magda steps forward, and he crouches on one knee and presents his offering to her.

"Sugar-free, of course," Milton declares, glancing at Vadim.

Magda takes it and eagerly rips off the wrapping, before taking a tentative lick. Her eyes practically light up even as she takes a step back from him. I watch in awe as she reaches out with her free hand, finding Vadim's pantleg. Their expressions mirror each other's for a split second—hers irritated by her seemingly overwhelming need to cling to him, while he seems overwhelmed all at once.

Rising to his feet, Milton maintains his polite, charming smile, but when his eyes meet Vadim's, something unspoken flashes between them. It's like I can sense the atmosphere shift in an instant.

"It was very nice to meet you, Magdalene," Milton says. "But right now, I'd like to borrow Vadim for a minute."

Vadim glances at Magda, and I can see the internal struggle as he wrestles with leaving her. But then he cuts his gaze to the other man. Again, some understanding flashes between them and his jaw clenches. Sighing, he captures the hand Magdalene has on his pant leg, and I can tell that nothing in the world pains him more than having to ease her away.

"I'll be back," he swears, stepping forward. "And I will bring you a reward fit for a conquering queen."

Whether the promise mollifies Magda or not, I can't tell. She's utterly stoic, watching as the two men head toward the study. I skip toward her, and I can't resist tugging on a dark curl even though she wrinkles her nose and turns away.

"Help me clean up, oh majesty?" I ask her before eyeing the fortune of fake money scattered over the floor.

She eyes me skeptically, crossing her arms. "Queens don't clean up."

"Hmm." I stroke my chin and nod. "Not normally. But they do if the treasury is at stake and a thief is on the loose, threatening their fiscal hold on the populous!"

I stoop for a fistful of money. Alarmed, Magda drops to her knees and attempts to grab as many bills as she can before I snatch them first. Within minutes, we've gathered up every last bit.

"I win," Magda declares as she places her haul back into the box.

I can't resist tugging on another curl though this time she doesn't seem to resist. "You did! Awesome job…"

I trail off, distracted by a sudden noise coming from the hall near the study. Angry, thumping, brutal noise. Smiling wider for Magda's benefit, I playfully tap the bridge of her nose with my finger. "Why don't you figure out how to set up for a second round, oh majesty? I'm going to go grab a pen so we can keep score."

I use that harmless lie as my excuse for tiptoeing down the hall. Not the urge to spy or eavesdrop. I need a pen. A pen that ceases to matter completely the second I catch Vadim's grated rasp.

"…and you still seem to hold out hope that we will reconcile?" he laughs. "I don't think so. Not after this."

"You did provoke him," Milton replies, his tone level. "You know how he can get. Like a dog with a bloody bone. Give him time to cool down."

"Time?" Vadim echoes coldly. "Don't play coy, Milton. You aren't a gossip, and you wouldn't be telling me of his little ultimatum if you didn't believe he was serious in this threat. What was it again? 'I leave within three days, or he will take *measures*.'" He laughs in that icy, beautiful way that resembles how I figure a fallen angel might. One seriously considering joining the ranks of Lucifer. "And you asked me why he will never see Magdalene?"

"Like I said, give him time to cool down," Milton insists. "Besides, he'll be gone for a few days. He's on his way to Moscow. Apparently, *someone* disrupted a supply chain of munitions he had stored there. Damn near took out an entire arm of his operation overnight. You wouldn't know anything about that, would you?"

Munitions? Supply chain? Something at the back of my brain tingles, filing away those terms for later. They sound far more sinister than the typical business venture, that's for damn sure.

"Would you be surprised if I did?" Vadim asks dryly. Gathering up the nerve, I creep forward enough to peek into the office through the cracked door. He's leaning over his desk, his eyes downcast.

Milton must be standing before him, his posture rigid. "No. Especially not after you accused him of disrupting your own business interests there—an accusation he denied, by the way. And you know he wouldn't shy away from claiming ownership if he had."

"Or maybe you've just grown too damn trusting," Vadim counters with a harsh laugh. "Would you believe me if I denied it? Perhaps a part of me gets some sick pleasure out of making little Maxi squirm?"

I shiver at the coldness in his tone. But just as quickly, his posture seems to slump, his body deflated.

"I've humored Maxim's hostility far longer than I should have," he says softly. "But I am telling you now, Milton. If he dares to do anything, I won't be so forgiving this time."

"He's all bluster," Milton says. "Between the shit going on in Russia and the shock of discovering your little secret, you might want to cut the man some slack. I will admit that I was skeptical at first myself. That you were planning one of your little mind games to drive the man insane. But, damn… She looks just like you." His voice deepens, conveying the depth of his awe.

"Which is why…" Vadim sighs. "Maxim can harbor his hatred toward me all he likes, but I will *never* let him hurt her—"

"And I would?" Milton counters, stepping forward to brace his hands over the desk. "Threatening children isn't Maxim's style, you know this. But I will suggest you consider moving anyway. Why provoke him further?"

"Why?" Vadim shakes his head, chuckling to himself. "You always take his side. I've ceded this city to Maxim for ten years. I've dwelt in the shadows and let him play king. Not anymore. I said it once, and I will say it again —I'm taking what I want. For myself and Magdalene. Her desire is my only concern, so if he wants to get in my way, let him try."

"Or," Milton says softly, "you two could finally put aside your petty feud and play happy families. Especially if you both are so intent on starting your own."

"Don't compare me to him." Vadim stands and turns his attention to the door just as I manage to scuttle away.

I find Magda seated at the dining table with a neatly arranged and reset monopoly board before her and a look of utter ferocity on her face.

"Ready for round two?" I ask, joining her with a forced grin.

She kicks my ass. In the end, I have to concede with shreds of my pride left intact.

"You are well on your way to world domination," I tell her as we clean up the game for good. "But I'm still the adult, and I will always have one superpower over you, even when you rule the world."

She raises an eyebrow. "What's that?"

"Bedtime."

I follow her upstairs and into her room, where I enter her closet. "I'll pick out your pajamas while you take your bath, okay?"

Surprisingly, she doesn't argue. Minutes later, she's dripping wet and freshly dressed in a pair of ivory silk pajamas that make her resemble a dark-haired variation of the porcelain doll tucked under her arm.

"Can I brush your hair?" I ask, moving toward her end table as I speak.

After a moment's hesitation, she nods and climbs beneath the covers while I sit beside her and tackle those gorgeous curls. This time, I deliberately ignore that warning voice telling me to back away. That I shouldn't be enjoying this.

Smoothing my fingers through her hair shouldn't feel this natural, neither should I take pride in how she relaxes against me.

I'm not her mother. It's wrong.

"I thought you might be asleep…"

I look over to find Vadim hovering in the doorway. His eyebrow raises as he spots me beside Magda, and I smooth one last curl into place before backing away. She's already slumped against the pillow, her eyes drifting shut. When she spots what Vadim holds in his hands, however, she bolts upright.

"I thought you might need this if you are to ride your pony tomorrow," he says, stepping forward to place a large, white box on the bed. It's wrapped neatly with a turquoise ribbon that Magda rips off before lifting the lid.

Her mouth drops open, and I can't smother a grin as she gingerly withdraws a sheet of tissue paper to reveal a pair of tan jodhpurs, a white riding blouse, and an ebony jacket, complete with a riding helmet.

"They're beautiful," I murmur as Magda runs her fingers over the material.

Though she doesn't admit it out loud, I can guess from her wide-eyed expression that she feels the same.

"I'll let you get some sleep," Vadim says, seemingly not expecting much more gratitude from her than that. "Goodnight."

My heart feels swollen as he leaves. I slip from the bed and make the mistake of looking back. Magda's already slumping sideways, her eyes falling shut even as she clutches the sleeve of her new jacket. I lift the box from her bed and set it aside before gently easing her beneath the blankets. I tell myself that the act is purely out of necessity—but brushing a stray curl behind her ear isn't.

Neither is making sure that both Biphany and It are within her reach before turning off the light and finally leaving her room.

The panic I feel is ten times stronger than the emotions I try to resist when it comes to Vadim. I've had my heart stomped on by a man before. As much as it stings, I can survive that pain again. But I don't think there's a cure for loving a child that isn't mine.

Don't do this to yourself, Tiffy.

I enter the master suite and find Vadim sitting on the bed as if waiting for me. He's removed his suit jacket, and the topmost buttons of his dress shirt are undone, revealing a tempting sliver of his chest. It's a fitting distraction from budding emotional turmoil. After locking the door behind me, I eagerly start to strip my dress.

"Wait." He stands and crosses to me. I've rarely seen him so tired, his lips pursed, eyes unreadable. Alarmed, I let my hands fall from the skirt of my dress as he captures each one, stroking the knuckles. "You are…incredible," he tells me.

But this confession feels different from his prior attempts at practicing praise. His voice reaches down into some secretive, innermost part of me, making it bloom despite myself. Swell. I feel my cheeks catch fire, my throat tightening. The feeling has nothing to do with selfish pride or gratitude—it's far simpler than that. It's a desperation I've been struggling to ignore. A desperation to feel useful to him. To help him. To make him feel safe enough to keep his wall down around me, even as I mutter something about needing to leave. Boundaries.

"*You* are incredible," I tell him, inching closer. I bury my nose into the crook of his shoulder, inhaling him as his arms encircle me, cradling me to his lean frame. I've never felt so safe before.

And so very exposed.

A FLURRY of commotion has me blinking my eyes open to a darkened room, my heart racing. Shadows flicker along the walls, cast by a quickly moving figure darting from the closet. Before the panic can crest, I recognize that surly frown, barely visible through the dark.

"Vadim?" My voice croaks, heavy with sleep. "What's going on?"

"Go back to sleep." I stiffen at the steel in his tone. He marches back into the closet, and I hear hangers clanging together. The clock on his nightstand reads that it's barely six a.m.

"You're leaving?" I murmur as he stumbles back into the room, wrenching on a pair of loafers.

His gaze cuts up to mine, constricted with visible torment. "I… I need to attend to something. Get some sleep—" He crosses to me, brushing his lips over my cheek in a hasty kiss. "I'll be back later today. If you need anything, I'll have Ena stay close by."

His wary grin struggles to convey a calmness that his stiff posture contradicts. Once he wrestles on his suit jacket and loops a tie into place, he practically races from the room.

Alone, I slump against the pillows, but it's impossible to fall back asleep. Eventually, I slip into a robe and head downstairs in a futile search for coffee. Vadim, it seems, is a tea man. After heating up a kettle on the stove, I make myself a cup of some fancy French blend I can't even begin to pronounce. Then I sit at the dining room table and watch the sunrise sluggishly over the water, my thoughts in turmoil.

To distract from his absence—and all the many potential causes for it—I scan the view beyond the window glass, pleasantly surprised.

Vadim's been making small improvements to the property day by day, it seems. The playground is nearly done, lacking only a completed swing set. Near the water, I can see that the docks now sport two small rowboats that instantly make me imagine lazy days on the water beside him, Magda in tow.

A dangerous fantasy to indulge for sure. One that seems more impossible to attain when tiny footsteps allude to the figure who prances into the kitchen.

The second I see Magda decked out in her riding outfit, my heart breaks. I can barely muster up the strength to meet her gaze, especially as her lips part into a rare, fleeting grin.

"Can we ride my pony now?" she asks. Her eyes excitedly scan the kitchen, presumably for Vadim. And my heart splinters all over again for them both.

"He had to go away on business, honey," I say thickly. "I'm sorry."

As if she inherited his internal emotional switch, her expression falls and hardens in a way that triggers a horrible sense of *déjà vu*. Just like Vadim, she knows how to erect a wall in a heartbeat, closing herself off.

"He'll take you as soon as he comes back," I insist, rising to my feet. "I promise."

But he won't be back anytime soon, I suspect—though I don't have the heart to say it out loud. I saw it in his face. The pain of being away from her, even for a short amount of time. Whatever drew him away, might keep him all day again.

And something tells me that Magda knows that as well as I do. She spins on her heel, racing from the kitchen.

"Honey, wait!" I follow her up the stairs, wincing as the door slams in my face. I test the handle, finding it unlocked, but when I finally push the door open, she's lying face down on her bed. Her shoulders shake though she's overall silent. Her pale skin reddens, and I imagine her biting her lip as hard as she can to keep any noise inside.

"I'm so sorry, honey." I sit on the edge of the bed and tentatively place my hand on her back. "I know you're disappointed—"

"I'm not!" She wrenches away from me and snatches the helmet off her head, throwing it across the room. Then she glares at me, her expression so fierce I suck in a breath.

Until, she breaks. Before my eyes, she transforms from a mini, ice-cold Vadim into a seven-year-old girl whose hopes have been dashed. Tears spill from her eyes, and I can't stop myself from snatching her into my arms. Boundaries be damned, I hold her even as she squirms until finally, she succumbs, sobbing openly against my shoulder.

"I know, honey. I know…" Helpless, I can only smooth my fingers down her back, letting her cry. A part of me suspects that this emotion has nothing to do with her pony and everything to do with something deeper. Something that makes her melt into my embrace, too exhausted to fight. I rock her, speaking reassurances that I doubt she even hears.

Eventually, I coax her into pulling back enough for me to see her face.

"How about we go pet your pony?" I suggest, wiping away some of her tears.

Her eyes blaze. "No!" She lunges from the bed, storming into a corner, her arms crossed.

"Okay." Sighing, I start to follow her only to change tact and enter her closet. "Let's go for a walk instead, hmm?" I take my time picking out the clothing I suspect were her favorites from our shopping trip. The red dress. The black faux fur stole. It doesn't matter if they're too extravagant, I help her dress in them as she allows me to stiffly manipulate her limbs, her expression blank.

I gingerly brush her hair and arrange her curls behind a red headband. Then I take her hand and lead her downstairs for a quick snack before we step out onto the terrace. It's a relatively beautiful day, though the sun is hiding behind a screen of overcast. Still, it's warm enough out, and a gentle breeze enhances the natural beauty of the property.

"Do you want to swim?" I ask, pointing to the pool.

Magda shakes her head, her wall still in place. She doesn't even show interest when I take her past the partially done playground and suggest she try out the jungle gym. It's only when we near the water's rocky edge—where a grunting Ena is adjusting the docked rowboats—that any semblance of curiosity shapes her otherwise flat expression.

Like a shark sensing blood, I latch onto the potential diversion. "Would you like to see if we can go out onto the water?"

After a second, she nods, and I nearly drag her over to Ena.

Forcing what I hope passes for a charming smile, I try to meet his gaze as he wrestles with a length of rope, securing it to a post on the dock.

"Mr. Vadim gone," he says gruffly before I can say a word. "All day."

"Do you think you could take us out?" I ask. I have to physically stop myself from batting my eyelashes in the hopes of cajoling a yes.

His lips part to deliver what I suspect is an automatic no. But then he makes the mistake of looking at Magda and something in his surly expression cracks.

"Okay." He sets his rope aside and lumbers into the boathouse, returning with two orange life vests. "You put on." He shoves the preserver at me but stoops into a crouch and takes his time assisting Magda. She stiffens, but gradually submits to his surprisingly gentle instruction.

The moment we're sufficiently dressed, Ena steps into one of the boats and helps us down from the dock. Taking up both oars, he sets us off while I settle in beside Magda.

That logical, nagging part of my brain picks up again, warning me against letting her sit too close—I don't move. But I should pull away when she nestles into me, shivering against the cooler air over the water. I shift an inch, putting space between us only to put my arm around her a heartbeat later. That little act of rebellion is the gateway drug to crossing even more boundaries. I smooth back her fluttering curls and stroke away one of the final tears as her expression brightens.

Even Ena seems to fall under her spell, and he keeps his pace steady, steering farther out into the bay. Eventually, her blank mask cracks, revealing genuine excitement beneath as she scans the shores and gentle roving waves.

She sits forward so suddenly the boat jolts beneath us. "Look!" She points to a spot along the left-hand beach. There, up on a ridge, appears a little white pony with a flowing mane. Riding him is a small girl with blond hair streaming from an ebony riding helmet. Spotting us, she waves, and to my surprise, Magda offers up a tentative one in return.

"It looks like you might have a friend to play with after all," I blurt. Only to feel the color drain from my face as a woman appears beside the girl, holding the pony's reins. She's slender, with long brunette hair, but even from this distance, I recognize her instantly.

Maxim's fiancée.

Ena too must sense the property he's unintentionally strayed into. Grunting with the effort, he immediately begins to turn the boat around.

"Can I play with her?" Magda tugs on my arm, and I can tell from her surly expression that she doesn't like to beg. Because that's what she's doing—begging. "Huh? Do you know where she lives? I bet I can find it!" She starts counting on her fingers, her lips moving wordlessly.

"Oh, honey…" I tuck a curl behind her ear, wrestling with indecision. In the end, my feelings match Ena's. "Let's go get some lunch, huh?"

Magda's frown returns, lasting the entire trip back to the house. When we enter the kitchen, I do my best to feign supreme excitement in finding something to eat amongst Ena's prepared meals. "How about some pizza, hmm?"

I fish out the meal and pop it in the oven while she watches me from the counter.

"Can I go wait upstairs until it's ready?" she asks.

I nod, relieved to leave the topic of our possible neighbors behind. "Go ahead. I'll get you when it's ready."

She scampers off while I set the table and fish some fresh orange juice from the fridge. Ena must stock it regularly, maintaining a methodical sense of order with just a few bare things he needs to keep Vadim, and now Magdalene, alive. It's such a contrast from my old fridge in the home I shared with Jim, when I had it stuffed with failed attempts at baking and cooking. All because he insisted I play the role of the perfect housewife.

He'd scoff in disgust if I ever had the nerve to serve him a previously frozen meal. The thought makes me frown. It's been at least a few days since I've thought of him. Why now? In an effort to distract myself, I rearrange one of the cupboards, moving around Vadim's already neatly composed collection of glass dishes. Then I grab the food from the oven and head upstairs to get Magda.

"Come and eat, it smells divine…" I push open her door only to find her room empty. So is her bathroom and the closet, and she isn't in the hallway. "Magda?" I check the master bedroom but don't find her there either. Returning downstairs, I scan the kitchen and the living room only to come up short.

My heart is starting to race, my palms slick with sweat. A barrage of worst-case scenarios crosses my mind as I race out onto the terrace and check the pool. Thank God, she's not there, but neither is she anywhere within view. A harsher sense of dread thickens my throat as I run to the dock. I'm almost too horrified to scan the water at first.

But…

The boats are still here, as are the lifejackets left inside the one we took out. I don't see any sign of a tiny body floating on the water. I'm so relieved that I have to bend over, bracing my hands over my knees. And then I hear it —faint, soft laughter, riding a gust of wind.

Out here with little noise on the property, sound travels far. Blindly, I plunge beneath the trees, following the laughter through brambles and faded trails for what feels like an eternity.

"Magda?" My heart is a constant hammering pulse by now. I feel like I might vomit, and a call to 911 is my next course of action until I spot a tiny flash of scarlet between two trees. "Magda!"

I throw myself into the underbrush and crash out on the other side.

"Oh, thank God!"

Magdalene stands just a few paces away, her red dress wrinkled, her shoes muddied. Otherwise, she looks none too worse for wear—as does the blond girl standing beside her. Both watch me, wide-eyed in a way that makes me question my own appearance. I'm panting, my skin slick with sweat.

"Sweetie, don't you ever take off like that again! I was worried sick! And I'm sure your mother is worried about you too," I tell the girl.

Magda shrugs, her tiny lips pursing. "Can I visit her pony?" she asks. After a moment's hesitation, she adds, "Please?"

"Yeah!" The little girl pitches in. She's beautiful—the blond equivalent to Magda's dark-haired visage. Her tiny riding habit is secured by a bright pink ribbon, the fabric every bit as expensive as the one Vadim bought Magda.

Something tells me that despite their feud, the two brothers share the same inclination when it comes to spoiling the children under their protection. "My house is right over there," the girl adds, pointing through the woods. "We can play whenever we want!"

"Ainsley!" In a scene that I assume must mirror my appearance just seconds ago, a woman staggers from a copse of trees. "Don't you ever run off like that. I—" She breaks off, her brown eyes flitting in my direction.

Again, I'm struck by just how young she is. Especially when paired with a man like Maxim, who—while no old man by any means—is certainly far older. And stronger. And bigger. I'm so lost in the mental comparisons that I barely notice when she speaks.

"Ainsley, come back to the house."

"And we should be leaving too." I step forward and take Magda's hand. Surprisingly, she doesn't resist.

Instead, she turns her eyes on me, deploying an as of yet unseen ability—puppy dog eyes brimming with as much intensity as her trademark icy glare.

"Can she come over to play? And see my pony? …please?"

"I, um…" I make eye contact with Maxim's fiancée. Francesca, I think that's her name. Without a word spoken, I sense that we share a mutual understanding— these children may be innocent in the affairs of the adults around them, but it's better not to touch that dynamic with a ten-foot pole. "We'll talk about it later, sweetie.

Come on, your lunch is getting cold. Maybe after we can go pet Dasha, hmm?"

She follows as I tug her along, but cranes her head back to watch as Francesca does the same to Ainsley. The two girls wave at each other while my insides squirm uncomfortably. How utterly cruel is it to deny a child a potential playmate merely because their guardians hate each other?

Very, I decide once we return to the house, and Magda's frown makes a dramatic reappearance. I cajole her into eating, and we're in the middle of another game of Monopoly when the front door opens. I turn only to choke on my relieved sigh; Vadim isn't the one who storms into the kitchen.

"Mr. Vadim no come back," Ena declares. "Business. Be back tomorrow."

"Tomorrow?" I try to keep the panic from my voice. "Can I call him? Do you have his number—"

"No call." Ena crosses his arms, and I have enough sense to suspect that point is non-negotiable. "He busy. You see him tomorrow."

"But what about…" I trail off, glancing at Magda. This isn't her fault. I can discuss the whole "how dare you abandon me with your child" issue with Vadim at a later date. Instead, I force a grin and pick up the dice. "Ready to get your butt kicked, kiddo?"

She smirks, apparently more than eager to accept the challenge.

CHAPTER FIFTEEN

I figure I should be far more pissed at becoming a forced babysitter than I actually am. Because that's what this is, isn't it? Babysitting?

Because, as I've told myself repeatedly, Magda isn't *mine*. I shouldn't enjoy losing to her at Monopoly for the umpteenth time. I shouldn't find an odd sense of pride in the fact that she allows me to pick out her pajamas—a pink, gossamer nightgown—while she takes her bath. Brushing her hair is far too personal a task for a glorified babysitter, as is tucking her in and ensuring that both of her dolls are within reach.

"Goodnight, sweetie."

I return to Vadim's room alone, finding the bed huge without him here. And as I huddle beneath the silken sheets, a wave of doubt crashes over me with such brutal intensity, I almost can't breathe beneath the onslaught. Where is he? Is he safe? Or has something happened?

Something that drove him off on one of those emotional benders he's hinted at?

I spend the night tossing and turning as those various fears torment me, robbing any anger I should feel of potency. I'm exhausted by the time I finally crawl out of the still-empty bed and get dressed. Downstairs, I make myself more tea and turn my sole focus to Magda.

Pushing any thoughts of boundaries aside, I make her a bowl of cereal for breakfast and pour her a fresh glass of juice. Then I head upstairs, relieved to find her still in bed.

Perched on the end of her mattress, I run my fingers through her hair until she wakes up. "Time to get the day started, kiddo."

Rubbing her eyes, she sits up and scuttles to the end of her bed, waiting expectantly. It's a belated second before I realize why. Following my unspoken cue, I enter her closet and pick out another outfit—a pair of jeans and a lime green sweater. After I braid her hair, she follows me downstairs and eats.

Then she fixes me with another disarmingly vulnerable glance I'm woefully unprepared for. "Can I go play with Ainsley?" Her eyes are so wide I feel swallowed by them, devoured by their openly pleading nature. "Please?"

I fumble for my glass of juice and promptly knock it over. "I... Um, we should wait for Vadim to get back." I force a grin, but her mouth falls flat in response. From her dour expression, I assume that she feels the same way on that prospect that I do deep down—who knows when that will be?

"I want to play," she says, folding her hands beside her bowl.

It's such a simple, plaintive statement that somehow slips through my defenses and cuts deep. Maybe because it's a different tact from her stoic persona. I'm just as vulnerable to her as I am to Vadim when he lets his true emotions slip through. Helpless.

"I... I'll be right back."

My mind spins as I leave the kitchen and head aimlessly for the foyer. Instead of Vadim returning, I find Ena standing guard, his arms crossed as I approach. And a split-second's decision forms in my brain too quickly to challenge.

"I want to make a deal," I tell him as he eyes me warily. "And I know you'll want to refuse it, but hear me out."

He cocks his head, his frown skeptical. "I listen."

"Magda wants to play with the little girl next door—" As far as mansions with acres of property go. "And I think she could. And yes, I am talking about Maxim's daughter."

Ena's nostrils flare, and I almost take a step back. He looks liable to hit me, revealing the true depths of his loyalty to Vadim. "No. No—"

"I'll take all responsibility," I insist, lifting my hands in a placating gesture. "Or... I'll tell Vadim that you let her wander onto his property unprotected. I found her there yesterday."

It's a low blow. One I would never resort to under different circumstances. Is a playdate even worth it?

No. Ena's furious expression warns me that making an enemy out of him is the worst possible act I could have taken.

"Look at her," I demand, trying another tack. "She's cooped up in a strange house, with strange people. The man who brought her here just disappeared to only God knows where. She's lonely. All she wants to do is play with a little girl her own age. Are you going to tell her no?"

He squares his jaw, and I have no doubt that he's capable of doing just that. He takes a step toward her, only to deflate, his shoulders slumping. Whirling on his heel, he jabs a finger at me.

"You take blame," he insists. "Ena knows nothing. You take girl on your own."

I sigh in relief. "Thank you—"

"No thank me." He laughs coldly, his upper lip quirked. But it's not a smug expression. It's pitying. "Mr. Vadim kill you."

And he may, I concede to myself. But not if I kill him first.

"Thank you." I race past Ena before he can change his mind and approach Magda. Any doubts I may have are instantly dashed when she gazes up at me, her wall lowered a fraction to reveal the little girl underneath.

Screw boundaries. If Vadim wants to leave me with his daughter overnight, then he would cede her to my authority. Gosh, I just hope that trust isn't misplaced.

"Ready to go on an adventure?" I run upstairs just to grab a jacket from the closet, then I open the door to the terrace and lead her outside. Taking her hand, I let her show me the route she took the other day.

"How did you even know where to go?" I ask, already hopelessly confused by the vast expanse of nature rendering this section of the grounds a virtual wilderness.

"Nautical navigation," she says, a rare hint of excitement seeping into her voice. She has Biphany clutched under one arm, but curiously it looks like she left It behind.

"Oh," I say, nodding. "Nautical navigation... Which in English means?"

She giggles in that rare, fleeting way. "Like the pirates used," she adds in response to my puzzled expression. Lifting her tiny fingers, she points in two opposing directions. "Longitude and latitude—the lines that go on a map like this. Then you use the position of the sun—" she points up above. "And cardinal directions, you know —east, west, north, south. You use those to estimate your position on the axis. Then you just calculate from there. If

I assume that we were fifty feet out on the water, then Ainsley lives roughly…" She counts on the fingers of her free hand. "One point seven five miles west of our house. See? It's easy." Whatever expression she sees on my face makes her giggle, shaking her head. "It's basic calculations. Even a baby could do it."

"Yeah," I say, almost stunned into silence. "Basic…"

Still grinning, she surges ahead, tugging me behind her, and all I can do is follow, seeing the world as a seven-year-old might. An exceptionally bright seven-year-old who is far too perceptive for her own good. Vadim and Maxim may have a proverbial ocean of emotional distance between them, but a child has no trouble cutting through the physical boundaries. Which isn't much. Once upon a time, these properties were connected, it seems, linked by a series of dirt paths that are now barely visible in the underbrush.

And yet, as a testament to the vastness of both properties, Maxim's is still a good twenty or thirty minutes' walk at the brisk pace of an eager seven-year-old. If Maxim is anything like Vadim in terms of security, I half-expect a gruff, gun-toting equivalent of Ena to come bursting from the shadows the second we breach the boundary of his land. Instead, we emerge from the woods relatively unscathed—though I sense eyes on the back of my neck with every step we take toward the modest, cozy-looking mansion on the hill.

Maxim's property is laid out much in the same way as Vadim's. There is a stable on the far edge, set amongst a series of sprawling, fenced-in fields. Beyond that is a rocky shore with its own private dock. The house even has a pool, barely visible from this angle.

Inhaling deeply, I take Magda around the perimeter of the property, heading toward the house proper. The second we step onto a paved stone path snaking to the front door, it opens, and a man in a suit steps out. He's dapper, with graying hair and gentle though guarded eyes. I recognize him instantly as the man who drove me home after Vadim made a spectacle of me at Maxim's dinner party.

Small world.

"May I help you?" he asks, smiling warmly. The politeness catches me off guard, and some of my unease dissipates a fraction.

But before I can open my mouth, Magda steps forward. "I want to play," she says. "Is Ainsley here, sir?"

I gape at her even as my heart melts at her sweet tone. Like father like daughter. She knows when to turn on the charm. It doesn't hurt that even in her more casual outfit, she still looks like a little princess with her braids adorned with green ribbon and Biphany tucked under her arm—I now suspect that leaving the less innocent-looking It at home was a calculated choice.

One that turns out to be devastatingly effective. The man blinks at the overload of girlish energy. But in a testament to his professionalism, he doesn't break completely.

"I'm not sure if Ms. Ainsley will be able to play today," he says carefully, cutting his gaze to me. "But I will ask."

He disappears inside the house, and not even a second later, the door flies open, and a tiny figure skips out.

"You came!" Ainsley bounds down the path, sporting a pink equivalent to Magda's casual sweater and jeans. Her loose hair flows over her shoulders as she bounds toward us. "Can we go play, Frankie? Huh?"

She directs the question toward the slender figure who appears in the doorway behind her. Cautiously, the woman's dark eyes meet mine, and I sigh in response.

"Can we talk?" I ask her as the girls ignore us, already skipping off together, holding hands. Their innocent joy makes it painfully apparent just how foolish this is—the adults being nervous at the prospect of a budding friendship merely because of two men who hate each other. It's laughable in theory. But not so trivial once I recall how the brothers react when in the same vicinity.

I feel like a general, going behind her leader's back to forge a truce behind enemy lines. Yes, on the one hand, every small ounce of peace is a victory within itself. On the other hand, treason is punishable by death, and even Ena didn't care to sugar coat things.

Mr. Vadim kill you.

But the time for any doubt has sadly passed. Tentatively stepping forward, Francesca nods, and I suspect she's of the same mind. In unison, we watch the girls giggle, muttering conspiratorially, and any lingering misgivings I may have held vanish.

"Come on, Ainsley," Francesca calls, her expression strained. "Let's go into the back yard."

IT IS a strange thing to sip lemonade behind enemy lines for the sake of a playdate. I add the experience to the growing list of *"things I thought I'd never do during my journey to sexual exploration."*

Stoically, Francesca sits beside me on a wooden lounger while we both watch the girls play on a section of grass across from a spacious pool. Here, the similarities between Maxim and Vadim's properties end. Maxim's is lived in, for one—a landscape of toys and skateboards bustling with activity. I catch several other faces peering out from the windows at times.

"I know this puts you in an awkward spot," I say to break the ice as Magda and Ainsley chatter away. "But when you have a seven-year-old stuck in the house for a week, it gets hard to deny her request for human interaction. And she's so darn cute." I crack a smile.

And so does my opponent. She really is beautiful in an understated way, with curling dark hair and brown eyes. *Haunted* eyes. A black dress with short sleeves reveals the bare skin of her arms—a sight I am desperately preventing myself from staring at.

They're covered in scars. Vicious, healed scars.

"You live with Dima?" she asks, her tone surprisingly neutral, given the nature of this war.

"Dima?" It takes me a second to remember Vadim's nickname. "I, um… Yes. For now. It's complicated."

Her lips form a wry frown. I sense her mulling over her next words carefully before she finally says, "He's dangerous."

I swallow at her tone. My gaze cuts to Ainsley, who seems merrily undisturbed, though, according to Maxim, Vadim kidnapped her. It's a horrible act for sure, and while I don't claim to know Vadim fully just yet—I *do* know him enough to understand why he might have done it. To test himself. To convince himself that he could interact with Magda. He all but told me, and I don't doubt that looking back at all he's done since.

"He's…complicated," I say in answer to Francesca's statement. "I won't pretend like he's not."

And hell, after today I may not have to—he'll kick me out. I try to feel more guilty, but as I watch Magda smile as she shows off Biphany, my heart swells up so big that there isn't room for any other emotion but relief.

"Complicated is one way to put it," Francesca says, her eyes narrowed in a way that makes me suspect she hasn't forgiven him. Not one damn bit.

"I know what he did was awful," I confess. "To Ainsley. I hope it didn't traumatize her, I truly do. But maybe Maxim should take a page from his book the next time he breaks into our home and terrorizes a little girl."

Oops, I realize as her eyes go wide. It seems Maxim didn't tell her that little detail.

"Dima brings out the worst in him," she says, her lips pursed. It's not an explanation—I don't think it's meant to be one. Not really.

It mirrors something Vadim told me once himself. These brothers, so hostile, and yet so damn similar. Will they ever be able to let go of whatever hatred is simmering between them?

"I think it's stupid that two little girls can't play because their fathers are insane," I blurt out loud.

Francesca eyes me for a moment. Slowly her small smile returns. "Maxim isn't her father," she says. "She's not even mine. She's my sister."

"Ah." I nod, and some of the uncomfortable tension between us eases. "Well, Magda's not mine, either."

Though you seem to think she is, a part of me hisses. *You're making decisions for her after all, behind her father's back.*

"But she's Vadim's, isn't she?" Francesca says with a sureness that alludes to the fact she too can see the resemblance. "I'm sorry, but he doesn't seem like the fatherly type."

"He's trying," I admit with a sigh. "He really is… I take it, you aren't his biggest fan, though?"

She bites her lip as if to stop herself from saying more. Then she shrugs. "I don't like being the recipient of his little mind games, that's for damn sure."

Yikes. I file away that assertion for later. Could Vadim be manipulative? Yes, case and point is my current predicament—despite all my insistence to the contrary, I'm watching his daughter while he gallivants off to only God knows where. But are said actions malicious? Francesca seems to think so.

She stares off into the distance, frowning as if at an unpleasant memory.

To change the subject, I blurt out the first thing that comes to mind. "Are you excited for your wedding?" It's the wrong topic, one I'm woefully unable to be objective about. To my own horror, judgment leeches into my voice, far too potent to go unnoticed. "I got married young," I confess apologetically. "It didn't end well. I'm a bit jaded about it. Please allow me to live vicariously through you, though."

Francesca eyes me warily, an eyebrow raised. "We haven't planned much," she admits.

From her tone, I suspect it's not by choice. Could the delay have something to do with whatever drew Maxim to Moscow? Rather than pry, I shrug.

"I remember my own wedding. I put so much effort into it, when I should have put more time and energy into planning my future, sans some self-centered asshole."

Ouch, Tiffy. This isn't about you. Once again, Jim rears his ugly head, and I don't know why. Why the hell would I bring up marriage at all? But my lips rebel against my brain, carrying on the conversation, "I *was* too young," I add, eyeing the woman up and down. "Twenty, barely out of high school. I had no clue. Not that there's anything wrong with getting married young, that is..."

Judging from the faint pink coloring Francesca's cheeks, she's not too far from the twenty-year age mark. Damn. I could kick myself for insinuating something so rude. "I'm sorry—"

"Don't be. I'm not ashamed of my relationship with Maxim," she says with a maturity that puts past Tiffy's mindset to shame. Her eyes take on that faraway look, betraying a difficult past I can only speculate on. "He's not perfect. I'm not either. But I don't have to justify that to anyone."

I tilt my glass, finding far more solidarity in her words than I care to admit to myself at the moment. "I'll drink to that."

We finish off our glasses, still watching the girls. They chase each other, each one cackling madly as if in a competition to prove who is having more of a blast. If mirth could be graded on the decibel scale, then I'll say this is one hell of a successful playdate.

"Ains doesn't really have anyone her age to play with outside of school," Francesca says after a moment's silence. Her voice is so soft, it's almost as if she's talking more to herself than to me. But that seemingly harmless statement opens the door to so much more.

And for Magda's sake, I step right on through. "We're just next door," I say carefully.

But we both leave it at that without crossing over that unspoken boundary.

Not yet.

Magda and I return to the house under the disapproving glare of Ena, who skulks off the second we're safely inside. Vadim hasn't returned yet, it seems. Sighing, I fix Magda a pre-prepared meal, and then we spar in another round of Monopoly.

Much to my utter joy, I don't get slaughtered minutes in. That little play date must have zapped Magda of her energy because I'm seconds away from beating her when the door opens. My body shivers in recognition of those slow, heavy footsteps before Vadim even appears in the doorway.

I gasp, alarmed at his appearance. Any irritation for his disappearance vanishes, and I lurch to my feet, staggering toward him. He's paler than ever, his features gaunt in a way that makes me suspect he might have gone both days without eating. His hair is mussed, his suit wrinkled, and those eyes wretchedly hollow. They flit over me with barely any recognition before latching onto Magda. He barrels past me, snatching her from her chair despite her shrieked protests. Sinking into a crouch, he holds her to his chest, smoothing his hands through her hair.

No matter how she struggles or resists, he doesn't let her go, his body trembling with tension. Eventually, she goes stiff with shock, enduring the contact.

"Vadim?" Alarm runs through me when he doesn't even react to the sound of my voice. I step forward, bracing my hand on his back—he's practically vibrating. "Vadim, what's wrong?"

He says nothing, so intent on Magda that I doubt he even heard me. It's only when she squirms against his grip that he finally lets her go. He stands as she darts across the kitchen and turns to me. Seconds later, I'm in his arms, his mouth capturing mine with a ferocity that leaves me breathless.

I arch into the kiss before common sense makes me draw back. "Wait. Baby, wait—"

He backs away, panting, swiping at his mouth. He blinks as if he's only now realizing where he is. Then he turns and heads for the stairs.

Shaken, all I can do is grasp at the pieces of the gameboard with trembling fingers. Magda watches me, her expression unguarded for once. She looks terrified.

Forcing a smile, I grasp a handful of fake money. "Let's clean up, shall we?"

She nods, her eyes still wide. Together we pack up the pieces and put the game away in silence.

"Why don't you go brush Biphany's hair, and I'll come to get you ready for bed, huh?" I force another grin that Magda doesn't return as she obediently heads upstairs.

Alone, I attempt to gather up the nerve to follow after her and approach the master bedroom. Vadim sits on the bed, his jacket on the floor, his dress shirt partially unbuttoned. As I approach, he meets my gaze, seeming more exhausted than ever.

"Are you okay?" I ask.

He glances away, running his fingers through his hair. "I'm fine. I'm sorry if I startled you."

"You are *not* fine." I stalk toward him and finger his wrinkled collar. My nostrils flare with his scent—all male musk. I doubt he's even showered since he left. "You look awful." I run my fingers through his hair, forcing him to look at me. "Tell me what's wrong."

His throat works to swallow. "I—"

"I'm ready for bed," a small voice declares. Startled, I lurch away from Vadim and turn to find Magda in the doorway her arms crossed, wall firmly in place. "Are you coming, *Tiffany?*"

"Yes… I'm coming, honey."

She nods and then pointedly glances at Vadim, her expression icy. Turning on her heel, she marches away, making her thoughts on his return abundantly clear.

"Damn it," he hisses, bracing both hands on his knees. He slumps forward, the picture of guilt, and some more of my irritation is chipped away. "The pony. I forgot…"

"I'll go put her to bed," I say, heading down the hall. "But when I come back, we need to talk."

I find Magda waiting for me on the edge of her bed. As I enter her closet to pick out a set of pajamas, I sense the unlikely start of a routine. One in which I return with her clothing and arrange it on the bed while she takes her bath. When she emerges dripping wet and draped in a robe, I brush her hair and braid it. Finally, I let her crawl beneath the blankets and tuck her in, placing her toys on either side of her.

"Night, sweetie." I linger far too long, smoothing my fingers over her hair until she finally drifts off. When I return to Vadim, he's pacing, still partially undressed, his expression even more constricted.

"I've fucked up," he declares the second I see his face. "She's angry with me."

"Yes," I say, choosing not to lie. "You disappointed her. And I'll tell you now that you'll have to work hard to make it up to her. No more just buying her things. Spend the day with her. That's what she wants—no, that's what she *needs* from you."

He sighs, his lips twisting into a frown. "And you are angry with me as well…"

"Pissed off, actually." I prance past him and lift my dress over my head, but I know my posture warns him from touching me. I am angry. I just didn't realize how strongly until now.

"I don't know what misconceptions you have, but I am not your employee," I tell him, my voice shaking. "You don't get to disappear and leave me with your henchman and your kid without even asking me to stay. You don't have that right, fake wife or otherwise."

"I know." I sense him come up behind me. When his fingers brush my sides, I don't pull away, leaning into him instead. Two days alone create an unfair disadvantage as far as maintaining a grudge is concerned. Luckily for me, I have one powerful bit of ammo in my holster. Best to get it out of the way now. "Before Ena spills the beans, I took Magda to play with Maxim's little girl."

He sucks in a breath, backing away from me. "You what?"

I swallow hard before facing him. Meeting his gaze, I square my chin—but it's a hard-fought bravery to keep up. I sway as his eyes touch on a terrifying shade of black. Soulless and cold at the threat of betrayal.

"You gamble her safety to punish me?"

"No! Of course not!" I scoff, insulted by the accusation. "I gambled your stupid pride and let your lonely daughter have some fresh air and play with a girl her own age because her father broke her heart over some stupid pony!"

He grunts as if struck, his gaze pained. I almost feel guilty for going there. Almost.

But if he wants to play the self-righteous indignation game, I can be just as petty. "Why did you go running off anyway? After how you made Magda feel, you better have one damn good reason—"

"I do." He's facing away from me, his tone hoarse. "I filed to adopt her the day she came here. The Robinsons had expressed no interest, and as her only previous foster family, I was assured that no one else could lay claim. I did everything in my power to expedite it legally."

I bite my lip. Could that explain his disappearance the other day on that mysterious "business?"

"So, what happened?" I ask. Something in his stance draws me to him. I place my hand on his forearm and gasp. He's trembling. "Vadim, tell me."

"My petition stalled. Blocked, in fact, though the reasoning why was unclear. My lawyers assured me they could have the hold-up dealt with swiftly... But the other day, I learned the real obstacle barring me."

He turns around, his expression shaped by such pain... I step into him, caressing the stern line of his jaw. I give him time to speak, sensing that whatever he means to say is hard for him to put into words.

"The person who blocked the adoption did so on the grounds of claiming to be Magda's biological mother."

"What?" My eyes go wide as a million implications come crashing down all at once. *Irina? Some other mysterious woman?* Overwhelmed, I stagger to the bed and sit down. "Is it the truth? C-can they prove it?"

"I don't know." He sits beside me and takes my hand, gripping it tightly. "I spent two days in the state of her birth, trying to learn the answers to those very questions. With all the fucking legal hurdles, I didn't get anywhere. But unless the petitioner comes forward and files in person, they still have no claim."

"But it's still a hurdle," I croak, panic constricting my throat. God, it's like what happened at my church all over again. An adoption ruined on a selfish whim—but not my own. Right? Wrong. Even after a few short days… "Could it be her?" I ask, my voice breaking. "Magda's mother? …Irina?"

He glances at me sharply, his eyes flashing with a million emotions ranging from suspicion to…resignation? I sense the bricks of his wall shifting, fighting to reform. At the last second, they fall, leaving his emotions accessible, as volatile as they are.

"So, you *did* hear," he says softly. "I don't know if it's her. But… She wasn't well back then—" He frowns at the memory as his grip on my hand grows firmer by the second, tightening to the point of pain. It takes everything I have not to pull away, for his sake. Lost among the shadows of his past, I sense he needs physical contact now more than ever.

"I wasn't either. You don't understand what it's like. I can't explain. But, if this is her, she isn't hiding out of shame I can tell you that. The girl I knew, she was broken. In her world, everything was a game. She needed that mindset, but I indulged her. Too much, I indulged her. If I had the choice, I'd pray to whatever God would listen that Magda *isn't* hers."

I swallow thickly. There goes my jealousy, at least, though I'm not sure if I like the emotion that replaces it. Fear? I listen to him ramble, hopelessly confused—but I don't have the heart to prod for more. This seems to be the only way he can explain this at all—in disjointed bursts of information with little context sprinkled in between.

"Could it be her?" He shakes his head slowly. "Who knows."

"But why not come see her? Why not visit her first? And if they aren't her mother, who would be so cruel?"

"I don't know," Vadim insists. "But one thing could strengthen my claim over her, biological mother or not."

"You mean claim that you're her father to the courts?"

"No. Something even better." He draws my hand to his mouth, planting a kiss over the knuckles. His eyes practically glow as they meet mine, brimming with conviction. Alarm bells go off at the back of my mind, even as my body heats in response to the naked passion conveyed in that one, searing glance.

Damn. I half-expect my clothing to melt, reduced to ashes by his desire alone.

"If I can prove that I can provide a stable home for her, no one could take her away," he says carefully. "And, if you join my adoption petition. Marry me for real…"

Mental overload. It's too much seriousness at one time. My brain can't cope. All I can do is laugh, pulling my hand away as I lurch to my feet.

"We could ask Maxim to make his wedding a double," I suggest, laughing. "His fiancée said they haven't planned much. I'm sure they'd be down for it."

I'm smiling, but as the seconds tick by, he doesn't return it.

"I would marry you in tandem with whoever you wanted," he swears in a voice that robs my lungs of air. "As long as you said yes."

I sway, stunned. He sounds too damn serious. Too convinced in the madness of his plan.

"Vadim… You don't even know me."

"I know enough to know I'm not making a rash decision," he insists, rising to his height, stepping into me. "I know that you care for Magda already. I know she's warming to you more than she ever might to me. I know I need you. And…I know that you care for me as well."

My cheeks flame. I can't even deny it. My only course of action is to parry his passion with logic. "So, you railroad me into another marriage without even feigning the guise of love first? At least Jim gave me that." I don't know why I'm so angry. Because I am. Angry and hurt and torn by his dilemma. Could I even refuse him in these circumstances? That's the scary part. I'm not sure I can. "You should have told me what was going on sooner," I insist, changing tact to something I feel more comfortable punishing him over. "I could have comforted you. I could have understood why you left, and I could have helped you smooth things over with Magdalene."

"I'm telling you now." His voice is sin, soothing through my frustration like a salve. Too fast. I'm melting into him before he even touches me, his hands finding my breasts, kneading them possessively. "And I am not looking to 'railroad' you. As always, when it comes to you, I'm being greedy. Shameless. You want love? What about *need*? I always need more of you."

"Smooth talker," I rasp. It's alarming how he always manages to say the right thing. Even as my brain struggles to counter him with logic. The more he touches me, the less my fears make sense. The world narrows to this—him and me. My body heats, my hips writhing shamelessly to soothe the ache building between my legs. A heat that catches fire as my piercing remains rigid against swelling flesh, applying incredible pressure.

"Will you kick me out of your bed tonight as punishment for aggravating you?" he wonders. His lips find the crook of my throat, pressing there in a teasing kiss. Then a harder, teasing bite. "Or can I find some way to make it up to you?"

Damn...

"I think you're heading in the right direction," I gasp as his hands skim down my hips, finding my thighs. I spread my legs, encouraging him to travel lower. A gasp rips from my throat as his fingers slip between my legs, teasing the very edge of my piercing. My eyelids flutter, and I'm leaning into him, relying on his support just to stay upright.

"Mmm, my beauty. Don't tell me you've neglected yourself while I've been gone?"

Neglected... My brain spins, dizzy at the thought of fingering myself thinking of him. I hadn't. Why? "You didn't leave your toy for me," I confess. "I don't like to tease myself when I know waiting for the real deal will feel so much better."

He murmurs his approval, sliding a finger between my folds, tempting me with the promise of fullness. I spin around to face him, snatching at his collar. Logic can wait. He's right—I need this. Him. All of him.

Desperate, I rub my hips shamelessly against his thigh, teasing a groan from his throat.

"Still so insatiable..." He guides me backward, letting me fall onto the mattress. I spread my legs for him, gasping as he cups me, encouraging me rock against his palm.

"You find pleasure in this?" he whispers as my eyes threaten to roll.

His voice does something to me, triggering an avalanche of emotions, too overwhelming to resist. My lips part, the truth spilling out before I can stop myself, "I find pleasure in *you.*"

"Prove it," he murmurs, nuzzling my neck, nipping intermittently with his teeth. "Show me how badly you crave this."

He bucks his hips, letting his cock graze my inner thigh.

How much do I crave him? Enough to lose my mind. Enough to forget my boundaries.

Enough to lose myself.

Enough to drown.

I wake up utterly content. Rolling onto my back, I open my eyes to a room filled with sunshine and the pleasant weight of Vadim's arm over my waist. I nestle into him, so relaxed that I almost miss the tiny figure standing at the end of our bed, watching us.

Puzzled, I blink, but the intruder doesn't disappear. In fact…

As my brain wakes up, more of her expression comes into painfully sharp focus.

"M-Magda!" I lurch upright, clutching the sheet over my front. Beside me, Vadim stirs, still asleep. "What is it, honey?"

She frowns, crossing her arms over her nightgown, her glare accusatory. "You didn't wake me up."

"Huh?" I glance at the clock, surprised to find that it's nearly noon. Though, after last night, it honestly is no shock. Even Vadim's still out. Turning to Magda, I can't escape a wave of guilt as every real-world concern comes slamming back to the forefront. Her supposed mother. Her father's demands. The fact that I'm naked.

"Did you eat breakfast yet?" I ask her, clutching the sheet even tighter.

She shakes her head, and I scramble to the edge of the mattress. "Let me get dressed, and I'll make you something to eat."

The second she leaves, I dart into the bathroom and change in record time. When I scramble into Magda's room, she's still wearing her pajamas. After muscling her into the bathroom, I lay out a fresh set of clothing on her bed. Only then do I stop to realize what I'm doing.

Coddling her? Or maybe there's a worse word for it in this context...

Mothering her.

Mrs. Robinson eat your heart out. It seems the busybody was wrong about Magdalene in more ways than one. Though...she *was* independent her first few days here, dressing without prompting. I sense this new insistence on having me assist her has nothing to do with laziness. Oh God, I think it's deeper than that. More terrifying than that.

Did the Robinsons ever attempt to do this for her? Did the mother even try to tuck her in and lay out her clothing? Something tells me no. Am I making a huge mistake by letting her get accustomed to this? To me?

"I can't wear that without pants," Magda says from the doorway of her bathroom, seemingly amused by the fact that I've only placed a yellow cashmere sweater on her bed and nothing else. She giggles—a sound so rare and fleeting that I promptly squash my doubts and force a grin.

"Right you are, smarty pants. But let's try a skirt today instead?" I pick out a tan tweed one and a baby blue headband. Once dressed, she hops onto the end of the bed, and I heed my cue, settling in to brush and braid her hair, securing it with a length of yellow ribbon.

Downstairs, I make her a bowl of cereal and warm up a piece of toast for Vadim, who stumbles downstairs not long after. I can tell that he showered, throwing on a pair of sweats in lieu of a suit. Looking beautifully dazed, he rakes his fingers through his damp hair, and once again, his thoughts are easier to read than ever. Like the fact that he's alarmed for one, unnerved at having slept for so long.

"Your food, good sir." I place a plate in front of him and feel my toes curl at the gracious look he shoots me. *Damn.* Boundaries are important—if only he didn't make domestic life so damn appealing to imitate.

But weddings can't be faked as easily as marriages can.

"Tiffany," Magda says after a bite of cereal. "Can we play Monopoly?"

"Yes, honey," I reply absently as I return to the counter and grab myself a croissant from Ena's customary breakfast basket.

"And can we go see my pony?"

"Yes, honey."

"And can we go in the boat?"

I frown at the prospect. "Only if Mr. Ena agrees to take us."

"I can take you," Vadim pitches in, his tone cautious. I glance over my shoulder and discover that his wariness is for a good reason. Magda's pleasant expression promptly sours.

"I don't want to go on the boat anymore," she declares, her tone an icy imitation of his cruelest drawl. Embodying his standoffish talent, she pushes back from the table and grabs It by his head, letting him dangle from her hand as she marches from the kitchen, presumably upstairs.

"Give her time," I warn him. Sure enough, when I turn around, he's frowning, his gaze distant.

"How could I be so foolish?"

"You were still worried about her," I point out. "She'll get over it. And…" I weigh my next words carefully and decide that they're relevant. "If you let her play with Ainsley again, she'll forgive you a lot faster."

He raises an eyebrow. "Are you suggesting bribery?"

I shrug and hold up my hands defensively. "What you call bribery, I call 'attending to her needs.' She's lonely. What will a little playdate hurt?"

"Try telling that to Maxim," he counters gruffly. "I'm sure he's convinced himself that I am Magdalene, playing dress-up in a child suit by now."

I have to snort at that, seriousness aside. "Save your feud with your brother for another day. As for now, give Magda time. You can start with not letting her scare you off. Take us on the water today."

"Will I be rewarded for being a good captain?" he wonders, his voice husky.

My cheeks catch fire, and it takes everything I have not to retort with something equally suggestive. "No sex talk around innocent ears," I warn, waggling my finger. "And we really need to come up with some kind of schedule or safe word if Magda is in the house. I'd rather not be startled awake in post-coital bliss by a seven-year-old again."

"Point taken. You go grab her, and I'll get the boat ready."

VADIM HAS an expert poker face when he wants to. His invisible wall can seem insurmountable, and I never want to taste a fraction of the wrath he directs Maxim's way.

Magda inherited all of his skills of icy brooding and then some.

She scowls during the entire boat ride, letting her guise slack only in the rare moments when she thinks no one is watching. Only then does awe peek through her icy exterior, triggered by some aspect of the scenery or another. The property itself really is beautiful—a paradise nestled in the shadow of the sprawling metropolis that is Fair Haven. There are so many ways for Vadim to enhance the place, creating an oasis for Magda to thrive in.

That is, if she'll let him.

She maintains her stony silence when we return to the house for dinner. When I grab the Monopoly box, she crosses her arms and storms upstairs once it's clear that Vadim plans to participate.

"I'll go get her," I volunteer with a sigh. But Vadim rises to his feet, passing me.

"No. I will."

I swallow hard and follow him up to her room. She's stewing on the bed, and her glare darkens when she sees him.

"We should talk," he says, sitting on the edge of her bed. "I'm sorry I disappointed you. I promised you I would take you riding. I should have upheld that promise. You have every right to be upset with me."

"Why?" Magda demands. I flinch at the venom in her tone.

"Because I want you to trust me," Vadim says firmly.

"Trust you?" she scoffs, her tiny body radiating with increasing fury. "I hate you!"

"Magda!" I step forward, but Vadim raises his hand, and I stop short.

"Why?" he asks. "You have every right to hate me, but I would like to know why." His tone is so unnervingly gentle. She can't resist it.

"*Why?* Because you're a liar!" She lurches to her feet. Even while standing on the bed, she barely manages to tower above him. "I'm not stupid!" she shrieks, her voice losing any aspect of maturity. In this moment, she is all of seven. A hurt, brooding, wounded seven.

"I'm not stupid! I'm not!" She brandishes It by his floppy head, his body jerking wildly.

"Of course, you're not," Vadim murmurs. "I know that—"

"No, you don't!" She grasps It's body in one hand and brutally rips off his head with the other. The violence is tempered only by the tears spilling down her cheeks. She throws the bear's head aside and plunges her hand into its limp body—but rather than stuffing, she withdraws a folded slip of paper. "I know who you are," she says, sobbing openly. "I know! I saw papers in Mr. Robinson's office. Money that he got from some stupid company. I googled it, and I saw your picture." She throws the slip of paper at Vadim.

His fingers shake as he unfurls it, revealing a faded printed photo of him in business attire.

"I waited for you," Magda snarls, her body heaving, her voice hitching. "I waited and waited and waited! You never came! You left me there! You left me with those people!" She puffs up, her face red, her expression so broken an answering tear falls down my cheek before I can wipe it away. "You didn't want me," she wails, pointing at him. "You didn't want me—"

"I wanted you." Vadim's tone is so fierce she falls silent in the face of it, her tiny shoulders slumping. I don't know who initiates the contact, but the next second, she's in his arms, her face in his chest, his fingers in her hair, loosening her braid. "More than anything," he grates against her scalp. "I wanted you..."

I back away the second Magda's tiny hands clutch him in return, sensing the need to make my exit. Downstairs I try to distract myself by cleaning up the table and the dirty dishes. Eventually, I wind up nursing a glass of wine, contemplating running.

This is best for everyone, right? A father and daughter reunited—no more need for an interloper...

After over an hour, I risk creeping up the stairs. A soothing, deep hum drifts from Magda's room. Singing?

Yes. God, I recognize the rasping, haunting voice as Vadim's. He has her sleeping in his arms, rocking her as he sings the same song he must have while she was in the hospital.

My heart aches as I leave them be and crawl into bed alone.

If I were a better woman, I would gather my things and leave now. Let them rebuild their bond in peace. It might hurt in the short-term, but in the long-term, they'd be better off. They belonged together—without me.

But as the minutes tick by, I don't get up.

I never pack my things.

I never leave.

CHAPTER EIGHTEEN

I wake up, alarmed to realize that Vadim isn't beside me. Judging from the state of the sheets, he never came to bed during the entire night, either. When I venture down the hall, my alarm eases. I find him still in Magda's room, in the same position I'd left them in last night.

His eyes meet mine tiredly as she slumbers in his arms, her head propped against his shoulder.

Again, I retreat and shower, taking my time. I get dressed, and when I finally reemerge, Magda's room is empty. I head downstairs, but they aren't in the kitchen either. Or on the terrace.

Confused, I wander the rest of the downstairs level, only to run into a scowling Ena when I reach the front door.

"Horse," he grunts, though I sense he regrets telling me even that much.

I head out to the stables. Sure enough, the beautiful Zzazza is in one of the fenced-in pastures, looking like something out of a fairytale. Riding her is Vadim, still in his rumpled sweats. Seated before him, in her riding outfit, helmet in place, is Magda. She sits stiffly as he murmurs instructions into her ear, explaining various aspects of riding.

But bit by bit, she obeys his gentle suggestions, adjusting her grip on the reigns. And every now again, her eyes dart to him for approval—which she finds every single time.

My chest aches as I creep to the fence and watch them. It's a night and day contrast to yesterday. They both look relaxed, for one, their expressions neutral. Still hesitant in some ways, but it's progress.

Spotting me, Magda cracks the tiniest hint of something that may or may not be a smile, and my heart soars. Above her, Vadim grins in that wary, breathtaking way.

And their fragile, fledgling joy resonates like sunlight, adding life to the overcast landscape.

ONLY ONCE NIGHT FALLS, and Magda is fast asleep do I finally meet with Vadim alone. He enters the bedroom awkwardly, having been the one on bedtime duty for once.

Our eyes meet, and words spill from my throat before I can hold them back. "I'm so happy for you," I tell him, my voice wrought with emotion. "I am. I'm so, so happy—"

"But you're doubting." His eyes narrow as he advances, pinning me in against the wall before I even realize what's happening. One shift of his body and I'm trapped. But this prison isn't one I'm eager to escape, no matter how fiercely every nerve in my body is urging me to run.

"My beauty…" My eyelids flutter as he grasps my chin, cradling my jaw against his palm. It should be illegal for one gesture to contain so much emotion. I sway, overwhelmed as he draws me to him, his mouth hovering near my throat.

"Gaining Magdalene was one obstacle I've surmounted," he tells me, his voice low with a determination that sets me alight. "I won't lose you. Whether I have to shackle you, or chastise or claim…" He captures my hips, grinding his touch into my flesh. "I refuse to relent. You *will* give in to me. I know it."

"Through marriage?" I ask softly.

He smiles, and my heart lurches, hammering madly. "Through corruption," he corrects, stroking my hair from my face. "I will corrupt you as thoroughly as you have tainted me, be it through marriage or otherwise."

"That sounds like a threat," I confess, even as I find myself lurching into him, manipulated by his groping touch.

"Take it as you will," he warns, his voice deepening with possession. "I will have you. No matter the cost. No matter the price. I will."

Whether I'm willing to be bought or not.

558

"That's another round lost for Tiffany," Vadim declares from over a stack of neatly arranged Monopoly money. "I think we might have to up the stakes."

"Like what?" Magda asks conspiratorially. They sit on the same end of the table, far too close for my liking. Something tells me that I'm woefully outmatched in this war.

"Like…" Vadim cuts his gaze to me. "If Tiffany loses again, we should devise a fitting punishment for her."

"No fair!" I snatch a handful of money from the till and throw it at him. "I forfeit!"

Vadim's grin is sinful. "Shall we let her?" he asks Magda, who gleefully shakes her head, her curls bouncing.

"Then, I declare…" He strokes his chin in chilling contemplation. "That she be tickled to death!"

He lunges for me, and I race away, cackling at the top of my lungs. "No! I'll never give in! Never—"

I break off as a knock sounds from the front door, and I skid to a stop at the mouth of the foyer.

Frowning, Vadim slips past me, the playful mood broken. Squaring his shoulders, he opens the door, and I can tell just from his posture alone who he expects to be on the other end. His brother. "Shit, Ena didn't tell me that anyone…"

He trails off at the sight of the figure on the other end. As he steps back, alarm shoots through me at his expression. I've never seen his eyes so wide. So…open. It's as if he's seen a ghost.

And maybe he has.

The beautiful woman in the doorway is pale enough to have come from some ethereal realm. Curling blond hair falls down her shoulders, stopping almost at her waist. Delicate features form a face of breathtaking perfection, crowned by two intense light-blue eyes that fixate solely on the man between us.

"Irina," Vadim croaks.

"Vadim," she says, her voice softly accented. "I came to see our daughter."

CONQUER

Conquer

Conquer By Lana Sky

Copyright © 2020 by Lana Sky
All rights reserved.

No part of this publication may be reproduced, distributed, or
transmitted in any form or by any means, including photocopying,
recording, or other electronic or mechanical methods, without the prior
written permission of the author.

This is a work of fiction. Names, characters, businesses, places, events and
incidents are either the products of the author's imagination or used in a
fictitious manner. Any resemblance to actual persons, living or dead, or
actual events is purely coincidental.

Cover Design and Interior Formatting by Charity Chimni
Proofreading by Charity Chimni

ACKNOWLEDGMENTS

Thanks so much to everyone who supported this draft along the way, including the many beta readers who provided encouragement along the way! Please keep in mind that this story includes dark, graphic, and explicit content matter that is not suitable for readers under the age of 18—or for readers who are uncomfortable with the following subject matter: explicit sex, mentions of sexual abuse, mentions of child abuse, graphic depictions of violence, and mentions of self-harm.

CHAPTER ONE

Insecurity thrives on doubt—but it doesn't help when reality reinforces every last one of those petty fears. Like when your new lover's ex-whatever-she-is-to-him comes back from the proverbial grave. It's easy to write off the concerns as paranoia at first, until the truth is staring you in the face, and there is no escaping it.

Knowing that Vadim had another woman in his life, no matter how he characterized her, scares me for reasons well beyond the obvious jealousy. Mainly because whenever I dare to picture such a woman…

One small consolation was that the mythical figure I'd conjured up seemed so unrealistic in my head, a part of me was convinced she couldn't possibly exist. She's always *beyond* beautiful—she had to be in order to become swept within the orbit of someone like him.

But here she is, in the flesh, and my self-deprecating fantasies didn't even do her justice. *Irina.* Tall and slender, her long, curling blond hair ends at her waist, and her beautiful features convey poise and confidence—high cheekbones, perfect pouty lips, and a figure to die for.

I self-consciously run my fingers over the skirt of my outfit, trying and failing to maintain my fake smile. My first thought is that she didn't come dressed to impress her daughter. A tight-fitting navy dress exposes a wealth of cleavage, clinging to her narrow hips, hugging every curve not shrouded by her tailored black jacket. I can't help but picture her with the man standing before me, their hands entwined…

And they look fucking perfect, despite the fact that Vadim is still wearing a pair of sweats, rumpled from riding.

My only consolation is an entirely selfish realization—she and Magda could be strangers for all the similarities they share. The latter is a damn near carbon copy of her father with his delicate bone structure, for one—even her expressions seem to mirror his. It could be safely assumed that Irina might not be related to her at all, save for their eyes.

Vadim had called it himself—*those eyes*. Ice-cold blue, their twin gazes tether them together more strongly than any one feature of his. And I hate myself for being so bothered by that fact.

Awkwardly, I linger at the back of the foyer while Vadim blocks the doorway, frozen solid. Some genuine sympathy creeps in, gnawing away at my nerves. For all of my selfish reservations, this woman has one title I can't deny—a mother. Who am I to blame her for coming to see her child, even if it's out of the gosh darn blue?

Channeling my own mother, I force a polite smile and try to meet her gaze. "Hello—"

"It's been a long time," Irina says softly without looking my way once. Her voice is lilting, tinged with a heavy accent I can't place—but I'm too distracted by where her gaze is focused to really give a damn. The way she eyes the man standing between us…

There is a word to describe it, I think. That longing, desperate expression.

If my brain weren't on red alert with dread, I'd be able to come up with the right description. Maybe *ownership*? That would certainly explain why my cheeks catch fire, and I sense my chin tilt defensively into the air. Stepping forward, I slip my hand into Vadim's—not jealously. Just… Reassuringly. A silent way to reinforce that I'm here on this battlefield with him.

Because, I sense, this very much is a battle.

Irina herself imparts the first warning shot as her gaze finally settles over me. Only my time with Magda helps me interpret the icy shift in those unsettlingly blue irises. *Annoyance.*

"I was hoping we could speak in private." Her gaze lowers to our clasped hands and Vadim's flex, gripping mine almost to the point of pain—but just as quickly, the tension loosens.

"Tiffany…" From this angle, I can't see his face. I don't need to in order to picture his expression. Haunting, dark eyes implicitly closed off. Before I know it, his wall goes up, solid stone against me—and that realization stings. Almost as much as the act of him slipping his hand from mine does. "Why don't you go for a walk?" he suggests without turning around.

Hurt sears through my chest a split second before my ears perk up, catching the subtle, deliberate inflection in his voice. *Walk.* In this context, that clearly means something else when paired with how his gaze flicks toward the kitchen—and the tiny, helpless figure still there, oblivious to our visitor's arrival.

"Okay." With difficulty, I turn away, sensing Irina enter the house—her presence is *that* overwhelming. Cloying rose-scented perfume itches my nostrils as her voice taunts me, a low hum.

"I've missed you, my Dima," she tells him in a way that makes my chest constrict. "God, how I've missed you…"

Only sheer pride prevents me from turning back to see their reunion unfold. Determined, I make it into the kitchen, and there I spot the true target of my so-called "walk." Instantly my priorities shift, and I bite back any lingering unease.

"You okay, honey?"

Magda watches me from the very back of the space, her arms crossed, her gaze wary. A tiny pang of panic makes me falter and brace my hand against the nearest counter. Did she see Irina? Hear her? Recognize her? If she has, I doubt even my mother's skills of social navigation will help me much in this instance…

"Is it the man?" she asks. In response to my raised eyebrow, she adds, "The big, scary man." Her tone strives to convey bravery. If only her eyes weren't bug-wide, her jaw clenched.

But at least her assumption is so far off base, I doubt she knows our visitor's true identity. Though, as for a big, scary man… *Maxim?* Forcing a smile, I shake my head. "No, honey. Just boring adult business. How about we go for a walk?"

"A walk?" she parrots suspiciously, her arms still crossed.

"Yes. I bet it's lovely out." I stroll boldly through the sliding glass door leading to the terrace and promptly feel my plan change on the fly once I realize that it's pitch-black dark outside.

"So…no walk," I confess. As my eyes scan the brightly lit terrace, they fall over one promising diversion, however. "What about a swim?"

"Now?"

I have to smirk at the alarm in Magda's tone. Like father like daughter. Reckless, impulsive decisions aren't her style.

"Yes," I say, strutting boldly to the edge of the pool. She lingers back, but I glance over my shoulder to find her watching me with avid interest, bathed in the glow of a few lamps placed strategically throughout the terrace. "You've never taken a night swim before?"

Her tiny lips press together, and I can practically see the gears in her brain whirling. Does she trust me enough to divulge whatever bit of information she's mulling over? Finally, she sighs. "I can't swim."

Her voice is so soft, so guarded. I suspect the lacking skill is a sore point for her, and I chalk it up as yet another failure of her last foster family.

"I can teach you," I suggest, fighting to keep the surprising amount of genuine desire from my voice. I actually want to—though with her birth mother seemingly back in the picture...

Who knows if I'll get the chance?

Be positive, Tiffy. Forcing yet another grin, I shrug. "I may be too rusty in riding to help you with your pony, but I, my girl, have swum to and fro many a yacht party in the middle of the night."

I look back again to find her lips twitching, fighting a smile. "What's a yacht party?"

It's my turn to be guarded. "I'll tell you when you're older."

Sighing, Magda wraps her arms around herself and rocks onto her heels. "I'm cold. Can we go back into the house now?"

Shit. Thinking quickly, I skip to the edge of the pool, say a prayer for this beautiful Chanel ensemble, and then I dive in. The water is a shock to the system, but nowhere near as cold as it could be—as I kick, I recall something Vadim said about it being heated. The second I break the surface, I'm faced with a tiny figure leaning eagerly over the edge of the pool.

With her wide-eyed, gleeful expression, I barely recognize the same surly little girl.

"You are going to get into *so* much trouble," she declares, sounding ecstatic at the prospect.

As I let my brain toy with what my potential punishments may be—at the hands of my handsome punisher, of course—I feel myself more than matching her excitement.

"God, I hope so."

"You're all wet," she adds more sternly. "And your clothes are all ruined. You'll probably catch a cold. I bet you'll get in *big* trouble too."

My lips twitch into a gleeful smile at the prospect of a disciplinarian Vadim. That is, if he isn't with Irina right now, bending her over the desk in his office, overcome with lust at her return. My gaze drifts to the house as I picture it…

There goes my smile. To hide my worried expression, I lean back, kicking my legs in an easy backstroke.

"Trouble? I laugh in the face of trouble! And what about you, little Miss? Don't tell me you're afraid?"

"I'm not!" She frowns and inches ever closer to the edge of the pool. As she eyes the water, her expression wavers in such a childlike display of hesitation that my heart swells at the adorableness of it all.

"Chicken?" I ask her playfully.

"I can't swim," she insists, sounding irritated at having to announce her weakness to the world a second time. So prideful, just like her father.

"I'll catch you," I suggest, swimming toward her. "I promise. Keep your feet together. Jump straight down—just whatever you do, don't panic. I've got you."

Her eyes narrow, her lips pursed in a damn near carbon copy of one of her father's wary expressions. "Promise?"

I stick out my pinky, deadly serious. "I promise."

Her eyes blaze as if she wants more than anything to deny that. Prove me wrong. So young, but so mistrustful already. I'm sure she'll refuse and go storming back into the house when she steps back, smoothing her hands over her beautiful new outfit.

"I'll always have your back," I tell her. "You can trust me."

She shoots me a fearful glance—glimpsed without her trademark mini-wall—and before I even have the chance to mull over the implications, she jumps into the pool. I lunge forward, slipping my arms around her the second I sense her start to flail. She claws at my arms, her tiny nails biting in, but I can tell that she's trying hard not to panic, even as she sputters at the air, her expression shocked.

"See?" Gently, I kick my legs, sending us further out into the water. "There's nothing to it."

She eyes me skeptically, her teeth chattering. But when I shift to let her kick on her own, she does, clinging to my arms as I steer her into the shallower end.

"Good job! It's not so bad, is it?" I praise as she paddles with all her might to stay afloat.

Her tiny lips twitch. Fighting a smile? A frown? In the end, an impishly self-satisfied grin shapes her mouth for just a second. I let her practice for a few more laps before bringing her to the end of the pool. The second she can touch down with her own feet, she lets me go, but her mouth is stretched wide. Definitely a smile this time.

"You'll teach me more?" she asks, barely managing to disguise her eagerness. "So, I can swim by myself?"

I nod and then playfully flick my wrist splashing her. "You've got it—"

"What on earth is going on here?"

We whip around to find Vadim standing at the opposite end of the pool, his arms crossed, the picture of playful discipline. I feel my toes curl, and my heart drop in the same conflicting motion. One might never guess that, seconds ago, he had to deal with a literal demon from his past. Staying in the pool feels preferable to confronting whatever reality might await inside the house.

His disarming smirk gives me no clue, only unnerving me further. "Whose idea was this?"

"She did it!" Magda scuttles from the water, waddling to his side as her sodden clothing clings to her tiny frame. Crossing her arms, she copies his posture, eyeing me disapprovingly. "I told her not to."

"And you were right," Vadim agrees, his tone ringing with authority. "Ena will kill me if you two track water throughout the house." His smile lessens the impact of that statement, however. Gone is the darkness I feel I should see in his gaze, and my unease nibbles deeper. Is Irina still here, lying in wait to meet her daughter?

Have they reconciled about her custody, already?

Together?

I try my damn hardest to make eye contact with Vadim as I swim to his corner, but his attention is fixated firmly on his daughter.

"What am I going to do with you?" He raises his hand to her, only to falter partway. Then something in his gaze hardens with resolve, and he tentatively ruffles one of her damp braids. Remarkably, she doesn't cringe from him—a fact that makes his dark eyes soften with such gentleness I bite back a groan. "You're soaked," he tells her, some real concern slipping into his teasing murmur. "Let's hope you don't catch a cold, *oui*?"

"Yeah," Magda says, wrinkling her button nose.

A teensy bit of guilt dampens my enthusiasm as I climb from the pool and rise to my feet. "Maybe you should grab us some towels? That way we won't make too much of a mess—"

"But I'm little," Magda says, shifting toward Vadim conspiratorially. She tugs on his pant leg like a queen commanding a servant. "You can pick me up, and I won't drip like *she* will."

The little minx. She's so intent on her apparent victory that she doesn't seem to notice she gave him permission to touch her. Permission he accepts with a strained look of awe so potent my heart aches.

"Right you are." He shrugs off his sweatshirt and drapes it over her before lifting her gingerly into his arms. She eyes me smugly from her new height, and I can't resist seizing a chunk of her hair as I come up beside them, giving it a tug.

"Tattletale."

She swats me off, and I finally meet Vadim's gaze from over her head. Only for him to turn away. "Let's head inside," he says.

I follow them into the house without complaint, and I'm relieved—yet unnerved—to find the lower level seemingly empty. Even Ena isn't lurking in view. Neither is a breathtaking blond with more of a claim to this budding family than I have.

But as we cross the foyer, Magda stiffens, clinging to Vadim to the point that he has to adjust her grip around his neck to keep her from accidentally choking him.

"What's wrong?" he asks, his expression drawn with concern.

She doesn't answer. Her eyes worriedly scan the corners of the foyer, her nostrils flaring. Out of fear of Maxim?

"No one's here, sweetheart," I say, stroking through her damp hair. As the words leave my mouth, however, I realize that I'm not even sure of that fact.

"That's right," Vadim insists, his tone hard. "No one."

He forges onward upstairs and pauses only to grab a towel for me from a hall closet before carrying Magda straight into her room. As he ushers her into the bathtub, it's as if his entire demeanor changes without him seeming to realize it. His voice deepens, soothing but stern as he urges her to wait while he runs the water until it's warm enough.

While I slip into her closet and procure a nightgown, he scours her bedroom for anything out of place and then turns back her blankets. By the time she emerges from the bath, bundled in a robe, he descends on her with an army of towels and patiently dries every last curl.

I'm completely enthralled. Like a shameless voyeur, I find myself leaning against the doorway to the closet, as he grabs her brush and diligently tackles her hair, braiding it with a skill that leaves me both awed and seething with jealousy. To think that only a few days ago, he'd been worried about failing her. As it turns out, he's damn good at this dad thing.

When Magda huddles beneath her blankets, freshly dressed and pampered, he starts to pull away.

"Wait!" She tugs at his hand until he stills. Then she scans her room with laser focus. Spotting her doll, Biphany, on the nightstand, she grabs it, tucking it under her arm. Vadim seems to read his cue and stoops to lift something else from the floor—two halves of a decapitated teddy bear.

Magda sighs with relief and eagerly grasps for the torn pieces.

"We should fix him, *non?*" Vadim suggests as he sits on the side of her bed.

Magda nods solemnly even as she crushes the deflated bear to her chest, damaged or not.

"He needs advanced surgery," she decides, eyeing It's head with a weary sigh. "Multiple stitches. A stuffing transfusion… You'll do it?" She looks so wary as she phrases the question, almost as if she's afraid he'll refuse.

And Vadim, well aware of the gravity of the task, nods with the demeanor of a world-renowned surgeon. "Of course. It will be a grueling surgery," he explains, stroking a bit of the bear's ivory fur. "But I'm sure that if he is a good lad, he'll come through. Maybe with a present to mark his bravery."

"Good." Magda closes her eyes, snuggling beneath her blankets. Within seconds, she's already drifting off.

Quietly, Vadim and I escape her room, shutting off the light and closing the door behind us. Once we reach the bedroom, however, Mommy and Daddy lose the "E for everyone" rating.

My thoughts instantly shift to Irina, and a question about her is already on the tip of my tongue when I sense Vadim come up behind me.

"*Merde.*" He grabs me, wrenching up my sodden dress and cups me directly between my legs. The desperation with which he does so tempers the answering lust sparking to life inside my belly. He's more possessive than sensual, yanking me around so swiftly I have to clutch his shoulders just to stay upright. His mouth finds my throat, lips parting, teeth latching with a searing nip that makes me gasp.

Lust ignites my blood like liquid fire—so potent that I almost forget the world-shattering event at the forefront. Almost.

"Irina," I rasp as he strokes me, applying devious pressure to my clit, enhancing the placement of my piercing. *Holy crap.* I nearly lose my train of thought, and then I realize as his eyes hungrily watch me bite down a moan—that's what he wants.

To distract me.

"Tell me what happened." With difficultly, I break away from him, backing up to put distance between us. My body hums, craving him, but I force myself to deny the desire and meet his gaze with what I hope passes for a stern expression. "Tell me. What did she want? Is she still holding up the adoption?"

He turns away, putting his back to me. A heavy sigh betrays the exhaustion he hid so well in front of Magda—and the alarming instability that has become his hallmark. How he rakes his hands through his hair. Trembles with emotion. Gets that hard, low note in his voice I've come to associate with some impulsive gesture—like tying me up. Twice.

"I will tell you everything," he swears, his shoulders hunched, body radiating tension. "If, you tell me something first…"

My breath catches as I advance a step toward him. "Anything."

"Tell me that you'll marry me." He whirls around, fixing me with the full intensity of his gaze, and I stagger backward. His eyes are so damn dark, so fucking earnest and determined all at once. My throat dampens, my body pulsating even as alarm bells go off at the back of my mind.

Only as he starts to advance do I fully register what he said. "Vadim—"

"Tomorrow," he interjects as he continues to approach, backing me into a corner. Within a heartbeat, I'm trapped, forced to crane my neck just to take him in. "I already have the paperwork drawn up. Together, we will file for joint custody over Magdalene—"

"Slow down!" I place my hand on his chest, my voice breaking.

"You will adopt her," he continues as if I'd never spoken. "My lawyer has already set plans in motion to expedite the request. All I need is your signature. I have a judge on my payroll, ready to validate them—"

"Wait!" I feel like I'm spinning, forced to brace myself against the wall just to gain some semblance of stability. "Tell me what happened. What did Irina—"

"Fuck Irina!" His voice booms, startling me with the ferocity. The vitriol. The...fear. Too late, he seems to realize his mistake. His eyes dart to the door, his head cocked to listen for any hint of Magda stirring.

While he's distracted, I take my chance and escape to the opposite end of the bed.

"Tell me what happened," I plead, making my voice as soothing as I can. "Talk to me—"

"She is irrelevant," he says coldly. "You tell *me*. Say yes."

"Vadim…" I lean against the wall, my face in my hands. "This is a lot to take in. Maybe if you explain what happened—"

"It doesn't matter what happened. You claimed you wanted a relationship with me. Or will you let a woman you've never even met be your excuse to run?"

I blink. "I'm sorry?"

He barks out a harsh laugh, pacing the length of the windows. "Sorry," he echoes, eyeing his hands as they curl and uncurl into fists. "You spend my money. Mother my daughter though you tease the idea of leaving when it suits you. Fuck me senseless. And yet, you won't marry me. You refuse to."

I gasp, stunned. "That's a bit of a low blow," I croak. A surprisingly painful one too. I place my hand over the center of my chest, startled by a real actual ache throbbing there. "Demanding a woman marry you after barely a month is a bit unprecedented. Especially when you won't tell me why—"

"You know I would do anything for you." He makes it sound like a crime on my part. Something awful and corrupting that I did to him. *This.* I made him break down his wall. I forced him to let me in. Let me see those dark, twisted parts of himself no one else ever has.

But from where I'm standing, he's not the one clutching at his literal heart, feeling it swell too big to fit in his chest.

"Tell me what you want, and you will have it," he demands. His voice, though softer, still resonates like thunder, radiating more conviction than I think I've heard from him until now. In so many ways, he reminds me of his brother. Where they lack in physical similarities, this is what they must share—a ruthless intensity when it comes to what they want.

No matter who stands in their way.

Something in me breaks in the face of this emotion, and I sway, forced to slump onto the end of the bed, too drained to stay standing.

"My money?" he prods, stepping forward. "You have it. My home? You have it. My—"

"I don't want anything from you," I confess in a whisper. As his expression falls, I race to add, "I mean, not physically. I don't want a transactional relationship with you. I want… Time. I just need *time*."

More time to heal from Jim. Time to think. Time to feel like being with him is my decision and not a product of hastiness or desperation—it shocks me to realize how much I truly want that—a natural progression with him. Nothing forced or faked.

I want this to be real.

"Just give me time." I gather the nerve to meet his expression and suck in a hopeful breath. His eyes are still narrowed, his jaw clenched—but that awful, bitter suspicion is gone, replaced by a hunger I'm too tired to deny. I raise my hands to the straps of my dress, guiding them down my shoulders as he tracks every bared bit of flesh with an expression that makes my toes curl. "Can you do that for me? Just give me time."

He doesn't answer. With one monstrous lunge on his part, I'm in his arms, swept toward the center of the bed. He strips my sodden clothing, groping the flesh underneath. I react to him wantonly, letting him drown my logical brain in friction and touching and heat.

But even as our lips meet, I sense that unspoken figure looming between us, growing harder to ignore with every surging beat of my pulse. *Irina.*

Irina. Irina. Irina!

Though I seem to be the only one in this bed haunted by her.

Vadim groans, sinking his fingers into my hair as he manipulates me beneath him—legs splayed, hips pinned against his. Gone is his usual restraint—he enters me with a commanding thrust, going so deep we both cry out. *Holy hell.* There isn't even time for my body to adjust to him before he rocks his hips, taking me whether I'm ready or not. Hungrily.

Recklessly.

His piercing batters my inner walls, his size straining my limits. It's a sensation almost verging on uncomfortable—and he moves in a way that makes me suspect, with a hint of alarm, that's just what he wants. To force me to focus on him, taking him fully. Lulled by his rhythm, my thoughts dissipate. Then reform, still fixated on that beautiful, mysterious blond.

But it's as if he knows the second my attention shifts from him. Growling, he reaches between us, his thumb grazing my clit, teasing me with the weight of my piercing.

I feel my head tip back, my eyes fluttering shut as the pleasure builds with every stroke.

More. More. More.

A burst of wetness eases his next stroke. The next… But that's where all similarities to carefree, normal sex end. The second he shifts, gripping my chin, his eyes boring into mine with more ferocity than his cock, I know…

This is something more.

Claiming.

Owning.

Dominating.

He slows his pace, making me arch into him, my eyes rolling, breaths feathering. I almost can't bear to meet his gaze like this, head-on. He looks at me so hauntingly. It's…insane.

Like I'm a lifeline he's clinging to, strengthening his grip with every thrust. Every startled moan he wrenches from my chest. Helpless, my knees curl around his waist, dragging him in despite the urgings of my brain to stop this. Resist. Fight.

But I can't.

He has me. All I can do is hold on, groaning as the pleasure builds and builds, and he times his movements with calculated, piercing thrusts. My orgasm is punishing—a wave that hits like a freight train, slamming into me before I realize it.

To savor his victory, his lips capture my startled cry, his body bucking against me as he strives toward his own release. All the while, he strokes me, cradles me to him. Cherishes me.

It's an intimacy I've never known. Not with any other man. Not even within myself during my deepest moments of self-reflection.

It's torture in its truest, rawest, most debasing form.

A pain I can't deny or escape.

A pleasure that will undo me.

CHAPTER TWO

He lets me rest, panting for air as he shifts to sit on the end of the bed, his back to me. Despite everything, I reach for him, sensing the bricks of his wall reforming too quickly to batter down.

What the hell happened in the space of time I was in the pool? Something vital. Something that's shaken him so thoroughly even sex can't clear his head.

Much like he did when Irina first inserted her presence into his life again, he's spiraling.

"Don't shut me out," I whisper, my voice rasping and broken. "This isn't a rejection. I promise. I promise—"

"Every time you look at me, I can see you plotting your escape." His voice. It's ice-cold, such a contrast to how he spoke to me just mere seconds ago. I go rigid, the air trapped in my chest, my hand frozen inches from him.

"You take what you can from me, but it is never enough, is it?" He stands, striding for the bathroom. His stiffened posture warns me not to follow. Regardless, his voice reaches back like the snap of a whip. "I prefer for you to spend my money."

"V-Vadim!" I watch him go, blinking frantically. It isn't until a searing warmth runs down my cheeks that I realize I'm crying, hurt by that implication way more than I want to be. It sounds so dirty. So vicious—using him. Maybe I have. Maybe I am.

But sometimes, manipulation is a two-way street.

I hear the water run, used as a barrier to disguise the sounds of what he's doing. Splashing water onto his face? Showering? The former, I suspect when he returns, dry save for his damp hair, mussed as if torn through by raking, ruthless fingers.

"What did she say to you?" I demand, alarmed by this shift in him. He isn't like this—driven by emotion. Wild.

Callous.

His eyes meet mine, so cold I gasp, shrinking in my seat. "What will it take?" he demands, stopping short just beyond the bed, utterly naked. When I sputter wordlessly, he crosses his arms, his chin cocked in that cruel, calculating way he does when only one thing is on his mind. Business. "Name your price. More money? Clothing? Shoes?"

"Don't do this." I shut my eyes just to get a reprieve from his icy exterior. "Don't hurt me. I am not rejecting you—"

"What do you call it then?" he counters. "When a man offers you the world, and you not only spit on his hand. You demand his thoughts. His secrets. You always ask for more."

I flinch. "I call it one thing—"

"What?"

"I'm scared!" My voice breaks, echoing so violently I'm sure Magda can hear it. We both wait, straining through the silence, but no other sound stirs. Just his frantic, furious—gosh, he's so angry—breaths, and my shallow whimpers as I fight back the tears I feel brewing.

"I'm scared, okay? I marry you in the heat of the moment when your thoughts are on your daughter—as they should be. But what happens in six months when the danger wears off?"

I draw my knees beneath my chin, hunched against the mattress as tears spill down my cheeks, wetting the sheets beneath me. "I'll tell you what. You realize that you're shackled to a…" My voice breaks. I'm channeling my ex-husband in this moment. What were the words he said to me on the eve of our divorce? "A lazy, selfish, self-centered, spoiled bitch who can't even run a home, let alone fend for herself. That's fine in a one-night stand," I add, laughing bitterly. "I know my limits. But do you? Do you want more children? I told you about my miscarriage, but I never told you why. It's not easy for me to get pregnant. Most doctors I consulted recommended IVF. Painful, expensive, grueling treatments that may or may not work. Are you willing to sign up for that? Are you willing to sign up for supporting someone who can't even hold a fucking job outside of one handed to her because her husband is prominent in a church? You claim I'm after your money? Money can only get you so far."

It can get you a life, beautiful on the outside, but jagged and agonizing within. A world wherein people only see your worth in a resume or who put a ring on your finger. A world I went on a wild, sexual goose chase just to escape.

"I'm not holding back out of fear for myself. I'm fearful for you! I don't… I don't want to disappoint you. I don't want you to wake up one day, bored, and go looking for another model. I don't want to be broken again. I *want* a relationship with you."

The mattress shifts. Warmth engulfs me, drawing me into a body that conforms to mine, strong and welcoming. He holds me so tightly I couldn't pull away, even if I wanted to. His voice bathes me in reassurance, so gentle that I relax instantly, my fear drained. He says something in French, too grated to decipher.

In this moment, I don't need to. I don't need anything from him but this. Silence. Nearness. Understanding.

I hide my face against his chest, seeking out any comfort in his embrace I can find. The real world can wait—because this conversation isn't over. Not by a long shot.

But for now, he relents.

And I have a fraction of more time.

I WAKE up before he does and escape into a robe, throwing on a nightgown underneath. Entering the hallway, I stop by Magda's room and peek in to find her still sleeping.

Thank God.

Craving silence, I steal into the kitchen and make myself a cup of tea.

I've barely taken a sip before my opponent appears across from me, dressed in a shirt and slacks that look as though he just tugged them on without any forethought. As he claims the seat at the end of the table, I sense the war horns being blown.

Another round is about to take place—because our battle isn't over.

"Look at me," he demands.

Because my gaze is on the window apparently, watching dawn claw across the horizon. When I risk sneaking a glance in his direction, I gasp, struck dumb by his expression. Gone is the icy rage from last night. He's too calm now.

Disarming in his persistence. He's brought weapons to this fight, I realize—a stack of documents that he places on the table and shoves toward me.

I glance at them, my heart racing. Sure enough, my worst fears are confirmed as I read the topmost line of the first page. *Petition to adopt...*

"Vadim—"

"I heard your concerns," he says, in a tone like thunder, though alarmingly quiet so as not to disturb anyone beyond this room. "Now, you hear mine. My daughter... You think I would offer her guardianship to you on a whim? That I would entrust her to anyone else? I've stood in the background of her life for too damn long, never would I jeopardize her safety or her trust. Never."

I set my tea aside, overwhelmed, and clutch my head in my hands, desperate to keep my thoughts focused. "Vadim, this is—"

"And I don't extend an offer of marriage lightly," he adds, easily cutting over me. "Do you know how many women have tried to seduce me? Fool me? Deceive me? I have seen through them all. Outsmarted them all." He's proud of that, I realize. Prideful, and defensive. "I knew from the second you approached me at that bar that you were different. Why? I wasn't your first choice," he says as if seeing right into my thoughts. My very soul. "I wasn't even your second or third. You approached me with no preconceived notions or deception, though I wanted to deny it. I did deny it. You approached me as a game," he says, his brow furrowing, eyes blazing. "To see if I could give you the fun you sought. Or not. You didn't care. If I failed, you would easily seek your fortune with someone else. It was so damn *easy* for you to find someone else."

His tone turns feral, and I picture him recalling all those men I'd taunted him with. Nearly run off to bed with. He's right, I'd treated it as a game—but only because he kept pushing me away. He hurt me, each time he did so.

"I had to fight to keep you entertained," he adds, gritting his teeth at the thought. Him, fight? As though he never has. Never sought a relationship with someone else before me—or maybe he *did*, I realize with growing horror…

Only for that person to reject him. Spurn him so badly he preferred to live his life closed-off, expecting only the worst from those who dared approach him. And the second he does let down his guard, that past rejection makes him spiral into paranoia.

Who was the culprit? Irina? Maxim? In this moment, I don't even think it matters who. They aren't the object of his focus now. His ire. His rage.

"I've plied you," he adds through gritted teeth. "Tempted you. Bought you. Fucked you. Tasted you. And yet it feels as if it's never enough. Like I'm always a heartbeat from losing you. You are still playing your game—"

"No!" I cringe at the woman he's describing and push back from the table. "I never manipulated you," I point out, shaking my head. "I never hurt you or tried to play mind games at your expense."

"Correct." He nods, his eyes are so dark I swear I can see myself reflected in them—a small, fragile woman on the verge of something both horrific and lifechanging. A realization. A mental breakdown. Who the hell knows?

"You just tease," he growls, palming the table with a quiet thud that sends my heart racing. "You give me a taste of everything I fucking never knew, and you threaten, every minute, to take it all away."

"Vadim…" I can't look at him anymore. I break, forfeiting the round to stare down at my hands. They're shaking. "What do you want from me?"

"I want everything." He sounds so hollow. So cold. A man denied warmth for so damn long he doesn't even remember what it feels like. Just that he craves it above all else. Jealously, he craves it. "Your body." But his tone implies something else. Something that makes me stiffen, desperate to head him off.

"Don't—"

"Your touch."

"Stop it—"

"Your taste. Your love—"

"Vadim!" I lurch to my feet, scrambling for the terrace door. My eyes are burning, vision blurring. Putting distance between us now is my only hope for escape. "I'm going for a walk."

"So you run," he snarls. "As is the case with everyone else, I am never enough to keep you."

I stagger, so wounded I nearly collapse right then and there. There's so much pain in his voice. Such awful, unending pain…

And a terrifying threat.

"Is this about whatever happened with Irina?" I say, deploying my own secret weapon. "Just tell me what she said—"

"You want time?" he questions. The telltale scrape of a chair over the flooring warns of him standing, his steps heavy. "You have it. But I suggest you not take too long. I am well used to the pain that comes from rejection by others—but Magdalene? My daughter will never know that pain again. *Never.* You can toy with me all you'd like, but I won't let you trap her in your web. Never will you be the one to take her happiness away."

His steps advance from the kitchen, moving toward the foyer.

"Leave or stay," he adds. "But know that I am done playing your game."

He retreats to some distant corner of the house, and I slump against the nearest wall, gasping for air. My chest feels so damn tight. Like it's caught in a vice, being crushed between desire and fear. Ultimatums are nothing new—Jim tossed out his fair share.

But none ever left me feeling like this…

Shaken to my fucking core. Beaten down to a fragile shell seconds from cracking. No one else in my entire life has ever left me so uncertain. Of myself. Of the world around me. Of my heart and every fiber making up the body I've spent twenty-eight years dwelling within.

I don't even process moving, but eventually, I find myself outside, sitting on the edge of the pool in the frigid morning air, shivering, my legs calf-deep in the water. I don't know how long I've sat like this. Just that my only tether to the real world comes in the form of a tiny, disapproving voice speaking to me from the direction of the house.

"Are you going to go swimming in your clothes again?"

I turn to find Magda watching me from the doorway of the kitchen. She's neatly dressed in a light blue skirt and magenta sweater. Someone took the time to brush her hair and braid it with meticulous care, securing two pigtails with pure white ribbons.

I don't know why I flinch at first. Vadim's her father, he should be the one to help her. And yet, I can't help but interpret the act as a threat, its warning simple. When it comes down to it, I'm not needed.

"No," I tell her, forcing a tired smile. "I'm just thinking." I kick my legs for emphasis, sending up a spray of water.

Warily, she slips from around the door and approaches me, her hands on her hips. "Can I play with Ainsley today?" she asks.

I sigh, turning my gaze to the churning waters of the bay beyond our quiet spot. "I don't know, honey. You'll have to ask your father—Mr. Vadim."

A glance from the corner of my eye reveals her pouting, but seemingly undeterred. "I'm hungry."

"Okay." I unfurl my sore limbs and follow her into the kitchen. There, I spot the time above the stove and realize that I've lost at least three hours, just staring into space. I'm freezing as a result, shivering violently as I adjust to the heat of the house.

After making Magda a bowl of cereal, I creep upstairs into the master bedroom, relieved to find it empty. I shower quickly and throw on a relatively casual outfit consisting of a light linen dress and a sweater. When I return downstairs, Magda's still seated at the table, but a larger figure dominates the space beside her.

He's adjusted his outfit, smoothing out the rumpled appearance to regain his polished composure. The only oddity to contrast his icy, businessman persona is the fact that he's manipulating a white teddy bear with utmost care.

It got a makeover, it seems. His fur is a brighter, cleaner white as if he took a trip through the washing machine. He's also been freshly stuffed, his head sewn back on and adorned with a tiny red scarf to hide the stitching around his neck.

"What do we think?" Vadim asks, holding the toy up for Magda's inspection.

She observes the bear critically and then nods in approval, reaching for it. Vadim watches as she tucks the bear under her arm, betraying a sentiment that makes my throat constrict.

It's like my torment alerts him to my presence before any other clue. His head jerks up, those dark eyes roving in my direction. Coldly, they graze over me before returning to his daughter as he smooths his fingers over one of her braids.

"Would you like to ride Dasha today?" he asks, referring to her pony.

She perks up. "Can we?" She's already lurching to her feet and bounding from the kitchen by the time he tells her yes. I step aside, my lips parting into a smile. But the expression lasts until the second I see Vadim's face.

Gone is the warmth he displayed around his daughter. That coldness sets in, hardening the line of his jaw and making his gaze so chilling, I'm frozen even in my sweater. The worst part is that his wall is down all the way, and there's nothing to temper the hostility. The raw pain he displays, making one fact overwhelmingly clear.

It's all my fault.

And yet, I can't seem to move. I'm frozen, caught like a deer in the headlights of this fragile truce until Magda comes racing back into the kitchen, her skirt swapped for jodhpurs, her riding helmet in place.

Like magic, Vadim's face transforms again, radiating warmth as he stands and follows her out. Before she steps over the threshold, however, she looks back, her gaze finding me.

"Are you going to come to watch?" she asks in that wary, hesitant tone. As if, like Vadim, she's guarding herself from me, still unsure.

I nod as enthusiastically as I can. "Of course!"

"Then come on." She squares her shoulders and marches off, her father in tow. And I promptly stagger to the nearest counter, gripping the edge so tightly my knuckles whiten.

Get it together, Tiffany, my inner bitch warns. But even she sounds shaken, a shadow of the guidance that has driven me since leaving Jim. That's the scary part. Everything I rebuilt of myself—everything I managed to salvage of the shadow I became—I can feel splintering around me, in danger of crumbling all over again. Will the resulting

Tiffany be stronger or worse off in the aftermath? I don't know.

I don't know anything about myself anymore. My thinking has been corrupted, shaped by a man who seems to crave me one minute, only to push me away the next. Then crave again, somehow making me feel as though it's my fault for letting him shove. And if he keeps on shoving, I'm going to fall eventually.

Right, a part of me hisses. *So, grit your teeth, dig your heels in and stand firm. What do you want?*

Him. But on my terms, with enough time to ensure that this is really what he wants as well. I rushed into marriage with Jim and look how that turned out? I deserve the chance to convince myself in every way that life with Vadim is worth the inherent risks.

Because Jim hurt me so badly, it took a reckless vow of sexual exploration to get me back on my feet. Vadim? I can feel the echoes of that old pain where he is concerned —tenfold. He won't just break me if I lose him the same way.

This man could utterly destroy me.

And yet it's almost too easy to plaster a fake smile onto my face and skip out to the stable as if nothing is wrong. In one of the fenced-in pastures, I spot Magda, sitting astride her pony as Vadim directs her from the center of the paddock, holding a pink lead rope.

Watching them interact is always engrossing, but now with the sun shining and both of them fighting back grins? I'm helpless to resist. Creeping forward, I slip my fingers through the wooden slats of the fence and watch, my heart aching, my thoughts in disarray.

They move together so well, a beautiful synchrony. With gentle words and reminders, he corrects her posture and offers encouragement. With every word from him, she sits straighter, her eyes brightening, her lips twitching until a genuine grin unfurls despite herself. The potential relationship building between them could be something fearsome to behold—a partnership no one could ever come in between. But one with room for anyone else?

That remains to be seen. And I'm not the only one mulling that very question, I suspect. In the snatches of time that Magda's back is to him, Vadim's expression slips, revealing a tumult of contradicting emotions. Every now and again, he'll look at me, his gaze still accusatory. Wounded. But the second he senses his daughter's attention on him, he suppresses the darkness, greeting her only with the light.

It's like being tortured, over and over again, leaving me grasping the paddock for sole support as I'm teased with the full extent of his happiness and then stabbed with his anger.

Again. Again. Again.

I barely notice the sound of approaching footsteps, until a childish bit of laughter reaches my ears. From Magda, I realize in shock. She's practically bouncing in her saddle, waving frantically at a pair of figures advancing across the fields behind me.

Our intruders somehow made it past Ena, given the unofficial seal of approval to cut into the property from its west end. One of the figures sprints ahead, her dirty-blond hair flying out like a missile behind her. Within seconds, she's at the paddock gates, cooing. "Wow! He's so pretty," she says with all of the solemn awe a child can possess.

Magda beams, so proud from her perch. "*She* is pretty," she corrects. "Want to pet her?"

Ainsley looks to Vadim for permission, who tightens his grip on the lead rope and helps Magda down. Then he approaches the gate, allowing Ainsley inside, and stands watch as the girls fuss over the pony. It's adorably cute in the brief moments those dark, storming eyes avoid meeting mine.

But then they do, and the resulting chill is enough to drive me back from the paddock altogether. Wrapping my arms around my torso, I turn and spot the lone figure lingering on the path, her gaze wary and watchful over the trio behind me.

Sighing, I advance toward her, forcing a neutral smile. "Hey!"

"Hey," Francesca replies, though she barely takes her eyes off her sister to greet me. Both enemy subjects are dressed warmly—Ainsley in a pink sweater and jeans, Francesca in a black woolen dress and jacket. Her dark hair frames her face, hanging down her shoulders.

"I'm glad you came over," I say, genuinely pleased for Magda.

Francesca's lips part into a small grin. "It's good for Ains to play with someone her own age. Someone other than her brother Eric, at least. And I could use a break from the fighting."

"I hear you on that," I murmur, glancing over my shoulder. Even while outnumbered, Vadim maintains his trademark charm. Always the master manipulator, he has the girls spellbound, teaching them various parts of the horse mingled with jokes and exaggerated expressions that have them giggling.

"Cover your mouth, Ains!" Francesca calls as the girl sneezes mid-cackle. Then she turns to me, and something in my expression must trigger her alarm. "Sorry. I think she may be coming down with a cold… Are you okay? This isn't a bad time—"

"No, of course not!" I make my grin wider, playing up my own social charms. "How about we let the girls play and have our own playdate? I have the best wine—" I eye her warily with what I hope passes for a friendly chuckle. "You are twenty-one, right?"

"I don't really drink…" Her gaze strays again to her sister. Is she worried about Vadim?

With an awkward bit of guilt, I remember the whole tiny detail about him having kidnapped Ainsley once upon a time.

"Right," I say nervously. "Well, we could just hang around, and—"

"No." Francesca shakes her head, forcing a heavy sigh. "No, you're right. A glass of wine sounds great."

"Good!" I'm so relieved, I sway. "I could use a bit of adult time, to be honest."

At least time with an adult who isn't intent on consuming me, body, and soul.

CHAPTER THREE

"I got married young," I blurt out once Francesca and I are settled into lounge chairs, positioned halfway between the house and the stable. From this position, we have a clear view of our charges, but are far enough back to let the girls play in peace.

In my hand is a glass of wine, while hers rests untouched, balanced on the arm of her chair. Lacking her restraint, I drink deeply as my eyes trace the contours of Vadim's silhouette, visible from here.

"I was too young," I add, lowering my voice for my audience of one. "So young, I had no idea who I was or what I even wanted out of life. I let the thrill of belonging to someone completely shape me. In the end, it almost destroyed me. But, you don't want to hear about that," I add with a forced, hollow laugh. "Listen to me, babble on about nothing. How are things on your end?"

"Good," she says. But her brown eyes trace mine, too damn alert. Aware. There's something in her expression that makes me squirm until, helpless, I find myself desperate to spill more.

"You're not afraid?" I ask. "Of marrying Maxim?"

She averts her gaze from me and lifts her glass, taking a sip. "I was," she confesses after swallowing. "I was terrified as hell."

"But?" I prod, already halfway through my glass. Thankfully, I brought the bottle, leaving it perched against my calf.

She frowns. "He gets me better than anyone. And I may be young, but I've been through a lot. He gets me."

I'm instantly drawn to the unapologetic nature in her tone. No bullshit, I suspect. No love-blind sugar coating. Just raw honesty.

He gets me.

"Does Maxim know you're here? I have to say that I'm surprised you came over."

A hint of unease slips into her weary grin. "He's out of town," she says. I remember the conversation I'd overhead a few days ago between Vadim and Milton—Maxim was in Russia apparently, dealing with some kind of business disruption. "I told him Ainsley, and I were going out today—but I didn't say to where. Ainsley's been begging me for the past two days, and Lucius promised to cover for me. We have about an hour before we need to head back, though."

Lucius, I suspect, is the kind, older man who allowed Magda and I onto their property the other day. And his sudden leniency most likely has everything to do with the former's charms. I look over to find her relishing in the attention from both her father and her new friend—a different girl from the surly, brooding figure who came here just over a week ago.

"Is there a reason you're thinking about marriage?" Francesca asks, her tone gently probing.

With another sip of wine and a sigh, I relent. "Yes. There is a reason. A twenty-four-carat reason." I'm eyeing the fake engagement ring on my finger, but who knows what Vadim would spring for as the real deal. Something obscenely expensive, I suspect, and the thought of it terrifies me. Denying him terrifies me. As afraid as I am of the potential downfalls, I'm quickly realizing that I don't want to lose him. Not like this.

Because as volatile as his mood has been these past twenty-four hours, something tells me that one culprit is behind the shift. *Irina.* She said something to set him on edge, making him jump to a hasty marriage as his only solution.

"But I'm not ready," I admit out loud. "I'm not."

"And if Dima is anything like Maxim, you feel like you don't have a choice," Francesca says softly.

There's lingering pain in her voice, alluding to a wound that I suspect is every bit as deep as the one festering in my heart at the moment. Sadly, I tilt my glass as my gaze finds the sole cause of my torment. "I'll drink to that—"

"But," Francesca adds without lifting her glass to her mouth, "You can't have a relationship built on just one person's rules. There has to be a give and take…" She trails off, her gaze fixated somewhere in the distance. After a few seconds, she shakes her head and sighs. "I don't think you should let anyone pressure you if you aren't ready. You'll only lose yourself in the end."

"It's not that," I say, feeling some need to defend Vadim from the picture my dancing around the subject is creating. "It's just…"

I'm not sure just what point I'm trying to make. To avoid the subject entirely, I down the rest of my glass as the girls scamper around the paddock.

But the niggling, defensive feeling won't leave. Finally, with a sigh, I'm forced to confront it. "I lost myself once," I admit. "I swore to myself I'd never let it happen again."

Francesca eyes me simply, her gaze conveying more maturity than her age should allow her to. "Then don't," she says, as if it's that easy.

But in the realm of Vadim Gorgoshev, I'm not sure that anything truly is.

THE SECOND, Francesca and Ainsley leave, Vadim helps Magda cool down and stable Dasha while I watch from the safety of my lounge chair. Together, we finally return to the house, and I sense an even firmer boundary settling between us.

An ocean of emotional distance separates me from Vadim as we file into the kitchen, and he heads to the fridge, presumably to make dinner. He doesn't look my way once, his shoulders rigid, his warm tone solely reserved for his daughter.

"Spaghetti?" he suggests to her while rummaging through various cupboards.

"Okay." She nods in agreement, clutching her riding helmet to her chest.

"I'll get it ready. You go get washed up, *oui*?"

"Okay!" She dutifully sets off, and I don't even realize I'm following after her until his voice reaches me, a cautious rasp.

"Tiffany…"

"I should help her get ready," I say, practically running for the stairs. Magda looks surprised when I enter her room, but like the princess she is, she promptly points to her closet.

"I want to wear my pink pajamas," she declares, and like a good servant, I rush to obey.

As she showers, I lay out the clothing on her bed. The moment she reappears, I make a show of fussing over her, helping her towel dry her hair and braid it.

"You took a very steamy shower, you lobster," I tease, running my hand over her scalp. "You're still boiling."

"Can you teach me to swim tomorrow?" she asks, her eyelids heavy.

"Sure," I say, oddly touched by the request. At least someone wants me around. "As long as it's not too cold out. Maybe we can go out on the boat, too?"

She holds out her tiny hand, raising her pinky. "Promise?"

Chuckling, I curl my own pinky around hers. "Promise. Now let's go eat."

Clutching the newly restored It to her chest, she bounds downstairs for dinner.

But I don't follow right away. Instead, I retreat into the bedroom and strip my own clothing. Then I enter the shower and linger until the water runs cold, and my shivering serves as a cover for my own silent sobs.

Get a grip, Tiffy, I try to tell myself. *You're a bad bitch, remember? Stop second-guessing yourself!*

But that's all I seem capable of doing while in the realm of Vadim Gorgoshev. Second-guessing. Fearing. Doubting. Questioning.

Something that can feel this damn good, and yet hurt this damn much... It can't be real, can it? Let alone healthy?

I haven't decided by the time I finally leave the shower and slip into a robe. The second I take a step over the threshold to the bedroom, however, I stop short, my gaze fixated on the creature watching me from the edge of the bed.

He's stripped his shirt, wearing just his slacks, his hair mussed like it is only when he's been tearing through it ruthlessly. Dark, his eyes track my every movement, hunting me with a predator's intensity as I tentatively take a step. Then another.

Still holding my gaze, he rises to his feet. His eyes blaze anger, but as they trace the low neckline of my robe, the lids lower, his lips parting. My heart hammers in response, and I don't shy away from his gaze, even with the tension simmering between us.

Lust is the one language we speak that transcends all others, and I'm so desperate for a connection...

It's like I lose control over my body. Myself.

With Jim, sex was always used as leverage. Or as a reward, if I'd jumped through various hoops and pleased him enough to deign indulging me in the moment.

With Vadim, sex is wild. Untamable. Communication. It is the only way I seem to be able to understand him. In groping, hungry touches the second I come close enough.

In a fierce, mind-melding kiss that renders me defenseless against him.

Hungrily, he grasps my hips, twisting around to shove me onto the bed. His gaze intent, he mounts the mattress after me. Hooking his fingers beneath my hips, he flips me onto my back, easing my legs apart before I can protest. This angle robs me of any leverage, forcing me to buck into him. Chase him. Crave him.

I shiver as he enters me, thrusting deep, taking what he can and battering down any resistance I may think to put up. His chest cages me in, his hands crushing me flat, controlling the pace. Angle. Everything. Mindless, I rock against him, letting him stretch me to my limits. Take me beyond them. Leave me quaking on the edge of sanity and then watch me fall.

This isn't over, I sense, even as we both gasp out in relief. Just a reprieve. A truce.

The real war is only beginning, and when he finally withdraws from me, spent, he collapses with his back to me, his shoulders rigid.

I go limp, panting against the sheets, my thoughts scattered, body still burning alight. If I had the strength to move, I would. Run far, far away—put distance between us any way I can.

Physically at least, because emotionally, we might as well be on different planets.

CHAPTER FOUR

I wake up, blinking at a partially darkened ceiling, though I'm not sure why. Closing my eyes, I'm already drifting back off when I hear it—a voice low with concern.

"Magda?" Vadim murmurs. I turn to find him rolling upright, dragging part of the sheet over his body. Magda stands on his end of the bed, her eyes half-closed, lips pursed. Seemingly in a daze, she tugs on his hand until he faces her.

"What is it, *ma chérie*?" Vadim questions, stroking her hair. But something makes him frown and press his palm to her forehead. "Shit! You're burning up." He lurches to his feet, snatching his pants from the floor. Once dressed, he lifts Magda into his arms, racing into the hall. "Ena!" I hear him shout. "Bring the car around! Now!"

"Vadim?" Shrugging off my exhaustion, I scramble to my feet and hunt for my discarded nightgown. By the time I make it downstairs, Vadim is already carrying Magda through the front entrance. Beyond them, a stern-faced Ena is waiting beside the compact gray car, opening the door to the backseat.

"Get her a change of clothes," Vadim commands, cutting his gaze to me. The raw, frantic desperation in his eyes takes my breath away, and I run off, anxious to help. Panting, I tear into Magda's room and find her gray suitcase under her bed. I snatch a change of clothing from her closet, along with pajamas and her toothbrush. Last but not least, I grab It and Biphany, still tucked beneath her blankets.

"I've got it!" I call as I peel down the stairs. But the front door is closed. When I wrench it open in confusion, I find the driveway empty.

And it's nearly a solid minute of staring before the truth sinks in.

They're gone.

And I've been left behind.

I spend all of five minutes searching the house for a phone before I realize that I don't even know Vadim's cell phone number should I find one. Or Ena's. Hell, I don't even know where the car keys are kept. A trip to the garage reveals nothing but mocking, empty vehicles I have no way of driving.

"Damn it!" I'm crying, I realize, as my hoarse sobs echo back to me. I'm not even hurt, not really. My overriding thought is that Magda needs her teddy bear. She needs her pajamas and a ribbon for her hair. She needs me to tuck her in—and God forbid she's sick enough to need intensive care…

I should be there.

I *need* to be there.

That driving thought has me running from the house on a whim, cutting through the woods that shroud the west side of the property. At the back of my mind, I try to imagine the picture I make—I'm barefoot, wearing only a thin nightgown, clutching a tiny suitcase to my chest. Only God knows how I appear to the older man approaching the edge of Maxim's property to meet me.

Lucius. He's wearing a suit, murmuring into an earpiece. "Stand down," he says to someone on the other end of the device before turning his attention to me. "Are you alright—"

"Please help me! I need to get to the hospital. Please. I need to be there. I don't know how. I don't…"

Lucius' expression shifts into one of stoic concern. As I shiver in anticipation of his reaction, he shrugs off his suit jacket and drapes it over me. Within minutes I'm being ushered into the back of a black car as he takes the wheel.

I barely even know what I'm saying. Just that Magda needs her bear. Her pajamas. Me.

"Do you know what hospital?" he asks gently.

I think I try to say something, but all I wind up doing is sobbing. Openly. Loudly. I don't even know why I'm upset. Maybe by the implicit understanding that this is it —my worst fear coming true. When hell breaks loose, I'm left behind, forced to scramble on my own. He didn't even think to wait for me, so used to forging ahead.

What kind of marriage would this be?

By the time we finally make it to the hospital, I'm resolved. Gritting my teeth, I swipe the tears from my face and school my expression into one of calm. I start to scramble from the backseat on my own, thanking Lucius profusely.

"Wait just a moment." He exits the car, but rather than open the door for me, he enters the hospital directly, leaving me to squirm and contemplate running in anyway. I deflate with relief, however, when he returns and presents me with not only a change of clothes—a sweater and pants with the price tags still on—but a sturdy pair of decent shoes and a visitor's badge with my name on it.

"She's in room 2207," he says after I quickly change in the backseat. How he knows as much is far too unsettling to question at the moment.

I'm more grateful than alarmed.

"Thank you," I tell him, grasping his hand. "Thank you so much!"

Inside, a woman at the front desk directs me to a set of elevators that bring me to the second floor. The moment I see the sign over the archway leading to the section of rooms Magda's belongs to, my heart sinks—Pediatric Intensive Care Unit.

When I gather the nerve to step over the threshold, I'm faced with yet another woman at the desk.

"Hello," I tell her, struggling to regain my charming persona. "I'm here to see the patient in 2207. My name is Tiffany Connors."

The woman nods and turns to her computer screen. Whatever she sees makes her frown and rise from her desk. "I'll be right back, Miss."

She disappears down a hallway only to return seconds later with Vadim in tow. He looks awful, a man apart from who he was only a few hours ago. The darkness once again has claimed his expression, but glimpsed without the filter of his wall...

It's terrifying.

"Thank you," he says to the clerk. Then he advances toward me and inclines his head to a small sitting room just off the unit entrance. "We need to talk."

I follow him, still clutching Magda's things to my chest. Before he can even say a word, I feel the need to place her suitcase on a nearby coffee table, open it and fish out It. "She needs this," I tell him, shoving the bear into his hands. "And I brought her brush and some ribbon."

He accepts the offering, but his expression doesn't ease one damn iota. If anything, the line of his jaw hardens against me. "You shouldn't have come."

I blink. "What... What do you mean? She needs her clothes and her bear, and—"

"I mean this is the time when she needs stability," Vadim says, his tone harsh. "A parent. Someone she can trust not to leave when she needs them the most. Someone who won't be cavalier with her health—"

"What..." I'm still processing his word usage. *Cavalier*—reckless. "What are you talking about?"

His eyes flash. In a violent motion, he tosses the bear across the room so hard it rebounds off a nearby couch, and I'm left stunned in the face of such a display.

"I mean, you refuse to adopt her," he growls, straining to keep his voice low. "You refuse to marry me. And now you want to tease her at a time when her health and safety is of the utmost importance? Was this your aim all along when you got her soaking wet in forty-degree weather? Slip out while she's rushed to the hospital? And what, you got cold feet and came back in guilt?"

I turn away from him, hunting for a chair, and I hurriedly perch myself on the edge of it. My brain is spinning, thoughts so tangled, it's almost painful to form coherence from his statements, pairing his anger with his words. But when I finally do, the resulting implication is soul-crushing.

"Are you saying I got her sick on purpose?" I whip my head around to face him. He doesn't even have the nerve to flinch. Look guilty. Anything but face me with such a cold, hostile expression.

I can feel something inside me crack—right in my chest. No therapy, sex, or wine could ever soothe this pain. And I know there's no way he could be doing this on purpose.

"You're upset," I say, staggering to my feet. "I can understand that. Let's just go see her—"

"No." He steps back, denying me the ability to reach for him. "You should leave."

A startled laugh escapes me before I can bite it back. "I'm not leaving her alone. No. I'm not." I picture the stoic figure who held a grudge against her father for leaving her in foster care, paired with the innocent girl who begged me to teach her to swim. "I'm not," I insist, shaking my head.

"She needs *me*," Vadim says, flicking his collar. "Someone she can trust."

"How…how dare you?" I can't breathe. My chest feels so damn tight. Looking at the man before me, I can't reconcile him with the figure who held me at night or bathed me with care. I'm numb, barely aware of the wetness sliding down my cheeks until my vision blurs, and I'm blinded by tears. "How dare you?"

"How dare I?" I sense him move—his shape distorted as more tears fall, impossible to stem. "You've already denied her once," he points out. "I think it's better if you leave now. Let her heal from your mistake, and your absence before your eventual departure hurts her more."

He grabs her suitcase and crosses the room, snatching It from the floor. Then he heads toward the unit, leaving me to scramble after him.

"Vadim, don't do this. Just let me see her—"

He stops short, so suddenly I nearly run into him. "I think it's best for everyone if you just go. Now. Ena will take you back to the house. Help yourself to what you wish. Just be gone by the time I return."

He marches forward, breezing past the front desk. When I try to follow, the woman seated there stands, her voice apologetic. "I'm sorry, Miss, but due to the nature of our unit, I can't let you by without permission from a parent or guardian."

I keep blinking at her as if that single action will make her disappear. Make this pain go away. I'll wake up in bed beside the Vadim I thought I knew, and this will all turn out to be some horrid nightmare.

I just keep blinking, as my legs move woodenly to navigate my way back into the elevator and down to the lobby. I keep blinking even as I find Ena waiting out front, his expression stern.

I just keep blinking.

But I never wake up from this nightmare.

CHAPTER FIVE

I n a daze, I return to the house, but I don't go upstairs to pack, even though I should. I find myself sitting at the dining room table instead, too numb to do anything but stare at a pile of mocking, goddamn documents. He made it sound so damn simple. Sign a piece of paper, claim joint custody of a little girl—like it was something people did on a daily basis.

On a whim.

Though in his world, maybe they do. Maxim did it? I wonder if that's where his anger truly stems from. Maxim supposedly didn't hesitate to take on six children when asked. But when it comes to his one?

I balk.

Because that's what normal people do when presented with the gravity of caring for a child, a part of me insists. *Leave, Tiffy. Run.*

Run…

I find the strength to stand and make it upstairs, but I don't enter the closet first. I stagger into the bathroom, alarmed by the woman I find watching me from the mirror's surface. Her eyes are bloodshot, her hair a mess, her outfit totally unfashionable.

She's a stranger—though not entirely. I've glimpsed her before, hunched over the sink, or cowering after a fight with Jim. After he made her feel so damn worthless…

And my already low mood plummets. What was that promise I made to myself all those months ago? Never again.

Bracing my hands over the countertop, I fight to take a deep breath. The moment I manage to drag in enough air, I release it slowly, tilting my head up to the ceiling. The last time I found myself in this position, I gave myself only a second to come up with a game plan. Back then, it was simple—live, kick ass, make my list. Fuck the world —literally.

But now?

This newer decision forms slowly, coming together as I strip my clothing and enter the shower, turning the water as hot as I can stand. Surrendering to the torrent, I let the heat and steam wash away my pain and hurt, watching it all circle the drain like blood. Then I towel off, and enter the closet, taking just one outfit from the hangers.

It's a modest gray dress. Without thinking, I select the matching jacket, and complete the outfit with a black leather purse and heels. The resulting effect is a more confident woman than the disheveled waif in gift shop clothing. And yet it's still not enough. I have to run a brush through my hair and carefully apply enough makeup to disguise the red blotches from crying. Then I line my eyes with liner and spread a soft pink lipstick on my lips.

Only now do I feel like myself again.

When I finally return downstairs, I'm surprised to find Ena leaning against the front door. Spotting me, he cocks his head, his expression wary.

"You go back?" His tone surprises me almost as much as his neutral gaze. It isn't hostile, for once.

I nod, and he grunts in reply, lumbering to open the door. "I bring car around."

"I'll be there in a moment." With my head held high, I take a detour into the kitchen, grabbing the handful of documents from the dining room table. I flip through them, picking out the adoption papers pertaining to Magda, ignoring the rest. He had this all planned out meticulously, it seems—the bastard even left his pen.

Lifting it, I give myself one last chance to second-guess the decision…

Before I sign my name on every last page. As I watch the ink dry, I rip off my fake engagement ring and leave it right by the unsigned marriage documents.

And don't regret a damn thing.

A DIFFERENT WOMAN claims the ICU reception desk when I approach. She takes one look at me, and her frown deepens as though she's recalling some warning about a woman matching my description.

The second I slam a stack of documents down before her, however, her frown fades.

"I'm here to see the patient in room 2207," I say in my chirpiest voice with my most charming smile. "I'm her legal guardian."

The woman nods and rises to her feet, but this time she beckons me after her, down a wide hallway and past an open nurse's station. Another woman is already advancing to meet us, her gray suit practical, a sturdy briefcase tucked under her arm.

"Mrs. Gorgoshev!" She extends her hand to me, her smile warm, and I vaguely recognize her as Magda's social worker. Ms. Anderson.

"I wish I could stay longer," she says with a small laugh. "Current circumstances aside, I'll confess that I don't think I've seen Magda look happier in a long time. I have the doctor's information, and they'll keep me posted on her condition…" She breaks off, scanning my face, and I sense her smile widen as if she's desperate to reassure me the same way she must soothe those in her care. "Don't worry now. She's a tough girl. And this visit is just a formality given her hospital admission. I have to get going, but I'll contact your husband about the next check-in. Have a wonderful day!"

She scampers off, leaving the nurse to continue forging the way through the small unit. There, in a room at the very back of the space, I find Magdalene, resting in bed, chatting animatedly to a figure who's seated beside her, holding her hand.

"…and then I wanna ride my pony, and—Tiffany!" Her tiny face breaks into a smile so wide it almost distracts from the alarming pallor of her skin. A sheen of sweat ghosts her forehead, gluing stray curls to the damp flesh. Gone are her neat braids, and the tousled style only enhances her similarities to the man nearby. While she may not be on a ventilator—thank God—a series of tubing extends from an IV. The mass of bandages looks monstrous encircling her fragile wrist. Not that the treatment has dampened her excitement any—she squirms, prevented from claiming the object I'm holding between two hands. "Is that for me?"

"It is," I tell her, placing a giant bear nearly as big as she is on the end of her bed. She beams, too exhausted I suspect, to feign disinterest.

The figure beside her quietly rises to his feet. I sense his eyes on me, unusually wide—with shock? It doesn't matter. In this moment, he doesn't exist, and I pour all of my attention into Magda as I pull up a free chair beside her.

"Where were you all day?" she demands, eyeing me with an eyebrow raised.

This time, I do make the mistake of glancing toward Vadim. His expression is guarded, impossible to read. I guess he spared Magdalene his little rant. He didn't even tell her I tried to visit.

But I don't have the heart to challenge that now—for Magda's sake. Instead, I smile and tug on one of her new bear's enormous arms. "I was trying to find the perfect friend to keep you company," I tease. "What shall you call him?"

"Hmmm." She bites her lip and shrugs. "I don't know yet."

"Well, you better think of something good." I slip out of my coat and fold it over the side of my chair.

"You're staying?" she asks, her expression brightening even more.

I nod. "Of course. In fact, I'm going to stay with you all night." As I speak, I fixate my gaze on the man standing near the doorway, letting every ounce of vitriol seep into my expression. It's so much I almost can't contain it without wanting to sob. Break.

But I don't.

"Whatever you need, I'm here. I'll always be here for *you.*"

Vadim says nothing until he finally crosses the threshold, his back to us. "I'll get you some more water, *chérie.*"

He leaves, and Magda promptly picks up whatever tale she was in the middle of conveying to him. Something about all of the things she wants to do once discharged from the hospital. Go on an airplane. See the beach. Ride her pony off the lead. Go bike riding. Eat ice cream.

I file away every request, determined to ensure she gets to do every last one.

"You came."

The grated voice draws me out of a light sleep, and I blink my eyes open to a spacious hospital room, lit only by a few dimmed lamps. Magda is sleeping, her chest rising and falling, her new bear practically swallowing her though she tried her damn hardest to wrestle it under one arm. It lies tucked beneath the blankets on her other side, with Biphany on her nightstand.

The sight of her erases any doubts that may have crept in as I slept. I have no regrets. Motherhood wasn't on my original list, but I can make an addendum. No relationships—*but* this one. For Magdalene.

As for her father?

I stiffen the second I sense him enter the room, his face in shadow, his posture rigid. "You signed the documents?" He doesn't sound doubtful—more prodding, as if this is his way of demanding proof.

Luckily for us both, I've come more than prepared to rub his nose in my decision.

Forcing out a cold laugh, I reach under my chair, snatching the adoption papers from my purse. I throw them at him, watching them scatter throughout the room like misshapen snowflakes.

"Yeah, I signed your fucking papers," I hiss.

Despite the vitriol, my voice is barely louder than a whisper, and I keep Magda in my line of sight, watching for any signs she might be awake. She looks so peaceful in this moment. So innocent. Even in my anger, I can't risk upsetting her. So, I direct every ounce of loathing I can into the harshest stage-whisper.

"But I did it for her," I croak, my throat tight. "Not you. As far as I'm concerned, I'm a single mother forced to share custody with an asshole who doesn't even have the privilege of being called my ex-husband. Congrats, Vadim. You're below Jim on the *people who have fucked me over* list. I hope you're pleased with yourself. Now take your fucking papers and get the hell out. In the morning, you can have time with her, considering you barred me all fucking day!"

He flinches so slightly it could be a trick of the light. Then that telltale muscle in his jaw twitches before his expression hardens with resolve. He crouches, carefully gathering up every last document. Then he tucks them under his arm and leaves.

And I'm more confused than ever, slumping in my seat, my eyes blinking fiercely. He should have been angry at my change of heart, right? Angry that I had the nerve to show up at all. Not…resigned?

Like baiting me into agreeing to take custody was his plan all along.

Because that would be far too cruel. Way too manipulative.

That would be unforgivable.

I wake up a second time to find Magda watching me from her bed, her blue eyes unreadable.

"How are you feeling?" I ask, placing my hand over one of hers.

"Better." She shrugs, ever the stoic. "But I'm hungry."

"Okay, honey." Yawning, I lurch to my feet and set off in search of a nurse. By the time her breakfast is served, and the nurse has finished her morning assessment—her vitals are improving, and pending another round of bloodwork, she could be discharged as early as tomorrow—Vadim arrives, and I promptly prepare to make my exit.

"You're leaving?" Magda watches me from over her breakfast tray, her eyes so wide that I assume she's been perfecting this innocent expression solely for moments like this. Gosh, she's so much like her father, but the comparison stings now more than it feels endearing.

An emotional terrorist with a devastating arsenal at her disposal.

"Yes, honey," I say, gathering up my coat as Vadim claims the chair on the opposite end of her bed. "I'll see you tonight."

I hesitate beside her only to change my mind at the last second. Boundaries be damned. Leaning down, I kiss her forehead. Her fever has broken, but she still feels clammy, her skin far too pale. "Don't have too much fun without me," I warn, tugging on one of her curls.

On my way out, I stop by the nurses' station and write down their number. Then I exit the hospital to find Ena waiting out front, as gruff as ever. But, as he steers the car back toward the house, he grunts in an uncharacteristic way. Then he speaks. "You no understand."

"I'm sorry?" I reply, aiming for politeness. I'm too tired to direct my anger at anyone but Vadim.

"You no understand," he insists, his jaw clenched as if speaking to me is an agonizing ordeal. And yet, he persists. "Mr. Vadim did not want to hurt you." He takes his time to phrase the words carefully. "He was scared. Scared of *her*."

"Irina?" I ask, my nostrils flaring. How could something as momentous as Magda's mother returning out of the blue go ignored until now? It just serves as a testament to the emotional roller coaster Vadim and his life have set me on. At this point, I'm no longer aware of which way is up or down. I'm trapped, along for the ride. "Magda's mother?"

Ena nods, snorting in disgust. "She crazy. Mr. Vadim only want to protect the girl."

Protect. It's a strong word to use in the context of a mother seeking to reconnect with her child. One that I suspect Ena isn't using lightly.

"Do you know her?"

He nods, and in the rearview mirror, I see his upper lip pull back from his teeth, his eyes narrowed. "I know her. She is viper. From the old days. Mr. Vadim never saw it, but Ena did." He nods, smug. And yet there's a hint of regret shaping his features. "She cannot have girl. He did it for her."

It being ban me from seeing Magda when she needed me the most. It as in turning the tables and yet demanding my trust. It as in shattering any hope of us ever being in a healthy relationship.

"He told you?" Ena demands. "Of the old days?"

He phrases it all so carefully that I recognize the sensitivity of the subject he's referring to—Vadim's past.

"Yes," I say thickly. "He told me. He told me… That you saved his life."

Ena's lips twitch into a scowl. "No. That place? It was hell. And Vadim, he good at pretending. They all did."

"Pretending?"

He shrugs, frustrated by my lack of understanding. "He was the only one to ask for help," he adds with deliberate slowness. "The others. They pretend. He didn't."

I say nothing, disturbed by the picture he paints. A hellscape of abused victims too conditioned to their ordeals to show their pain. The one time Vadim did—allow himself to be vulnerable—he expected to die soon after.

But what does he expect from me?

Ena doesn't give me any insight on that front, falling silent—though I sense he wants to say more. Maybe I should let him? About Irina and Vadim and their murky past, clouding everyone's judgment.

Or I can seethe and wallow, and try to lick my wounds in peace.

God, I need to be angry with him. Hate him. I don't think I'll have anything left in me otherwise.

Once we reach the house, I grab some food from the kitchen and shower. Then I leave the master bedroom, slip on my coat, and head out onto the terrace. It's freezing out, but I ignore the chill and curl up on a wooden-framed lounger overlooking the water. Not for the first time, I indulge in the idea of leaving. Running away. Ignoring Vadim and his fucked-up life and going back to California.

It startles me to realize how much I miss it. My old family home in the heart of wine country. My parents, whom I've been avoiding pretty much since my divorce out of shame. A sudden longing for home rises up so swiftly I sob silently in the face of it, and I decide on the spot to stop letting guilt and manipulation run my life.

Vadim won. He got his way to an extent—but I plan on taking my power back tenfold. He wanted me to be a mother to his daughter, then fine. But that means nothing as far as *he* is concerned.

And it's best I prove that fact to us both.

Sooner rather than later.

CHAPTER SIX

I don't know how, but I must fall asleep because I startle to awareness as a shadow falls over me. It's cast by a suit jacket, I realize, one someone is in the process of draping over me. My eyes drift up, spotting a beautiful face, so haggard my heart aches in sympathy. No man should carry such scars so openly—such pain.

But then I blink, and reality comes surging back. I remember, and I nearly fall off the lounger in my rush to get away from him.

"Don't touch me!"

"I apologize." Vadim recoils, his expression shifting, his wall lifting. "I didn't mean to scare you." He sounds so damn defensive. As if I don't have the right to shrug off his jacket and lurch to my feet, marching as far from him as the terrace space will allow.

Only now—as my legs buckle beneath me—do I realize that I'm freezing. That my fingers are numb, my teeth chattering so fiercely my jaw aches.

"You can have the bed," Vadim says, his tone eerily level. Ice. "I'll sleep in my office—"

"I don't want to sleep anywhere you've been," I hiss.

He nods. "I'll have a guest bedroom made up for you, then."

"Fuck off!" I cross my arms, storming to the end of the pool. "I'm sure you're so twisted in the head that you think I'd rather freeze to death on purpose. Catch a cold like I supposedly infected Magda?"

From the corner of my eye, I see him flinch as if struck. "I'm sorry," he grates. "I didn't mean—"

"Don't talk to me about mean! I will never forgive you for this. Never." My eyes burn, and the desperate need to salvage my pride makes me reckless enough to risk adding, "So I hope you're prepared to do long-distance parenting."

My threat takes a second to register. The moment it does, his entire posture shifts, his height lengthening, eyes narrowing. "Long-distance?"

I shiver at the subtle way his voice drops a dangerous octave.

"How is Magda?" I demand, picking another battle to fight—the one regarding my leaving can wait. Preferably when my bags are already packed and a plane ticket booked. Even now, I still hear his voice, persistent. *You haven't asked yourself, will I let you go?*

I'm trapped in the memory—and now his past words feel more of a threat than anything else.

"She's fine," Vadim says, drawing my attention back to him. "The doctor believes it is a minor infection, but given her history, they decided to monitor her more carefully. She's improving, at least. If her vital signs are stable by the morning, and if she continues to take her antibiotic, she can be discharged within a few days."

"Good." I suck in a breath and face him fully, squaring my shoulders. Screw waiting. Reclaiming my independence is now or never. "Because when she's out of the hospital, I'm going back to California."

I can't explain the way his expression shifts. It's like watching a violent storm roll across the landscape. His eyes flash, posture sways, voice booming like thunder.

"So, you *still* leave—"

"Leaving you, yes," I say nastily. "But you wanted me to have joint custody of Magda? Well, you got your wish, because I'm taking her with me. One week. I'll bring her back after that, but that's how we'll do this from now on. I can't live with you anymore."

His eyes turn so damn cold I stiffen in the face of his anger. But suddenly, he deflates. Boneless, he staggers to a nearby chair and collapses onto the end of it. Both hands shake as he tears them through his hair, sending the dark curls flying in every direction. "You would take her from me?"

He sounds so damn hurt at the mere prospect. So wounded, that even in my rage I can't relish in causing him this kind of pain.

"No. I'm not taking her from you. But you wanted me to be a mother to her? This is what happens when there is no trust between two parents. They separate. I want to go home. You forced me into this. Besides, don't my parents deserve to meet the new grandchild they had no clue existed when I left? Magda deserves to spend time with me, in my home. Or was that all a lie, and all you wanted was yet another toy in your game?"

"No!" He forms a first, slamming it onto the cushioned surface beneath him. "Fine. You want to take her? Fine. You want to leave me? *Fine.* But then admit it. All you wanted from me was to take, wasn't it? My money. My lust. Now my child—"

"No!" I'm blinking rapidly, but nothing can stop the tears from falling. "I wanted to love you! I could have if you just trusted me! Gave me time, like I asked."

It terrifies me to realize how close I'd been to getting there. Falling in love with him. Only now can I admit it to myself.

All along, I'd been on the edge of abandon.

"*You* ruined us, not me." I push past him and storm into the house. I navigate the layout in a blur and find Ena waiting for me out front, already in the driver's seat of the gray car. When I slip into the backseat, Vadim appears in the doorway of the house, his expression stricken.

I watch him as the car finally pulls off, but I fight back any more tears and angrily swipe away those already fallen. By the time I reach the hospital, I've nearly regained my composure, and when I enter Magda's room, I'm my charming, carefree self once more.

And no one will ever knock her down again.

MAGDA ISN'T DISCHARGED until a full four days after her admission. Though the doctor approves her traveling via plane, he cautions against an excess of sugar or exercise, at least for a week.

The latter prescription she takes the most umbrage at.

"I feel fine," she insists as I bundle her into the backseat while Ena watches on, his arms crossed. In our wake, Vadim follows at a safe distance, packing her things into the trunk. It's the first time in days that we've managed to be together in her presence for longer than the few tense seconds it takes to trade-off.

God, I can't even look at him.

"I should be able to ride my pony," Magda insists as I slide onto the seat beside her. "Right?" She glances mournfully at Vadim as he enters the front passenger's side.

"I'm afraid not, *chérie*," he says, calmly but firm. "But once you're fully recovered, I'll take you riding every day, *ça va?*"

"Okay." That seems to mollify her, and she sits back in her seat, clutching It to her chest. Despite her ever-growing collection, that bear is the one toy she's rarely without, battered to hell and back with signs of her affection.

Does that bother me? Maybe. Even if I'm determined to cut Vadim out of my life, as long as she's a part of it, he'll always be there. A festering wound encased in synthetic fucking fur.

"What's wrong?" Magda asks, adjusting her grip on It.

Forcing a grin, I shake my head. "N-Nothing!"

When we reach the house, Vadim heads for the trunk while I take Magda inside. As we head up to her room, I finally gather up the nerve to speak.

"Honey…" I guide her to the bed and crouch down as she sits on the edge of the mattress. Taking both her hands in mine, I force her to meet my gaze. "I've decided that I need to go back home, to where I'm from. All this cold is giving me wrinkles."

She frowns and wriggles her hands away. For a split second, she can't disguise the panic that shapes her features, widening her eyes and making her lips part. "Why?" she demands, crossing her arms, strangling her bear in the process. "Why are you leaving?"

I playfully tug on one of her braids. "I miss the sun, honey. And I think we could both use a walk along the beach. That's why I want you to come with me."

"Really?" Her expression brightens before something quickly makes her temper her excitement. "Is Vadim coming?" She says his name so carefully—as though she's deliberately avoiding calling him anything else. And the wary note in her voice paired with another uneasy frown makes me realize that she *does* want him to come. Even if she won't admit it.

Damn.

"Not at first," I say, with an enthusiasm I don't feel. "He has some business, and we need a girl's trip anyway. But maybe later in the week. Besides, you'll be back before you know it, and you can ride Dasha by then. At least this way, you won't be tempted."

She frowns, the gears in her brain turning. Then she nods. "Okay! When are we going?"

"Tomorrow."

She shrugs, kicking her legs, but doesn't argue. Feeling brave enough to risk it, I head into her closet and rifle through the hangers. "What would you like to bring?"

"Hmm…" She bounds to her feet and marches past me. "My sweater," she declares, fingering a turquoise ensemble. "And this."

"Okay."

We have an armful of items assembled by the time Vadim appears in the doorway, her suitcase in hand. He sets it on the floor, his jaw rigid as he spots the clothing I promptly place on the bed. I start folding various items, aware of his gaze boring a hole through the back of my neck.

When Magda shuffles from the closet carrying a stack of nightgowns, she inclines her head in his direction. "When are you coming?" Another rare hint of unease creeps into her voice.

"I… I'm not sure yet, *chérie*," he admits. From the corner of my eye, I see him crouch down to her level, his expression pained but neutral for her sake. His eyes dart toward me, and I turn away, folding a dress into thirds. "I have a lot of business to attend to. But I want you to have this. I promise to call you every single day."

"A phone?" Magda exclaims. I turn to find her brandishing a blue model with a touch screen. Wide-eyed, she meets his gaze, and he ruffles her hair.

"I am always just one call away," he tells her, cutting his gaze to me. "Always."

"Can we go swimming in the ocean?" she asks, her eyes still on her phone. I don't know if she's directing the question at him or me.

"Maybe," Vadim says before I can form a reply. "But anything you do will be a lot easier if you have this, hmm?" He pulls yet another present from nowhere—a blue and white polka dot fanny pack. Magda snatches for it, her eyes bug-wide.

"You can keep your phone in it, as well as your insulin supplies," Vadim explains while helping her strap the bag around her waist. "It is very important that you keep them safe. Especially when you play. No one else should ever take your medicine but you. Understood?"

She nods solemnly.

"And don't worry about your pony." He breaks his stern, fatherly character long enough to ruffle her braids, his smile strained. "Mr. Ena will take care of all of the horses while you're gone."

"Okay!" She climbs onto the bed, looking nothing like the sickly girl rushed to the hospital four days ago.

"Help me finish packing," I say to her gently. "And then we can eat dinner. We have an early flight tomorrow."

"Flight? We're going on an airplane?" Judging from her tone, a plane ride seems almost as appealing as riding her pony.

"Yes," Vadim cuts in before I can reply. "Your very own private plane, all to yourself."

I stiffen, biting back a retort. So much for the two commercial flights I'd booked last night. I know without bothering to ask that the bastard took the "liberty" of canceling them. I want to be pissed. Furious, even—but in this case, logic counters my irritation. It's probably not good for Magda to be squeezed onto a plane with hundreds of other people, anyway. So, I force a grin.

"You'll love it, honey. Now, why don't you go get washed up for dinner? Vadim and I will be downstairs."

I push past him and enter the doorway before I can fully process his startled grunt. He's on my heels, his breaths tainting the air, steps unsteady.

"Finally," he rasps once we reach the first floor. "We can talk—"

"No talking," I hiss, striding into the kitchen. "Just boundaries. You don't come near my parent's home without permission. You don't come near me. If you want to see Magda, you make arrangements for somewhere else, and I will bring her to you. Understood?"

I whirl to face him and suck in a breath. *Damn.* His expression is too open, and I'd give anything for the shelter of his wall. In lieu of it, the full extent of his gaze renders me weak. He's never looked so open as his dark eyes blaze with hurt. My knees buckle, throat hitches. I can't face him like this—so I turn to the row of windows overlooking the bay instead.

"I mean it," I whisper, my gaze on the churning waters in the distance. "You don't follow me—us. You don't pop up unannounced. If I didn't already tell Magda you'd come, I'd request you stay away from California entirely—"

"So you think to ban me from your world?" he demands, his tone that stormy, grated cadence that makes me quiver. "Rather than talk to me? I am sorry that I—"

"Sorry doesn't cut it!" My voice breaks, and I hate myself. Still, it's too late now, blinking back tears, I soldier on. "You accused me of trying to kill your daughter through reckless intent. Then you barred me from her hospital room. You told me to leave. Well, this is me, *leaving*."

"If you would just listen to reason, I wouldn't be forced to such measures," he growls—yet in a tone far too low for Magda to hear from upstairs. Regardless, his heavy footsteps resonate like gunshots, advancing toward me.

I scramble to a distant corner, but he's right on my heels. Too fast. I'm defenseless as he seizes my wrist in an iron grip, his breath fire against my ear.

"All I wanted was for you to hear me out," he growls, his chest hard against my back, his hips pressing against my ass. "But it seems you only want to take from me—"

"I'm hungry."

We both whirl around to find Magda standing in the doorway, holding It crushed to her chest, her new fanny pack still slung around her waist. And it's as if we both flip some internal switch. I slap on a fake grin while Vadim swallows his fearsome scowl in favor of a neutral smile. He heads for the freezer while I turn on the oven and usher Magda to the dining room table.

"What are you in the mood for, honey?" I ask, ruffling her hair.

She taps her chin with a tiny finger and then shrugs. "Pizza?"

"Pizza it is." Vadim diligently sets about warming her a meal while I cajole her into a conversation that I pray distracts her from whatever she might have overheard.

When the food is finally ready, we eat in a terse, awkward silence broken only by Magda's oblivious, innocent chatter.

And I realize that my divorce from Jim, as painful as it was, was a cakewalk compared to this.

This is torture.

Unbearable agony.

Because in this case, I can't just walk away.

Ena drives us to the airport in the morning, and we arrive in Cali by noon. It's a surreal experience, returning to my home state via a private runway rather than a commercial queue. Unsurprisingly, Vadim arranged for a car to pick us up, but as I hasten Magda into the backseat, I realize that I never even told my parents I was coming.

In fact, I haven't spoken to them at all in roughly…

A month? Two months? It's amazing what shame will do to a person, driving them from even their most cherished relationships. I toy with the idea of calling them now, only to chicken out.

An hour's heads up is the least of my concerns when it comes to them, all things considered. As the driver takes off, I wrestle with the best way to spring my new life choices on my parents. Well, I'm alive for one. And, I'm not destitute, pregnant, or addicted to drugs—but in some ways, I'm no better off. Pseudo-married to a billionaire, the newly adoptive mother of his daughter, and I'm addicted to *him*. Vadim Gorgoshev.

Which reality might cause my parents less stress?

"You lived here?" Magda asks, drawing my attention to her. She has It balanced on her lap, still wide-eyed from the plane ride. If I weren't too busy seething, I'd wish Vadim could have seen her reactions—utter fascinated interest—to the inner workings of the takeoff and landing. I think in addition to her interest in boats, planes are a newfound discovery as far as her hobbies are concerned.

"Yes," I tell her, smoothing back her tousled braids. "I used to live here."

Until a brooding businessman and his magic cock lured me away into a world of manipulation and mind games. It all has the makings of some sordid fairytale.

Too enthralled by the landscape beyond the windows, Magda falls silent until the car pulls up before a set of wrought iron gates, adorned with the phrase *"Connors Residence"* in elegant script.

"You lived *here?*" She sounds far more skeptical now, and I bristle at the doubt.

"Yes, I lived here." But, as I join her in gaping out of the window, I can admit that the place is impressive when glimpsed from the outside.

My father's estate is a minor offshoot of his brother's—my uncle Conroy—vineyard, which supplies a world-renowned label internationally. By virtue of its location, the property is impressive, though it has nothing on the rustic charm of Vadim's place.

Still, I didn't grow up a pauper, to be sure. Our house, my mother's pride and joy, is a four-story white stone Victorian style villa draped in rose vines and oodles of prestige that come with being "old money." Or so my father used to say.

Everything looks nearly the same as when I left it. The rose bushes, and begonias lining the paved stone paths. The tennis courts beyond the house and the acres of wine country looming just beyond the front walkway. I've never appreciated it more. In fact, I think I'm more eager than Magda to escape the car and stretch my legs. First things first, I circle around to the trunk and assist the driver with her bags. The second I lift Magda's gray suitcase, a familiar booming voice calls out.

"Tiffy? Sweetheart? Is that you?"

"Daddy!" I run to the front porch as he descends the few steps to meet me. Within seconds, I'm in his arms, inhaling his trademark scent of cologne, whiskey, and cigar smoke. He's wearing his typical polo and light wash jeans, I find as I pull back, his graying blond hair windswept back from his face.

"Where the hell have you been?" he asks with mock seriousness, his blue eyes twinkling. "I think your mother was about to send in the national guard."

"Tiffany?" As if on cue, a slender woman with reddish curls appears in the entryway, her hair coiffed, her outfit one-hundred-percent authentic vintage Chanel. Her eyes widen dramatically as she spots me, her lips breaking into one of her signature charming grins.

At least until she spots Magda scuttling up the steps after me and said grin slips at the edges.

"This is Magdalene," I say, getting it out of the way now. Sighing, I glance from Daddy to my mother and shrug. "It's a long story."

"It's a good thing you came during my afternoon wine," my mother snipes from over her half-empty glass. We're in the sunroom overlooking the garden while Magda inspects the blooming flowerbeds under my father's watchful eye.

"This situation may be far harder to understand otherwise, darling." Tilting her head back, my mother promptly drains her glass and smacks her lips. Satiated, she reaches for a nearby bottle and pours herself a refill. "Now tell it again, from the beginning."

"I'm dating someone," I reiterate, choosing the safest of options to describe Vadim. "Magda is his daughter.

He's…away on business. I decided to give us the week off and come spend time with you guys."

"Hmph." Fifty-four years of well honed-bullshit detecting are concentrated in the look my mother levels my way. Desperate to escape her scrutiny, I stand and approach one of the screen windows, watching Magda dutifully follow my father from bed to bed. He entrusted her with a watering can it seems, his voice a soothing hum audible even from here. Gently, he tells her how much or how little to give each plant, sprinkling every bit of advice with charming jokes. The familiarity hits me like a kick in the gut, and I realize just how much I've missed this. Missed them.

At least, when they aren't playing detective into my personal life.

"Did you hear me, Tiffany Ann?" My mother snaps in her no-nonsense chirp deployed only in emergencies. "I insist we must meet him this… What was his name again?"

"Vadim," I rasp without turning to face her. "And I told you, he's on business—"

"Poppycock. He can't spare a few hours to come to visit you? Or meet the strangers forced to accommodate his child? What kind of man is this?"

I bite my lip. Disparaging Vadim as some kind of deadbeat, absentee father too busy for social connections could help in the long run when I later tell them that I'm co-parenting Magda and separated from him. But…

I can't lie about his character, not even as angry as I am.

"He's busy, but if I ask, I'm sure he'll make the time," I say, conceding the point to her.

She nods and savors her victory by topping up her glass of wine yet again. "Well, I'll run off and find Gwendolyn so that she can prepare a guest bedroom. I wish you would have informed us sooner. We could have prepared toys or something… Honestly, it's as if you enjoy taunting me. I know I've been asking for a grandchild, but I'd prefer a teensy bit of notice." She sniffs, takes another sip, and all is forgiven. With a wave of her hand, she clears the air. "I'll see you at dinner, dear. Though if you want to rest, I can excuse you this once." She hesitates and reaches out, fingering a lock of my hair. "You look exhausted, darling. Have you been moisturizing? Your skin is—"

"I'm just tired from the flight," I say with a forced smile. "Thanks for accommodating us on such short notice."

"Anything for you, dear." She saunters off to find Gwen, our maid who's been with the family for over a decade. In her absence, I stand and creep back to the screen partition separating this space from the outside. Magda and my father have taken a break from flowering, it seems. They sit back to back on a decorative stone stool, each tearing into a fresh orange picked from one of the trees scattered throughout the yard.

Squaring my shoulders, I step out and join them.

"Ah, Tiffy, just in time!" Daddy rises to his feet, wiping his hands on his jeans. "I need to go get some fertilizer from the shed. You can keep the little miss company, and both of you can prepare to get your hands dirty." He winks and takes off in the direction of the tennis courts where the garden shed is.

Sighing, I claim his spot on the stool and watch Magda gingerly peel her orange and take a tentative bite.

"Good, huh?" I ask as her nose wrinkles in pleasure. "I used to love mornings here. We'd always have fresh juice for breakfast."

Something in my tone must make her frown, the orange paused midway to her mouth. Setting the fruit on her lap, she crosses her legs, her eyes downcast. "Are you never coming back?" I barely recognize the small voice as belonging to the same bold girl I've gotten to know these past few days. "Back home?"

I stiffen, my lips parting as I fight to find the right words. In the end, all I can say is, "What makes you ask that?"

She shoots me a funny look, her eyebrow raised defiantly. "I'm not a baby," she declares, her tone its usual haughty cadence. "I heard you fighting."

"Ah…" I lean back, nudging her shoulder. "Eavesdropper. What did you hear?"

"I know you're angry with Vadim," she says, resuming her inspection of the orange. "I know he made you sign legal papers, even though you didn't want to."

Damn. I grit my teeth, my cheeks flaming. "So, you weren't sleeping then, either."

She makes a small noise in her throat and meets my gaze. "He made you say you'll take care of me," she says, a childish summary of what really transpired. Still, the hurt in her voice reveals that she understood as much all the same. "You didn't want to?"

"Oh, no. Honey..." I turn around and grab her shoulders, forcing her to face me. "It's not you. I will always be there for you, got it?"

She nods, swayed by the conviction in my voice—almost as much as I am.

"What's happening between Vadim and me... It's grown-up stuff, and you know better than anyone that grown-ups are stupid."

She cocks her head, seeming to mull it over. Then she nods and takes a bite from her orange. "Stupid," she agrees with her mouth full.

I chuckle and tug a lock of her hair, but her revelation as a grade-A spy leads to far more questions. The main one revolving around the fuzzy, white bear resting on the ground between her legs. I let her go and lift It by his battered body. Vadim did a careful, precise job re-stuffing him. A loving job, betraying so much care for its owner, my heart throbs in the face of it.

"You knew who Vadim was to you before you went to the Robinsons, didn't you?" I ask as my fingers trace the nearly invisible row of stitches hiding beneath It's new scarf.

Magda takes her time peeling a fresh section of orange and takes a bite. Then she nods. "Last time I was sick…" She trails off, her nose wrinkling, and I suspect those memories aren't ones she likes to relive. Much like her father, she compartmentalizes her emotions, preferring to maintain control over them in lieu of expressing too much. "When I woke up, one of the nurses asked me if I like the bear my Daddy left me—" she nods to It. "She had been on vacation, I think. She later came back and told me she'd made a mistake, and it had been donated, but I knew she was lying."

And she knew that her father had vanished after that point, leaving her alone in foster care. I can't resist stroking my hand along one of her pigtails. Surprisingly she doesn't cringe from the contact. "I'm so sorry, honey," I tell her.

I can't imagine the pain she must have felt being so young, trying to process such conflicting emotions. But if she remembers Vadim, I have to wonder if she remembers anyone else.

"Can I ask you another question?"

She nods, her expression guarded.

"Do you know anything about your mother? Your birth mother?" I'm trying my damned hardest to keep any hint of jealousy or emotion from my voice. But I must fail because she goes rigid, her tiny shoulders stiff. Frowning, I add, "Anything before you went to the—"

"No! I don't remember." She turns away, crossing her arms. The reaction is so out of character for her, I'm taken aback.

"Okay." I can take a hint—an off-limits topic. For now. "I'm sorry if I upset you. We don't have to talk about anything you don't want to."

To cement our truce, I stroke her back until her posture relaxes, and she starts to kick her legs again.

Sensing another opportunity, I decide to aim for a seemingly safer topic next. "I heard you singing a song," I add carefully, easing my fingers through her braid. This approach seems to land with less of a defensive reaction. "Where did you learn it?"

She shrugs and kicks her legs out before her one by one. "It was always in my head. After I woke up, I mean. It's nice."

And the man who spent ten straight days singing it to her still has no clue just how much it meant to her. How much *he* meant to her.

"I don't want to come in between you and your dad," I tell her, my voice thick. Only belatedly do I realize that it's the first time I referred to Vadim's identity out loud in explicit terms.

She stiffens, but says nothing, still peeling her orange.

"I don't want you to think I'm trying to pretend to be your mother, either," I add, though I'm not sure why I feel the need to say it. Maybe for my own peace of mind? "But I'll be here, no matter what you need from me. Always. You're stuck with me, kiddo—" I nudge her with my elbow. "Whether you like it or not."

She carefully works away the last bit of her orange peel. Then she takes the sizeable remainder of fruit and shoves it into her mouth. Her cheeks bulge, barely able to contain it, and I make a show of fussing over her, swiping at her face with the end of my shirt.

"Messy girl!"

We break into laughter, so loud and raucous that I don't notice my father returning until he sets a crate of ripe fertilizer right at our feet. I cringe, but Magda lurches upright, her gaze inquisitive.

"Is that animal feces?" she asks, with awe coloring her voice rather than the disgust I think would be standard for a girl of her age. "Like cow poop?"

"Genuine, goddamn cow shit," Daddy says with a chuckle. "Don't go repeating that. This stuff we put on the flowers though, not in the vegetable garden. But it makes the flowers bloom really nice, especially those damn crotchety lilies."

Magda listens to him wide-eyed, absorbing every detail. When she looks up and spots my expression, she giggles. "It's like plant food," she explains, revealing a hint of her intellect. "It contains nutrients and microbes that help them grow."

"Right you are, Missy," Daddy says. "Why don't you come with me and we'll sprinkle this around. Let's let Tiffy go get some rest—" he shoots me an apologetic glance. "You look wrecked, sweetheart."

"Thanks, Daddy…"

Considering that both parents have mentioned my appearance in a negative way, I decide to take the hint and enter the house, heading up for my old room. In so many ways, it's just as I left it. Juvenile—decorated in shades of bright pink—childish, and superficial. The girl who once slept beneath this frothy, bubblegum-colored canopy spent her final nights here dreaming of what life would be like as Mrs. James Walker. Boy, what a letdown that turned out to be.

Nearly ten years later and this Tiffy has learned her lesson. Dreaming is for fools. But even as I strip my clothing, change into a nightgown, and crawl beneath my old hot pink comforter, a man sneaks into my head regardless.

His presence is more consuming than Jim could ever hope to be.

He's insistent, promising me the world…

But all I seem capable of doing is spitting onto his hand.

CHAPTER EIGHT

I had forgotten how hard it can be to sleep alone. To forgo the teasing warmth of another figure, their body close to yours, their touch pervasive—as if they can't bear to let you go.

I wake up somehow more exhausted than I was when I laid down in the first place. My nap, it seems, has stretched way beyond dinner, I realize as I scramble to my feet and view the world beyond my windows. Not only did I sleep through the evening meal, but I also tossed and turned right through the night, and it now looks to be mid-morning.

In a daze, I stagger into my old bathroom and try to wake up with a hot shower. Afterward, I brush my teeth, blow out my hair, and skip one of my Chanel ensembles in favor of an old T-shirt and jeans fished from my closet.

By the time I scramble downstairs, Gwen is in the kitchen preparing what looks like lunch.

"Hello, Ms. Tiffany," she calls as I scramble past, following the faint sounds of girlish chatter into the sunroom.

Sure enough, Mother and Daddy are in the garden, fussing about their plants while a tiny figure races between them, carrying out various tasks with an eagerness that betrays yet another newfound interest to add to Vadim's list. A gardener in the making, Magda beams with unabashed joy as she chases my father with a water pail before fetching a pair of pruning shears for my mother.

And she isn't the only one uncharacteristically animated. My mother hasn't graced the garden with her presence in about fifteen years since one of the influential socialites in her country club declared gardening passé. Though I doubt the flowers are what drew her out into the fresh air and unfashionable sunlight.

Magda is wearing an outfit I know for a fact I didn't buy for her—an adorable, frilly white dress with frothy sleeves that makes her look more like a little princess than ever— even with her polka dot fanny pack strapped to her waist. Someone elaborately braided her hair as well, adorning it with flowers and an excess of yellow ribbon. In fact, she resembles a seven-year-old Tiffy—whose tortured visage could be found in one of many portraits hanging throughout the house—whose mother enjoyed dressing her up like a doll. Magda, however, doesn't seem to mind the fuss.

Her cheeks glow a healthy pink, her eyes shining as Daddy speaks to her, no doubt explaining gardening techniques and the process behind their actions. And while my mother appears to be pruning one of the rose bushes, I realize that more often than not, those freshly trimmed roses seem to wind up in Magda's hair.

When I finally leave the house and join them, my mother jumps so badly she nearly drops her shears like a criminal caught in the act.

"Tiffy," she says shrilly. "We thought you were still sleeping. We went ahead and had breakfast already, but I had Gwen save you a plate."

"We had pancakes!" Magda pitches in from across the lawn, where my father is instructing her on how to best tell if the oranges on the tree are ripe enough to pick.

"Pancakes?" Horror constricts my voice. "Magda has diabetes—"

"We know," Daddy says. "Little Missy was very informative and gave us a list of her dietary restrictions, and we had Gwen whip up the best goddamn healthy nut pancakes a girl could ask for."

"Language, Harold," my mother sniffs.

"I'm sorry. I didn't think I'd sleep that long…" I falter, unsure of why I even feel the sense of guilt that I do. "It looks like you guys made out okay without me."

"Yes," Daddy says in that reassuring way only he can. "We got little Missy to bed, and even made sure she got her phone call."

I raise an eyebrow. "Phone call?"

"With her father, darling," Mother interjects, her tone suspicious.

"Oh, right…"

"Don't tire yourself out too much," she adds. "I was planning on showing Magdalene all of your old pageant dresses. Oh, I'm sure she'll look just darling in that old blue one with the silk, and that imported bit of lace. You remember the one."

"I don't think her father will be putting her in any pageants," I point out.

But Mother rolls her eyes. "She can use them for dress-up, darling. I've already offered her the pick of the lot. And she promised to take very good care of them, haven't you, sweetheart?"

"Yes, Ma'am." Magda nods, the picture of pure charm. I realize in horror that she's every bit as much of a social chameleon as Vadim. It's an awe-inspiring and yet terrifying skill to witness in action. Especially considering that my mother once threatened to stab a mover who made the mistake of assuming a box of my old pageant dresses was meant for Goodwill. She clung to those damn things with such sentiment I was sure she'd insist on them all following her into the grave.

"If you're planning on sticking around, Tiffy, then why don't you give us a hand?" Daddy asks. "Magdalene here wants to try whipping up her own batch of fresh OJ. You used to be a damn good little picker. Let's see if you still got it in you."

I approach them warily and yet find myself biting back a smile. The cynical part of me warns that the fact that she isn't mine by blood means I shouldn't take such pride in watching her eyes light up with joy as she finds a ripe fruit on her first try. I shouldn't relish how seamlessly she's blending into my family, or that she seems to love my childhood home already.

I shouldn't be skipping ahead, envisioning Christmases or other holidays spent here with her. And I definitely shouldn't be picturing another figure alongside her, imagining how he'd look with his lips wet with fresh orange juice, his dark curls filled with roses.

But I do.

And I am.

And nothing I tell myself seems capable of stopping it.

BY THE TIME NIGHT FALLS, Magda is the one who tires out first. She barely manages to keep her eyes open during dinner. I feel the need to take her hand once her plate is cleared away just to make sure I can get her upstairs without her falling asleep along the way.

As we leave the dining room, my mother's voice chases me, one of her stern reminders. "Don't forget, Tiffy, darling! We need to meet this businessman of yours. Preferably before the end of the week. He wouldn't want to make a bad impression, now would he?"

I do my best to ignore her as I lead Magda into the guest bedroom and help her dress in a fresh nightgown and braid her hair. She's seemingly on the verge of drifting off when suddenly she bolts upright and scrambles for something on her nightstand—her fanny pack, from which she withdraws her blue cell phone. As I watch in confusion, she dials a number and holds the receiver to her ear.

The moment I assume someone picks up on the other end, her body relaxes, and she slumps against the pillows, It clutched in her free hand.

"Yes, I had fun," she says tiredly, her words slurring. But I can sense the effort she makes to keep talking, humoring the figure speaking to her in a gentle, insistent hum. But eventually, her replies come further apart until I feel the urge to gingerly pry the phone from her grasp before she nods off altogether.

"Goodnight, *ma chérie*," a gruff voice urges from the other end, so gentle and soothing I nearly break in the face of it.

"Wait," I croak before he can hang up.

I hear his breath catch, and the seconds tick by as I gather up the nerve to keep speaking. "I… My parents want to meet you," I blurt in a rush. "I think it's best, even if… They should meet you. For Magda's sake. Later we can come up with a lie to—" I break off, my eyes on a drowsy, barely coherent Magda. After what she overheard the last time, I've learned my lesson about speaking freely around her. "We can devise an *explanation* for how things really are," I say, changing tact. "But not now. They deserve to at least get to know you first."

Silence, so thick I can feel it constricting my throat falls. Just when I'm on the verge of suffocating, his voice returns, far more cautious than the warm, honeyed tone he used with Magda.

"I can be on the plane within the hour."

"Okay?" My tongue stiffens, making the word an awkward question.

"Goodnight," Vadim says.

"Bye." I hang up and drop the phone back on the nightstand as if burned. After kissing Magda on the cheek and ensuring her toys are within her reach, I creep from her room and enter mine. My mother—as knowing as she is—ensured that Magda had the suite just one door down.

THIS TIME, I don't sleep deeply enough to miss the telltale patter of her getting up hours later. Yawning, I wash up and get dressed and manage to catch her just as she pads out of her room, fully clothed, fanny pack in place, her curls tousled.

"I'm supposed to help with the weeding today," she tells me, her expression so serious that I can't resist ruffling her messy hair.

"What about some braids first, sleepyhead?" She follows me into my old room, and I set her up at my vanity, watching her scan our surroundings with barely concealed interest.

"This was your room?" she asks, sounding skeptical once more.

I nod, but even I can admit that the décor and color scheme is a little outdated. "Sit still."

I smooth a brush through her hair, and I'm finishing the second plait when I realize a fact that makes me stiffen. "Vadim is coming today," I confess, surprised by how her features light up for a split second before she reigns in any excitement behind one of her neutral masks. "But my parents don't really know the full…details."

She nods, and I'm sure that a child as perceptive as she is picked up on way more nuances about those "details" than anyone else has.

"Lying is wrong," I say to preface my next request. "But, probing questions are annoying, and my mother is the queen of them."

"So, we have to pretend?" Magda inquires, an eyebrow raised. *Damn.* She's copied her father's inflection—when he's in the middle of devising a devious twist or laying the foundation of some mind game or another. As if she's testing me, waiting to see if I'll say the right thing.

Or fail entirely.

"Not pretend," I say softly.

To stall for time, I rifle through the drawers of my vanity, finding an old stash of hair ribbon. I select two light blue strands and weave them through the ends of her braids, tying them into bows.

"Let's think of it more as…evading. Whatever we're comfortable defending, we defend. And what we're not, we compromise on. And not by lying," I add, turning her chair so that she faces me. "But just by cleverly avoiding the truth. For now."

My convoluted way of explaining that while Vadim and I may pretend to be a couple now, the reality couldn't be further from the truth.

She nods, appearing to mull it over. Then she squares her shoulders and hops from the chair.

"Can I go to the garden now? I wanted to help out early."

"Sure." I tug one of her braids and watch her skip off. Then I claim her vacated seat and try to give myself my own "lying is for the benefit of society" pep talk. I don't think I've made much progress by the time a commotion rising from downstairs warns of the impending approach of yet another visitor.

Much to my mother's chagrin.

"Tiffy," she scolds as I descend the stairs and—sure enough—discover an unfamiliar black car cruising up the driveway. "Is it too much to ask for a bit of forewarning as to when we can expect your guests?"

I murmur some form of an apology as I slip through the front door, beating the pack just in time to head off the figure climbing from the vehicle's driver's seat. Vadim, it seems, took the tactical approach of driving himself rather than hiring a driver to do so. His outfit also strikes me as deliberately calculated—a casual mixture of a less formal dark brown suit with a looser white dress shirt underneath and no tie.

The result is a man who looks no less approachable than any other suitor hoping to make a good first impression, be them a billionaire or not.

God. It's unfair. I can sense every little extent he's gone through to ensure as much. He probably forced himself to eat something during the plane ride because he isn't shaking, his features refreshed after days of chronic lack of sleep. His hair has been neatly arranged, and I can imagine him having to physically stop himself from raking his fingers through it.

He eyes me warily as I circle the car and approach him, my arms crossed.

"You don't plan on staying long?" I ask when he doesn't move to grab a suitcase from the trunk. His nostrils twitch—he didn't miss the audible relief in my voice.

"I booked a hotel," he says. "I was able to schedule some business meetings while I'm here."

Though he avoids mentioning a timeframe as to when he'll depart. I sense myself frown, but I decide to leave that battle for another day.

"Tiffy?" I hear my mother calling from the front steps. "Are you going to introduce your gentleman caller or have him stand out in the hot sun all day?"

Here goes nothing... I inhale raggedly. Then I extend my hand for Vadim's. Any shock he might feel at the gesture is damn near instantly suppressed, replaced by one of his light, quick smiles. He grabs for me in return, and his heat runs through me like a lance, enhancing the aches and pains I'd been able to ignore until this moment.

The soreness of tossing and turning at night—too many nights—while in bed alone. The throbbing awareness of how long it's been since I've had him inside me—such a strange thing to notice, all things considered. A reprieve from passionless sex was one of the many benefits of my separation from Jim, but this…

Being taunted with Vadim's nearness is a torture I wouldn't wish upon anyone.

Though maybe I'm alone in that regard. He loosens his grip on my hand, releasing me and turns his attention to the backseat of the car. I'm surprised to find that—in lieu of a suitcase—he did bring a few items with him. A bouquet of gorgeous roses that must have cost a fortune, as well as three neatly wrapped boxes.

I'm flashed back to when I accompanied him to his brother's home, insisting upon bringing presents. I think I'd explained it away as social etiquette—but I have a feeling he took those words to heart, studying such a concept as thoroughly as his foray into kink.

"Help me with these?" he asks, his tone soft—but he isn't speaking to me. A small figure bounds to his side, her smile beaming.

"Okay!" she chirps, playing the role of a precocious innocent so thoroughly I almost forget that I'd asked her to. She holds her arms out while Vadim piles each present on top of the other. Then she leads the way into the house as my parents watch on.

I think it should bother me a little, the approval I find in my mother's eyes as she takes in Vadim's slender frame and handsome visage. My father, on the other hand, seems more interested in studying the quality of his tailored suit and rented car.

"Mother, Daddy, this is Vadim," I say once we're all crowded into the foyer.

"Welcome!" My mother exclaims, drifting forward to plant a French-style kiss on each of his cheeks. "I apologize for the lack of proper fanfare. If I would have known you were coming so soon—" She breaks character just long enough to shoot me a glare, "I would have prepared better. Regardless, I'll have Gwen whip up a marvelous lunch. Do you plan on staying long?"

"As long as I'm welcome to," Vadim says, his accent adding an extra flair to his usual charm. "Though, I do have business that may call me away later, unfortunately."

Smart man, laying the foundation for an easy escape route should the need arise.

"Welcome, Vadim," Daddy says, eyeing him skeptically. As Magda hovers near his side, I finally make out the telltale signs of dirt stains on the cuffs of their jeans, their hands equally filthy.

"Looks like someone's been having fun," Vadim remarks, inspecting his daughter from head to toe.

"I've been helping," she says in response to his questioning look. Her eyes brim with excitement, and I don't think I've ever seen her so animated. "We're waging war against those goddamn caterpillars—"

"And, she's been a good little gardening assistant," my father says quickly. He places his hand on her shoulder and shoots her a conspiratorial wink.

Meanwhile, my mother's cheeks flush blood-red, and I half-expect her to faint. "Please, come and sit—Tiffy, show him into the sunroom, will you? I'll have Gwen prepare some tea. I'm sure you're exhausted."

"That would be lovely, thank you," Vadim says, his smile so breathtaking that even my mother's nerves seem put at ease. For now, at least. "And please, accept these small tokens of my appreciation for taking such good care of Magdalene."

He offers my mother the roses, and she simpers. Internally, I know that, like me, she's tallied up the potential cost of such a gesture and is more than pleased with her estimate. Material value means little to her, but in terms of hospitality, every good hostess appreciates being rewarded for her efforts.

And she shoots me yet another glare before flouncing off, murmuring something about needing Grandmamma's old crystal vase.

Two of the presents, Vadim has divided between my parents, saving the final one for Magdalene.

"I thought I heard you mention something the other day about working in the garden," he says teasingly as she rips open her package to discover a blue apron, complete with her own miniature gardening tools. She flashes one of those rare grins and throws her arms around his waist in the semblance of something that could be called a hug before she takes off, dragging my father with her.

Alone with Vadim, the awkward tension sets in, too potent for even my mother's best hosting abilities to conquer.

"I... I'll show you to the sunroom," I tell him before guiding him through the house and out into the sun-dappled space. Beyond the screen walls, we can make out

Magda standing patiently by as my father crouches on a gardening pad, cursing up a storm.

Rather than sit, Vadim strips his suit jacket and escapes into the fresh air to join them, much to Magda's apparent delight.

I hang back, observing from a safe distance as he crouches down, no doubt ruining his priceless suit, and watches intently as she shows him how to use her new tools, her laughter infectious, smile contagious.

Soon my own lips are twitching despite myself, my heart throbbing as I watch them interact, easily including my father into their beautiful dynamic. Almost like…

Almost like a real family. The thought unfurls, too dangerous to indulge in. But I'm weak in this fight, and the fantasies persist.

I think my only saving grace when it comes to the potential of my mother murdering me in a fit of rage and burying me out in the garden is that Vadim doesn't plan on spending the night—thus sparing her the trouble of having to scramble to prepare another guest bedroom. Instead, she whips poor Gwen into a frenzy in her attempt to produce a meal "worthy" of our guests.

The result is a grand affair of roasted chicken, vegetables, and a dessert catered specifically to both Magda and Vadim's dietary needs. Somehow, Mother manages to arrange all of this while seeming as though meticulously planned meals and priceless, antique cutlery are trivial things someone might pull out as an everyday occurrence. In other words, I'm rendered inadequate, watching a master at work.

She somehow manages to get Vadim to let his guard down in ways that I suspect even he isn't comfortable with—not intentionally. There's a softness to his posture I'm not used to glimpsing in the presence of others. He's still without his suit jacket, having had to change into a spare pair of my father's slacks after his became coated in muck from the garden.

"Do tell us how you met Tiffany," my mother instructs as she savors her third glass of wine for the evening. Ruthlessly, she inspects him in between swallows, hunting for any minor flaw to seize upon. "Our dear girl has her charms, but I'm curious as to what might attract someone of your…caliber." It's a testament to her skill of social navigation that she somehow manages to make the insult both sting and sound endearing all at once. I'm still not forgiven for the lack of notice, it seems.

"What might attract me?" Vadim laughs, and his eyes take on a soft, faraway gleam I'm sure is one-hundred percent intentional. It has to be. "Your daughter is…"

His gaze finds me, hesitant, and clouded with uncertainty. I can imagine him agonizing over the right words to say. How to say them. In the end, he clearly states, "When I met her, I noticed her instantly—the moment she entered the room, every other man did as well." That hard note betrays a jealousy only I know the true extent of. An envy that led him to foil any attempt I made to forge a connection with another man. "She nearly slipped past me without a second glance," he admits. "But, I was determined to earn her attention."

His tone… His expression.

My throat goes dry, and I grapple for my own wine glass, inhaling the liquid within.

"That's our Tiffy," Daddy pitches in with a bellowing laugh. "She can be a whirlwind. Let's just hope you haven't gotten a taste of her temper yet. She's an ace sulker —can hold a grudge for days. But just when you think she'll hate you forever, she bakes you the most terrible cake you ever did taste as a peace offering. And you know what they say about redheads…"

He winks.

My mother fans herself.

Magda grins mischievously. It doesn't escape my notice that she managed to wedge herself in between my father and Vadim. Both of them seem intent on "accidentally" slipping extra slices of sugar-free cake onto her plate. I don't think there's another little girl alive in danger of being so thoroughly spoiled.

"What *do* they say about redheads, Harold?" My mother lobbies him with a barely concealed bit of bait.

Bait that he wisely sidesteps with a contrite nod of his head. "That they are beautiful, intelligent creatures worthy of utter worship and devotion, sweetheart," he says.

Satisfied, she takes a congratulatory sip of wine.

"How long did you say you were planning on staying, Vadim?" she asks a second time. "We would love to have you. Tomorrow, Magdalene is going to model some of Tiffy's old pageant dresses. As long as I have your permission, she can have as many of them as she'd like. They were all handmade by some of the best designers of the time. I'm sure she'll look just darling in them."

"I agree," Vadim says earnestly. His eyes, however, cut toward me, cautiously guarded. If he's looking for a clue as to how to reply, I look down at my hands rather than convey an answer either way. Left to scramble for his own response, he says, "But I'm afraid my business may call me away."

"What is it you do exactly?" Daddy asks, raising an eyebrow. "I'm in investments, myself."

"I work in pharmaceuticals," Vadim explains. "Mainly German-based companies. Have you heard of Eingel Industries?"

My father's eyes widen—he's impressed. "Heard of it? I have stock in it!" He laughs heartily, smacking his hand on the table. "Damn, it's been performing like a beauty these past few quarters. Son of a bitch—"

"Harold!" My mother sniffs in disgust.

"It's one of many entities under my control," Vadim confesses. "Lately, I will admit that I've been trying to take a lighter approach to the business aspect, however, so that I can spend as much time as possible with Magdalene."

Both of my parents nod in approval, and I sense that we're nearing a dangerous line that I doubt we ever crossed with Jim. They like him. They *really* like him.

God, they like him too much.

And when his voice takes on that deep, disarming rasp, I know I'm royally screwed.

"I want to thank you for your hospitality," he says. While his voice resonates throughout the room, loud enough for everyone to hear, I feel like it's directed solely toward me, running down my spine in an ominous thrill of vibration. "For my daughter, especially. I can't tell you what your kindness means to us both."

"Oh, it's nothing, darling." My mother dabs at her lips with a napkin, her cheeks pink, and my father coughs in that way he does when things become too emotional for his comfort.

"It's no problem," he declares, rising from his chair. "How about us three interlopers go sip lemonade and watch the stars while Tiffy and Vadim get reacquainted, huh?"

"Okay!" Magda lurches to her feet, following at his heels while my mother reluctantly rises as well.

"Night darling," she murmurs to me, planting a kiss on my cheek. In a voice too low for Vadim to hear, she whispers, "Very good catch, darling."

And I want to melt into a puddle of shame as they finally leave the dining room.

"I don't have to stay," Vadim says, rising to his feet. "I'll be in town at least until it's time for Magda to come home. Then I'll—"

"Wait." I suck in a breath and let it out slowly while parsing my options. Finally, I make up my mind and face him. Self-preservation trumps pride, and I eye his collar rather than meet his gaze. I'm not brave enough. "We need to talk."

Preferably—given how our last few conversations have gone—somewhere far out of my parents' earshot. And Magda's for that matter.

Vadim frowns and, for the first time, a teeny hint of unease gnaws through my wall of anger. Could his hesitation be because he'd already picked up some floozy who—as I was in our first days of meeting—is now lounging around his suite, waiting for her next delivery of designer clothing? I let myself indulge in the possibility as though it were real.

And jealousy claws through my chest so violently I have to smother a gasp. Could I even blame him if he did have another woman in the wings? *No,* I realize as I scan his face and catch the glimpses of exhaustion, he's so cleverly disguised until now. I couldn't, even if I wanted to.

And maybe he *has,* merely to drive that stake through my chest—punish me. "If you've already made plans—"

"No," he says quickly, though his frown only deepens. "No... It's that my hotel suite this time isn't what you're used to."

I raise an eyebrow, my dread building, jealousy seething. "Oh?"

He seems to deflate and rakes his fingers through his hair, disrupting yet another aspect of his polished façade. "It's just that, I wasn't planning on sharing it with anyone."

"I'm not staying," I add, even as my curiosity is piqued tenfold. "We just need to discuss some logistics."

"Alright." He stands, and we take a detour into the sunroom to reclaim his jacket. In the distance, Magda is barely visible, sitting on my father's lap, pointing up at the stars in the sky as both he and my mother babble on.

It's a heartwarming sight even I can't deny.

Vadim, however? His expression melts, conveying such tenderness…

I have to turn away and nearly run out to his car just to escape it. His hotel, I quickly realize, is on the outskirts of my old hometown, about ten minutes from my family's home—the narrowest adherence to my previous guidelines regarding his distance from me. And he wasn't lying about his room.

I'm taken aback as I follow him into the narrow, efficient setup. Gone is the sprawling, luxurious penthouse booked by a bachelor accustomed to picking up escorts at random when the urge struck. This small, yet comfortable, suite is the preference for a man solely intent on business over pleasure. Even the bed is a modest full instead of a massive king.

Instead, the star attraction is a sleek modern style office in the corner, complete with a mini, circular conference table.

I take up one end while Vadim collapses onto a chair across from me. His stricken expression makes something inside me flinch, and I hesitate, unsure of what to say. He looks so damn tired. Exhausted. Like a man waiting for his execution to finally commence. He's had enough of this torture.

But so have I.

"Tell me something that will make me forgive you," I demand, letting every ounce of raw anger and pain seep into my voice. "Though believe me when I say that I don't ever think I can."

The pure intensity of my emotions seems to take him back. His posture sprawls out without an ounce of poise to guide it, his fingers raking through his hair—in this moment, comfort takes precedence over putting on a show. He's fully unguarded, his wall in shambles, and my heart sinks. I'm not sure if I'm well equipped enough to face him like this.

Gritting my teeth, I'm willing to try, though. "You hurt me," I add before he can say a word in his own defense. "You really did. How dare you accuse me of wanting to harm Magda?" I'm blinking furiously, desperate to keep from crying. "How dare you?"

"I'm not sorry for what I did," he admits, his tone firm. Stubborn, even. The blatant honesty tempers the pain ripping through my chest—at least he's not lying or trying to manipulate. It's the truth. "I will always put Magdalene first. Always. But… It wasn't until I saw you upset that I realized I should have gone about it differently. I know you would never purposefully hurt her." It seems to kill him to admit as much—the calculating, manipulative Vadim fucked up. He went too far to reach his aims. "You were supposed to demand money," he continues, his voice lacking any inflection. He could seem robotic if it weren't for the vast wealth of emotion contorting his expression. His hair is a mess, his eyes fixated on something beyond me. "Money or something else of value to you—"

"You think I'm that much of a gold-digging bitch?" I lurch to my feet and spin around, definitely on the verge of tears now.

"But I've seen how you are with her," he mutters as if oblivious to my reaction. He's speaking without his filter this time—saying plainly whatever thoughts are in his head. A man with nothing left to lose and the world to gain. "You could extort me, but I know you wouldn't do the same to her. I could live with that. I had to live with that. You weren't supposed to…"

"What?" I whirl to face him, my arms crossed, posture livid.

"Want *me*," he confesses, his eyes meeting mine without an ounce of anger or defensiveness. "My money, material things, yes. I told myself I could lose your interest, if it meant keeping you for Magdalene. It would damn near kill me," he adds, his hand at his throat, stroking the remnants of his scar. "But I could endure it. I could forfeit your body. This game. But never, would I gamble something more."

"I don't know what kind of women you usually consort with," I croak through clenched teeth, "but most don't shack up with a man they barely know and fall in love with his daughter for money. Most women don't forgive mind game, after mind game for money! Most women don't beg for more from a man only to get his fucking money!"

"But most people are more than content to use *me*," he counters, snarling. Lunging.

We're toe to toe in an instant, and I'm woefully unprepared for the vitriol in his voice. His gaze. All of it directed at me. Beyond me. At the whole damn world, he's raging.

"My mother? A whore who sold me into slavery for the price of a year's worth of rent," he snarls. "My father was a monster who inducted me into his family of vipers, pitting me against his true heir every fucking waking moment. My whole life has been spent at the whims of others. Trying to assume what it is they want. How to achieve it. How to prostrate myself for their fucking benefit. No one has ever offered me their love—"

"You're wrong," I say, standing fearlessly in the midst of his tirade. Even as his eyes take on that cold, mistrustful gleam, his teeth bared. I don't look away. "Everyone loves you! Ena. Milton. Your old partner, Hiram. Even Maxim, I think, loves you in his own way."

Why else would his henchman drive me to the hospital at five in the morning? Lucius may be kind, but I doubt his concern would extend beyond the boundaries of what his employer would allow.

The fact that he greeted me at all was testament enough—Maxim permitted him to.

"You're just too blind to see it. Your instinct is to always assume the worst. Always lash out when you feel stretched too thin."

"My instinct?" he echoes in a dangerous, vicious hum. His hand raises to my throat, his thumb tracing a quivering artery. I shiver, a heartbeat away from backing down…

But I stay, enduring the ominous caress, even as he curls his fingers around my neck entirely.

"My instinct is telling me that you're lying," he tells me softly. "You only aim to get inside my head. Because, your love? I want it," he admits in a growl so resonating I sway. "But I am not stupid enough to think I could ever have it. Ever have you. Not without a price."

"Why?" I counter, forcing myself to meet his gaze. The more I challenge him, the more unsteady his dark irises become, glazed over and unfocused. Crazed. "Why can't I *just* love you? Why can't you *just* trust me? Like when the mother of your child comes calling, and all I want is to know how to help you—"

"Because…" He encircles my throat in his fist, applying pressure…pressure. More. As I gasp, his eyes flash, nostrils flaring. Like my fear is a welcome addition to this tension —something he's used to navigating. Manipulating. "Because who could love me?" He says it all so fervently… I think he means it.

Every last word.

As if in emphasis, he tightens his grip slowly, letting me feel the flesh of my throat conform around his fingers. Collapse. My breaths feather at first, followed by that terrifying constriction of my windpipe. The building terror that he's cutting off my air. Choking me—but in the gentlest, lingering of ways.

Because I'm not resisting him. A fact he only realizes just as my breathing wheezes, a hair's breadth from being cut off completely.

"*Merde!*" He lets me go, staggering away from me, horrified. Panting, he stares down at his hands, his voice a broken rasp, "I'm sorry—"

"Don't be," I say, my voice surprisingly strong even as my throat aches slightly with the remnants of his touch. "At least you aren't hiding how *you* really feel for fucking once. Is that what you want to do to me? Hurt me?"

"No!" His eyes flash at the mere idea of it. "Never—"

"But you have," I cut over him. "You are. Every fucking time you push me away. Play with my mind. How can I trust you if you won't even trust me?"

"I've let you into my life," he points out, regaining his stiff, imposing posture. At his sides, his fingers curl and uncurl again—a mere hint as to the extent of his frustration. "I've let you around my daughter. You don't call that trust?"

"I don't know anymore," I admit, my voice breaking. "But I trusted *you*. That is what love is. Sometimes, it means being a petty bitch and second-guessing everything, but in the end, I trusted you."

Despite how he fucks with my head. Plays with my soul. Makes me hate him. Want him. Crave him.

"So now what?" he wonders with a cold, harsh laugh. "You leave after tempting me with the one thing I will never have?"

"No!" I scoff in exasperation. I think I even stomp my foot, I'm so frustrated. "You always had it!" I practically shout at him. "Always! You were just too fucking paranoid to see it."

And I refused to. Why? Who falls in love with a stranger after barely a few weeks?

But how many strangers are like Vadim?

As tormented as him?

As beautiful as him?

As utterly frustrating as him?

"But what was I to you, huh?" I demand nastily. "Collateral? A tramp you could just throw away—"

"Never!" He's before me in an instant, his hands cupping my skull, drawing me into him. Near my ear, he croaks, his voice hoarse, "You were what happiness always was to me. A futile dream always out of reach. At least before…"

"Before what?" I'm trying so damn hard to maintain my composure. My anger. My hurt. But it's splintering, breaking apart with every second his breath bastes my throat. With his fingers caressing my skin. His gaze so deep and unending I'm drowning in it.

"Before you taunted me with it." His eyes slide shut as his mouth grazes my lower jaw brazenly, his lips parted, tasting me. Inhaling me. "That's what you've done, isn't it? Tease me. Dangle a world I never imagined for myself, but you never reveal the fucking price—"

"Because there isn't one!" My voice lacks any real anger. I'm lost in the urgency of his touch, my hips arching into him before I can help it. "You can't buy love."

"Only take it," he says with a fervor that leaves me reeling. Hungry, he grips me tighter, drawing me further against him. "Claim it—"

"No. You *earn* it," I snap, devastated by the fact that he truly seems to mean those words. A man so lost he sees affection as something worth stealing, never his to take without a struggle. "It is given freely. Like when you let a man put his hands around your throat because you know he won't hurt you."

He blinks, his eyes fluttering open, dark with confusion. As I watch, they glaze over, hardened with resolve.

"I *will* earn you," he tells me. But when he presses his mouth to mine, I doubt a verbal confession is on his mind.

Because conversation never gets us very far in the long run. Only one form of communication seems to supersede all others when it comes to the two of us.

And he initiates this discussion with his touch sliding down to my ass, snatching me into him. Gasping, I run my hands down his chest, letting my nails rake at the fabric of his shirt, gouging the flesh underneath. He sucks in a startled breath, his gaze radiating confusion—but the confusion quickly morphs into something else when I keep traveling lower, finding the fastenings of his pants.

With a deftness I didn't even know I was capable of, I unhook the front clasp and yank down the zipper. Waiting beyond the barrier is his cock, stiffening against me, pulsating so strongly I swear I can count his heartbeat like this.

His very being is in the palm of my hand.

And groaning, he submits to me, letting me cradle him… and then tighten my grip so firmly he lurches, a growl revving in his throat. His hands grip me in retaliation, snatching me to him, grinding me over the contours of his body.

And we both cry out.

Days without him and my body reacts as though I've committed a crime. The ultimate act of self-harm—denying myself of this. Him.

Sensation returns like a gut punch, drowning me in a heat so potent it's like I'm burning alive.

But in this instance, I'm not suffering alone.

He grunts at the feel of me as if punched with every grasping handful. Ruthless, his lips capture mine, his hands roving, nails scraping. Groping. Claiming. I'm putty in his hands, a slave to his whims as he drags me toward the bed. Only to change tact at the last minute and shove me against the window instead.

He spins me to face the glass as his body cages me in from behind. I feel his hands in my hair, working their way down to my shoulders. My throat. He encircles it, gripping it again, tightening those slender fingers. Tighter. Tighter. At the same time, I feel him grinding himself shamelessly against my lower back, teasing his erection to the point of straining against the confines of his boxers.

It has to be uncomfortable, I realize somewhere at the back of my mind. Painful. But it's like he waits until the second I'm writhing, my thighs grinding together just to find relief.

The second I do, he cradles my throat, guiding my head back until our gazes connect from this angle—me straining up, him staring down, his eyes unfocused, glazed with lust.

A silent understanding passes between us. One that makes me buck into his grip and brace my hands over the window glass. Without hesitation, he plunges his hand beneath the skirt of my dress, finding my thong, wrenching it down my legs.

I writhe shamelessly, arching into his touch. Gasping out when his grip on my throat cinches—tighter than before. My eyes water, my lungs straining, lips parting.

But at the same time, he brushes his thumb over my clit, pairing the physical discomfort with pleasure and…

Holy, gosh darn *kink.*

My brain melts, every nerve going haywire. There is something inherently sinful when he stops holding back. Reacts without calculation or forethought. Adjusting his grip on me with one hand, he wrenches me onto him, plunging inside me on the first thrust.

It's fire.

The force and pressure apply friction to my piercing from the inside, and I yelp at the sensation, feeling an orgasm build damn near instantaneously.

Rather than feed the flames, he rocks his hips, withdrawing just as swiftly. His grip on my throat returns, applying more pressure as his lips feather kisses down my collar. The conflicting actions make my body go limp, my eyes rolling as he slams back in.

In.

Again.

Again.

I let him pin me against the window glass, murmuring praises. Gasps. *Nothing* as he controls my intake of air, teasing me with just enough space to gasp before his fingers clench. Body rocks. Cock thrums against my inner walls.

Rippling convulsions assault me, contorting my body from the inside out.

Never in my life have I come so violently before. I almost fear the incredible rise because I know the fall could be deadly. Only his grip serves as my sole safety net as the pleasure ebbs and flows in shattering waves.

"You *do* want something from me," he grates into my ear as I mewl wordlessly, on the brink of another earth-shattering release. "My love, is that it? I can't give it," he confesses, bucking so hard I'm sandwiched between him and the window glass, my body bared for anyone passing by who happens to look up.

My addled, deranged mind skips ahead, envisioning a future with him. Exhibition with him, letting the world watch him take me like this. Claim me like this…

Pain sears through my earlobe, and with difficultly, I refocus my waning senses on him. His teeth nip me again, ensuring he has my full attention.

"My love? You've already taken it from me," he growls, his body thrumming as he jerks, spilling himself inside me, heightening the depths of his confession. "*Always*. From the first fucking time you teased me with your praise. You've taken this from me…"

His bed, as it turns out, is too damn small for us to even lay on comfortably. We wind up lying naked on a sheet spread before the window, watching the world advance beyond this realm, bathed in darkness.

In the dizzying comedown, he only moves to salvage something from his pants, pressing it to his ear in the dark. "Goodnight, *ma chérie*," I hear him murmur, revealing the sole person worthy of drawing his attention in this moment. Even now, he strives to keep his promise to her, always. "I will see you tomorrow. Please tell Tiffany's parents she decided not to return too late and risk waking anyone. Goodnight."

He hangs up and settles down beside me, forcing a physical connection I have no chance of resisting—his arms encircle me, a prison of heat.

Silence falls again. Finally…

"I guess this means no more trolling the bars for fake wives. No more bringing strange women to your penthouse suites," I tell him, stroking his bare chest, loving how the moonlight paints him in silvery tones. "It seems as though you may be a family man now."

"What a fate," he says mournfully. One of his hands runs through my hair while the other possessively cups my hip. "And you can no longer flaunt your skills at attracting a variety of different men, it seems. Never will anyone else have you."

"Never ever," I agree with playful despondence. "But…"

I shift, craning my neck to see his face more clearly. The man is the picture of contentment, his eyes gleaming in the dark, his lips devoid of their natural resting frown. If I squint, his expression could almost be deemed a smile, soft and curling like the fall of his hair.

"There is one obstacle we need to overcome," I tell him sternly.

He raises an eyebrow. "Oh."

"Yes." Sighing, I collapse against him, nestling into his touch. "We need to get you a million more books on kink. All the research you could ever need."

Holy crap. My throat still aches, but damn was it worth it. Already, my body is humming at whatever tricks the man could have in store. I'm tempted to risk pissing him off again if only to experience the depths of his depravity all over again. Jim made normal sex into an ordeal.

With Vadim, makeup sex is a world unto itself, let alone the vanilla stuff. A woman could get seriously drugged on his cock. Though, I could think of far worse fates.

Like being stupid enough to lose him for good.

"I'm an idiot for bringing this up now, I know I am," I confess, apologizing in advance with a kiss pressed against his nipple. "But I need to know…"

The one question I've been avoiding up until this moment, dancing around my feelings for him—as well as the shadows looming in his past.

"Who is Irina? Who was she to you? What did she say?"

"Irina…" He sighs, and rolls onto his side, capturing me in his arms, drawing me against him, my back against his chest. His mouth settles against the back of my skull, his hands on my breasts. The heaviness in his voice tempers any lust the position inspires. In some ways, I feel like what It is to Magda—a security blanket, being crushed for comfort. "We were not lovers," he says into my hair. "I need you to understand that, because when I describe our relationship… It was never sexual. But given the nature of our environment at the time, sex with another was not a necessity."

I wince, my heart aching for him, as it does every time I try to picture the horrific trappings of his childhood.

"Emotional connection, however?" he continues gruffly. "That was a commodity we both sought with an almost addicted fervor. But not in the way you are thinking.

More like… The need to feel superior. Challenged. Our games revolved around the manipulation of others. Our captors. Our clients. We were damn good at utilizing those we could control to the fullest extent—and relishing in that power. It was all we had."

I slip my arms from his protective cocoon and tentatively stroke the length of his arm, sensing his need for something reassuring. Something to tether him from that darkness. He grunts, gripping me even tighter while lowering his mouth to my throat.

"We were kept like dolls," he explains, his tone empty. Lifeless. "Locked into rooms for clients to pick from the way one might select a garment from a rack. Those who couldn't learn to turn off their pain—perform and endure —didn't last. But I endured, and Irina? She *thrived*. We were both young when we came to him. I might have been thirteen? Fourteen? She wasn't much older, a beauty from Eastern Europe trafficked by her own family to pay off gambling debts. We were…*favorites,* of our owner," he says, his voice hitching over the word. *Favorites.* He's used it before I realize, and I suspect that term means more than the superficial definition. It was a shackle.

"The sick bastard used us more than the others. Demanded more from us. He dangled our appeal before his most prized clients, and we did what we could to beat each other at the game. If she could learn political secrets from one powerful dignitary, then I would learn firsthand intelligence from another. If she gained a necklace as a token, then I would cajole a more expensive trinket from my own abuser. We traded knowledge and money and companionship, each of us fighting to cement their role as the better player. The strongest. The coldest. We were just children," he admits, his voice deepening. "Surviving the only way we knew how. And that way involved backstabbing and intrigue. If Irina were assigned to a client she didn't like, I would be manipulated to perform in her place. If there were a punishment awaiting her for food she'd stolen, or rules she'd broken, I somehow would be the one to wind up lashed. I let her use me as her scapegoat," he adds, his voice thickening as if only now can he admit that to himself. "I let her take from me. Toy with me… Abandon me when she saw her own escape."

And in the process, he learned to mistrust those around him, seeing any and all forms of communication as strictly transactional.

"I never begrudged her then," he admits, flexing his fingers over my breasts, making me shiver in a tormented mixture of pleasure from his touch and disgust at his words. "But our owner, the Collector… He enjoyed his favorites too much, and so sick a man he was… He aimed to breed us—but not on our own terms, mind you. I don't even know how advanced the technology was back then, but one by one, we were dragged off to the medical suite. Strapped down. Prodded. Poked. Our liberties and DNA taken as though we were animals in a kennel, matched with the intent for our offspring to be bought and sold. My turn came not long before I escaped," he adds coldly. "I was sure I'd torched the place to ashes, burning all traces of those experiments."

"So…you think Irina took your 'samples' for Magda?" I don't know how to say it without sounding foolish. A naïve innocent crudely narrating the darkest details of his past as though they're a spectacle to gape over.

But if anything, some of the tension from him eases, his lips nuzzling my heated flesh. And for the first time, I reconcile the fact that he's holding me at all—not staring into place, numbly recounting this like the few other times we've broached this topic.

"Irina was always cunning," he says. "Cunning and calculating. Those times she used me to her own ends? She always had a token on the other end to make up for it, or so she saw them as. For instance, after I'd be whipped for her crimes, she'd sneak a priceless jewel into my chambers. Or a sweet. Though those gifts were always predicated by a desire on her part to use me again. They always carried a price."

And thus, a brooding, ice-cold transactional man was born from the darkness of such a cruel life.

"If she did manage to get a hold of our 'samples.' Have Magdalene… To her, the girl would only ever be a token. A means to an end—and by dangling her before me, eventually, there will be a price to be paid in return."

But in the case of his daughter, I don't think he'll hesitate to pay it, whatever it may be.

"What did she want when she came by the house?" I ask warily.

"Nothing," he rasps, but his voice is gruff with unease. Unsteady. "*Nothing.* She told me she 'missed me,' then she left. No mention of Magdalene. Not even a fucking confirmation or a threat. And *that* is what…frightens me. She always wants something. Everything is a means to an end."

"But Magda isn't a token," I whisper, matching his apparent protectiveness.

"Nor a toy," he agrees. "And I am not the same broken little boy she left behind."

I shiver at the ferocity in his tone, my heart aching for him. Thinking quickly, I resist his grip enough to twist around to face him and loop my arms around his neck. Desperate to distract him, I kiss a path up from his collar bone to his mouth, grinding my hips with every teasing peck.

He lunges into the kiss, pinning me beneath him, easily parting my legs.

And this time, I let him take from me.

Whatever he needs.

All that he can salvage.

Everything.

CHAPTER TEN

We return to my parents' house in the morning to find Magda once again in the garden, but this time sampling frozen treats—sugar-free I see at a glance—on a picnic blanket spread out beneath one of the orange trees. Mother and Daddy sit on either side of her, each cajoling her into trying a new delicacy, their laughter carefree.

My heart swells in my chest. I don't think I've ever seen them so relaxed—let alone my mother willingly sit so close to the actual earth. Her eyes sparkle as she runs her fingers through Magda's loose curls as Daddy shapes orange peels with his tongue to make her giggle.

"Your kid is a master manipulator," I tell Vadim in awe as we watch her work from the obscurity of the sunroom. "I think someone will wind up with a very good haul at Christmas."

His jaw clenches at that, his gaze constricted with an emotion I can't read just yet. Something every bit as tender and delicate as the freshly blooming flowers spreading their petals throughout the garden. If I stumble too close to it now, I might wind up crushing it.

So instead, I coax him out where we join the makeshift picnic much to Magda's delight. Soon enough, rather than just two peons to fawn over her, her court grows to four, and every bit the little princess, she plays her role to the fullest extent.

"Can we go to the beach?" she asks, once we've eaten lunch and my parents have gone off in search of more things to placate her with—my father with the promise of showing her his power tools once he's cleaned the shed, and my mother in the process of fetching every dress I'd ever worn from storage.

"The beach…" Vadim locks eyes with me, conceding the decision to my discretion, I suspect. Something tells me he's well aware of the sensitive ground venturing into town treads upon for me.

But my past wounds aren't Magda's problem.

"I can show you my old haunts," I tell her, tugging at a curl. "I loved hanging out on Faraday beach."

Just like that, we bundle into the car and enter the town I haven't stepped foot in since my divorce was finalized over six months ago. It's one of those small, overly beautiful, secretly judgmental, and cloistered coastal towns with none of the allure of say, Orange County, but twice the charm.

I'm pleased to find most of my old favorite cafes and boutiques are still in business, gearing up for the peak tourist season.

"You lived here," Magda says, this time with utter confidence, her eyes on a gaggle of giggling blond teens decked out in matching designer fashions.

"Hey!" I elbow her in the shoulder as we leave the car parked beyond the boardwalk. "I would never walk in an identical cluster. I was the trendsetter, not the follower."

Her sly grin tells me she doubts that assessment.

Still, we trailblaze our own path through the beach bum clones, lazily patrolling the boardwalk before skimming past the water as Magda skips through the waves, her sandals in hand, her smile infectious.

"Something tells me you're considering investing in a beach house," I taunt Vadim once I spy the way he's watching her. Avidly, like a man who thought he'd never see the sun experiencing a full-on supernova up close and personal.

"Already in the process of closing on one," he admits, running his finger along the collar of his casual button-down. "Seeing your family's home sold me on vacationing in wine country."

I have to wonder if this purchase came before or after our makeup session last night. Judging from his smirk, he won't tell.

I lean against him rather than prod, slipping my hand in his as his other arm goes around me. I crave this nearness now more than ever—because as much as I hate to admit it, there is a reason I preferred to stay on the East coast, shacking up with a sexy, handsome billionaire rather than come back home.

Being here still stings.

We've passed the seaside diner Jim took me to early on in our relationship. And the spot on the beach where he proposed—but with a stand-in ring because his father's credit line at the jewelry store hadn't gone through at the time. Now, we're nearing the overlook where he liked to stroll, showing me off like arm candy before he tired of me.

I'm doing my best to ignore the poisonous nostalgia, but my mood must plummet to the point that even Vadim senses it.

"Let's take a break," he suggests, stopping short before a row of white picnic tables positioned with a view of where the boardwalk intersects the beach. "How about some ice cream?"

"Okay!" Magda takes his hand without a second thought, and they head off toward a frozen treat stand a few paces away. I find myself scanning the stream of traffic combing through the boardwalk as I wait, letting my brain run rampant with vicious scenarios.

I wonder if Jim is enjoying life with his new baby and harlot. If he takes her here, to these places, and she's dumb enough to assume they belong to her alone. If they both expect that I'm somewhere in hiding, living off his alimony payments and seething with jealousy.

I think that's the part that alarms me the most. I'm *not* seething. I'm pissed—so very pissed with myself and the fact that I suffered for so long. Lied to myself for so long.

And all for what?

To discover that the world beyond my marriage could be ten times more beautiful, and sexier and fulfilling. And I never had to change the person I was—not really. Dumb, lazy Tiffy could thrive when given the chance, with or without a relationship to assign her value.

Fuck Jim, may he rot in marital bliss.

But, because the world is cruel, I think I wind up conjuring him from thin air.

I almost mistake him for another balding, beer-gut sporting beachgoer at first. But no. No one else could sport that smug posture, like a peacock strutting, wanting the whole world to see the gussied-up, naïve little hen he'd cajoled into marrying him. His hen looks even younger than Francesca when glimpsed out in the open and not scurrying from me in the church corridors or cowering in Jim's shadow.

She's slender, with ginger waves curling down her back, a baby balanced on her hip. He has his arm around her, showing off the sexy young piece of ass a washed-up man his age managed to score.

But shock isn't what has me lurching to my feet, toying with the idea of running back to the car. Just pain. Because I recognize that look on her face—the thin-lipped smile, and simpering expression. God, how could I face myself in the mirror every day and not see it before?

But they see me. Jim cocks his head, frowning once he spots an unwelcome addition to his fawning crowd. He squints as if unsure if it really is me—dressed in a sexy, A-line beige sundress, my hair hanging loose in the style he never liked, my makeup bold and obvious.

His lips twitch in that ugly way, a hallmark of his irritation. Most often glimpsed when I said the wrong thing or seemingly embarrassed him, and he felt the need to "set me straight" with some cruel tirade. Rather than approach me, he tugs his new bride closer, almost protectively.

Because in his tiny brain, I'm still in love with him. Still pining for him. I bet he thinks I followed him here on purpose, waited for him.

Fuck him.

I don't even realize I'm taking a step forward until a pair of tiny arms goes around my waist. "Mommy!" a little girl chirps, clamoring for my attention. "We got you ice cream! Do you like it?"

A masculine arm encircles my shoulders, as the child—who I'm startled to recognize as Magda—flanks my opposite side.

"Here you go, baby," Vadim murmurs, pressing a cone piled high with strawberry ice cream into my hand, his lips soft on my cheek. And yet his voice is loud enough for anyone within ten yards to easily here. "It's about time we got back, don't you think?"

Like orderlies guiding a wayward patient, he and Magda block me in, forcing me down the length of the boardwalk. Purposefully I suspect. And yet, I can't resist glancing back, just enough to see Jim's face.

"Keep walking," Vadim tells me, his tone gently insistent. "Let's savor this moment."

Savor…

He couldn't know who Jim is, could he? I look over to find him and Magda trading conspiratorial winks, and then it clicks. Hell, yes, he knows.

And he intervened to give me a revenge too sweet to have devised on my own.

"You two and your mind games," I murmur, equally awed and impressed.

Poor Jim. He'll probably spend all night wondering if it really was me he saw—the woman he supposedly defeated

—or a stranger with a beautiful life he could only dream of.

I've never dreaded leaving my parents' home more. Even Magda seems to sulk at the prospect after a week spent gardening and playing dress up in my old wardrobe. Vadim, ever the resigned stoic, is the one level-headed enough to muster us to the airport after three days spent in utter bliss.

"I mean it, Tiffy," my mother scolds as she and Daddy follow us out to the car. "We expect you back for the summer holidays. And Magdalene, darling, I'll take you to all of the clubs once they open. Oh, all of the girls will find you so darling, and we can get you into tennis lessons, and maybe if your father *does* decide to try out a pageant or two—"

"Stay in the muck, kid," Daddy says with a knowing wink. "You'll learn more rooting through the dirt than you ever could in some fancy dress."

"Oh, Harold," my mother whines in exasperation.

They fuss as Vadim claims the driver's seat, and we make our escape. In the end, the journey home isn't anywhere near as daunting as I'd initially thought. Travel with one stoic—and a mini-stoic in tow—is an experience in of itself. Especially when Magda struggles to hide her excitement during her second plane trip, and Vadim loses himself in the pure joy of watching her eagerly prattle about plane engines and aerodynamics.

When she finally tires out, I find myself seated beside him, my head on his shoulder, his fingers lazily parting my hair.

"How did you know?" I ask, eyeing the clouds rolling beneath us beyond the windows. "About my ex?"

He shrugs, his expression neutral. "I noticed you were uncomfortable, and I made a logical leap to the obvious conclusion."

Fair enough. But as I submit to his gentle stroking, he adds, "And, I may or may not have researched the man the second I learned you were divorced."

"Oh," I croak, stunned by the implications of that confession. Seemingly harmless. But seemingly *not*, considering Vadim's wealth of resources. Not to mention his knack for manipulation.

"I don't think your arrival caused his ill mood, however," he explains, going a step further in his assessment of my ex's mental state than even I did. "It seems that persistent rumors of his infidelity may have reached the leadership of your old parish. Poor James may have been relieved of his duties for the time being, given the rumor of impropriety."

I gasp and bolt upright, placing my hand on his chest. "You didn't! You devil!" I'm grinning ear to ear, though, even as I feign utter shock. "I, good Sir, am a lady far beyond the machinations of revenge."

"Of course," he concedes, drawing me back to him, his lips brushing my forehead. "As am I. As am I…"

Hours later, when we finally pull up to the house, I'm alarmed to find that I'm not anywhere near as homesick as I'd assumed I would be. My family home in California is a beautiful oasis, but when glimpsed in the dappling evening sunset that reflects like embers over the water, I have to admit that Vadim's home has a certain charm to it.

Even Magda seems affected, skipping up the front walkway, It dangling from her hand. She moves assuredly, with the knowledge that this is hers. Her *home*.

But somewhere between the last section of the path and the front door, she stops short. The color drains from her face, and Vadim is before her instantly.

"What's wrong?" He crouches down, fervently feeling along her forehead. Then he frowns. "Look at me, *chérie*."

Magda doesn't even seem to realize he's there. Her nostrils flare, her chest heaving as if she's struggling for air. Desperate to breathe.

"Magdalene," Vadim says in a stern tone. She blinks, startled, and refocuses on his face.

"I smelled something," she says, her voice devoid of its usual charm. The resulting effect is a hollow, broken tone that makes me approach her, sinking down beside Vadim. "Do you smell it?"

I sniff and shrug. "Roses?"

Her eyes widen, and she nods, clutching It so tightly her knuckles are white.

"Oh." Vadim chuckles, ruffling her hair. "Ena has a secret green thumb," he explains, rising to his feet. "Give him time, and this house will resemble the garden at Tiffany's family home."

That seems to mollify her. As if flipping that pesky internal switch, she's back to her animated self, rearing to enter the house.

"Can we see my pony?" she asks as Vadim gathers our bags and finally unlocks the front door.

"Of course," he says indulgently. "Let's put our things away quickly, *non*? I'm sure we can make it out to our friends before dark."

They both hasten inside while I take my time savoring the view. Could I learn to call this place home as well? The second I see Magda bound up the stairs, filling the hall with childish clatter, I start to believe I could.

"I'll make dinner," I call as Vadim returns downstairs, dressed in a casual pair of slacks and a loose-fitting dress shirt while Magda scampers after him in her riding gear. They race out onto the terrace, Magda's giggles lingering long after they fade from view.

Left alone, I decide to hone my domestic skills and consider whipping up a meal from scratch. What might I cook safely without risking everyone's health? Frowning, I open the fridge and peruse the ingredients that Ena's stocked it with. Finding nothing promising—other than a potential salad—I start toward the pantry, hoping for more convenient options. Like cereal.

Intent on my task, I slip past the fridge, skirting the counter...

And promptly stop short.

A woman is seated at the dining room table, her legs crossed, her slim fingers—each tipped with a sharpened ruby fingernail—tracing patters over the glass surface, her expression the picture of contemplation.

My blood runs cold as she looks up, meeting my gaze.

"I'm surprised, to be honest," she says, her voice an odd mixture of cutting notes and lilting cadence. Shifting to face me fully, she crosses her arms, observing me with a judgmental flick of her gaze. Her navy dress helps her blend into the monochromatic background, and I wonder, horrified, just how long she's been sitting here.

Did Magda run right by her?

Or Vadim...

"Dima was always so secretive about his ideal type of woman," Irina continues, her pink lips quirked in a smirk that doesn't reach her gaze. Regardless, I stagger back, putting the counter between us, my fingers inching toward one of the drawers containing utensils. The sharp kind.

"How did you even get in here—"

"I'd assumed, it was because his standards were higher than he'd care to admit," she says, continuing as if I'd never spoken. "He was always so…obsessive with perfection." She frowns wistfully, her head cocked, gaze reflective. Then she shakes her head, sending her blond waves tumbling down her shoulders. "I will admit that it is disappointing to realize that I was wrong. The boy he was could never resist a sweet. Cheap, tawdry, fleeting joy."

I stiffen, recognizing an insult when I hear it. Squaring my shoulders, I swallow hard, schooling my expression into a mask of cool politeness. At the same time, my eyes dart to the glass door, hunting for Vadim. Ena. *Anyone.*

But with no witness in sight, my only course of action is to stay on guard. "You should go—"

"You asked me how I got in," Irina says, rising to her feet. With enviable grace, she smooths her hands down her front, drawing attention to her ample curves and tiny waist. Deliberately, I suspect—and just as she intends, I brush my hand along my simple dress skirt, mentally comparing the contrasting picture we must make.

As if aware of the thought, she smiles. "I'm sure you're smart enough to figure it out."

I flinch. "I'm guessing it wasn't with the permission of security."

Though she looks so slender in comparison to Ena's bulk, could she have incapacitated the bodyguard somehow? My stomach twists into knots at the thought—as surly as he can be, Vadim wouldn't want him hurt.

Neither do I.

"Security," Irina parrots, purring the word. "As in Boris Ena. Trust Vadim to draw the iciest, most ruthless bastard of the lot to his side. Luckily for me, I remember his… blind spots."

She winks, her eyelids lowered. At the back of my mind, I recognize the expression as a cruel imitation of one of Magda's. Her surly, brooding look when she's mulling over how to get her way during a round of monopoly. The second I see it, I know she's already won.

And I back up another hasty step. "Did you hurt him?"

She shrugs as her eyes scan the room while her body languidly approaches the counter. Frowning, she swipes her finger over the polished surface, scowling at imaginary dust. "I don't have to hurt him," she says, her voice alarmingly soft. "Just outsmart him. And you insinuated permission, I'm assuming. Well, there you have it—" She spreads her arms wide as if to exclaim, *ta da!* In the process, a whiff of her perfume teases my nose, the deceptively sweet scent of roses. "Vadim knows better than anyone my skills of evasion," she boasts. "Take his hiding behind such lax 'security' as proof that he knew I'd return. He all but asked me to."

I back up another step as she slips onto a stool. With my hand extended behind me, I finally manage to grasp the handle of a drawer. Yanking it open, I feel through the assorted cutlery, finding nothing useful. Forks…spoons—no knives.

"You're saying Vadim invited you here?" I ask, desperate to feign nonchalance.

Her expression flattens, her gaze clouding over. "You're mouthier than I'd assume he could tolerate." Only a subtle, harsh note of inflection reveals her anger.

And yet it's as bracing as touching a hot stove—every nerve prickles with awareness, warning that I'm in danger of being burned.

"Are you here for Magda, then?" I ask, mainly to keep her talking as I inch back another step, feeling the edge of the drawer brush my lower back.

But if I'd wanted to distract her, I've succeeded. She scoffs. "Magdalene? Magdalene is…flawed." She flicks her fingers as if swatting the mere idea of the girl away. "I can give Dima other children. Perfect children. But can you?"

I'm too stunned by her words—and their disturbing implications—that I barely notice her slip around the counter, her gaze fixated on me. And then my brain finally processes her insult and the sheer, cruel accuracy with which it was aimed.

"Tiffany Connors," she says as crisply as if reciting from a book. "Your gynecologist has quite the extensive record on you. Endometriosis. Poly Cystic Ovarian Syndrome. The occasional hormone imbalances. Even if you weren't on birth control, Dima could fuck you raw for a month, and you still wouldn't conceive, would you?"

Fire sears my cheeks. I blink, too startled to move, even as she slinks closer, her smile knowing.

"And I'm sure he has been fucking you." She reaches out, swiping the tip of her nail along my cheek.

I recoil so violently I wind up slamming the drawer over my wrist. Only gritting my teeth can keep me from crying out. "D-Don't touch me—"

"*Touch* you. Have you ever asked yourself why Vadim can? Why he does?" Her smile is feral, her eyes glittering in the shadow cast by the light falling onto her face from this angle. "It doesn't come naturally to him, but you know that. He's pretending, winding you up, his little toy. He'll watch you spin and spin until you serve your purpose. He's always been that way. Cruel. I suppose it explains why he's gotten as far as he has. Amassed the empire he has. I doubt you even know the true extent of it..." Her tone shifts as she glances down, her teeth clenched.

"What do you mean?" I ask, tentatively licking my lips.

She cackles. "You don't, do you? My resourceful boy's all grown up, but I'll admit that he's turned out far more ruthless than I could imagine. Though considering who his mentor was, how could he not?"

Mentor? Hiram, the man who rescued him?

"What are you saying?"

"Oh, darling…" Her eyes gleam with mock pity. "Have you ever stopped to ask yourself how a man his age could amass such a fortune so quickly? Especially given his lack of…let's call it a traditional upbringing. Has he told you of his family? Their legacy? Don't tell me you are so naïve to believe he could rise above it all unscathed?"

Denying her is my first instinct. I even start to, my lips parting. But something stops me, and another question forms on my tongue instead. "Why do you care? If he is toying with me? If you don't want Magdalene, then why are you here?"

"Why?" She chuckles, and leans back against the island, her hair spilling down her shoulders, her body positioned provocatively. "Because after more than ten damn years, my Dima has finally grown bored of waiting for me," she declares. "He is *provoking* me. Drawing me out the way he knew how to all along." She traces her bottom lip with the wet tip of her tongue, her gaze distant. "By daring to pretend I don't exist. By replacing me with puppets."

She rights herself, pushing past me for the foyer. "But I will remind him soon enough. This was always a game, my darling. You're just a pawn in it…"

Her steps fade, and I crane my neck to watch her vanish around the corner. *Damn.* I'm shaking, my knees buckling, my wrist throbbing as I wrench it from the painful clutches of the drawer.

Then I'm already halfway to the terrace door, my fingers grasping at the handle. My first fully coherent thought is to run to the stable. Warn Vadim.

And I don't even see the blow coming.

A force slams into me from behind, and I go down hard, landing on my side in the shadow of the dining table. Dazed, I turn, scrambling for purchase over the flooring. I only catch a glimpse of silver, flashing through the air before...

Pain!

It's so sharp and all-consuming I can't breathe. The air leaves my lungs, my body drained of everything but fiery agony centered around my left shoulder. Again. Again.

A distant thudding registers with the remaining logical part of my brain—pairing the sickening sound with that of a butcher, plunging a blade into a hunk of meat. Stabbing through it.

I can't move.

I can't even scream.

But my only coherent thought is of Vadim.

And Magda.

God, I can sense them, tramping across the terrace, their laughter raucous as my attacker retreats. I hear Magda first, her tiny voice high-pitched with excitement. "Can we have pizza again?"

"Of course," Vadim says, sounding closer. "Go get washed up—"

"Don't!" It takes everything I have to claw at the floor and drag myself behind the counter and out of view. "Vadim, don't let her in!"

Silence falls with the swiftness of a candle being blown out. Or maybe I'm just losing consciousness? Either way, I feel like I'm hearing everything as if from underwater, muffled, and distant.

"*Chérie*," Vadim says, his voice garbled. "I left my…at…stable…go fetch for me?"

A heartbeat later, heavy footsteps rush to my side, and I sense warm fingers prodding my forehead. "Look at me," Vadim urges in a tone so hoarse it makes my heart ache. "Look at me!"

But I can't.

My vision is already blurring, darkening around the edges…

Until I can't see anything at all.

I feel so warm. So peaceful. I almost dread opening my eyes because it feels damn good to just float in this colorless ether. At least until I hear the voice.

His voice.

"Look at me, beautiful," he commands in a tone that cuts through the peaceful haze like a knife. "Open your eyes. Please, open your eyes."

When I do, the world returns in blurred snippets of color and contrasting shadow. Even in this dreamy state, I'm convinced the face coming into focus will from here on out be the most beautiful sight I've ever witnessed.

Dark eyes framed by dizzyingly long eyelashes fixate on me, narrowed with worry. That same concern tightens the line of a gorgeous mouth, the lips so pink. The face of an angel, his expression contorts with relief as I blink to take more of him in.

"Thank God." He seems closer, his gaze tortured. "Can you speak? Say something."

A tattered giggle edges his words. From me? My body feels loosely connected, as if threaded together with the thinnest string. Somehow, I manage to make my lips move, my voice high-pitched and breathy.

"You are so pretty," I tell him seriously. "The prettiest person *ever*. Like ever. In forever…"

He frowns, glancing beyond me. "What did you give her?"

"Due to the position of the wounds, the doctor ordered a mildly strong sedative to prevent further trauma during the suturing process," a woman explains in crisp, hilarious tones. "The effects will wear off in a few hours." Her voice drifts away, and another tattered giggle bubbles from my chest.

"Drugged?" I ask Vadim, amused by his worried frown. He's sexy in his normal resting state, but when emotionally aroused—even with concern—the man looks divine. "I probably would have married you if you asked nicely," I blurt, too warm and comfy to care about how the confession may land. "You didn't have to drug me."

"Drug you? I should have *protected* you." He smooths his fingers through my hair as more of our surroundings come into focus. We're in a room—plain, with light blue walls—but I don't recognize the style as belonging to his house. Or his bedroom, for that matter…

And I have tentacles, I realize with a dazed, childish bit of horror. Tubes snake out of both my arms, feeding into various blinking, beeping machines.

"Uh, oh," I say, still giggling harder now than ever. "Did I have an accident?"

"Get some sleep," Vadim urges, apparently deciding that the hazy, dreamy darkness is the best place for me to be. "Sleep. I'll be here. Always, I'll be here."

But will he? A voice in my head is telling me no, using one painful fact as the winning argument.

"I could give you a baby," I tell him out loud, watching his face change as the boast registers. Rather than hopeful, he looks stricken. Like I've struck him. Mortally wounded. Because he knows I might be lying? But deep down, I don't think I am.

Even if I may or may not be totally high.

"I could," I insist, my voice breathier than ever. "I mean it. I *want* to—"

"Stop talking, beauty," he commands, stroking his fingers through my hair. "All I need now is for you to rest. That is all I want from you. Your health. Nothing else."

I nod obediently, letting my eyes close as exhaustion washes over me like a wave—but one last thought tickles my conscious mind before I can drift off completely.

"Are you shady, Vadim?" I ask him sleepily. For some reason, a bitchy voice is in my head, implying as much. Taunting as much. "Do you do bad things—"

"Sleep." His voice resonates with way more authority this time.

But even as I comply, I sense his presence surround me persistently, more potent than any drug.

MY SECOND ATTEMPT at waking up isn't as fun as the first. I groan even before I blink my eyes open to a dimly lit room and a tired, handsome face.

"Better?" Vadim asks, his fingers stroking my cheek.

I nod and wince. "I'm not high anymore," I confess, my voice rasping. "But the tradeoff is that I feel like I got hit by a truck."

And in a way, I have—a psychotic, blond, beautiful truck my memories tell me. I shiver at reliving them, choosing to focus on Vadim instead. He's frowning, his jaw clenched, that muscle twitching.

"Four stab wounds. Fifty-two stitches in total," he confesses, his tone blunt. "Spanning from your left shoulder down to your hip. They are deep, but all avoided any vital organs, thank God. Still, you will need to take care to ensure you heal without any complications. An infection could be difficult to recover from, and the surgeon warned that, given that the injuries to your shoulder sliced through muscle, you will be in pain."

I wince. "That sounds about right."

"Should I get the nurse?"

Grunting with the effort, I shake my head. "No. I'll live…" Though a part of me shudders at the realization that Irina didn't intend as much by accident. She *deliberately* avoided killing me. Why?

One look at the man across from me, and I can guess the answer—this was merely a warning, to him alone.

"Where is Magda?" I ask, alarmed when I don't see her.

The hint of a smile sneaks into the corner of his mouth, so beautiful and unexpected that my physical pain is all but forgotten. "Charming your nurses into giving her more crayons, I suspect. She already has them wrapped around her finger." His gaze softens a fraction, and I sense a part of him takes pride in his socially adept offspring. Like father like daughter.

Or could such skill stem from her mother?

I suck in a breath as my brain finally dares to connect the dots of the pain searing through my left side to the vague images circling my scattered memories. Fifty-two stitches. That beats my previous record—stemming from a drunken yacht accident—by double digits.

"Irina," I croak, and Vadim stiffens, his gaze unreadable. But this time, he isn't hiding behind his wall. "*She* attacked me—"

"I don't know how she got in," he swears, leaning forward to grip my hand, unconsciously pressing my fingers against his chest, near his heart. He's seated beside me, his rumpled dress shirt betraying at least a few hours of vigil by my bedside—and something inside me heats and melts. At least in the brief second wherein I forget his psycho ex-partner in crime.

A horrible, sobering thought makes me slip my hand from his and utilize what little energy I have to brush his cheek, seeking out the contours of his haggard expression. "She doesn't want Magda," I tell him softly, a relief within itself. And, in so many ways, a tragedy for a child who, some might say, was abandoned by both parents at some point. "She wants *you*."

His eyes blaze, his throat constricting around a hard swallow. And... I think, deep down, he already knew that.

He was afraid of that very reality.

"I don't know how she got past Ena," he says hoarsely. "He didn't even see her. He was beside himself..." He sighs and runs the fingers of his free hand through his already mussed hair. "I hired ten more guards to cycle out at random intervals. I'm selling the house. Our new location is somewhere unlisted, impossible to trace. She won't come near you again."

I sink against my pillows, overwhelmed by the raw note of possession in his voice. The conviction with which he swears something so assuredly. Its power.

"Did Magda see…"

"No. I heard your warning." He takes my hand again, bringing it to his mouth, running his lips over my knuckles. "I entered the house first and distracted her before she saw anything. As far as she knows, you opened a cupboard of glass dishes with a faulty shelf, fell over and cut yourself—but she is intelligent," he admits, sadness crossing his features. "Too intelligent. Your parents, however, received the same story. I believe they accepted it, for what it's worth."

"Thank you…" The thought of him reaching out to my parents, given his lack of familial ties, means more to me than I would have expected.

But my relief is countered by concern for Magda. My heart aches for her—and pounds ferociously in the same breath. I don't think I've ever felt a desire to protect another so strongly before. Every time I think of her in danger…my blood boils.

"Irina doesn't want her," I reiterate, my voice cold. "She said she was…flawed—"

"She won't ever touch her." Vadim stands, turning his back to me, both hands in his hair, his posture rigid. Slowly, he starts to pace the length of the room, and my pulse flutters the more I watch him. Gone is the pain—

replacing it is steely, terrifying anger. "Never. I will kill her before I let that happen—"

"You knew." Gingerly, I shift around, groaning as fire shoots through my side. It's intense—I can feel each, individual puncture wound. Four, he said? Their placement makes it hard to find a comfortable position without being reminded of my injuries every time I take a breath. Intentionally, I suspect. And if Vadim really grew up with Irina as he claimed, then he most likely is well aware of her capabilities. "*That's* why you really tried to push me away. Not only for Magda."

In his own, twisted, broken logic—he wanted me to run. But in me, the master manipulator met his match.

His hands fall as he turns to face me, his eyes scanning my battered frame. "How do you feel?" he asks, a deliberate change in subject.

I wince and twist my hips into a slightly more comfortable position. "Not dead, at least." I force a laugh that he doesn't return. "What happened? When you found me."

He crosses over to a single window betraying a view of the darkening sky. "Magda raced me back to the house, but I started inside before she did. I saw the blood first," he confesses. "I sent her back to the stable to fetch something. Called Ena. I held you down to apply pressure to your wounds while he raced us to the hospital."

"And Magda? Don't tell me you left her there alone."

He cocks his head, his frown deepening. Layers enhance the tormented expression, creating a grimace shaped by both pain and…confusion. "Not quite—"

"Tiffany!" Magda waltzes into the room as if on cue, armed with a massive box of crayons and a stack of printer paper. I'm not sure how much time I've lost being stuck in this bed already—a day, maybe longer? Someone, however, took up my hair brushing duties in my absence, as well as dressed her in a lilac dress—though it clashes with her trusty fanny pack—complete with matching hair ribbons. The only detail glaringly out of place is a massive amount of glittery, unicorn stickers climbing up the length of her left arm.

"Pretty," I say, as she marches to my side, squeezing past Vadim. Reaching out, I stroke the gaudiest sticker—a pink unicorn bunny with big blue eyes. "Where did you get such swag, honey?" Call it a hunch, but they don't quite seem like Vadim's style.

She shoots her father a wary glance, but I can tell she's bursting at the seams with this new secret. "Ainsley gave them to me," she says, flashing that rare, ripe grin as she shows off her decked-out arm. "We had a sleepover."

"A sleepover?" I feel my eyebrows shoot up as I glance at Vadim while seriously considering the fact that I may actually still be high.

He doesn't meet my gaze, his frown surly, though as he looks down on Magda—and her obvious joy—his lips soften again. "A sleepover," he concedes.

That's it. I *am* hallucinating. As quickly as I dare, I sit upright, making him face me. He looks on edge, as if I've caught him with his pants down. Or, even worse in his mind, I caught him at a moment when he'd been desperate enough to go to the one person he seems to hate more than anyone.

Solely for Magda's sake.

"*Francesca* watched over her," he finally admits. "And her siblings."

But not the main, dominant member of that household—his brother Maxim. Not too long ago, he was out of the country. Could he still be gone?

Yet, the idea of Vadim crossing the invisible boundary between the property is a sight so unexpected—and at its core, so damn selfless, with such tender motivations—my heart almost can't contain it.

"Can I go back tonight?" Magda asks. She's curled up on his vacated chair, her gaze fixated on a drawing she's in the process of scribbling with a red crayon. At a glance, she's the picture of childish nonchalance—but her eyes betray her. Every few seconds, she glances hopefully at Vadim, her bottom lip dangerously close to a pout.

"Not tonight, *ma chérie*," Vadim says, moving toward her to ruffle her hair. She deflates, but relents to his touch, her nose wrinkling. "We're going to our new home tonight, remember? So that we can get it ready for Tiffany's return."

She nods, turning her attention to me. "No glass this time," she says solemnly. But damn…

Much like Vadim, I sense she's well versed in doublespeak —and my heart swells again. Literally.

A series of beeping machines goes off, and Vadim scrambles for a nurse. After checking my vital signs, she deems me no closer to dying than at any other moment throughout the day. Still, he's frowning, unconvinced.

"You need rest," he declares, brushing his lips over my forehead. "I'll come back tonight after Magda's in bed. Ena will watch over her this time. You'll have three guards on you at all times. You're safe." He sounds so confident in that fact, but as he pulls away, I suspect his reassurances were more for himself than me. He looks so exhausted as the waning daylight casts shadows over his haggard features. Worn. And yet, as he hasn't failed to do since her arrival, he swallows down any discomfort as he faces Magda.

"Let's go, *chérie*," he calls to her. "I'm sure Tiffany appreciates your many creations."

As battered as he is, the man cracks a tired smile at the sight of her drawings scattered all over my side table. I spot one and reach for it, wincing with the effort.

"This is lovely," I croon, glancing over a misshapen blob formed of black crayon that may or may not be an animal of some kind.

"It's It," Magda says seriously. She slips from the chair and gathers her belongings. Squished into the cushions of the seat behind her is a small white bear that she clings to even while juggling her pilfered art supplies. "He can protect you. From falling onto glass."

I laugh, but when I look up from the page, her eyes... They bore into mine so fiercely I flinch. Oblivious, Vadim comes to relieve her of her artistic burden and heads for the door. "Let's go."

She follows him, but when she glances back, I nearly lunge from the bed to grab her, barely able to suppress a fierce desire to hold her in my arms until she never sports such an expression again. Fear. Raw, naked terror so potent I'm rendered silent in the face of it.

CHAPTER TWELVE

I barely have the chance to mourn his absence before I sense Vadim return just as I'm dozing off. He slips into the room without a word, reclaiming his post beside me. I shiver, content, as warmth feathers my forehead—the shadow of a chaste kiss.

As I continue to feign sleep, his fingers capture mine, lifting them from my crumpled blankets. I make myself limp, my breathing steady. Maybe I'm curious as to what he'll do? And he doesn't disappoint.

With breathtaking care, he brings my fingers to his mouth, or so I assume from the warm bursts of air ghosting my knuckles. The feel of his lips a second later—grazing the back of my hand reverently—makes me shiver. Damn this man...

He gently strokes whatever parts of me he can reach. Runs through my hair with aching gentleness. He lavishes me in silent praise, all in secret without an audience to preen for. And even though my eyes remain closed, I know that this is *him*—a man Irina was never, ever privy to.

The real, unfiltered Vadim.

I WAKE up to find a watchful gaze directed my way, its owner wearing another stripped-down suit—this time with a navy dress shirt and no jacket. The moment I start to lift my head from the pillows, he races to get me a pitcher of water and small pieces of fruit, fussing to make sure I'm hydrated and fed.

Once my nurse comes in and performs her assessment, then the doctor—who deems me stable enough to leave— I find myself discharged and promptly carried into a waiting car a little after noon.

"Where's Magda?" I ask once I find the backseat empty.

Vadim's chosen to drive us himself, and he chuckles as he settles into the driver's seat, his lip twitching. "Forcing Ena to teach her gardening techniques. Well, perhaps not necessarily against his will." His expression turns wistful as he navigates the steering wheel with one hand, the other placed firmly on my knee. "I don't think I've ever seen the bastard smile," he admits. "At anyone."

Satisfied, I sit back in my seat, oddly amused by the prospect. But then my thoughts turn to more dangerous topics as my injuries throb, even after a dose of—much less potent than my initial dosage—pain medication.

"How did she get past him?" I ask, eyeing Vadim warily. "Irina?"

He frowns, all traces of joy vanishing from his face. "I suspect she timed it. Watched him long enough to know his schedule—when he'd be the easiest to circumvent. She was always like that. Cunning."

An assessment that brings up another chilling suspicion circling my brain. "Magda... Do you think she remembers Irina?"

He cocks his head, his brow furrowing. If he's considered such a possibility himself, I can't tell. "What makes you ask that?"

Several reasons come to mind. Her aversion to roses, for one. Not to mention her almost obsessive need for her teddy bear—a bear, that I'm starting to realize, may symbolize more to her than just a sentimental gift. A fact bolstered by a certain picture she'd chosen to hide within it.

He can protect you, she told me after giving me her drawing—which I've kept tucked within my discharge paperwork.

For all of her intellect, she's still seven at heart. A child prone to magical beliefs of monsters and mystery—and one who trusts in Vadim's presence so strongly that, in her mind, he could protect her from anything. Even her worst nightmares...

"It's nothing," I finally say, rather than bother him with a bunch of random observations that may not mean anything. "But have you talked to her yet? About what she might remember of her life before you found her?"

It's a topic that feels far too intimate for me to broach again. Only her father should have reign over that arena.

…Shouldn't he?

"No," he confesses. "I haven't. Not yet. According to her records, she had decent nutrition and healthcare prior to being discovered. But…" He frowns and lifts his hand from me, stroking it through his hair.

"But?" I prod when he falls silent.

"Her diabetes was newly onset, so her blood sugars had been wildly uncontrolled—but that is typical with this illness. Otherwise, there wasn't a mark on her."

But I know firsthand that abuse can extend far beyond the physical. Some of the worst wounds are the ones inflicted upon your soul. As strange as it feels to admit, even to myself, Irina's attack—while hurting like a bitch—doesn't sting anywhere near as badly as some of the verbal blows Jim dished out. Injuries to my self-esteem that I'm still recovering from years later.

The thought of Magda suffering even a fraction of the same…

"She doesn't *need* Irina," Vadim says, injecting himself into my scattered thoughts. "Irina's heart has only ever had room for herself. But you? Bleeding and injured, your sole concern was that Magda didn't see you in such a state."

Awe colors his voice, making my cheeks catch fire. He makes it sound so momentous—so unfathomable to him. That the welfare of another could supersede even someone's personal pain.

Not that I'm the only one capable of that kind of selflessness.

"You're such a good dad to her," I tell him once the internal rage has worn off, and I can objectively review his actions over the past few days. "To Magda. She adores you—"

"And you," he says almost hesitantly as if he's not sure how I'll handle that knowledge. His gaze finds me warily though he keeps most of his attention on the road. "I can't get her to stop asking when we'll go to California again."

I laugh, wincing as my left side twinges. "If my parents have their way, then probably for every major holiday at least. A few of the minor ones too. You do realize they'll be expecting us for Christmas, don't you?"

A smile softens the line of his mouth, and it is breathtaking. I sense him sneak another peek at me and his eyes brim with a hint of something that may or may not be…hope?

"Another chance to practice my gift-giving skills," he says earnestly.

"Wine for my mother. Beer for my father. And as long as you don't buy the entire toy store for Magda, I think you'll do just fine."

It's only when I see the pained edge to his expression that I realize something I don't have the heart to ask out loud. Has he ever spent a Christmas with family? With anyone other than Ena?

I make a mental note to myself to spoil him lavishly when the time comes—shower blow jobs galore. When I'm through, he'll look forward to the holiday season with a childlike sense of joy.

I'll fix all of the broken memories his childhood denied him.

Even if it kills me.

It isn't until Vadim parks in an unfamiliar driveway—one barricaded behind a high stone wall and wrought iron gate—that I recognize the stout, clinical gray mansion as our new home.

In so many ways, it's not as impressive as the last.

Dour and relatively plain, it lacks the charm of the beautiful house overlooking the cove—instead, commanding a ruthlessly manicured plot of land cast in shadow by that massive wall spanning the entire perimeter. Once inside, I find the décor seriously lacking. Or, as my mother would say, "Where is the sunlight, darling?"

Without the aid of bay windows to provide said natural light, or a view of a body of water, Vadim's dour color scheme creates an almost prison-like atmosphere. One bolstered by the strange men I spot patrolling various sections of the property.

Gone are the days of Ena's out of sight, out of mind approach to security, it seems.

We find the old bodyguard himself sitting at a square table in a spacious dining room at the center of the floor plan. In addition to his typical battered leather jacket, he sports a new, unusual accessory draped around his neck— a bright pink feathery boa. Across from him sits Magda, her gaze intent on what looks to be a pink tea set arranged in between them. Carefully, Magda lifts an empty cup and places it before Ena.

"You drink it," she says as if narrating a play.

He nods. "Okay."

"And now you're poisoned," Magda says, deadpanned. "So…you have to die."

Ena shrugs. "Okay."

"That's it?" Magda purses her lips, fighting to maintain her serious frown. Despite her best attempts, a smile breaks through within seconds. "You're supposed to be *dead*," she exclaims, throwing her hands into the air. "Try making death noises or something! Play pretend. Let's go again—"

"It looks like the queen needs to work on her poisoning skills," I call from the doorway as Vadim comes up behind me.

Magda looks up, her smile unfurling in full. "Tiffy!"

"Easy, *chérie*," Vadim scolds gently as she races over and snatches my hand, tugging me to her makeshift royal tea party. "She's still very sore."

"Never too sore for palace intrigue," I say, forcing a grin as Magda ushers me into the chair beside Ena.

Once she reclaims her throne, she glances at the bodyguard, her frown apologetic. "You're not the princess anymore," she tells him, though judging from his stoic expression, I doubt the man is too heartbroken by his demotion in status.

Something far more serious seems to be on his mind. Guilt? His dark eyes shift toward me and quickly dart away. "Okay," he grunts, starting to rise to his feet.

"*But,*" Magda says, making him pause mid-motion. "You can be my royal henchman. Tiffy will play the princess. Now, henchman—" Her eyes take on a gleeful, calculated gleam. "Pour the tea!"

What unfolds next is an enthralling, heart-stopping game of royal politicking during which I die five times, and Ena has to robotically endorse the maniacal musings of his mad queen. All the while, Vadim hovers in the background, his expression guarded and yet completely decipherable.

He watches his daughter, his gaze soft with a love no one would deny. He smiles when she squeals in delight during the twists and turns of her "game," and I think he's spellbound by every machination of her imagination. But pretty soon, I'm equally as enthralled by him.

As much as I try to deny it, Irina's petty jabs *did* sting. They still do—and entirely not out of concern for Vadim and his potential motives either. He may want another child one day, but so do I. *Badly,* I'm starting to realize. More than I thought I ever would.

"Pay attention, Tiffany," Magda scolds as the daylight wanes beyond the windows. Already, Vadim had to switch on an overhead lamp just to provide enough illumination for us to see by. "I've just declared you an illegitimate heir to the throne. You are banished from the kingdom, and my evil henchman has come to take you away forever! What do you do?"

I frown, thinking it over. Then I tap my chin. "I think I'll ask, why I've been banished," I decide.

But Magda's expression falls flat. "Because you're sick," she says tonelessly. "And no one wants you anymore."

I stiffen, my gaze darting around the room. Vadim's vanished—presumably to make dinner—and Ena already managed to escape his role nearly an hour ago. There's no one else left to witness the pain transforming her features, and I have a suspicion that our "game" isn't so hypothetical anymore.

If it ever were, to begin with.

"The *queen* is saying this?" I say cautiously, twisting my pink teacup between my fingers.

She nods.

"Hmm. And what about the king?"

She looks away, her expression distant. "He doesn't want you either. So the mean men come to take you away…"

My throat is dry, my heart pounding at the sheer horror I suspect I'm only getting the faintest glimpse of. Is *that* why Irina abandoned her? Because of her illness? A condition that she clearly inherited from Vadim?

Not to mention Magda's obvious fear of men built like Maxim. How had she described him? *"Is the big scary man here?"*

Did that fear also stem from Irina? Had the woman arranged for some brutal henchman to yank Magda from whatever home she'd known, dumping her at an orphanage? It would certainly explain her reaction to Maxim, and Milton to an extent.

And, that obvious atrocity aside, my worst fear is that Magda knows well enough of her mother's intentions. All along, she's known. Even more tragic, she's carried that pain believing the worst—Vadim didn't want her. Irina *told* her he didn't want her.

When I find my voice again, I clear my throat to banish any traces of anger. "You know what I'd do?" I set my teacup aside, fold my hands and lean forward, forcing her to meet my gaze head-on. "I'd tell the queen to shove it. I am a princess, and I have more powers than she could ever dream of."

She raises an eyebrow, her lips quirked downward. "Like what?"

"Like…" *Make this good, Tiffy.* "I'm charming, and pretty, and I'm damn good at shopping. I'll scour the whole damn world and hunt down a cure. Then I'll use my wits to secure a lifetime supply of it. Cursed or not, I'm stronger for it either way."

She wrinkles her nose, unconvinced.

"*And,*" I add, thinking fast. My eyes settle on a tuft of white centered on her lap, barely visible above the table. "I know that I'm never alone in my adventures. Because the king *does* want me—more than anything else in the world. In fact, he sent me a protector to always look out for me when I'm afraid, or lonely. And since the evil queen is a liar, I'll know that he must have been cursed too. That's why he isn't there," I add as she shifts, her fingers creeping toward It, burying in his plush fur. "And that when he wakes up, he'll find me. He will always find me, no matter what."

"Why?" she asks, her voice so hollow that I nearly lunge across the table to grab one of her hands, gripping it tightly.

"Because he loves *you,*" I tell her so fiercely, my voice cracks. "He will always love you. Always."

Silently, she wrangles her fingers from mine. Then, she slips from her chair and scurries around the table. Before I have the sense to steel myself, she's climbing onto my lap, burying her face in the crook of my shoulder.

"Oh, honey…" Without a thought given for my stitches, I wrap my arms around her, squeezing as tight as I'm able to. "And when the king does find you, he'll have a crazy bitch girlfriend who will stab the queen's eyes out if she ever comes near you again. You hear me?"

She says nothing, but I rock her in silence, inhaling the scent of her hair and the fruity shampoo Vadim must have bought for her. I stroke my fingers through her braided curls and reassure her in every way I can that my words are more than just a boastful fairytale.

I will personally fight to make them true.

AFTER PUTTING MAGDA TO BED, I'm limping when I finally creep into a master suite—admittedly nowhere near as spacious or appealing as the old one. There I find Vadim hovering near the bed. The second he spots me, he's by my side, lifting me into his arms.

"You've overexerted yourself," he scolds, carrying me over to the bed. "Lie still. I need to check if you've broken any sutures."

I pout and submit to his inspection. With utmost care, he strips my clothes, leaving them on the floor and manipulates me until I'm lying face down, his fingers gingerly peeling back my bandages.

"No damage," he declares after a moment. "But, I'm inclined to put you on mandatory bed rest."

I lift my head hopefully. "Sexy bedrest?"

He shakes his head, stroking down my lower back in a way that inspires thoughts of *anything* but resting. "I'm afraid not," he says, contradicting the desire conveyed by every swipe of his fingers. "You will have to go without until your wounds heal. That is final."

"Is that so?" I play dirty and reach out, inching toward the front of his slacks.

"Very final," he insists, groaning as I cup him, finding him straining the tailored fabric.

I'm not the only one who will go without, it seems. Still teasing him, I flex my fingers, watching his expression shift as he turns onto his side, facing me.

"Where did you go after dinner?" I ask cautiously. Once mine and Magda's tea party ended, he'd served us another one of his delicious homemade meals and then vanished, leaving us to play a round of monopoly—during which I got my ass thoroughly kicked.

He frowns and captures my rebellious hand, moving it to settle on his chest. "Something you said piqued my curiosity," he admits. "I made another round of calls to my contacts in the hopes of finding out more about Magda's origins. Anything I can use to—" He breaks off, his jaw clenched, but I can guess the words he's holding back.

He's tracking down anything he can use against Irina. At least in her legal battle if she persists in her quest to block his custody.

"Any luck?" I ask hopefully, but he shakes his head.

"No. It's like she appeared from thin air. And I'll be honest…" He rakes one of his hands through his hair, sighing in exasperation. "Hiram was the one behind most of the arrangements in those early days when I was alerted to her existence. I still don't know many of the details. I doubt Magda remembers much, either—though how can I ask her to? She was so young."

Meeting his gaze, I flex my fingers over his chest. "I think Magda remembers her," I tell him. "I think… I think she's *afraid* of her. Terrified. I can't really explain it in much detail, but I think Irina abandoned her the second she became diagnosed with diabetes."

Or, in her twisted, sick opinion—*flawed.*

"It's possible," he grates, his eyes flashing. "But what makes you say that?"

"Call it a hunch," I say wistfully. "Or, to be more accurate, fairytale logic. You know how Magda likes to play games of the queen and the princess? What if they aren't games to her at all?"

And one overarching theme becomes painfully apparent the more I think on it. *You've been poisoned,* she declared to preface almost every one of her "tea parties." *Poisoned by the queen…*

Could Irina have drugged her? Or, given her a drink of some kind that her childish brain interpreted as much. I'm so lost in the thought that I barely notice I'm in Vadim's arms until his voice drips into my ear, sensually low.

"I say that Magdalene's past is the past," he growls, his tone both stern and husky. "I will strive to make her future so bright she looks back on any prior memories as a faint shadow. A beautiful future. One in which she has everything she could ever ask for or need—while her parents are forced to sneak away every now and again to indulge in their filthiest desires."

I swallow hard. Parents? Not to mention the way the man can utter the word "filthy." An answering ache resonates down my spine, and I pout. No fair.

"Where will we sneak to?" I ask him, reaching up to run my fingers through his abused, wild curls.

His lips twitch thoughtfully. "I may have to declare my renewed interest in the club," he suggests, nuzzling at the nape of my neck. "I'm envisioning a private suite filled with those apparatuses I ordered for you."

My toes curl. I could squeal in excitement, and the potential of healing has never seemed better. "Well then, you better get building," I tell him, slapping his chest playfully. "Though I insist on watching. But, that means you may have to make up with your brother, if only to prevent the off chance of you killing each other should you enter the same vicinity."

His eyes darken at the prospect, though I figure I'm more amused than alarmed at the display. He reminds me almost of a stubborn child, refusing to end a grudge too soon, if only to salvage his pride.

"I once promised I'd smooth things over between you two, didn't I?" I point out. Poor, naïve past Tiffy. She had no fucking clue. "What happened between you and him? Maxim?"

That muscle in his jaw twitches, his gaze drifting away from me—at the last second, however, something draws him back. "We grew up in hell," he states, encasing me in his arms. "But for whatever reason, Maxim showed me kindness more than once." His voice is gruff, as if the confession physically hurts him to voice. "But unlike you, he didn't boldly acknowledge his actions. It's more like… he strived to punish me for them. For wanting to reciprocate them. As a result, we've spent almost thirty fucking years spitting on each other. I don't think even he understands why."

It's such a raw admission from him. One I don't take lightly. Bracing my hand over his chest, I risk planting a kiss over his heart, letting my breath warm that precious space.

"I will *always* acknowledge you," I tell him. "Always. As long as you keep me well supplied with sex—but it won't be transactional. What you give, I will gladly reciprocate."

He laughs in that beautiful, haunting way. "And what you wish, you shall receive."

I nestle against him, lulled into a daze by the thrum of his heartbeat. I know that—despite all of our pillow talk—there's so much more between us awaiting to be addressed. Nuances, we need to put into words. Boundaries that need adjusting.

But, as I allow him to redress me and then drift off, I have to admit that I'm more than looking forward to it.

Each grueling, sweaty, sensual bit of "negotiation."

CHAPTER FOURTEEN

The door to our room flies open with a bang, rousing me from a light sleep and making Vadim lurch upright, wrenching the covers back. His rigid posture conveys power—a desire to protect so vicious I'm awed in the face of it.

But just as quickly he transforms as our intruder makes herself known in frantic little steps, her braids askew, her bear dangling from one hand.

"*Chérie?*" He reaches for her hesitantly, his brows drawn. "What's wrong—"

"I don't like it here," she declares, lunging onto the bed. As I watch in shock, she squirms in between us, curling into a ball, her face buried in the body of her bear. "I hate this place. I want to go home."

"Home?" Vadim asks, as if horribly confused by the prospect. He reaches out, stroking her back. When she doesn't recoil, he tentatively braces his arm around her, and almost instantly, she's burrowing into his chest, her tiny limbs shaking.

"*Home*," she insists plaintively, in a tone I've never heard her use. "I want to go home! With my pony. I want my old room. I don't like it here!"

"Alright. Alright..." He relents with little resistance, petting through her hair. His expression is puzzled—confused even. As if he isn't quite sure of the allure that would drive a child to his arms in the middle of the night. Or why she might instinctively love the home he labored to prepare for her. But I think he's catching on quickly.

His eyes meet mine, alight with the beginnings of a life-altering revelation. With Magda in between us, I risk reaching over her to stroke his chest and nod in encouragement.

"Super dad," I mouth to him, much to his surprise.

Slowly, he settles her tiny figure against him, cradling her carefully, his gaze awestruck. I realize now that—not even in his most optimistic of potential futures—did he envision a moment like this. One so sweet, *I* almost feel like the intruder...

Until Magda hooks her tiny hand around my wrist as if sensing the possibility that I might pull away. I surrender to her grasp, thanking my lucky stars that Vadim and I are at least clothed during this midnight intrusion.

It seems our forced abstinence worked out for the best, in the end.

And, I suspect judging from Vadim's wistful gaze, better than he could have ever dared to hope.

Despite Vadim's prior intention to sell the house, "home" turns out to be pretty much as we'd left it. As I peer into the foyer, I have a mental image of him studiously overseeing a team of movers, ensuring they replaced everything in the same exact position—minus any bloodstains in the kitchen or signs of a psychotic blond.

Even so, I'm surprised by just how strongly a sense of dread paralyzes me as I linger on the threshold. Especially considering that I had no problem entering the home I shared with Jim after he *figuratively* stabbed me in the back.

But now?

My hands shake, and breathing becomes a struggle. If I'm honest with myself, I know exactly why I'm on edge. It's not fear of Irina that makes me linger in the fresh air, unable to enter those four walls. It's the crushing reality of who might never come to exist to fill this home at all. The rooms beside Magda's that might never gain an occupant. The wonderful, albeit lonely life she'll have as an only child—spoken from experience.

Unless, of course, her father remarried someone else capable of expanding his family tenfold.

"Are you alright?" Vadim wonders, his gaze intense with concern, his hand on my lower back.

Forcing a smile, I nod. "Yeah… Besides, it looks like someone's happy."

Oblivious to my discomfort, Magda tears through the lower level, a whirlwind of energy. Her joy gives me the courage necessary to cross the threshold, and I find myself caught in her wake, laughing as she eagerly unpacks her clothes in her room.

"Can I go play with Ainsley?" she asks Vadim once our things are put away, and we've had lunch at the dining room table. "Please?" She bats her eyelashes, playing his heartstrings like a fiddle. I almost feel bad for the man.

Helpless, he looks to me, but I shrug innocently, leaving him to drown.

"I…"

"Ena will take," a firm voice pitches in before the bodyguard himself marches into the kitchen. "And there is cake. In fridge." He looks at me, his gaze conveying something unspoken that catches me off guard. I vaguely remember Vadim mentioning something about a special chocolate cake Ena sometimes bakes. Dare I hope for a truce?

The old bodyguard turns away before I can be sure, shuffling to the sliding glass door leading to the terrace.

"Come," he grunts, his tone unusually soft, directed at the tiny figure leaping to her feet.

"Really?" Magda skips toward him, clutching It to her chest. No one would ever know that a horrific attack took place in this very room just a few days ago. At least, if it weren't for the way she's starting to carry her bear almost every waking moment. She's already worn at It's newly sewn head, and I'm sure he'll wind up decapitated again before long.

And yet, she beams as she glances at Vadim. "Can we? Please?"

Sighing, he gives a nod of approval. "Alright."

She races off, her loyal henchman in tow. The second they slip beyond view, I rise from my chair and slink toward Vadim. Given the fact that I'm still very much in pain—my muscles stiff with disuse—I wind up lurching toward him more than anything sensual. Still, he reaches for me, settling me gingerly onto his lap.

"We should have some alone time," I declare, pressing my lips to the side of his throat. Against his flesh, I murmur, "I declare our brief abstinence officially over."

He chuckles, his hands on my hips, his expression pained once I slip my hand between us and cup the front of his slacks. "You've barely healed," he points out as I flinch the second I strain my side too much.

Shrugging him off, I persist, rocking my palm against him until he groans in capitulation. "Be naughty with me for just a moment," I beg, shamelessly licking a path down to his collar bone. "I'll even let you have a slice of my cake after. I promise it'll be worth it…"

"Not if I cause you any pain, it won't," he warns, always the stoic. Still, when I start to work my fingers into the clasp of his pants, he stands, lifting me in his arms. Before I regain my bearings, he carries me to the center island. Dazed, I grip the edge of the marble surface as he sinks to his knees, cursing under his breath.

I'm not the only one impatient, it seems.

"Don't move," he commands as his fingers creep beneath the waistband of my "healing attire"—a pair of his sweats. I shiver in anticipation, my eyelids threatening to shut as his heat bastes my belly and below.

A true torturer, he takes his time, unwrapping me as meticulously as one would a cherished present. I can't prevent a moan from escaping my throat as I'm fully bared to him, deliciously exposed.

With his gaze fixated on my flesh, he grunts in appreciation. "And to think," he murmurs, more to himself than to me. "I was almost foolish enough to risk losing this…"

This. A prize that he claims with a single, devastating stroke of his thumb, making me lurch into his touch, a gasp breaking loose.

"Beautiful." He sounds like a repentant sinner, more than ready to prostrate himself before an altar in a quest for redemption. And damn, does he endeavor to earn every ounce of mercy…

I gasp as his lips nudge my inner thigh, swiftly inching downward, forcing me to cling to the counter. As a result, I wind up opening myself to him further—a vulnerability that he eagerly takes advantage of. Soft, his tongue feathers over my piercing first in teasing, slight swipes. Followed by his lips. His teeth.

Everything.

I whine, gripping the counter to the point of pain, too far gone to feel the discomfort in my back as I arch into his embrace. Holy crap, he's gotten too damn good at this since the last time. Far too soon, I'm nearing the brink, drowning in the quick, searing glances he throws my way in between every tasting lick and nibble.

Like I'm his alone…

To consume.

Own.

Destroy.

When my orgasm finally arrives with the strength of a freight train slamming into me, I moan shamelessly, my voice echoing throughout the room. The only way to save face is to fist my hand in his hair and tug, drawing him to his feet. Still holding him captive, I spin, switching positions.

Taking care not to rip my sutures, I sink down carefully, relying on his touch to steady me. Then I impatiently tug his pants down and eagerly return the favor.

"*Merde!*" He hisses as I flick the end of his piercing with my tongue and suckle, swallowing him whole, holding his gaze as I do so.

His eyes flicker, unfocused, and heavy-lidded. One flick of my tongue, and he's experiencing another revelation, after revelation, after *revelation*. Before me, the man is born anew, empowered with a lifetime's worth of pleasure he's spent so long denying himself.

Soon, he's rocking into me, grating out various broken bits of French. I make a mental note to do everything I can to learn the language as I suck, sending him spiraling into his own release. Spent, I lean against his thigh, stroking patterns into his perfect flesh. It's so easy to just coexist with him, even in the aftermath of such a filthy, intimate act.

There is no shame between us. No more boundaries. Just silence, and understanding, and a peace so heavy it hurts.

And to think, I've spent so damn long denying myself of this. Will I let a bitch like Irina barge in and take this fragile calm away?

Hell no.

But a part of me warns that I may not have a choice…

"Shit!" Vadim jolts to attention, gently helping me to my feet, before scrambling to adjust his pants and wash his hands in the sink. Confused, I copy him, even as my brain struggles to process what set him off.

"What's wrong?" I follow the line of his gaze and quickly discover the source of his alarm.

A tiny figure races across the terrace—but gone is her exuberant energy from earlier. Tears spill down her cheeks, her cries audible even before Vadim lurches to the door and wrenches it open. He has her in his arms in an instant, and as I follow him out, I spot two figures hurrying from the woods in her wake.

One is a huffing Ena, his gaze alert despite the obvious exertion of having run after a seven-year-old.

By his side is a tiny blond, her expression constricted with concern. Spotting me, she sighs in exasperation. "He didn't mean to! I tried to tell her that he only *looks* scary—"

"What's wrong, *ma chérie?*" Vadim murmurs to Magda, stroking her hair. "What happened?"

She shakes her head, hiding her face in the crook of his shoulder. Frowning, he glances at Ena, who shrugs.

"I know." With a maturity well beyond her young years, the smaller girl steps forward, her gaze focused on her friend. "Max came home," she explains. "I tried to tell her that he only looks scary. Come back, and you'll see, Mags.

Promise! I bet he'll even play tea party with us if we ask him to—"

"No! I don't want to go away!" I barely recognize the childish whimper as belonging to Magda. She's trembling, her chest heaving with choking, gasping sobs. "I don't. Don't let me," she wails, clinging to Vadim, who looks stricken in the face of her fear. "Don't let him take me—"

"No one is taking you anywhere," Vadim insists. He cuts his gaze to Ena, radiating authority. "Secure the perimeter."

The man nods and marches off. "Yes, Sir."

Left behind is Ainsley, her bottom lip trembling, her eyes welling. Before another disaster can ensue, I step forward and gingerly link my hand in hers.

"I'll take her home," I say, starting off in the direction of Maxim's property before Vadim can argue.

I glance over my shoulder to find him carrying Magda into the house, speaking to her calmly all the while.

"I'm sorry," Ainsley whines, her nostrils flaring. "He's not mean, honest!"

"I believe you, honey." Though internally, I'm questioning a little girl's interpretation of "mean" where a man as imposing as Maxim is concerned. Halfway to the house, we're met by a panting figure who races from the underbrush.

"Thank God!" Francesca exclaims, clutching at her chest. She races to her sister's side, bundling the girl in her arms. Despite my best efforts, Ainsley is crying soon enough, and my heart breaks for both girls for very different reasons.

"Mind if I join you?" I ask Francesca as she starts back toward her house. She looks alarmed and glances warily over her shoulder—but eventually, she nods. "Sure."

She comforts her sister the entire trip back, and the girl sports the beginnings of a smile by the time the house looms above. A towering figure stands waiting to greet her near the edge of the terrace.

She squirms from her sister's arms and races over, tugging insistently on the pantleg of a man most would eagerly avoid. Dressed in black from head to toe, he stands with his arms crossed, his blond hair streaming loosely behind him, his gaze on me.

"I'm sorry," Ainsley tells him, her voice hitching. "I don't know why she got so scared."

But I do. Stepping forward, I force myself to meet the man's steely gaze. "Can we talk?"

From the corner of my eye, I see Francesca stiffen, but Maxim? He eyes me for so long I nearly sway with relief when he finally nods and turns into the house. Inside, I'm once again reminded of the glaring similarities—and differences—between the two brothers.

This house has a softness to it Vadim's lacks. Perhaps it lies in the pops of color sprinkled throughout the relatively muted color scheme—hints of red, yellow, and blue in the form of pillows or throw blankets or potted plants. Or the scattered toys that hint toward a bustling family life. Or it could just be that Maxim, as foreboding as he seems, dominating this spacious room, has settled into a relationship that may or may not have softened some of his harsher edges. At least where Ainsley is concerned. Maybe even Magdalene?

Clearing my throat, I face him. *Here goes nothing.* "Vadim needs you," I blurt in a rush. "Now, more than ever. I don't know what's between you two." Something tells me that Maxim's tale of their feud may differ slightly from the one Vadim told. The details don't matter. "He needs you. Your niece, needs you."

He flinches as something unreadable crosses over his dark, unsettling eyes. "Niece?" He grunts as his rumbling voice echoes through the room. "You believe that?"

"I know it," I counter swiftly. Crossing my arms, I level him with an eyebrow cocked, ignoring the fire searing through my shoulder. "Do you really want to deny that? You can look at her and see for yourself. And you can see that they both need you."

"Is that so?" He lumbers to a far corner of the room, turning his back to me. Without the distracting intensity of facing him head-on, I'm left to inspect the rest of his bulk, adding up more clues to cement the brothers' strange idiosyncrasies. Their panache for tailored, Italian-style suits for one. Maxim's is black, and yet despite wearing it, there's a primal intensity to his form that doesn't portray quite the level of icy businessman Vadim can. This man looks less business and more…not legal. I recall a hint of a conversation I heard between Vadim and his friend Milton. I'm more convinced than ever—Maxim —much in the way Irina hinted about Vadim—doesn't play by anyone's rules.

Hopefully, not Irina's.

"Someone is trying to hurt him," I say in response to his obvious skepticism. Vadim once joked that Maxim probably thought he was Magdalene in a child-sized suit, and I'm starting to realize that statement might not have been entirely an exaggeration. "Someone is trying to hurt his *daughter.* Does that mean anything to you? Or do you enjoy having little girls run from you in terror?"

He grimaces, and I have my answer. *No.*

"Vadim may need you when the time comes," I add, taking a step toward him. "If you give a damn at all, you'll answer the door when he does."

"Oh?" Maxim scoffs, whirling to face me. I assume some form of an insult is poised on his tongue when he stiffens, his eyes homing in on my left hip. "You're bleeding," he says.

Shit. Sure enough, without the overriding concern for Ainsley or Magda clouding my senses, I can feel the fiery pain ripping down my left side in full force now. A glance downward reveals a splotch of scarlet seeping through the gray fabric of my borrowed sweatshirt.

After trudging over a mile through the woods, it's not surprising to assume I may have ripped some of my stitches.

"Well…" Wincing, I start for the back door, praying to God that I don't track blood all over the floor. "I'll be leaving—"

"No." The big man rocks on his heels as if wrestling with indecision. Finally, he sighs and cocks his head. "Lucius!"

As if conjured from thin air, the kind, older gentleman, who I'm beginning to suspect may be a saint, appears near the doorway leading to the foyer. "Sir?"

Maxim nods curtly in my direction and then marches for the terrace. "Take her home."

"Yes, Sir." Lucius beckons me forward only to pale when he sees the blood staining my ensemble.

"It's just a scratch," I insist with a faint grin.

Minutes later, I'm racing up the front path and barreling into Vadim's house. I find him in the process of leaving Magda's room, closing the door softly behind him. From beyond his shoulder, I see her asleep on her bed, clutching It to her chest with one hand, while her other stuffed toys form a protective perimeter around her. Courtesy of her father, I suspect.

His eyes meet mine, brimming with a tenderness that makes my chest tighten. At least until he notices the blood and yanks me into his arms. Dazed, I find myself being lowered onto the bed seconds later, wrenched to lie face down as he draws my sweatshirt up.

"Damn it," he hisses in disgust. "You've ripped them."

I sigh dejectedly, pouting. "Are you going to play sexy doctor and stitch me back up?"

"No," he says without an ounce of humor. Rising to his full height, he draws a cell phone from his pocket. "This is well beyond my skill set."

A hint of unease seeps in at the thought of being poked and prodded by a real doctor. "What if I promise never to get up again?" I say mournfully.

"Nice try." He shoots me a stern look before dialing a number into his phone and bringing the device to his ear. "I need your help," he says to someone I suspect most definitely isn't Maxim. "Preferably now."

As it turns out, he called Milton. The man must be a doctor of some kind because he stitches me back up in no time, but with a stern warning as he packs up his supplies. "Rip these, and you'll have a nasty set of scars to look forward to."

Adequately cowed, I lie flat as the two men exit the bedroom, heading downstairs.

And the second they're out of earshot, I slither onto the floor and practically crawl to the mouth of the stairs, straining my ears to listen.

"So, I'm beginning to suspect that you *didn't* cause Maxim's headaches in Moscow," Milton declares, his voice drifting from the direction of the kitchen. "The attack was too vicious. Even you aren't *that* bloody ruthless. He managed to salvage what he could of the supply, but the setback will take months to fully recover from. I suspect that was the aim all along—he'll be distracted for a while, at least."

"Good," Vadim says with chilling vitriol. "Maybe the bastard will finally realize that I'm not the only Boogeyman lurking in the shadows."

"Trust me," Milton insists with a harsh laugh, "he is well aware of that. Anatoli is still 'lurking' as you put it. Even now, I bet the old fucker is itching to get back into the game. Especially after losing Sevastyn."

"Dear old grandfather?" Vadim says with a hostility that makes me suspect he doesn't cherish this particular family member the way I do my old "Pop-Pop." "I will admit I've left the old bastard alive solely because he torments little Maxi so damn well. And, perhaps I'd been arrogant enough to assume that, with Sevastyn dead, he couldn't get up to much trouble on his own."

The viciousness in his tone is chilling—a reminder of the cold aspects of his personality the fatherly tendencies in him obscure so well.

"Enough," Milton scolds. "Let me tell you why I'm here. You remember when you told me about your problem?"

"Irina," Vadim hisses. "You've tracked her?"

"Someone who goes by that name anyway, yes. You won't like what I've learned, though," he adds gruffly. "Especially where your daughter is concerned."

Vadim sucks in a breath, and I imagine his eyes taking on that cold, ruthless gleam I've wisely grown wary of. "Tell me."

"She's a prominent player in the Circle. What's left of it, anyway. You mentioned Sevastyn? Well, without him at its head, the trade's been all but splintered," Milton says, his voice wracked with utter loathing.

And my stomach turns. *Circle. Trade.* Do they mean the horrific crimes Vadim suffered as a child? A slave trade.

"Your Irina's found herself scrambling for territory," Milton continues. "Though, her come-up was relatively quick, to begin with. The bitch got her hands on a large sum of money in a fairly short timeframe a few years back. Now, she runs her own ring—not with children, but women. All unwilling, exploited, or sold, nonetheless. She trades them to the highest bidder and has made quite the name for herself, mainly using aliases, mind you, but my contacts are clever. I'm sure it's her. She prefers to operate primarily under the name 'The Madam.'"

"*Fils de pute!* Son of a bitch," Vadim snarls. A faint thud resonates throughout the house as if he slammed his fist against a firm surface like a table. Or the wall. "And she has the nerve to seek me out? To toy with *me*. I'll kill her—"

"You may not have to," Milton suggests. "She's made plenty of enemies for herself. Give me time, and I'm sure I can spin the right kind of trap. Hell, you might be able to sell *her* for a profit."

My heart stops. Given the man's grim tone, something tells me that wasn't a figurative statement.

"Don't joke," Vadim counters, and I manage to breathe again. He sounds disgusted by the suggestion, at least. Or is that pure rage coloring his voice? "My only concern is Magdalene. I won't let that bitch harm her—"

"Neither will I," Milton swears, his voice hard. "If you're antsy, I was able to track down a lead on the orphanage she came from. Ask around, and you may find more information. The identity of who alerted you to her, at least… Because here is the part you really won't like—two years ago, rumor is 'The Madam' was looking to traffic a little girl. Caused quite the stir if you can imagine. Her aim wasn't the trade, mind you. Just the black-market adoption circuit—"

"Like that makes it any fucking better!" Vadim's voice breaks. He sounds horrified. Gutted. It takes everything I have—and the fact that I'm terrified to stand up—not to run down to him, eavesdropping be damned. "I was hoping the bitch had given her up out of…I don't know, *love*? For Magdalene's sake. How can a child face the fact that their own mother wanted to sell her like chattel?"

"*We* did," Milton says in a tone that makes me suspect he too has a traumatic past behind him. One comparable to Vadim's. Or worse. "And we fucking survived, didn't we? So will she. She has you. And if you want this information, maybe you can find out who did rescue her. And why."

He leaves the offer in the air, and by the time the two men return to the foyer, I'm not sure whether Vadim has accepted the information or not.

As Milton leaves, I slither back toward the bedroom as quickly as I dare. I nearly make it to the bed when a set of heavy footsteps breaches the threshold, and a disapproving voice rings out, "Caught you."

"Damn it." I risk glancing at him, my eyes bug-wide, my lower lip protruding. Somehow, it's easy to suppress the horror of what I've heard. Too easy. Denial. "*Please* don't punish me. Too hard. We can start with a spanking."

"Insolent witch." He cracks a smile despite the concern twisting his features into a haggard, grim expression that tugs at my heart like nothing else. Crossing to me, he takes me into his arms but doesn't set me down right away. His eyes stare into mine, demanding an answer to a question he doesn't ask out loud just yet.

Did I overhear?

And if so…

Am I bothered by what I've learned?

I match his silence with my own nonverbal answer. Arching toward him, I let our lips meet. He stiffens in response, his lips parting. The second they do, I loop my hand around his neck, extending the kiss as much as I dare. When he finally pulls back, I'm panting, both thrilled and wary.

"I heard everything," I confess, my stomach heavy as those dark revelations loom overhead.

He sighs, averting his gaze from me. "And?"

"I want you to explain it to me," I say, surprised by how calm I sound, all things considered.

That muscle in his jaw twitches as he sets me down onto the edge of the bed. Then he starts to pace, his hands sinking into his hair. "Explain. The supposed mother of my child trades in women the same way *we* were traded. She wanted to sell her own daughter. And I didn't know a damn thing until someone literally dropped the news of her existence into my lap. At every turn, I seem to keep failing her—"

"You haven't," I insist, my voice breaking. He's distant again, glowering into his past, swaying with the weight of it all. "You're angry," I add, stating the obvious. In some ways, it helps to say as much out loud. To acknowledge his obvious disgust at these dark, twisted things. Even though, from his scattered conversations with Milton, I sense that he's more familiar with these horrific aspects of the world than I can even imagine.

Irina all but taunted as much.

"You should follow-up on the information Milton offered you," I say softly, skirting the larger question of his real identity. For now. "For your sake."

Because he needs this, I realize. Answers—even if they're offered on a fragile bit of thread. If anything, he needs them for Magda. Her peace of mind. Her sanity.

But as stubborn as he is, I don't think he can admit it out loud just yet. So he sinks onto the bed, reaching for me. Again, our lips collide, his tongue stealing deep. I grasp at him, surrendering myself to every searching kiss. Every groan he utters into my open mouth. Soon enough, we wind up tangled together, though he makes sure that I'm on top of him, lying on my stomach so as to not risk my stitches.

Groaning, he nuzzles the nape of my neck, smoothing his hands down my hips. "I will think about your suggestion," he finally says. "It would require traveling upstate. Arrangements would have to be made, appointments organized." He frowns at the prospect, and I can't tell what he's decided upon when he sighs in defeat. "Give me a few days to decide."

"Okay." I seal the promise with a kiss and rest my face against his chest, listening to his heartbeat. "I'm sorry for spying. But," I add in my own defense, "I was just being a good fake wife, after all."

"Don't be," he says, deceptively soft. "Because when you heal, I fully intend to punish you."

I flinch, utterly thrilled by the threat. "Then add another crime to the tally, good Sir, because…" I suck in a breath and sneak a peek at his face. He looks so beautiful, so calm. I savor the expression selfishly before I confess, "I spoke to Maxim."

He hisses out a breath, his nostrils flaring. Anger, yes—but nowhere near the extent I might have expected.

"Did he scare her purposefully?" he asks in a tone so murderous my toes curl.

"No," I say quickly. "He didn't. But… I think I know why she might have reacted to seeing him the way she did."

The same way she's reacted to him since their very first—albeit traumatic for Magda—meeting.

"Because of Irina?" Vadim questions coldly, his eyes fixated on something in the distance. Years away, I suspect, far in the past. "I'm sure she kept goons around who frightened her. She kept begging me not to let her be taken from me—" He breaks off, scowling, and I almost regret breaching the topic at all.

"But you won't," I say confidently. "You won't let anyone frighten her ever again."

"You're right," he agrees, pressing his lips against my forehead. "Because I aim to cut off the source of her fears. Right at the fucking head."

I cringe at the ferocity in his voice—not that I can blame him for the violent imagery.

Such a fate would be a fitting end for Irina's figurative role as Magda's mad queen.

CHAPTER SIXTEEN

We must fall asleep with our limbs entwined, still fully dressed, because I'm startled to awareness when Vadim's arms stiffen around me as the door to the room swings open. Once again, we've been interrupted by a small figure who doesn't wait for an invitation.

Instead, she lurches onto the bed and burrows her way in between us, seeking out the safety of Vadim's arms, which I'd been enjoying until now. As a result, I'm forced to make room as she slithers in to take my place.

Her father, however, has already switched into dad mode. "What's wrong?" he murmurs to her, so gently that even I'm soothed by his tone. "I thought you liked the house?"

"I do," Magda insists against his chest. "But it's too dark in my room."

I raise an eyebrow. "Too dark?"

"We can turn on the lights, *chérie*," Vadim offers. His confusion matches mine.

"No," Magda whines the second he starts to pull away. "I don't want to."

The independent girl who first came here a few weeks ago had no problem sleeping on her own. Though, back then, she wasn't reminded of the aspects of her past that still obviously scare her. This new aversion, I suspect, has everything to do with what happened with Maxim. Whatever memories seeing him triggered, haunt her badly enough that she'll risk her pride just to find safety in her father's arms.

It would be heart-warming if it weren't so tragic. I can't stop myself from stroking my hand down her back, sensing her trembling beneath her nightgown.

"It's dark," she repeats, still clinging to Vadim, her body curled into a stubborn ball. "I want to sleep *here*."

She doesn't bother asking, not that the man holding her would ever have the heart to refuse her if she did. Sighing, I crack a smile and shift over to make room.

"I guess it's okay for tonight," I say.

Always prepared, Vadim repositions himself to somehow embrace us both on either side of him. Like leeches, we nestle into his warmth, draining him of all the comfort he has to offer.

And, he seems to possess more than enough for us both. When morning finally comes, he disentangles from our mass of limbs long enough to return minutes later with breakfast food piled on a tray and a jug of orange juice.

Sensing a shift in the mood, we eat in silence and wind up lounging in the master bed, sandwiched together—Vadim in the middle—with Magda and me on opposite ends. And, of course, It somewhere in between. For the first time, I realize that the bedroom even has a flat-screen television affixed to the far wall, defaulted to the news station. After flipping through the channels, we settle on watching cartoons and promptly vegetate the rest of the day.

The time spent in this way reveals a strange new aspect of our dynamic. The doting father. The clingy daughter. The pseudo-mother popping pain pills every few hours just to stay coherent. When evening comes, Vadim retreats again to bring back pizza, and we only leave at various intervals to get ready for bed—him assisting Magda—before we all wind up back in the master suite.

This time, she doesn't even bother to give an excuse before burrowing beneath the blankets, not that Vadim or I ask for one. With her nestled in between us, we fall asleep in the middle of a show about rambunctious undersea critters and wake up to very much the same routine. Again, the cycle repeats the next day.

And the next.

By the end of the week, I'm forced to confront a horrible realization as I wake up with Magda's foot in my stomach and Vadim's breath fanning over my forehead. We've barely left the room, let alone the house in days. Our only outside interaction at all came in the form of Milton stopping by to remove my stitches.

Otherwise, we've been on an island unto ourselves—and I think Magda's fingers are starting to leave permanent marks on Vadim's forearms.

There is no dancing around it—we haven't just been indulging in the lazy inclinations of a seven-year-old. We've been *coddling* her. In essence, we've become *those* people. One of those weird families so fearful of the outside world and the danger it may bring that they collapse in on themselves. Eventually, we'll have Magda encased in bubble wrap and only leave the house to fetch the mail. Though, with Ena around, we may not even get to do that.

Somewhere during Vadim rousing himself like a zombie to trudge down to the kitchen, I come to a conclusion.

"Rise and shine, princess!" I ruffle Magda's hair until she blinks up at me, deliriously innocent and half asleep. "You too, Sir." I slap Vadim on the ass as he rises to his feet.

Then I shimmy to the edge of the mattress and tentatively stand. After days of being damn near bedridden, I have to sway just to regain my balance. Once I do, I'm surprised to find my left side feels marginally better. Enough that I can march into the bathroom, leaving my bedmates staring after me. When I emerge—having brushed my teeth and run my wet fingers through my hair—I snap to command their attention.

"Hop to it! We're going riding."

Vadim raises an eyebrow. "Do you want to injure yourself again?" he asks, ever the spoilsport.

Undeterred, I wiggle my arms and only wince a little. "I'm nearly healed," I say. "As long as we go slow, I'll be fine. And the fresh air will do us all some good."

He doesn't look fully convinced. Nonetheless, he copies my lead, heading toward the closet.

But he's not the only one needing persuading, it seems.

"Why?" Magda wonders, her voice bordering on a whine. With It against her chest, she burrows beneath the blankets and promptly disappears beneath them, she's so tiny in such a large bed. "I don't want to," she declares, her voice muffled.

"Sure, you do." I shuffle forward and yank the blankets from over her, revealing her pouting at me with an intensity that makes my heart soften and melt.

"Can't we watch more cartoons?" she asks plaintively. "I don't *want* to go outside."

Her eyes flicker in the direction of a certain neighbor's property, and I sigh in exasperation. The entire display is almost enough to make me give in. Almost…

But then I envision myself as a helicopter mom with badly permed hair leading Magda around by a child leash and promptly change my mind.

"No. Come on, you love riding," I say, doing my best to cajole her. Judging from her stubborn frown, it's going to be an uphill battle. "You can show me how to ride Magnus," I add, naming the horse Vadim procured for me. "I haven't even gotten to test him out yet."

"And," Vadim pitches in, returning from the closet fully dressed in a pair of jodhpurs and a black T-shirt, "we can race her on my Zzazza. With you as my copilot, I'm sure we'll win, even at a slower pace."

I look at him in mock indignation. "You're on! What do you say, Mags?"

She eyes us warily, mulling it over. Finally, she crawls off the bed and marches toward her room, her head down, her shoulders slumped in defeat. I follow and make a show out of rifling through her riding outfits—mysteriously, it seems at least ten more sets have joined the first one Vadim bought her since the last time she's ridden—settling on a bold, scarlet jacket, white blouse, and black pants.

The clothing tempts her when even my best jokes don't. She's still brooding during our quick breakfast and the entire walk out to the stable. I almost fear I've made a mistake, but the second she spots the face of her pony peeking eagerly from over the door of her stall, her entire face brightens.

By the time the three of us are out on the trail—me riding my black stallion Magnus, with Vadim and Magda astride his beautiful Zzazza—I have no more doubts. We needed this, all of us. Fresh air. Peace. The tranquility we find in exploring the furthest reaches of the property by horseback.

Vadim picked his property well. It spans way more ground than one would think when observing the space solely from the house. Alone, he commands a good bit of the waterfront and the surrounding woods. A series of old paths lend themselves well to becoming decent trails with a bit of work to flesh them out.

Something even Magda picks up on. "Could I ride my pony here one day with Ainsley?" she asks midway in. It's the first complete sentence she's said since leaving the house, but her expression has brightened at least. Gone is the surly frown, and her eyes gleam as she looks back to find Vadim nodding.

"Of course, *chérie.* I'm sure you could."

Content with that answer, she settles against his chest. By the time we return to the house, she's almost fully shaken the foul mood entirely. After dinner, I help her up to bed and promptly discover that Vadim has made some minor changes to our previous routine.

"You have to brush it *this* way," Magda commands, showing me how to coax the brush through her hair, supposedly the same way her father does. Once I've finally arranged the braids to her liking and tucked her beneath the blankets, I retreat for the door.

"Oh!"

I turn around to find her lurching upright, riffling through her end table until she withdraws her cell phone from a drawer. As I watch her dial a number in confusion, she looks up and says, "I promised Harry and Gigi I'd call them once a week."

"Harry and Gigi?" She mentions the prospect of calling these mystery people with such earnest seriousness that I'm at a complete loss. Until I realize. "You mean my parents?"

She nods and settles against her pillow with the phone pressed to her ear. "Vadim said I could. Harry is going to tell me about his strawberry plants, and Gigi said she was going to send me dress-up clothes—" She breaks off, cocking her head to listen, and I'm promptly forgotten. "Hi," she says in her charming way, so similar to Vadim's disarming cadence. It's like she's studied his tactics for manipulation as an art form. "Yes, I've been in the muck…"

I leave her to it, escaping down to the kitchen to find Vadim washing the dishes, looking deliciously domestic.

"You gave her permission to call my parents once a week?" I ask, slipping my arms around him from behind. "How very kind of you. They're smitten. I think they might have kidnapped her if we didn't leave when we did." My voice turns wistful as I reflect on just how quickly my parents have taken to her. To him.

Jim was lucky to get a Christmas card and a coupon in the mail for his birthday.

"She insisted," Vadim says, frowning. He turns to face me, cupping my chin against his palm. "But… I've decided. She deserves her answers, and I intend to find them."

"I think you should," I say softly.

His furrowed brows betray that he doesn't fully like the prospect, but his fingers part my hair, tilting me back for a searching, slow kiss. "And, though I'm not sure how long it will take, I believe you may be safer with me," he adds.

I feel my nose wrinkle. "What about Magda?"

His gaze darkens as he contemplates the possibility of leaving her behind, even for a little while. "Ena will watch over her."

"Or," I say, tentatively licking my lips. "She can still have Ena's protection, *and* the benefit of being around someone who can actually participate in a game of tea party."

He raises an eyebrow. "Oh?"

I nod. "And an uncle who, admittedly, is big and scary enough to protect her from anyone who might harm her, let alone Irina—"

"You want me to leave my daughter with Maxim?" He breaks away from me, scowling at the mere idea.

But I don't relent, following him into his study. "What scenario do you think will benefit her more in the long run? Having a friend her own age to play with, and getting to know her uncle—learning not to fear him to the point that she can't even sleep in her own bed for a week—or huddling here with Ena watching cartoons all day and trying to make him pretend to be a princess? By the time we come back, I'm sure she'll be starting to put down roots into the flooring."

He scoffs, unconvinced. "What makes you think he would even agree to it?" He whirls to face me, but rather than angry, he just looks…helpless. Like a drowning man who knows a lifeline is within reach—but he's afraid it will vanish the second he grasps it.

"I think he will," I say, stepping into him, letting our bodies connect and collide. "If you *ask* him to."

He's still frowning, embodying Magda's surly, brooding mood from this morning. But eventually, he sighs, wrapping his arms around me—though taking care with my injuries. "Maybe. But…"

I rest my head on his chest, wiggling into his touch. "But?"

"But if Maxim refuses to watch Magdalene, then *you* have to tell Ena he'll be on tea party duty."

I giggle, picturing the image in my head. "Deal."

SENDING Magda to Maxim's for a harmless playdate, during which she can bond with both her uncle and pseudo-cousin, sounded promising in theory. A win-win, actually. The reality, however, turns out to be a lesson in child wrangling as Magda refuses to get out of the car once she recognizes the house we're parked in front of.

With her arms crossed, her persistent utterances of "No," quickly devolve to high-pitched shouting. Soon, her stoic façade gives way entirely to wracking sobs and real, enormous tears spilling down her cheeks as Vadim finally coaxes her from the backseat.

"Oh, *ma chérie...*" He rocks her in his arms, murmuring soothingly to her in French while, from the house, a curious press of faces watches us from the windows.

"Look at me," Vadim finally urges in a tone stern enough to make her risk lifting her head from his shoulder. Her bloodshot eyes scan his imploringly as her white-knuckled hands grip his forearms to what I'm sure is the point of pain. "I will never put you in danger," Vadim tells her. "Do you believe that? That I will always do what is best for you?"

Slowly, Magda nods even as her eyes continue to spill over. Her bottom lip trembles, her expression so stricken...

I relent first. "Maybe we should go back—"

"No." Vadim crouches down, settling his daughter on his knee. Gingerly he wipes away her tears and smooths the wild curls back from her face. She has no choice but to quiet down and listen to him. "My brave girl is going to wait here while I go inside, *oui?*"

He sounds so confident and assured for her. When I can tell from how the muscle in his jaw twitches that inside, he's thinking—*I'll go inside, and hopefully, Maxim refuses to take you, and this is all rendered moot, and we can watch cartoons for the rest of the week.* And yet, he does his best not to reveal his doubts. He smothers his own unease, entirely for her.

"Why don't you stay with Mr. Ena?"

Following his cue, Ena steps forward to take her hand, and she promptly clings to his hip, the princess, and her trusty henchman.

Together Vadim and I approach the house only to have the door opened from within the moment we reach it. Lucius isn't the one standing guard on the other end, this time. A wary Francesca greets us instead, her eyes guarded as they flick over Vadim.

And looming behind her, the picture of brute strength, is Maxim, his posture tense, dark eyes flashing. I sense myself instinctively step back, letting the brothers square each other up in their unique, calculating ways. Maxim glowers while Vadim eyes him coldly, his unease painfully apparent.

"Hello," Francesca says softly, and yet her voice alone seems to crack the tension enough that Maxim uncurls his hands out of fists. "What brought you over?" she prompts, her eyes on me.

Sighing, I take my cue and forge a path inside, leaving Vadim to follow in my wake. "We wanted to see if Magda could spend the day while we—"

"She can sense your hostility, you do realize," Vadim says in a deadly quiet tone. My alarm bells go off, and I instantly regret suggesting this option. Nothing, it seems, can ease thirty years of animosity overnight. Not even the welfare of a little girl.

"Your hatred toward me," Vadim continues in a hiss, still positioned in the doorway, his head cocked, gaze ice-cold. "You scared the hell out of her. We couldn't get her out of bed for a week. She would rather hide inside than feel safe venturing out of her own home. Because of *you*."

For all of his coldness…

Something in Maxim's expression gives for a split second, and I know the accusation hit home. His jaw twitches, his lips parting before slamming shut into a fearsome scowl.

"So what?" he tosses back, his accent thick. "You demand I leave? Try to buy this property out from under me, again?"

Vadim grits his teeth, and I sense something in him falter. Spite? Guilt? He's wavering on a precipice, and one wrong act will send him hurtling over it—both of them.

The only way to salvage this, I suspect, is to throw caution to the wind and lay the cards on the table.

"Magda wants to spend the day with Ainsley," I blurt out. "Vadim and I will be out of town for a few hours, if you wouldn't mind her playing here."

"It will be good for them," Francesca pitches in. Following my lead, she steps forward, bracing her hand on Maxim's forearm and bit by bit some of the crackling tension eases. A minuscule bit. "They can play outside—"

"But can *he* refrain from taking out his hatred toward me on a child?" Vadim wonders, though I suspect that question is directed more at himself than anyone else. And I can tell from the set of his jaw alone that he wants to believe it. He does. But he's spent so much of his life expecting the worst from those around him.

His first instinct is always to suspect.

"Can you?" he demands of Maxim.

The other man grits his teeth. "Can I trust you not to steal a child?" he counters. "Related to you by blood or not."

They eye each other fiercely, but as the seconds pass, they don't come to blows at least.

Finally, I can't take the silence anymore.

"I'll go get Magda."

I race for the door as both men swivel in my direction with equally fierce expressions. Vadim flinches toward me. To stop me?

"Yes," Francesca encourages from beyond the fray before he can voice any refusal out loud. "I'll go get Ains."

Taking my cue, I hasten outside and find Magda still clinging to Ena's pantleg so tightly the bodyguard has to adjust his posture just to withstand her weight thrown against his one leg. Her eyes dart to the house—searching for Vadim?

When I reach for her, though, she takes my hand and reluctantly follows me inside. My heart pounds, my throat tightening as I realize that bringing a traumatized seven-year-old into the thick of a brooding feud between two powerful men may not be the best course of action.

But right when I hesitate, Vadim appears in the doorway to the house. Gone is his hateful mask. He looks neutral again, his composed, poised self.

Meeting his daughter's gaze, he inclines his head for her to follow. Her trust in him is apparent solely in the fact that she does, even as her grip on me tightens to the point I feel myself wince.

Maxim is no longer in view, I realize, as we cross the spacious living room for a door leading out to their terrace. It seems the other man has migrated outside, his posture tense, his back to us as we step out to join him.

When he turns to face Magda, I exhale sharply. A blind man could sense the sheer amount of discipline he's utilizing to keep his expression neutral. Some of the ice leaves those cold, dark eyes, rendering him slightly less "big and scary." But apparently not enough.

Releasing me, Magda contorts herself to cling to Vadim's leg, forcing him to stop short. It's such a striking contrast to the brave little girl who had spurned him just a few short weeks ago. Though I think this new display of emotion is merely a testament to how much she's opened herself up to him. How much she's learning to trust him.

And Vadim's pained frown tells me that he is well aware of that fragile bond. Sighing, he sinks down to her level and cradles her chin against his palm, urging her to meet his gaze.

"I know you're afraid." He brushes some of her tears away and smooths back her curls. "But you don't need to be. Here, you can play with your friend and focus on your tea parties."

She shakes her head. "Why are you leaving me? Again!"

"I'm not," he says firmly. "I will never leave you. Besides, Mr. Ena whom I trust more than anyone else in the world will stay with you, yours to command. I'll return as soon as I can, and you have your cell phone, yes?" He brushes his hand along the fanny pack that's become a near-permanent fixture around her waist. "If you ever feel unsafe, I will return within an instant."

He sounds so damn reassuring, his expression persistently calm. Even she can't resist. Her bottom lip trembles, her eyes still watering, but she loosens her grip on him enough for him to point to Maxim.

"And I'm not leaving you with just anyone," he says, his voice a deep, soothing hum. "This is your uncle, *chérie*. He will protect you while I'm gone. And if he doesn't…" His eyes flash. "Then he will answer to me."

If Maxim takes offense to the threat, he surprisingly doesn't say as much. With his face still arranged in that careful, neutral mask, he stalks forward and crouches, extending his hand in Magda's direction, even as she flinches back.

"I hear you like ponies," he says, his accent sounding more charming than threatening. "Would you like to see mine?"

Magda glances warily at her father, who nods in encouragement. "It's okay."

Slowly, she places her tiny hand on Maxim's enormous one and allows him to lead her toward the edge of the terrace. Even so, she looks back at Vadim, her bloodshot eyes frantic.

"It will be alright," he says so fiercely even her fear can't withstand his assurance. "I promise you."

She nods and turns back to Maxim. To the man's credit, he meets her gaze with gentle acknowledgment, and something in my heart twists a little. These brothers…

It's like they were designed to repel all assumptions of care, empathy, or compassion, only to reveal an uncanny knack for emoting all three when pushed to do so. At least by those they deemed worthy of such emotions.

Case and point, a tiny figure races from the house and snatches up Maxim's other hand without an ounce of fear.

"Wait for me!" Surging ahead, Ainsley winds up pulling her two companions behind her, forging the way to the stable. "I can't wait for you to see my pony," she prattles to Magda. "You'll love him!"

"Score one for super dad," I murmur as Vadim rises to his feet, his expression constricted. I know that nothing in the world was probably harder for him to endure than this moment—save leaving Magda in the first place, of course. Regardless, his jaw is clenched with resignation as we exit the house and return to the car.

"She'll be fine," I insist as he glances back at the house at least ten times before finally climbing into the driver's seat.

Without looking my way, he mutters under his breath, "She better be."

CHAPTER SEVENTEEN

For some reason—despite the fact that he's rarely relied on a massive show of security in the time I've known him—I'm surprised to discover our road trip seems to consist of just me and him. No driver. No Ena.

His trusted friend hasn't been sidelined, of course, but merely reassigned to cover a target Vadim values above all else. And yet, his seemingly second most important target, he's decided to guard personally.

It betrays such a confidence in his own skillset, and a level of concern for me—one declared without him having to strut down a boardwalk to show me off. With his actions alone, he proves the lengths he's willing to go.

But have I been willing to do the same?

"Don't tell me you're so far unimpressed by our solo excursion," Vadim remarks dryly, drawing my attention to him. He's smiling, I find, his lips in a rare, lazy grin that makes my heart sputter further. At the same time, he looks so tired.

His eyes are bloodshot, his expression haggard. A sudden thought hits me—he probably hasn't slept much at all these past few days. With Magda in his arms, maybe he'd been too afraid to—too worried about failing her trust in him to ever drop his guard.

So, he put her first over his own discomfort.

"I'm more than impressed," I confess, though our impending destination is far from my mind.

He frowns, stroking the back of my hand. "And here I was, assuming you were disappointed we've forsaken the private jet."

I puff up with mock indignation. "I'm with you for the designer clothing, remember? Not the limitless travel."

He laughs, but something darkens his expression. Doubt?

"And, I'm with you for the sex," I add, nestling against him before his paranoia can fester. "And your patience. Your kindness. And your ass. And…" I bring my mouth near his ear, my voice husky. "Your filthy brain."

His posture relaxes, a sly grin playing over his lips. But even dirty talk can't seem to placate him for long. Within seconds, he's scowling again—but before I can even prompt him for a reason, he sighs. "There is always one possibility," he says softly. "One I've considered since the day I learned of Magda's existence."

"Oh?" His expression warns me that whatever his suspicion, it doesn't inspire warm and fuzzy feelings.

He cocks his head, meeting my gaze, still stroking my hand. "There is always the chance that she isn't mine. That Irina crafted an elaborate deception just to convince me she was. I had test results commissioned from a private laboratory, but..." He shrugs. "I am not so foolish to believe that even my most rigorous testing is infallible."

I don't know what to say, so I bite my lip and try to see the dilemma from his angle. It *is* possible—in the mind of a paranoid man so mistrustful of the world around him. But even so, there are aspects of Magda too authentically him to have been faked. Her mannerisms. Her facial features. Her illness.

"I think she's yours through and through," I tell him. "Biologically or not." But another realization makes me observe him from the corner of my eye. "Is that why you were afraid to adopt her before now?"

He flinches. "No! I mean..." He rakes a hand through his hair, disrupting the mussed curls. "It isn't easy for me to let people into my life," he confesses. "I know Irina. I know her games. And I knew that I couldn't survive letting a child in—mine or not—and losing her. Or worse, having her utilized as a pawn. If I kept her at a distance, it would be better for us both..."

Until he couldn't. Until the desire for a family got the best of him, and he took on that risk. Whatever Irina's plan may be, he won't give up Magda without a fight.

"She *is* mine now," he says as if reading my mind. His eyes brim with a raw emotion I can't name. Devotion? Love? Desperation? "No one will take her from me. No one."

I can't resist slipping my hand within his as a silent gesture of reassurance. But I know, as a sleepy, small town appears on the horizon, that my vulnerable Vadim will have to take a backseat to his more ruthless personality.

And that I better hold on for the ride.

THE BUILDING where Magda was abandoned turns out to be a small, modest brick-and-mortar front for what seems to be a nonprofit child advocacy program.

"The United States no longer relies on the traditional concept of an orphanage," a woman explains as she leads us on a tour of a spacious series of wide, open rooms decorated with framed photos of children, seemingly from all over the world.

"That's why I remember it so clearly, the day Magdalene showed up," she says. "I couldn't fathom it—someone just dropping a little girl here, all alone, without even checking to make sure staff were even on the property. Thank God a janitor saw her when he did. Naturally, we called the police, but we do have the capacity to take in children in emergency situations, so she stayed here in the facility for a few days as they attempted to establish her identity. You know, I was sure that she had been kidnapped. A little girl so well-groomed and impeccably dressed. I think her clothing was worth more than my salary." She breaks off with a nervous laugh and shakes her head, her smile fading. "But… She didn't cry like you'd think a normal child might. She didn't ask for her mother or father, or anything of the sort. It was almost as if she knew."

"Knew what?" Vadim prompts. I've never seen his expression so rigid, his eyes dark and distant.

"That she had been abandoned," the woman says with an apologetic nod. "Honestly, I haven't stopped thinking about her since. I'm so glad that she's found an adoptive family—"

"How did you learn her name?" Vadim demands, so lost in his own thoughts that I doubt he realizes that he interrupted the woman at all. "Her birthday?" I can tell from the set to his jaw that it's physically paining him to ask more. Questions I suspect he already knows the answer to.

Did you learn anything about her mother? Her father? Her origins?

"She told us her name," the woman says, wrinkling her mouth. "Though, she had a slip of paper in her clothing. It had her name written on it, along with her birthday and immunization records—all validated, of course."

"A slip of paper?" Vadim raises an eyebrow, and I recognize the intense set to his jaw. He wasn't aware of that detail.

"Yes. The police took it in their initial investigation," the woman admits. "But… I made a copy. I'm not sure why, it all felt so strange. I think I felt compelled to remember it somehow. If you wait right here, I'll be back."

She disappears down a winding hallway while Vadim starts to pace, stroking his jaw, the gears in his brain whirring. I watch him, even as I find myself imagining this place two years ago, with a five-year-old Magda walking haughtily through its halls. She would have been even smaller, twice as frail, and under the assumption that neither parent wanted her. My heart breaks for that girl, and I'm more resolved now than ever to live up to the commitment Vadim admittedly goaded me into. Adopting her—no matter who may stand in the way.

"Here it is!" The woman returns brandishing a slip of neatly folded photocopy paper. Vadim scans the surface, his eyes widening.

"That logo…"

"You recognize it?" The woman tilts her head thoughtfully. "Eingel Industries is one of our main contributors. In fact, for well over a decade, their donation has far exceeded all others. It was an odd coincidence, but there's a factory not too far from here, and the workers tend to scatter their promotional materials all over. I'd thought her parents may have worked there, but honestly, it could have been taken from the local library just as plausibly."

Something I sense Vadim doubts. His hands shake as he scans the page over and over again. From over his shoulder, I make out a few lines written in crisp, neat handwriting. A series of unique flourishes make the style stand out—far more elegant than one might suspect of a desperate guardian dropping off an abandoned child.

Does he recognize it as Irina's?

"May I have this?" he asks of the woman.

"Of course. I'm so glad to hear that Magdalene is safe and thriving. I think about her often. I wonder… Does she still have that quirk when it comes to roses?"

Vadim frowns, still reading the note. "Roses?" From his tone, I doubt he understands the significance of that one statement.

But I do.

"Quirk?" I ask, turning my full attention toward the woman.

She purses her lips, wringing her hands. "It was around Valentine's day when she arrived—which was why I couldn't imagine someone bringing her *here*. It was freezing. Anyway, we host a few children's groups throughout the year, and we prepare crafts for them to complete during the holidays. That month, we had them design rose vases that we displayed throughout the facility.

They truly were beautiful." She smiles faintly, only for the expression to drain from her face, replaced by utter confusion. "When poor little Magdalene stepped foot inside, she vomited. It was one of the first things she said —not to ask for her parents, but simply *I hate that smell.* We had to clear away any trace of the flowers from the area we kept her in. I was wondering if she had grown out of the aversion."

In some ways, she has. While playing with my parents in their garden, she can frolic amongst a sea of roses unbothered. But when sensed while caught off guard, she panics. So much so that she crawls into her father's bed at night and breaks down at the mere thought of someone taking her from him.

"Thank you for your help," Vadim says, leading the way to the door. I follow him out, and as we enter the car, I notice that he still has that note clenched in his fist, his gaze unfocused.

"What's wrong?" I ask, bracing my hand over his forearm as he settles beside me. "Is that handwriting... Is it Irina's?"

"No," he says hoarsely, looking hopelessly confused. "It's not."

I frown. "Do you think she had someone else—"

"Irina didn't write this," he says, as if he has to repeat it just to drill the fact into his own understanding. "But I know who did."

"Who?" I ask.

Carefully, he folds the paper and slips it into his breast pocket. With his gaze on the window nearest him, he says, so softly, I almost don't hear him, "Hiram Gorgoshev."

CHAPTER EIGHTEEN

The weight of his statement casts a pall over the entire mood of our impromptu trip. I'm at a loss for words, truly unsure of what to say.

Not that anything I could voice would be able to penetrate the cloud of unease hanging over Vadim. It's so heavy I feel as though if I reach out to touch him, I'll feel an invisible barrier barring my path—his wall, rebuilt higher than ever.

Hiram, his mentor, and father figure who entrusted his business to him… *That* man had somehow written a note that wound up on Magdalene the day she arrived at the crisis center. A crisis center primarily funded by said company.

It's almost too convoluted a web to unravel all at once.

And Vadim especially seems perplexed by this new twist in the puzzle that is Magdalene's past. By the time we're nearly an hour into our drive, he finally speaks.

"I knew there were things he never told me," he says gruffly. "I'm not a fool. But this… Did he plan this with that bitch? Goad me to take in Magdalene for his own gain?" His voice trembles, coarse with anger, and my heart aches for him. Cracks.

In his mind, such a betrayal makes sense—it's the only way he's learned to see the world. Always on the defense. But something tells me that the explanation may not be so simple. Maybe reinforced simply by the fact that a man who would do so much for a young, tormented boy to cross his path—even going so far as to give him his name —wouldn't be so cruel as to gamble that trust on a reckless whim. Would he?

"He's probably laughing at me from the grave," Vadim adds with a harsh, callous scoff. "I've still carried his name all this time. I was going to give my daughter *his* name."

He glowers, his hands clenched over the steering wheel, his eyes flashing a vitriol he doesn't even display toward his brother. All I can do is place my hand on his shoulder and let him rage.

"Is there anything he left you that might give you a clue as to his motives?" I ask, gingerly giving Hiram the benefit of the doubt.

Vadim blinks as if he didn't think to consider the possibility for himself. "I had most of his estate liquidated," he explains, raking a hand through his hair repeatedly. "But some personal effects I had shipped to the city and placed in storage. I never had the heart to go through them."

"So let's do it now," I suggest, hoping I sound braver than I feel. "Together."

He eyes me warily, and I see the faintest hint of his wall starting to splinter. I feel so attuned to him in this moment, I swear I'm reading his mind. Once again, he's grappling with his decision to trust me. Hiram supposedly betrayed him, am I next?

I meet his gaze unflinchingly, hoping that whatever he finds gives him enough reassurance to trust me. At least for now.

After a few tense seconds, he sighs and steers the car onto an off-ramp heading toward Fair Haven. Sensing the need to remain silent, I let him stew for nearly the entire drive.

It's only when we arrive before a prestigious bank in the heart of the city that I manage to blurt, "So this is where billionaires get all those fancy limitless cards from."

My awe is quickly tempered, however, when Vadim exits the car, stone-faced, and reaches back for me. Together, we enter a minimally designed lobby where a teller guides us to a private room supposedly designed to store personal effects.

As we wait on leather loungers, the woman returns with a few small items balanced on a silver tray.

"Take all the time you need," she explains as she sets the tray onto a wooden table before us.

The second she's gone, I sit forward and eagerly peruse each object. There isn't much—perhaps Vadim's ruthless minimalism isn't a trait he picked up on his own, but one he learned from Hiram? A leather-bound journal, a gold-set watch on a leather band, and finally, a black metal lockbox make up the bulk of his few personal effects.

The last item draws my interest the most, but I sit back as Vadim takes his time inspecting the arrangement. Finally, he reaches out, fingering the watch first.

"He told me once, he'd leave this to me," he says, more to himself than to anyone else. Sighing, he turns his attention to the notebook, warily flipping through the first few pages. With a pained expression, he sets it aside and then finally opens the lockbox.

I find myself leaning forward, eagerly peering within— only to frown in confusion. Hiram Gorgoshev cherished few things in life, it seems. A small stack of documents, and a selection of glossy snapshots tied together with a delicate strip of ribbon. But not just any photos.

I recognize the little girl staring plaintively from the topmost one—so does Vadim. He snatches the entire stack and spreads them out over the table, his expression increasingly constricted. Magda stars in every last one, spanning at least most, if not her entire short lifespan. A wide-eyed, stoic baby. A blankly staring toddler. A presumably five-year-old girl photographed without flashing so much as a smile.

Vadim lifts that one, his hand shaking so badly. It slips through his grasp and lands face-down, revealing a slash of cruelly elegant script written on the back: *Proud of your creation?* Every picture sports some variation of a message, each one seemingly more mocking than the last.

So innocent. So perfect. How many such well-bred creatures did you deny the world when you grew a soul, Hiram?

Do you see his face? I do. What would he say?

And finally…

Do you deny she's a result of your 'research?' Flawed, like everything you touch.

The author of these cruel messages needs no explanation. Irina wrote them, using the pointed language to taunt Hiram. Blackmail him? And the last one, adorning the oldest photo of Magda, mentioned that damn, hateful word. Flawed.

In disgust, Vadim swipes his hand over the photos, scattering them further. Then he snatches the remaining stack of documents from the lockbox and scours them with a deepening frown.

"What is it?" I ask as he lurches to his feet, his gaze on one page in particular.

He shakes his head rather than tell me. Then he retreats to a corner of the room while withdrawing a cell phone from his pocket. In hushed tones, he relays something fervently to whoever is listening on the other end, but I only manage to catch snippets. "…Verify. The one Hiram used. Yes. See if you can track him down."

As I strain my ears to listen, I reach for one of the documents he'd left behind. All it contains is an itemized list. An invoice? I struggle to decipher the final details. A series of names… Countries? Each one is followed by a date and a scribbled response in different handwriting that makes me suspect they had been written in after the fact.

Gone.

Left in June.

No sign.

Witnesses saw a child but no sign.

Was Hiram tracking someone? Someone with a child who apparently bounced from city to city—even country to country. And judging from the number of invoices, his surveillance of that mysterious figure spanned months if not years.

"He knew," Vadim rasps. I look up to find him stowing his cell phone in his pocket, apparently speaking to me now. "Irina kept in contact with him. The bastard even had her traced. Put a bounty on her head—"

"I'm sorry." I rise to my feet and approach him. Everything we've learned takes a backseat to the betrayal I know he's feeling. And I'm already steeling myself to withstand his instinctive way of reacting when hurt.

His eyes cut down to mine, blazing with mistrust. "How do I know you aren't working with her as well?" he demands. "Am I supposed to believe it was a coincidence that you appeared in my life when you did? How good you are with her. It could be an act. It could…" He deflates, raking his hands through his hair, his gaze unreadable. "No," he decides, shaking his head. "No."

What exactly about me makes him change his mind, he doesn't say. Instead, he sinks onto the edge of the leather chaise and sighs.

"Hiram's man was the one who brought Magda to the crisis center." He tosses the crumbled invoice onto the table, eyeing it in disgust. "He tracked Irina to Fair Haven of all places. His mercenary took Magda—terrified her in the process—and then…he abandoned her."

"And then that man sent you that note?" I ask cautiously.

He shrugs. "It makes sense. Or at least it would if Hiram were the kind of man who thrived in deceit."

"But he wasn't," I say, going off his obvious distress. "So there must be another explanation." Desperate to help him find one, I grab the journal and flip through the pages. Hiram was a man of few words, most of them spent reflecting on his take on the current stocks, or his viewpoint on the current events that day. I'm starting to feel my search is in vain when I stumble across a page near the very end that isn't like the others.

It's longer for one, with Vadim's name sprinkled throughout. It's a summary of his accomplishments at the time, more like an exhaustive list. His ascent in the biotechnical industry. His many accolades regarding his education and various business acquisitions. And at the very end, he'd written simply—*he is ready for anything.*

My throat constricts at the realization of just how true those words are, but for whatever reason, I can't bring myself to voice them.

"Let's go." Vadim stands, leaving everything on the table but the stack of invoices. "If we leave now, we can make it back before dark. I'll call Magdalene."

He's already in the hallway by the time I manage to stand. Before I leave the room, however, I can't stop myself from gathering everything into the lockbox and tucking it under my arm. When I rejoin Vadim out in the car, he spots my bounty, but he already has his cell phone against his ear, and the person on the other end takes precedence over all else.

"Having fun?" he asks in a jovial tone that's such a startling contrast to his glowering expression. The man sure can turn on the charm when he needs to. Even I would be convinced if I didn't happen to be staring directly at him. Whatever Magda says makes some warmth creep back into his gaze even as his frown deepens. "You want to stay the night," he says, sounding surprised by that fact. His eyes meet mine, wavering with indecision. "I…"

"Yes." I gently ease the phone from his grasp. Magda's excited chirping is audible even before I fully press the device against my ear.

"…and we went hiking. And they said we could camp in the backyard! Can I stay? Please?"

I barely recognize this little girl, brimming with the full extent of a seven-year-old's excitement. Even Vadim seems to realize that, despite his feelings toward Maxim, raining on her parade now would be cruel.

"That sounds great, honey," I say, deciding for him. "Of course, you can stay. We'll pick you up first thing in the morning."

Vadim eyes me both grudgingly and with a hint of something that might be relief as I return the phone to him. After talking to Magda for a few more minutes, he finally hangs up.

"This is a good thing," I insist in response to his distant gaze. "She gets to spend time with her family, and you get to digest what you've learned. You deserve to feel betrayed. But, you also deserve to think things through and have doubts about what the information may seem to present. It's okay to not want to believe the worst in anyone."

"Is it?" he wonders, flicking his gaze toward me.

"Yes." I nod. "And, it's especially easy to when you have a diversion. Let's take advantage of the absence of little ears and paint the town red."

I feel so smug with my offer, but Vadim's lips don't even twitch in the hint of a smile.

"Red with Irina's blood?" he wonders in a tone that makes me suck in a breath.

"N-Not quite. More like…dinner and wine?"

He sighs but starts driving, presumably toward a restaurant here in the city. After settling Hiram's estate on the floor of the car—and conveniently out of sight—I lean against him, slipping my hand in his.

He doesn't pull away at least, but by no means is he content with any of the events today has brought his way. Were I not here, I think he'd go off on his own and brood. Maybe spiral into one of the dark moods I've briefly witnessed, and that Ena has warned me about.

And I make a promise to myself to do everything within my power to prevent that from happening.

No matter the cost.

CHAPTER NINETEEN

Vadim's version of wining and dining centers around a gorgeous French restaurant in the heart of the city. The food is amazing, the wine even better, and as we sit at a private table amongst beautiful ambiance, one could easily assume it'd make for the most romantic tension ever.

Or not.

My date scowls during the entire meal and barely touches his food, too distracted by the thoughts in his head. It's like I can see them, dancing across his expression one by one. Fear of losing Magda. Anger at Irina. Pain at the thought of Hiram's betrayal.

By the time our waiter clears away our plates, I'm resigned to what I feel is my only course of action left, other than to let him brood.

"Talk to me," I demand, reaching across the table to clasp one of his hands. He stiffens, refocusing on me. It's like he forgot I was even here, so lost in his own torment. "Tell me what you're feeling. Or…" I lick my lips, recalling the one method of communication between us that never seems to fail. "You can show me."

He raises an eyebrow and lifts his hand from beneath mine only to capture my wrist. Curiosity alights those dangerous eyes, and I feel a thrill shoot through me.

"Show?" he wonders gruffly.

I nod and casually finger the low neckline of my dress with my free hand, deliberately drawing his attention downward. "If you don't want to talk to me, then show me. Let me feel what you're feeling."

His lips press together in a thoughtful gesture. "Sexual torment?" he muses in a tone so dark… I almost—*almost* have second thoughts. If only the logical part of my brain isn't instantly drowned out by the lustful part, who relishes the avenues ventured by his twisted whims.

"I'm here for you," I tell him, sounding more earnest than I think I have about anything in my life—other than when I said the same to Magda. "Let me be here."

He stands, pulling me to my feet. In a whirlwind blur, we leave the restaurant and return to the car. It isn't long into the drive that I become eerily familiar with the direction we're headed in.

But before anything of note appears on the horizon, Vadim makes time for something far more important than sex.

"Goodnight, *ma chérie*," he says into his cell phone, once again speaking to Magda. My heart swells as some softness seeps into the hardened lines of his expression as he lets her regale him with more of her day. But I think real tears prick my eyes as, instead of hanging up, he offers the phone to me.

"Goodnight, honey," I tell her, sensing from her slurred reply that she's already half asleep.

The brief, domestic moment makes for a startling contrast to our eventual destination—an infamous club that happens to be partially owned by the man beside me.

An ominous shiver runs down my spine as he takes my hand, and we exit the car. Once inside the familiar ebony walls, Vadim leads me boldly through an archway in the direction opposite the club floor. It doesn't appear to lead to the upstairs level either, but some new taboo section, and I have to admit my interest is piqued.

"I mentioned to Milton that I wished to expand my private use of the club," he explains as my eyes excitedly scan the corners, hunting for any hint of where we might be headed. So far, all that greets me is a long, winding hallway draped in shadow. "He and Maxim both have rooms here," he adds, steering me forward as the corridor begins to curve. "He granted my request."

That being his own "private space," presumably lurking beyond a massive ebony door waiting up ahead. That ominous tingle strengthens, turning into a shudder I can't suppress. Excitement becomes a palpable thing—I can almost taste it.

Dark, dangerous kink.

Still, I try my best to cut the tension. "Milton granted your request," I parrot, leaning against him playfully. "Is he in charge?"

"No," Vadim says, his tone suddenly serious. He brings me to a stop as we reach the door. With one hand, he pushes it open, while the other captures the side of my face, forcing me to meet his gaze directly. "*You* are in charge," he tells me huskily. Before I've even processed those words, he gently shoves me back, forcing me to stagger over the threshold of the room. "Always… Of how much of yourself you are willing to submit. Of how far you'll allow me to go. Of your trust. Of *me*."

Sensory overload. Especially as I find myself turning to take in the room we're in—a beautiful, haunting space decorated almost entirely in hues of black and navy. The man has certainly researched kink down to an art form. I blink as my brain races to take in every last detail.

There are windows, large and rectangular with a view overlooking what appears to be an enclosed courtyard complete with a bubbling, black marble fountain. Plush, ebony carpeting lends to a mysterious aura only enhanced by matching curtains. A lone leather chaise positioned near the windows serves as the sole piece of traditional furniture.

Because everything else is so very NSFW.

"Holy crap," I whisper as my eyes fall over one promising structure directly ahead. Extending from the ceiling in a display of expert craftsmanship is a round, circular base hung upright with two strips of material dangling from the bottom. Longer, larger sections dangle directly from the ceiling, framing it at all four corners.

It's a fancy version of a sex swing.

Beyond it, I recognize the pillory from the house, along with a few hanging cabinets, no doubt containing more goodies.

"A fitting enough playground?" Vadim wonders, coming up behind me. I'm too busy staring to answer him right away. Awed, I continue to take in the meticulously compiled décor—and all the while, his hands slide down my shoulders, removing my dress as they go.

I'm only vaguely aware of the material falling to my hips —and promptly tugged down the rest of the way. All I can do is surrender to his touch as my attention fixates back on the swing. My thoughts whirl, quickly envisioning how many naughty, twisted things he could do to me on it.

But, as he runs his fingers through my hair, smoothing the strands back from my neck, I suspect that I haven't even come close to what he's planned. Not by a longshot.

"Do you trust me?" he asks near my ear, his voice a low rasp.

My heart stutters. Breaths quicken. Excitement builds, nearly impossible to contain.

"Yes," I croak, sensing him lower something from above my head. His hands brush my cheeks as I blink to recognize a black strip of silk being positioned before my eyes. His tie?

Make that a makeshift blindfold, in this instance.

I don't resist as he loops the silk around my head, tying it in the back. Warm and dangerously soft, I sense the shape of his fingers dance down my forearms, finding my wrists next. With gentle pressure, he urges me forward, forcing me to follow his prompting blind.

And it is an experience unto itself. Trust had a different meaning before this moment—being naked, at his mercy, completely under his control.

At the same time, he tied the blindfold loosely enough that I have to keep my head still to prevent it from slipping. An oversight? Or by intention…

The latter, I suspect, predicated on one twisted bit of reasoning. If I want to see where this new game goes, I have to commit fully. There is no room for doubt or hesitation. The second I falter, his illusion will quite literally fall as well.

Sneaky devil.

The implicit insinuation is that every step, every bit of obedience to his touch, is entirely of my own free will and completely at his discretion.

"Kneel," he whispers against the column of my throat, his voice sensually warm.

I start to obey before he even finishes getting the word out, sinking to my knees on the plush carpeting.

"So beautiful," he praises thickly, sounding somewhere above me, still behind. "Now lie flat, onto your stomach."

My unease only grows in the most delicious of ways. Taking care with my back, I ease myself down onto my belly. From this position, I'm painfully aware of just how vulnerable I am. Open and naked to any assault he deigns to dish out.

For now, he seems content to make me wait. I breathe in and out, my face pressed against the flooring, him presumably watching down on me. Surprisingly, I feel anything but degraded. I know without even having to see his face, his expression is only one of lust.

And desire.

But just as I start to relax, I sense movement near my right. His footsteps? They're muffled, harder to track. I can only interpret him moving maybe a few feet away before he returns. A hiss of air betrays him sinking to his knees, I think, his fingers trailing down to my wrist. Something softer than flesh replaces his touch a heartbeat later. Silk? He loops it around, securing it tightly, but the sensation is nowhere near painful.

With a deliberate series of movements, he does the same to my other wrist. A subtle bit of tensing makes me suspect that my binds aren't manacles this time. They don't feel secured together, or even to the floor or any nearby surface. From up above instead?

I'm distracted from my suspicions as my ankle is next to receive the mysterious silk treatment. Then the other. Finally, his hands rove up to my waist, smoothing over the bones in my hips.

"Beautiful," he breathes before silken fabric brushes over my lower back in a teasing swipe. The gesture urges me to arch inward, allowing him to loop the fabric underneath. When I lie back down, I sense a swath of the silken material wide enough to stretch from my upper thighs to my navel.

"Do you trust me?" he asks again, but this time his tone makes me shiver in anticipation. It's low. Hoarse. Alluring.

And too damn smug beneath it all.

"Y-Yes," I whisper. The word barely escapes my lips before…

Ascent. Glorious, heart-stopping, mind-bending ascent. I don't know how he does it. The fabric carefully looped around my limbs goes taut, but not constricting, Regardless, the sudden tension lifts me from the floor completely—my belly first, then my wrists and ankles, suspending me seemingly by a thread.

A startled gasp escapes my throat. I can't even tell how high up I am—or if there is anything beneath me should I fall. But before I can voice my doubts fully, a stern voice reminds me, "You trust me."

That's all he has to say for it to click. So, *this* is the swing he envisioned for us—a completely different concept to the sturdy, more traditional base I helped him build what feels like a lifetime ago. Even now, I'm swaying, my body lying limp in this virtual harness.

But the logistics of my predicament aside, his care for me is readily apparent. He made sure there is no pressure on my back, for one. The position of the strap beneath my hips is expertly placed, ensuring that the tension is spread out evenly, preventing any one limb from taking too much stress.

It betrays an impeccable attention to detail, and I have a feeling that—as he has with most of his toys—he ensured this was designed with my specific measurements in mind.

"Are you afraid?" Vadim wonders, sounding somewhere in front of me. I almost reach out for him, feeling disarmingly unmoored. Lost. But his voice is like an anchor, imparting a calmness that heats me down to my core. "Don't be," he urges in a tone like sin. So deep, rumbling in earnest. "You never need to fear me. That isn't what I crave from you. But do you know what I *do* crave?"

My belly flips, sensing him even closer. A prickle of heat along my cheek alludes to his nearness. Then…

Whoosh!

I fall.

Stop short.

Raise again even higher.

Descend twice as fast.

It's *almost* too much. Almost. But the tension of the fabric is just a hairsbreadth on the side of more restraining than restricting. My body feels unnaturally loose—less like I'm a fly stuck in a spider's web, but more as though I am the spider. One whose web is being meticulously manipulated by a beast with devious intentions in mind.

But in the end, I still have some level of control.

Or not.

A featherlight touch along my jaw has me inclining my head toward the source, desperate for any clue of what lies in store.

"So beautiful," I hear Vadim say, his voice throaty and gruff. That gentle touch steadily inches downward, brushing the trembling column of my throat. "You wanted me to show you how I feel?" What I think is his thumb caresses my windpipe. "This."

Again, my binds are manipulated. The world shifts, and in a dizzying display of motion, I sense that I'm now suspended at an angle, slanted with my head downward judging from the blood rushing toward it. The strip beneath my belly still provides enough support that I don't feel in danger of falling. Just disoriented like hell.

"Always on edge," Vadim explains, his voice even closer. A prickling heat over my shoulder blades makes me envision him standing before me, stroking his fingers through my hair. "Like everything I knew no longer provides the same structure. The same support. You've taken that away from me."

Have I? I suck in a breath, mulling over the description.

"No one else would ever dare," he adds in a dangerous murmur. The air shifts again as the binds around my wrist tighten while the ones around my ankles loosen. My stomach flips as I wind up upright, leaning slightly against the strip across my belly, my hands stretched above me, while my legs are slightly bent behind me.

I definitely hear him now, moving to stand nearby. Then I feel him. A slow, hungry kiss against my eager mouth. Groping fingers cupping my breasts.

But, even as my body melts beneath his ministrations, I'm painfully aware of the fact that I'm unable to touch him in return. A shudder runs through me as I recall his deliberate phrasing. *You've taken that away from me.* So, he's retaliated by robbing me of any chance to turn the tables. Taking away my own sense of support.

But damn is it a glorious exchange. In return, he gives me a teasing, sparse bit of contact I never knew I needed. My body contorted like this, every nerve and sensation are enhanced tenfold. I can feel every ridge of his fingers. The softness of his tongue. Being helpless is surprisingly…

Kinky.

But I never forget his grated statement, or the way he said it. *You've taken…*

And in return, he devours. I'm never sure of where he's standing or how exactly he's touching me. Just that he is—near, there, everywhere somehow all at once. I'm a puppet on his strings, capable of moving only as much as he'll allow.

It's so disorienting. I lose track of up and down. Left and right. Gravity. My sense of direction comes solely from him. His mouth, grazing my jaw, inching down to my breast, encasing the nipple. Sucking…pain. Warmth of his tongue to soothe the sting. Then again.

Again.

Again.

I don't realize how turned-on I am until he adjusts my legs, making them chafe and bringing painful awareness to the moisture gathering there—that's how distracted he has me. I'm feeding off every bit of physical contact he's willing to give. I'm thriving on it. Growing mad on it…

But it's as if he's avoiding true stimulation on purpose, making me wait. Ache. Throb in a way I never have. My thoughts start to dissipate, scattered by his searching, grasping fingers. Down to my hips. Up across my ribcage and around to my healing scars. One by one, he gives every wound his own unique brand of attention, caressing the flesh around each with worshiping reverence before turning to my breasts again. Lower.

But never too low.

I'm biting my lip so hard I taste blood just to keep from voicing a plea. Sweat slicks my skin, making the fabric chafe with every swaying motion, but the slight friction only enhances my sensitivity more. A moan breaks loose before I can help it, but the low sound seems to trigger something in him.

Finally, his touch slips between my splayed legs, his voice dripping into my ear. "I have you," he tells me throatily as one of his fingers invades, working past my contracting muscles. "Don't I? I have you."

Mindless, I nod, lost to the feeling of his touch.

"You will never leave me."

Never, a part of me whispers as he thrusts that invading digit, making my eyes roll back into my head. It's like he's drugging me with every deliberate motion, making me susceptible to any command he dishes out.

"And you will finally tell me what you've danced around confessing all this time, won't you?"

Tell? Then it clicks. My eyelids flutter against the fabric of his makeshift blindfold. "Let me see you," I whisper, my voice hoarse. "Please. I need to see you."

I sense him hesitate, presumably unsure of my motives—always battling that closed-off, paranoid part of himself. Finally…

His fingers brush the planes of my cheeks before the blindfold is lifted away, and I can take in his face. Those beautiful dark eyes watch me warily, still too proud to beg. So he demands instead, stroking me from the inside out, wringing a strangled gasp from me in lieu of words.

He wanted me to feel what he does? I show him, arching shamelessly into his touch, forcing my body to sway, at the mercy of his contraption. I let his fingers work their magic, turning my insides to putty, my brain to mush. I allow any lingering doubts to drain away, my blood drugged on lust as our gazes meet.

"I love you," I tell him, meaning every word. The conviction in my own voice terrifies me, but I can't deny it any longer.

And this is true surrender.

And corruption.

"I love you—"

Growling, he steps into me, at the same time reaching up to snatch one of the strips holding my wrists aloft. The sharp shift in angle draws me against him, and his free hand grips my hip, snatching me the rest of the way. His lips pry mine apart, his tongue plunging in between as his finger strokes a brutal friction that makes me moan openly, senseless.

He's still fully dressed, I realize somewhere at the back of my mind. A fact he quickly rectifies, snatching open his slacks with a sharp tug of his free hand while his opposite fingers withdraw from me.

Bucking his hips, he enters me hard, lowering his mouth to my throat, his teeth catching the tender flesh there. "Again," he rasps in between harsh thrusts that leave me reeling. "Again—"

"I love you." I marvel at how easily the words come now. No hesitation. No shame. I'm as locked into the confession as I am to the apparatus he's created for me, surrendering of my own free will.

CHAPTER TWENTY

I'm only vaguely aware of the moment he releases me from the straps, cradling me into his arms. His jacket encases me, a prison of tailored cotton, as he carries me from the room and then the club entirely. I can sense the change in the atmosphere—the sensual tension traded for welcome calm—right up until the moment he finally brings me over the threshold of our home and utter contentment sets in. Now I know why Magda missed it so much during our brief absence—the smell. The familiar feeling in the air that makes me relax into his arms as he takes me into our room.

We're on the bed, my limbs still slick with sweat when he drags me closer, his lips pressed to my forehead. "I love you," he tells me in a low, fierce hum more beautiful than any other sound in the world. "I love you."

MAGDA GETS the benefit of having her playdate extended to midafternoon as I spend the morning recovering in bed, and Vadim pampers me with mind-blowing attention to detail. He bathes me first, then feeds me a hot breakfast of eggs and toast—I'm starting to appreciate how his research has broadened into culinary skills. When we finally get dressed and drive the short distance to Maxim's home, Vadim's still so relaxed there's barely any clue as to his unease.

It's only when he finally parks in the driveway and steps from the car that a frown tugs on his mouth as his gaze fixates on the front door. His right hand sinks into his pocket, and I envision him grasping his cell phone, ready to call Magda the second he doesn't catch sight of her.

But as the seconds pass, he doesn't take a step toward the house.

"Come on, Mr. Brooding," I tease, stepping forward to slip my hand in his. But inside, I'm just as uneasy.

Can the brothers extend their terse truce for longer than a few seconds at a time?

God only knows.

I aim for optimism, however, as we approach the front door. I think it's the first time that it isn't automatically opened from the inside. Instead, we're forced to knock, and Vadim's wary expression deepens into flat out dread.

Seconds pass in silence before audible footsteps approach from inside the home. Finally, the door cracks, revealing an unfamiliar face so unexpected that I blink.

"They're in the back," a teenager declares, his dark hair shaggy and untamed. He must be sixteen or seventeen, at least, nearly as tall as Vadim. Is he one of Francesca's siblings? I think I vaguely recognize him from the "party" I attended all those weeks ago.

Without a more thorough introduction, he inclines his head for us to follow him inside and leads the way out onto the terrace.

One look at what awaits us on the lawn, and I feel my eyes threaten to fall from my head. Beside me, Vadim's jaw tightens, his gaze unreadable.

"Off with his head!" Magda shrieks. Somehow she got a hold of one of my old pageant dresses—a bright pink chiffon that hangs on her tiny frame, clashing with her fanny pack. Wearing an equally extravagant dress is Ainsley, crouched beside her, cackling maniacally.

Both girls look poised to lunge at the poor, unfortunate figure caught in their midst.

"Get him!" Ainsley calls, leading the charge.

Both girls proceed to throw themselves at their victim— the only fact impeding their attack is that their opponent dwarfs them in both size and stature. Nonetheless, he's a good sport and playfully keels over to accept his fate.

All circumstances aside, it's an oddly heartwarming thing to witness. Maybe I'm not the only one who feels as much—Vadim's watching as well, his expression blank. Mistrustful, still? Even if he is, he doesn't march forward to draw Magda's attention.

He merely watches the scene unfold, and I imagine him envisioning all the many ways he was denied one similar to it. A peaceful, happy childhood spent playing games with his brother on their lawn, safe and protected.

The longer he observes them, the more pained his expression becomes until, finally, I feel compelled to brace my hand over his shoulder.

"Let's give her a little bit more time, huh?"

His only sign of acknowledgment is a terse nod before he turns on his heel, retreating inside the house. I spare the trio one last glance—they're so caught up in their game, Maxim it seems has turned the tables on his two charges, lifting them into the air one by one. Neither one seems to notice our arrival or our absence.

We retreat back to the house, and by the time Magda finally returns, courtesy of Ena, she's a rumpled, exhausted shadow of the earlier, energetic princess. She can barely keep her eyes open during dinner, and Vadim has to carry her up to bed.

Once she's down, I follow him into the master suite, but even as I run my hands down his back, inching toward his front, I sense he's not fully here. Especially when I tug at the fastenings of his pants, and he doesn't react.

"Earth to Vadim," I murmur against the back of his neck, but I'm worried. I'd almost forgotten just how far away he can seem when his thoughts are focused inward. Like we're miles apart, separated by infinity. "Tell me what's wrong," I urge him, moving my hands to cup his hips.

"Maxim," he says coldly, but his voice lacks the vitriol I'm used to hearing where his brother is concerned. "Given how much you've been eavesdropping, you're probably aware, but someone has been causing his business interests trouble in Russia. I'll spare you the nitty details—let's just say that everything my brother has a hand in isn't necessarily legal, so his position is a bit more precarious than you'd think."

"Legal," I say, tasting the word carefully. It tastes dangerous. Like a trigger to a potential avalanche of unwelcome information—like the aspects of him that Irina alluded to. Mocked me over. "And what about you?" I ask him softly, my eyes on the line of his jaw—it tightens. "Is everything you do *completely* legal?"

He sighs and grasps my hands, spinning around to face me in the same motion. I wind up caught in his embrace, forced to crane my neck to meet his gaze. Gone is any ounce of a barrier—he lets me see all of him clearly. The shadows bathe his beautiful features in a mixture of darkness and light. Much like who he is at his core, I suspect. A man capable of the tenderest love imaginable…

And yet equally ruthless, shaped by the hell he grew up in. Is it fair to even expect such a creature to play by the rules of the very world that chewed him up and spit him out?

I can't decide as his eyes scan mine, hunting for a reaction. I'm not sure what he finds. Dread? Concern? Desperation just to learn more about him?

"I would lie to you," he tells me as his thumb ghosts my cheek in a reverent caress. "I would. If I knew that it would shape your opinion of me… I would lie merely to keep you. But in the end, it wouldn't. Trust?" He makes the word sound more foreign to him than any other concept, flicking his tongue along his lower lip just to sample the aftermath. Lowering his mouth to my ear, his arms shift around me, crushing me against him. "That's what you want, isn't it? My trust. I could entrust the truth to you. But warn me now if it could change this. Us."

I inhale sharply, startled by the raw heat in his voice. What the hell could he reveal? And would anything truly change my opinion of him? It could. That's the scary fucking part—never mind my trust in him, do I trust my heart to have picked the right man to claim it?

It didn't do so good of a job the last time.

"It could," I confess, flinching as he stiffens. "But you need to trust me to handle the truth."

"So ask me," he commands, his voice concealing the hint of a dare. "I will tell you anything you want to know."

I swallow hard; the gravity of the offer isn't lost on me. Tentatively, I decide to start with the obvious, horrible suspicion tossing around my brain ever since Irina first implied it. "Do… Do you hurt people?" I don't even know how else to phrase it. "Like how you were—"

"No!" He wrenches back from me, his expression pained. "I do not trade in people. Never."

"Okay," I murmur, smoothing my fingers along his jaw until he stills, his nostrils flaring at the mere suggestion. "So, what is it you do, then?"

Illegal or not, anything has to be better than human trafficking.

Right?

"You need to understand something about my family…" He moves to the bed, sitting on the edge with his back to me. His shoulders are rigid, his posture taking on the tense, stone-like stiffness that's become a hallmark of when he reflects on his past. I can't imagine how painful this is for him to face—and the true magnitude of darkness those memories may hold. "My father belonged to a family well-known in Russia and beyond for their ruthless grip on power. The *Koslovs*."

He says that name the same way he referred to Irina and her exploits while speaking to Milton. With utter disgust and loathing.

"Various branches dabble in their own aspects of crime—some so evil you couldn't fathom them. As far as Maxim and I are concerned, our father dealt primarily in weapons. Stealing them from various military strongholds or manufacturers and then selling them to the highest bidder on the black market. Whether it be to mercenaries, or crime lords terrorizing parts of Africa, money dictates the sale rather than morality."

"So, is that what Maxim does?" I ask, advancing toward him. "He sells weapons?"

"And more." He inclines his head as if gauging for himself just how much more I'm willing to hear. In the end, he says, "His club? He uses it primarily as a front to swindle blackmail and favors from powerful clients or rivals. He doesn't employ the same tactics my old master did, mind you, but the aim is the same."

"I might have been able to guess that much eventually," I admit, thinking of Geoff, the man I met there. He made scoring entry to the club sound comparable to winning the lottery, though he had also implied the shadowy nature of Maxim and his operations. "So what is it you do?"

"Me?" He sighs, and from this angle, I catch how his eyes flicker toward the windows, cold and distant. "I have a stranglehold on one of the premier pharmaceutical manufacturers in the world. When I took control, Eingel was little more than a blip on the map—a small, though pioneering, biotechnical firm. Now, they corner the lion's share of the market. Insulin. Lab equipment. Research studies regarding various vaccines to illnesses, some of them newly discovered. But one drug that makes up most of our portfolio is one used by paramedics to treat heroin overdoses. It's a fairly new delivery system, allowing it to be given with the same ease one might use to administer an epinephrine pen."

"But?" I croak, sensing a horrible caveat looming on the horizon.

He shifts to face me, his expression open and wary. It's his unease that makes me steel myself against the truth. His seeming resignation to the fact that whatever he's about to reveal, I won't accept. And yet he's taking the risk to trust me with it, all the same.

"The drug is a form of Naloxone, engineered to be effective within seconds of administration. But I ensure its demand more than matches the supply."

He pauses deliberately, as if forcing me to ask the magic words.

"How?"

"By taking steps to ensure the flow of heroin continues unabated," he says. "Using my influence to ensure incoming shipments into the city aren't entirely seized by law enforcement, for one. Supplying dealers through untraceable methods. No matter how fierce a campaign some praise-hungry politician mounts against 'the war on drugs,' my interests are never threatened."

He sounds ice-cold. No bluster. No bravado. One hundred percent honest.

And I feel *punched*. Swaying, I grapple for the edge of the mattress and sink onto it. "We can't mention that to my parents at Christmas dinner," I croak. I'm surprised when I blink to find moisture building behind my eyes. Out of shock? Fear? Or perhaps just pure sadness for the fact that someone as beautiful, and intelligent can never rise fully above the darkness that bore him.

"Tell me why," I whisper before the horror can build to an unbearable level. "I want to hear you explain it to me."

The bed shifts as he stands, his steps heavy. "Maxim was given control of our family's assets from the time he was ten years old," he confesses. "I was given *nothing*. Always, I had to fight and scrape to gain a fraction of what the chosen heir had handed to him on a silver platter. Always. You don't understand… In our world, power is money. Money is *life*. If I couldn't outwit them, garner my own resources to stay ahead, I would have drowned before I realized the water was even above my head. It is a cruel world, and cruel measures are required to survive in it. I refuse to lie down like a good dog. Never again will I be used as a toy in another's game."

His voice… That isn't Vadim talking. I imagine it's his father, or worse—some other phantom who threatened or harmed him in the past. Even now, seemingly successful with more money than any man could ask for, he's still running. Still fighting.

Can he ever truly be at peace?

"I can't pretend like I agree with any of this," I admit, my eyes welling, throat constricting. "I can't. I can't understand it—but I can admit that I have never been faced with what you have. You want my trust, then you have it. That doesn't mean acceptance."

He stops, his back to me. "So what does it mean?"

I suck in a breath at the ice in his tone. It's not the chilling, detached way he's spoken to me when cutting me off from Magda or accusing me of wanting to use him. This anger, I suspect, is fully focused inward, solely at the boy he used to be, desperate to outwit his brother at every turn. Craving to prove his worth in any way he could. A part of me wants to…

But in the end, I can't blame that little boy for who he is now.

I don't have that right.

"Should I prepare the plane to fly you to California?" he wonders. But he sounds so hollow, I doubt he's joking. Resigned. He's *that* convinced I'll leave him merely for hearing the truth.

"I'm not running, am I?" I ask hoarsely. "I'm listening. I'm processing…" Sighing, I rise to my feet, advancing toward him on trembling limbs. "I love you."

The space where his arm meets his shoulder is a refuge I seek out, burying my face in that hollow as my arms go around him to settle over his stomach. "That means facing the good and the bad. You're more than the person I met in a bar on a whim. I can't expect everything about you to be tailor-made for my life and expectations. But... Neither can you when it comes to me. So I'm asking for the same mercy. Be honest with me."

His fingers flutter over mine, hesitant as if he's not fully convinced I won't pull away. "Anything."

"What do you really expect from us? I need to know. Is it children? B-Biological children—" God, how selfish is it that this topic stings more than the reality of him supplying an entire illegal drug trade to spur the sales of his company's assets. Damn Irina. Her smug grin is in my head, her snide accusations ever looming. I can't escape them no matter how hard I fucking try. Walking away from a glorified drug dealer due to my own moral compass is one thing. Having him cast me aside because of the failings of my own body is another.

It's so selfish...

But there it is.

"I want to hear it from you," I tell him, my words muffled by the fabric of his suit jacket. "Please. Just tell me—"

"I don't deserve one child." His voice resonates throughout his entire body, guttural with pure conviction. "Let alone more. I'm not so arrogant as to *demand* more."

He shifts, prying me from him only to spin me into the embrace of his chest. With utter gentleness, his fingers brush my chin, coaxing me into facing him. Those eyes swallow me whole, absolving my guilt, my fear.

He looks at me like someone seeing sunlight after years spent in the dark. With too much awe, he looks at me—more than any one woman could ever deserve. Ever live up to.

But he doesn't make it feel unwarranted—and that's the terrifying part.

"Love," he murmurs, trailing his lips across my forehead. Then down. Over my cheek and against my mouth. "I won't demand more from you than what you can offer. Again."

I sway, seeking out the contours of his body for stability.

"Push me away like that again, and I'll kill you," I tell him seriously. "Your reputation or not."

"My reputation..." He chuckles, and some of that persistent pain leaves his gaze. Just enough to make him seem more exhausted than calculating for once. A man so used to going to war with the world, he's still mistrustful of peace. "But that is why Irina's recent actions don't make sense," he admits, his lips contorting into a frown as the pressing reality at the forefront asserts itself again. "I never told her about Maxim. To go after him, she has an aim in mind far beyond aggravating me."

In a funny way, it's striking that he can only realize as much now, with a tiny fraction of his animosity toward Maxim cooled for Magda's sake.

"Like?" I press.

His brow furrows, revealing a mere glimpse of a man ruthless enough to rebuild the world around him as he saw fit. "Like… She dug too deep into my past and decided to make a deal with the devil."

I feel my eyebrow raising. "Don't tell me Lucifer himself is another relative."

"My grandfather," he says, without missing a beat. The scary part? He doesn't sound like he's joking. "Anatoli Koslov. A bastard cruel enough to sow an empire of thieving, scheming degenerates. Maxim defied him. I'd thought he'd slunk off to Moscow by now."

"You think Irina…made a deal with him somehow?"

"No," he says quickly, but he frowns, raking a hand through his hair. "Unless… Fuck!" He turns, pacing with renewed focus. "How the fuck didn't I see it before? Why would a woman like Irina have a child? *My* child. I can tell you she never expressed a maternal interest before. But to the Koslovs? A child is a commodity," he says darkly, his hands curling into fists. "One easily bought and sold. My past? I still have yet to tell you the full extent."

He inhales raggedly, his body swaying, his eyes unfocused.

"I'm here," I say, bracing my hand against his chest. "I'm here."

"My mother sold me to my father. To the Koslovs," he says. "And when I failed to challenge Maxim, I was given to our uncle, Sevastyn. *His* realm was far different than trading in guns," he admits, his voice rasping. "Through him… I was sold to The Collector."

"Oh my god…" It's too horrifying to fathom. I refuse to, pressing my face against his chest, sensing his heart pound frantically underneath.

"Maxim has not always played by our grandfather's rules," he adds. "Securing an heir should have been his primary focus the moment he came of age—but he hasn't. Deliberately, I suspect, though the bastard would never admit as much to me. As far as Anatoli is concerned, having a child of Koslov blood—no matter their origins—would be a preferable backup. Even the child of a worthless bastard long since sold."

My heart breaks for him. As cold as he sounds, and as ruthless as he can be, admitting as much guts him. I know it does.

"You think that's why Irina had Magda? To sell her to your family?"

"If she is prominent in the trade, then she knew Sevastyn," he grates, his expression horrified. "No one could enter that realm without kissing that bastard's ring. But if that was her aim, to curry favor with a child, they would have no interest in a girl."

And, in a cruel twist of fate, once Magda became diagnosed with diabetes, Irina had no interest in her either.

"But why keep her?" I ask, more to myself than him. "If the Koslovs didn't want her, and obviously her bond to her wasn't that strong considering she abandoned her, why keep her at all for the first five years of her life?"

Something in Vadim's expression shifts. He's having one of his many revelations, but this one is different. It crushes him. "Money," he rasps. "Money she could extort via blackmail."

"From you?"

He shakes his head. "Of the man whose research may have led to her creation being possible in the first place. Irina somehow stole the remnants of our employer's sick experiments—but those experiments were only possible due to Hiram Gorgoshev and his expertise."

And once selling Magda to the Koslovs was no longer an option, Irina decided to use her as a cash cow instead, extorting money from Hiram to keep her child's origins secret. My heart throbs for her, Magda. I can't imagine anyone ever treating their own child so callously.

But at least in her case, she wound up in the arms of someone who will go to the ends of the earth to protect her.

"I know what the bitch wants," Vadim growls. "Why she's chosen now to come back. Sevastyn's dead. Without him, I'm sure her sick fucking realm is in shambles. She wants to ally with the Koslovs to ensure her revenue isn't affected."

And she'll use her own daughter as a bargaining chip to do so. It's such a sad, selfish motive, but something warns me that it's only a fraction of what may be really driving Irina. I can't ignore how she looked when speaking about him. That possessiveness.

And pain at the thought of being forgotten by him.

"What are you going to do?" I ask, running my fingers over the planes of his chest.

He catches my wrist, his expression softening as he forces his attention outward.

"Irina would only feel bold enough to go after Maxim if she assumed I wouldn't put the pieces together in time."

"I guess your relationship must not be a secret then."

"But if I go to him directly… If we combine our resources…" He frowns, not liking the idea even as the words leave his mouth. "He'd never agree to it."

"But if he did?" I prod.

He grimaces at the mere thought and strokes his chin. "We could head her off. Formulate countermeasures to wipe out her and the fucking ring while we're at it. Milton would help."

"So then ask him." I plant my lips against his jaw and feather a path of them down to the center of his chest. "If you need a better reason, I promise to reward you handsomely after."

"That is a tempting offer..." He captures my waist, anchoring me against him. In this position, I've never felt smaller in his shadow, nestled against him like something cherished and delicate. Protected.

"Whatever you do, I'll support you."

Even if it means accepting the unforgivable.

CHAPTER TWENTY-ONE

He wakes up early, rolling away from me without a word. I can tell from the set of his jaw alone not to question. Not to speak. Instead, I watch from the safety of the blankets as he stands and enters the bathroom. Minutes later, he emerges dripping wet, his gaze set in a grim mask of determination.

Lost in his thoughts, he takes his time picking out his suit, and when I finally rise and join him, I find him scouring his selection of hanging ties.

"This one," I say, stepping forward to gently remove a navy blue one from the rack. I loop it around his neck as he watches me, his gaze so open my toes curl the few times I sneak a glimpse at it directly.

Once he's fully dressed, I stand on tiptoe and plant a kiss against his pursed lips.

"I'll be waiting for you when you come back," I tell him huskily.

Though for what exactly? Those plans seem up in the air as tiny footsteps approach from down the hall, and the door is opened from the outside.

"Can we go swimming today?" Magda asks, still half asleep, her braids crooked, It tucked under one arm.

Vadim chuckles, his expression softening as he takes her in. "As long as it's not too cold out," he says, smoothing his hand over one of her braids. His touch lingers, eventually finding her chin—gently, as if giving her every opportunity to pull away. When she doesn't, he tilts her head back to face him. "You need all the practice you can get if we're to summer at the beach, *oui?*"

Her smile is so damn ripe even her stoic nature isn't enough to suppress it. "Really?"

He nods, drawing his hand away to adjust his collar. "I'm looking into a boat as well. Would you like to fish?"

She eyes him warily and nods, padding after him into the hall. "Can we get a yacht? And have a party on it…"

"A yacht?" Vadim sounds utterly perplexed by the request, and I feel my cheeks flush. Note to self—watch my terminology around the child next time.

I slip into a robe and follow, my lips stretched into a grin as I watch them interact. Once we've had breakfast, Vadim leaves, no doubt heading to face a challenge far more intimidating than lounging by the pool.

And I try not to stress over the possibilities of what could happen between him and his brother. Luckily, the sun is shining, and it's warm enough out that I feel brave enough to risk another shot at swimming lessons.

"What do you say?" I ask my co-pilot, posted beside me, as I wash the dishes. "How about a swim?"

She darts off while I take my time entering the master suite, trying to pick which one of my outfits I'll sacrifice to the waters of the pool. I've barely begun perusing my options when I spot a luxurious black shopping bag I definitely do not remember purchasing myself. Inside, I find not one, but several beautiful, stylish swim sets to choose from.

The bastard even got me a particularly risqué bikini in emerald green.

I'm smiling as I pick a modest navy-blue one-piece for now, and I've just managed to get it on when a tiny voice calls from the mouth of the closet. "Are you ready yet?"

I peek out to find that I'm not the only one who found a few presents in her wardrobe. Magda's fully decked out in a charming yellow one-piece decorated with white polka-dots, complete with a matching set of sunglasses and her fanny pack.

"Hold your horses, sailor-girl," I tell her playfully. "And you don't want your phone to get wet. Leave the bag in your room, and go wait for me downstairs. I'll be there in a second."

"Five minutes?" she prods, every bit as manipulative as her father.

I relent with a sigh. "Five minutes."

Within two, I already hear frantic shouting coming from down below.

"I'm coming," I call out. "Just give me one second." With a pile of towels slung over my arm, I pad down the stairs. As I round the corner of the kitchen, I call out, "I hope you're ready to learn how to doggie paddle—"

A piercing scream cuts me off mid-sentence, followed by a monstrous splash. My heart stops. Before I know it, I'm racing onto the terrace. My eyes fixate on the pool—and the tiny figure flailing in the center.

I stop thinking. The next second I'm in the water, diving down just as she slips beneath the surface. Adrenaline and instinct control my limbs, giving me a strength I didn't know I possessed to grab her in my arms and spring toward the surface.

I gulp at the air, kicking toward the edge of the pool on autopilot as my attention turns to the girl in my arms. She's quiet. Too quiet.

"Magda!" I spin her around, my thoughts racing as I struggle to recall the first steps of CPR. Two large blue eyes blink up at me, stunned but alert.

I manage to haul her onto the edge of the pool and climb out after her before relief barrels through me like a sucker punch. My hands shake as I stroke the hair from her face, my eyes on her chest. Only when my voice reaches back to me—high pitched and frantic—do I realize that I've been speaking to her this whole time.

"What were you thinking, coming out here without me? Are you okay? Magda! Say something."

But she's silent, even though—physically at least—she seems to be okay. I draw her into my arms anyway, squeezing so tightly I think she'd protest if she weren't in shock. Soon any anger I may have felt turns to a crippling, overwhelming sense of guilt. I stroke my hands down her back, my voice soothing. "It's okay, honey. You're okay…"

But she isn't.

"What the hell?" Red splotches mar her left arm, noticeable only when I start to pull back. Alarm shoots through me like a lance. They don't look like a rash or a harmless reaction to the water. They're scratches. As if someone grabbed her there. Brutally.

"Honey…" I force her to face me. "Tell me what happened."

I've never seen her like this. Dazed. Distant. Much like Vadim in his very worst of mind states. When it seems like nothing short of screaming can reach him. When his past has all but consumed him.

I snatch Magda into my arms and carry her back into the house, my heart pounding. I wrench the sliding glass door shut and lock it. Then I race to the cutlery drawer and grab the biggest knife I can. Brandishing it in one hand, I curl my free arm around Magda—though she's clinging to me so tightly on her own.

At first glance, nothing looks out of place. The kitchen is as pristine as always, the dining table cleared of dishes or dust for that matter. The heightened sense of unease that has me scanning the corners could be attributed to paranoia.

But then I hear it. Laughter. Faint and distant, it comes from the direction of the terrace. I whip around to find a beautiful blond lazily skirting around the pool. In her hand is a pistol, aimed squarely at the glass door.

There isn't time to panic. I just run, barreling upstairs before I even process why. In Magda's room, I rip her from me, crouching down to her level.

"Get your cell phone, honey," I tell her, making my voice as stern as I can. "Call your dad and hide. No matter what, stay hidden, okay?"

She nods, and some twisted semblance of relief eases my fear. I stroke her hair and then close the door, returning downstairs. It's stupid. I should be hiding too. Running in search of a guard or wait for Vadim.

But deep down, I know in the pit of my gut that nothing I do will deter Irina for long. She doesn't want a chase.

She wants a fight.

The kitchen is her battlefield. She sits at the dining table amid a sea of shattered glass—remnants of the sliding glass door. She eyes me from above her neatly folded hands, the gun out of sight.

"You've called him already, I'm sure," she says, her lips parted into a beautiful smile. Her outfit this time is a ruby red dress that enhances her curves, playing off the gold in her hair. "Good. It's best we keep this quick—"

"Keep what quick?" I counter, adjusting my grip on the knife. I stride toward the counter, putting it in between us, my eyes on her hands. If she goes for her gun, I might be able to duck quickly enough to avoid the first bullet.

But the longer I keep her talking, the more time Magda has to hide.

"You don't want your daughter," I point out, cocking my head with a confidence I don't feel. "You already had the chance to kill me, and you didn't take it. What now?"

"Now?" She giggles, her eyes sparkling. "*You* were never a factor," she tells me. "Just a toy. A diversion. And Magdalene, while I may have no use for her, she does serve one purpose..."

"Vadim," I croak. "You know he'd do anything for her. So why try to drown her?" Anger makes my voice tremble in a way I've never heard it before. I barely recognize this woman.

But embodying her gives me an insight I'd never have before my brief introduction into Vadim's world.

"You didn't," I say, changing my opinion as Irina's eyes darken with disgust. Annoyance.

And then it hits me. The red marks. Magda's fear. It all paints a horrifying picture—rather than let her mother drag her away, she jumped into a pool, knowing she couldn't swim. Or, even more chilling, she made the most noise she could, trusting me to hear her. Save her.

"Do you think Vadim will really allow you to hold her life over him?" I ask incredulously. "He'll kill you."

"Perhaps." She shrugs, but in a fluid, graceful motion, she snatches the gun from its hiding place on her lap and aims it squarely in my direction. "Or, he may be too distracted by grief at your death. I'm curious to see it. Something tells me that he'll get over you quickly." She smiles wickedly, her eyes gleaming. "Magdalene or no, he could have a flawless child to dote over soon enough."

It takes everything I have in me to let the barb go unchallenged. Distracting me is what she wants. Instead, I try to read between the lines, finding the meaning in what she *isn't* saying.

"You must be desperate for money," I decide, honing in on her clenching jaw. *Bingo.* "To come crawling to him after a decade. What? Did the amount you blackmailed from Hiram run dry?"

Her eyes narrow; I've caught her off guard again. "Hiram. You say the man's name as if you know him. But you don't, do you? No. And neither did Vadim." She stands, still aiming the gun, though she twirls it by the handle, around and around—a twisted game of roulette.

"Hiram was too smart for his own good. So smart, he accepted the challenge set down by a monster—help him preserve his toys so that he could make more whenever the mood struck him. Children that he wouldn't have to go through the trouble of buying on the black market, stealing or smuggling. Homegrown stock. I don't think the old man knew the full extent of what he'd signed up for," she acknowledges with a shrug. "I'm sure he couldn't face his shame before his perfect little Dima. That he was the one behind the program that saw him strapped down, his essence ripped away. And for what? A broken little girl child so genetically flawed, she carried on his curse."

"You mean you couldn't sell her," I snap, my voice shaking with anger. "To his family. That's the real reason why you gave birth to her, isn't it?"

She raises an eyebrow, and I know I've hit a bullseye. "His family... Do you even know a hint of their reputation? I think not, or you wouldn't mention them so cavalierly." Smug once more, she cocks her chin, a smirk playing over her red lips. "So what if I aimed to give them a child? They would have welcomed Dima back into the fold then. He might have thanked me."

"But Magda was a girl," I point out. "So, you blackmailed Hiram for money instead."

"Hiram, Hiram." She sadly shakes her head. "A poor man, so wracked with guilt and fear of what his poor Vadim would do if he knew his savior contributed to the hell we lived through. He was pathetic."

Or he was human. A human who loved a man like his son, enough that he'd do anything to protect him the only way he knew how.

"Why now?" I demand. "Why come back now?" But then I remember something Vadim voiced, his own suspicion. "Your sick little sex ring is in jeopardy? You need more money. How disgusting."

"You are *very* mouthy," she spits, her eyes flashing. "It seems even Dima fed you tidbits to keep you quiet. Though you still have no idea, do you? His world. The crimes he's ingrained himself within. The darkness that lurks inside of him. One day, he'll give you a real taste— but I don't think you'll enjoy it much."

She pivots to face me, her expression cold. "You will never know him. No matter what lies he spins to placate you, you will never know the full extent. Money? That man commands more than money—"

"Power," I finish for her. "Is that it? You want protection." She flinches, and I know I've hit a sore spot. Like a shark sensing blood, I latch on, caution be damned. "The little boy you used and threw away now runs the world. But he doesn't even want you. He's had plenty of time to seek you out. Plenty of resources. He's used them to claim his daughter, but never you. Why?"

She flicks her wrist, pointing the gun at me once more. "Should I kill you quickly?" she muses, tilting the barrel toward my head. "Or slowly?" She turns her attention to my chest and licks her lips. "*Slow*, I think—"

"Mommy!"

God, no... In slow motion, I turn to the foyer, helpless to stop a tiny figure from racing into the room. Shouting, I lunge from behind the counter, but she's too fast. As I watch in horror, she runs up to her mother...

And throws her arms around her waist.

"Mommy," she wails plaintively, her face in Irina's hip, her tiny hands fisting in her skirt. "Mommy..."

It's a display that shouldn't sting nearly half as much as it does. Doubt creeps in, stealing away my resolve. Could I truly fight this battle with Magda as a bystander? Especially if—instead of fearing—she actually loves her mother?

The answer is simple—no.

And well aware of that fact, Irina faces me, her gaze alight with triumph. She lowers her free hand toward her daughter's head, her fingers unnaturally stiff. Then she flinches and shoves her off so violently her tiny body goes flying into the row of counters with a sickening thud.

"No!" I run to her, wrapping her in my arms, using my body as a barrier between her and our assailant.

"Little bitch," Irina hisses, swatting at her side. "Enough of this game—"

She aims her gun, heedless of the child in view—and I push all concern for myself out of my brain. Pushing Magda out of range, I pivot on my heel and lunge, swinging with the knife recklessly. Sheer surprise works to my advantage. I catch her off guard, knocking her against the table. The gun flies from her hand, but she lashes out, swiping her nails through the flesh of my cheek.

Growling, she kicks me back and scrambles for her gun. But before she can grab it, she staggers. Falls. Convulses, her eyes rolling.

A monstrous shout resonates from the foyer before I can even process what's happening. A heartbeat later, Vadim races into the room, Maxim hot on his heels. He takes one look at Irina and then me, his posture tense.

"Get the gun," he snaps to his brother—an act of trust so startling that I don't think he even realizes what he's done. His sole focus is on his daughter, overriding even a decades' long feud. He lunges for her over the sea of broken glass, stopping short only when he notices me. "Are you alright?"

I nod. "I'm fine."

With that, we both turn to Magda, and my heart sinks. She's hunched on the floor, staring blankly.

Vadim tentatively takes a step toward her. "Magdalene?"

She inclines her head toward him, but her blue eyes are fixated on her mother's body, watching as the woman's limbs contort uncontrollably. A brief stint of binge-watching medical dramas gives me a vague clue as to what's happening—she's seizing.

"She's not shot," Maxim declares, his tone cold. He's standing over Irina, scanning her body with a predatory intensity that makes me shiver. Meeting Vadim's gaze, he extends her discarded gun.

Vadim steps forward and takes it, hissing in disgust. "What the hell happened—"

I have no idea why or how—but in response to Vadim's concerned frown, Magda lifts her hand. In it is a tiny syringe, and a horrible explanation for Irina's state becomes clear.

"You gave her insulin?" Vadim's expression shifts as he crosses to her, crouching before her. Gingerly, he strokes her cheeks, forcing her to face him. "How much did you give her? How much?" he asks gently.

Magda shrugs and drops the syringe at his feet.

"The whole thing?" Vadim looks at Irina, his gaze unreadable.

"What does that mean?" Maxim demands, seemingly as confused as I am. But then something Vadim told Magda echoes in my mind—*no one else should ever take your medicine but you...*

"It means… We need to call Milton. Now." Standing, Vadim forces himself to leave his daughter, turning to the unconscious blond. "Tiffany. Can you take her upstairs to dry off?"

I force myself to move, gathering Magda into my arms. I carry her past Maxim, slipping upstairs. Once we're in her room, however, I can't seem to let her go.

"What were you thinking, huh?" I demand against her scalp. "You could have been hurt, honey. I told you to hide. I told you…"

She doesn't say anything, but her arms go around me in return, holding me just as tightly.

And *neither* of us can seem to let go.

Hours later, Vadim and Ena have temporarily boarded up the terrace door. Irina is gone to only God knows where and Magda—somehow—is sleeping in her bed. I linger near her more than I should, planting kisses over her forehead and smoothing my hands along her back until I'm sure she's asleep.

When I creep downstairs to check the progress of the cleanup, I find Vadim, leaning against a counter, his face in his hands. "She killed two guards," he explains, fixing me with a haggard, exhausted expression.

"Is she dead?"

He sighs. "No. Though she easily could be, with the amount of insulin in her system. But… I couldn't let Magdalene grow up believing she killed her own mother. Irina doesn't deserve to impact her life any more than she already has."

"So where is she?" I gather up the nerve to ask, fearful of the answer.

And he knows it. "Do you want me to say I let her go?" he wonders tiredly, shooting me a searching glance. "That she repented and is in prison forever and will never harm another soul? I will not lie to you—"

"And I don't want you to. So, tell me the truth," I prod.

"Why? Do you want to be disgusted? Do you want to hear that I sold her to the highest bidder? That the bitch will suffer for ever daring to touch my daughter? My family? Would that bother you?"

"It might," I admit. "But I think I'll get over it."

He cocks his head, not expecting that answer. Maybe he can hear it in my voice—I'm not lying. Compelled to explain, I let the true depth of my conflicted emotions wash over me. Disgust. Fear. Hate.

All of those things old Tiffy—even in the midst of her divorce—could never imagine feeling to this extent.

"Magda jumped in the pool just to keep Irina from taking her away." I can't disguise my horror. "How can a seven-year-old be forced to choose between drowning or her own mother? She can't swim. She was *that* afraid of her. If I didn't hear her… If I didn't get to her in time…"

"She's intelligent," Vadim states. I'm in his arms before I know it, crushed to his chest, and I relent to the embrace. "She *knew* you'd get to her in time."

And she must have known that Irina wouldn't even bother. The thought is so grim that any lingering unease I may have felt at her fate is instantly washed away.

As the Sunday school teacher deep within me might say— an eye for an eye.

But I appear to be the only one in a grudge-holding mood —one glaring event of the day stands out, and I rear back, poised to watch his expression.

"You and Maxim…"

He winces, his lips curling.

But I'm ruthless. "You brought *Maxim* with you. He *helped* you." I sound so childish, like I'm taunting him— but I can't help the silly glee that has me grinning. "You two were quite the dynamic duo—"

"I met him at the club," Vadim says, his tone far more somber than mine. "I intended to discuss our mutual headache. As it seems, our interests converged far more quickly than I initially thought."

Some of my excitement deflates at his frown. His eyes take on that distant gleam that they do when only one person is on his mind. "Magda called you," I say, my voice rasping. "God, she must have been terrified."

His brow furrows in surprise. "Commanding actually," he says, a rare smile sneaking onto his mouth. "She demanded I come to rescue you. I tried to convince her to hide somewhere safe and wait for me, but she hung up." He looks torn between fear and grudging admiration.

"It seems she didn't just inherit your good looks," I tease, stepping into him again, letting my head rest against his chest. "She got your stubbornness too."

Chuckling, he brings his hand to my scalp, cradling me against him. "It seems she picked up some traits from you as well," he murmurs, sounding amused once more. "Your remarkable ability to enthrall those around you, for one. I only had to say her name for Maxim to come."

His voice deepens, revealing just how much that confuses him. His brother came when he needed him the most.

Could the rift between those two ever be mended?

I picture two beautiful little girls, and I'm hopeful that they might be up to the task.

It should be impossible to expect things to return to normal after the events of the past few days. In some ways, they still aren't. Vadim and I wake up to find Magda squirming in between us, her bear firmly wedged under her arm, her fanny pack still on.

But she's the first one to spring from the mattress, padding downstairs, chattering excitedly.

"Can Ainsley sleep over here today?" she asks over a bowl of cereal. She seems oblivious to the fact that Vadim and I are perched on opposite ends of her, waiting for the second we might have to swoop in and comfort her.

The pink sundress she's wearing exposes her arms—and the mottled bruises down the length of one. Vadim was concerned enough by them to have Milton come over in the middle of the night and examine her. Supposedly, there is no lasting damage.

She'll be fine.

But she doesn't even seem to notice. "Huh?" she prods after shoveling a spoonful of cereal into her mouth. She eyes Vadim questioningly until he snaps to awareness.

"Yes, *ma chérie?*"

"Can we go back to California soon? I want to be on a boat."

"Of course. We can leave by the end of the week," he ruffles her braids, but the line of his jaw betrays concern. He didn't miss the same note in her voice that I did—the same way she'd "asked" to sleep in our bed for a week after being spooked by Maxim.

But once she finishes her food and skips off to the garden —watched over by Ena, there's no sign of trauma at all. Which is a testament to childish fortitude because I can't even look at the terrace door—newly replaced overnight —without flinching.

"I asked Milton for recommendations for a child psychologist," Vadim tells me as we clear the dishes.

"Once we settle on one, I'll have her start regular sessions." He moves toward the stairs next, and I find myself following him, too distracted by my own worries for Magda.

"What if Irina comes after us again?" It's a fear that won't stop nibbling, and it leads my thoughts down a dark path. Like the musing that next time, Magda won't be the one to inject the bitch with a lethal dose of insulin.

"She won't," Vadim says. He sounds so damn sure of that. I start to question, but something in his gaze warns me not to. Some aspects of his world, I'm better off not knowing about.

So I turn my attention to what I'd much rather study—him. He grunts in surprise when I slink toward him and press my body against the hardness of his. We're in the bedroom, and the row of windows makes for a fitting surface for him to push me against while ensuring we can both still see Magda frolicking about her budding garden, Ena in tow.

I stand on tiptoe and nibble along his jaw, tugging at the front of his slacks.

"Wait." He looks pained as he grasps my wrists, halting my assault. His eyes take on that dark, wary gleam as if he's hesitating on the verge of a decision. Sighing, he relents and releases me to reach into his pocket. "I haven't asked you to marry me," he states while presenting a small black box balanced on the center of his palm. "I still won't. Not until you're ready. But…"

He lifts the lid of the box, and I sway at the sheer opulence of what lurks beneath it. A ring—but one so delicately, beautifully crafted that I know it received the same careful attention to detail that his kinky endeavors did. It's beyond anything I could have imagined, and my throat tightens.

"Vadim…"

"I want you to know what awaits you if you do accept," he explains, his gaze alight with such raw emotion my heart swells, unable to contain it all.

Gently, I place my hand over his, forcing him to lower the ring. "I can't accept this," I tell him, hating the tension that tightens his jaw—the disappointment he can't even try to hide.

Disappointment that turns to confusion as I sink to my knees and return my attention to the front of his slacks.

"I do believe that it is *my* turn to propose." I free his cock and promptly tease the tip of his piercing with my tongue. "Mr. Vadim Gorgoshev," I declare in between devious tastes of him. "Will you marry me?"

I think he says yes, nearly drowned out by his groans as I take him as far into my mouth as I can.

When I draw back, he looks dazed. Like a man trapped in a dream, one he definitely doesn't want to wake up from.

"There is one condition," I tell him, though I'm not even sure how serious a thought it is. "I've always wanted a double wedding."

He raises an eyebrow, but when I curl my fist around him and press my lips against the crown, he promptly loses his ability to argue.

And if this proposal is anything to go off of, this marriage won't be anything like my last. My heart swells with that knowledge, and I watch him through my lashes, prepared to earn the ring I know lurks in the box still clenched in his fist. His face is the picture of awe. Rapture...

Horror.

"Damn," he whispers a split second before my ears pick up the noise triggering his alarm—tiny footsteps skipping down the hall in our direction. I barely manage to lurch to my feet—while he wrestles himself back into his pants —before the door opens and Magda marches in.

"Mr. Ena wants you," she says to Vadim, her button nose wrinkled in confusion as Vadim staggers to her side, still smoothing his clothing into place.

"H-He told you to tell me?"

Magda nods while I suppress a grin. Sending a child to do his dirty work could be a hallmark of the old bodyguard slacking—or his knowledge of what he might have interrupted as well as the inkling that his employer would spare poor Magda his wrath. Which he does with a wry grin that warms me down to my core. Taking her hand, he leads the way downstairs, where Ena lurks in the kitchen, scowling at the scene visible through the newly replaced terrace door.

"Ainsley!" Shirking her father's grasp, Magda surges forward, and Ena has just enough time to wrench open the sliding glass door before she can career right through it.

Sure enough, her target is already racing to meet her, her blond hair flying out behind her. Smiling, I scan her wake for a familiar figure and promptly feel my mouth drop open.

"Jesus Christ," I whisper. I have to resist the urge to rub my eyes just to make sure the stoic figure striding across the lawn is real.

"What the hell does he want?" Vadim murmurs, though he sounds genuinely curious rather than hostile—another fact contributing to my dropped jaw.

But his question winds up presenting its own answer—it's obvious to anyone watching just what Maxim wants.

"Uncle Max!" Magda's voice is audible from here, chirpy in the familiar way that took her own father weeks of trust-building to achieve. She skips to him, looping her hand within his, chatting animatedly the entire while.

And as his dark eyes take her in, they ignite with a warmth I figure might be visible from space. His posture relaxes as his lips quirk in the semblance of an expression that on any other man could be called a smile.

As Ainsley claims his other hand, I'm convinced that, foreboding figure or not, his heart has been stolen more than once.

As has the love of the man standing beside me. His hand flattens against my waist as if anchoring me to him is the only way he can stop himself from marching forward. Mistrust is always his first instinct—especially where Maxim is concerned—but in this case, I can sense the effort he exerts to stay still.

To watch.

To let his brother enjoy the simple gift they've both been denied for so long—family.

Did you enjoy the final installment of Vadim and Tiffany's Trilogy? Sign up to be alerted about all things Club XXX!

Hey there!

Thank you so much for reading! If you enjoyed the story, please leave a review and recommend the book to any friend you think would love this twisted world. You'd have my eternal gratitude. Even a short sentence goes a long way!

Then, come join the rest of us dark romance lovers in my Facebook Group where you can get snippets, sneak peeks of upcoming books and even help vote on aspects of future novels.

Come to the dark side:
https://www.facebook.com/
groups/lanasbeautifulmonsters/

WANT MORE STUFF TO READ?
Join my newsletter and get a **free book**! Plus, you get to

stay updated with any new releases, random giveaways
and exclusive sneak peeks!
https://www.lanaskybooks.com/newsletter

Other Novels: https://lanaskybooks.com/

ABOUT THE AUTHOR

Lana Sky is a reclusive writer in the United States who spends most of her time daydreaming about complex male characters and parenting her Cockapoo Joey. She writes dark, twisted romance across several genres. Her titles include everything from mafia romance to vampires.

facebook.com/AuthorLanaSky

twitter.com/lanasky101

amazon.com/author/lanasky

pinterest.com/lanasky101

goodreads.com/lanasky

instagram.com/lanasky101

bookbub.com/authors/lana-sky

www.ingramcontent.com/pod-product-compliance
Lightning Source LLC
Chambersburg PA
CBHW060740210726
48292CB00012B/11